Praise

W9-AGO-456

"Cronin's masterly prose and intricate plotting bring an entire world to life. . . . The vast scope of his story begs favorable comparisons to epics such as J.R.R. Tolkien's *The Lord of the Rings* and Stephen King's *The Stand*. Readers left hanging at the end of the first book will find some resolution here, but also twists, turns, and new developments that will make them desperate for book three."
—*Library Journal*

"I hate to use the word 'perfection.' But . . . I can't imagine a better book than *The Twelve*. . . . A remarkably frightening and tense novel."
—*National Post*

"Cronin's books, for all their brutality, have an ethereal quality that most other apocalypse books I've read lack. He has created a dark and brutal world, but his monsters are linked by dreams. . . . Cronin's skill as a storyteller keeps us immersed in their strange long dream."
—*The Millions*

"Cronin writes scenes of palpably growing terror and manages to keep up intense pacing and characterization. *Passage* fans will be clamoring for this one."
—*Booklist*

"*The Twelve* is even better than *The Passage*. . . . Cronin's apocalypse novels prove that good writers needn't stay mired in realism. And make no mistake. Cronin is a very good writer indeed."
—*The Plain Dealer*

"There is no question that this book is a compulsive read. . . . [Cronin's] world, a second time around, still feels fresh and surprising. . . . His vision of post-apocalyptic America is meticulously realized. . . . Cronin's world remains as satiating as a pint of O-positive."
—*San Francisco Chronicle*

"Like the bloodsucking virals in the storyline, this trilogy is something new, something unique, something evolved. . . . Mark my words on this: when all is said and done, Cronin's *Passage* saga will be remembered as a classic trilogy of novels—by fans of post-apocalyptic fiction, vampire fiction, and literary fiction alike. . . . Prepare to be blown away."
—Barnes & Noble Explorations

"Cronin is a prophetic and passionate writer and beneath its weight *The Twelve* is an undeniable and compelling epic. . . . Cronin boldly matches form and content."
—*Milwaukee Journal Sentinel*

"Cronin is one of those rare authors who works on two different levels, blending elegantly crafted literary fiction with cliffhanger thrills and spine-tingling 'gotcha' scares."
—*Fort Worth Star-Telegram*

"This dazzling sequel offers horrific scenes of demonic lords driving hordes to attack ever-diminishing outposts of a lost mankind."
—*The Oklahoman*

"If *The Passage* is the trilogy's Genesis, this second book, *The Twelve,* is its Exodus, a complex narrative of flight and forgiveness, of great suffering and staggering loss, of terrible betrayals and incredible hope. . . . If *The Twelve* is humanity's wandering in the proverbial wasteland, then the novel's ending suggests the final book in the trilogy will be a revelation."
—Minneapolis *Star Tribune*

Praise for *The Passage*

"[A] magnificent beast of a new novel . . . What makes *The Passage* special is the extraordinary level of verbal craft and psychological insight Cronin brings. . . . Cronin has taken his literary gifts, and he has weaponized them. . . . *The Passage* can stand proudly next to Stephen King's apocalyptic masterpiece *The Stand*, but a closer match would be Cormac McCarthy's *The Road:* a story about human beings trying to generate new hope in a world from which all hope has long since been burnt."

—Time

"[Cronin] artfully unspools his plot's complexities, and seemingly superfluous details come to connect in remarkable ways. . . . *The Passage,* then, is fundamentally an investigation into the creation and destruction of a flawed race."

—The New York Times Book Review

"Part apocalyptic tale, part allegory, and all great storytelling . . . vital, tender, and compelling."

—O: The Oprah Magazine

"Cronin has given us what could be the best book of the summer."

—USA Today

"A heavyweight in more ways than one . . . involving and immediate . . . magnificently unnerving."

—Entertainment Weekly

"Cronin's unguessable plot and appealing characters will seize your heart and mind."

—Parade

"Owing a debt, and paying homage, to such classics as *Earth Abides* and Stephen King's *The Stand,* Cronin's apocalyptic thriller hits all the right notes. . . . *The Passage* will likely join King's end-of-the-world opus and books like Robert McCammon's *Swan Song* in the pantheon of genre classics. . . . Cronin gets everything right the first time out. . . . Nearly every chapter increases the narrative momentum, and readers will find themselves hard-pressed not to stay up for a twenty-four- or forty-eight-hour marathon reading session. . . . The first serious contender of the twenty-first century worthy of sitting alongside apocalyptic/post-apocalyptic fiction classics. . . . Cronin nails the ending. . . . Many people

feel this will be the 'it' book of the summer; there's little reason to disagree."
—*The Denver Post*

"An epic narrative . . . a story that's equal parts supernatural thriller and chronicle of survival . . . an enthralling narrative about the evolution of a new world."
—Minneapolis *Star Tribune*

"An epic . . . a character-driven apocalyptic road trip of a novel that takes us on a journey both physical and metaphysical. His writing transcends genre in every way. . . . Cronin has given his readers a feast here and they'll need time to digest it before he delivers the next course."
—California Literary Review

"*The Passage* is indeed all that. . . . Cronin gets it just right; the combination of attentive realism and doomsday stakes makes for a mesmerizing experience."
—Salon

"The first installment of Cronin's post-apocalyptic trilogy has the advantage of a whole lot of story and a handful of well-drawn characters. . . . Cronin's clean, elegant writing will lure the literati."
—*Houston Chronicle*

"In this staggering book of speculative fiction, Cronin has proven that he can transcend genre and, with his power of language, create a distant world that feels close and credible. . . . Cronin's sense of place; of time; of timelessness; and his magnificent explorations of memories; of memories folded and unfolded and twisted in time; and of the self and the Shadow self are examples of his bridges from genre to literature."
—MostlyFiction Book Reviews

"A wild, headlong, sweeping extravaganza of a novel . . . a bona fide thriller that is sharply written, deeply humane, ablaze with big ideas, and absolutely impossible to put down."
—JENNIFER EGAN, author of *The Keep*

"Addictive, terrifying, and deeply satisfying . . . Not only is this one of the year's best thrillers; it's one of the best of the past decade—maybe one of the best ever."
—*Men's Journal*

"A postapocalyptic epic . . . our summer escape!"
—*Elle*

"Imagine Michael Crichton crossbreeding Stephen King's *The Stand* and *Salem's Lot* in that lab on *Jurassic Park,* with rich infusions of Robert McCammon's *Swan Song, Battlestar Galactica* and even Cormac McCarthy's *The Road.*"
—*The Washington Post*

"*The Passage* is a real manly man's monster novel, a call back to the good old days of *Jaws* and *The Andromeda Strain.*"
—The *Daily Beast*

"The monsters in this compulsive nail biter are the scariest in fiction since Stephen King's vampires in *Salem's Lot.* . . . Cronin is a master at building tension, and he never wastes words. Shout it from the hills! This exceptional thriller should be one of the most popular novels this year and will draw in readers everywhere."
—*Library Journal* (starred review)

"Not only is *The Passage* compulsive reading, but it's carried off with more literary flair . . . than King's best. . . . The kind of novel that keeps you flipping pages without ever looking to see what page you're on."
—Boulder *Daily Camera*

"Fans of vampire fiction who are bored by the endless hordes of sensitive, misunderstood Byronesque bloodsuckers will revel in Cronin's engrossingly horrific account of a post-apocalyptic America overrun by the gruesome reality behind the wish-fulfillment fantasies. . . . Manages to engage the reader with a sweeping epic style."
—*Publishers Weekly* (starred review and pick of the week)

"A creation story for this millennium, a heroic tale filled with battles between good and evil and struggles with the supernatural . . . What is *The Passage*? It's speculative fiction at its finest."

—*Milwaukee Journal Sentinel*

"A smart, addictively page-turning blockbuster . . . a novel with heart and intelligence . . . one of the best books I've read in 2010."

—SFFWorld

"Intricate and complex but seamless plotting . . . There is adventure, apocalyptic vistas, small moments of humor, battle, death, love requited and un-, heroism, pain, terror, and surprise."

—*The Buffalo News*

"A riveting tale."

—Fredericksburg *Free Lance–Star*

"This book could eat up your whole summer."

—*Lincoln Journal Star*

"I dare you to crack open *The Passage* and read page one. . . . Suspenseful and surprising."

—*BookPage*

"Cronin has imagined a frighteningly believable future. . . . Cronin's psychological insight and detailed writing style make these characters far fuller than genre fiction needs them to be. . . . *The Passage* is the perfect summer read, the kind that obliterates life outside its pages."

—Bloomberg

"One of the better instances of someone taking the time to do popcorn fiction right . . . Cronin never does the expected. . . . The writing quality is really what makes the novel worth reading."

—The Onion A.V. Club

"If you are looking for a compelling and colossal beach read, *The Passage* will not disappoint."
—*Bucks Local News*

"The type of big, engrossing read that will have you leaving the lights on late into the night."
—*The Dallas Morning News*

"A plot that grabs readers by the scruff of the neck and holds them until the very last page, this brilliantly written novel is destined to create much-deserved buzz and even more new readers for this extraordinary writer."
—*Tucson Citizen*

"Impossible-to-put-down."
—*Philadelphia Weekly Press*

"*The Passage* has a blend of Tolkien, Cormac McCarthy and Stephen King's *The Stand*. . . . Cronin is just a superb storyteller."
—*The Madison County Herald*

"A sprawling work of suspense."
—Bookslut

"If you read one book this year, Justin Cronin's *The Passage* should be it. . . . A thriller, an adventure, a horror story. . . . *The Passage* could very well be the best book this year."
—*Las Vegas Review-Journal*

"If you're looking for a gripping and totally absorbing summer read, then pick up *The Passage*. Just be sure to clear your calendar for a few days so you won't be interrupted. Oh, and don't expect to sleep well."
—*Glens Falls Post-Star*

ALSO BY JUSTIN CRONIN

The Summer Guest
Mary and O'Neil

IN *THE PASSAGE* TRILOGY

The Passage

Books published by The Random House Publishing Group are
available at quantity discounts on bulk purchases for premium,
educational, fund-raising, and special sales use. For details,
please call 1-800-733-3000.

THE TWELVE

THE TWELVE

A NOVEL

JUSTIN CRONIN

BALLANTINE BOOKS
NEW YORK

The Twelve is a work of fiction. Names, characters, places, and incidents are products of the author's imagination or are used fictitiously. Any resemblance to actual events, locales, or persons, living or dead, is entirely coincidental.

2013 Ballantine Books International Edition

Copyright © 2012 by Justin Cronin

All rights reserved.

Published by Ballantine Books, an imprint of The Random House Publishing Group, a division of Random House, Inc., New York.

BALLANTINE and colophon are registered trademarks of Random House, Inc.

Originally published in hardcover in the United States by Ballantine Books, an imprint of The Random House Publishing Group, a division of Random House, Inc.

Grateful acknowledgment is made to the following for permission to reprint previously published material:

Alfred A. Knopf, a division of Random House, Inc.: "In the Afterlife" from *Almost Invisible* by Mark Strand, copyright © 2012 by Mark Strand. Reprinted by permission of Alfred A. Knopf, a division of Random House, Inc.

ISBN 978-0-553-84074-2
eBook ISBN 978-0-345-53489-7

Cover design: Belina Huey
Cover illustration: Tom Hallman

Printed in the United States of America

www.ballantinebooks.com

9 8 7 6 5 4 3 2 1

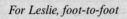
For Leslie, foot-to-foot

She stood beside me for years, or was it a moment? I cannot remember. Maybe I loved her, maybe I didn't. There was a house, and then no house. There were trees, but none remain. When no one remembers, what is there? You, whose moments are gone, who drift like smoke in the afterlife, tell me something, tell me anything.

—MARK STRAND, "IN THE AFTERLIFE"

CONTENTS

PROLOGUE

From the Writings of the First Recorder ("The Book of Twelves")
Presented at the Third Global Conference on the North American Quarantine Period
Center for the Study of Human Cultures and Conflicts
University of New South Wales, Indo-Australian Republic
April 16–21, 1003 A.V.

[Excerpt begins.]

CHAPTER ONE

1. For it came to pass that the world had grown wicked, and men had taken war into their hearts, and committed great defilements upon every living thing, so that the world was as a dream of death;

2. And God looked upon his creation with a great sadness, for his spirit no longer abided with mankind.

3. And the LORD said: As in the days of Noah, a great deluge shall sweep over the earth; and this shall be a deluge of blood. The monsters of men's hearts shall be made flesh, devouring all in their path. And they shall be called Virals.

4. The first shall walk among you disguised as a virtuous man, concealing the evil within him; and it shall come to pass that a sickness will befall him, such that he is made into the likeness of a demon, terrible to gaze upon. And he shall be the father of destruction, called the Zero.

5. And men shall say: Would not such a being make the mightiest of soldiers? Would not the armies of our enemies lay down their weapons to cover their eyes at the very sight of him?

6. And a decree shall go forth from the highest offices that twelve criminals shall be chosen to share of the Zero's blood, becoming demons also; and their names shall

be as one name, Babcock-Morrison-Chávez-Baffes-Turrell-Winston-Sosa-Echols-Lambright-Martínez-Reinhardt-Carter, called the Twelve.

7. But also I will choose one among you who is pure of heart and mind, a child to stand against them; and I will send a sign so that all may know, and this sign shall be a great commotion of animals.

8. And this was Amy, whose name is Love: Amy of Souls, the Girl from Nowhere.

9. And the sign went forth in the place of Memphis, the beasts howling and screeching and trumpeting; and one who saw was Lacey, a sister in the eyes of God. And the LORD said to Lacey:

10. You too are chosen, to be as a helpmate to Amy, to show her the way. Wither she goes you shall go also; and your journey shall be a hardship, lasting many generations.

11. You shall be as a mother to the child, whom I have brought forth to heal the broken world; for within her I shall build an ark to carry the spirits of the righteous.

12. And thus did Lacey according to all that God commanded her, so did she.

CHAPTER TWO

1. And it came to pass that Amy was taken to the place of Colorado to be the captive of evil men; for in that place the Zero and the Twelve abided in chains, and Amy's captors intended that she should become one of them, joining to them in mind.

2. And there she was given the blood of the Zero, and fell into a swoon as unto death; but neither did she die, nor acquire monstrous form. For it was not the design of God that such a thing should come to pass.

3. And in this state Amy lingered through a period of days, until a great calamity occurred, such that there should be a Time Before and a Time After; for the Twelve escaped and the Zero also, unleashing death upon the earth.

4. But one man befriended Amy, and took pity upon her, and stole her away from that place. And this was Wolgast, a man righteous in his generation, beloved of God.

5. And together Amy and Wolgast made their way to the

place of Oregon, deep in the mountains; and there they abided in the time known as the Year of Zero.

6. For in that time the Twelve beset the face of the world with their great hunger, killing every kind; and those they did not feed upon were taken up, joining to them in mind. And in this manner the Twelve were multiplied one million–fold to form the Twelve Viral Tribes, each with his Many, who roamed the earth without name or memory, laying waste to every living thing.

7. Thus did the seasons pass; and Wolgast became as a father to Amy, who had none, nor he a child of his own; and likewise did he love her, and she him.

8. And also did he see that Amy was not as he was, nor like any living person upon the earth; for neither did she age, nor suffer pain, nor seek nourishment or rest. And he feared what would become of her, when he himself was gone.

9. And it came to pass that a man came to them from the place of Seattle; and Wolgast did slay him, lest the man should become a demon in their midst. For the world had become a place of monsters, none living but they.

10. And in this manner they remained as father and daughter, each attending to the other, until a night when a blinding light filled the sky, too bright to gaze upon; and in the morning the air was foul with a rank odor, and ashes descended upon every surface.

11. For the light was the light of death, causing Wolgast to fall ill with a lethal sickness. And Amy was left to wander the ravaged earth alone, with none but the Virals for company.

12. And in this manner time passed, four score and twelve years in sum.

CHAPTER THREE

1. So it was that in the ninety-eighth year of her life in the place of California Amy came upon a city; and this was The First Colony, four score and ten souls abiding within its walls, the descendants of children who had made their way from the place of Philadelphia in the Time Before.

2. But at the sight of Amy the people became frightened, for they knew nothing of the world, and many words were spoken against her, and she was imprisoned; and

much confusion occurred, such that she was forced to flee in the company of others.

3. And these were Peter, Alicia, Sara, Michael, Hollis, Theo, Mausami, and Hightop, eight in sum; and each had a cause of righteousness in his heart, and desired that they should see the world outside the city where they dwelled.

4. And among them Peter was first in name, and Alicia second, and Sara third, and Michael fourth; and likewise were the others blessed in the eyes of God.

5. And together they left that place under cover of dark to find the secret of the world's undoing, in the place of Colorado, a journey of one-half year in the wilderness, enduring many tribulations; and the greatest of these was The Haven.

6. For in the place of Las Vegas they were taken as captives to stand before Babcock, First of Twelve; for the dwellers of that city were as slaves to Babcock and his Many, and would sacrifice two of their number for each new moon, so that they might live.

7. And Amy and the others were cast into the place of sacrifice, and did battle with Babcock, who was terrible to behold; and many lives were lost. And together they fled from that place, lest they too should die.

8. And one among them fell, who was the boy, Hightop; and Amy and her fellows buried him, marking it as a place of remembrance.

9. And a great grief was upon them, for Hightop was the most beloved of their number; but tarry could they not, for Babcock and his Many did pursue them.

10. And after more time had passed Amy and her fellows came upon a house, untouched by time; for God had blessed it, making it hallowed ground. And this was known as the Farmstead. And there they rested in safety, seven days in sum.

11. But two among them chose to stay in that place, for the woman was with child. And that child was to be born Caleb, who was beloved of God.

12. Thus the others continued while two remained behind.

CHAPTER FOUR

1. And it came to pass that Amy and her fellows made their way through the days and nights to the place of

Colorado, where they came into the company of soldiers, five score in sum. And these were known as the Expeditionary, from the place of Texas.

2. For Texas was in that time a place of refuge upon the earth; and the soldiers had traveled abroad to fight the Virals, each taking a pledge to die for his fellows.

3. And one among them chose to join their ranks, becoming a soldier of the Expeditionary; and this was Alicia, who was to be called Alicia of Blades. And one of the soldiers elected to join with them in turn; and this was Lucius the Faithful.

4. And there they would have tarried, but winter was upon them; and though four of their number desired to travel with the soldiers to the place of Texas, Amy and Peter chose to press on alone.

5. And it came to pass that the pair arrived at the place of Amy's making, and there atop the highest peak they beheld an angel of the LORD. And the angel said to Amy:

6. Fear not, for I am the same Lacey whom you remember. Here have I waited through the generations to show you the way, and to show Peter also; for he is the Man of Days, chosen to stand with you.

7. For as in the time of Noah, God in his design has provided a great ship to cross the waters of destruction; and Amy is that ship. And Peter shall be the one to lead his fellows to a place of dry land.

8. Therefore will the LORD make whole what is broken, and bring comfort to the spirits of the righteous. And this shall be known as The Passage.

9. And the angel Lacey summoned Babcock, First of Twelve, from out of the darkness; and a great battle was joined. And with a burst of light did Lacey slay him, casting her spirit to the LORD.

10. And thus were Babcock's Many set free of him; and likewise did they remember the people they had been in the Time Before: man and woman, husband and wife, parent and child.

11. And Amy moved among them, blessing each in turn; for it was the design of God that she should be the vessel to carry their souls through the long night of their forgetting. And thereupon their spirits departed the earth, and they died.

12. And in this manner, Amy and her fellows learned what lay before them; though the way of their journey was steep, and only just beginning.

I

THE GHOST

SUMMER, 97 A.V.

FIVE YEARS AFTER THE FALL OF FIRST COLONY

Remember me when I am gone away,
Gone far away into the silent land.

—CHRISTINA ROSSETTI,
"REMEMBER"

I

ORPHANAGE OF THE ORDER OF THE SISTERS, KERRVILLE, TEXAS

Later, after supper and evening prayer, and bath if it was bath night, and then the final negotiations to conclude the day (*Please, Sister, can't we stay up a little longer? Please, one more story?*), when the children had fallen asleep at last and everything was very still, Amy watched them. There was no rule against this; the sisters had all grown accustomed to her nighttime wanderings. Like an apparition she moved from quiet room to quiet room, sidling up and down the rows of beds where the children lay, their sleeping faces and bodies in trusting repose. The oldest were thirteen, poised at the edge of adulthood, the youngest just babies. Each came with a story, always sad. Many were thirdlings left at the orphanage by parents unable to pay the tax, others the victim of even crueler circumstances: mothers dead in childbirth, or else unwed and unable to bear the shame; fathers disappeared into the dark undercurrents of the city or taken outside the wall. The children's origins varied, yet their fates would be the same. The girls would enter the Order, giving their days to prayer and contemplation and caring for the children they themselves had been, while the boys would become soldiers, members of the Expeditionary, taking an oath of a different but no less binding nature.

Yet in their dreams they were children—still children, Amy thought. Her own childhood was the most distant of memories, an abstraction of history, and yet as she watched the sleeping children, dreams playfully flicking across their slumbering eyes, she felt closer to it—a time when she herself was just a small being in the world, innocent of what lay ahead, the too-long journey of her life. Time was a vastness inside her, too many years to know one from the other. So perhaps that was why she wandered among them: she did it to remember.

It was Caleb whose bed she saved for last, because he would be waiting for her. Baby Caleb, though he was not a baby anymore but a boy of five, taut and energetic as all children were, full of surprise and humor and startling truth. From his mother he had taken the high, sculpted cheekbones and olive-hued complexion of her clan; from his father the unyielding gaze and dark wonderings and coarse black cap, shorn close, that in the familial parlance of the Colony had been known as "Jaxon hair." A physical amalgamation, like a puzzle assembled from the pieces of his tribe. In his eyes Amy saw them. He was Mausami; he was Theo; he was only himself.

"Tell me about them."

Always, each night, the same ritual. It was as if the boy could not sleep without revisiting a past he had no memory of. Amy took her customary position on the edge of his cot. Beneath the blankets the shape of his lean, little-boy's body was barely a presence; around them, twenty sleeping children, a chorus of silence.

"Well," she began. "Let's see. Your mother was very beautiful."

"A warrior."

"Yes," Amy replied with a smile, "a beautiful warrior. With long black hair worn in a warrior's braid."

"So she could use her bow."

"Correct. But most of all she was headstrong. Do you know what that means, to be headstrong? I've told you before."

"Stubborn?"

"Yes. But in a good way. If I tell you to wash your hands before dinner, and you refuse to do it, that is not so good. That is the wrong kind of stubborn. What I'm saying is that your mother always did what she believed was right."

"Which is why she had me." He focused on the words. "Because it was . . . the right thing to bring a light into the world."

"Good. You remember. Always remember you are a bright light, Caleb."

A warm happiness had come into the boy's face. "Tell me about Theo now. My father."

"Your father?"

"Pleeease."

She laughed. "All right, then. Your father. First of all, he was very brave. A brave man. He loved your mother very much."

"But sad."

"True, he was sad. But that was what made him so brave,

you see. Because he did the bravest thing of all. You know what that is?"

"To have hope."

"Yes. To have hope when there seems to be none. You must always remember that, too." She leaned down and kissed his forehead, moist with childlike heat. "Now, it's late. Time for sleep. Tomorrow is another day."

"Did they . . . love me?"

Amy was taken aback. Not by the question itself—he had asked this on numerous occasions, seeking assurance—but by his uncertain tone.

"Of course, Caleb. I have told you many times. They loved you very much. They love you still."

"Because they're in heaven."

"That's right."

"Where all of us are together, forever. The place the soul goes." He glanced away. Then: "They say you're very old."

"Who says so, Caleb?"

"I don't know." Wrapped in his cocoon of blankets, he gave a tiny shrug. "Everyone. The other sisters. I heard them talking."

It was not a matter that had come up before. As far as Amy was aware, only Sister Peg knew the story.

"Well," she said, gathering herself, "I'm older than you, I know that much. Old enough to tell you it's time for sleep."

"I see them sometimes."

The remark caught her short. "Caleb? How do you see them?"

But the boy wasn't looking at her; his gaze had turned inward. "At night. When I'm sleeping."

"When you're dreaming, you mean."

The boy had no answer for this. She touched his arm through the blankets. "It's all right, Caleb. You can tell me when you're ready."

"It's not the same. It's not like a dream." He returned his eyes to hers. "I see you too, Amy."

"Me?"

"You're different, though. Not how you are now."

She waited for him to say more but there was nothing. Different how?

"I miss them," the boy said.

She nodded, content for the moment to let the matter pass. "I know you do. And you will see them again. But for now you have me. You have your uncle Peter. He'll be coming home soon, you know."

"With the . . . Expe-dishunary." A look of determination glowed in the boy's face. "When I grow up, I want to be a soldier like Uncle Peter."

Amy kissed his brow again, rising to go. "If that's what you want to be, then that is what you'll be. Now, sleep."

"Amy?"

"Yes, Caleb?"

"Did anyone love you like that?"

Standing at the boy's bedside, she felt the memories wash over her. Of a spring night, and a wheeling carousel, and a taste of powdered sugar; of a lake and a cabin in the woods and the feel of a big hand holding her own. Tears rose to her throat.

"I believe that they did. I hope they did."

"Does Uncle Peter?"

She frowned, startled. "What makes you ask that, Caleb?"

"I don't know." Another shrug, faintly embarrassed. "The way he looks at you. He's always smiling."

"Well." She did her best to show nothing. Was it nothing? "I think he is smiling because he's happy to see you. Now, sleep. Do you promise?"

He groaned with his eyes. "I promise."

Outside, the lights were pouring down: not a brightness as total as the Colony's—Kerrville was much too big for that— but, rather, a kind of lingering dusk, lit at the edges with a crown of stars above. Amy crept from the courtyard, keeping to the shadows. At the base of the wall she located the ladder. She made no effort to conceal her ascent; at the top she was met by the sentry, a broad-chested man of middle years with a rifle held across his chest.

"What do you think you're doing?"

But that was all he said. As sleep took him, Amy eased his body to the catwalk, propping him against the rampart with his rifle across his lap. When he awoke he would possess only a fragmented, hallucinatory memory of her. A girl? One of the sisters, wearing the rough gray tunic of the Order? Perhaps he would not awaken on his own but would be found by one of his fellows and hauled away for sleeping at his post. A few days in the stockade but nothing serious, and in any event, no one would believe him.

She made her way down the catwalk to the empty observation platform. The patrols moved through every ten minutes; that was all she had. The lights spilled their beams onto the ground below like a shining liquid. Closing her eyes, Amy cleared her mind and directed her thoughts outward, sending them soaring over the field.

—Come to me.

—Come to me come to me come to me.

They came, gliding from the blackness. First one and then another and another, forming a glowing phalanx where they crouched at the edge of the shadows. And in her mind she heard the voices, always the voices, the voices and the question:

Who am I?

She waited.

Who am I who am I who am I?

How Amy missed him. Wolgast, the one who had loved her. Where are you? she thought, her heart aching with loneliness, for night after night, as this new thing had begun happening inside her, she had felt his absence keenly. Why have you left me alone? But Wolgast was nowhere, not in the wind or the sky or the sound of the earth's slow turning. The man he was, was gone.

Who am I who am I who am I who am I who am I who am I?

She waited as long as she dared. The minutes ticked away. Then, footsteps on the catwalk, coming closer: the sentry.

—You are me, she told them. You are me. Now go.

They scattered into the darkness.

2

SEVENTY-SIX MILES SOUTH OF ROSWELL, NEW MEXICO

On a warm September evening, many miles and weeks from home, Lieutenant Alicia Donadio—Alicia of Blades, the New Thing, adopted daughter of the great Niles Coffee and scout sniper of the Second Expeditionary Forces of the Army of the Republic of Texas, baptized and sworn—awakened to the taste of blood on the wind.

She was twenty-seven years old, five foot seven, solidly built in the shoulders and hips, red hair shorn close to her scalp. Her eyes, which had once been only blue, glowed with an orange hue, like twin coals. She traveled lightly, nothing wasted. Feet shod in sandals of cut canvas with treads of vulcanized rubber; denim trousers worn thin at the knees and seat; a cotton jersey with the sleeves cut away for speed. Crisscrossing her upper body she wore a pair of leather bandoliers with six steel blades ensheathed, her trademark; at her back, slung on a lanyard of sturdy hemp, her crossbow. A Browning .45 semiautomatic with a nine-shot magazine, her weapon of last resort, was holstered to her thigh.

Eight and one, was the saying. Eight for the virals, one for yourself. Eight and one and done.

The town was called Carlsbad. The years had done their work, sweeping it clean like a giant broom. But still some structures remained: empty husks of houses, rusted sheds, the becalmed and ruined evidence of time's passage. She had spent the day resting in the shade of a filling station whose metal awning somehow still stood, awakening at dusk to hunt. She took the jack on her cross, one shot through the throat, then skinned it and roasted it over a fire of mesquite, picking the stringy flesh from its haunches as the fire crackled beneath it.

She was in no hurry.

She was a woman of rules, rituals. She would not kill the virals while they slept. She would not use a gun if she could help it; guns were loud and sloppy and unworthy of the task. She took them on the blade, swiftly, or on the cross, cleanly and without regret, and always with a blessing of mercy in her heart. She said: "I send you home, my brothers and sisters, I release you from the prison of your existence." And when the killing was done, and she had withdrawn her weapon from its lethal home, she touched the handle of her blade first to her brow and then her chest, the head and heart, consecrating the creatures' deliverance with the hope that, when that day should come, her courage would not fail her and she herself would be delivered.

She waited for night to fall, doused the flames of her fire, and set out.

For days she had been following a broad plain of lowland scrub. To the south and west rose the shadowed shape of mountains, shoulders shrugging from the valley floor. If Alicia had ever seen the sea, she might have thought: That's what this place is, the sea. The floor of a great, inland ocean, and the mountains, cave-pocked, time-stilled, the remains of a giant reef from a time when monsters unimaginable had roamed the earth and waves.

Where are you tonight? she thought. *Where are you hiding, my brothers and sisters of blood?*

She was a woman of three lives, two befores and one after. In the first before, she had been just a little girl. The world was all lurching figures and flashing lights, it moved through her like a breeze in her hair, telling her nothing. She was eight years old the night the Colonel had taken her outside the walls of the Colony and left her with nothing, not even a blade. She'd sat under a tree and cried all night, and when the morning sun found her, she was different, changed; the girl she'd been was no more. Do you see? the Colonel asked her, kneeling before her where she sat in the dust. He would not hold her for comfort but faced her squarely, like a soldier. Do you understand now? And she did; she understood. Her life, the meager accident of her existence, meant nothing; she had given it up. She had taken the oath that day.

But that was long ago. She had been a child, then a woman, then: what? The third Alicia, the New Thing, neither viral nor human but somehow both. An amalgamation, a composite, a being apart. She traveled among the virals like an unseen spirit, part of them but also not, a ghost to their ghosts. In her veins was the virus, but balanced by a second, taken from Amy, the Girl from Nowhere; from one of twelve vials from the lab in Colorado, the others destroyed by Amy herself, cast into the flames. Amy's blood had saved her life, yet in a way it hadn't. Making her, Lieutenant Alicia Donadio, scout sniper of the Expeditionary, the only being like herself in all the living world.

There were times, many times, all the time, when Alicia herself could not have said precisely what she was.

She came upon a shed. A pockmarked and pitted thing, half-buried in the sand, with a sloping metal roof.

She . . . *felt* something.

Which was strange, nothing that had happened before. The virus had not given her that power, which was Amy's alone. Alicia was yang to Amy's yin, endowed with the physical strength and speed of the virals but disconnected from the invisible web that bound them together, thought to thought.

And yet, did she not? Feel something? Feel *them*? A tingling at the base of her skull, and in her mind a quiet rustling, faintly audible as words:

Who am I? Who am I who am I who am I who am I . . . ?

There were three. They had all been women, once. And even more: Alicia sensed—how was it possible?—that in each one lay a single kernel of memory. A hand shutting a window and the sound of rain. A brightly colored bird singing in a cage. A view from a doorway of a darkened room and two small children, a boy and a girl, asleep in their beds. Alicia received each of these visions as if it were her own, its sights and sounds and smells and emotions, a mélange of pure existence like three tiny fires flaring inside her. For a moment she was held captive to them, in mute awe of them, these memories of a lost world. The world of the Time Before.

But something else. Wrapping each of these memories was a shroud of darkness, vast and pitiless. It made Alicia shudder to the very core. Alicia wondered what this was, but then she knew: the dream of the one called Martínez. Julio Martínez of El Paso, Texas, Tenth of Twelve, sentenced to death for the murder of a peace officer. The one Alicia had come to find.

In Martínez's dream, he was forever raping a woman named Louise—the name was written in a curling script on the pocket of the woman's blouse—while simultaneously strangling her with an electric cord.

The door of the shed was hanging kitty-corner on its rusted hinges. Tight quarters: Alicia would have preferred more room, especially with three. She crept forward, following the point of her cross, and eased into the shed.

Two of the virals were suspended upside down from the rafters, the third crouched in a corner, gnawing on a hunk of meat with a sucking sound. They had just fed on an antelope; the desiccated remains lay sundered on the floor, clumps of hair and bone and skin. In the dazed aftermath of feeding, the virals took no notice of her entry.

"Good evening, ladies."

She took the first one in the rafters with her cross. A thud and then a squeal, abruptly squelched, and its body crashed to the floor. The other two were rousing now; the second released its hold on the rafter, tucked its knees to its chest, and rolled in the midst of its descent to land on its clawed feet, facing away. Dropping the cross, Alicia drew a blade and in a single liquid motion sent it spinning into the third, which had risen to face her.

Two down, one to go.

It should have been easy. Suddenly it wasn't. As Alicia drew a second blade, the remaining viral turned and swatted her hand with a force that sent the weapon spiraling into the dark. Before the creature could deliver another blow, Alicia dropped to the floor and rolled away; when she rose, fresh blade in hand, the viral was gone.

Shit.

She snatched her cross from the floor, loaded a fresh bolt, and dashed outside. Where the hell was it? Two quick steps and Alicia launched herself to the roof of the shed, landing with a clang. Quickly she surveyed the landscape. Nothing, no sign.

Then the viral was behind her. A trap, Alicia realized; it must have been hiding, lying flush to the far side of the roof. Two things happened simultaneously. Alicia spun on her heels, aiming the cross instinctively; and with a sound of splintering wood and tearing metal, the roof gave way beneath her.

She landed face-up on the floor of the shed, the viral crashing on top of her. Her cross was gone. Alicia would have drawn a blade, but both of her hands were now occupied in the stalemated project of holding the viral at arm's length. Left and right and left again the creature darted its face, jaws snapping, toward the curve of Alicia's throat. An irresistible force meeting an immovable object: how long could this go on? The children in their beds, Alicia thought. That's who this one was. She was the woman looking through the doorway at her sleeping children. Think about the children, Alicia thought, and then she said it:

"Think about the children."

The viral froze. A wistful expression came into its face. For the thinnest instant—not more than half a second— their eyes met and held in the darkness. Mary, Alicia thought. Your name was Mary. Her hand was reaching for her blade. *I send you home, my sister Mary,* thought Alicia. *I release you from the prison of your existence.* And with an upward thrust she sank her blade, tip to hilt, into the sweet spot.

Alicia rolled the corpse away. The others lay where they had fallen. She collected her blade and bolt from the first two, wiped them clean, then knelt by the body of the last. In the aftermath Alicia usually felt nothing beyond a vague hollowness; it surprised her now to discover that her hands were shaking. How had she known? Because she had; with absolute clarity, she had known that the woman's name was Mary.

She pulled the blade free, touched it to her head and heart. *Thank you, Mary, for not killing me before my work is complete. I hope you are with your little ones now.*

Mary's eyes were open, gazing at nothing; Alicia closed them with her fingertips. It wouldn't do to leave her where she was. Alicia hoisted the body into her arms and carried it outside. A rind of moon had risen, washing the landscape in its glow, a darkness visible. But moonlight wasn't what Mary needed. A hundred years of nighttime sky were enough, Alicia thought, and laid the woman on a patch of open ground where, come morning, the sun would find her and cast her ashes to the wind.

Alicia had begun to climb.

A night and a day had passed. She was in the mountains now, ascending a dry creekbed through a slim defile. The feeling of the virals was stronger here: she was headed toward something. *Mary,* she thought, *what were you trying to tell me?*

It was nearly dawn by the time she reached the top of the ridge, the horizon jumping away. Below her, in the wind-scraped blackness, the valley floor unfurled, none but the stars for company. Alicia knew it was possible to parse discrete figures from their arbitrary-seeming arrangement, the shapes of people and animals, but she had never learned to do this. They appeared to her only as a random scattering, as if each night the stars were flung anew against the sky.

Then she saw it: a gaping maw of blackness, set in a bowl-like depression. The opening was a hundred feet tall or more. Curved benches, like an amphitheater, carved from the rocky face of the mountain, were situated at the cave's mouth. Bats were flicking through the sky.

It was a door to hell.

You're down there, aren't you? Alicia thought, and smiled. *You son of a bitch, I've found you.*

II

THE FAMILIAR

SPRING
YEAR ZERO

'Tis now the very witching time of night,
When churchyards yawn and hell itself breathes out
Contagion to this world.

—SHAKESPEARE,
HAMLET

Denver Police Dept.
Case File 193874
District 6
Transcript of Interview with Lila Beatrice Kyle
VIA: Det. Rita Chernow
3 May 4:17 A.M.

RC: Let the record show that the subject has been fully apprised of her rights and has declined to have an attorney present at this interview. Questioning conducted by Detective Rita Chernow, Denver PD, District Six. The time is four-seventeen A.M. Dr. Kyle, would you please state your full name?

LK: Lila Beatrice Kyle.

RC: And you're an orthopedic surgeon at Denver General Hospital, is that correct?

LK: Yes.

RC: And do you know why you're here?

LK: Something happened at the hospital. You wanted to ask me some questions. What is this room? I don't know it.

RC: We're in the police station, Dr. Kyle.

LK: Am I in trouble?

RC: We talked about this, remember? We're just trying to figure out what happened in the ER tonight. I know you're upset. I have just a few questions for you.

LK: There's blood on me. Why is there blood on me?

RC: Do you recall what happened in the ER, Dr. Kyle?

LK: I'm so tired. Why am I so tired?

RC: Can we get you something? Coffee maybe?

LK: I can't drink coffee. I'm pregnant.

RC: Water, then? How about some water?

LK: Okay.

(*Break.*)

RC: So let's start at the beginning. You were working in the emergency room tonight, is that correct?

LK: No, I was upstairs.

RC: But you came down to the ER?

LK: Yes.

RC: At what time?

LK: I'm not sure. Sometime around one A.M. They paged me.

RC: Why did they page you?

LK: I was the orthopedist on call. They had a patient with a broken wrist.

RC: And was that patient Mr. Letourneau?

LK: I think so, yes.

RC: What else did they tell you about him?

LK: Before I went downstairs, you mean?

RC: Yes.

LK: He had some kind of animal bite.

RC: Like a dog bite?

LK: I suppose so. They didn't say.

RC: Anything else?

LK: He had a high fever. He'd vomited.

RC: And that's all they told you?

LK: Yes.

RC: And what did you see when you got to the ER?

LK: He was in the third bed. There were only a couple of other patients. Sunday's usually quiet.

RC: What time would this be?

LK: One-fifteen, one-thirty.

RC: And did you examine Mr. Letourneau?

LK: No.

RC: Let me rephrase. Did you see the patient?

(*Pause.*)

RC: Dr. Kyle?

LK: I'm sorry, what was the question?

RC: Did you see Mr. Letourneau tonight in the ER?

LK: Yes. Mark was there, too.

RC: Are you referring to Dr. Mark Shin?

LK: He was the attending. Have you talked to him?

RC: Dr. Shin is dead, Dr. Kyle. He was one of the victims.

LK: (inaudible)

RC: Could you speak up, please?

LK: I just . . . I don't know. I'm sorry, what did you want to know?

RC: What can you tell me about Mr. Letourneau? How did he seem?

LK: Seem?

RC: Yes. Was he awake?

LK: He was awake.

RC: What else did you observe?

LK: He was disoriented. Agitated. His color was strange.

RC: How do you mean?

(*Pause.*)

LK: I have to go to the bathroom.

RC: Let's just get through some questions first. I know you're tired. I promise I'll get you out of here as quickly as I can.

LK: Do you have children, Detective Chernow?

RC: I'm sorry?

LK: Do you have any children? I was just curious.

RC: Yes, I have two boys.

LK: How old? If you don't mind my asking.

RC: Five and seven. I have just a few more things to ask you. Do you think you're up to that?

LK: But I bet you're trying for the girl, aren't you? Believe me, there's nothing like having a baby girl of your own.

RC: Let's focus on Mr. Letourneau for now, would that be okay? You said he was agitated. Can you elaborate on that?

LK: Elaborate?

RC: Yes. What did he do?

LK: He was making a funny noise.

RC: Can you describe it?

LK: A clicking sound, in his throat. He was moaning. He seemed to be in a great deal of pain.

RC: Had they given him anything for the pain?

LK: They'd given him Tramadol. I think it was Tramadol.

RC: Who else was there besides Dr. Shin?

(*Pause.*)

RC: Dr. Kyle? Who else was there when you examined Mr. Letourneau?

LK: One of the nurses. She was trying to calm him down. He was very upset.

RC: Anyone else?

LK: I don't remember. An orderly? No, two.

RC: What happened then?

LK: He started to seize.

RC: The patient had a seizure, you mean?

LK: Yes.

RC: What did you do then?

LK: Where's my husband?

RC: He's right outside. He came with you. Don't you remember?

LK: Brad is here?

RC: I'm sorry. Who's Brad?

LK: My husband. Brad Wolgast. He's with the FBI. Maybe you know him?

RC: Dr. Kyle, I'm confused. The man who came with you is named David Centre. He's not your husband?

(*Pause.*)

RC: Dr. Kyle? Do you understand what I'm asking you?

LK: Of course David is my husband. What a strange thing for you to say. Where did all this blood come from? Was I in an accident?

RC: No, Dr. Kyle. You were at the hospital. That's what we're talking about. Three hours ago, nine people were killed in the ER. We're trying to figure out how that happened.

(*Pause.*)

LK: It looked at me. Why did it just look at me?

RC: What looked at you, Dr. Kyle?

LK: It was horrible.

RC: What was?

LK: It killed the nurse first. There was so much blood. Like an ocean.

RC: Are you speaking of Mr. Letourneau? He killed the nurse? I need you to be clear.

LK: I'm thirsty. Can I have some more water?

RC: In a minute. How did Mr. Letourneau kill the nurse?

LK: It happened so fast. How could anybody move that fast?

RC: I need you to focus, Dr. Kyle. What did Mr. Letourneau use to kill the nurse? Was there a weapon?

LK: A weapon? I don't remember a weapon.

RC: How did he do it then?

(*Pause.*)

RC: Dr. Kyle?

LK: I couldn't move. It just . . . looked at me.

RC: Something looked at you? Was there somebody else in the room?

LK: He used his mouth. That was how he did it.

RC: Are you saying that Mr. Letourneau bit the nurse?

(*Pause.*)

LK: I'm expecting, you know. I'm going to have a baby.

RC: I can see that, Dr. Kyle. I know this is very stressful.

LK: I need to rest. I want to go home.

RC: We'll try to get you out of here as quickly as we can. Just to clarify, is it your statement that Mr. Letourneau bit the nurse?

LK: Is she all right?

RC: She was decapitated, Dr. Kyle. You were holding the body when we found you. Don't you remember?

LK: (inaudible)

RC: Can you speak up, please?

LK: I don't understand what you want. Why are you asking me these questions?

RC: Because you were there. You're our only witness. You saw nine people die tonight. They were ripped apart, Dr. Kyle.

LK: (inaudible)

RC: Dr. Kyle?

LK: Those eyes. It was like looking into hell. Like falling forever into darkness. Do you believe in hell, Detective?

RC: Whose eyes?

LK: It wasn't human. It couldn't have been human.

RC: Are you still speaking of Mr. Letourneau?

LK: I can't think about this. I have to think about the baby.

RC: What did you see? Tell me what you saw.

LK: I want to go home. I don't want to talk about this anymore. Don't make me.

RC: What killed those people, Dr. Kyle?

(*Pause.*)

RC: Dr. Kyle, are you all right?

(*Pause.*)

RC: Dr. Kyle?

(*Pause.*)

RC: Dr. Kyle?

4

Bernard Kittridge, known to the world as "Last Stand in Denver," realized it was time to leave the morning the power went out.

He wondered what had taken so long. You couldn't keep a municipal electrical grid running without people to man it, and as far as Kittridge could tell from the nineteenth floor, not a single human soul was left alive in the city of Denver.

Which was not to say he was alone.

He had passed the early hours of the morning—a bright, clear morning in the first week of June, temperatures in the mid-seventies with a chance of bloodsucking monsters moving in toward dusk—sunning on the balcony of the penthouse he had occupied since the second week of the crisis. It was a gigantic place, like an airborne palace; the kitchen alone was the size of Kittridge's whole apartment. The owner's taste ran in an austere direction: sleek leather seating groups that were better to look at than sit on, gleaming floors of twinkling travertine, small furry rugs, glass tables that appeared to float in space. Breaking in had been surprisingly simple. By the time Kittridge had made his decision, half the city was dead, or fled, or missing. The cops were long gone. He'd thought about barricading himself into one of the big houses up in Cherry Creek, but based on the things he'd seen, he wanted someplace high.

The owner of the penthouse was a man he knew slightly, a regular customer at the store. His name was Warren Filo. As luck would have it, Warren had come into the store the day before the whole thing had broken to gear up for a hunting trip to Alaska. He was a young guy, too young for how much money he had—Wall Street money, probably, or one of those high-tech IPOs. On that day, the world still cheerily humming along as usual, Kittridge had helped Warren carry his purchases to the car. A Ferrari, of course. Standing beside it, Kittridge thought: Why not just go ahead and get a vanity plate that says, DOUCHE BAG? A question that must have been plainly written on his face, because no sooner had it crossed Kittridge's mind than Warren went red with embarrassment. He wasn't wearing his usual suit, just jeans and a T-shirt with SLOAN SCHOOL OF MANAGEMENT printed on the front. He'd wanted Kittridge to see his car, that was obvious, but now that he'd allowed this to happen, he'd realized how dumb it was, showing off a vehicle like that to a floor manager at Outdoor World who probably made less than fifty grand a year. (The number was actually forty-six.) Kittridge allowed himself a silent laugh at that—the things this kid didn't know would fill a book—and he let the moment hang to make the point. *I know, I know,* Warren confessed. *It's a little much. I told myself I'd never be one of those assholes who drive a Ferrari. But honest to God, you should feel the way she handles.*

Kittridge had gotten Warren's address off his invoice. By the time he moved in—Warren presumably snug and safe in Alaska—it was simply a matter of finding the right key in the manager's office, putting it into the slot in the elevator panel, and riding eighteen floors to the penthouse. He unloaded his gear. A rolling suitcase of clothes, three lockers of weaponry, a hand-crank radio, night-vision binoculars, flares, a first-aid kit, bottles of bleach, an arc welder to seal the doors of the elevator, his trusty laptop with its portable satellite dish, a box of books, and enough food and water to last a month. The view from the balcony, which ran the length of the west side of the building, was a sweeping 180 degrees, looking toward Interstate 25 and Mile High field.

He'd positioned cameras equipped with motion detectors at each end of the balcony, one to cover the street, a second facing the building on the opposite side of the avenue. He figured he'd get a lot of good footage this way, but the money shots would be actual kills. The weapon he'd selected for this task was a Remington bolt-action 700P, .338 caliber—a nice balance of accuracy and stopping power, zeroing out at three hundred yards. To this he'd affixed a digital video scope with infrared. Using the binoculars, he would isolate his target; the rifle, mounted on a bipod at the edge of the balcony, would do the rest.

On the first night, windless and lit by a waning quarter moon, Kittridge had shot seven: five on the avenue, one on the opposite roof, and one more through the window of a bank at street level. It was the last one that made him famous. The creature, or vampire, or whatever it was—the official term was "Infected Person"—had looked straight into the lens just before Kittridge put one through the sweet spot. Uploaded to YouTube, the image had traveled around the globe within hours; by morning all the major networks had picked it up. Who is this man? everyone wanted to know. Who is this fearless-crazy-suicidal man, barricaded in a Denver high-rise, making his last stand?

And so was born the sobriquet, Last Stand in Denver.

From the start he'd assumed it was just a matter of time before somebody shut him down, CIA or NSA or Homeland. He was making quite a stir. Working in his favor was the fact that this same somebody would have to come to Denver to pull the plug. Kittridge's IP address was functionally untraceable, backstopped by a daisy chain of anonymizer servers, their order scrambled every night. Most were overseas: Russia, China, Indonesia, Israel, Sudan. Places beyond easy reach for any federal agency that might want to pull the plug. His video blog—two million hits the first day—had more than three hundred mirror sites, with more added all the time. It didn't take a week before he was a bona fide worldwide phenomenon. Twitter, Facebook, Headshot, Sphere: the images found their way into the ether without his lifting a finger. One of his fan sites alone had more than two million subscribers; on eBay, T-shirts that read, I AM LAST STAND IN DENVER were selling like hotcakes.

His father had always said, *Son, the most important thing in life is to make a contribution.* Who would have thought Kittridge's contribution would be video-blogging from the front lines of the apocalypse?

And yet the world went on. The sun still shone. To the west, the mountains shrugged their indifferent rocky bulk at man's departure. For a while, there had been a lot of smoke—whole blocks had burned to the ground—but now this had dissipated, revealing the desolation with eerie clarity. At night, regions of blackness blotted the city, but elsewhere, lights still glittered in the gloom—flickering streetlamps, filling stations and convenience stores with their distinctive fluorescent glow, porch lights left burning for their owners' return. While Kittridge maintained his vigil on the balcony, a traffic signal eighteen floors below still dutifully turned from green to yellow to red and then to green again.

He wasn't lonely. Loneliness had left him, long ago. He was thirty-four years old. A little heavier than he would have liked—with his leg, it was hard to keep the weight off—but still strong. He'd been married once, years before. He remembered that period of his life as twenty months of oversexed, connubial bliss, followed by an equal number of months of yelling and screaming, accusations and counteraccusations, until the whole thing sank like a rock, and he was content, on the whole, that this union had produced no children. His connection to Denver was neither sentimental nor personal; after he'd gotten out of the VA, it was simply where he'd landed. Everyone said that a decorated veteran should have little trouble finding work. And maybe this was true. But Kittridge had been in no hurry. He'd spent the better part of a year just reading—the usual stuff at first, cop novels and thrillers, but eventually had found his way to more substantial books: *As I Lay Dying, For Whom the Bell Tolls, Huckleberry Finn, The Great Gatsby.* He'd spent a whole month on Melville, drilling his way through *Moby-Dick.* Most were books he felt he ought to read, the ones he'd somehow missed in school, but he genuinely liked most of them. Sitting in the quiet of his studio apartment, his mind lost in tales of other lives and times, felt like taking a long drink after years of thirst. He'd even enrolled in a few classes at the community college, working at Outdoor World during the day, reading and writing his papers at night and on his lunch hour. There was something in the pages of these books that had the power to make him feel better about things, a life raft to cling to before the dark currents of memory washed him downstream again, and on brighter days, he could even see himself going on this way for some time. A small but passable life.

And then, of course, the end of the world had happened.

* * *

The morning the electricity failed, Kittridge had finished uploading the previous night's footage and was sitting on the patio, reading Dickens's *A Tale of Two Cities*—the English barrister Sydney Carton had just declared his everlasting love for Lucie Manette, the fiancée of the haplessly idealistic Charles Darnay—when the thought touched him that the morning could only be improved by a dish of ice cream. Warren's enormous kitchen—you could run a five-star restaurant out of the thing—had been, unsurprisingly, almost completely bereft of food, and Kittridge had long since thrown away the moldy take-out containers that had constituted the meager contents of the fridge. But the guy obviously had a weakness for Ben and Jerry's Chocolate Fudge Brownie, because the freezer was crammed with the stuff. Not Chunky Monkey or Cherry Garcia or Phish Food or even plain old vanilla. Just Chocolate Fudge Brownie. Kittridge would have liked some variety, considering there was going to be no more ice cream for a while, but with little else to eat besides canned soup and crackers, he was hardly going to complain. Balancing his book on the arm of his chair, he rose and stepped through the sliding glass door into the penthouse.

By the time he reached the kitchen, he had begun to sense that something was off-kilter, although this impression had yet to coalesce around anything specific. It wasn't until he opened the carton and sank his spoon into a soft mush of melted Chocolate Fudge Brownie that he fully understood.

He tried a light switch. Nothing. He moved through the apartment, testing lamps and switches. All were the same.

In the middle of the living room, Kittridge paused and took a deep breath. Okay, he thought, okay. This was to be expected. If anything, this was long overdue. He checked his watch: 9:32 A.M. Sunset was a little after eight. Ten and a half hours to get his ass gone.

He threw together a rucksack of supplies: protein bars, bottles of water, clean socks and underwear, his first-aid kit, a warm jacket, a bottle of Zyrtec (his allergies had been playing hell with him all spring), a toothbrush, and a razor. For a moment he considered bringing *A Tale of Two Cities* along, but this seemed impractical, and with a twinge of regret he put it aside. In the bedroom he dressed himself in a wicking T-shirt and cargo pants, topping this off with a hunting vest and a pair of light hikers. For a few minutes he considered which weapons to take before settling on a Bowie knife, a pair of Glock 19s, and the retrofitted Polish AK with the folding stock: useless at any kind of range but reliable close in, where he expected to be. The Glocks fit snugly in a cross-draw holster. He filled the pockets of his vest with loaded magazines, clipped the AK to its sling, hoisted the backpack over his shoulders, and returned to the patio.

That was when he noticed the traffic signal on the avenue. Green, yellow, red. Green, yellow, red. It could have been a fluke, but he doubted it.

They'd found him.

The rope was anchored to a drainage stack on the roof. He stepped into his rappelling harness, clipped in, and swung first his good leg and then his bad one over the railing. Heights were no problem for him, and yet he did not look down. He was perched on the edge of the balcony, facing the windows of the penthouse. From the distance he heard the sound of an approaching helicopter.

Last Stand in Denver, signing off.

With a push he was aloft, his body lobbing down and away. One story, two stories, three, the rope smoothly sliding through his hands: he landed on the balcony of the apartment four floors below. A familiar twang of pain shot upward from his left knee; he gritted his teeth to force it away. The helicopter was closing in now, the thrum of its blades volleying off the buildings. He peeled off his harness, drew one of the Glocks, and fired a single shot to shatter the glass of the balcony door.

The air of the apartment was stale, like the inside of a cabin sealed for winter. Heavy furniture, gilt mirrors, an oil painting of a horse over the fireplace; from somewhere wafted the stench of decay. He moved through the becalmed space with barely a glance. At the door he paused to attach a spotlight to the rail of the AK and stepped out into the hall, headed for the stairs.

In his pocket were the keys to the Ferrari, parked in the building's underground garage, sixteen floors below. Kittridge shouldered open the door of the stairwell, quickly sweeping the space with the beam from the AK, up and down. Clear. He withdrew a flare from his vest and used his teeth to unscrew the plastic top, exposing the igniter button. With a combustive pop, the flare commenced its rain of sparks. Kittridge held it over the side, taking aim, and let go; if there was anything down there, he'd know it soon. His eyes followed the flare as it made its descent, dragging a contrail of smoke. Somewhere below it nicked the rail and bounced out of sight. Kittridge counted to ten. Nothing, no movement at all.

Three flares later he reached the bottom; a heavy steel door with a push bar and a small square of reinforced glass led to the garage. The floor was littered with trash: pop cans, candy bar wrappers, tins of food. A rumpled bedroll and a pile of musty clothing showed where someone had been sleeping—hiding, as he had.

Kittridge had scouted out the parking garage the day of his arrival. The Ferrari was parked near the southwest corner, a distance of approximately two hundred feet. He probably should have moved it closer to the door, but it had taken him three days to locate Warren's keys—who kept his car keys in a bathroom drawer?—by which time he'd already barricaded himself inside the penthouse.

The fob had four buttons: two for the doors, one for the alarm, and one that, he hoped, was a remote starter. He pressed this one first.

From deep within the garage came a tart, single-noted bleep, followed by the throaty roar of the Ferrari's engine. Another mistake: the Ferrari was parked nose to the wall. He should have thought of that. Not only would this slow his escape; if the car had been facing the opposite way, its headlights would have given him a better look at the garage's interior. All he could make out through the stairwell door's tiny window was a distant, glowing region where the car awaited, a cat purring in the dark. The rest of the garage was veiled in blackness. The infected liked to hang from things: ceiling struts, pipes, anything with a tactile surface. The tiniest fissure would suffice. When they came, they came from above.

The moment of decision was upon him. Toss more flares and see what happens? Move stealthily through the darkness, seeking cover? Throw open the door and run like hell?

Then, from high overhead, Kittridge heard the creak of an opening stairwell door. He held his breath and listened. There were two of them. He stepped back from the door and craned his neck upward. Ten stories above, a pair of red dots were dancing off the walls.

He shoved the door open and ran like hell.

He had made it halfway to the Ferrari when the first viral dropped behind him. There was no time to turn and fire; Kittridge kept on going. The pain in his knee felt like a wick of flame, an ice pick buried to the bone. From the periphery of his senses came a tingling awareness of beings awakening, the garage coming to life. He threw open the door of the Ferrari, tossed the AK and rucksack onto the passenger seat, got in, and slammed the door. The vehicle was so low-slung he felt like he was sitting on the ground. The dashboard, full of mysterious gauges and switches, glowed like a spacecraft's. Something was missing. Where was the gearshift?

A *wang* of metal, and Kittridge's vision filled with the sight of it. The viral had bounded onto the hood, folding its body into a reptilian crouch. For a frozen moment it regarded him coolly, a predator contemplating its prey. It was naked except for a wristwatch, a gleaming Rolex thick as an ice cube. *Warren?* Kittridge thought, for the man had been wearing one like it the day Kittridge had walked him to the car. *Warren, old buddy, is that you? Because if it is, I wouldn't mind a word of advice on how to get this thing in gear.*

He discovered, then, with the tips of his fingers, a pair of levers positioned on the undersides of the steering wheel. Paddle shifters. He should have thought of that, too. Up on the right, down on the left, like a motorcycle. Reverse would be a button somewhere on the dash.

The one with the R, genius. That one.

He pushed the button and hit the gas. Too fast: with a squeal of smoking rubber, the Ferrari jolted backward and slammed into a concrete post. Kittridge was hurled back into his seat, then tossed forward again, his head smacking the heavy glass of the side window with an audible thud. His brain chimed like a tuning fork; particles of silver light danced in his eyes. There was something interesting about them, interesting and beautiful, but another voice inside him said that to contemplate this vision, even for a moment, was to die. The viral, having tumbled off the hood, was rising from the floor now. No doubt it would try to take him straight through the windshield.

Two red dots appeared on the viral's chest.

With a birdlike quickness, the creature broke its gaze from Kittridge and launched toward the soldiers coming through the stairwell door. Kittridge swung the steering wheel and gripped the right paddle, engaging the transmission as he pressed the accelerator. A lurch and then a leap of speed: he was thrust back into his seat as he heard a blast of automatic weapon fire. Just when he thought he'd lose control of the car again he found the straightaway, the walls of the garage streaming past. The soldiers had bought him only a moment; a quick glimpse in the rearview and Kittridge beheld, in the glow of his taillights, what appeared to be the detonation of a human body, an explosive strewing of parts. The second soldier was nowhere visible, though if Kittridge had to bet, he'd say the man was surely dead already, torn to bloody hunks.

He didn't look back again.

The ramp to the street was located two floors above, at the far end of the garage. As Kittridge downshifted into the first corner, engine roaring, tires shrieking, two more virals dropped from the ceiling, into his path. One fell under his wheels with a damp crunch, but the second leapt over the roof of the barreling Ferrari, striding it like a hurdler. Kittridge felt a stab of wonder, even of admiration. In school, he had learned that you couldn't catch a fly with your hand because time was different to a fly: in a fly's brain, a second was an hour, and an hour was a year. That's what the infected were like. Like beings outside of time.

They were everywhere now, emerging from all the hidden places. They flung themselves at the car like suicides, driven by the madness of their hunger. He tore through them, bodies flying, their monstrous, distorted faces colliding with the windshield before being hurled up and over, away. Two more turns and he'd be free, but one was clinging to the roof now. Kittridge braked around the corner, fishtailing on the slick cement, the force of his deceleration sending the viral rolling onto the hood. A woman: she appeared to be wearing, of all things, a wedding gown. Gouging her fingers into the gap at the base of the windshield, she drew herself onto all fours. Her mouth, a bear trap of blood-lined teeth, was open very wide; a tiny golden crucifix dangled at the base of her throat. *I'm sorry about your wedding,* Kittridge thought as he drew one of the pistols, steadied it over the steering wheel, and fired through the windshield.

He blasted around the final corner; ahead, a shaft of golden daylight showed the way. Kittridge hit the ramp doing seventy miles an hour, still accelerating. The exit was sealed by a metal grate, but this fact seemed meager, no obstacle at all. Kittridge took aim, plunged the pedal to the floor, and ducked.

A furious crash; for two full seconds, an eternity in miniature, the Ferrari went airborne. It rocketed into the sunshine, concussing the pavement with a bone-jarring bang, sparks flying from the undercarriage. Freedom at last, but now he had another problem: there was nothing to stop him. He was going to career into the lobby of the bank across the street. As Kittridge bounced across the median, he stamped the brake and swerved to the left, bracing for the impact. But there was no need; with a screech of smoking rubber, the tires bit and held, and the next thing Kittridge knew he was flying down the avenue, into the spring morning.

He had to admit it. What had Warren's exact words been? *You should feel the way she handles.*

It was true. Kittridge had never driven anything like it in his life.

5

For a time, a long time, which was no time at all, the man known as Lawrence Grey—former inmate of Beeville Men's Correctional Facility and registered sex offender of the Texas Department of Public Safety; civilian employee of Project NOAH and the Division of Special Weapons; Grey the Source, the Unleasher of Night, Familiar of the One Called Zero—was nowhere at all. He was nothing and no place, a being annihilated, possessing neither memory nor history, his consciousness dispersed across a shoreless sea of no dimension. A wide, dark sea of voices, murmuring his name. *Grey, Grey.* They were there and not there, calling to him as he floated alone, one with the darkness, adrift in an ocean of forever; and all above, the stars.

But not just the stars. For now had come a light—a soft, golden light that swelled above his face. Blades of shadow moved across it, gyring like a pinwheel, and with this light a sound: aortal, heartlike, a *thrum-thrum-thrum* that pulsed to the rhythm of its turning. Grey watched it, this wonderful, gyring light; and the thought crept into his consciousness that what he beheld was God. The light was God in his heaven above, moving over the waters, brushing the face of the world like the hem of a curtain, touching and blessing his creation. The knowledge blossomed inside Grey in a burst of sweetness. Such joy! Such understanding and forgiveness! The light was God and God was love; Grey had only to enter it, to go into the light, to feel that love forever. And a voice said:

It's time, Grey.

Come to me.

He felt himself rising, lifted up. He rose and as he rose the sky spread its wings, receiving him, carrying him into the light, which was almost too much to bear and then was: a brightness blinding and obliterating, like the sound of a scream that was his own.

Grey, ascending. Grey, reborn.

Open your eyes, Grey.

He did; he opened his eyes. His vision crawled into focus. A dark form was whirling unpleasantly above his face.

It was a ceiling fan.

He blinked the grime away. A bitter taste, like wet ashes, painted the walls of his mouth. The room where he lay possessed the unmistakable sense of a chain motel—the scratchy coverlet and cheap foam pillow, the cratered mattress below and popcorn ceiling above, the smell of recycled, overused air in his nostrils. His brain felt as empty as a leaky pail, his body a shapeless mass, vague as gelatin. Even to move his head seemed to require a feat of strength beyond his power. The room was lit with a sticky yellow daylight filtered through the drapes. Above his face, the fan spun and spun, rocking on its bracket, its worn-out bearings rhythmically creaking. The sight was as abrasive to his senses as smelling salts, and yet he could not look away. (And wasn't there something about a thrumming sound, something in a dream? A brilliant light, lifting him up? But he no longer recalled.)

"Good, you're awake."

Sitting on the edge of the second bed, eyes downcast, was a man. A small, soft man, filling out his jumpsuit like a sausage in its casing. One of the civilian employees of Project NOAH, known as sweeps: men like Grey whose job it was to clean up the piss and shit and back up the drives and watch the sticks for hours and hours, slowly going loony; sex offenders to a one, despised and forgotten, men without histories anyone cared to remember, their bodies softened by hormones, their minds and spirits as neutered as a spayed dog.

"I thought the fan would do it. Tell you the truth, I can't even look at the thing."

Grey tried to respond but couldn't. His tongue felt toasted, as if he'd smoked a billion cigarettes. His vision had gone all watery again; his goddamned head was splitting. It had been years since he'd drunk more than a couple of beers at a time—with the drugs, you were too sleepy and pretty much lost interest in everything—but Grey remembered what a hangover was. That's how this felt. Like the worst hangover in the world.

"What's the matter, Grey? Cat got your tongue?" The man

chuckled at some private joke. "That's funny, you know. Under the circumstances. I could go for a little cat tartare right now." He turned toward Grey, his eyebrows arcing. "Don't look so shocked. You'll see what I mean. Takes a few days but then it kicks in, real hard."

Grey remembered the man's name: Ignacio. Though the Ignacio that Grey remembered was older, more worn-down, with a heavy, creased brow and pores you could park a car in and jowls that sagged like a bassett hound's. This Ignacio was in the pink of health—literally *pink,* his cheeks rouged with color, skin baby smooth, eyes twinkling like zircs. Even his hair looked younger. But there was no mistaking who it was, on account of the tat—prison ink, blurred and bluish, a hooded snake rising up his neck from the open collar of his jumpsuit.

"Where am I?"

"You're a regular riot, you know that? We're at the Red Roof."

"The what?"

He made a little snort. "The fucking Red Roof, Grey. What did you think, they'd send us to the Ritz?"

They? Grey thought. Who were *they*? And what did Ignacio mean by "send"? Send for what purpose? Which was the moment Grey noticed that Ignacio was clutching something in his hand. A pistol?

"Iggy? What are you doing with that thing?"

Ignacio lazily raised the gun, a long-barreled .45, frowning at it. "Not much, apparently." He angled his head toward the door. "Those other guys were here for a while, too. But they're all gone now."

"What guys?"

"Come on, Grey. You know those guys. The skinny one, George. Eddie whatzisname. Jude, with the ponytail." He looked past Grey toward the curtains. "Tell you the truth, I never did like him. I heard about the stuff he did, not that I'm anyone to talk. But that man, he was flat-out disgusting."

Ignacio was talking about the other sweeps. What were they all doing here? What was *he* doing here? The gun wasn't a good sign, but Grey couldn't call up a single memory of how he'd come to be where he was. The last thing he recalled was eating dinner in the compound cafeteria: beef bourguignon in a rich gravy, with a side of scalloped potatoes and green beans and a Cherry Coke to wash it all down. It was his favorite meal; he always looked forward to beef bourguignon. Though as he thought about it, its greasy taste, his stomach clamped with nausea. A squirt of bile shot up his throat. He had to take a moment just to breathe.

Ignacio gave his pistol a halfhearted wave toward the door. "Look yourself if you want. But I'm pretty sure they're gone."

Grey swallowed. "Gone where?"

"That depends. Wherever they're supposed to go."

Grey felt totally at sea. He couldn't even figure out what questions to ask. He was pretty sure he wouldn't like the answers, though. Maybe the best thing was to lie quietly. He hoped he hadn't done something terrible, like in the old days. The days of the Old Grey.

"Well," Ignacio said, and cleared his throat, "as long as you're awake, I guess I better be moving on. I've got a long walk ahead of me." He rose and held out the gun. "Here."

Grey hesitated. "What do I want a gun for?"

"In case you feel like, you know, shooting yourself."

Grey was too stunned to reply. The last thing he wanted was a gun. Somebody found a gun on him, they'd send him back to prison for sure. When he made no move to accept the weapon, Ignacio placed it on the bedside table.

"Give it some thought, anyway. Just don't drag your feet like I did. It gets harder the longer you wait. Now look at the fix I'm in."

Ignacio moved to the door, where he turned to cast his gaze a final time around the room.

"We really did it. In case you were, you know, wondering." He took a long breath, blowing out the air with puffed cheeks, and angled his face toward the ceiling. "Funny thing is, I really don't see what I did to deserve this. I wasn't so bad, not really. I didn't mean to do half those things. It was just the way I was built." He looked at Grey again; his eyes were filmed with tears. "That's what the shrink always said. Ignacio, it's just the way you're built."

Grey had no idea what to say. Sometimes there was nothing, and he guessed this was one of those times. The look on Ignacio's face reminded him of some of the cons he'd known in Beeville, men who'd been inside so long they were like zombies in some old movie. Men with nothing but the past to dwell on and, ahead, an endless stretch of nothing.

"Well, fuck it." Ignacio sniffled and rubbed his nose with the back of his wrist. "No use complaining about it now. You make your bed you have to lie in it. Think about what I said, okay? Be seeing you, Grey." And with a wash of light from the open door, he was gone.

What to make of that? For a long time Grey lay still, his mind spinning like a bald tire on ice. Part of him wasn't sure if he was awake or still sleeping. He reviewed the facts to give his mind a point to fix on. He was on a bed. The bed was in a motel, a Red Roof. The motel was somewhere in Colorado, probably, assuming he hadn't gone far. The light in the windows said morning. He didn't appear to be injured. Sometime in the last twenty-four hours, maybe more and maybe less, but probably not more than a day, he'd blacked out.

He'd have to go from there.

He drew himself up on his elbows. The room reeked of sweat and smoke. His jumpsuit was stained and torn at the knees; his feet were bare. He gave his toes a wiggle, the joints cracking and popping. Everything seemed to be working.

And come to think of it, wasn't it true that he was feeling better? And not just better—a lot better. The headache and dizziness were gone. His vision had cleared. His limbs felt firm and strong, full of fresh, coiled energy. His mouth still tasted foul—finding a toothbrush or a pack of gum was job one—but other than that, Grey felt right as rain.

He swiveled his feet to the floor. The room was small, just space enough for the beds, with their brown-and-orange coverlets, and a little table with a television. But when he picked up the remote to turn it on, all he got was a blue screen with a sound like a dial tone. He flipped through the channels; the network affiliates, CNN, the War Channel, GOVTV—all were blued out. Well, didn't that just figure. He'd have to tell the manager about that. Though as far as he recalled he hadn't paid for the room, and his wallet had been confiscated months ago, when he'd first arrived at the compound.

The compound, Grey thought, the word dropping to his gut like a rock. Whatever else was true, he was in a heap of trouble. You didn't just up and leave. He remembered Jack and Sam, the two sweeps who'd gone AWOL, and how pissed off Richards had been. Who was not somebody you wanted to piss off, to put it mildly. Just a glance from the man made Grey's bowels twist.

Maybe that's why the sweeps had all run off. Maybe it was Richards they were afraid of.

His thirst hit him then—a mad, crazy thirst, like he hadn't had a drink in days. In the bathroom he jammed his face under the tap, gulping fiercely, letting the water stream over his face. Slow down, Grey, he thought, you're going to make yourself sick if you drink like this.

Too late; the water hit his stomach like a crashing wave, and the next thing he knew he was on his knees, clutching the sides of the toilet bowl, all the water coming up.

Well, that was dumb. He had no one to blame but himself. He stayed on his knees a moment, waiting for the cramping to pass, breathing in the stink of his own vomit—mostly water, but in the final instance a gooey, yolk-like glob, no doubt the undigested remnants of the beef bourguignon. He must have strained something, too, because his ears were ringing: a faint, nearly subaural whine, like the sound of a tiny motor whirring deep inside his skull.

He struggled to his feet and flushed the puke away. On the vanity he saw a little bottle of mouthwash in a tray with soaps and lotions, none of it touched, and he took a swig to clear the taste in his mouth, gargling long and hard and spitting into the sink. Then he looked at his face in the mirror.

Grey's first thought was that somebody was playing a joke on him: an elaborate, unfunny, improbable joke, in which the mirror had somehow been replaced by a window, and on the far side stood a man—a much younger, better-looking man. The urge to reach out and touch this image was so strong he actually did it, the man in the mirror perfectly mimicking his movements. What the fuck? Grey thought, and then he said it: "What the fuck?" The face he beheld was slim, clear-skinned, attractive. His hair brushed over his ears in a lush mane, its tone a rich chestnut. His eyes were clear and bright; they actually sparkled. Never in his life had Grey looked so good.

Something else drew his eye. Some sort of mark on his neck. He leaned forward, tilting his head upward. Two lines of symmetrical beadlike depressions, roughly circular in their arrangement, the top of the circle reaching to his jaw-line, the bottom skimming the curve of his collarbone. The wound had a pinkish color, as if only lately healed. When the hell had this happened? As a kid he'd been bitten by a dog once; that was what this looked like. A surly old mutt-dog from the pound, but still he'd loved it, it was something that was his, until the day he'd bitten Grey on the hand—no good reason for it; Grey had only meant to give him a biscuit—and his father had dragged him to the yard. Two shots, Grey recalled that clearly, the first followed by a yelping squeal, the second dimming the dog forever into silence.

The dog's name was Buster. Grey hadn't given him a thought in years.

But this thing on his neck. Where had it come from? There was something familiar about it—a feeling of déjà vu, as if the recollection had been stored in the wrong drawer in his mind.

Grey, don't you know?

Grey spun from the mirror.

"Iggy?"

Silence. He returned to the bedroom. He opened the closet, knelt to look beneath the beds. No one.

Grey. Grey.

"Iggy, where are you? Quit fucking with me."

Don't you remember, Grey?

Something was wrong with him, really wrong. It wasn't Iggy's voice he was hearing; the voice was in his *head.* Every surface that met his eyes seemed to throb with vividness. He rubbed his eyes, but it only got worse. It was as if he weren't just seeing things, but touching and smelling and tasting them too, as if the wires in his brain had crossed.

Don't you remember . . . dying?

And all at once he did; the memory pierced him like an arrow to the chest. The aquatic blue of the containment chamber, and the slowly opening door; Subject Zero rising above him, assuming his full and terrible dimensions; the feel of Zero's jaws on the curve of his neck and the clamp of boring teeth, picketed row upon row; Zero gone, leaving him alone, and the blare of the alarm and the sound of gunfire and the screams of dying men; his stumble into the hall, a vision of hell, blood everywhere, painting the walls and floor, and the grisly remains, a slaughterhouse of legs and arms and torsos with their roping entrails; the sticky, arterial spurt through his fingers where he held them to his throat; the air whooshing out of him, and his long slide to the floor, blackness enveloping him, his vision swimming; and then the letting go.

Oh God.

Come to me, Grey. Come to me.

He tore from the room, daylight blasting his eyes. It was crazy; he was crazy. Across the parking lot he ran like a great, lumbering animal, sightless and without direction, his hands clamped to his ears. A few cars dotted the lot, parked at haphazard angles, many with their doors standing open. But in its white-hot state, Grey's mind failed to register this fact, just as it failed to note other troubling details: the smashed front windows of the hotel; the highway on which not a single vehicle could be seen to move; the vacant filling station across the access road, its windows smeared with red, and the body of a man slumped against the pump in the manner of an impromptu siesta; the wrecked McDonald's, its chairs and tables and ketchup packets and Happy Meal toys and patrons of various ages and races hurled through the windows in violent disgorgement; the plume of chemical smoke from the still-burning wreckage of a tractor-trailer two miles away; the birds. Great wheeling clouds of large, black birds, crows and ravens and buzzards, the scavengers, idly spinning overhead. All of it suspended like the aftermath of a terrible battle, bathed with pitiless summer sunshine.

Do you see, Grey?

"Stop it! Shut up!"

He stumbled on something soft. Organically damp and squishy, under his feet. It sent him crashing to his hands and knees, skidding on the blacktop.

See the world that we have made.

He squeezed his eyes shut. He was heaving for breath. He knew without looking that the squishy thing was a body. *Please,* he thought, not sure whom or even what he was addressing. Himself. The voice in his head. God, whom he'd never quite believed in but was willing to believe in now. *I'm sorry for whatever I did. I'm sorry, I'm sorry, I'm sorry.*

By the time he finally looked, all hope had left him. The body was a woman. The flesh of her face was sucked so tightly to the bones it was hard to tell how old she was. She was dressed in sweatpants and a scoop-necked T-shirt with a little frill of pink lace at the neckline; Grey supposed she'd been in bed and had come out to see what was happening. She was splayed on the pavement, her back and shoulders twisted. Flies were buzzing over her, dipping in and out of her mouth and eyes. One arm lay outstretched on the pavement, palm up; the other was bent across her chest, the tips of her fingers touching the wound at her throat. Not a cut or gash, nothing as tidy as that. Her throat had been chomped away, down to the bone.

She was not the only one. Grey's vision widened, like a camera lifting over the scene. To his left, twenty feet away, a Chevy half-ton was parked with the driver's door open. A heavyset man in suit pants with suspenders had been pulled from his seat and now hung half in and half out of the truck, dangling head-down over the running board, though his head wasn't there; his head was somewhere else.

More bodies lay near the hotel entrance. Not bodies, strictly speaking—more like a zone of human parts. A woman police officer had been eviscerated as she'd stepped from her cruiser. She rested with her back propped against the fender, pistol still clutched in her hand, her chest opened like the flaps of a trench coat. A man in a shiny purple tracksuit, wearing enough gold around his neck to fill a pirate chest, had been hurled upward, his torso lodging like a kite in the limbs of a maple tree; his bottom half had come to rest on the hood of a jewel-black Mercedes. The man's legs were crossed at the ankles, as if the lower half of his body hadn't heard it was missing the rest.

By this time, Grey knew himself to be in something close to a trance. You couldn't look at something like this and allow yourself to feel anything.

The one that finally did it was the one that wasn't there. Two vehicles, a Honda Accord and a Chrysler Countryside, had collided head-on near the exit, their front ends crumpled into each other like the bellows of an accordion. The driver of the sedan had been shot through the windshield. The sedan was otherwise untouched, but the minivan looked ransacked. Its sliding door had been ripped away and hurled across the parking lot like a Frisbee. On the pavement by the open door, in a plume of debris—suitcases, toys, a jumbo pack of diapers—lay the prostrate body of a woman; just beyond the reach of her outstretched hand, tipped on its side, was an empty baby carrier. *What happened to the baby?* Grey thought.

And then: *Oh.*

Grey chose the pickup. He wouldn't have minded driving the Mercedes, but he guessed a truck would be more sensible. He'd owned a Chevy half-ton, back in a life that didn't seem to matter now, so the pickup was something familiar to cling to. He eased the decapitated driver free and laid him on the pavement. It was troubling, not having the head to give back to the poor guy. It didn't seem right to leave him there without it. But the head was nowhere obvious, and Grey had seen enough. He looked around for a pair of shoes his size—13EEE; whatever Zero had done to him, it hadn't shrunk his feet any—and finally chose a pair of loafers from the feet of the man on the Mercedes. They were Italian lambskin, soft as butter, and a little narrow in the toe box, but leather like that would stretch. He got in the truck and started the engine. There was a little more than three-quarters of a tank of gas; Grey figured that would get him most of the way to Denver.

He was about to pull away when a last thought occurred to him. He put the vehicle in park and returned to the room. Holding the pistol a little distance from his body, he walked back to the truck and deposited it in the glove compartment. Then, with only the gun for company, he put the truck in gear and drove away.

6

Momma was in the bedroom. Momma was in the bedroom, not moving. Momma was in the bedroom, which was forbidden. Momma was dead, precisely.

After I'm gone, remember to eat, because you sometimes forget. Bathe every other day. Milk in the fridge, Lucky Charms in the cupboard, and hamburger casseroles to reheat in the freezer. Put them in at 350 for an hour, and remember to turn off the oven when you're done. Be my big boy, Danny. I love you always. I just can't be afraid anymore. Love, Momma.

She'd left the note tucked beneath the salt and pepper shakers on the kitchen table. Danny liked salt, but not pepper, which made him sneeze. Ten days had gone by—Danny knew this from the marks he put on the calendar every morning—and the note was still there. He didn't know what to do with it. The whole place smelled something awful, the way a raccoon or possum did when it had been run over again and again for days.

The milk was no good, too. With the electricity off, it had gone sour, warm and unpleasant in his mouth. He tried the Lucky Charms with water from the tap, but it wasn't the same, nothing was the same, everything was different because Momma was in the bedroom. At night he sat in the dark in his room with the door closed. He knew where Momma kept the candles, they were in the cupboard over the sink where she kept her bottle of Popov for when her nerves got to her, but matches were nothing for him. They were on the list. It wasn't an actual list, it was just the things he couldn't do or touch. The toaster, because he kept pushing the button back down and burning the toast. The pistol in Momma's nightstand, because it wasn't a toy, it could shoot you. The girls on his bus, because they wouldn't like it, and he wouldn't get to drive the No. 12 anymore, which would be bad. That would be the worst thing in the world to Danny Chayes.

No electricity meant no TV, so he couldn't watch Thomas, either. Thomas was for little boys, Momma had told him so a million times, but the therapist, Dr. Francis, said it was okay to watch it as long as Danny tried other things, too. His favorite was James. Danny liked his red color and matching tender, and the sound of his voice the way the narrator did it, so soothing it made his throat tickle at the top. Faces were hard for Danny, but the expressions on the Thomas trains were always precise and easy to follow, and it was funny, the things they did to each other, the pranks they liked to play. Switching the tracks so Percy would run into a coal loader. Pouring chocolate all over Gordon, who pulled the express, because he was such a haughty engine. The kids on his bus sometimes made fun of Danny, calling him Topham Hatt, singing the song with not-nice words in place of the real ones, but for the most part Danny tuned this out. There was one kid, though. His name was Billy Nice, and nice was not what he was. He was a sixth grader, but Danny thought he'd probably been held back a few times, on account of he had a body like a full-grown man's. He boarded each morning without so much as a book in his hands, sneering at Danny as he mounted the steps, high-fiving and what-upping the other boys as he sauntered down the alley between the seats, dragging a smell of cigarettes.

Hey, Topham Hatt, how are things going on the Island of Sodor today? Is it true that Lady Hatt likes to take it in the caboose?

Har-har-har, Billy laughed. Har-har-har. Danny never said anything back, because it would only make things worse; he'd never told Mr. Purvis anything, because he knew what the man would say. *Goddamnit, Danny, whatcha let the little shit treat you like that for? Lord knows you're one weird duck, but you've got to stand up for yourself. You're the captain of that ship. You allow a mutiny and the next thing you know everything goes in the dumper.*

Danny liked Mr. Purvis, the dispatcher. Mr. Purvis had always been a friend to Danny, and Momma, too. Momma was one of the cafeteria ladies, so that was how they knew each other, and Mr. Purvis was always coming around the house, fixing things, like the disposal or a loose board on the porch, even though he had a wife of his own, Mrs. Purvis.

He was a big bald man who liked to whistle through his teeth and was always hitching up his pants. Sometimes he visited at night, after Danny was in bed; Danny would hear the TV going in the living room, and the pair of them laughing and talking. Danny liked those nights. They gave him a good feeling in his mind, like the happy-click. When anybody asked, Momma always said that Danny's father "wasn't in the picture," which was precisely true. There were pictures of Momma in the house, and pictures of Danny, and pictures of the two of them together. But he'd never seen one with his father in it. Danny didn't even know the man's name.

The bus had been Mr. Purvis's idea. He'd taught Danny to drive in the parking lot at the depot, and went with him to get his Class B license, and helped him fill out the application. Momma hadn't been so sure at first, on account of her needing Danny to help around the house, being a useful engine, and the Social Security, which was money from the government. But Danny knew the real reason, which was the different and special way he was. The thing with a job, Momma had explained, using her careful voice, was that a person needed to be "adaptable." Things would happen, different things. Take the cafeteria. Some days they would serve hot dogs, and some days lasagna, and other days chicken cutlets. The menu might say one thing, but it turned out to be another; you couldn't always know. Wouldn't that upset him?

But a bus wasn't a cafeteria. A bus was a bus, and it ran on a schedule, precisely. When Danny got behind the wheel, he felt the happy-click bigger and deeper than he'd ever felt in his life. Driving a bus! A big yellow one, all the seats in their orderly rows, the gearshift with its six speeds and reverse, everything laid out nice and neat before him. It wasn't a train but it was close, and each morning as he pulled away from the depot, he always imagined he was Gordon or Henry or Percy or even Thomas himself.

He was always on time. Forty-two minutes from depot to drop-off, 8.2 miles, nineteen stops, twenty-nine passengers, precisely. *Robert-Shelly-Brittany-Maybeth-Joey-Darla/ Denise (the twins)-Pedro-Damien-Jordan-Charlie-Oliver (O-Man)-Sasha-Billy-Molly-Lyle-Dick (Dickhead)- Richard-Lisa-Mckenna-Anna-Lily-Matthew-Charlie-Emily- JohnJohn-Kayla-Sean-Timothy.* Sometimes a parent would wait with them on the corner, a mother in a housecoat or a father in a jacket and tie, holding a mug of coffee. *How's it going today, Danny,* they might say, wearing a good-morning smile on their faces. *You know, a person could set their watch by you.*

Be my useful engine, Momma always said, and that's what Danny was.

But now the children were gone. Not just the children: everyone. Momma and Mr. Purvis and maybe all the people in the world. The nights were dark and still, no lights burning anywhere. For a while there had been a lot of noise—people yelling, sirens wailing, Army trucks roaring down the street. He'd heard the pop of guns. *Pop!* went the guns. *Pop-pop-pop-pop!* What are they shooting at, Danny wanted to know, but Momma wouldn't say. She told him to stay inside, using her strong voice, and not to watch TV, and to keep away from the windows. What about the bus, Danny asked, and Momma only said, Damnit, Danny, don't worry about the bus now. School's out today. What about tomorrow, Danny asked. And Momma said, It's out tomorrow, too.

Without the bus, he didn't know what to do with himself. His brain felt as jumpy as corn in a hot pan. He wished Mr. Purvis could come over and watch TV with Momma, it always made her feel better about things, but the man never did. The world went quiet, the way it was now. There were monsters out there. Danny had figured that out. As a for instance, there was the woman across the street, Mrs. Kim. Mrs. Kim taught the violin, kids coming over to her house for their lessons, and on summer days when the windows were open Danny could hear them playing, twinkle-twinkle and Mary-had-a-little-lamb and other things he didn't know the names of. Now there was no violin and Mrs. Kim was hanging over the porch railing.

And then one night Danny heard Momma crying in the bedroom. Once in a while she cried like this, all alone, it was normal and natural and nothing for Danny to worry about, but this felt different. For a long time he lay in his bed listening, wondering what that must be like, to feel something so sad it made you cry, but the idea was like something on a shelf he couldn't reach. Sometime later he awoke in the dark to the feel of someone touching his hair and he opened his eyes to see her sitting there. Danny didn't like to be touched, it gave him the.jangly feeling something awful, but it was okay when Momma did it, mostly, on account of he was used to it. What is it, Momma? Danny said. What's wrong? But all she said was Hush now, hush now, Danny. Something was resting in her lap, folded in a towel. I love you, Danny. Do you know how much I love you? I love you, too, Momma, he said, because that was the right answer when someone said I-love-you, and to the feel of her hand caressing him he fell asleep, and in the morning her bedroom door was closed and never opened and Danny knew. He didn't even have to look.

He decided to drive the bus after all.

Because maybe he wasn't the only person still living. Because it gave him the happy-click, driving the bus. Because he didn't know what else to do with himself, with Momma in the bedroom and the milk spoiled and all the days gone by.

He'd laid out his clothes the night before the way Momma always did, a pair of khakis and a white collared shirt and brown tie shoes, and packed a lunch. There wasn't much left to eat except for peanut butter and some graham crackers and a bag of stale marshmallows, but he'd saved a bottle of Mountain Dew, and he put it all in his backpack with his pocket knife and his lucky penny, then went to his closet to get his hat, the blue-striped engineer's cap that Momma had bought him at Traintown. Traintown was a park where kids could ride the trains, just like Thomas. Danny had gone there since he was little, it was his favorite place in the world, but the cars were too tight for Danny to fit in with his big legs and long arms, so he liked to watch the trains go round and round with their little puffs of smoke chuffing from their stacks. Except for trips to Traintown, Momma didn't let him wear the hat outside the house, on account of she said people would make fun of him, but Danny figured it would be okay to wear it now.

He set out at dawn. The bus's keys were in his pocket, flat against his thigh. The depot was 3.2 miles away, precisely. He hadn't walked a block before he saw the first bodies. Some were in their cars, others were lying on their lawns or draped over garbage cans or even hanging in the trees. Their skin had turned the same blue-gray color as Mrs. Kim's, their clothing stretched tight over limbs that had swollen in the summer heat. It was bad to look at, bad but strange and also interesting; if he'd had more time, Danny would have stopped to get a closer look. There was a lot of litter, bits of paper and plastic cups and fluttering grocery sacks, which Danny didn't like. People shouldn't litter.

By the time he got to the depot, the sun was warm on his shoulders. Most of the buses were there but not all. They were parked in rows with empty spaces, like a mouth with missing teeth. But Danny's bus, the No. 12, was waiting in its usual spot. There were many different kinds of buses in the world, shuttle buses and charter buses and city buses and coaches, and Danny knew about them all. That was something he liked to do—to learn everything there was to know about one thing. His bus was a Redbird 450, the Foresight model. Built to the most exacting engineering standards, with all-permanent frame fixtures, Easy Hood Assist™, an advanced driver's information display providing a wealth of system knowledge to both the operator and service technicians, and the purpose-built, single-scope Redbird Comfortride™ chassis, the 450 was the number one choice for safety, quality, and extended life-cycle value in the industry today.

Danny climbed aboard and wedged the key into the ignition; as the big Caterpillar diesel roared to life, a warm surge filled his belly. He checked his watch: 6:52. When the big hand hit the twelve, he put the bus in gear and pulled away.

It seemed odd at first, driving through empty streets with no one around, but by the time Danny was approaching his first stop—the Mayfields', Robert and Shelly—he'd settled into the rhythms of the morning. It was easy to imagine that today was just an ordinary day. He brought the bus to a halt. Well, Robert and Shelly were sometimes late. He'd honk the horn and they'd come dashing out the door, their mother calling after them to be good, have fun, and sending them off with a wave. The house was a bungalow not much bigger than the one Danny lived in with Momma but nicer, painted the color of a pumpkin and sitting behind a wide front porch with a swing. In spring there were always baskets of flowers hanging off the rails. The baskets were still there, but the flowers had all wilted. The lawn needed mowing, too. Danny craned his neck to look up through the windshield. A window on the second floor looked like it had been ripped from its frame. The blind was still hanging in the space where the window used to be, lolling out of it like a tongue. He honked the horn and waited a minute. But still nobody came.

Seven-oh-eight. He had other stops to make. He pulled away from the corner and guided the bus around a Prius lying on its side. He came to other things in the road. An overturned police car, smashed flat. An ambulance. A dead cat. A lot of the houses had X's spray-painted on their doors, with numbers and letters in the spaces. By the time he arrived at his second stop, a townhouse complex called Castle Oaks, he was already running twelve minutes late. *Brittany-Maybeth-Joey-Darla/Denise.* He gave the horn a long honk, then another. But there wasn't any point. Danny was just going through the motions now. Castle Oaks was a smoking ruin. The entire complex had burned to the ground.

More stops: all were the same. He guided the bus west into Cherry Creek. The houses were bigger here, set back from the road behind wide, sloped lawns. Big leafy trees draped curtains of dappled shade over the street. There was a quiet feeling here, more peaceful. The houses looked like they always did, and there were no bodies that Danny could see. But still there were no children.

By now his bus would have had twenty-five kids in it. The silence was unnerving. The noise in the bus always built along the route, each stop adding a little more with every kid who got on, the way music rose in a movie, approaching the final scene. The final scene was the bump. A speed bump on Lindler Avenue. *Do the bump, Danny!* they'd all cry out. *Do the bump!* And though he wasn't supposed to, he'd give the bus a little extra gas, jolting them from their seats, and for that one moment he'd feel himself to be a part of them. He'd never been a kid like they were, just a kid going to school. But when the bus went over the bump, he was.

Danny was thinking about this, missing the children, even Billy Nice and his stupid jokes and har-har-har, when up ahead he saw a boy. It was Timothy. He was waiting with his older sister at the end of their driveway. Danny would have known the boy anywhere, on account of the cowlick—two spikes of hair that stuck up from the back of his head like antennae on a bug. Timothy was one of the youngest kids, second grade or maybe third, and small; sometimes the housekeeper waited with him, a plump brown woman in a smock, but usually it was the boy's older sister, who Danny guessed was in high school. She was a funny girl to look at, not funny ha-ha but funny strange, with hair streaked the color of the Pepto that Momma gave him when his stomach got nervous from eating too fast and heavy black eyeliner that made her look like one of those paintings in a scary movie, the kind with eyes that moved. She had about ten studs in each ear; most days she was wearing a dog collar. A dog collar! Like she was a dog! The odd thing was that Danny thought she was sort of pretty, if not for all the weird stuff. He didn't know any girls her age, or any age, really, and he liked the way she waited with her brother, holding his hand but letting it go as the bus approached so the other kids wouldn't see.

He drew up to the end of the driveway and pulled the lever

to open the door. "Hey," he said, because that was all he could think of. "Hey, good morning."

It seemed like their turn to talk, but they didn't say anything. Danny let his eyes quickly graze their faces; their expressions were nothing he could read. None of the trains on Thomas ever looked like these two did. The Thomas trains were happy or sad or cross, but this was something else, like the blank screen on the TV when the cable wasn't working. The girl's eyes were puffy and red, her hair kind of smooshed-looking. Timothy had a runny nose he kept rubbing with the back of his wrist. Their clothing was all wrinkled and stained.

"We heard you honking," the girl said. Her voice was hoarse and shaky, like she hadn't used it in a while. "We were hiding in the cellar. We ran out of food two days ago."

Danny shrugged. "I had Lucky Charms. But just with water. They're no good that way."

"Is there anybody else left?" the girl asked.

"Left where?"

"Left alive."

Danny didn't know how to answer that. The question seemed too big. Maybe there wasn't; he'd seen a lot of bodies. But he didn't want to say so, not with Timothy there.

He glanced at the boy, who so far had said nothing, just kept nervously rubbing his nose with his wrist. "Hey, Timbo. You got allergies? I have those sometimes."

"Our parents are in Telluride," the boy stated. He was looking at his sneakers. "Consuela was with us. But she left."

Danny didn't know who Consuela was. It was hard when people didn't answer your question but instead answered some other question you hadn't even thought of.

"Okay," said Danny.

"She's in the backyard."

"How can she be in the backyard if she left?"

The boy's eyes widened. "Because she's *dead.*"

For a couple of seconds, nobody said anything. Danny wondered why they hadn't gotten on the bus yet, if maybe he'd have to ask them.

"Everybody's supposed to go to Mile High," the girl said. "We heard it on the radio."

"What's at Mile High?"

"The Army. They said it's safe there."

From what Danny had seen, the Army was pretty much dead, too. But Mile High would give them someplace to go. He hadn't really thought of that before. Where was he going?

"I'm April," the girl said.

She looked like an April. It was funny how some names were like that. They just seemed to fit.

"I'm Danny," he said.

"I know," said April. "Just please, Danny? Get us the hell out of here."

7

The color wasn't right, Lila decided. No, it wasn't right at all.

The shade was called "buttercream." On the sample from the store it was a soft, faded yellow, like old linen. But now, as Lila stood back to inspect her work, dripping roller in hand—honestly, she was making such a mess; why couldn't David do these things?—it looked more like: well, what? A lemon. An *electrified* lemon. Maybe in a kitchen it would have been all right, a bright, sunny kitchen with windows looking out to a garden. But not in a nursery. My God, she thought, a color like that, the baby wouldn't sleep a wink.

How depressing. All her hard work wasted. Hauling the ladder up the stairs from the basement, laying the drop cloths, lowering herself onto her hands and knees to tape off the baseboards, only to find she'd have to go back to the store and start over. She'd planned to have the room done by lunch, leaving enough time for the paint to dry before she hung the wallpaper border, a repeating pattern of scenes from Beatrix Potter. David thought the border was silly—"sentimental" was the word he'd used—but Lila didn't care. She'd loved the stories of Peter Rabbit when she was a girl, crawling onto her father's lap or snuggling down in bed to hear, for the hundredth time, the tale of Peter's escape from Mr. McGregor's garden. The yard of their house in Wellesley had been bordered by a hedgerow, and for years—long after she should have stopped believing in such things—she'd patiently searched it for a rabbit in a little blue jacket.

But now Peter Rabbit would have to wait. A wave of exhaustion enfolded her; she needed to get off her feet. The fumes were making her dizzy, too. Something seemed to be wrong with the AC, although with the baby, she always felt a little overheated. She hoped David would get home soon. Things were crazy at the hospital. He'd called her once to let her know he'd be late, but she hadn't heard from him since.

She made her way downstairs to the kitchen. The place was an awful mess. Dishes piled in the sink, counters stained, the floor beneath her bare feet tacky with grime. Lila stopped in the doorway, feeling puzzled. She hadn't realized how badly she'd let things go, and what had happened to Yolanda? How long since she'd been here? Tuesdays and Fridays were the housekeeper's regular days. What was today? To look at this kitchen, thought Lila, you'd think Yolanda hadn't been to the house in weeks. Okay, the woman's English was not the best, and sometimes she did strange things, like confusing the teaspoons with the tablespoons—how David grumbled about that—or depositing the bills, unread, straight into the recycling bin. Annoying things like that. But Yolanda wasn't one to miss even a day of work. One winter morning she'd shown up with a cough so bad that Lila could hear it from upstairs; she'd practically had to pry the mop from the woman's hands, saying, *Por favor, Yolanda, let me help you, I'm a doctor. Soy médico.* (Of course it was bronchitis; Lila had listened to the woman's chest right there in the kitchen and written the prescription for amoxicillin herself, knowing full well that Yolanda probably didn't even *have* a doctor, let alone insurance.) So, okay, she sometimes threw the mail away and mixed up the silverware and put the socks in the underwear drawer, but she was a hard worker, tireless really, a cheerful and punctual presence they depended on, what with their crazy schedules. And now not even a call.

Which was another thing. The phone didn't seem to be working, on top of which there was no mail. Or newspaper. But David had told her not to go outside under any circumstances, so Lila hadn't checked. Maybe the newspaper was sitting in the driveway.

She fetched a glass from the cabinet and turned on the faucet. A groan from below, a burp of air, and . . . nothing. The water, too! Then she remembered; the water had been out a while. Now she'd have to call a plumber on top of everything else. Or would have, if the phones were working. Wasn't it just like David to be away when everything went to hell in a handbasket. That had been one of Lila's father's favorite expressions, hell in a handbasket. A curious turn of phrase, now that Lila thought about it. What exactly was a handbasket, and how was it different from a regular basket? There were lots of phrases like that, even just simple words that could suddenly look strange, as if you'd never seen them before. Diaper. Misled. Plumber. Married.

Had that really been her idea, to marry David? Because she didn't remember thinking, *I will marry David.* Which a person *should* think, probably, before they went ahead and did it. Strange how one minute life was a certain way and then it was another, and you couldn't remember what you'd done to make it all happen. She wouldn't have said that she loved David, exactly. She *liked* him. She *admired* him. (And who could fail to admire David Centre? Chief of cardiology at Denver General, founder of the Colorado Institute of Electrophysiology, a man who ran marathons, sat on boards, held season tickets to both the Nuggets and the opera, who daily hauled his patients from the very brink of death?) But did these feelings add up to love? And if not, should you actually marry such a man because you were carrying his child—nothing planned, it had simply happened—and because, in a moment of characteristically David nobility, he had announced that he intended to "do the right thing"? What *was* the right thing? And why did David sometimes seem not like David but someone *resembling* David, *based on* David, a man-sized, David-like object? When Lila had told her father the news of their engagement, she'd seen it in his face: he knew. He was sitting at his desk in his study, surrounded by the books he loved, stroking glue onto the bowsprit of a model ship. In just the tiniest lift of his generous eyebrows, the truth was written. "Well," he said, and cleared his throat, pausing to screw the top onto the little jar of glue. "I can see how, under the circumstances, you might want to. He's a good man. You can do it here if you like."

Which he was, and which they had, flying off to Boston on the front edge of a spring blizzard, everything rushed and jammed into place, just a handful of relatives and friends able to make it at the last second to stand awkwardly in the living room while vows were exchanged (it had taken all of about two minutes) before making their excuses. Even the caterer had left early. It wasn't the fact that Lila was pregnant that made it all so awkward. It was, she knew, that someone was missing.

Someone would always be missing.

But never mind. Never mind David, and their awful wedding (really, it had felt more like a wake), with its piles of leftover salmon and the snow and all the rest. The important thing was the baby, and taking care of herself. The world could go to hell in a handbasket if it wanted to. The baby was what mattered. She would be a girl; Lila had seen her on the ultrasound. A baby girl. Tiny hands and tiny feet and a tiny heart and lungs, floating in the warm broth of her body. The baby liked to hiccup. *Hiccup!* went the tiny baby. *Hiccup! Hiccup!* Which was a funny word as well. The baby breathed the amniotic fluid in and out, contracting the diaphragm, causing the epiglottis to close. A synchronous diaphragmatic flutter, or singultus, from the Latin *singult,* "the act of catching one's breath while sobbing." When Lila had learned this in medical school, she'd thought: Wow. Just, wow. And of course she had immediately started to hiccup herself; half the students had. There was a man in Australia, Lila knew, who had been hiccupping continuously for seventeen years. She'd seen him on *Today.*

Today. What was today? She had made her way to the front hall, becoming gradually aware, as if her mind were lifting on tiptoes to peer above a ledge, that she had drawn the curtain aside to take a look outside. Nope, no newspaper. No *Denver Post* or *New York Times* or that trashy little neighborhood thing that went straight into the bin. Through the glass she could hear the high, tree-borne buzz of summer insects. Usually you'd see a car or two gliding by, the postman whistling his way down the block, a nanny pushing a stroller, but not today. *I'll be back when I know more. Stay inside, lock the doors. Don't go out under any circumstances.* Lila remembered David saying these things to her; she remembered standing at the window to watch his car, one of those new hydrogen-powered Toyotas, zip silently down the drive. Good God, even his car was virtuous. The pope probably drove one just like it.

But wasn't that a dog? Lila pressed her face closer to the glass. The Johnsons' dog was toddling down the middle of the street. The Johnsons lived two doors away, a pair of empty nesters, the daughter off married somewhere, the son away at college. MIT? Caltech? One of those. Mrs. Johnson ("Call me Sandy!") had been the first neighbor to show up at their door the day they'd moved in, all bundt cake and big hellos, and Lila saw her nearly every evening when she wasn't on call, sometimes in the company of her husband, Geoff, out walking Roscoe, a big grinning golden retriever so submissive he'd hurl himself tummy-up on the pavement when anyone approached. ("Excuse my fucking fairy of a dog," Geoff said.) That was Roscoe out there, but something wasn't right. He didn't look the same. His ribs were sticking out like the keys on a xylophone (Lila was touched, fleetingly, by a memory of playing the glockenspiel in grammar school, and the tinkling melody of "Frère Jacques"), and he was walking in a disconcertingly aimless manner, gripping something in his mouth. Some sort of a . . . floppy thing. Did the Johnsons know he'd gotten loose? Should she telephone them? But the phones weren't working, and she'd promised David she'd stay indoors. Surely someone else would notice him and say, Why, that's Roscoe; he must have gotten out.

Goddamn David, she thought. He could be so stuck on himself, so inconsiderate, out doing God knows what when here she was, no water and no phone and no electricity and the color in the nursery all wrong. It wasn't even close! She was only twenty-four weeks along, but she knew how the time raced by. One minute you were months away and the next thing you knew you were hustling out the door in the dead of night with your little suitcase, driving pell-mell to the hospital, and then you were on your back beneath the lights, huffing and puffing, the contractions roaring down upon you, taking you over, and nothing else would happen until you had the baby. And through the fog of pain you would feel a hand in your own and open your eyes to see Brad beside you, wearing a look on his face you had no name for, a beautiful terrified helpless look, and hear his voice saying, *Push, Lila, you're almost there, one more push and you'll be done,* and so you would: you would reach inside yourself and find the strength to do this one last thing and push the baby out. And in the stillness that came after, as Brad handed you the magical swaddled present of your baby, rivers of happiness running down his cheeks, you would feel the deep and permanent rightness of your life, knowing that you had chosen this man above all others because you were simply meant to, and that your baby, Eva, this warm new creature you had made together, was just that: the two of you, made one.

Brad? Why was she thinking about Brad? *David.* David was her husband, not Brad. Pope David and his popemobile. Had there been a Pope David? Probably. Lila herself was a Methodist. She wasn't the person to ask.

Well, she thought, Roscoe having wandered out of sight, enough was enough. She'd had it with being trapped in a filthy house. David could do as David liked; she saw no reason to sit out this perfectly beautiful June day, not with so much to do. Her trusty old Volvo awaited her in the driveway. Where was her purse? Her wallet? Her keys? But here they were, sitting on the little table by the front door. Just where she had left them some period of time ago.

Upstairs, she went to the bathroom—my God, the toilet

was in such a state, she didn't even want to *think* about that—and examined her face in the mirror. Well, that was not so good. You'd think she'd been in a shipwreck—her hair a rat's nest, her eyes sunken and bleary-looking. Her skin was all washed out, like it hadn't seen the sun in weeks. She wasn't one of those women who needed an hour to primp before leaving the house, but even so. She would have liked a shower, but of course that was impossible; she settled for washing her face with water from one of the jugs on the sink, using a washcloth to scrub her skin pink. She ran a brush through her hair, applied blush to her cheeks, stroked mascara onto her lashes, and put on a bit of lipstick. She was wearing only a T-shirt and panties in the heat; she retreated to the bedroom, with its guttered candles and heaps of dirty laundry and the musty smell of unwashed sheets, and pulled one of David's long-tailed shirts from the closet. What to wear below this was a problem—nothing really fit anymore. She settled on a pair of loose jeans she could wriggle into if she didn't do the top button, and a pair of sandals.

Once more to the mirror. Not bad, Lila concluded. A definite improvement. It wasn't like she was going anyplace special, after all. Although it might be nice to stop for lunch, once her errands were done. She certainly had earned it after all this time indoors. Someplace nice, where she could eat outside. Few things were nicer than a glass of tea and a salad, sitting outdoors on a spring afternoon. Café des Amis—that was just the ticket. They had a marvelous patio draped with vines of fragrant flowers, and the most wonderful chef—he had visited their table once—who had trained at Cordon Bleu. Pierre? François? The man could do the most amazing thing with sauces, teasing the deepest flavors from even the simplest dishes; his coq au vin was to die for. But the desserts were what Des Amis was known for, especially the chocolate mousse. Lila had never tasted anything so heavenly in her life. She and Brad always shared one after dinner, spooning it into each other's mouths like a couple of teenagers so besotted that the world barely existed beyond the two of them. Such blissful days—courtship days, all the promises of life opening before them like the pages of a book. How they'd laughed when she'd damn near swallowed the engagement ring he'd tucked within its airy cocoa folds, and again on the night when Lila had sent Brad out into the pouring rain—anything would do, she told him, a Kit Kat or Almond Joy or a plain old Hershey's—and awakened an hour later to see him standing in the doorway of the bedroom, soaked to the bone, wearing the most hilarious smile on his face and bearing a giant Tupperware container of François's—Pierre's?—famous chocolate mousse, enough to feed an army. Which was just the kind of man Brad was. He'd gone around to the back, where a light was still burning, and pounded on the door until somebody came to receive his rain-drenched fifty-dollar bill. Which was the sweetest thing of all. *My God, Lila,* Brad said as she spooned a mouthful to her lips, *the way you're going, this baby is going to be born half chocolate.*

But there she went again. *David.* David Centre was her husband now. Lila really had to get a handle on that. Not that she and David had ever shared a chocolate mousse or been to Café des Amis or done anything remotely of the kind. The man didn't have one romantic bone in his body. How had she let a man like that talk her into marriage? As if she were merely one more item on a glorified to-do list? Become a famous doctor, check. Get Lila Kyle pregnant, check. Do the honorable thing, check. He hardly seemed to know who she was.

Down the stairs she went. Outside the sun was pouring down, filling the hall like a golden gas. By the time she reached the door, a pure excitement was coursing through her. What sweet release! After so much time cooped up, to venture out at last! She could only imagine what David would say when he found out. *For God's sake, Lila, I told you it's not safe. You have to think of the baby.* But it was the baby she was thinking of; the baby was the reason. That's what David didn't understand. David, who was too busy off saving the world to help with the nursery, who drove a car powered by asparagus, or pixie dust, or wholesome thoughts, or whatever it was, and who had left her here alone. Alone! And what was worse, really the worst thing of all, was that he didn't even *like* Peter Rabbit. How was it possible she was going to have a baby with a man who didn't like Peter Rabbit? What did that say about him? What kind of father would he be? No, it was none of David's business what she did, Lila concluded, lifting her purse and keys from the hallway table and unbolting the door. It was none of his business if she went outside, or if she painted the nursery chartreuse, or vermilion, or puce. David could go screw himself. That's what David could do.

Lila Kyle would buy the paint herself.

8

It was not a good day in the office of the deputy director. Today, May 31—Memorial Day, not that it mattered—was an end-of-the-world kind of day.

Colorado was gone, basically. Colorado was kaput. Denver, Greeley, Fort Collins, Boulder, Grand Junction, Durango, the thousand little towns in between. The latest aerial intel looked like a war zone: cars crashed on the highways, buildings burning, bodies everywhere. During daylight hours, nothing seemed to be moving except the birds, huge spiraling swarms of them, like the word had gone out from Vulture Central Command.

Would somebody please tell him whose idea it had been to kill the entire state of Colorado?

And the virus was moving. Spreading in every direction, a twelve-fingered hand. By the time Homeland had sealed off the major interstate corridors—those dithering assholes couldn't get themselves out of a burning house—the horse was already galloping from the barn. As of this morning, the CDC had confirmed cases in Kearney, Nebraska; Farmington, New Mexico; Sturgis, South Dakota; and Laramie, Wyoming. And those were just the ones they knew about. Nothing yet in Utah or Kansas, though that was a matter of time, maybe just hours. It was five-thirty in northern Virginia, three hours till sundown, five in the west.

They always moved at night.

The briefing with the Joint Chiefs had not gone well, though Guilder hadn't expected it to. To begin with, there was the whole "problem" of Special Weapons. The military brass had never been particularly comfortable with, or especially clear on, what DSW did, or why it existed outside any military chain of command, drawing its budget from, of all things, the Department of Agriculture. (Answer: Because nobody gave a shit about agriculture.) The military was all about hierarchies, who urinated highest on the hydrant, and as far as the brass could see, Special Weapons answered to no one, its pieces cobbled together from a dozen other agencies and private contractors. It resembled nothing so much as a game of sidewalk three-card monte, the queen always moving, not quite where you thought it would be. As for what DSW actually did, well, Guilder had heard the nicknames. "Distraction from Serious Warfare." "Department of Silly Wingnuts." "Deep-Shit Weirdness." And his personal favorite: "Discount Shoe Warehouse." (Even he had started calling it the Warehouse.)

So it was that Deputy Director Horace Guilder (were there any actual directors anymore?) had found himself sitting before the Joint Chiefs (enough stars and bars around the table to start a Girl Scout troop) to offer his official assessment of the situation in Colorado. (Sorry, we made vampires; it seemed like a good idea at the time.) A full thirty seconds of dumbfounded silence ensued, everyone waiting to see who would speak next.

Let me see if I have you right, the chairman intoned. He leaned his folded hands over the table. Guilder felt a bead of sweat drop from his armpit to slither the length of his torso. *You decided to reengineer an ancient virus that would transform a dozen death row inmates into indestructible monsters who live on blood, and you didn't think to tell anybody about this?*

Well, not exactly "decided." Guilder hadn't been with DSW at the outset. He'd come in at the change of administration, so much money and so many man-hours already down the rat hole that he couldn't have put the brakes on if he tried. Project NOAH was under a chain of command so obscure, even Guilder didn't know where it had originated—probably NSA, though he'd gotten the sense it might have gone even higher than that, even to the White House itself. But sitting before the Joint Chiefs, he understood that this distinction was pointless. Guilder had spent three decades working in agencies where so much was a secret that nobody was actually responsible for anything. Ideas seemed to flower of their own accord. *We did what? No, we didn't.* And so, off into the shredder it went. Which was exactly what was about to happen to Special Weapons; probably even to Guilder himself.

But in the meantime, there was blame to be doled out. The meeting had quickly devolved into a shouting match, Guilder taking verbal punch after verbal punch. He felt relieved when he was banished from the room, knowing that the situation was out of his hands. Henceforth, the military would deal with this the way they dealt with all problems: by shooting everything in sight.

In hindsight, Guilder might have put the situation more

diplomatically. But the CDC's projections spoke for themselves. Three weeks, four at the outside, and the virus would take out Chicago, St. Louis, Salt Lake. Six weeks and they were looking at the coasts.

Vampires, for Christ's sake. What had he been thinking? What had *everyone* been thinking?

And yet there was no doubt that Lear had been on to something. The great Jonas Lear—even Guilder was intimidated by the man, a Harvard biochemist with an IQ of a zillion who had, for all intents and purposes, invented the field of paleovirology, retrieving and resuscitating ancient organisms for modern use. Within his professional circle it was generally assumed that Lear was a shoo-in, someday, for a Nobel Prize. Okay, maybe using death row inmates hadn't been the smartest move. They'd gotten ahead of themselves there. And certainly Lear wasn't rowing with his oars entirely in the water. But you had to admit the idea had possibilities. Such as, for instance, not dying. Ever. A matter in which Guilder had lately found himself holding a not-inconsiderable personal stake.

His only hope was the girl.

Amy NLN. The thirteenth test subject, snatched from a convent in Memphis, Tennessee, where her mother had abandoned her. Guilder hadn't felt exactly comfortable signing off on that. A kid, for the love of God. Somebody was bound to notice, and they had; by the time Wolgast had brought her in, everybody from the Oklahoma Highway Patrol to the U.S. Marshals was scouring the country for her, and Richards, that lunatic, had left a trail of bodies a mile wide. The nuns at the convent, shot in their sleep. A pair of small-town cops. Six people at a coffee shop whose only mistake was coming in for breakfast at the same time as Wolgast and the girl.

But the request for the girl, which had come from Lear himself, was nothing Guilder could make himself refuse. Each of the cons had been infected with a slightly altered variant of the virus, though the effects had been the same. Illness, coma, transformation, and the next thing you knew they were hanging upside down from the ceiling, gutting a rabbit. But the Amy variant was different. It hadn't come from Fanning, the Columbia biochemist who'd been infected on Lear's misbegotten excursion to Bolivia; it had come from the group of tourists who'd started the whole thing—terminal cancer patients on a lark in the jungle with an ecotour group called Last Wish. They'd all died within a month: stroke, heart attack, aneurysm, their bodies blowing apart. But in the meantime, they'd shown remarkable improvements in their condition—one man had even grown back a full head of hair—and they'd all died cancer-free. Reading Lear's mind was a fool's errand, but he'd come to believe this variant was the answer. The trick was keeping the first test subject alive. For this he'd chosen Amy, a young, healthy girl.

And it had worked. Guilder knew it had worked. Because Amy was still alive.

Guilder's office, on the third floor of an otherwise nondescript low-rise federal office building in Fairfax County—DSW shared space with, among other entities, the Office of Technology Assessment, the Department of Homeland Security Special Energy Task Force, the National Oceanic and Atmospheric Administration, and a day care—looked out on Interstate 66. Monday of Memorial Day weekend, yet there was almost no traffic. A lot of people had left the city already. Guilder imagined a lot of chits were being called in. A mother-in-law in upstate New York. A friend with a cabin in the mountains. But with all air transportation grounded, people could get only so far, and it wouldn't make much difference in the end. You couldn't hide from nature forever. Or so Horace Guilder had been told.

The girl had made it out of Colorado somehow. They'd caught her signature in southern Wyoming in the first few hours. Which meant she was in a vehicle, and not alone—somebody had to be driving. After that, she'd disappeared. The transmitter in her biomonitor was short-range, too weak for the satellites; she had to be within a few miles of a cell tower, and not some rural co-op but one connected to the federal tracking network. Which, in southern Wyoming, as long as you stayed off major highways, would be easy to avoid. She could be anywhere now. Whoever was with her was smart.

A knock at the door broke his train of thought; Guilder swiveled from the window to see Nelson, the department's chief technical officer, standing in the doorway. Christ, what now?

"I have good news and bad news," Nelson announced.

Nelson was dressed, as always, in a black T-shirt and jeans, his dirty feet shoved into a pair of flip-flops. A fast-talking Rhodes scholar with not one but two PhDs from MIT—biochemistry and advanced information systems—Nelson was the smartest guy in the building by a mile, a fact that he knew only too well. He still had the young person's predisposition to regard the world as a series of vaguely irritating problems created by people less cool and smart than he was. Though their relationship was cordial, Nelson had a habit of treating Guilder like a doddering elderly parent, a figure of respect but no longer quite worthy—which was exasperating, coming from a guy who seemed to comb his hair every fourth day, though not, Guilder had to admit, entirely unwarranted. He was twenty-eight to Guilder's fifty-seven, and everything about Nelson conspired to make him feel old.

"Any sign of her?"

"Nada." Nelson scratched his scraggly beard. "We're not getting any of them."

Guilder rubbed his eyes, which stung of sleeplessness. He needed to go home for a shower and a clean suit. He hadn't left the office in two days, grabbing only a few winks on the couch and living on junk from the vending machines. He was having trouble with his fingers, too. Numbness, tingling.

"You said something about good news?"

"Depends on how you look at it. From a free-speech point of view, probably it's not the best, but it looks like somebody finally shut down that lunatic in Denver. My guess would be NSA, or else one of Lear's little pets finally got to him. Either way, the dude's off-line in a permanent way."

Last Stand in Denver: Guilder had watched his videos, like everybody else. You had to hand it to the guy for balls. Theories abounded about his identity, the general consensus being that he was ex-military, Special Forces or SEALs.

"So what's the bad?"

"New numbers just came in from the CDC. It seems the original algorithm failed to take into proper account just how much these things like to eat. Which I could have told them if they'd asked. Either that or some summer intern moved a decimal place when he was daydreaming about the last time he boned his girlfriend."

Sometimes talking with Nelson felt like trying to corral a five-year-old. A genius five-year-old, but still. "Please, just spit it out."

Nelson shrugged. "As it now stands, based on the most recent projections, it appears we're looking at a more succinct timeline. Something on the order of thirty-nine days."

"For the coasts you mean?"

"Um, not exactly."

"What then?"

"The entire North American continent."

A gray shadow swooped over Guilder's vision; he had to sit down.

"A response is already in the works at Central," Nelson continued. "My guess is they'll try to burn it out. Major population centers first, then anyone else who gets left behind."

"Christ almighty."

Nelson frowned. "Small price to pay, on the whole. I know what I'd do if I were, say, the president of Russia. No way I'd let this jump the pond."

The man was right, and Guilder knew it. He realized his right hand had begun to tremble. He reached for it with his left, trying to bring the spasms under control while also making the gesticulation seem natural.

"You okay there, boss?"

His right foot had begun to shake as well. He felt the incomprehensible urge to laugh. Probably it was the stress. He swallowed effortfully, a taste of bile in his throat.

"Find that girl."

Once Nelson was gone, Guilder sat in his office for a few minutes, trying to collect himself. The trembling had passed, but not the impulse to laugh—a symptom euphemistically known as "emotional incontinence." Finally he just gave in, ejecting a single, cleansing bark. Jesus, he sounded possessed. He hoped nobody outside had heard.

He departed the building, got his car from the garage— a beige Toyota Camry—and drove to his townhouse in Arlington. He wanted to clean himself up, but this suddenly seemed like work; he poured himself a Scotch and flipped on the TV. It hadn't taken long for each of the networks, right down to the Weather Channel, to brand the emergency with a catchy slogan ("Nation in Crisis," etc.), and all the broadcasters looked harried and sleep-deprived, especially the ones reporting from beside a highway somewhere—a cornfield in the background, long lines of vehicles creeping past, everybody pointlessly honking. The whole country was seizing up like a bad transmission. He checked his watch: 8:05. In less than an hour, the middle of the country would go dark.

He heaved his disobedient body from the couch and climbed the stairs. Stairs—that had been a concern for the future. What would he do when he could no longer climb the stairs? But it hardly mattered now. In the master bath he turned on the shower and stripped to his shorts, standing before the mirror while the water heated. The funny thing was, he didn't look especially sick. A little thinner, perhaps. There was a time when he'd thought of himself as athletic— he'd run cross-country at Bowdoin—though those days were long past. His line of work, with its attendant demands for secrecy, had made marriage impossible, but well into his forties Guilder had managed—well, if not to turn heads exactly, then at least to keep himself occupied. A series of discreet affairs, everyone apprised of the facts. He had prided himself on the well-managed quality of these encounters, but then one day it had all simply stopped. Glances that might have been returned slid past him, conversations that before had merely served as elaborate preambles went no place. Inevitable, Guilder supposed, but nothing to cheer about. He surveyed his reflection, taking stock. A square-jawed face that had once looked rugged but had long since sagged at the jowls. A scrim of thinning hair swept back over his scalp, trying not quite successfully to conceal the ghostly white presence of his scalp. Bags of skin beneath his eyes, a rubbery paunch at the waist, legs skinny and insubstantial looking. Not a pretty sight, but nothing he hadn't accepted as the inescapable degradations of late middle age.

To look at him, you'd never know he was dying.

He showered and changed into a clean suit. His closet contained almost nothing else; an understated two-button— dark navy usually but sometimes gray with a subtle pinstripe, occasionally khaki poplin in summer—paired with a shirt of powder blue or starched white and a tie as neutral as Switzerland, was so closely aligned with his sense of himself that he felt naked without one. Minding his balance, he descended the stairs to the living room, where the television was dutifully barking out its parade of bad news. Though he possessed no appetite, he heated up a frozen lasagna in the microwave, standing before it as the seconds ticked away. He sat at the table and did his best to eat, but the diazepam made everything taste bland and vaguely metallic, and the tightness in his throat had not abated, as if he were wearing a collar two sizes too small. His doctor had suggested he try milk shakes, or something soft like macaroni, but resorting to kiddie food was nothing he could face. From there, everything would go downhill.

He dumped the unfinished lasagna down the disposal and checked his watch again. A little after nine. Well, whatever was happening in the middle of the country was happening. Nelson would call if he needed him.

He left the townhouse and drove to McLean. What lay ahead was a grim duty, but Guilder was the only one to do it. The facility was set back from the road behind a sweeping green lawn; by the driveway a sign read, SHADOWDALE CONVA-LESCENT CENTER. At the check-in desk, Guilder presented his driver's license to the nurse, then proceeded down the medicinal-smelling hallway, past its mass-produced paintings of green fields and summer sunsets. The place was quiet, even for the hour; usually there were orderlies around, and patients in the common room, those who still got some benefit from human company. Tonight the place was a tomb.

He came to his father's room and gently knocked, opening the door without waiting for an answer.

"Pop, it's me."

His father was propped in his wheelchair by the window. His jaw drooped open, the muscles of his face as slack as pancake batter. A pendulum of spittle dangled from his mouth to the paper bib around his neck. Somebody had dressed him in a stained sweat suit and orthopedic shoes with Velcro tabs. He gave no sign of recognition as Guilder stepped into the room.

"How you doing, Pop?"

The air around his father tanged of urine. The Alzheimer's had progressed to a point where he recognized no one, but still one had to go through the motions. How terrifying it was, Guilder thought, the solitude of the mind. Yet his father's silence, the feeling of absence, was nothing new. In life—as now, in death—he had been a man of almost reptilian coldness. Guilder knew that this was just the way his father had been raised—the son of small-town dairy farmers who'd attended church three times weekly and slaughtered their own hogs—yet still he couldn't bring himself to put aside his resentments for a boyhood spent hoping to win the attention of a man who was simply incapable. It had been a small thing, a natural thing, what he'd asked of his father, simply by being born: to treat him like a son. A game of catch on a fall afternoon, a word of praise from the side-lines, an expression of interest in his life. Guilder had done everything right. The good grades, the dutiful performances in auditoriums and on athletic fields, the full ride to college and swift ascent into a useful adulthood. Yet his father had had virtually nothing to say about any of this. Guilder could not, in fact, recall a single instance when his father had told him he loved him, or touched him with affection. The man just didn't care.

Hardest of all had been the toll it had taken on Guilder's mother, a naturally sociable woman whose loneliness had driven her to the alcoholism that eventually killed her. In later life, Guilder came to believe that his mother had sought comfort elsewhere, that she had had affairs, probably more than one. After his father had been moved to Shadowdale, Guilder had cleaned out the house in Albany—an absolute mess, every drawer and cabinet crammed with stuff—and discovered, in his mother's dressing table, a velvet Tiffany box. When he'd looked inside he'd found a bracelet—a *diamond* bracelet. Probably it had cost as much as his father, a civil engineer, had made in a year. It was nothing he could have afforded, and the box's location—concealed in the back of a drawer beneath a pile of moldering gloves and scarves—had told Guilder what he was looking at: a lover's gift. Who had it been? His mother had been a legal secretary. One of the lawyers at her firm? Somebody she had met in passing? A rekindled romance of her youth? It had gladdened him to know that his mother had found some happiness to brighten her lonely existence, yet at the same time this discovery had sunk him into a depression that had continued unabated for weeks. His mother was the one warm memory of his childhood. But her life, her real life, had been a secret from him.

Always these visits to his father brought these memories to the surface; by the time he left, he was often so dispirited, or else seething with unexpressed rage, that he could barely think straight. Fifty-seven years old, yet still he craved some flicker of acknowledgment.

He positioned the room's only chair in front of his father. The old man's head, bald as a baby's, was tipped at an awkward angle against his shoulder. Guilder retrieved a rag from the bedside table and wiped the spit from his chin. An open container of vanilla pudding sat on a tray with a flimsy metal spoon.

"So how you feeling, Pop? They treating you okay?"

Silence. And yet Guilder could hear his father's voice in his head, filling in the spaces.

Are you kidding me? Look at me, for Christ's sake. I can't even take a proper shit. Everyone talking to me like I'm a child. How do you think I am, sonny boy?

"I see you didn't eat your dessert. You want some pudding? How would that be?"

Fucking pudding! That's all they give me around this place. Pudding for breakfast, pudding for lunch, pudding for dinner. The stuff's like snot.

Guilder tucked a spoonful between his father's teeth. Through some autonomic reflex, the old man smacked his lips and swallowed.

Look at me. You think this is a picnic? Drooling on myself, sitting in my own piss?

"Don't know if you've been following the news lately," Guilder said, delivering a second spoonful into his father's mouth. "There's something I thought you should know about."

So? Say your piece and leave me alone.

But what did Guilder want to say? I'm dying? That everyone was dying, even if they didn't know it yet? What purpose could this information possibly serve? A chilling thought occurred to him. What would become of his father when everyone was gone, the doctors and nurses and orderlies? With everything that had happened in the last few weeks, Guilder had been too preoccupied to consider this eventuality. Because the city was emptying out; soon, in weeks or even days, everyone would be running for their lives. Guilder remembered what had happened in New Orleans in the aftermath of the hurricanes, first Katrina and then Vanessa, the stories of elderly patients left to wallow in their own waste, to perish slowly of hunger and dehydration.

Are you listening to me, sonny boy? Sitting there with that big dumb look on your face. What's so all-fired important that you came here to tell me?

Guilder shook his head. "It's nothing, Pop. Nothing important." He spooned the last of the pudding into his father's mouth and wiped his lips with the rag. "You get some rest, okay?" he said. "I'll see you in a few days."

Your mother was a whore, you know. A whore a whore a whore . . .

Guilder stepped from the room. In the vacant hallway, he paused to breathe. The voice wasn't real; he understood that. But still there were times when it felt as if his father's mind, departed from his bodily person, had taken up residence inside his own.

He returned to the front desk. The nurse, a young Hispanic woman, was penciling in a crossword puzzle.

"My father needs his diaper changed."

She didn't look up. "They all need their diaper changed." When Guilder didn't move, her eyes darted upward from the page. They were very dark, and heavily lined. "I'll tell someone."

"Please do."

At the door he stopped. The nurse had already resumed working on her puzzle.

"So *tell* someone, goddamnit."

"I said I'd get to it."

A fierce protective urge came over him. Guilder wanted to shove her pencil down her throat. "Pick up the fucking phone if you're not going to do it yourself."

With a huff she lifted the phone and dialed. "It's Mona at the front. Guilder in 126 needs changing. Yes, his son is here. Okay, I'll tell him." She hung up. "Happy?"

The question was so absurd he didn't know where to begin.

Guilder wouldn't die like his father—just the opposite. ALS: amyotrophic lateral sclerosis, more commonly known as Lou Gehrig's disease. Major motor function would be the first to go, the muscles spasming and dimming into uselessness, followed by speech and the ability to swallow. The spontaneous laughing and crying were a mystery—nobody knew quite why this happened. Ultimately he would die on a respirator, his body utterly stilled, unable to move or speak. But worst of all was the fact that he would experience no diminishment of his ability to think or reason. Unlike his father, whose mind had failed first, Guilder would live every moment of his decline with full awareness. A living death, no one but some sulky nurse for company.

It was clear to him that in the aftermath of his diagnosis, he had gone through a period of profound shock. That was the explanation he gave himself for the foolish thing he'd done with Shawna—though, of course, that wasn't even her real name. For two years Guilder had been visiting her on the second Tuesday of each month, always at the apartment provided by her employers. She was dark-skinned and slim, with subtly Asiatic eyes, and young enough to be his daughter, though this was not the attraction—if anything, he would have preferred that she were older. He had originally found her through a service, but after a probationary period he had been permitted to call her directly. The first time, he had been as nervous as a college boy. It had been a while since he'd been with a woman, and he'd found himself worrying that he wouldn't measure up—in hindsight, a preposterous concern. But the girl had quickly put him at his ease, taking command of the occasion. Always the ritual was the same. Guilder would ring the bell outside; the buzzer would sound; he would mount the stairs to the apartment, where she would be waiting in the open door, wearing a welcoming smile and dressed in a black cocktail dress beneath which lay an erotic treasure of lace and silk. A few pleasantries, as might be exchanged by any two lovers meeting in the afternoon, followed by the unremarked-on placement of the envelope of cash on the dresser; then on to the thing itself. Always Guilder undressed first, then watched as she did so herself, allowing the cocktail dress to fall to the floor like a curtain before stepping regally away from it. She made love to him with an enthusiasm that seemed neither manufactured nor overly professional, and for those slender minutes, Guilder's mind found a serenity that nothing else in his life came close to matching. At the moment of his release, Shawna would say his name over and over, her voice losing itself in a wholly persuasive facsimile of womanly satisfaction, and Guilder would find himself floating on these sounds and sensations, riding them like a surfer onto a tranquil shore.

Why don't I see you more often? she would ask him after. Are you happy with the things I do? There isn't anybody else, is there? I want to be your only one, Guilder. Very happy, he would say, stroking her velvety hair. I couldn't be happier than I am with you.

He knew nothing about her at all—at least, nothing real. Yet in the weeks that followed his diagnosis, the only refuge his mind could take was in the absurd idea that he was in love with her. The memory embarrassed him now, and the psychological subtext was obvious—he didn't want to die alone—but at the time, he'd been utterly convinced. He was madly, hopelessly in love, and wasn't it possible, likely even, that Shawna shared his feelings? Was that what she meant when she said she wanted to be his only one? Because what they did and said to each other *couldn't* be false; those things occurred on a plane that only two people who were truly connected could share.

On and on like this, until he had worked himself into such a state that Shawna was all he thought about. He decided he would give her something—a symbol of his love. Something expensive and worthy of his feelings. Jewelry. It had to be jewelry. And not something new from a store, but something more personal: his mother's diamond bracelet. Energized by this decision, he wrapped the Tiffany box in silver paper and drove to Shawna's apartment. It wasn't Tuesday, but that didn't matter. What he felt wasn't anything a person could schedule. He rang the bell and waited. Minutes passed, which was strange; Shawna was always very prompt about the bell. He rang again. This time the speaker made a little burst of static and he heard her voice. "Hello?"

"It's Horace."

A pause. "I don't have you in the book. Do I? Maybe this is my fault. Did you call?"

"I have something for you."

The speaker seemed to go dead. Then: "Hang on a second."

A few minutes passed. Guilder heard footsteps descending the stairs. Perhaps the buzzer wasn't working; Shawna was coming down to open the door. But the figure that turned the corner wasn't Shawna. It was a man. He looked about sixty, bald and heavyset, with the piggish face of a Russian gangster, wearing a rumpled pin-striped suit, his necktie loosened. The implications were obvious, yet in its agitated state, Guilder's mind refused them. The man stepped through the door, giving Guilder a cursory glance as he passed.

"Lucky you," he said, and winked.

Guilder hurried up the stairs. He knocked three times, waiting with buoyant anxiety; at last the door swung open. Shawna wasn't wearing the dress, just a silk robe cinched at the waist. Her hair was disheveled, her makeup smeary. Perhaps he'd caught her taking a nap.

"Horace, what are you doing here?"

"I'm sorry," he said, suddenly breathless. "I know I should have called."

"To tell you the truth, it's not really the best time."

"I'll only be a minute. Please, can I come in?"

She eyed him skeptically, then seemed to soften. "Well, all right. It'll have to be quick, though."

She stood aside to let him enter. Something felt different about the apartment, though Guilder couldn't say exactly what. It seemed dirty, the air unpleasantly dense.

"Now, what's this I see?" She was eyeing the silver-papered box. "Horace, you shouldn't have."

Guilder held it out to her. "This is for you."

With a warm light dancing in her eyes, she undid the wrapping and removed the bracelet.

"Isn't that thoughtful. What a pretty thing."

"It's an heirloom. It belonged to my mother."

"That makes it even more special." She kissed him quickly on the cheek. "You give me a minute to clean up and I'll be right with you, baby."

A titanic wave of love broke over him. It was all he could do not to throw his arms around her and press his mouth to hers. "I want to make love to you. Real love."

She glanced at her watch. "Well, sure. If that's what you want. I don't have the full hour, though."

Guilder had begun to undress, madly unbuckling his belt, yanking off his wingtips. But something was wrong. He sensed her hesitation.

"Isn't there something you're forgetting?" she asked.

The money. That's what she was asking for. How could she think about money at a time like this? He wanted to tell her that what they shared couldn't be counted in dollars and cents, words along those lines, but all he managed to say was "I don't have it with me."

She frowned. "Honey, that's not how this works. You know that."

But by this time Guilder was so frantic he was barely processing any of it. He was also standing in front of her wearing only his boxers and undershirt, his pants bunched around his ankles.

"Are you all right? You don't look so good."

"I love you," he said.

She gave an airy smile. "That's sweet."

"I said, I love you."

"Okay, I can do that. That's no problem. Put the money on the dresser and I'll say anything you want."

"I don't have any money. I gave you the bracelet."

Suddenly there was no sign of warmth or even friendship in her eyes. "Horace, this is a cash business, you know that. I don't like the way you're talking."

"Please, let me make love to you." Guilder's pulse was throbbing in his ears. "You can sell the bracelet if you want. It's worth a lot of money."

"Baby, I don't think so." She held it out to him with unconcealed contempt. "I hate to break it to you, but this is glass. I don't know who sold it to you, but you should get your money back. Now go on, be sweet. You know the drill."

He had to make her understand how he felt. In desperation he reached for her, but his feet were still tangled up in his trouser legs. Shawna released a yelp; the next thing Guilder knew, he was sprawled on the floor. He raised his face to discover a pistol aimed at his head.

"Get the fuck out."

"Please," he moaned. His voice was thick with tears. "You said you wanted to be my only one."

"I say a lot of things. Now get out of here with your crappy goddamned bracelet."

He rose heavily to his feet. Never had he experienced such humiliation. And yet what he mostly felt was love. A helpless, melancholy love that would devour him whole.

"I'm dying."

"We're all dying, baby." She waved the pistol at the door. "Do like I say before I shoot your balls off."

He knew he could never face her again. How could he have been so stupid? He drove to his townhouse, pulled into the garage, shut off the engine, and sealed the door with the remote. He sat in his car for a full thirty minutes, unable to muster the energy to move. He was dying. He had made a fool of himself. He would never see Shawna again, because he meant nothing to her.

Which was when he realized why he was still sitting in the Camry. All he had to do was turn the engine back on. It would be like falling asleep. He'd never have to think about Shawna again, or Project NOAH, or live in the prison of his own failing body, or visit his father at the convalescent center—none of it. All his cares lifted, just like that. Following an impulse he could not explain, he removed his watch and took his wallet from his back pocket, placing them on the dashboard—as if he were getting ready for bed. Probably it was customary to write a note, but what would he say? Who would the note be for?

Three times he tried to make himself turn the key. Three times his resolve failed him. By then he had begun to feel silly, sitting in his car—one more humiliation. There was nothing left to do but put his watch back on and return his wallet to his pocket and go into the house.

As Guilder was driving home from McLean, his handheld buzzed. Nelson.

"They're on the move."

"Where?"

"Everywhere. Utah, Wyoming, Nebraska. A large group massing in western Kansas." He paused. "That's not why I called."

Guilder drove straight to the office. Nelson met him in the hallway. "We picked up the signal a little before sunset. Grabbed it off a tower west of Denver, a town called Silver

Plume. It took some doing, but I was able to call in some favors at Homeland and reroute one of the drones to see if we could get a picture."

At his terminal he showed Guilder the photograph, a grainy black and white. Not the girl; it was a man. He was standing beside a pickup truck parked on the side of the highway. It looked like he was taking a leak.

"Who the hell is this? One of the docs?"

"It's one of Richards's guys."

Guilder was perplexed. "What are you talking about?"

For a moment, Nelson appeared faintly embarrassed. "Sorry, I thought you were in the loop on this. They're paroled sex offenders. One of Richards's little projects. For security reasons, all sixth-tier civilian personnel were harvested from the national registry."

"You're shitting me."

"I shit you not." Nelson tapped the image on the screen. "This guy? Our lone survivor of Project NOAH? He's a fucking pedophile."

9

The pickup gave out late on the morning of Grey's second day on the road.

The hour was just shy of noon, the sun high in the sky. After a restless night in a Motel 6 near Leadville, Grey had picked up I-70 near Vail, then made his descent toward Denver. As far east as the town of Golden, the interstate corridor had been mostly clear, but as he moved into the city's outer suburban ring, with its huge shopping centers and sprawling subdivisions, things began to change. Portions of the highway were choked with abandoned cars, forcing him onto the access road; the vast parking lots lining the highway were scenes of frozen disorder, store windows smashed, merchandise strewn over the pavement. The stillness was different here, too—not a simple absence of sound but something deeper, more ominous. A lot of the bodies he saw were headless, like the suspendered man at the Red Roof. Grey guessed maybe Zero and the others liked to take the heads.

He did his best to keep his eyes on the road, forcing the carnage to the fringes of his vision. The weird, buzzing energy he'd felt at the Red Roof had not abated; his brain was humming like a plucked string. He hadn't slept in a day and a half, but he wasn't tired. Or hungry, which wasn't like him at all. Grey used to slam it down, but for some reason the thought of food wasn't remotely appealing. In Leadville he'd gotten a Baby Ruth from a vending machine in the lobby of the Motel 6, thinking he should try to put something in his stomach, but he couldn't get the damn thing past his nose. Just the odor of it made his insides clench. He could practically smell the preservatives in the thing, a nasty chemical stink, like industrial floor cleaner.

By the time the city's core rose into view, Grey knew he would have to abandon the interstate. There was simply no way around the cars, and the situation was only going to get worse the closer he got. He drew the truck into the parking lot of a 7-Eleven and checked his map. The best route would be circling downtown to the south, he decided, though this was just a guess; he didn't know Denver at all.

He veered south, then east again, picking his way through the suburbs. Everywhere was the same, not a living soul about. He wished he could at least have had the radio for company, but when he scanned up and down the dial, all he could get was the same empty wash of static he'd heard for a day and a half. For a while he honked the truck's horn, thinking this might alert anyone left alive to his presence, but eventually he gave up. There was no one left to hear it. Denver was a crypt.

By the time the engine died, Grey had entered a state of such complete despair that for several seconds he actually failed to notice. So disturbing was the silence that it had begun to seem possible that he would never see a living soul again—that the whole world, not just Denver, had been swept clean of humanity. But then he realized what was happening, that the engine had lost power. For a few seconds the truck coasted on its own momentum, but the steering had locked up, too; all Grey could do was sit and wait for it to glide to a halt.

Christ, he thought, this is all I need. Sliding Iggy's gun into the pocket of his jumpsuit, he climbed out and lifted the hood. Grey had owned enough junky cars in his day to know a broken fan belt. The logical step would have been to abandon the truck and find another vehicle with the keys in it. He was on a wide boulevard of big-box retail outlets: Best Buy, Target, Home Depot. The sun was glaring down. Each lot had a scattering of cars in it. But he had no heart to look inside them, knowing what he would find. He'd swapped out a fan belt lots of times. All he needed was the belt and a few basic tools, a screwdriver and a couple of wrenches to adjust the tensioner. Maybe the Home Depot had auto parts. It couldn't hurt to look.

He crossed the highway and headed for the door, which stood open. The cage of propane tanks by the entrance had been pried open, all the canisters taken, but otherwise the front of the store appeared undamaged. A phalanx of lawn mowers, chained together, rested undisturbed by the doorway, as did a display of patio furniture dusted with yellow pollen. The only other sign that anything was amiss was a large square of plywood propped against the wall, spray-painted with the words NO GENERATORS LEFT.

Grey drew the pistol from his pocket, wedged the door open, and stepped inside. The power was out, but a semblance of order had been maintained; a lot of the shelves had been stripped bare, though the floor was mostly clear of debris. Holding the gun out before him, he advanced cautiously along the front of the store, his eyes scanning the signs over the aisles for one that said AUTO PARTS.

He had made it halfway down the rows when Grey stopped in his tracks. From ahead and to his left he heard a quiet rustling, followed by a barely audible murmuring. Grey took two steps forward and peered around the corner.

It was a woman. She was standing in front of a display of paint samples. She was dressed in jeans and a man's dress shirt; her hair, a soft brown, was swept behind her ears, fixed in place by a pair of sunglasses perched on top of her head. She was also pregnant—not have-the-baby-right-this-second pregnant, but pregnant enough. While Grey watched, she pulled a little square of color from one of the slots and angled it first this way and then the other, frowning pensively. Then she returned it to its slot.

So unexpected was this vision that Grey could only gaze at her in mute astonishment. What was she doing here? A full thirty seconds passed, the woman taking no notice of his presence, wholly engaged by her mysterious business. Not wanting to frighten her, Grey gently placed the gun on an open shelf and took a cautious step forward. What should he say? He'd never been good at icebreakers. Or even talking to people, really. He settled for clearing his throat.

The woman glanced at him over her shoulder. "Well, it's about time," she said. "I've been standing here for twenty minutes."

"Lady, what are you doing?"

She turned from the display. "Is this or is this not the paint department?" She was holding out a group of sample chips, fanned like a deck of playing cards. "Now, I'm thinking maybe Garden Gate, but I'm worried it will be too dark."

Grey was utterly dumbfounded. She wanted him to help her pick paint?

"Probably nobody ever asks your opinion, I know," she continued briskly—a little too briskly, Grey thought. "Just put it in a can and take my money, I'm sure that's what everybody says. But I value the judgment of someone who knows his business. So, what do you think? In your professional opinion."

Grey was standing within just a few feet of her now. Her face was fine-boned and pale, with a subtle fan of crow's-feet at the corners of her eyes. "I think you're confused. I don't work here."

She narrowed her eyes at him. "You don't?"

"Lady, no one works here."

Confusion swept over her face. But just as quickly it disappeared, her features reorganizing into a look of irritation. "Oh, you hardly need to tell me that," she said, tossing his words away. "Trying to get a little help around this place is like pulling teeth. Now," she went on, "as I was saying, I need to know which of these would go best in a nursery." She gave a bashful smile. "I guess it's no secret, but I'm expecting."

Grey had known some crazy people in his days, but this woman took the cake. "Lady, I don't think you should be here. It's not safe."

Another little hitch of time passed before she answered; it was as if she was processing his words and then, in the next instant, rewriting their meaning.

"Honestly, you sound just like David. To tell you the truth, I've had just about enough of this kind of talk." She sighed heavily. "So, Garden Gate it is then. I'll take two gallons in an eggshell finish, please. If you don't mind, I'm in kind of a hurry."

Grey felt completely flustered. "You want me to sell you paint?"

"Well, are you or aren't you the manager?"

The manager? When had that happened? The fact was dawning on him that the woman wasn't just pretending.

"Lady, don't you know what's going on around here?"

She pulled two cans from the shelves and held them out. "I'll tell you what's going on. I'm buying some paint, and you're going to mix it for me, Mr.— Now, I don't believe I got your name."

Grey swallowed. Something about the woman seemed to make him absolutely powerless, as if he were being dragged by a runaway horse. "It's Grey," he said. "Lawrence Grey."

She pushed the cans toward him, forcing him to take them. Christ, she practically had him filling out an employment application. If this went on much longer, he'd never get a fan belt. "Well, Mr. Grey. I'd like two gallons of Garden Gate, please."

"Um, I don't know how."

"Of course you do." She gestured toward the counter. "Just put it in the whatchamacallit."

"Lady, I can't."

"What do you mean, you can't?"

"Well, just for starters, the power's out."

This remark seemed to have some beneficial effect. The woman tilted her face toward the ceiling.

"Now, I think I did notice that," she said airily. "It does seem a little dim in here."

"That's what I was trying to tell you."

"Well, why didn't you just say so?" she huffed. "So, no Garden Gate. No color at all, from what you're saying. I have to tell you this comes as a disappointment. I was really hoping to get the nursery done today."

"Lady, I don't think—"

"The truth is, David should really be the one doing this, but oh no, he has to go off and save the world and leave me stuck in the house like a prisoner. And where the hell is Yolanda? Pardon my French. You know, after everything I've done for her, I'd expect a little consideration. Even just a call."

David. Yolanda. Who were these people? It was all completely baffling, and not a little weird, but one thing was obvious: this poor woman was completely alone. Unless Grey found a way to get her out of here, she wouldn't last long.

"Maybe you could just paint it white," he offered. "I'm sure they got lots of that."

She looked at him skeptically. "Why would I want to paint it white?"

"They say white goes with anything, right?" For the love of God, listen to him; he sounded like one of those fags on TV. "You can do anything with white. Maybe add something else with color in the room. The curtains and stuff."

She hesitated. "I don't know. White does seem a little

plain. On the other hand, I did want to get the painting done today."

"Exactly," Grey said, and did his best to smile. "That's just what I'm saying. You can paint it white, then figure out the rest when you see how it looks. That's what I'd recommend."

"And white does go with anything. You're correct about that."

"You said it was a nursery, right? So maybe later you could add a border, to jazz it up a little. You know, like bunnies or something."

"Bunnies, you say?"

Grey swallowed. Where had that come from? Bunnies were the glowsticks' all-time favorite food. He'd watched Zero gobble them down by the cartload.

"Sure," he managed. "Everybody likes bunnies."

He could see the idea taking hold of her. Which raised another question. Assuming the woman agreed to leave, what then? He could hardly let her go off on her own. He also wondered just how pregnant she was. Five months? Six? He wasn't a good judge of these things.

"Well, I think you really may have something there," the woman said with a nod from her fine-boned chin. "We really seem to be on the same wavelength, Mr. Grey."

"It's Lawrence," he said.

Smiling, she held out her hand. "Call me Lila."

It wasn't until he was sitting in the woman's Volvo—Lila had actually left a wad of cash at one of the registers, with a note promising to return—that Grey realized that somewhere between his carrying the cans to the car and loading them into the cargo area, she had successfully maneuvered him into agreeing to paint the nursery. He didn't recall actually doing this; it just kind of happened, and the next thing he knew they were driving away, the woman steering the Volvo through the abandoned city, past wrecked cars and bloated bodies, overturned Army trucks and the still-smoking rubble of gutted apartment complexes. "Really," she remarked, guiding the station wagon around the burned-out hulk of a FedEx delivery truck with barely a glance, "you'd think people would have the sense to call a wrecker and not just leave their cars sitting in the road." She also chattered on about the nursery (he'd hit pay dirt with the bunnies), tucking in more snide asides about David, who Grey figured was her husband. Grey guessed the man had gone off somewhere, leaving her alone in her house. Based on the things he'd seen, it seemed likely he'd gotten himself killed. Maybe the woman had been crazy before, but Grey didn't think so. Something bad had happened to her, really bad. There was a name for this, he knew. Post-traumatic something. Basically the woman knew but didn't know, and her mind, in its terrified state, was protecting her from the truth—a truth that, sooner or later, Grey would have to tell her.

They arrived at the house, a big brick Tudor that seemed to soar above the street. He'd already guessed the woman was well-off from the way she'd spoken to him, but this was something else. Grey retrieved the supplies from the Volvo's cargo area—in addition to the paint, she'd selected a package of rollers, a tray, and an assortment of brushes—and mounted the steps. At the front door, Lila fumbled with her keys.

"Now, this always sticks a little."

She shouldered the door open to a wash of stale air. Grey followed her into the foyer. He had expected the interior of the house to be like something in a castle, all heavy drapes and overstuffed furniture and dripping chandeliers, but it was the opposite, more like some kind of office than a place people actually lived. To his left, a wide arch led to the dining room, which was occupied by a long glass table and some uncomfortable-looking chairs; to the right was the living room, a barren expanse interrupted only by a low-slung couch and a large black piano. For a moment Grey just stood there, dumbly holding the cans of paint, trying to put his thoughts together. He smelled something, too—a pungent whiff of old garbage coming from deep within the house.

As the silence deepened, Grey scrambled for something to say. "Do you play?" he asked.

Lila was depositing her purse and keys on the little table by the door. "Play what?"

Grey gestured at the piano. She swiveled her head to look at the instrument, seeming vaguely startled.

"No," she answered with a frown. "That was David's idea. A little pretentious, if you ask me."

She led him up the stairs, the air thickening as they made their ascent. Grey followed her to the end of the carpeted hall.

"Here we are," she announced.

The room felt disproportionately snug, considering the dimensions of the house. A ladder stood in one corner, and the floor was covered by a plastic drop cloth taped to the baseboards; a roller sat in a tray of paint, hardening in the heat. Grey moved farther in. The room's original tone had been a neutral cream, but someone—Lila, he guessed—had rolled broad, haphazard stripes of yellow up and down the walls, following no organized pattern. It would take him three coats just to cover it.

Lila was standing in the doorway with her hands on her hips. "It's probably pretty obvious," she said with a wince, "I'm not much of a painter. Certainly not a professional such as yourself."

This again, Grey thought. But as long as he'd decided to play along, he saw no reason to disabuse her of the notion that he knew what he was doing.

"Do you need anything else before you get started?"

"I guess not," Grey managed.

She yawned into her hand. A sudden weariness seemed to have overcome her, as if she were a slowly deflating balloon. "Then I suppose I'll leave you to it. I'm going to get off my feet for a bit."

With these words, she left him alone. Grey heard the snap of a door closing down the hall. Well, wasn't this the damnedest thing, he thought. Painting a baby's room in some rich lady's house certainly wasn't anything he'd imagined himself doing when he'd woken up at the Red Roof. He listened for more sounds from her but heard nothing. Maybe the funniest thing of all was that Grey didn't mind, not really. The woman was as nutty as they came, and not a little bossy. But it wasn't as if he'd deceived her about who he was, since she'd never even asked. It felt good to be trusted by someone, even if he didn't deserve it.

He retrieved his supplies from the foyer and got to work. Painting wasn't anything he'd ever done much of, but it was hardly rocket science, and he quickly settled into its rhythms, his mind a pleasant blank. He could almost forget about waking up at the Red Roof, and Zero and Richards and the Chalet and all the rest. An hour passed, and then another; he was cutting in the edges along the ceiling when Lila appeared in the doorway, bearing a tray with a sandwich and a glass of water. She had changed into a high-waisted denim maternity dress that, despite its roominess, made her appear even more pregnant.

"I hope you like tuna."

He climbed off the ladder to receive the tray. The bread was covered with furry green mold; there was a smell of rancid mayonnaise. Grey's stomach flipped.

"Maybe later," he stammered. "I want to do a second coat first."

Lila said nothing more about this, instead stepping back to look around the room. "I have to say, this really looks better. *So* much better. I don't know why I didn't think of white before." She pointed her eyes at Grey again. "I hope you don't think me too forward, Lawrence, and I don't want to assume anything, but you don't by chance need a place to stay the night?"

Grey was caught short; he hadn't thought that far ahead. He hadn't thought ahead at all, as if the woman's delusional state were contagious. But of course she'd want him to stay. After so many days alone, there was no way she was letting him get loose now—keeping him here was the point. And besides, where would he go?

"Good. It's settled then." She gave a nervous laugh. "I have to say, I'm very relieved. I feel so guilty, dragging you into this, never even asking if you have someplace else to be. And after you've been so helpful."

"It's okay," Grey said. "I mean, I'm glad to stay."

"Don't mention it." The conversation seemed over, but at the doorway Lila turned, wrinkling her nose with distaste. "Sorry about the sandwich. I know it probably isn't very appetizing. I keep meaning to get out to the market. But I'll make you a nice dinner."

Grey worked through the afternoon, completing the third coat as the sun was setting in the windows. He had to say, the room didn't look half bad. He deposited his brushes and rollers in the tray, descended the stairs, and followed the central hallway back to the kitchen. Like the rest of the house, the room had a spare, modern appearance, with white cabinets, black granite countertops, and appliances of gleaming chrome, the effect marred only by the garbage bags that were piled everywhere, reeking of old food. Lila was standing at the stove—the gas appeared to be working—and stirring a saucepan by candlelight. The table was set with china, napkins, and silverware, even a tablecloth.

"I hope you like tomato," said Lila, smiling at him.

Lila directed him to a small room behind the kitchen with a utility sink. There was no water to wash the brushes, so Grey left them in the basin and used a rag to clean his hands as best he could. The idea of tomato soup repelled him, but he would have to do a convincing job of trying to eat—there was simply no way to avoid it. By the time he returned, Lila was ladling the steaming soup into a pair of bowls. These she carried to the table with a plate of Ritz crackers.

"Bon appétit."

The first spoonful nearly made him gag. It didn't even seem like food. Against every instinct, he managed to swallow. Lila appeared to take no notice of his distress, breaking the crackers into her soup and spooning it into her mouth. By sheer force of will, Grey took another spoonful, then a third. He could feel the soup lodging at the base of his gut, an inert mass. As he attempted a fourth, something viselike clamped inside him.

"Excuse me a second."

Trying not to run, he retreated to the utility room, arriving at the sink in the nick of time. Usually he made a racket when he puked, but not now: the soup seemed to fly effortlessly out of his body. Christ, what was the matter with him? He wiped his mouth, took a moment to steady himself, and returned to the table. Lila was looking at him with concern.

"Is the soup all right?" she asked gingerly.

He couldn't even look at the stuff. He wondered if she could smell the puke on his breath. "It's fine," he managed. "I'm just . . . not very hungry, I guess."

The answer appeared to satisfy her. She regarded him for a long moment before speaking again. "I hope you don't mind my asking, Lawrence. But are you looking for work?"

"More painting, you mean?"

"Well, certainly there's that. But other things, too. Because I have the impression, and forgive me if I'm leaping to conclusions, that you may be a little bit . . . at loose ends. Which is fine. Don't get me wrong. Things happen to people." She squinted across the table. "But you don't really work at Home Depot, do you?"

Grey shook his head.

"I thought so! Really, you had me going for a while there. And regardless, you've done a beautiful job. A *beautiful* job. Which only proves my point. If you see what I'm saying. Because I'd like to help you get back on your feet. You've been so helpful, I'd like to return the favor. God knows there's plenty that needs doing around here. There's putting up the border, and of course the problems with the AC, and the yard, well you've seen the yard . . ."

If he didn't stop her now, Grey knew, he'd never get her out of here. "Lady—"

"Please." Holding up a hand, she gave him a warm smile. "It's Lila."

"Lila, okay." Grey drew a breath. "Have you noticed anything . . . strange?"

A puzzled frown. "I don't know what you mean."

Best to back in slowly, Grey thought. "Like, take the electricity, for instance."

"Oh that," she said, and waved a hand dismissively. "You already mentioned that, at the store."

"But doesn't it seem odd that it's still out? Don't you think they would have fixed it by now?"

A vague disturbance moved across her face. "I haven't the foggiest. Honestly, I don't see where you're going with this."

"And David, you said he hasn't called. How long has it been?"

"Well, he's a busy man. A very busy man."

"I don't think that's the reason he hasn't called."

Her voice was absolutely flat. "You don't."

"No."

Lila's eyes narrowed suspiciously. "Lawrence, do you know something you're not telling me? Because if you're a friend of David's, I hope you would have the decency to tell me."

Grey might just as well have tried to snatch a fly out of the air. "No, he's not a friend of mine. I'm just saying . . ." There was nothing to do but just come out with it. "Have you noticed there aren't any people?"

Lila was staring at him intently, arms crossed above her pregnant belly. Her eyes held a look of barely contained rage. She rose abruptly, snatched her bowl from the table, and carried it to the sink.

"Lila—"

She shook her head emphatically, not looking at him. "I won't have you talk this way."

"We have to get out of here."

With a clatter she tossed the bowl into the sink and turned on the tap, violently pumping the lever back and forth, to no avail. "Goddamnit, there's no water. *Why is there no fucking water?*"

Grey got to his feet. She spun to face him, her fists balled with anger.

"Don't you understand? I can't lose her again! I can't!"

Did she mean the baby? And what did she mean by "again"?

"We can't stay." He took another cautious step, as if approaching a wary animal. "It's not safe here."

Furious tears began to spill down her cheeks. "Why do you have to do this? Why?"

She lurched toward him, fists raised like hammers. Grey was thrust back on his heels. She began to pummel his chest as if she were trying to break down a door. But her attack wasn't organized; it was an expression of pure panic, of the storm of emotion breaking inside her. As she reared back again, Grey regained his balance and pulled her into him like a boxer into a clinch, encircling her upper body and pinning her arms to her sides. The gesture was reflexive; he didn't know what else to do. "Don't say that," Lila pleaded, thrashing inside his grip. "It isn't true, it isn't true. . . ." Then, with a rush of breath and a whimper of surrender, the air let out of her and she collapsed against him.

For a period that might have been a full minute they stayed that way, locked in an awkward embrace. Grey couldn't have been more astonished—not by her violent reaction, which he could have foreseen, but by the mere presence of a woman's body in his arms. How slight she was! How different from himself! How long had it been since Grey had hugged a woman, hugged anyone? Or even been touched by another person? He could feel the hard roundness of Lila's belly pressed against him, an insistent presence. A baby, Grey thought, and for the first time, the full implications of this fact dawned in his mind. In the midst of the chaos and carnage of a world gone mad, this poor woman was going to have a baby.

Grey relaxed his grip and backed away. Lila was looking at the floor. The brisk, officious woman he'd met in the paint aisle was gone; in her place stood a frail, diminished creature, almost childlike.

"Can I ask you something, Lawrence?" Her voice was very small.

Grey nodded.

"What did you do before?"

For a moment he didn't understand what she was asking; then he realized she meant what job. "I cleaned," he said, and shrugged. "I mean, I was a janitor."

Lila considered his statement without expression. "Well, I guess you've got me there," she said miserably. She rubbed her nose with the back of her wrist. "To tell you the truth, I don't think I was anything at all."

Another silence descended, Lila staring at the floor, Grey wondering what she would next say. Whatever it was, he sensed their survival depended on it.

"I lost one before, you see," Lila said. "A baby girl."

Grey waited.

"Her heart, you understand," she said, and placed a hand against her chest. "It was a problem with her heart."

It was strange; standing in the quiet, Grey felt as if he'd known this about her all along. Or, if not the thing itself, then the kind of thing. It was as if he were looking at one of those pictures that made no sense when you saw it up close, but then you backed away and suddenly it did.

"What was her name?" Grey asked.

Lila raised her tear-streaked face. For a moment she just looked at him, her eyes pulled into an appraising squint. He wondered if he'd made a mistake, asking this. The question had just popped out.

"Thank you, Lawrence. Nobody ever asks me that. I can't tell you how long it's been."

"Why wouldn't they?"

"I don't know." Her shoulders lifted with a tiny shrug. "I guess they think it's bad luck or something."

"Not to me."

A brief silence passed. Grey didn't think he'd ever felt so awful for anybody in his life.

"Eva," Lila said. "My daughter was Eva."

They stood together in the presence of this name. Outside, beyond the windows of Lila's house, the night was pressing down. Grey realized it had begun to rain—a quiet, soaking, summer rain, pattering the windows.

"I'm not really who you think I am," Grey confessed.

"No?"

What did he want to tell her? The truth, surely, or some version of it, but in the last day and a half, the idea of truth seemed to have slipped its moorings completely. He didn't even know where to begin.

"It's all right," Lila said. "You don't have to say anything. Whoever you were before, it doesn't make much difference now."

"It might. I've had . . . some troubles."

"So that would make you just like the rest of us, wouldn't it? One more person with a secret." She looked away. "That's the worst part, really, when you think about it. Try as you might, nobody will ever truly know who you are. You're just somebody alone in a house with your thoughts and nothing else."

Grey nodded. What was there to say?

"Promise me you won't leave," Lila said. "Whatever happens, don't do that."

"Okay."

"You'll look after me. We'll look after each other."

"I promise."

The conversation seemed to end there. Lila, exhaling a weary breath, pushed her shoulders back. "Well. I guess I'd better turn in. I expect you'll want to be leaving first thing in the morning. If I'm reading you correctly."

"I think that's best."

Her eyes wistfully traveled the room with its shiny appliances and overflowing trash bags and dirty dishes in piles. "It's too bad, really. I did want to finish the nursery. But I guess that will have to wait." She found his face again. "Just one thing. You can't make me think about it."

Grey understood what she was asking. *Don't make me think about the world.* "If that's what you want."

"We're just . . ." She looked for the words. "Taking a drive in the country. How does that sound? Do you think you can do that for me?"

Grey nodded. The request struck him as strange, even a little silly, but he would have put on a clown suit if that's what it took to get her out of there.

"Good. Just so long as that's settled."

He waited for her to say something more, or else leave the room, but neither thing happened. A change came into Lila's face—a look of intense concentration, as if she were reading tiny print that only she could see. Then, abruptly, her eyes grew very wide; she seemed about to laugh.

"Oh my goodness, what a scene I made! I can't believe I did that!" Her hands darted to her cheeks, her hair. "I must look terrible. Do I look terrible?"

"I think you look fine," Grey managed.

"Here you are, a guest in my home, and off go the waterworks. It drives Brad absolutely crazy."

The name wasn't one he'd heard from her before. "Who's Brad?"

Lila frowned. "My husband, of course."

"I thought David was your husband."

She gave him a blank stare. "Well, he is. David, I mean."

"But you said—"

Lila waved this away. "I say a lot of things, Lawrence. That's one thing you'll have to learn about me. Probably you think I'm just some crazy woman, and you wouldn't be wrong."

"I don't think that at all," Grey lied.

An ironic smile creased her fine-boned face. "Well. We both know you're only saying that because you're being nice. But I appreciate the gesture." She surveyed the room again, nodding vaguely. "So, it's been quite a day, don't you think? I'm afraid we don't really have a proper guest room, but I made up the couch for you. If you don't mind, I think I'll just leave the dishes for the morning and say good night."

Grey had no idea what to make of any of this. It was as if Lila had broken her trance of denial, only to slip back into it again. Not slip, he thought; she had done this to herself, forcing her thoughts back into place with an act of will. He watched in dumb wonder as she made her way to the doorway, where she turned to face him.

"I'm so very glad you're here, Lawrence," she said, and smiled emptily. "We're going to be good friends, you and I. I just know it."

Then she was gone. Grey listened to her slow trudge down the hallway and up the stairs. He cleared the rest of the dishes from the table. He would have liked to wash them, so she could come down to a clean kitchen in the morning, but there was nothing he could do but deposit them in the sink with the others.

He carried one of the candles from the table to the living room. But the minute he lay down on the sofa, he knew sleep was out of the question. His brain was bouncing with alertness; he still felt a little nauseated from the soup. His mind returned to the scene in the kitchen, and the moment when he'd put his arms around her. Not a hug, exactly; he'd just been trying to get Lila to stop hitting him. But at some point it had become something hug*like*. It had felt good—more than good, actually. The feeling wasn't anything sexual, not as Grey recalled it. Years had gone by since Grey had experienced anything that even approximated a sexual thought— the anti-androgens saw to that—on top of which, the woman was pregnant, for God's sake. Which, come to think of it, was maybe what was so nice about the whole thing. Pregnant women didn't just go hugging people for no reason. Holding Lila, Grey had felt as if he'd stepped into a circle, and within this circle there were not just two people but three—because the baby was there, too. Maybe Lila was crazy and maybe she wasn't. He was hardly the person to judge. But he couldn't see that this made a difference one way or the other. She'd chosen him to help her, and that was exactly what he'd do.

Grey had almost talked his way into sleep when the silence was cut by an animal yelp. He lurched upright on the couch, shaking off his disorientation; the sound had come from outside. He hurried to the window.

That was when he remembered Iggy's gun. He'd been so distracted, he'd left it at the Home Depot. How could he have been so dumb?

He pressed his face to the glass. A dog-sized hump was lying in the middle of the street. It didn't seem to be moving. Grey waited a moment, his breath suspended. A pale shape bounded through the treetops, the image fading, then gone.

Grey knew he wouldn't shut his eyes all night. But it didn't matter. Upstairs Lila slept, dreaming of a world that was no more, while outside the walls of the house, a monstrous evil lurked—an evil Grey was part of. His mind returned to the scene in the kitchen, and the image of Lila, standing at the sink, desperate tears flowing down her cheeks, her fists clenched with rage. *I can't lose her again, I can't.*

He would stand guard at the window till morning, and then, come sunrise, get them the hell out of here.

Lila Kyle was brooding in the dark.

She'd heard the yelp from outside. A dog, she thought; something had happened to a dog. Some thoughtless motorist, speeding down the street? Surely that was what had happened. People should be more careful with their pets.

Don't think, she told herself. Don't think don't think don't think.

Lila wondered what it would be like, being a dog. She could see how there might be some advantages. A purely thoughtless existence, nothing on one's mind but the next pat on the head, a walk around the block, the sensation of food in one's belly. Probably Roscoe (because it *was* Roscoe she had heard; poor Roscoe) hadn't even known what was happening to him. Maybe a little bit, at the end. One minute he was snuffling down the street, searching for something to eat—Lila recalled the floppy thing she'd seen in his mouth that morning, instantly pushing this unpleasant memory aside—and the next: well, there was no next. Roscoe was sailing into oblivion.

And now there was this man. This Lawrence Grey. About whom, Lila realized, she knew exactly nothing. He was a janitor. He cleaned. What did he clean? Probably David would have a conniption if he knew she'd let a total stranger into the house. She would have liked to see the look on David's face. Lila supposed it was possible she'd misjudged the man, this Lawrence Grey, but she didn't think so. She'd always been a good judge of character. Granted, Lawrence had said some disturbing things in the kitchen—*very* disturbing. About the lights being out and people missing and all the rest. (Dead, dead, everyone was dead.) He'd certainly gotten her upset. But to be fair, he'd done a wonderful job with the nursery, and she could tell just by looking at him that his heart was in the right place. Which was another of her father's favorite expressions. What did it mean, exactly? Could the heart be anywhere else? Daddy, I'm a doctor, she'd told him once, laughing; I can tell you for a fact, the heart is where it is.

Lila heard herself sigh. Such an effort, just to keep everything straight in her mind. Because that was what you had to do; you had to look at things in a certain light and no other, and no matter what happened, you couldn't break your gaze away. The world could overwhelm you otherwise, it could drown you like a wave, and then where would you be? The house itself was nothing she would miss; she had secretly hated it from the moment she'd stepped inside, its show-offy dimensions and too-many rooms and gaseous yellow light. It wasn't at all like the one that she and Brad had lived in on Maribel Street—snug, homey, full of the things they'd loved—but how could it be? What was a house but the life it contained? This pompous monstrosity, this museum of nothing. It had been David's idea, of course. The House of David: wasn't that something from the Bible? The Bible was full of houses, the house of so-and-so and the house of such-and-such. Lila remembered being a little girl, snuggled up on the sofa to watch *A Charlie Brown Christmas*—she'd loved Snoopy almost as much as Peter Rabbit—and the moment when Linus, the smart one, the one who was really just a man pretending to be a boy with his blanket, stepped downstage to tell Charlie Brown what Christmas was all about. *And there were in that same country shepherds abiding in the field, keeping watch over their flocks by night. And lo, the angel of the Lord came upon them, and the glory of the Lord shone round about them, and they were sore afraid. And the angel said unto them, Fear not, for behold, I bring you good tidings of great joy, which shall be to all people. For unto you is born this day in the city of David a Savior, which is Christ the Lord.*

City of David, House of David.

But the baby, Lila thought. The baby was where her

thoughts belonged. Not with the house, or noises from outside (there were monsters), or David not coming home (dead David), or any of the rest. All the literature had clearly shown, indisputably shown, that negative emotions affected the fetus. It thought as you thought, it felt as you felt, and if you were frightened all the time, what then? Those upsetting things Lawrence had said in the kitchen: the man meant well, he was only trying to do what he thought was best for her and Eva (Eva?), but did these things have to be true, simply because he'd said them? They were *theories*. They were just his *opinions*. Which wasn't to say she disagreed. Probably it was time to go. It had gotten awfully quiet around this place. (Poor Roscoe.) If Brad were here, that's what he would have said to her. Lila, it's time to go.

Because sometimes, lots of times, all the time, it felt to Lila Kyle as if the baby growing inside her wasn't somebody new, a whole new person. Since the morning she'd squatted on the toilet with the plastic wand between her thighs, watching in mute wonderment as the little blue cross appeared, the idea had taken root. The baby wasn't a new Eva, or a different Eva, or a replacement Eva: she *was* Eva, their own little girl, come home. It was as if the world had righted itself, the cosmic mistake of Eva's death undone.

She wanted to tell Brad about it. More than wanted: his name produced a longing so powerful it brought tears to her eyes. She hadn't meant to marry David! Why had Lila married David—sanctimonious, overbearing, eternally do-gooding David—when she was already married to Brad? Especially now, with Eva on the way, coming to make them a family again?

Lila still loved him; that was the thing. That was the sad and sorrowful mystery of it all. She'd never stopped loving Brad, nor he her, not for a second, even when their love was too much pain for either to carry, because their little girl was gone. They had parted as a way to forget, neither being able to accomplish this in the company of the other—a sad, inevitable sundering, like the primordial separation of continents. Until the very end they'd fought it. The night before he'd moved out, his suitcases in the hall of the house on Maribel Street, the lawyers properly apprised, so many tears having been shed that no one even knew what they were crying about anymore—a condition as general as the weather, a world of everlasting tears—he'd come to her in the bedroom he had long since vacated, slid beneath the covers, and for a single hour they'd been a couple again, silently moving together, their bodies still wanting what their hearts could no longer bear. Not a word had passed between them; in the morning Lila awoke alone.

But now all of that had changed. Eva was coming! Eva was practically here! She would write Brad a letter; that's what Lila would do. Surely he was going to come look for her, it was just the kind of man he was, you could always count on Brad when things went to hell in a handbasket, and how would it be for him to find she wasn't there? Her spirits restored by this decision, Lila crept to the little desk under the windows, fumbling in the drawer for a pencil and a sheet of notebook paper. Now, what words to choose? *I am going away. I don't know quite where. Wait for me, my darling. I love you. Eva will be here soon.* Simple and clear, elegantly capturing the essence of the thing. Satisfied, she folded the paper into thirds, slid it into an envelope, wrote "Brad" on the outside, and propped it on the desk so she would see it in the morning.

She lay back down. From across the room, the letter watched her, a rectangle of glowing whiteness. Closing her eyes, Lila let her hands drift down to the hard curve of her belly. A feeling of fullness, and then, from within, a gaseous twitch, then another and another. The baby was hiccupping. *Hiccup!* went the tiny baby. Lila closed her eyes, allowing the sensation to wash over her. Inside her, in the space beneath her heart, a small life was waiting to be born, but even more: she, Eva, was coming home. The day was catching up to her, Lila knew; her mind was riding the currents of sleep like a surfer paddling on the curve of a wave; in another moment the wave would wash over her, taking her under. Eva had quieted under her fingertips. I love you, Eva, thought Lila Kyle, and with that she fell asleep.

10

It was nearly ten A.M. by the time they got to Mile High. Driving into downtown, Danny found himself caught in a maze of barricades: abandoned Humvees, machine-gun positions with their piles of sandbags, even a few tanks. A dozen times he was forced to backtrack in search of an alternate route, only to find his passage blocked. Finally, as the last of the morning haze was burning off, he found a clear path under the freeway and ascended the ramp to the stadium.

The parking area was a grid of olive-green tents, eerily becalmed under the morning sun. Surrounding this was a ring of vehicles, passenger cars and ambulances and police cruisers, many of them looking half-crushed: windows smashed, fenders torn from the frames, doors ripped off their hinges. Danny brought the bus to a halt.

They disembarked into a stench of decay so thick that Danny nearly gagged. Worse than Momma, worse than all the bodies he'd seen that morning, walking to the depot. It was the kind of smell that could snake inside you, into your nose and mouth, and linger there for days.

"Hello!" April called. Her voice echoed across the lot. "Is anybody here? Hello!"

Danny had a bad feeling in the pit of his stomach. Some of this was the smell, but some wasn't. He had the jangly feeling all over.

"Hello!" April called again, her hands cupped around her mouth. "Can anyone hear me?"

"Maybe we should go," Danny suggested.

"The Army's supposed to be here."

"Maybe they left already."

April removed her backpack, unzipped the top, and withdrew a hammer. She gave it a swing, as if to test its weight.

"Tim, you stay by me. Understand? No wandering off."

The boy was standing at the base of the bus's steps, pinching his nose. "But it smells gross," he said in a nasal voice.

April slid her arms into the straps. "The whole *city* smells gross. You'll just have to deal with it. Now come on."

Danny didn't want to go either, but the girl was determined. He followed the two of them as they made their way into the maze of vehicles. Step by step, Danny began to comprehend what he was seeing. The cars had been positioned around the tents as a defense. Like in pioneer times, the way settlers would circle the covered wagons when the Indians attacked. But these weren't Indians, Danny knew, and whatever had happened here, it looked to be long over. There were corpses, somewhere—the smell seemed to intensify the farther they went—but so far they'd seen no trace of them. It was as if everyone had vanished.

They came to the first of the tents. April entered first, holding the hammer up before her, ready to swing. The space was a mess of overturned gurneys and IV poles, debris strewn everywhere—bandages, basins, syringes. But still there were no bodies.

They looked in another tent, then a third. Each was the same. "So where did everybody go?" April said.

The only place left to look was the stadium. Danny didn't want to, but April wouldn't take no for an answer. If the Army said to come here, she insisted, there had to be a reason. They moved up the ramp toward the entrance. April was leading the way, clutching Tim with one hand, the hammer with the other. For the first time, Danny noticed the birds. A huge black cloud wheeling over the stadium, their hoarse calls seeming to break the silence and to deepen it at the same time.

Then, from behind them, a man's voice:

"I wouldn't go in there if I were you."

The Ferrari had died as Kittridge was pulling into the parking area. By this time the car was bucking like a half-broke horse, plumes of oily smoke pouring from the hood and undercarriage. There was no mistaking what had happened: Kittridge's rocket ride out of the parking ramp—that leap into space and then the hard bang on the pavement—had cracked the oil pan. As the oil had drained away, the motor had gradually overheated, metal expanding until the pistons had seized in their cylinders.

Sorry about your car, Warren. It sure was good while it lasted.

After what he'd seen in the stadium, Kittridge needed some time to collect himself. Jesus, what a scene. It wasn't anything he couldn't have predicted, but staring it in the face was something else. It sickened him to the core. His hands were actually shaking; he thought he might be ill. Kittridge had seen some things in his life, horrible things. Bodies in pits lined up like cordwood; whole villages gassed, families lying where they'd fallen, their hands reaching out in vain for the last touch of a loved one; the indecipherable remains of men and women and children, blasted to bits in a marketplace by some lunatic with a bomb strapped to his chest. But never anything even remotely on this scale.

He'd been sitting on the hood of the Ferrari, considering his options, when in the distance he'd heard a vehicle approaching. Kittridge's nerves snapped to attention. A large diesel engine by the sound of it: an APC? But then, lumbering up the ramp, came the surreal vision of a big yellow school bus.

How about that, Kittridge thought. Holy son of a bitch. A goddamned school bus, like a class trip to the end of the world.

Kittridge watched as the bus came to a stop. Three people emerged: a girl with a streak of pink in her hair, a knobby-kneed boy in a T-shirt and shorts, and a man in a funny-looking hat, whom Kittridge guessed was the driver. Hello! the girl called out. Is anybody here? A moment of conferral, then they advanced into the tangle of vehicles, the girl leading the way.

Probably it was time to say something, Kittridge thought. But alerting them to his presence could incur a host of obligations he'd vowed to avoid from the start. Other people weren't part of the plan; the plan was to get gone. Travel light, stay alive as long as possible, take as many virals with him as he could when the end came. Last Stand in Denver making his bright, meteoric descent into the void.

But then Kittridge realized what was about to happen. The three of them were headed straight for the stadium. Of course that's where they'd go; Kittridge had done the same. These were *kids,* for God's sake; plan or no plan, no way could he let them go in there.

Kittridge grabbed his rifle and hustled to head them off.

At the sound of Kittridge's voice, the driver reacted so violently that Kittridge was momentarily frozen into inaction. Erupting with a yelp, the man lurched forward, stumbling over his feet while simultaneously burying his face in the crook of his elbow. The other two scurried away, the girl yanking the little boy protectively to her waist, swiveling toward Kittridge with a hammer held before her.

"Whoa, steady there," Kittridge said. Pointing the rifle skyward, he raised his hands. "I'm one of the good guys."

Kittridge saw that the girl was older than he'd first guessed, seventeen or so. The pink hair was ridiculous, and both her ears had so many studs in them they looked like they'd been riveted to her head, but the way she regarded him, coolly and without a hint of panic, told him she was more than she appeared. There was no doubt in his mind that she'd use the hammer on him, or try to, if he went another step. She had on a tight black T-shirt, jeans worn to threads at the knees, a pair of Chuck Taylors, and bracelets of leather and silver up and down both arms; a backpack, crime-scene yellow, hung from her shoulders. The boy was obviously her brother, their familial connection evident not only in the unmistakable arrangement of their features—the slightly too-small nose with its buttony tip, the high, sudden planes of the cheekbones, eyes of the same aquatic blue—but also in the way she had reacted, shielding him with a fierce protectiveness that struck Kittridge as distinctly parental.

The third member of their group, the driver, was harder to quantify. Something was definitely off about the guy. He was dressed in khakis and a white oxford shirt buttoned to the collar; his hair, a reddish-blond mop peeking from the sides of his peculiar cap, looked like it had been cut by pinking shears. But the real difference wasn't any of these things. It was the way he held himself.

The boy was the first to speak. He had just about the worst cowlick Kittridge had ever laid eyes on. "Is that a real AK?" he said, pointing.

"Quiet, Tim." Drawing him closer, the girl lifted the hammer, ready to swing. "Who the hell are you?"

Kittridge's hands were still raised. For the moment, the notion that the hammer presented an actual threat was something he was willing to indulge. "My name's Kittridge. And yes," he said, speaking to the boy, "it's a real AK. Just don't go thinking I'll let you touch it, young man."

The boy's face lit with excitement. "That's *cool.*"

Kittridge lifted his chin toward the driver, who was now gazing intently at his shoes. "Is he okay?"

"He doesn't like to be touched is all." The girl was still studying Kittridge warily. "The Army said to come here. We heard it on the radio."

"I expect they did. But it looks like they've flown the coop on us. Now, I don't believe I caught your names."

The girl hesitated. "I'm April. This is my brother, Tim. The other one is Danny."

"Pleased to meet you, April." He offered his most reassuring smile. "So do you think it would be all right with you if I put my hands down now? Seeing as we've all been properly introduced."

"Where'd you get that rifle?"

"Outdoor World. I'm a salesman."

"You sell guns?"

"Camping and fishing gear, mostly," Kittridge replied. "But they give a nice discount. So what do you say? We're all on the same team here, April."

"What team's that?"

He shrugged. "The human one, I'd say."

The girl was weighing him with her eyes. A cautious one,

this April. Kittridge reminded himself that she wasn't just a girl; she was a survivor. Whatever else was true, she deserved to be taken seriously. A few seconds passed, then she lowered the hammer.

"What's in the stadium?" Tim asked.

"Nothing you want to see." Kittridge looked at the girl again. She seemed like an April, he decided. Funny how it sometimes worked that way. "How'd you all get by?"

"We were hiding in the wine cellar."

"What about your folks?"

"We don't know. They were in Telluride."

Jesus, Kittridge thought. Telluride was ground zero, the place where everything had started.

"Well, that was smart. Good thinking." He gestured toward Danny again. He was standing ten feet off to the side with his hands in his pockets, looking at the ground. "What about your friend?"

"Danny was the one who found us. We heard him honking."

"Well, good for you, Danny. I'd say that makes you the hero of the day."

The man gave Kittridge a darting, sidelong glance. His face bore no expression at all. "Okay."

"Why can't I see what's in the stadium?" Tim cut in again.

A look passed between April and Kittridge: *Not a good idea.*

"Never mind about the stadium," April said. She returned her attention to Kittridge. "Have you seen anybody else?"

"Not for a while. That doesn't mean there aren't any."

"But you don't think so."

"Probably it's wisest if we assume we're alone."

Kittridge could see where this was all headed. An hour ago he'd been riding down the side of a building, fleeing for his life. Now he was facing the prospect of looking after two kids and a man who couldn't even meet his eye. But the situation was what it was.

"That your bus, Danny?" he said.

The man nodded. "I drive the blue route. Number twelve."

A smaller vehicle would have made more sense, but Kittridge had the feeling the man wouldn't be leaving without it. "Feel like maybe driving us out of here?"

The girl's expression hardened. "What makes you think you're coming with us?"

Kittridge was taken aback; he hadn't considered the possibility that the three of them wouldn't want his help.

"Actually, nothing, you put it that way. I guess you'd have to invite me."

"Why can't I *see*?" Tim whined.

April rolled her eyes. "For fuck's sake, Tim, just shut up about the stadium, will you?"

"You said the F word! I'm telling!"

"And who are you going to tell?"

The boy was suddenly on the verge of tears. "Don't say that!"

"Listen," Kittridge cut in, "this really isn't the time. By my count we've got eight hours of daylight left. I don't think we want to be anywhere near here after dark."

Which was when the boy, sensing his opening, spun on his heels and bolted up the ramp.

"Shit," Kittridge said. "Both of you stay here."

He took off at a hobbling run, but with his leg, he was in no condition to close the gap; by the time Kittridge caught up to the boy, he was standing in the open mouth of one of the gates, staring dumbly at the field. Just a few seconds, but it was enough. Kittridge snatched him from behind and hoisted him to his chest. The boy went limp, collapsing against him. He made no sound at all. Jesus, Kittridge thought. Why had he let the kid get the jump on him like that?

By the time he reached the base of the ramp, Tim had begun making a sound that was half hiccup, half whimper. Kittridge lowered him to the ground in front of April.

"What do you think you were doing?" Her voice was thick with angry tears.

"I'm . . . s-sorry," the boy stammered.

"You can't go running off like that, you *can't*." She shook him by the arms, then pulled him into a desperate hug. "I've told you a thousand times, you stay with me."

Kittridge had moved to where Danny was standing, gazing at the ground with his hands in his pockets.

"They were really all alone?" he asked quietly.

"Consuela was with them," Danny stated. "But she left."

"Who's Consuela?"

He gave a loose-limbed shrug. "She waits with Tim at the bus sometimes."

There wasn't much else to say on the subject. Maybe Danny wasn't all there, but he'd rescued two helpless kids whose parents were almost certainly dead. It was more than Kittridge had done.

"So how about it, my friend," Kittridge said. "Feel like firing up that bus of yours?"

"Where are we going?"

"I was thinking Nebraska."

11

They left an hour after dawn. Grey took whatever he could find in the kitchen that still looked edible—a few remaining cans of soup, some stale crackers, a box of Wheaties, and bottles of water—and loaded it into the Volvo. He didn't have so much as a toothbrush of his own, but then Lila appeared in the hall with two wheeled suitcases.

"I took the liberty of packing you some clothes."

Lila was dressed as if leaving on vacation, in dark leggings paired with a crisply-starched, long-tailed shirt. A brightly colored silk scarf lay over her shoulders. She'd washed her face and brushed her hair, and was even wearing earrings and a bit of makeup. The sight of her made Grey realize how dirty he was. He hadn't washed in days; probably he didn't smell the best.

"Maybe I should clean up a bit."

Lila directed him to the bathroom at the head of the stairs, where she'd already laid out a change of clothes for him, neatly folded on the toilet seat. A brand-new toothbrush, still in its wrapper, and a tube of Colgate rested on the vanity beside a jug of water. Grey peeled off his jumpsuit and washed his face and splashed his armpits, then brushed his teeth, facing the broad mirror. He hadn't looked at his reflection since the Red Roof, and it still came as a shock, how young he looked—skin clear and taut, hair growing lushly over his scalp, eyes radiating a jewel-like glitter. He looked like he'd lost a lot of weight, too—not surprising, since he'd eaten nothing in two days, but the degree to which this had occurred, both in quantity and kind, was startling. He wasn't just thinner; it was as if his body had rearranged itself. Turning to the side, holding his gaze on his reflection, he ran a hand experimentally over his belly. He'd always run on the chubby side; now he could discern the taut outline of muscles. From there it was a small step to flexing his arms, like a kid admiring himself. Well, look at that, he thought. Actual biceps. God damn.

He put on the clothing Lila had left for him—white boxers, a pair of jeans, and a checked sport shirt—discovering, to his continued amazement, that it all fit rather well. He took one last look at himself in the mirror and descended the stairs to the living room, where he found Lila sitting on the sofa, paging through a *People* magazine.

"Well, there you are." She regarded him up and down, smiling in her airy way. "Don't you look nice."

He wheeled the suitcases to the Volvo. The morning air was weighted with dew; birds were singing in the trees. As if the two of them were just taking a drive in the country, Grey thought, shaking his head. Yet as he stood in the driveway wearing another man's clothes, this almost seemed true. It was as if he had stepped into a different life—the life, perhaps, of the man whose jeans and sport shirt now graced his newly slender, muscled body. He took a deep sniff, expanding his chest. The air felt fresh and clean in his lungs, full of scent. Grass, and new green leaves, and damp earth. It seemed to contain no trace of the terrors of the night before, as if the light of day had cleansed the world.

He sealed the hatch and looked up to see Lila standing at the front door. She turned the lock, then removed something from her purse: an envelope. She withdrew a roll of masking tape from her purse and taped the envelope to the door, standing back to look at it. A letter? Grey thought. Who would it be for? David? Brad? One of these, probably, but Grey still had no idea who was who. The two seemed virtually interchangeable in Lila's mind.

"There," she announced. "All set." At the Volvo, she handed him the keys. "Would it be all right if you drove?"

And Grey liked that, too.

Grey decided it would be best to stay off the main roads, at least until they were out of the city. Though this fact was unstated, it also seemed part of his agreement with Lila that he should avoid passing the sorts of things that might upset her. This turned out not to matter: the woman barely looked up from her magazine. He picked his way through the suburbs; by midmorning, they were in a parched, rolling land of empty fields the color of burnt toast, moving east on a rural blacktop. The city faded away behind them, followed by the blue bulk of the Rockies, vaporizing in the haze. The scene around them possessed a barren, forgotten quality—just a scrim of feathery clouds high overhead, and the dry fields, and the highway unspooling under the Volvo's wheels. Eventually Lila gave up her reading and fell asleep.

The oddness of the situation was inarguable, yet as the miles and hours passed, Grey felt a swelling rightness in his chest. Never in his life had he really mattered to anyone. He searched his mind for something, anything to compare the feeling to. The only thing he could come up with was the story of Joseph and Mary and the flight into Egypt—a boyhood memory, because Grey hadn't been to church in years. Joseph had always seemed like an odd duck, taking care of a woman who was carrying somebody else's baby. But Grey was beginning to see the sense in it, how a person could become attached just by being wanted.

And the thing was, Grey liked women; he always had. The other thing, with the boys, was different. It wasn't about what he liked or didn't like but what he *had* to do, because of his past and the things that had been done to him. That was how Wilder, the prison shrink, had explained it. The boys were a compulsion, Wilder told him, Grey's way of returning to the moment of his own abuse, to reenact it and, in so doing, seek to understand it. Grey no more decided to touch the boys than he decided to scratch an itch. A lot of what Wilder said sounded like bullshit to Grey, but not that part, and it made him feel a little better, knowing he wasn't entirely at fault. Not that it let him off the hook any; Grey had beaten himself up plenty. He'd actually felt relieved when they sent him away. The Old Grey—the one who'd found himself lingering on the edges of playgrounds and cruising slowly past the junior high at three o'clock and dragging his feet in the locker room at the community swimming pool on summer afternoons—*that* Grey was nobody he ever wanted to know again.

His mind returned to the hug in the kitchen. It wasn't a boy-girl thing, Grey knew that, but it wasn't nothing either. It made Grey think of Nora Chung, the one girl he'd dated in high school. She hadn't been a girlfriend, exactly; they'd never actually done anything. The two of them were in the band together—for a brief period, Grey had gotten it in his head to play the trumpet—and sometimes after practice Grey would walk her home, the two of them not even touching, though something about those walks made him feel for the first time that he wasn't alone on the earth. He wanted to kiss her, but he'd never summoned the courage; eventually she'd drifted away. Curious that Grey should remember her now. He hadn't so much as thought her name in twenty years.

By noon, they were approaching the Kansas border. Lila was still sleeping. Grey himself had lapsed into a half-dream state, barely paying attention to the road. He'd managed to avoid towns of any considerable size, but this couldn't last; they'd need gas soon. Ahead he saw a water tower poking from the plain.

The town was named Kingwood—just a short, dusty main street, half the store windows papered over, and a few blocks of dismal houses on either side. It looked harmlessly·abandoned; the only evidence that anything had happened was an ambulance parked in front of the fire station with its rear doors hanging open. And yet Grey sensed something, a tingling at his extremities, as if their progress was being observed from the shadows. He cruised the length of the town, finally coming to a filling station on its eastern edge, an off-brand place called Frankie's.

Lila stirred when Grey shut the engine off. "Where are we?"

"Kansas."

She yawned, squinting through the windshield at the desolate town. "Why are we stopping?"

"We need gas. I'll just be a sec."

Grey tried the pump, but no dice: the power was off. He'd have to siphon some off somehow, but for that he'd need a length of hose and a can. He stepped into the office. A battered metal desk, covered with stacks of paper, stood by the front window; an old office chair rested behind it, rocked back on its hinges, giving the ghostly impression of having only recently been vacated. He moved through the door that led to the service bays, a cool, dark space that smelled of oil. A Cadillac Seville, late-'90s vintage, was perched on one of the lifts; the second bay was occupied by a Chevy 4x4 with a jacked-up suspension and fat, mud-choked tires. Resting on the floor was a five-gallon gas can; on one of the workbenches, Grey located a length of hose. He severed off a six-foot section, slid one end into the 4x4's fuel port, drew in a sip that he spat away, and began to siphon gas into the can.

The can was nearly full when he heard a scuffling above his head. Every nerve in his body fired simultaneously, clenching him in place.

Slowly he lifted his face.

The creature was suspended from one of the ceiling beams, hanging upside down with its knees folded over the strut like a kid on monkey bars. It was smaller than Zero, more human-seeming. As their eyes locked, Grey's heart froze between beats. From deep inside the creature's throat came a trilling sound.

You don't have to be afraid, Grey.

What the fuck?

His feet tangled under him as he lurched backward, sending him pitching to the hard concrete. He snatched the gas can off the floor, fuel still gushing from the siphon, and charged from the service bay into the office and out the door. Lila was standing with her back braced against the car.

"Get in," he said breathlessly.

"You didn't notice if they had a vending machine inside? I'd really like to get a candy bar or something."

"Damn it, Lila, get in the car." Grey threw open the Volvo's hatch, tossed the can inside, and slammed it closed. "We have to go *right now*."

The woman sighed. "Fine, whatever you say. I don't see why you have to be so rude about it."

They raced away. Only when they were a mile from town did Grey's pulse begin to slow. He let the Volvo coast to a stop, threw the door open, and stumbled from the car. Standing at the side of the road, he placed his hands on his knees, breathing in huge gulps of air. Jesus, it was like the thing had *spoken* to him. Like those clicks were a foreign language he could understand. It even knew his name. How did it know his name?

He felt Lila's hand on his shoulder. "Lawrence, you're bleeding."

He was. His elbow looked ripped open, a flap of skin dangling. He must have done it in the fall, although he'd felt nothing.

"Let me look."

Wearing an expression of intense concentration, Lila gently probed the edges with her fingertips. "How did it happen?"

"I guess I tripped."

"You should have said something. Can you move it?"

"I think so, yeah."

"Wait here," Lila commanded. "Don't touch it."

She opened the hatch of the Volvo and began to rummage through her suitcase. She removed a metal box and a bottle of water and dropped the tailgate.

"Let's sit you down."

Grey positioned himself on the tailgate. Lila opened the box: a medical kit. She rubbed a dab of Purell into her hands, removed a pair of latex gloves, snapped them onto her hands, and took his arm again.

"Do you have any history of excessive bleeding?" she asked.

"I don't think so."

"Hepatitis, HIV, anything like that?"

Grey shook his head.

"How about your last tetanus shot? Can you remember when that was?"

What Lila was this? Who was Grey seeing? Not the lost woman of the Home Depot, or the defeated soul in the kitchen; this was someone new. A third Lila, full of efficiency and competence.

"Not since I was a kid."

Lila took another moment to examine the wound. "Well, it's a nasty gash. I'm going to have to suture it."

"You mean like . . . stitches?"

"Trust me, I've done it a million times."

She swabbed the wound with alcohol, removed a disposable syringe from the box, filled it from a tiny vial, and tapped the needle with her forefinger.

"Just a little something to numb you up. You won't feel a thing, I promise."

The prick of the needle and in just a few seconds, Grey's pain melted away. Lila unfolded a cloth onto the tailgate, laying out a pair of forceps, a spool of dark thread, and a tiny scissors.

"You can watch if you want, but most people prefer to look away."

He felt a series of tiny tugs but that was all. Moments later, he looked down to see the gash and its flap of skin replaced by a tight black line. Lila spread ointment over it, then dressed it with a bandage.

"The stitches should dissolve in a couple of days," she said as she was snapping off her gloves. "It may be a little itchy, but you can't scratch it. Just leave it alone."

"How did you know how to do that?" Grey asked. "Are you a nurse or something?"

The question appeared to catch her short. Her mouth opened like she was about to say something; then she closed it again.

"Lila? Are you okay?"

She was sealing up the kit. She returned her supplies to the Volvo and closed the hatch.

"We better be going, don't you think?"

Just like that, the woman who'd stitched his arm was gone, the moment of her emergence erased. Grey wanted to ask her more but knew what would happen if he did. The pact between them was clear: only certain things could be said.

"Do you want me to drive?" Lila asked. "It's probably my turn."

The question wasn't really a question, Grey understood. It was the natural thing to ask, just as it was his job to decline the offer. "No, I can do it."

They got back in the Volvo. As Grey put the car in gear, Lila took up her magazine from the floor.

"If it's all right with you, I think I'm going to read a bit."

A hundred and twelve miles to the north, traveling east on Interstate 76, Kittridge had also begun to worry about fuel. The bus had been full when they'd started; now they were down to a quarter tank.

With a few minor detours, they'd managed to stay on the highway since Fort Morgan. Lulled by the motion of the bus, April and her brother had fallen asleep. Danny whistled through his teeth while he drove—the tune was nothing Kittridge recognized—gamely spinning the wheel and working the brakes and gas, hat tipped to his brow, his face and posture as erect as that of a sea captain facing down a gale.

For the love of God, Kittridge thought. How in the hell had he ended up in a school bus?

"Uh-oh," said Danny.

Kittridge sat up straight. A long line of abandoned vehicles, stretching to the horizon, stood in their path. Some of the cars were lying upside down or on their sides. Bodies were scattered everywhere.

Danny stopped the bus. April and Tim were awake now as well, gazing out the windshield.

"April, get him out of here," Kittridge directed. "Both of you to the back, now."

"What do you want me to do?" Danny asked.

"Wait here."

Kittridge stepped down from the bus. Flies were buzzing in vast black swarms; there was an overwhelming odor of rotten flesh. The air was absolutely still, as if it couldn't bring itself to move. The only signs of life were the birds, vultures and crows, circling overhead. Kittridge moved up the line of cars. Virals had done this, there was no mistaking it; there must have been hundreds of them, thousands even.

What did it mean? And why were the cars all together like this, as if they'd been forced to stop?

Suddenly Danny was beside him.

"I thought I told you to wait with the others."

The man was squinting into the sunlight. "Wait." He held up a hand, then said, "I hear something."

Kittridge listened. Nothing at all, just the creak of the crickets in the empty fields. Then it came: a muffled pounding, like fists on metal.

Danny pointed. "It's coming from over there."

The sound became more distinct with each step. Somebody was alive out there, trapped inside the wreckage. Gradually its components began to separate, the pounding underscored by a strangled echo of human voices. *Let us out! Is somebody out there? Please!*

"Hello!" Kittridge called. "Can you hear me?"

Who's out there? Help us, please! Hurry, we're cooking to death!

The sound was coming from a semitrailer with the bright yellow FEMA insignia printed on its sides. The pounding was frantic now, the voices a shrill chorus of indistinguishable words.

"Hang on!" Kittridge yelled. "We'll get you out!"

The door had been knocked kitty-corner in its frame. Kittridge looked around for something to use as a lever, found a tire iron, and wedged the blade under the door.

"Danny, help me."

The door refused them at first; then it began, almost imperceptibly, to move. As the gap increased, a line of fingers appeared beneath the lip, attempting to draw it upward.

"Everybody, on three," Kittridge commanded.

With a screech of metal, the door ascended.

They were from Fort Collins: a couple in their thirties, Joe and Linda Robinson, the two of them still dressed for a day at the office, with a young baby they called Boy Jr.; a heavy-set black man in a security guard's uniform, named Wood, and his girlfriend, Delores, a pediatric nurse who spoke with a thick West Indian accent; an elderly woman, Mrs. Bellamy—Kittridge was never to learn her first name—with a nimbus of blue-rinsed hair and an enormous white purse that she kept clutched to her side; a young man, maybe twenty-five, named Jamal, with a tight fade haircut and brightly colored tattoos winding up and down his bare arms. The last was a man in his fifties with the coarse gray hair and barrel-shaped torso of an aging athlete; he introduced him-self as Pastor Don. Not an actual pastor, he explained; by trade, a CPA. The nickname was a leftover from his days coaching Pop Warner football.

"I always told them to pray we didn't get our asses kicked," he told Kittridge.

Though Kittridge had initially assumed they'd traveled to-gether, they had wound up with one another by accident. All told versions of the same story. They'd fled the city only to be stopped by a long line of traffic at the Nebraska border. Word passed down from car to car that there was an Army roadblock ahead, that nobody was being let through. The Army was waiting for word to let people pass. For a whole day they'd sat there. As the light had ebbed, people had begun to panic. Everyone was saying the virals were coming; they were being left to die.

Which was, more or less, what happened.

They arrived just after sunset, Pastor Don said. Some-where ahead in the line, screaming, gunshots, and the sound of crunching metal; people began to tear past him. But there was nowhere to run. Within seconds, the virals were upon them, hundreds blasting out of the fields, tearing into the crowd.

"I ran like hell, just like everybody else," Pastor Don said.

He and Kittridge had stepped away to confer; the others were sitting on the ground by the bus. April was passing out bottles of water they'd collected at the stadium. Pastor Don removed a box of Marlboro Reds from his shirt pocket and shook two loose. Kittridge hadn't smoked since his early twenties, but what could it hurt now? He accepted a light and took a cautious drag, the nicotine hitting his system in-stantly.

"I can't even describe it," Don said, ejecting a plume of smoke. "Those goddamn things were everywhere. I saw the truck and decided it was better than nothing. The others were already inside. How the door got jammed I don't know."

"Why wouldn't the Army let you through?"

Don shrugged philosophically. "You know how these things work. Probably somebody forgot to file the right form." He squinted at Kittridge through a trail of smoke. "So what about you, you got anybody?"

He meant did Kittridge have a family, somebody he had lost or was looking for. Kittridge shook his head.

"My son's in Seattle, a plastic surgeon. The whole package. Married his college sweetheart, two kids, a boy and a girl. Big house on the water. They just redid the kitchen." He shook his head wistfully. "The last time we spoke, that's what we talked about. A fucking kitchen."

Pastor Don was carrying a rifle, a .30-.06 with three rounds remaining. Wood was carrying an empty .38. Joe Robinson had a .22 pistol with four cartridges—good for killing a squirrel, maybe, but that was about all.

Don glanced toward the bus. "And the driver? What's his story?"

"A little off, maybe. I wouldn't try to touch him—he'll just about have a seizure. Otherwise he's okay. He treats that bus like it's the *Queen Mary*."

"And the other two?"

"They were hiding in their parents' basement. I found them wandering around the parking lot at Mile High."

Don took a last, hungry drag and crushed the butt underfoot. "Mile High," he repeated. "I'm guessing that was nothing nice."

There was no way around the wreckage; they would have to backtrack and find another route. They scavenged what supplies they could find—more bottles of water, a couple of working flashlights and a propane lantern, an assortment of tools, and a length of rope that had no obvious use but might find some purpose later on—and boarded the bus.

As Kittridge mounted the bottom step, Pastor Don touched him on the elbow. "Maybe you should say something."

Kittridge looked at him. "Me?"

"Somebody has to be in charge. And it's your bus."

"Not really. Technically, it's Danny's."

Pastor Don met Kittridge's eye. "That's not what I mean. These people are worn out and frightened. They need somebody like you."

"You don't even know me."

He gave a cagey smile. "Oh, I know you better than you think I do. I was in the reserves myself, way back when. Just doing the quartermaster's books, but you learn to read the signs. I'm guessing ex–Special Forces. Rangers, maybe?" When Kittridge said nothing, Pastor Don shrugged. "Well, that's your business. But you obviously know what the hell you're doing better than anyone else around here. This is your show, my friend, like it or not. My guess is, they're waiting to hear from you."

It was true, and Kittridge knew it. Standing in the aisle, he surveyed the group. The Robinsons were seated up front, Linda holding Boy Jr. on her lap; directly behind them was Jamal, sitting alone; then Wood and Delores. Don took the bench across the aisle. Mrs. Bellamy sat at the rear, clutching her big white purse with both hands, like a retiree on a casino junket. April was sitting with her brother on the driver's side, behind Danny. Her eyes widened as their glances met. *What now?* they said.

Kittridge cleared his throat. "Okay, everybody. I know you're scared. I'm scared, too. But we're going to get you out of here. I don't know just where we're going, but if we keep heading east, sooner or later we're going to find safety."

"What about the Army?" Jamal said. "Those assholes left us here."

"We don't really know what happened. But to be on the safe side, we're going to keep on back roads as far as we can."

"My mother lives in Kearney." This was Linda Robinson. "That's where we were headed."

"Jesus, lady." Jamal scoffed. "I told you, Kearney's just like Fort Collins. They said so on the radio."

In every group, Kittridge thought, there was always one. This was all he needed.

Linda's husband, Joe, twisted in his seat. "Close your mouth for once, why don't you?"

"I hate to break it to you, but her mother's probably hanging from the ceiling right now, eating the dog."

Suddenly everybody·was speaking at once. Two days in the truck, Kittridge thought. Of course they'd be at one another's throats.

"Please, everybody—"

"And just who put you in charge?" Jamal jabbed a finger at Kittridge. "Just because you're all, like, strapped and shit."

"I agree," said Wood. It was the first time Kittridge had heard the man's voice. "I think we should take a vote."

"Vote on what?" Jamal said.

Wood gave him a hard look. "For starters, whether or not we should throw you off this bus."

"Fuck you, Rent-a-Cop."

In a flash, Wood was up. Before Kittridge could react, the man gripped Jamal in a headlock; in a flurry of arms and legs, they went tumbling over the bench. Everyone was shouting. Linda, clutching the baby, was trying to scamper away. Joe Robinson had joined in the fray, attempting to grip Jamal around the legs.

A gunshot slapped the air; everyone froze. All eyes swiveled to the rear of the bus, where Mrs. Bellamy was pointing an enormous pistol at the ceiling.

"Lady," Jamal spat, "what the *fuck*."

"Young man, I think I speak for everyone when I say I'm tired of your crap. You're just as afraid as the rest of us. You owe an apology to these people."

It was completely surreal, Kittridge thought. Part of him was horrified; another part wanted to laugh.

"Okay, okay," Jamal sputtered. "Just put that cannon away."

"I think you can do better than that."

"I'm sorry, okay? Quit waving that thing around."

She thought a moment, then lowered the pistol. "I suppose that will have to do. Now, I do like the idea of a vote. This nice man in the front— I'm sorry, my hearing isn't what it used to be—what did you say your name was?"

"Kittridge."

"Mr. Kittridge. He seems perfectly capable to me. I say all in favor of his running things, let's see a show of hands."

Every hand went up except Jamal's.

"It would be nice if it could be unanimous, young man."

His face was burning with humiliation. "Christ, you old bag. What else do you want from me?"

"Forty years of teaching public school, believe me, I've dealt with more than my share of boys like you. Now, go on. You'll see how much better you feel."

With a look of defeat, Jamal raised his hand.

"That's better." She directed her attention at Kittridge again. "We can go now, Mr. Kittridge."

Kittridge glanced at Pastor Don, who was trying not to laugh.

"Okay, Danny," Kittridge said. "Let's turn this thing around and find a way out of here."

12

They'd lost him. How the good Christ had they lost him?

Last they knew, Grey had been driving into Denver. He'd dropped off the screen at that point—the Denver network was a mess—but a day later they'd picked up his signature from a Verizon tower in Aurora. Guilder had asked for another drone to sweep the area, but they'd found nothing; and if Grey had gotten off the interstates, as now seemed likely, and headed into the sparsely populated eastern half of the state, he could travel for miles without leaving a mark.

And no sign at all of the girl. For all intents and purposes, she'd been swallowed by the continent.

With little to do but wait for news from Nelson, Guilder had plenty of time to ponder Grey's file, including the psychiatric workup from the Texas Department of Criminal Justice. He wondered what Richards had been thinking, hiring men like this. Human disposables—although that was, Guilder supposed, the point; like the original twelve test subjects, Babcock and Sosa and Morrison and all the creepy rest, the sweeps were no one anybody was ever going to miss.

To wit: Lawrence Alden Grey, born 1970, McAllen, Texas. Mother a homemaker, father a mechanic, both deceased. The father had served three tours in Vietnam as an Army medic, honorably discharged with a bronze star and a purple heart, but it had done the guy in anyway. He'd shot himself in the cab of his truck, leaving Grey, just six years old, to find him. A series of common-law stepfathers followed, one drunk after another by the looks of it, a history of abuse, etc.; by the time Grey was eighteen, he was on his own, working as a roughneck in the oil fields near Odessa, then on rigs in the Gulf. He'd never married, though that was no big shocker; his psychiatric profile was a bag of problems, everything from OCD to depression to traumatic disassociation. In the shrink's opinion, the guy was basically heterosexual, but with so many hang-ups it didn't even figure; the boys had been Grey's way of reliving his own childhood abuse, which his conscious mind had repressed. He'd been arrested twice, the first time for exposure, which he'd pled down to a misdemeanor, the second for aggravated sexual assault. Basically, he'd touched the kid—not exactly a hanging offense, but nothing nice, either. With the first conviction on his sheet the judge had sentenced him to the max, eighteen to twenty-four years, but nobody did the full bid anymore, and he'd been paroled after ninety-seven months.

After that, there wasn't much of a story. He'd moved back to Dallas, done little bits of work but nothing steady, met with his PO every two weeks to pee in a cup and swear eight ways to Sunday he hadn't set foot within a hundred yards of a playground or school. His court-ordered regimen of anti-androgens was standard, as was a fresh psychiatric evaluation every six months. By all accounts, Lawrence Grey was a model citizen, at least as far as a chemically neutered child molester could be.

None of which did anything to tell Guilder how the man had survived. Somehow he'd escaped the Chalet; somehow he'd managed to avoid getting himself killed since then. It simply made no sense.

Nelson's new plan was to retraffic all the cell towers in Kansas and Nebraska, shutting down both states for a period of two hours and trying to isolate the signal from Grey's chip. Under usual circumstances, this would have required a federal court order, a pile of paperwork ten miles high, and a month's lead time, but Nelson had used a back channel at Homeland, which had agreed to issue a special executive order under Article 67 of the Domestic Security Act—more commonly known in the intelligence community as the "Do Whatever the Fuck You Want" Act. The chip in Grey's neck was a low-wattage transmitter at 1432 megahertz; once everything else was cleared out, and assuming Grey passed within a few miles of a tower, they could triangulate his position and retarget a satellite to get a picture.

The shutdown was scheduled for eight A.M. Guilder had come in at six to find Nelson typing away at his terminal. A buzz of music was leaking from the earbuds stuffed in the sides of his head.

"Let Mozart work," he said, shooing Guilder away.

Guilder was running on coffee and adrenaline; he went down to the break room to get something to eat. All they had were vending machines; he'd already paid his three dollars for a Snickers when he realized it would take too much effort to swallow. He tossed it in the trash and got a Reese's, but even that, with the sticky peanut butter, was difficult. He snapped on the TV, tuned it to CNN. New cases were suddenly popping up all over: Amarillo, Baton Rouge, Phoenix. The U.N. was vacating its New York headquarters, relocating to The Hague; once martial law was declared, the military would be recalled from overseas. What a fiasco that would be. It would make Pandora's box look like a picnic basket.

Nelson appeared in the door. "Bow down," he declared with a grin. "Houston, we have a sex offender."

Nelson had already targeted the satellite. By the time they reached the terminal, the image was coming in.

"Where the hell is this?"

Nelson worked the keyboard, bringing the picture into focus. "Western Kansas."

A grid of cornfields came into aerial view and, at the center, a long, low-slung building with a grid of parking spaces in front. A single vehicle, some kind of station wagon, was in the lot. A figure stepped from the building, pulling a suitcase.

"Is that the same guy?" Nelson asked.

"I'm not sure. Bring it in closer."

The image faded, then resolved again, assuming an approximate aerial distance of eighty feet. Now Guilder felt certain he was looking at Lawrence Grey. He'd changed out of his jumpsuit, but it was him. Grey returned to the building; a minute later he reemerged with a second suitcase, which he deposited in the car's cargo compartment. He stood a moment, as if lost in thought. Then a second figure emerged from the building, a woman. A little heavy, with dark hair; she was wearing slacks and a light-colored blouse.

What the hell?

They had less than thirty seconds left. Already the picture had begun to lose its crispness. Grey opened the passenger door; the woman lowered herself into the car. Grey glanced around the parking lot one more time—as if, thought Guilder, he knew he was being watched. He got into the vehicle and drove away, just as the image dissolved into sparkles of static.

Nelson looked up from his terminal. "Looks like our target made a friend. From the psych workup, I have to say I'm a little surprised."

"Call back the last shot with the woman in it. See if we can enhance it."

Nelson tried, but the results were only a modest improvement.

"Can we figure out what that building is?"

Nelson had slid his chair to an adjacent terminal. "Thirty-eight-twelve Main Street, Ledeau, Kansas. A place called Angie's Resort."

Who was she? What was Lawrence Grey doing with a woman? Was she from the Chalet?

"Which direction was he going?"

"Looks like straight east. He's headed right into the thick of it. If you want to grab him, we'd better move."

"Locate our nearest asset. Something outside the quarantine line."

More taps of the keys; then Nelson said, "The closest for something like this would be the old NBC lab in Fort Powell. The Army shut it down three years ago, when they moved everything to White Sands, but it should be an easy matter to get the lights turned on."

"What else is around there?"

"Not a lot except for Midwest State, which is about three miles east. It's your basic football factory with a few classrooms attached. Otherwise you've got a National Guard armory, some hog and cattle processing, a little light manufacturing. There's a small IAC hydroelectric facility, but it was mothballed when they built a larger one downstream. Pretty much the only reason the place exists is the college."

Guilder took a moment to think. They were the only ones who knew about Grey, at least so far. Probably it was time to bring in the CDC and USAMRIID.

Yet he hesitated. Partly because of the bad taste in his mouth from his meeting with the Joint Chiefs. How would it go down when Central Command learned that they'd put Lear's monstrosities under the surveillance of a bunch of paroled sex offenders? He'd never hear the end of it.

But that wasn't the real reason.

A cure for everything. Weren't those Lear's exact words? Wasn't that where the whole misbegotten thing had begun? And if Grey was infected but for some reason hadn't flipped, was it possible that the virus in his blood had changed somehow, achieving the very result Lear had hoped for? That he was in every way a prize as valuable as the girl? And wasn't it also true that, although death was everyone's problem, especially now, it was for Guilder just as pressing and personal—even more so, because the fate that awaited him left nothing to chance? Didn't he have some right to muster whatever resources he could on behalf of his own survival? Wouldn't anybody do the same?

We're all dying, baby. Fair enough. But some of us more than others.

Maybe Grey was his answer, and maybe he wasn't. Maybe he was just some lucky schmuck who'd managed to claw his way out of a burning building and avoid the glowsticks long enough to make his way to Kansas. But the more Guilder ruminated over it, the more he didn't think so. The odds were simply too long. And once he turned the man over to the military, he doubted they'd hear anything from Grey, or this mystery woman, again.

Which wasn't going to happen. Horace Guilder, deputy director of the Division of Special Weapons, would keep Lawrence Grey for himself.

"So? What do you want me to do?"

Nelson was staring at him. Guilder calculated the mechanics. Who else did he need? Nelson wasn't somebody Guilder would have described as loyal, but for the time being he could appeal to the man's naked self-interest, and he was the best person for the job, a one-man band of biochemical know-how. Sooner or later he'd catch wind of what Guilder was up to, and decisions would have to be made, but that was a bridge Guilder would cross when he came to it. As for making the pickup: there was always somebody off the books for tasks like that. One phone call and everything would be set in motion.

"Pack your things," he said. "We're going to Iowa."

13

Sunrise of the second day: they were deep into Nebraska now. Danny, hunched over the wheel, his eyes stinging with sleeplessness, had driven through the night. Everyone except for Kittridge had fallen asleep, even the obnoxious one, Jamal.

It felt good to have people on his bus again. To be useful, a useful engine.

They'd found more diesel at a small airport in McCook. The few towns they'd passed through were empty and abandoned, like something from a movie about the Old West. Okay, so maybe they were lost, kind of. But Kittridge and the other man, Pastor Don, said it didn't matter, as long as they kept heading east. That's all you got to do, Danny, Kittridge said. Just keep us headed east.

He thought of what he'd seen on the highway. That was really something. He'd seen a lot of bodies in the last couple of days, but nothing as bad as that. He liked Kittridge, who sort of reminded him of Mr. Purvis. Not that he *looked* like Mr. Purvis, because he didn't at all. It was the way the man spoke to Danny—as if he mattered.

While he drove, he thought about Momma, and Mr. Purvis, and Thomas and Percy and James and how useful he was being. How proud of him Momma and Mr. Purvis would be now.

The sun was peeking over the horizon, making Danny squint into its brightness. Before long, everyone would be awake. Kittridge leaned over his shoulder.

"How we doing on gas?"

Danny checked. They were down to a quarter tank.

"Let's pull over and refill from the cans," Kittridge said. "Let folks stretch their legs a bit."

They pulled off the road, into a state park. Kittridge and Pastor Don checked the bathrooms and gave the all clear.

"Thirty minutes, everyone," Kittridge said.

They had more supplies now, boxes of crackers and peanut butter and apples and energy bars and bottles of pop and juice and diapers and formula for Boy Jr. Kittridge had even gotten Danny a box of Lucky Charms, though all the milk in the grocery store's cooler had spoiled; he'd have to eat it dry. Danny, Kittridge, and Pastor Don unloaded the jugs of diesel from the back of the bus and began to pour it into the tank. Danny had told them that the bus had a fifty-gallon capacity, precisely; each full tank would get them about three hundred miles.

"You're a very precise guy," Kittridge had said.

When they'd finished refueling, Danny took the box of Lucky Charms and a can of lukewarm Dr Pepper and sat under a tree. The rest were seated around a picnic table, including Jamal. He wasn't saying much, but Danny had the feeling that everyone had decided to let bygones be bygones. Linda Robinson was diapering Boy Jr., cooing to him, making him wiggle his arms and legs. Danny had never been around babies much. He'd been led to understand that they cried a lot, but so far Boy Jr. had kept quiet as a mouse. There were good babies and there were bad babies, Momma had said, so Boy Jr. must be one of the good ones. Danny tried to remember being a baby himself, just to see if he could do it, but his mind wouldn't go back that far, not in any orderly way. It was strange how there was this whole part of your life you couldn't recall, except in little pictures: sunshine flaring on a windowpane, or a dead frog squashed in the driveway by a tire tread, or a slice of apple on a plate. He wondered if he'd been a good baby, like Boy Jr.

Danny was watching the group, feeding fistfuls of Lucky Charms into his mouth and swilling them down with the Dr Pepper, when Tim rose from the table and walked over to him.

"Hey, Timbo. How you doing?"

The boy's hair was standing all whichaway from his sleeping on the bus. "Okay, I guess." He gave a loose-boned shrug. "Mind if I sit with you?"

Danny scooched over to make room.

"I'm sorry the other kids tease you sometimes," Tim said after a minute.

"That's okay," said Danny. "I don't mind."

"Billy Nice is a real dickhead."

"He picks on you, too?"

"Sometimes." The boy frowned vaguely. "He picks on everybody."

"Just ignore him," Danny said. "That's what I do."

After a minute, Tim said, "You really like Thomas, huh?"

"Sure."

"I used to watch him. I had, like, this huge layout of Thomas trains in my basement. The coal loader, the engine wash, I had all that stuff."

"I'd like to see that," said Danny. "I bet that was great."

A brief silence followed. The sun was warm on Danny's face.

"You want to know what I saw in the stadium?" Tim asked.

"If you want."

"Like, a thousand million dead people."

Danny wasn't sure what to say. He guessed Tim had needed to tell someone; it wasn't the kind of thing you should keep bottled up inside.

"It was pretty gross."

"Did you tell April?"

Tim shook his head.

"You want to keep it a secret?"

"Would that be okay?"

"Sure," said Danny. "I can keep a secret."

Tim had scooped up a little bit of dirt from the base of the tree and was watching it sift through his fingers. "You don't get scared much, do you, Danny?"

"Sometimes I do."

"But not now," the boy stated.

Danny had to think about that. He supposed he should be, but he just wasn't. What he felt was more like *interested*. What would happen next? Where would they go? It surprised him, how adaptable he was being. Dr. Francis would be proud of him.

"No, I guess I'm not."

In the shade of the picnic area, everyone was packing up. Danny wished he could find the words to make the boy feel better, to wipe the memory of what he'd seen in the stadium from his mind. They were walking back to the bus when the idea came to him.

"Hey, I've got something for you." He reached into his pack and removed his lucky penny and showed the boy. "You hold on to that, I promise, nothing bad can happen to you."

Tim took the coin in his palm. "What happened to it? It's all squished."

"It got run over by a train. That's what makes it lucky."

"Where'd you get it?"

"I don't know, I've just always had it." Danny dipped his head toward the boy's open hand. "Go ahead, you can keep it."

A moment's hesitation, then Tim slipped the flattened penny into the pocket of his shorts. It wasn't much, Danny knew, but it was something, and there were times like these when just a little thing could help. As a for-instance: Momma's Popov, which she visited when her nerves got bad, and the visits from Mr. Purvis on the nights when Danny could hear them laughing. The roar of the Redbird's big caterpillar diesel coming to life when he turned the key each morning. Driving over the bump on Lindler Avenue, and all the kids hooting as they shot from the benches. Little things like that. Danny felt pleased with himself for thinking of this, like he'd passed along something he knew that maybe not everybody did, and as the two of them stood together in the morning sunshine, he detected, from the corner of his eye, a change in the boy's face, a kind of lightening; he might have even smiled.

"Thanks, Danny," he said.

Omaha was burning.

They saw it first as a throbbing glow over the horizon. It was the hour when the light had flattened. They were approaching the city from the southwest, on Interstate 80. Not a single car was on the highway; all the buildings were dark. A deeper, more profound abandonment than anything they'd seen so far—this was, or should have been, a city of nearly half a million. A strong odor of smoke began to flow through the bus's ventilation. Kittridge told Danny to stop.

"We have to get over the river somehow," Pastor Don said. "Go south or north, look for a way across."

Kittridge looked up from the map. "Danny, how are we doing for gas?"

They were down to an eighth of a tank; the jugs were empty. Fifty more miles at the most. They'd hoped to find more fuel in Omaha.

"One thing's for sure," said Kittridge, "we can't stay here."

They turned north. The next crossing was at the town of Adair. But the bridge was gone, blasted away, no part left standing. Only the river, wide and dark, ceaselessly flowing. The next opportunity would be Decatur, another thirty miles to the north.

"We passed an elementary school a mile back," said Pastor Don. "It's better than nothing. We can look for fuel in the morning."

A silence descended over the bus, everyone waiting for Kittridge's answer.

"Okay, let's do it."

They backtracked into the heart of the little town. All the lights were out, the streets empty. They came to the school, a modern-looking structure set back from the road at the edge of the fields. A marquee-style sign at the edge of the parking area read, in bold letters: GO LIONS! HAVE A GREAT SUMMER!

"Everybody wait here," Kittridge said.

He moved inside. A few minutes passed; then he emerged. He exchanged a quick look with Pastor Don, the two men nodding.

"We're going to shelter here for the night," Kittridge announced. "Stay together, no wandering off. The power's out, but there's running water, and food in the cafeteria. If you need to use the facilities, go in pairs."

In the front foyer they were met by the telltale scents of an elementary school, of sweat and dirty socks, art supplies and waxed linoleum. A trophy case stood by a door that led, presumably, to the main office; a display of collages was hung on the painted cinder-block walls, images of people and animals fashioned from newspaper and magazine clippings. Beside each of them was a printed label bearing the age and grade of its creator. Wendy Mueller, Grade 2. Gavin Jackson, Grade 5. Florence Ratcliffe, Pre-K 4.

"April, go with Wood and Don to find some mats to sleep on. The kindergarten rooms should have some."

In the pantry behind the cafeteria they found cans of beans and fruit cocktail, as well as bread and jam to make sandwiches. There was no gas to cook with, so they served the beans cold, dishing everything out on metal cafeteria trays. By now it was dark outside; Kittridge distributed flashlights. They spoke only in whispers, the consensus being that the virals might hear them.

By nine o'clock, everyone was bedded down. Kittridge left

Don to keep watch on the first floor and climbed the stairs, carrying a lantern. Many of the doors were locked but not all; he selected the science lab, a large, open space with counters and glass cabinets full of beakers and other supplies. The air smelled faintly of butane. On the whiteboard at the front of the room were written the words "Final review, chaps. 8–12. Labs due Wednesday."

Kittridge stripped off his shirt and wiped himself down at the washbasin in the corner, then took a chair and removed his boots. The prosthesis, which began just below his left knee, was constructed of a titanium alloy frame covered in silicone; a microprocessor-controlled hydraulic cylinder, powered by a tiny hydrogen cell, adjusted fifty times per second to calculate the correct angular velocity of the ankle joint, imitating a natural gait. It was the very latest in prosthetic limb replacements; Kittridge didn't doubt it had cost the Army a bundle. He rolled up his trousers, peeled off the mounting sock, and washed his stump with soap from the dispenser by the basin. Though heavily callused, the skin at the contact point felt raw and tender after two days without care. He dried the stump thoroughly, allowed it a few minutes of fresh air, then fixed the prosthesis back in place and drew down his pant leg.

He was startled by a sound of movement behind him. He turned to find April standing in the open doorway.

"Sorry, I didn't mean—"

He quickly drew on his shirt and rose to his feet. How much had she seen? But the light was dim, and he'd been partially concealed by one of the counters.

"It's no problem. I was just getting cleaned up a little."

"I couldn't sleep."

"That's okay," he said. "You can come in if you want."

She advanced uncertainly into the room. Kittridge moved to the window with the AK. He took a moment to quickly scan the street below.

"How's everything outside?" She was standing beside him.

"Quiet so far. How's Tim doing?"

"Out like a light. He's tougher than he looks. Tougher than I am, anyway."

"I doubt that. You seem pretty cool to me, considering."

April frowned. "You shouldn't. This calm exterior is what you'd call an act. To tell you the truth, I'm so scared I don't really feel anything anymore."

A wide shelf ran the length of the room beneath the windows. April hoisted herself onto it, bracing her back against the frame and pulling her knees to her chest. Kittridge did the same. They were face-to-face now. A stillness, expectant but not uncomfortable, hovered between them. She was young, yet he sensed a core of resilience in her. It was the kind of thing you either had or you didn't.

"So, do you have a boyfriend?"

"Are you auditioning?"

Kittridge laughed, felt his face grow warm. "Just making talk, I guess. Are you like this with everybody?"

"Only the people I like."

Another moment passed.

"So how'd you get the name April?" It was all he could think to say. "Is that your birthday?"

"It's from 'The Waste Land.'" When Kittridge said nothing, she raised her eyebrows dubiously. "It's a poem? T. S. Eliot?"

Kittridge had heard the name, but that was all. "Can't say I got to that one. How's it go?"

She let her gaze flow past him. When she began to speak, her voice was full of a rich feeling Kittridge couldn't identify, happy and sad and full of memory. "'April is the cruellest month, breeding/Lilacs out of the dead land, mixing/Memory and desire, stirring/Dull roots with spring rain . . .

"Winter kept us warm, covering
Earth in forgetful snow, feeding
A little life with dried tubers.
Summer surprised us, coming over the Starnbergersee
With a shower of rain . . ."

"Wow," said Kittridge. She was looking at him again. Her eyes, he noted, were the color of moss, with what looked like flecks of shaved gold floating atop the surface of her irises. "That's really something."

April shrugged. "It goes on from there. Basically, the guy was totally depressed." She was tugging a frayed spot on one knee of her jeans. "The name was my mother's idea. She was an English professor before she met my stepdad and we got all, like, rich and everything."

"Your parents are divorced?"

"My father died when I was six."

"I'm sorry, I shouldn't have—"

But she didn't let him finish. "Don't be. He wasn't what you would call an admirable sort. A leftover from my mother's bad-boy period. He was totally loaded, drove his car into a bridge abutment. And that, said Pooh, was that."

She stated these facts without inflection; she might have been telling him what the weather was. Outside, the summer night was veiled in blackness. Kittridge had obviously misjudged her, but he had learned that was the way with most people. The story was never the story, and it surprised you, how much another person could carry.

"I saw you, you know," April said. "Your leg. The scars on your back. You were in the war, weren't you?"

"What makes you think that?"

She made a face of disbelief. "Gosh, I don't know, just everything? Because you're the only one who seems to know what to do? Because you're all, like, super-competent with guns and shit?"

"I told you. I'm a salesman. Camping gear."

"I don't believe that for a second."

Her directness was so disarming that for a moment Kittridge said nothing. But she had him dead to rights. "You're sure you want to hear it? It isn't very nice."

"If you want to tell me."

He instinctively turned his face to the window. "Well, you're right, I was. Enlisted straight out of high school. Not Army, Marines. I ended up as a staff sergeant in the MPs. You know what that is?"

"You were a cop?"

"Sort of. Mostly we provided security at American installations, airbases, sensitive infrastructure, that kind of thing. They moved us around a lot. Iran, Iraq, Saudi. Chechnya for a little while. My last duty was at Bagram Airfield, in Afghanistan. Usually it was pretty routine, verifying equipment manifests and checking foreign workers in and out. But once in a while something would happen. The coup hadn't happened yet, so it was still American-controlled territory, but there were Taliban all over the place, plus Al Qaeda and about twenty different local warlords duking it out."

He paused, collecting himself. The next part was always the hardest. "So one day we see this car, the usual beat-up piece of junk, coming down the road. The checkpoints are all well marked, everybody knows to stop, but the guy doesn't. He's barreling straight for us. Two people in the car that we can see, a man and a woman. Everybody opens fire. The car swerves away, rolls a couple of times, comes to rest on its wheels. We're thinking it's going to blow for sure, but it doesn't. I'm the senior NCO, so I'm the one who goes to look. The woman's dead, but the man is still alive. He's slumped over the steering wheel, blood all over. In the back-seat is a kid, a boy. He couldn't have been older than four. They've got him strapped into a seat packed with explosives. I see the wires running to the front of the vehicle, where the dad is holding the detonator. He's muttering to himself. *Anta al-mas'ul,* he's saying. *Anta al-mas'ul.* The kid's wailing, reaching out for me. This little hand. I'll never forget it. He's only four, but it's like he knows what's about to happen."

"Jesus." April's face was horrified. "What did you do?"

"The only thing I could think of. I got the hell out of there. I don't really remember the blast. I woke up in the hospital in Saudi. Two men in my unit were killed, another took a piece of shrapnel in the spine." April was staring at him. "I told you it wasn't very nice."

"He blew up his own *kid*?"

"That's about the size of it, yeah."

"But what kind of people would do that?"

"You've got me there. I never could figure that out."

April said nothing more; Kittridge wondered, as he always did, if he'd told too much. But it felt good to unburden himself, and if April had gotten more than she'd bargained for, she had a way of hiding it. In the abstract, Kittridge knew, the story was inconsequential, one of hundreds, even thousands like it. Such pointless cruelty was simply the way of the world. But understanding this fact was a far cry from accepting it, when you'd lived it yourself.

"So what happened then?" April asked.

Kittridge shrugged. "Nothing. End of story. Off to dance with the virgins in eternity."

"I was talking about you." Her eyes did not move from his face. "I think I'd be pretty screwed up by something like that."

Here was something new, he thought—the part of the tale that no one ever asked about. Typically, once the basic facts were laid bare, the listener couldn't get away fast enough. But not this girl, this April.

"Well, I wasn't. At least I didn't think I was. I spent about half a year in the VA, learning to walk and dress and feed myself, and then they kicked me loose. War's over, my friend, at least for you. I wasn't all bitter, like a lot of guys get. I didn't dive under the bed when a car backfired or anything like that. What's done is done, I figured. Then about six months after I got settled, I took a trip back home to Wyoming. My parents were gone, my sister had moved up to British Columbia with her husband and basically dropped off the map, but I still knew some people, kids I'd gone to school with, though nobody was a kid anymore. One of them wants to throw a party for me, the big welcome-home thing. They all had families of their own by now, kids and wives and jobs, but this was a pretty hard-drinking crowd back in the day. The whole thing was just an excuse to get lit, but I didn't see the harm. Sure, I said, knock yourself out, and he actually did. There were at least a hundred people there, a big banner with my name on it hung over the porch, even a band. The whole thing knocked me flat. I'm in the backyard listening to the music and the friend says to me, Come on, there are some women who want to meet you. Don't be standing there like a big idiot. So he takes me inside and there are three of them, all nice enough. I knew one of them a little from way back when. They're talking away, some show on TV, gossip, the usual things. Normal, everyday things. I'm nursing a beer and listening to them when all of a sudden I realize I have no idea what they're saying. Not the words themselves. What any of it *meant*. None of it seemed connected to anything else, like there were two worlds, an inside world and an outside world, and neither had anything to do with the other. I'm sure a shrink would have a name for it. All I know is, I woke up on the floor, everybody standing over me. After that, it took me about four months in the woods just to be around people again." He paused, a little surprised at himself. "To tell you the truth, I've never told anybody that part. You would be the first."

"Sounds like a day in high school."

Kittridge had to laugh. "Touché."

Their gazes met and held. How strange it was, he thought. One minute you were all alone with your thoughts, the next somebody came along who seemed to know the deepest part of you, who could open you like a book. He couldn't have said how long they'd been looking at each other. It seemed to go on and on and on, neither possessing the will, or the courage, or even the desire, to look away. How old was she? Seventeen? And yet she didn't seem seventeen. She didn't seem like any age at all. An old soul: Kittridge had heard the term but never quite understood what it meant. That's what April had. An old soul.

To seal the deal between them, Kittridge removed one of

the Glocks from his shoulder holster and held it out to her. "Know how to use one of these?"

April looked at it uncertainly. "Let me guess. It's not like it is on TV."

Kittridge dropped the magazine and racked the slide to eject the cartridge from the pipe. He placed the gun in her hand, wrapping her fingers with his own.

"Don't pull the trigger with your knuckle, the shot will go low. Just use the pad of your fingertip and squeeze, like so." He released her hand and tapped his breastbone. "One shot, through here. That's all it takes, but you can't miss. Don't rush—aim and fire." He reloaded the gun and handed it back. "Go on, you can have it. Keep a round chambered, like I showed you."

She smiled wryly. "Gee, thanks. And here I don't have anything for you."

Kittridge returned the smile. "Maybe next time."

A moment passed. April was turning the weapon around in her hand, examining it as if it were some unaccountable artifact. "What the father said. *Anta*-something."

"Anta al-mas'ul."

"Did you ever figure out what it meant?"

Kittridge nodded. "'You did this.'"

Another silence fell, though different from the others. Not a barrier between them but a shared awareness of their lives, like the walls of a room in which only the two of them existed. How strange, thought Kittridge, to say those words. *Anta al-mas'ul. Anta al-mas'ul.*

"It was the right thing, you know," April said. "You would have been killed, too."

"There's always a choice," Kittridge said.

"What else could you have done?"

The question was rhetorical, he understood; she expected no reply. *What else could you have done?* But Kittridge knew his answer. He'd always known.

"I could have held his hand."

He kept his vigil at the window through the night. Sleeplessness was not a problem for him; he had learned to get by on just a few winks. April lay curled on the floor beneath the window. Kittridge had removed his jacket and placed it over her. There were no lights anywhere. The view from the window was of a world at peace, the sky pinpricked with stars. As the first glow of daylight gathered on the horizon, he let himself close his eyes.

He startled awake to the sound of approaching engines. An Army convoy was coming down the street, twenty vehicles long. He unsnapped his second pistol and passed it to April, who was sitting up now as well, rubbing her eyes.

"Hold this."

Kittridge quickly made his way down the stairs. By the time he burst through the door, the convoy was less than a hundred feet away. He jogged into the street, waving his arms.

"Stop!"

The lead Humvee jerked to a halt just a few yards in front of him, the soldier on the roof tracking his movements with the fifty-cal. The lower half of his face was hidden by a white surgical mask. "Hold it right there."

Kittridge's arms were raised. "I'm unarmed."

The soldier pulled the bolt on his weapon. "I said, keep your distance."

A tense five seconds followed; it seemed possible that he was about to be shot. Then the passenger door of the Humvee swung open. A sturdy-looking woman emerged and walked toward him. Up close her face appeared worn and lined, crackled with dust. An officer, but not one who rode a desk.

"Major Porcheki, Ninth Combat Support Battalion, Iowa National Guard. Who the hell are you?"

He had only one card to play. "Staff Sergeant Bernard Kittridge. Charlie Company, First MP Battalion, USMC."

Her eyes narrowed on his face. "You're a Marine?"

"Medically discharged, ma'am."

The major glanced past him, toward the schoolhouse. Kittridge knew without looking that the others were watching from the windows.

"How many civilians do you have inside?"

"Eleven. The bus is almost out of gas."

"Any sick or wounded?"

"Everybody's worn out and scared, but that's it."

She considered this with a neutral expression. Then: "Caldwell! Valdez!"

A pair of E-4s trotted forward. They, too, were wearing surgical masks. Everyone was except Porcheki.

"Let's get the refueler to see about filling up that bus."

"We're taking civilians? Can we do that now?"

"Did I ask your opinion, Specialist? And get a corpsman up here."

"Yes, ma'am. Sorry, ma'am."

They jogged away.

"Thank you, Major. It was going to be a long walk out of here."

Porcheki had removed a canteen from her belt and paused to drink. "You're just lucky you found us when you did. Fuel's getting pretty scarce. We're headed back to the guard armory at Fort Powell, so that's as far as we can take you. FEMA's set up a refugee-processing center there. From there you'll probably be evaced to Chicago or St. Louis."

"If you don't mind my asking, do you have any news?"

"I don't mind, but I'm not sure what to tell you. One minute these goddamned things are everywhere, the next nobody can find them. They like the trees, but any sort of cover will do. The word from CENTCOM is that a large pod's massing along the Kansas-Nebraska border."

"What's a pod?"

She took another gulp from the canteen. "That's what they're calling groups of them, pods."

The corpsman appeared; everyone was filing out of the school. Kittridge told them what was happening while the soldiers established a perimeter. The corpsman examined the civilians, taking their temperatures, peering inside their mouths. When everyone was ready to go, Porcheki met Kittridge at the steps of the bus.

"Just one thing. You might want to keep the fact that you're from Denver under your hat. Say you're from Iowa, if anyone asks."

He thought of the highway, the lines of torn-up cars. "I'll pass that along."

Kittridge climbed aboard. Balancing his rifle between his knees, he took a place directly behind Danny.

"God *damn*," Jamal said, grinning ear to ear. "An Army convoy. I take back everything I said about you, Kittridge." He poked a thumb toward Mrs. Bellamy, who was dabbing her brow with a tissue taken from her sleeve. "Hell, I don't even mind that old broad taking a shot at me."

"Sticks and stones, young man," she responded. "Sticks and stones."

He turned to face her across the aisle. "I've been meaning to ask you. What is it with old ladies and the snot-rag-in-the-sleeve thing? Doesn't that strike you as just a little unsanitary?"

"This from a young man with enough ink in his arms to fill a ditto machine."

"A ditto machine. What century are you from?"

"When I look at you, I think of one word. The word is 'hepatitis.'"

"Christ, the two of you," Wood moaned. "You really need to get a room."

The convoy began to move.

14

The plan was in motion. His team was assembled, the jet would meet them at dawn. Guilder had been in touch with his contact at Blackbird; everything had been arranged. The server and the hard drives at the warehouse had all been wiped. Go home, he'd told the staff. Go home and be with your families.

It was after midnight when he drove to his townhouse through quiet, rain-slickened streets. On the radio, a continuous stream of bad news: chaos on the highways, the Army regrouping, rumblings abroad. From the White House, words of calm assurance, the crisis was in hand, the best minds were at work, but nobody was fooling anybody. A nationwide declaration of martial law was sure to come within hours. CNN was reporting that NATO warships were churning toward the coasts. The door would slam on the North American continent. The world might despise us, Guilder thought; what will it do when we're gone?

As he drove, he kept a watchful eye on the rearview. He wasn't being paranoid; it was just how things tended to unfold. A roar of tires, a van pulling in front of him, men in dark suits emerging. *Horace Guilder? Come with us.* Amazing, he thought, that it hadn't happened already.

He pulled into the garage and sealed the door behind him. In his bedroom, he packed a small bag of essentials—a couple of days' worth of clothes, toiletries, his meds—and carried it downstairs. He fetched his laptop from the study and placed it in the microwave, sizzling its circuitry in a cloud of sparks. His handheld was already gone, tossed from the window of the Camry.

In the living room he doused the lights and peeled back the drapes. Across the street, a neighbor was loading suitcases into the open hatch of his SUV. The man's wife was standing in the doorway of their townhouse, clutching a sleeping toddler. What were their names? Guilder either had never known or couldn't remember. He'd seen the woman from time to time, pushing the little girl in a brightly colored plastic car up and down the driveway. Watching the three of them, Guilder was touched by a memory of Shawna—not that last, terrible encounter but the two of them lying together in the aftermath of lovemaking, and her quiet, whispering voice, tickling his chest. *Are you happy with the things I do? I want to be your only one.* Words that weren't anything more than playacting, a bit of cheap theatrics to crown a dutiful hour. How stupid he'd been.

The man accepted the child from his wife's arms and gently lowered her into the backseat. The two of them got in the car. Guilder imagined the things they'd be saying to each other. *We'll be all right. They have people working on it right now. We'll just stay at your mother's a week or two, until this all blows over.* He heard the engine turn over; they backed from the drive. Guilder watched their taillights vanish down the block. Good luck, he thought.

He waited five more minutes. The streets were silent, all the houses dark. When he was satisfied he wasn't being watched, he carried his bag to the Camry.

It was after two A.M. when he got to Shadowdale. The parking area was empty; only a single light burned by the entrance. He stepped through the door to find the front desk unmanned. An empty wheelchair sat beside it, a second in the hall. There were no sounds anywhere. Probably there were security cameras watching him, but who would examine the tapes?

His father was lying on his bed in darkness. The room smelled awful; nobody had been in for hours, perhaps as long as a day. On the tray by his father's bed, somebody had left a dozen jars of Gerber's baby food and a pitcher of water. A spilled cup told him his father had attempted the water, but the food was untouched; his father couldn't have opened the jars if he'd tried.

Guilder didn't have long, but it was not an occasion to rush. His father's eyes were closed, the voice—that hectoring voice—silenced. Better that way, he thought. The time for talk was over. He searched his memory for something nice about his father, however meager. The best he could come up with was a time when his father had taken him to a park when Guilder was small. The recollection was vague and impressionistic—it was possible it had never happened at all—but that was all he had. A winter day, Guilder's breath clouding before his face, and a view of bare trees bobbing up and down as his father had pushed him on a swing, the man's big hand at the center of his back, catching him and launching him into space. Guilder recalled nothing else about that day. He might have been as young as five.

When he slid the pillow from beneath his father's head, the man's eyes fluttered but didn't open. Here was the precipice, Guilder thought, the mortal moment; the deed, that, once done, could never be undone. He thought of the word *patricide*. From the Latin *pater*, father, and *caedere*, to cut down. He had lacked the courage to kill himself, yet as he placed the pillow over his father's face, he experienced no hesitation. Gripping the pillow by the edges, he increased the pressure until he was certain no air could reach his father's nose or mouth. A minute crept by, Guilder counting out the seconds under his breath. His father's hand, lying on the blanket, gave a restive twitch. How long would it take? How would he know when it was over? If the pillow didn't work, what then? He watched his father's hand for additional movement, but there was none. Gradually it came to him that the stillness of the body beneath his hands meant only one thing. His father wasn't breathing anymore.

He drew the pillow away. His father's face was just the same; it was as if his passage into death represented only the subtlest alteration in his condition. Guilder gently placed his palm beneath his father's head and moved the pillow back into place. He wasn't trying to hide his crime—he doubted anybody would be around to examine the situation—but he wanted his father to have a pillow to lie on, especially since, as now seemed likely, he would be lying there for a very long time. Guilder had expected a rush of emotion to overcome him at this moment, all the pain and regret unloosed inside him. His awful childhood. His mother's lonely life. His own barren and loveless existence, with only a hired woman for company. But all he felt was relieved. The truest test of his life, and he had passed it.

Outside, the hallway was quiet, unchanged. Who could say what degradations lay behind the other doors, how many families would be facing the same cruel decision? Guilder glanced at his watch: ten minutes had passed since he'd entered the building. Just ten minutes, but everything was different now. He was different, the world was different. His father was nowhere in it. And with that, tears came to his eyes.

He strode briskly down the hallway, moving past the empty common room and the vacant nurse's station and farther still, into the early morning.

15

It was late on the second day, approaching the Missouri border, that Grey saw an obstruction ahead. They were in the middle of nowhere, miles from any town. He brought the car to a halt.

Lila looked up from the magazine she was reading: *Today's Parenting.* Grey had gotten it for her at a mini-mart in Ledeau, with a pile of others. *Family Life, Baby and Child, Modern Toddler.* In the last day, her attitude toward him had shifted somewhat. Perhaps it was the mental effort of maintaining the fiction that their journey was nothing out of the ordinary, but she was becoming increasingly impatient with him, speaking to him as if he were an uncooperative husband.

"Will you look at that." She dropped the magazine to her lap. On the cover was the image of a ruddy-cheeked girl in a pink jumper. WHEN PLAY DATES GO BAD, the caption read. "What *is* that?"

"I think it's a tank."

"What's it doing there?"

"Maybe it's lost or something."

"I don't think they just *lose* tanks, Lawrence. Like, excuse me, have you seen my tank anyplace? I know it was around here somewhere." She sighed heavily. "Who just parks a tank in the road like that? They'll have to move it."

"So you're saying you want me to ask them," Grey stated.

"Yes, Lawrence. That's exactly what I'm saying."

He didn't want to, but to say no seemed impossible. He exited the car into the falling dusk. "Hello?" he called. He glanced back at Lila, who was watching him with her head angled through the open passenger window. "I think it's empty."

"Maybe they just can't hear you."

"Let's just turn around. We can find another road."

"It's the principle of the thing. They can't just block the road like that. Try the hatch. I'm sure there has to be somebody inside."

Grey doubted this, but he didn't want to argue. He clambered up on the exposed treads and hoisted himself to the top of the turret. He positioned his face above the hatch, but it was too dark to see anything down there. Lila had exited the Volvo and was standing at the base of the tank, holding a flashlight.

"I'm not sure this is such a good idea," Grey said.

"It's just a tank, Lawrence. Honestly. Sometimes you men are all the same, you know that?"

She passed him the flashlight. There was nothing to do now but look inside. Grey pointed the beam through the hatch.

Jesus fuck.

"So? What's down there?"

Grey guessed there had probably been two of them. It wasn't the easiest thing to sort out, visually. It looked like somebody had dropped a grenade, that's how torn up the soldiers were. But it wasn't a grenade.

Do you see, Grey?

He startled, as if hit by a jolt of current. The voice. Not like the one in the garage; the voice was in his head. The voice of Zero. Lila was staring at him from the base of the tank. He tried to say something, to warn her, but no words would leave his mouth.

Are you . . . hungry, Grey?

He was. Not just hungry: famished. The sensation seemed to take hold of every part of him, each cell and molecule, the tiniest atoms whirring inside him. Never in his life had he felt a hunger so profound.

It is my gift to you. The gift of blood.

"Lawrence, what's the matter?"

He swallowed. "I'll be . . . just a sec."

Down the hole he went. He had dropped his flashlight, but that didn't matter; the tank's dark interior was bright to his eyes, each surface glowing with its beautiful coating of blood. A titanic need seized him, and he pushed his face against the cold metal to drag his tongue along it.

"Lawrence! What are you doing in there?"

He was on his hands and knees now, licking the floor, burying his face in the syrupy remains. So wonderful! As if he hadn't eaten for a year, a decade, a century, only to be presented with the richest banquet in the history of the world! All the joys of the body rolled into one, a trance of purest pleasure!

The spell was broken by a violent boom. His fingers were

in his mouth; his face was covered in blood. What the hell was he doing? And what was that sound, like thunder?

"Lawrence! Come quick!"

Another boom, louder than the first. He scrambled up the ladder. Something was wrong with the sky; everything seemed lit by a fiery glow.

Lila took one look at his bloody face and began to scream.

A pair of jets roared low overhead, splitting the air with their velocity; a violent white sheen lit the sky, and Grey was slapped by a wall of heated air that knocked him off the roof of the tank. He landed hard, the wind sailing out of him. More planes shot past, the sky to the east flashing with light.

Lila was backing away from him, her hands held protectively before her face. "Get away from me!"

There was no time to explain, and what would he have said? It was clear what was happening now, they had wandered into the war. Grey grabbed her by the arm and began to drag her to the car. She was kicking, screaming, thrashing in his grip. Somehow he managed to open the passenger door and shove her in, but then he realized his mistake: the instant he closed the door, Lila hit the locks.

He pounded on the glass. "Lila, let me in!"

"Get away, get away!"

He needed something heavy. He scanned the ground near the car but found nothing. In another moment Lila would realize what she had to do; she would take the wheel and drive away.

He couldn't let that happen.

Grey reared back, squeezing his hand into a fist, and sent it plunging into the driver's window. He expected to be met by a wall of pain, all the bones of his hand shattering, but that didn't happen; his hand passed through the glass as if it were made of tissue, detonating the window in a cascade of glinting shards. Before Lila could react, he opened the door and wedged himself into the driver's seat and jammed the car into reverse. He spun into a 180, shifted into drive, and hit the gas. But the moment of escape had passed; suddenly they were in the midst of everything. As more planes rocketed past, a wall of fire rose before them; Grey swung the wheel to the right, and in the next instant they were barreling through the corn rows, the tires spinning wildly in the soft earth, heavy green leaves slapping the windshield. They burst from the field and, too late, Grey saw the culvert. The Volvo rocketed down, then up, the car going aloft before crashing onto its wheels again. Lila was screaming, screaming-screaming-screaming, and that was when Grey found it: a road. He yanked the wheel and shoved the accelerator to the floor. They were racing parallel with the culvert; the sun had dipped below the horizon, sinking the fields into an inky blackness while the sky exploded with fire.

But not just fire: suddenly the car was washed with a brilliant light.

"Stop your vehicle."

The windshield filled with an immense dark shape, like a great black bird alighting. Grey jammed his foot on the brake, pitching both of them forward. As the helicopter touched down on the roadway, Grey heard a tinkle of breaking glass and something dropped into his lap: a canister the size and weight of a soup can, making a hissing sound.

"Lila, run!"

He threw the door open, but the gas was already inside him, in his head and heart and lungs; he made it all of ten feet before he succumbed, the ground rising like a gathering wave to meet him. Time seemed undone; the world had gone all watery and far away. A great wind was pushing over his face. At the edge of his vision he saw the space-suited men lumbering toward him. Two more were dragging Lila toward the helicopter. She was suspended face-down, her body limp, her feet skimming the ground. "Don't hurt her!" Grey said. "Please don't hurt the baby!" But these words seemed not to matter. The figures were above him now, their faces obscured, floating bodiless over the earth, like ghosts. The stars were coming out.

Ghosts, Grey thought. *I really must be dead this time.* And he felt their hands upon him.

16

They drove through the day; by the time the convoy halted, it was late afternoon. Porcheki emerged from the lead Humvee and strode back to the bus.

"This is where we leave you. The sentries at the gate will tell you what to do."

They were in some kind of staging area: trucks of supplies, military portables, refuelers, even artillery. Kittridge guessed he was looking at a force at least the size of two battalions. Adjacent to this was a gated compound of canvas tents, ringed by portable fencing topped with concertina wire.

"Where are you off to?" Kittridge asked. He wondered where the fight was now.

Porcheki shrugged. *Wherever they tell me to go.* "Best of luck to you, Sergeant. Just remember what I said."

The convoy drew away. "Pull ahead, Danny," Kittridge said. "Slowly."

Two masked soldiers with M16s were positioned at the gate. A large sign affixed to the wire read: FEDERAL EMERGENCY MANAGEMENT AGENCY REFUGEE PROCESSING CENTER. NO REENTRY. NO FIREARMS PAST THIS POINT.

Twenty feet from the entrance, the soldiers motioned for them to halt. One of the sentries stepped to the driver's window. A kid, not a day over twenty, with a spray of acne on his cheeks.

"How many?"

"Twelve," Kittridge answered.

"City of origin?"

The tags had long since been stripped from the bus. "Des Moines."

The soldier stepped back, mumbling into the radio clipped to his shoulder. The second was still standing at the sealed gate with his weapon pointing skyward.

"Okay, kill the engine and stay where you are."

Moments later the soldier returned with a canvas duffel bag, which he held up to the window. "Put any weapons and cell phones in here and pass it to the front."

The ban on weapons Kittridge understood, but cell phones? None of them had gotten a signal in days.

"This many people, the local network would crash if people tried to use them. Sorry, those are the rules."

This explanation struck Kittridge as thin, but there was nothing to be done. He received the bag and moved up and down the center aisle. When he came to Mrs. Bellamy, the woman yanked her purse protectively to her waist.

"Young man, I don't even go to the beauty parlor without it."

Kittridge did his best to smile. "And right you are. But we're safe here. You have my word."

With visible reluctance she withdrew the enormous revolver from her purse and deposited it with the rest. Kittridge toted the bag to the front of the bus and left it at the base of the stairs; the first soldier reached inside and whisked it away. They were ordered to disembark with the rest of their gear and stand clear of the bus while one of the soldiers searched their luggage. Beyond the gate Kittridge could see a large, open shed where people had gathered. More soldiers were moving up and down the fence line.

"Okay," the sentry said, "you're good to go. Report to the processing area, they'll billet you."

"What about the bus?" Kittridge asked.

"All fuel and vehicles are being commandeered by the United States military. Once you're in, you're in."

Kittridge saw the stricken look on Danny's face. One of the soldiers was boarding the bus to drive it away.

"What's with him?" the sentry asked.

Kittridge turned to Danny. "It's okay, they'll take good care of it."

He could see the struggle in the man's eyes. Then Danny nodded.

"They better," he said.

The space was packed with people waiting in lines before a long table. Families with children, old people, couples, even a blind man with a dog. A young woman in a Red Cross T-shirt, her auburn hair pulled back from her face, was moving up and down the lines with a handheld.

"Any unaccompanied minors?" Like Porcheki, she'd given up on the mask. Her eyes were harried, drained by sleeplessness. She looked at April and Tim. "What about you two?"

"He's my brother," April said. "I'm eighteen."

The woman looked doubtful but said nothing.

"We'd like to all stay together," said Kittridge.

The woman was jotting on her handheld. "I'm not supposed to do this."

"What's your name?" Always good, Kittridge thought, to get a name.

"Vera."

"The patrol that brought us in said we'd be evacuated to Chicago or St. Louis."

A strip of paper slid from the handheld's port. Vera tore it off and passed it to Kittridge. "We're still waiting on buses. It shouldn't be long now. Show this to the worker at the desk."

They were assigned a tent and given plastic disks that would serve as ration coupons, then moved into the noise and smells of the camp: wood smoke, chemical toilets, the human odors of a crowd. The ground was muddy and littered with trash; people were cooking on camp stoves, hanging their laundry on tent lines, waiting at a pump to fill

buckets with water, stretched out in lawn chairs like spectators at a tailgate party, a look of dazed exhaustion on their
faces. All the garbage cans were overflowing, clouds of flies
hovering. A cruel sun was beating down. Apart from the
Army trucks, Kittridge saw no vehicles; all the refugees appeared to have come in on foot, their gasless cars abandoned.

Two people had already been billeted in their tent, an
older couple, Fred and Lucy Wilkes. They were from California but had family in Iowa and had been visiting for a
wedding when the epidemic hit. They'd been in the camp six
days.

"Any word on the buses?" Kittridge asked. Joe Robinson
had gone off to find out about rations, Wood and Delores to
see about water. April had let her brother run off with some
children from the adjacent tent, warning him not to wander
far. Danny had accompanied him. "What are people saying?"

"Always it's tomorrow." Fred Wilkes was a trim man of at
least seventy, with bright blue eyes; in the heat he'd removed
his shirt, displaying a fan of downy white chest hair. He and
his wife, as generously proportioned as he was undersized—
Jack Sprat and the missus—were playing gin rummy, sitting
across from each other on a pair of cots and using a cardboard box as a table. "If it doesn't happen soon, people are
going to lose patience. And what then?"

Kittridge stepped back outside. They were surrounded by
soldiers, safe for the time being. Yet the whole thing felt
stopped, everyone waiting for something to happen. Infan-
trymen were stationed along the fence line at one hundred
meter intervals. All of them were wearing surgical masks.
The only way in or out seemed to be the front gate. Abutting
the camp to the north he saw a low-slung, windowless building without visible markings or signage, its entrance flanked
by concrete barricades. While Kittridge watched, a pair of
sleek black helicopters approached from the east, turned in
a wide circle, and touched down on the rooftop. Four figures
emerged from the first helicopter, men in dark glasses and
baseball caps and Kevlar vests, carrying automatic rifles.
Not military, Kittridge thought. Blackbird, maybe, or Riv-
erstone. One of those outfits. The four men proceeded to
take up positions at the corners of the roof.

The doors of the second helicopter opened. Kittridge
placed a hand to his brow to get a better look. For a moment, nothing happened; then a figure emerged, wearing an
orange biosuit. Five more followed. The rotors of the heli-

copters were still turning. A brief negotiation ensued, then the biosuited figures removed a pair of long steel boxes from the helicopter's cargo section, each the approximate dimensions of a coffin, with wheeled frames that dropped from their undercarriages. They guided the two boxes to a small, hutlike structure on the roof—a service elevator, Kittridge guessed. A few minutes passed; the six reappeared and boarded the second helicopter. First one and then the other lifted off, thudding away.

April came up behind him. "I noticed that, too," she said. "Any idea what it is?"

"Maybe nothing." Kittridge dropped his hand. "Where's Tim?"

"Already making friends. He's off playing soccer with some kids."

They watched the helicopters fade from sight. Whatever it was, Kittridge thought, it wasn't nothing.

"You think we'll be okay here?" April asked.

"Why wouldn't we be?"

"I don't know." Though her face said she did; she was thinking the same thing he was. "Last night, in the lab . . . What I mean is, I can be like that sometimes. I didn't mean to pry."

"I wouldn't have told you if I didn't want to."

She was somehow looking both toward him and away. At such moments she had a way of seeming older than she was. Not seeming, Kittridge thought: being.

"Are you really eighteen?"

She seemed amused. "Why? Don't I look it?"

Kittridge shrugged to hide his embarrassment; the question had just popped out. "No. I mean yes, you do. I was just . . . I don't know."

April was plainly enjoying herself. "A girl's not supposed to tell. But to put your mind at ease, yes, I'm eighteen. Eighteen years, two months, and seventeen days. Not that I'm, you know, counting."

Their eyes met and held in the way they seemed to want to. What was it about this girl, Kittridge wondered, this April?

"I still owe you for the gun," she said, "even if they took it. I think it might be the nicest present anybody ever gave me, actually."

"I liked the poem. Call it even. What was that guy's name again?"

"T. S. Eliot."

"He got any other stuff?"

"Not much that makes sense. You ask me, he was kind of a one-hit wonder."

They had no weapons, no way to get a message to the outside world. Not for the first time, Kittridge wondered if they shouldn't have just kept driving.

"Well, when we get out of here, I'll have to check him out."

17

Grey.

Whiteness, and the sensation of floating. Grey became aware that he was in a car. This was strange, because the car was also a motel room, with beds and dressers and a television; when had they started making cars like this? He was sitting on the foot of one of the beds, driving the room—the steering column came up at an angle from the floor; the television was the windshield—and seated on the adjacent bed was Lila, clutching a pink bundle to her chest. "Are we there yet, Lawrence?" Lila asked him. "The baby needs changing." The baby? thought Grey. When had that happened? Wasn't she months away? "She's so beautiful," said Lila, softly cooing. "We have such a beautiful baby. It's too bad we have to shoot her." "Why do we have to shoot her?" Grey asked. "Don't be silly," said Lila. "We shoot all the babies now. That way they won't be eaten."

Lawrence Grey.

The dream changed—one part of him knew he was dreaming, while another part did not—and Grey was in the tank now. Something was coming to get him, but he couldn't make himself move. He was on his hands and knees, slurping the blood. His job was to drink it, drink it all, which was impossible: the blood had begun to gush through the hatch, filling the compartment. An ocean of blood. The blood was rising above his chin, his mouth and nose were filling, he was choking, drowning—

Lawrence Grey. Wake up.

He opened his eyes to a harsh light. Something felt caught in his throat; he began to cough. Something about drowning? But the dream was already breaking apart, its images atomizing, leaving only a residue of fear.

Where was he?

Some kind of hospital. He was wearing a gown, but that

was all; he felt the chill of nakedness beneath it. Thick straps bound his wrists and ankles to the rails of the bed, holding him in place like a mummy in a sarcophagus. Wires snaked from beneath his gown to a cart of medical equipment; an IV was threaded into his right arm.

Somebody was in the room.

Two somebodies in fact, the pair hovering at the foot of the bed in their bulky biosuits, their faces shielded by plastic masks. Behind them was a heavy steel door and, positioned high on the wall in the corner, watching the scene with its unblinking gaze, a security camera.

"Mr. Grey, I'm Horace Guilder," the one on the left said. His tone of voice struck Grey as oddly cheerful. "This is my colleague Dr. Nelson. How are you feeling?"

Grey did his best to focus on their faces. The one who'd spoken looked anonymously middle-aged, with a heavy, square-jawed head and pasty skin; the second man was considerably younger, with tight dark eyes and a scraggly little Vandyke. He didn't look like any doctor Grey had ever met.

He licked his lips and swallowed. "What is this place? Why am I tied up?"

Guilder answered with a calming tone. "That's for your own protection, Mr. Grey. Until we figure out what's wrong with you. As for where you are," he said, "I'm afraid I can't tell you that just yet. Suffice it to say that you're among friends here."

Grey realized they must have sedated him; he could barely move a muscle, and it wasn't just the straps. His limbs felt like iron, his thoughts moving through his brain with a lazy aimlessness, like guppies in a tank. Guilder was holding a cup of water to his lips.

"Go on, drink."

Grey's stomach turned—just the smell of it was revolting, like some hideously overchlorinated pool. Thoughts came back to him, dark thoughts: the blood in the tank, and Grey's face buried greedily in it. Had that actually happened? Had he dreamed it? But no sooner had these questions formed in his mind than a kind of roaring seemed to fill his head, a vast hunger lurching to life inside him, so overwhelming that his entire body clenched against the straps.

"Whoa now," Guilder said, backing away suddenly. "Steady there."

More images were coming back to him, rising through the fog. The tank in the road, the dead soldiers, and explosions all around; the feel of his hand crashing through the Volvo's window, and the fields detonating with fire, and the car sailing through the corn, and the bright lights of the helicopter, and the space-suited men, dragging Lila away.

"Where is she? What have you done with her?"

Guilder glanced toward Nelson, who frowned. *Interesting,* his face seemed to say.

"You needn't worry, Mr. Grey, we're taking good care of her. She's right across the hall, in fact."

"Don't you hurt her." His fists were clenched; he was straining against the straps. "You touch her and I'll—"

"And you'll what, Mr. Grey?"

But there was nothing; the straps held firm. Whatever they had given him, it had taken his strength away.

"Try not to excite yourself, Mr. Grey. Your friend is perfectly fine. The baby, too. What we're a little unclear on is just how the two of you came to be together. I was hoping you might help us with that."

"Why do you want to know?"

One eyebrow lifted incredulously behind the faceplate. "For starters, it seems that the two of you are the last people to come out of Colorado alive. Believe me when I tell you, this is a matter of some interest to us. Was she at the Chalet? Is that where you met her?"

Just the word made Grey's mind clench with panic. "The Chalet?"

"Yes, Mr. Grey. The Chalet."

He shook his head. "No."

"Then where?"

He swallowed. "At the Home Depot."

For just a moment, Guilder said nothing. "Where was this?"

Grey tried to put his thoughts together, but his brain had gone all fuzzy again. "Denver someplace. I don't know exactly. She wanted me to paint the nursery."

Guilder quickly turned toward the second man, who shrugged. "Could be the fentanyl," Nelson said. "It may take him a little while to sort things out."

But Guilder was undeterred. There was something more forceful about the man's gaze now. It seemed to bore right into him. "We need to know what happened at the Chalet. How did you get away?"

"I don't remember."

"Was there a girl there? Did you see her?"

There was a girl? What were they talking about?

"I didn't see anyone. I just . . . I don't know. It was all so confusing. I woke up at the Red Roof."

"The Red Roof? What's that?"

"A motel, on the highway."

A puzzled frown. "When was this?"

Grey tried to count. "Three days ago? No, four." He nodded his head against the pillow. "Four days."

The two men looked at each other. "It doesn't make sense," Nelson said. "The Chalet was destroyed twenty-two days ago. He's not Rip Van Winkle."

"Where were you for those three weeks?" Guilder pressed.

The question made no sense. Three weeks?

"I don't know," Grey said.

"I'll ask you again, Mr. Grey. Was Lila at the Chalet? Is that where you met her?"

"I told you," he said. He was pleading now, his resistance gone. "She was at the Home Depot."

His thoughts were swirling like water going down a drain. Whatever they'd given him, it had screwed him up good. With a thump in his gut, Grey realized what the straps were all about. They were going to study him. Like the sticks. Like Zero. And when they were done with him, Richards, or somebody like him, would put the red light on Grey, and that would be the end of him.

"Please, it's me you want. I'm sorry I ran away. Just don't hurt Lila."

For a moment the two men said nothing, just stared at him from behind their faceplates. Then Guilder turned toward Nelson, nodding.

"Put him back under."

Nelson took a syringe and a vial of clear liquid from the cart. While Grey looked on helplessly, he inserted the needle into the IV tube and pushed the plunger.

"I just clean," Grey said feebly. "I'm just a janitor."

"Oh, I think you're much more than that, Mr. Grey."

And with these words in his ears, Grey slipped away again.

Guilder and Nelson stepped through the air lock into the decontamination chamber. First a shower in their biosuits; then they stripped and scrubbed themselves head to foot with a harsh, chemical-smelling soap. They cleared their throats and spat into the sink, gargling for a minute with a strong disinfectant. A cumbersome ritual but, until they knew more about Grey's condition, one they were wise to observe.

Just a skeletal staff was present in the building: three lab technicians—Guilder thought of them as Wynken, Blynken, and Nod—plus an MD and a four-man Blackbird security team. The building had been constructed in the late eighties to treat soldiers exposed to nuclear, biological, or chemical agents, and the systems were buggy as hell—the above-ground HVAC was on the fritz, as was video surveillance for the entire facility—and the place had a disconcertingly deserted feel to it. But it was the last place anybody would look for them.

Nelson and Guilder stepped into the lab, a wide room of desks and equipment, including the powerful microscopes and blood spinners they'd need to isolate and culture the virus. While Grey and Lila were still unconscious, they'd each had a CT scan and blood drawn; their blood tests had been inconclusive, but Grey's scan had revealed a radically enlarged thymus, typical of those infected. And yet as far as Nelson and Guilder could discern, he'd experienced no other symptoms. In every other way he appeared to be in the pink of health. Better than that: the man looked like he could run a marathon.

"Let me show you something," Nelson said.

He escorted Guilder to the terminal in an adjacent office where he'd set up shop. Nelson opened a file and clicked on a JPEG. A photo appeared on the screen of Lawrence Grey. Or, rather, a man who *resembled* Grey; the face in the photograph looked considerably older. Sagging skin, hair a thin flap over his scalp, sunken eyes that gazed into the camera with a dull, almost bovine look.

"When was this taken?" Guilder asked.

"Seventeen months ago. These are Richards's files."

God damn, Guilder thought. It was just like Lear had said.

"If he's got the virus," Nelson said, "the question is why it's acting differently in his body. It could be a variant we haven't seen, one that activates the thymus like the others and then goes dormant somehow. Or it could be something else, particular to him."

Guilder frowned. "Such as?"

"Your guess is as good as mine. Some sort of natural immunity seems the likely culprit, but there's no way of really knowing. It might have something to do with the anti-androgens he was taking. All the sweeps were taking pretty big doses. Depo-Provera, spironolactone, prednisone."

"You think the steroids did this?"

Nelson shrugged halfheartedly. "It could be a factor. We know the virus interacts with the endocrine system, same as the anti-androgens." He closed the file and turned in his chair. "But here's something else. I did a little digging on the woman. Not much to find, but what there is is mighty interesting. I printed it up for you."

Nelson presented him with a fat file of papers. Guilder opened to the first page.

"She's an MD?"

"Orthopedic surgeon. Keep going."

Guilder read. Lila Beatrice Kyle, born September 29, 1974, Boston, Massachusetts. Parents both academics, the father an English professor at BU, the mother a historian at Simmons. Andover then Wellesley, followed by four years at Dartmouth-Hitchcock for her medical degree. Residency and then a fellowship in orthopedics at Denver General. All impressive, but telling him nothing. Guilder turned to the next page. What was he looking at? The first page of an IRS form 1040, dated four years ago.

Lila Kyle was married to Brad Wolgast.

"You're kidding me."

Nelson was wearing one of his victorious grins. "I told you that you were going to like it. *The* Agent Wolgast. They had one child, a daughter, deceased. Some kind of congenital heart defect. Divorced three years later. She got remarried four months ago to a doctor who works at the same hospital, some big cardiologist. There's a few pages on him, too, though it doesn't really add anything."

"Okay, so she's an MD. Is there any record of her at the Chalet? Was it possible she was on the staff?"

Nelson shook his head. "Nothing. And I seriously doubt Richards would have missed this. As far as I can see, there's no reason not to think Grey found her just like he said."

"She could have been in the truck in that first aerial we got. We wouldn't have seen her."

"True. But I don't think Grey's lying about where he met her. The story's just too weird to make up. And I checked: her Denver address puts her within just a couple of miles of a Home Depot. The way Grey was headed, he would have gone right through there. You've talked to her. She seems to think Grey is some kind of handyman. I don't think she has a clue what's going on. The woman's crazy as a bedbug."

"Is that your *official* diagnosis?"

Nelson shrugged. "There's no history of psychiatric illness in the paperwork, but consider her situation. She's pregnant, hiding, on the run. People are getting ripped to shreds. Somehow she manages to stay alive, but she gets left behind. How would you feel? The brain's a pretty nimble organ. Right now it's rewriting reality for her, and doing a hell of a good job. Based on Grey's file, I'd say she's got plenty in common with the guy, actually."

Guilder thought a moment and returned the file to the desk. "Well, I'm not buying it. What are the chances that these two would simply bump into each other? It's too big a coincidence."

"Maybe," Nelson said. "Either way, it doesn't tell us much. And the woman might be infected, but we're just not seeing it. Maybe her pregnancy masks it somehow."

"How far along is she?"

"I'm no expert, but from fetal size, I'd say about thirty weeks. You can check with Suresh."

Suresh was the MD Guilder had brought in from USAM-RIID. An infectious diseases doc, he'd been tasked to Special Weapons only six months ago. Guilder had told him little, only that Grey and the woman were "persons of interest."

"How long before we can get a decent culture from him?"

"That depends. Assuming we can isolate the virus at all, somewhere between forty-eight and seventy-two hours. If you're really asking my opinion, the wisest course would be to pack him off to Atlanta. They're the ones who are best equipped to handle something like this. And if Grey's immune, I can't see why they wouldn't just let bygones be bygones. Not with so much at stake."

Guilder shook his head. "Let's wait until we have something solid."

"I wouldn't wait long. Not with the way things are going."

"We won't. But you heard the guy. He thinks he's been sleeping in a motel. I doubt anybody's going to take us seriously if that's all we've got. They'll lock us both up and throw away the key if we're *lucky.*"

Nelson frowned, touching his beard with a thoughtful gesture. "I see your point."

"I'm not saying we won't tell them," Guilder offered. "But let's move cautiously. Seventy-two hours, then I'll make the call, all right?"

A frozen moment followed. Had Nelson bought it? Then the man nodded.

"Just keep digging." Guilder clapped a hand on Nelson's shoulder. "And tell Suresh to keep the two of them sedated for the time being. If either of them flips, I don't want to take any chances."

"You think those straps will hold?"

The question was rhetorical; both men knew the answer.

Guilder left Nelson in the lab and rode the elevator to the roof. His left leg was dragging again, a hitch in his step like a hiccup. Outside, the Blackbird officer in charge, named Masterson, nodded a terse greeting but otherwise left him alone. Vintage Blackbird, this guy: built like a dump truck with arms as thick as hydrants and a face petrified into the self-satisfied sneer of an overgrown frat boy. In his wrap-around sunglasses and baseball cap and body armor, Masterson seemed less a person than an action figure. Where did they get these characters? Were they grown on some kind of farm? Cultured in a petri dish? They were thugs, pure and simple, and Guilder had never liked dealing with them—Richards being Exhibit A—though it was also true that their almost robotic obedience made them ideally suited for certain jobs; if they didn't exist, you'd have to invent them.

He moved to the edge of the roof. It was just past noon, the air breathless under a shapeless white sun, the land as flat and featureless as a pool table. The only interruptions to the perfectly linear horizon were a gleaming domed building, probably something to do with the college, and, just to the south, the bowl-like shape of a football stadium. One of those kinds of schools, Guilder thought—a sports franchise masquerading as a college where criminals drifted through phony courses and filled the coffers of the alumni fund by pounding their opposite numbers to pieces on autumn afternoons.

He let his eyes peruse the FEMA camp below. The presence of refugees was a wrinkle he hadn't anticipated, and initially it had concerned him. But when he'd considered the situation more closely, he couldn't see how this made any difference. The word from the Army was that in a day or two they'd all be gone anyway. A group of boys were playing near the wire, kicking a half-deflated ball around in the dirt. For a few minutes Guilder watched them. The world could be falling apart, and yet children were children; at a moment's notice they could put all their cares aside and lose themselves in a game. Perhaps that was what Guilder had felt with Shawna: a few minutes in which he got to be the boy he never was. Maybe that was all he'd ever wanted—what anybody ever wanted.

But Lawrence Grey: something about the man nagged at him, and it wasn't just his incredible story or the improbable coincidence of the woman in question being Agent Wolgast's wife. It was the way Grey had spoken of her. *Please, it's me you want. Just don't hurt Lila.* Guilder never would have guessed Grey was capable of caring about another person like that, let alone a woman. Everything in his file had led Guilder to expect a man who was at best a loner, at worst a sociopath. But Grey's pleas on Lila's behalf had obviously been heartfelt. Something had happened between them; a bond had been forged.

His gaze widened, then taking in the entirety of the camp. All these people: they were trapped. And not merely by the wires that surrounded them. Physical barricades were nothing compared to the wires of the mind. What had truly imprisoned them was one another. Husbands and wives, parents and children, friends and companions: what they believed had given them strength in their lives had actually done the opposite. Guilder recalled the couple who lived across the street from his townhouse, trading off their sleeping daughter on the way to the car. How heavy that burden must have felt in their arms. And when the end swept down upon them all, they would exit the world on a wave of suffering, their agonies magnified a million times over by the loss of her. Would they have to watch her die? Would they perish first, knowing what would become of her in their absence? Which was preferable? But the answer was neither. Love had sealed their doom. Which was what love did. Guilder's father had taught that lesson well enough.

Guilder was dying. That was inarguable, a fact of nature. So, too, was the fact that Lawrence Grey—this disposable nobody, this goddamn janitor, a man who had in his pathetic life brought nothing but misery to the world—was not. Somewhere in the body of Lawrence Grey lay the secret to the ultimate freedom, and Horace Guilder would find it, and take it for his own.

18

The days crawled past. And still no word on the buses.

Everyone was restless. Outside the wire, the Army came and went, its numbers thinning. Each morning, Kittridge went to the shed to inquire about the situation; each morning, he came away with the same answer: the buses are on the way, be patient.

For a whole day it rained, turning the camp into a giant mud bath. Now the sun had returned, cooking every surface with a crust of dried earth. Each afternoon more MREs appeared, tossed from the back of an Army five-ton, but never any news. The chemical toilets were foul, the waste cans overflowing with trash. Kittridge spent hours watching the front gate; no more refugees were coming in. With each passing day, the place had begun to feel like an island surrounded by a hostile sea.

He'd made an ally of Vera, the Red Cross volunteer who had first approached them in the check-in line. She was younger than Kittridge had first thought, a nursing student at Midwest State. Like all the civilian workers, she seemed utterly drained, the days of strain weighing in her face. She understood his frustration, she said, everyone did. She had hoped to take the buses, too; she was stranded like the rest of them. One day they were coming from Chicago, then next from Kansas City, then from Joliet. Some FEMA screwup. They were supposed to get a bank of satellite phones, too, so people could call their relatives and let them know they were okay. What had happened to that, Vera didn't know. Even the local cell network was down.

Kittridge had begun to see the same faces: an elegantly dressed woman who kept a cat on a leash, a group of young black men all dressed in the white shirts and black neckties of Jehovah's Witnesses, a girl in a cheerleading outfit. A listlessness had settled over the camp; the deflected drama of nondeparture had left everyone in a passive state. There were rumors that the water supply had become contaminated, and now the medical tent was full of people complaining of stomach cramps, muscle aches, fever. A number of people had radios that were still operating, but all they heard was a ringing sound, followed by the now-familiar statement from the Emergency Broadcast System. *Do not leave your homes. Shelter in place. Obey all orders of military and law enforcement personnel.* Another minute of ringing, and the words would be repeated.

Kittridge had begun to wonder if they were ever getting out of there. And all night long, he watched the fences.

Late afternoon of the fourth day: Kittridge was playing yet another hand of cards with April, Pastor Don, and Mrs. Bellamy. They'd switched from bridge to five-card poker, betting ludicrous sums of money that were purely hypothetical. April, who claimed never to have played before, had already taken Kittridge for close to five thousand dollars. The Wilkeses had disappeared; nobody had seen them since Wednesday. Wherever they'd gone, they'd taken their luggage with them.

"Jesus, it's roasting in here," Joe Robinson said. He'd barely been off his cot all day.

"Sit in a hand," Kittridge suggested. "It'll take your mind off the heat."

"Christ," the man moaned. The sweat was pouring off him. "I can barely move."

Kittridge, with only a pair of sixes, folded his cards. April, wearing a perfect poker face, raked in another pot.

"I'm bored," Tim announced.

April was sorting the slips of paper they used for chips into piles. "You can play with me. I'll show you how to bet."

"I want to play crazy eights."

"Trust me," she told her brother, "this is a lot better."

Pastor Don was dealing a fresh hand when Vera appeared at the flap of the tent. She quickly met Kittridge's eye. "Can we talk outside?"

He rose from the cot and stepped into the late-day heat.

"Something's going on," Vera said. "FEMA just got word that all civilian transportation east of the Mississippi has been suspended."

"Are you certain?"

"I overheard them talking about it in the site director's office. Half the FEMA staff has bugged out already."

"Who else knows about this?"

"Are you kidding? I'm not even telling you."

So there it was; they were being abandoned. "Who's the officer in charge?"

"Major something. I think her name is Porcheki."

A stroke of luck. "Where is she now?"

"She should be in the shed. There was some colonel, but he's gone. A *lot* of them are gone."

"I'll talk to her."

Vera frowned doubtfully. "What can you do?"

"Maybe nothing. But at least it's worth a try."

She hurried away; Kittridge returned to the tent. "Where's Delores?"

Wood lifted his eyes from his cards. "I think she's working in one of the medical tents. The Red Cross put out a call for volunteers."

"Somebody go get her."

When everyone was present, Kittridge explained the situation. Assuming Porcheki would provide fuel for the bus—a big if—they would have to wait to leave until morning, at the earliest.

"Do you really think she'll help us?" Pastor Don asked.

"I admit it's a long shot."

"I say we just steal it and get the hell out of here," Jamal said. "Let's not wait."

"It may come to that, and I'd agree, except for two things. One, we're talking about the Army. Stealing it sounds like a good way to get shot. And two, we've got at most a couple of hours of light left. It's a long way to Chicago, and I don't want to try this in the dark. Make sense?"

Jamal nodded.

"The important thing is to keep this quiet and stick together. Once this thing gets out, all hell's going to break loose. Everybody stay close to the tent. You, too, Tim. No wandering off."

Kittridge had stepped from the tent when Delores caught up with him. "I'm concerned about this fever," she said quickly. "The med tents are being completely overrun. All the supplies are used up, no antibiotics, nothing. This thing is getting out of hand."

"What do you think it is?"

"The obvious culprit would be typhus. The same thing happened in New Orleans after Hurricane Vanessa. This many people crammed in, it was just a matter of time. If you ask me, we can't leave fast enough."

Another worry, Kittridge thought. Quickening his stride, he made his way to the shed, past overflowing dumpsters where crows were picking at the garbage. The birds had showed up the prior evening, attracted, no doubt, by the reek of accumulating trash. Now the place seemed full of them, so brazen they would practically snatch food from your hand. Never a good sign, he thought, when the crows showed up.

At the command tent, Kittridge chose the most direct approach, doing nothing to announce his presence before stepping inside. Porcheki was seated at a long table, speaking into a satellite phone. Three noncoms occupied the room, a densely packed jumble of electronic equipment. One of the soldiers yanked off his headset and shot to his feet.

"What are you doing in here? This area is restricted, no civilians."

But as the soldier stepped toward Kittridge, Porcheki stopped him.

"It's all right, Corporal." Her face a mask of weariness, she put down the phone. "Sergeant Kittridge. What can I do for you?"

"You're pulling out, aren't you?" The idea had formed in his mind even as he'd spoken the words.

Porcheki weighed him with her eyes. Then, to the soldiers: "Would you excuse us, please?"

"Major—"

"That's all, Corporal."

With visible reluctance, the three exited the tent.

"Yes," Porcheki said. "We've been ordered back to the Illinois line. The entire state goes under quarantine at eighteen hundred hours tomorrow."

"You can't just leave these people. They're totally defenseless."

"I know that, too." She was looking at him closely. She seemed on the verge of some announcement. Then: "You were at Bagram, weren't you?"

"Ma'am?"

"I thought I recognized you. I was there, with the Seventy-second Medical Expeditionary Group. You wouldn't remember me, I don't think." Her eyes darted downward. "How's the leg?"

Kittridge was almost too stunned to reply. "I get around okay."

A faint nod and, on her troubled face, what might have passed for a smile. "I'm glad to see you made it, Sergeant. I heard about what happened. That was a terrible thing, with the boy." Her officious manner returned. "As for the other, I've got two dozen coaches en route from the arsenal at Rock Island and a pair of refuelers. Plus your bus, that makes twenty-five. Not enough, obviously, but it's what I could put together. This is not for general consumption, mind you. We don't want to start a panic. I'd be lying to you if I didn't say I'm going way off the reservation here. Are we clear?"

Kittridge nodded.

"When those buses pull in, you'll want to be ready. You know what these things are like. You keep control as long as you can, but sooner or later it gets ragged around the edges. People will do the math, and you can bet nobody's going to want to be left behind. We should have time to make four trips before the border closes. That should do it, but we'll have very little margin. You have a driver for your bus?"

Kittridge nodded again. "Danny."

"The one with the hat? Forgive me, Sergeant, I mean no disrespect to the man. But I need to be sure he can handle this."

"You won't do better than him. You have my word."

A quick hesitation, then she agreed. "Have him report here at oh-three-hundred. The first load departs at oh-four-thirty. Just remember what I said. You want to get your people out of here, get them on those buses."

The next thing surprised Kittridge most of all. Porcheki leaned down, opened the bottom drawer of her desk, and removed a pair of pistols. Kittridge's own Glocks, still in their holsters. She handed him a blue windbreaker with FEMA stenciled on the back.

"Just keep them under wraps. Report to Corporal Danes outside and he'll escort you to the armory. Take all the rounds you need."

Kittridge slid his arms through the straps and put on the jacket. The woman's meaning was plain. They were behind the lines; the front had passed them by.

"How close are they?" Kittridge asked.

The major's expression darkened. "They're already here."

Lawrence Grey had never known such hunger.

How long had he been here? Three days? Four? Time had lost all meaning, the passage of hours broken only by the visits of the space-suited men. They came without warning, apparitions emerging from a narcotic haze. The hiss of the air lock and there they were; then the prick of the needle and the slow filling of the plastic bag with its crimson prize. Something was in his blood, something they wanted. Yet they never seemed satisfied; they would drain him like a slaughtered steer. *What do you want?* he pleaded. *Why are you doing this to me? Where's Lila?*

He was famished. He was a being of pure need, a man-sized hole in space needing only to be filled. A person could go mad with it. Assuming he *was* a person, still, which hardly seemed likely. Zero had changed him, altered the very essence of his existence. He was being brought into the fold. In his mind were voices, murmurings, like the buzz of a distant crowd. Hour by hour the sound grew stronger; the crowd was closing in. Against the straps he wriggled like a fish in a net. With every stolen bag of blood his strength drained away. He felt himself aging from within, a precipitous decline, deep in the cells. The universe had abandoned him to his fate. Soon he would vanish; he would be dispersed into the void.

They were watching him, the one named Guilder and the one named Nelson; Grey sensed their presence lurking behind the lens of the security camera, the probing beams of their eyes. They needed him; they were afraid of him. He was like a present that, when opened, might burst forth as snakes. He had no answers for them; they'd given up asking. Silence was the last power he had.

He thought of Lila. Were the same things happening to her? Was the baby all right? He had wanted only to protect her, to do this one good thing in his wretched little life. It was a kind of love. Like Nora Chung, only a thousand times deeper, an energy that desired nothing, that took nothing; it wanted only to give itself away. It was true: Lila had come into his life for a purpose, to give him one last chance. And yet he had failed her.

He heard the hiss of the air lock; a figure stepped through. One of the suited men, lumbering toward him like a great orange snowman.

"Mr. Grey, I'm Dr. Suresh."

Grey closed his eyes and waited for the prick of the needle. Go ahead, he thought, take it all. But that didn't happen. Grey looked up to see the doctor withdrawing a needle from the IV port. With careful movements he capped the needle and deposited it in the waste can with a clang. At once Grey felt the fog lift from his mind.

"Now we can talk. How are you feeling?"

He wanted to say: How do you think I'm feeling? Or maybe just: Fuck you. "Where's Lila?"

The doctor withdrew a small penlight from a pouch on his biosuit and leaned over Grey's face. Through the faceplate of his helmet his features swam into view: a heavy brow, skin dark with a yellowish cast, small white teeth. He waved the beam over Grey's eyes.

"Does it trouble you? The light."

Grey shook his head. He was becoming aware of a new sound—a rhythmic throbbing. He was hearing the man's heartbeat, the pulsing swish of blood through his veins. A blast of saliva washed the walls of his mouth.

"You have not had a bowel movement, yes?"

Grey swallowed and shook his head again. The doctor moved to the foot of the bed and withdrew a small silver probe. He scraped it quickly along the soles of Grey's bare feet.

"Very good."

The examination continued. Each bit of data was jotted onto a handheld. Suresh pulled Grey's gown up over his legs and cupped his testicles in his hand.

"Cough, please."

Grey managed a small one. The doctor's face behind his faceplate revealed nothing. The throbbing sound filled Grey's entire brain, annihilating any other thought.

"I am going to check your glands."

The doctor reached his gloved hands toward Grey's neck. As the tips of his fingers made contact, Grey darted his head forward. The action was automatic; Grey couldn't have stopped it if he'd tried. His teeth bore into the soft flesh of Suresh's palm, clamping like a vise. The chemical taste of latex, profoundly revolting, then a burst of sweetness filled his mouth. Suresh was shrieking, struggling to break free. His free hand pushed on Grey's forehead, fighting for leverage; he reared back and struck Grey across the face with his fist. Not painful but startling; Grey broke his hold. Suresh stumbled backward, clutching his bloody hand at the wrist, thumb and forefinger wrapping it like a tourniquet. Grey expected something large to happen, the sound of an alarm, men rushing in, but nothing of the kind occurred; the moment felt frozen and, somehow, unobserved. Suresh backed away, staring at Grey with a look of wide-eyed panic. He stripped off his bloody glove and moved briskly to the sink. He turned on the tap and began to scrub his hand fiercely, muttering under his breath:

"Oh God, oh God, oh God."

Then he was gone. Grey lay still. In the struggle, his IV had torn loose. There was blood on his face, his lips. With slow pleasure he licked them clean. The merest taste, but it was enough. Strength flowed into him like a tide upon the shore. He tensed against the straps, feeling the rivets start to give. The air lock was another matter, but sooner or later it would open, and when it did, Grey would be waiting. He would alight like an angel of death.

Lila, I am coming.

19

0330 hours: The group was gathered at the tent, gear packed, awaiting the dawn. Kittridge had told them they should sleep, to prepare for the journey ahead. Shortly after midnight, the promised buses had appeared outside the fence, a long gray line. From the Army, no announcement, but their arrival hadn't escaped attention. All through the camp the talk was of leaving. Who would get to go first? Were more buses coming? What about the ill? Would they be evacuated separately?

Kittridge had gone with Danny to the command tent for Porcheki's briefing. What was left of the civilian staff, FEMA and Red Cross, would directly supervise the loading, while the last of Porcheki's men, three platoons, would manage the crowds. A dozen Humvees and a pair of APCs would wait on the far side of the fence to escort the convoy. The trip to Rock Island would take a little under two hours. Assuming everything went as planned, the last of the four loads would reach Rock Island by 1730, just under the deadline.

When the meeting broke up, Kittridge took Danny aside. "If anything happens, don't wait. Just take what you can carry and go. Stay off the main roads. If the bridge at Rock Island is closed, head north, like we did the last time. Follow the river until you find an open bridge. Got that?"

"I shouldn't wait. Stay off the main roads. Go north."

"Exactly."

The other drivers were already headed for the buses. Kittridge had only a moment to say the rest.

"Whatever happens, Danny, we wouldn't have gotten this far without you. I'm sure you know it, but I wanted to say so."

The man nodded tightly, his gaze slanted away. "Okay."

"I'd like to shake on it. Do you think that would be all right?"

Danny's brow furrowed with an expression, almost, of pain. Kittridge was worried he'd overstepped when Danny extended his hand with furtive quickness, the two men's palms colliding. His grip, though hesitant, was not without strength. A vigorous pump; for a second Danny met his eye; then it was over.

"Good luck," said Kittridge.

He returned to the tent. Nothing to do now but wait. He sat on the ground with his back against a wooden crate. A few minutes passed; the flaps of the tent parted. April lowered herself beside him, drawing her knees to her chest.

"You mind?"

Kittridge shook his head. They were looking toward the

compound's entrance, a hundred yards distant. Under a blaze of spotlights, the area around it glowed like a brightly lit stage.

"I just wanted to thank you," April said. "For everything you've done."

"Anybody would have."

"No, they wouldn't. I mean, you'd like to think so. But no."

Kittridge wondered if this was true. He supposed it didn't matter. Fate had pushed them together, and here they were. Then he remembered the pistols.

"I've got something of yours."

He reached under his jacket and pulled one of the Glocks free. He racked the slide to chamber a round, turned it around in his hand, and held it out to her.

"Remember what I told you. One shot in the center of the chest. They go down like a house of cards if you do it right."

"How did you get it back?"

He smiled. "Won it in a poker game." He nudged it toward her. "Go on, take it."

It had become important to him that she have it. April took it in her hand, leaned forward, and slid the barrel into the waistband of her jeans, resting against her spine.

"Thanks," she said with a smile. "I'll use it in good health."

For a full minute, neither spoke.

"It's pretty obvious how all this is going to end, isn't it?" April said. "Sooner or later, I mean."

Kittridge turned his face to look at her; her eyes were averted, the lights of the spots glazing her features. "There's always a chance."

"That's nice of you to say. But it doesn't change a thing. Maybe the others need to hear it, but I don't."

A chill had fallen; April leaned her weight against him. The gesture was instinctive, but it meant something. Kittridge draped his arm around her, drawing her in for warmth.

"You think about him, don't you?" Her head lay against his chest; her voice was very soft. "The boy in the car."

"Yes."

"Tell me."

Kittridge took a long breath, exhaling into the darkness. "I think about him all the time."

A deeper silence fell. Around them the camp had fallen quiet, like the rooms of a house after everyone had gone to bed.

"I'd like to ask a favor," April said.

"Name it."

Kittridge felt her body tense just slightly. "Did I mention I was a virgin?"

Despite himself, he laughed; and yet this did not seem wrong. "Now, I think I'd remember something like that."

"Yeah, well. There haven't been what you'd call a lot of men in my life." She paused, then said, "I wasn't lying about being eighteen, you know. Not that it matters. I don't think this is a world where stuff like that means much anymore."

Kittridge nodded. "I guess maybe it doesn't."

"So what I'm saying is, it doesn't have to be any big thing."

"It's always a big thing."

April wrapped his hand with her fingers, slowly brushing her thumb over the tops of his knuckles. The sensation was as light and warm as a kiss. "It's funny. Even before I saw your scars, I knew what you were. Not just the Army—that was obvious to everyone. That something had happened to you, in the war." A pause, then: "I don't think I even know your first name."

"It's Bernard."

She pulled away to look at him. Her eyes were moist and shining. "Please, Bernard. Just please, okay?"

It was not a request that could be refused; nor did he want to. They used one of the adjacent tents—who knew where its occupants had gone? Kittridge was out of practice but did his best to be kind, to go slow, watching April's face carefully in the dim light. She made a few sounds, but not many, and when it was done she kissed him, long and tenderly, nestled against him, and soon was fast asleep.

Kittridge lay in the dark, listening to her breathe, feeling her warmth where their bodies touched. He'd thought it might be strange but it wasn't strange at all; it seemed a natural part of all that had occurred. His thoughts drifted, touching down here and there. The better memories; the memories of love. He didn't have many. Now he had another. How foolish he'd been, wanting to give away this life.

He had just closed his eyes when from beyond the gate came a roar of engines and a flare of headlights. April was stirring beside him. He dressed quickly and parted the flaps as he heard, coming from the west, a roll of thunder. Wouldn't you know they'd be leaving in the rain.

"Are they here?" Rubbing his eyes, Pastor Don was emerging from the tent. Wood was behind him.

Kittridge nodded. "Get your gear, everybody. It's time."

* * *

Where the hell was Suresh?

Nobody had seen the man for hours. One minute he was supposed to be examining Grey; the next he'd vanished into thin air. Guilder had sent Masterson to search for him. Twenty minutes later, he'd come back empty-handed. Suresh was nowhere in the building, he said.

Their first defection, Guilder thought. A crack like that would widen. Where could the man hope to get to? They were in the middle of a cornfield, night was pressing down. The days had passed in futility. Still they had failed to isolate the virus, to draw it forth from the cells. There was no doubt that Grey was infected; the man's enlarged thymus told them so. But the virus itself seemed to be hiding. Hiding! Those were Nelson's words. How could a virus be hiding? Just fucking find it, Guilder said. We're running out of time.

Guilder was spending more of his time on the roof, drawn to its sense of space. Past midnight once again, and here he was. Sleep was only a memory. No sooner would he drift off than he would jolt awake, the walls of his throat closing in. The seventy-two-hour deadline had come and gone, Nelson only raising his eyebrows: *Well?* Guilder's windpipe was so tight he could barely swallow; his left hand fluttered like a bird. One whole side of his body was dragging as if a ten-pound dumbbell were tied to his ankle. There was no way he could hide the situation from Nelson much longer.

From the rooftop, Guilder had watched the Army's ranks diminishing over the days. How far away were the virals? How much time did they have?

His handheld buzzed at his waist. Nelson.

"You better come see this."

Nelson met him at the door of the elevator. He was wearing a dirty lab coat, his hair askew. He handed Guilder a sheaf of paper.

"What am I looking at?"

Nelson's face was grim. "Just read."

DEPARTMENT OF THE ARMY
U.S. CENTRAL COMMAND
7115 SOUTH BOUNDARY BOULEVARD
MACDILL AFB, FL 33621-5101

010500JUN16
USCENTCOM OPERATION ORDER—IMMACULATA

REFERENCES: EXECUTIVE ORDER 929621, 1st HL Recon BDE OPORD 18–26, Map Sheet V107

TASK ORGANIZATION: Joint Task Force (JTF) SCORCH, including elements of: 388th Fighter Wing (388 FW), 23rd Fighter Group (23 FG), 62nd Homeland Aerial Defense Group (62 HADG), Colorado Army National Guard (CO ANG), Kansas Army National Guard (KS ANG), Nebraska Army National Guard (NE ANG), and Iowa Army National Guard (IA ANG)

1. SITUATION
  a. Enemy Strength: Unknown, +/- 200K
  b. Terrain: Mixture of high plains/grasslands/urban
  c. Weather: Variable conditions, moderate day visibility, limited night visibility, low to no moonlight
  d. Enemy Situation: As of 010500JUN16, 763 infected person groups ("pods") observed massed in Designated Areas 1–26. Enemy movement expected immediately following sunset (2116).

2. MISSION
JTF SCORCH conducts combat operations from 012100JUN16 through 052400JUN17 within designated Quarantine Zone in order to destroy all infected persons.

3. EXECUTION
Intent: JTF will conduct air and ground combat operations within Quarantine Zone. Priority task for JTF SCORCH is elimination of all infected personnel within Quarantine Zone. *All personnel, including civilians, within Quarantine Zone are assumed to be infected and are authorized for elimination in accordance with Executive Order 929621. End state is elimination of all infected personnel within Quarantine Zone.*

Concept of the Operation: This will be a two-phase operation:

PHASE 1: JTF deploys tactical air units of the 388 FW, 23 FG, and 62 HADG 012100JUN16 to conduct massed bombing of Designated Areas 1–26. PHASE 1 complete with 100% bombing saturation of Quarantine Zone. PHASE 2 will commence immediately following PHASE 1 complete.

PHASE 2: JTF will deploy 3 Mechanized Infantry Divisions from tactical ground units of the CO ANG, KS ANG, NE ANG, IA ANG to conduct free-fire assaults on remaining enemy forces within Designated Areas 1–26. PHASE 2 complete with 100% infected personnel destroyed within Quarantine Zone.

It went on from there: logistics, tactical, command, and signal. The bureaucratese of war. The upshot was clear: anyone behind the quarantine line was now forfeit.

"Jesus."

"I told you," Nelson said. "Sooner or later, this was bound to happen. It's less than two hours till dawn. We're probably okay for the night, but I don't think we should wait."

Just like that, the clock had run down to zero. After all he'd done, to accept defeat now!

"So what do you want me to do?"

Guilder took a breath to steady himself. "Evacuate the techs in the vehicles, but keep Masterson here. We can box up Grey and the woman ourselves and call for pickup."

"Should I notify Atlanta? You know, so they're at least aware of the situation."

It was, he thought, to Nelson's credit that he didn't indulge himself with a second I-told-you-so. "No, I'll do it."

There was a secure landline in the station chief's office. Guilder made his way upstairs and down the empty hallway, his left leg dragging pitifully. All the offices had been stripped bare; the only things in the room were a chair, a cheap metal desk, and a telephone. He lowered himself into the chair and sat there, staring at the phone. After some time he realized his cheeks were wet; he had begun to weep. The strange, emotionless weeping that had come to seem like a harbinger of his fate, and the body's unbidden confession of his wretched little life. As if his body were saying to him: Just you wait. Just you wait and see what I've got in store for you. A living death, sonny boy.

But this would never happen; once he picked up the phone, it would all be over. A small comfort, to know that at least he wouldn't live long enough to suffer the full brunt of his decline. What he had failed to accomplish that day in the garage would now be done for him.

Mr. Guilder? Come with us. A hand on his shoulder, the march down the hall.

No.

20

By the time they reached the buses, the soldiers had established a perimeter. A crowd was forming in the predawn darkness. Danny's bus was in the third slot; Kittridge glimpsed him through the windshield, hat wedged onto his head, hands clamping the wheel. Vera stood at the base of the steps, holding a clipboard.

God bless you, Danny Chayes, Kittridge thought. This is going to be the ride of your life.

"Please, everyone, keep calm!" Porcheki, moving up and down the line of buses behind the barrier of soldiers, was yelling through a megaphone. "Form an orderly line and load from the rear! If you don't get a seat, wait for the second load!"

The soldiers had erected barriers to serve as a kind of gate. The mob was pressing behind them, funneling toward the gap. Where were they going? people were asking. Was the destination still Chicago, or somewhere else? Just ahead of Kittridge's group was a family with two children, a boy and girl, wearing filthy pajamas. Dirty feet, matted hair—they couldn't have been older than five. The girl was clutching a naked Barbie. More thunder rolled in from the west, accompanied by flashes of light at the horizon. Kittridge and April were both keeping a hand on Tim, afraid the mob would swallow him.

Once through the gap, the group moved quickly to Danny's bus. The Robinsons and Boy Jr. were the first to board; at the bottom of the steps were Wood and Delores, Jamal and Mrs. Bellamy. Pastor Don brought up the rear, behind Kittridge, Tim, and April.

A burst of lightning, ghostly white, ignited the air, freezing the scene in Kittridge's mind. Half a second later, a long peal of thunder rolled. Kittridge felt the impact through the soles of his feet.

Not thunder. Ordnance.

A trio of jets shot overhead, then two more. Suddenly everyone was screaming—a high, shrill sound of undammed panic that built from the rear, engulfing the crowd like a wave. Kittridge turned his face toward the west.

He had never seen the virals in a large group before. Sometimes, from his perch on the tower, he had seen three of them together—never less or more—and of course there'd been the ones in the underground garage, which might have numbered as many as twenty. That was nothing compared to this. The sight suggested a flock of earthbound birds: a coordinated mass of hundreds, thousands even, rushing toward the wire. *A pod,* Kittridge remembered. *That's what they're calling them, pods.* For a second he felt a kind of awe, a pure breathtaken wonder at its organic majesty.

They'd sweep over the camp like a tsunami.

Humvees were racing toward the western wire, roostertails of dust boiling from their wheels. Suddenly the buses were unguarded; the crowd surged toward them. A great human weight crashed into Kittridge from behind. As the crowd enveloped him, he heard April scream.

"Tim!"

He dove toward her voice, fighting his way through the mob like a swimmer against the current, tossing bodies aside. A clot of people were trying to jam themselves into Danny's bus, pushing, shoving. Kittridge saw the man who had been ahead of them in line holding his daughter over his head. He was yelling, "Please, somebody take her! Somebody take my daughter!"

Then Kittridge saw April, caught in the crush. He waved his hands in the air. "Get on the bus!"

"I can't find him! I can't find Tim!"

A roar of engines; at the back of the line, one of the buses drew clear, then another and another. In a burst of fury, Kittridge rammed his way toward April, grabbed her by the waist and plunged toward the door. But the girl would have none of it; she was fighting him, trying to break his grip.

"I can't leave without him! Let me go!"

Ahead he saw Pastor Don at the base of the steps. Kittridge shoved April forward. "Don, help me! Get her on the bus!"

"I can't leave, I can't leave!"

"I'll find him, April! Don, take her!"

A final thrust through the melee, Don reaching forward, finding April's hand, pulling her toward the door; then she was gone. The bus was only half full, but there was no time to wait. Kittridge's last glimpse of April was her face pressed to the window, calling his name.

"Danny, get them out of here!"

The doors closed. The bus pulled away.

In her basement chamber of the NBC facility, Lila Kyle, who had spent the last four days in a state of narcotic suspension—a semiconscious twilight in which she experienced the room around her as if it were but one of several movie screens she was viewing simultaneously—was asleep, and dreaming: a simple, happy dream in which she was in a car at night, being driven to the hospital to have her baby. Whoever was driving the car, Lila couldn't see; the fringes of her vision were draped in blackness. Brad, she said, are you there? And then the blackness lifted, like the curtain over a stage, and Lila saw that it *was* Brad. A shimmering golden joy, weightless as June sunlight, thrummed through her entire being. We'll be there soon, my darling, Brad said. We'll be there any second. This isn't all going to hell in a handbasket. You just hold on. The baby is coming. The baby is practically here.

And those were the words Lila was saying to herself—the baby is coming, the baby is coming—when the room was buffeted by a violent explosion—glass shattering, things falling, the floor beneath her lurching like a tiny boat at sea—and she began to scream.

21

The viral pod that swarmed the eastern Iowa refugee-processing center in the early morning hours of June 9 was part of a larger mass gathering out of Nebraska. Estimates made later by the joint task force, code-named JTF Scorch, differed on its size; some believed it was fifty thousand, others many more. In the days that followed, it would convene with a second, larger pod, coming north out of Missouri, and a third, larger still, moving south from Minnesota. Always their numbers increased. By the time they reached Chicago, they were half a million strong, penetrating the defensive perimeter on July 17 and overwhelming the city within twenty-four hours.

The first virals to breach the wires of the refugee-processing center arrived at 4:58 CDT. By this time, extensive aerial operations in the central and eastern portions of the state had been under way for eight hours, and, in fact, all but one of the bridges over the Mississippi—Dubuque—had already been destroyed; the timing of the quarantine had been deliberately misreported by the task force. It was generally believed by the leaders of the task force—a conclusion supported by the combined wisdom of the American military and intelligence communities—that a concentrated human presence within the quarantine zone acted as a lure to the infected, causing them to coalesce in certain areas and thus make aerial bombardment more effective. The closest analogue, in the words of one task force member, was using a salt lick to hunt deer. Leaving behind a population of refugees was simply the price that needed to be paid in a war that lacked all precedent. And in any event, those people were surely dead anyway.

Major Frances Porcheki of the Iowa National Guard—in her civilian life, a district manager for a manufacturer of women's sporting apparel—was unaware of the mission of JTF Scorch, but she was no fool, either. Though a highly trained military officer, Major Porcheki was also a devout Catholic who took comfort in, and guidance from, her faith. Her decision not to abandon the refugees under her protection, as she had been ordered to do, followed directly from this deeper conviction, as did her choice to devote the final energies of her life, and those of the soldiers still under her command—165 men and women, who, nearly to a one, took up positions at the western wire—to provide cover for the escaping buses. By this time, the civilians who had been left behind were racing after the vehicles, screaming for them to stop, but there was nothing to be done. Well, that's it, Porcheki thought. I would have saved more if I could. A pale green light had gathered to the west, a wall of quivering radiance, like a glowing hedgerow. Jets were streaking overhead, unleashing the fury of their payloads into the heart of the pod: gleaming tracers, spouts of flame. The air was split with thunder. Through a gauntlet of destruction the pod emerged, still coming. Porcheki leapt from her Humvee before it had stopped moving, yelling, "Hold your fire, everyone! Wait till they're at the wire!," then dropped to a firing position—having no more orders to give, she would face the enemy on the same terms as her men—and began to pray.

* * *

Time itself acquired a disordered feel. Amid the chaos, lives were overlapping in unforeseen ways. In the basement of the NBC facility, a bitter struggle was ensuing. At the very moment that the Blackbird helicopter was alighting on the rooftop, Horace Guilder, who had been hiding from Nelson in the office when the assault commenced, his decision not to telephone his counterparts at the CDC having lifted one burden from his mind only to create another (he had no idea what to do next), had descended the stairs to the basement with considerable difficulty to find Masterson and Nelson frantically cramming blood samples into a cooler packed with dry ice, yelling words to the effect of "Where the hell have you been?" and "We have to get out of here!" and "The place is coming down around our ears!" But these sentiments, reasonable as they were, touched Guilder only vaguely. The thing that mattered now was Lawrence Grey. And all at once, as if he'd been slapped in the face, Guilder knew what he had to do.

There was only one way. Why hadn't he seen it all along?

His whole body was poised on the verge of paralyzing spasms; he could barely draw a breath through the narrowing tube of his throat. And yet he mustered the will—the will of the dying—to reach out and seize Masterson's sidearm and yank it free of its holster.

Then, amazing himself, Guilder shot him.

Kittridge was being trampled.

As the buses pulled away, Kittridge was knocked to the ground. As he attempted to rise, somebody's foot caught him in the side of his face, its owner tumbling over him with a grunt. More pummeling feet and bodies; it was all he could do to assume a posture of defense, pressing himself to the ground with his hands over his head.

"Tim! Where are you?"

Then he saw him. The crowd had left the boy behind. He was sitting in the dirt not ten yards away. Kittridge hobbled to his side, skidding in the dust.

"Are you okay? Can you run?"

The boy was holding the side of his head. His eyes were vague, unfocused. He was crying in gulps, snot running from his nose.

Kittridge pulled him to his feet. "Come on."

He had no plan; the only plan was to escape. The buses were gone, ghosts of dust and diesel smoke. Kittridge hoisted Tim at the waist and swung him around to his back and told him to hold on. Three steps and the pain arrived, his knee shuddering. He stumbled, caught himself, somehow stayed upright. One thing was certain: with his leg, and with the boy's added weight, he wouldn't make it far on foot.

Then he remembered the armory. He'd seen an open-backed Humvee parked inside. Its hood had been standing open; one of the soldiers had been working on it. Would it still be there? Would it function?

As the soldiers at the western wire opened fire, Kittridge gritted his teeth and ran.

By the time he reached the armory, his leg was on the verge of collapse. How he'd made it those two hundred yards, he had no idea. But luck was with him. The vehicle was parked where he'd seen it, among the now-empty shelves. The hood was down—a good sign—but would the vehicle run? He lowered Tim to the passenger seat, got behind the wheel, and pressed the starter.

Nothing. He took a breath to steady himself. Think, Kittridge, think. Hanging beneath the dash was a nest of disconnected wires. Somebody had been working on the ignition. He pulled the wires free, picked two, and touched the ends together. No response. He had no idea what he was doing—why had he thought this would work? He arbitrarily selected two more wires, red and green.

A spark leapt; the engine roared to life. He jammed the Humvee into gear, aimed for the doors, and shoved the accelerator to the floor.

They barreled toward the gate. But a new problem lay before them: how to make it through. Several thousand people were trying to do the same thing, a roiling human mass attempting to wedge itself through the narrow exit. Without taking his foot off the gas, Kittridge leaned on the horn, realizing too late what a bad idea this was—that the mob had nothing to lose.

It turned. It saw. It charged.

Kittridge braked and swung the wheel, but too late: the hordes swallowed the Humvee like a breaking wave. His door flew open, hands pulling at him, trying to break his grip on the wheel. He heard Tim scream as he fought to keep control. People were lunging at the vehicle from all directions, boxing him in. A face collided with the windshield, then was gone. Hands were reaching over his face from behind, clawing at him, more pulling at his arms. "Get off me!" he yelled, trying to bat them away, but it was no use. There were simply too many, and as more bodies rolled over the windshield and under the vehicle's tires and the Humvee began to tip, he reached for Tim, bracing for the crash; and that was the end of that.

Meanwhile, at a distance of three miles, the line of buses—carrying a total of 2,043 civilian refugees, 36 FEMA and Red Cross workers, and 27 military personnel—was roaring eastward. Many of the people on board were sobbing; others were locked in prayer. Those with children were clutching them fiercely. A few, despite the earnest pleas of their fellows to shut the hell up, were still screaming. While a handful were already undergoing the wrenching self-reproach of having left so many behind, the vast majority possessed no such misgivings. They were the lucky ones, the ones who'd gotten away.

At the wheel of the Redbird, Danny Chayes was experiencing, for the first time in his life, an emotion that could only be described as a magnificent wholeness of self. It was as if he had lived all of his twenty-six years within an artificially narrow bandwidth of his potential personhood, only to have the scales fall abruptly from his eyes. Like the bus whose course he guided, Danny had been shot forward, propelled into a new state of being in which a range of contrary feelings, in all their distinctive contours, existed simultaneously in his mind. He was afraid, genuinely and soulfully afraid, and yet this fear was a source of not paralysis but power, a rich well of courage that seemed to rise and overflow within him. *You're the captain of that ship,* Mr. Purvis said, and that's what Danny was. Over his left shoulder, Pastor Don and Vera were talking away, speaking in urgent tones about this and that and the other; behind them, on the benches, the others were huddled together in pairs. The Robinsons with their baby, who was making a kind of mewing sound; Wood and Delores, who were holding hands as they prayed; Jamal and Mrs. Bellamy, the two of them actually hugging; April, sitting woefully alone, her face too stunned for tears. Their deliverance had become the sole purpose of Danny's life, the fixed point in his personal cosmos around which everything else revolved, yet in the excitement of the moment and Danny's discovery of the amazing fact of his aliveness, their presence was a pure abstraction. At the wheel of his Redbird 450, Danny Chayes was in union with himself and with the universe, and when he saw, as no doubt the drivers of the other buses did as well, the second mass of virals rising from the predawn darkness to the south, and then the third, coming from the north, and discerned in his mind's eye with swift three-dimensional calculation that these two bodies would subsequently unite to form a single encircling mass that would swarm over the buses like hornets loosed from a nest, he knew what he had to do. Swinging the wheel to the left, he broke free from the convoy and jammed the accelerator to the floor, soaring past the other buses in the line. Seventy, seventy-five, eighty miles an hour: with every ounce of his being, he willed the bus to go faster. What are you doing? Pastor Don yelled. For the love of God, Danny, what are you doing? But Danny knew just what he was doing. His goal was not evasion, for there could be none; his goal was to be the first. To hit the pod at such barreling velocity that he would sail right through it, carving a corridor of destruction. The space behind him had erupted in a chorus of screams; beyond his windshield the pods were merging, a swelling legion of light. His knuckles were white on the wheel.

"Get down, everyone!" he yelled. "Get down!"

"What the fuck!"

Nelson was backing away, holding his hands protectively before his face. Guilder realized the man pretty much expected him to shoot him, too. Which was nothing he was particularly averse to, though in the near term he had other requirements.

"Get the woman," he said, gesturing with the pistol.

"There's no time! Christ, you didn't have to kill him!"

There were more concussions from above. The air was swirling with dust. "I'll be the judge. Move."

Later, Guilder would have cause to wonder how he'd known to get the woman first, one of the more fateful decisions of his life. He might have chosen to leave her, bringing about an altogether different outcome. Intuition, perhaps? Sentimentality for the bond he'd discerned between her and Grey—a bond that had eluded him all his life? Pushing Nelson forward at the end of his pistol, he crossed the lab to the door of Lila's chamber.

"Open it."

Lila Kyle, aroused by the explosions, had given herself over to incoherent and terrified screaming; she had no idea where she was or what was happening. She was strapped to a bed. The bed was in a room. The room and everything in it were moving. It was as if she'd awakened from one dream to find herself lost in another, each equally unreal, and she experienced only a partial awareness of Nelson and Guilder as they entered the room. The two men were arguing. She heard the word "helicopter." She heard the word "escape." The smaller of the two was plunging a needle into her arm. Lila could offer no resistance, yet the instant the needle pierced her skin a jolt of energy hit her heart, as if she'd been connected to a giant battery. Adrenaline, she thought. I have been sedated, and now they are injecting me with adrenaline, to wake me up. The smaller man was hauling her to her feet. Beneath her gown, a cold nakedness prickled her skin. Could she stand? Could she walk? Just get her out of here, the second man said.

With a tremendous urgency she could not make herself share, he half-dragged, half-carried her across the wide room, some kind of laboratory. The lights were out; only emergency beams shone from the corners. In the distance, a series of roars, and after each a moment of prolonged shuddering, like an earthquake. Glass was jostling, making a pinging sound. They came to a heavy door with a metal ring, like something on a submarine. The smaller man swung it open and stepped inside. She was being held by the larger man now; he was brandishing a pistol. He gripped her from behind, one hand wrapping her waist, the other pressing the barrel to her midsection. Her thoughts were coming clearer now. Her heart was clicking like a metronome. What would emerge from the door? She could smell the man's breath close to her face, a warm rottenness. She felt his fear in his grip; his hands, his whole body were trembling. "I'm pregnant," Lila said, or started to say, thinking this might alter the situation. But her voice was cut short as, from the far side of the door, came a womanly sound of shrieking.

The aerial operations over western and central Iowa on the night of June 9 were not without risks. Chief among them was that the pilots might fail to carry out their orders, and, in fact, some did not: seven flight crews refused to deploy their payloads over civilian targets, while three more claimed to have suffered mechanical malfunctions that prevented them from doing so, an operational failure rate of six percent. (Of these ten flight crews, three were court-martialed, five were reprimanded and returned to duty, and two dropped to the deck and were never seen again.) In the coming weeks, as the mission of JTF Scorch expanded to include centers of population throughout the nation's middle section and the Intermountain West, members of the task force would recall this statistic with something like nostalgia—the good old days. By the first of August, so many aviators were either sitting in the stockade as prisoners of conscience or had vanished with their aircraft into the skies above the dying continent that it became increasingly difficult to mount a coherent aerial offensive, casting the very mission of JTF Scorch into doubt. These difficulties were compounded by secessionist movements in California and Texas, both of which proceeded to declare themselves sovereign and appropriate all federal military resources within their borders, effectively daring Washington to stop them by force—a remarkably shrewd gambit, both militarily and politically, as by this time the situation was in pure free fall. Much bluster ensued on both sides, culminating in the Battle of Wichita Falls and the Battle of Fresno, in which vast numbers of American military, both on the ground and in the air, threw in the towel, laid down their arms, and asked for sanctuary. Thus, by mid-October of the year that came to be known by subsequent generations as the year zero, the nation known as the United States could be said to exist no more.

But in the early morning hours of June 9, beneath a moonless Iowa sky, JTF Scorch was still on-line, enjoying the full, or nearly full, cooperation of its assets. In confirmation of the task force's projections, great masses of Infected Persons had collected in four distinct hot spots across the state: Mason City, Des Moines, Marshalltown, and the FEMA refugee-processing facility in Fort Powell. By 0200, the first three had been dispensed with; Fort Powell was the final prize. A combination of A-10 Warthogs and F-18 fighter-bombers began the assault; concurrently a C-130 transport was inbound from MacDill. Within its bay lay an explosive device called a GBU-43/B Massive Ordnance Air Blast Bomb, or MOAB. Containing 18,700 pounds of H6 high explosive, the MOAB was the largest non-nuclear bomb in the United States military arsenal, capable of producing an impact crater five hundred feet in diameter and a blast wave sufficient to level an area the size of nine city blocks; its fires would burn for days.

When Nelson bent to undo Grey's straps—straps no longer attached to anything—Grey lurched forward, seizing him by the biceps and burying his teeth in the man's neck. A deep bite: he felt Nelson's windpipe being crushed beneath his jaws. As the two tumbled backward over the bed, Grey shook him like a wolf with a rabbit in its teeth; a jet of hot blood filled Grey's mouth. They were on the floor now, Nelson face-up, Grey above him. An agonal twitch of Nelson's hands and feet, and that was all. Grey burrowed his jaws deeper, into the soft meat.

He drank.

Had it been this easy for Zero, Grey wondered, this pleasurable? A rich vitality poured through him, a glorious immensity of pure sensation. With a final, soul-satisfying inhalation of blood, Grey pulled his face away. He allowed himself a couple of seconds to regard the corpse on the floor. The flesh of Nelson's face looked as if it had been shrink-wrapped to its underlying structure; his eyes, like the eyes of the woman in the parking lot of the Red Roof, bulged reptilianly from their bony orbits, staring into the heart of eternity. Grey searched his mind for some emotion that corresponded to his actions—guilt, perhaps, or pity, or even disgust. He was a murderer, a man who had killed. He had stolen the life of another. But he felt none of these things. He'd done what he had to do.

The door to his chamber stood open. Lila, he thought, I am coming to save you—all that has happened has ordained it.

He stepped through.

What emerged from the door was a man. The figure was backlit, sunk in shadow. As he advanced, beams from the emergency lights slanted across his face. His gown was bathed in blood.

Lawrence?

"Don't." The man with the gun was dragging Lila backward, jabbing its barrel deep into her ribs. His steps were uncertain, fluttering. His whole body was shaking like a leaf. It seemed that any second he might fall. "Keep your distance."

Grey reached his bloody hands plaintively forward. "Lila, it's me."

Horror, revulsion, a protective mental numbness at the violent swiftness of events—all combined in Lila's mind to grip her in a frozen, focusless terror in which her body and her brain seemed like only tangentially associated phenomena. Through the fog she realized what the screams from the chamber meant. If the state of his gown was any indication, Lawrence had not merely killed the small man but torn him to pieces. Which made a kind of sense; Lila should have seen this coming. She remembered the tank. She remembered

Lawrence's face, a mask of gore like some Halloween horror, as it popped from the hatch, and the glass of the Volvo's window splintering under his fist. Lawrence had become a monster. He had become one of those . . . things. (Poor Roscoe.) And yet there was something about his eyes, which she could not look away from, that told her not to be afraid. They seemed to bore straight into her, shining with an almost holy light.

"Don't you know what's happening?" the man barked. "We have to get out of here."

"Let her go."

Another blast from above and a lurching wave passed through the floor. Glass was falling; everything was caving in. The gun's barrel was pressed against her ribs like a cold finger pointing at her heart. The man angled his head toward a corner of the room.

"Up the stairs. There's a helicopter waiting."

"Put the gun down and I'll go with you."

"Goddamnit, there's no time for this!"

Something was happening to her. A kind of awakening, and it wasn't just the gun. It was as if she were returning to consciousness after years of sleep. How foolish she'd been! Painting the nursery, of all things! Pretending they were taking a drive in the country, as if that could change anything! Because David was dead, and Eva was dead, and Brad, whose heart she had broken; she had convinced herself the world wasn't ending, because it already had. And here was this man, this Lawrence Grey, who had come upon her like a redeemer, an angel to lead her to safety, as if the baby she carried were his own, and she knew what she had to say.

"Please, Lawrence. Do what he asks. Think about our baby."

A fraught moment followed, so suspended as to seem outside the flow of time. Lila could read the question on Lawrence's face. Could he get to the pistol before the man fired? And if he could, what then?

"Show us the way out of here."

By the time they reached the roof, the helicopter's blades were turning, casting a whirling wind across the rooftop. The sky was glowing with an eerie, emerald-tinged light, like the insides of a greenhouse. It seemed the helicopter would leave without them, a final irony, but then Lila saw the pilot urgently waving to them from the cockpit. They climbed aboard; Guilder slammed the door behind them.

Upward.

* * *

Kittridge became aware that he was face-down in the dirt. A taste of blood was in his mouth. He tried to get to his feet but realized he had only one; his prosthesis was gone. He lifted his face to see the Humvee tipped on its side a hundred yards away, like a beached sea creature. Its windshield was smashed; steam was pouring from its hood and undercarriage. The mob had fallen on it like a pack of animals; some were attempting to rock it back onto its wheels, but the effort was disorganized, coming from all sides. Others were standing on the top, shoving and kicking competitors away, defending their positions as if the mere possession of such a thing might offer some protection.

Kittridge crawled to where Tim lay. The boy was breathing but unconscious—a small mercy. His body was splayed at a tortured angle; his hair was matted with blood. More was running from his mouth and nose. Kittridge realized the shooting had stopped. Soldiers were tearing past, but there was nowhere to run. A mass of virals lay at the wire, felled by the soldiers' bullets, but as his eyes scanned the scene, Kittridge understood that the attack had been a test, an advance force sent to exhaust the soldiers' defenses. A second, vastly larger pod was now amassing. As it roared toward them, the image stretched, flowing like a shimmering green liquid as it surrounded the encampment. The final assault would come from all directions.

He lifted Tim's body by the shoulders and held his chest against his own. They were in the midst of chaos, people running, voices shouting, bombs falling; yet as they crouched in the dust, a bubble of silent inactivity seemed to encase them, protecting them from the destruction. Kittridge turned his face toward the east. For a brief moment he imagined he could see Danny's bus streaming away in the darkness, though this was an illusion, he knew. By now they were gone, far beyond the reach of his vision. *Godspeed to you, Danny Chayes.* A deep stillness wrapped his being and, with it, a feeling of the past, an experience like déjà vu: he was where he was but also not, he was here and also there, he was a boy at play and a man at war and the third thing he'd become. Images flashed through his consciousness: the viral in her wedding dress clinging to the hood of the Ferrari; a view of sparkling sunlight on a river he had fished for years; April, on the night when they had sat together in the window of the school, watching the stars, and the look of quiet peace on her face as the two of them made love; the boy in the car, his eyes full of a terrible knowledge, and his hand—his little boy's hand—desperately reaching, then gone. All of these and more. He recalled his mother, singing to him. The warmth of her breath on his face, and the feeling of being very small, a new being in the world. *The world is not my home,* she sang in her silky voice, *for I'm just passing through. The treasures are laid up somewhere, high beyond the blue. The angels beckon me from heaven's open door, and I can't feel at home in this world anymore.*

Tim had begun to make a choking sound; his eyes flickered, fought to open, then stilled. The virals, having completed their encirclement, were surging toward the wire. Kittridge became aware of an absence of sound around them. The battle was over; the planes had broken away. Then, in the quiet, he detected, high above, the drone of a heavy aircraft. Kittridge angled his face to the sky. A C-130 transport, coming from the south. As it passed overhead an object released from its belly, its dive abruptly stalled by the puff of a parachute. The plane climbed away.

Kittridge closed his eyes. So, the end. It would happen instantaneously, a painless departure, quicker than thought. He felt the presence of his body one last time: the taste of air in his lungs, the blood surging in his veins, the drumlike beating of his heart. The bomb was dropping toward them.

"I've got you," he said, hugging Tim fiercely; and again, over and over, so that the boy would be hearing these words. "I've got you, I've got you, I've got you, I've got you."

The blast wave from the MOAB struck the helicopter carrying Grey and Lila broadside: a blinding sheen of light, followed by an earsplitting slap of heat and sound. As if lifted on the crest of a wave, the helicopter lurched forward, its nose pointed earthward at a forty-five-degree angle, rocketed up again and began to spin, its angular momentum accelerating like a line of skaters wheeling on an ice rink. It spun and as it spun the pilot pitched to the side, his neck broken by the force of impact with the windshield; but by this time, between the sound of the alarm—a harsh blaring—and the centrifugal force of their velocity, nobody inside the helicopter was thinking very much at all. The forces that had held them aloft were gone, and nothing else would happen until they reached the ground.

Lawrence Grey experienced the crash itself as a severing in time: one moment he was pressed against the wall of the helicopter in its death spiral, the next he was lying in the

wreckage. He felt but did not specifically recall the moment
of impact; it had lodged in his body as a ringing sensation,
as if he were a bell that had been struck. There was a smell
of fuel, and hot insulation, and an electrical crackling sound.
Something heavy and inertly soft was lying on top of him. It
was Guilder. He was breathing but unconscious. The helicopter, what was left of it, lay on its side; where the roof
should have been was now the door.

"Lawrence, help me!"

The voice came from behind him. He shoved Guilder's
body off his chest and felt his way to the rear of the helicopter. One of the benches had twisted loose, pinning Lila to the
floor, crushing her at the waist. Her bare legs, the flimsy fabric of her gown—all glistened with a heavy, dark blood.

"Help me," she choked. Her eyes were closed, tears squeezing from the corners. "Please, God, help me. I'm bleeding,
I'm bleeding."

He tried to pull her free by her feet, but she began to shriek
in agony. There was no other way; he'd have to move the
bench. Gripping it by its frame, Grey began to twist. A
groan and then a pop and it broke away from the decking.

Lila was sobbing, moaning in pain. Grey knew he shouldn't
move her, but he had no choice. Positioning the bench beneath the open door, he hoisted her to his shoulder, stepped
up, and laid her gently on the roof. He followed, climbing up
the opposite side. He slid down the fuselage, circled back,
and reached up to receive her, easing her body down the side
of the helicopter.

"Oh, God. Please, don't let me lose her. Don't let me lose
the baby."

He lowered Lila to the ground, which was strewn with
rubble from the destroyed laboratory—twisted girders, concrete blasted into chunks, shards of glass. He was weeping,
too. It was too late, he knew; the baby was gone. Gouts of
blood, clotted with black, were spilling from between Lila's
legs, an unstoppable flow. In another moment she would follow her baby into darkness. A childhood prayer found
Grey's lips and he began to murmur, again and again, "Holy
Mary, Mother of God, pray for us sinners, now and at the
hour of our death, amen. Holy Mary, Mother of God, pray
for us sinners, now and at the hour of our death, amen. . . ."

Save her, Grey.

You know what to do.

He did; he knew. The answer had been inside him all

along. Since the Red Roof and Ignacio and the Home Depot and Project NOAH and long before.

Do you see, Grey?

He lifted his face to behold them. The virals. They were everywhere and all around, emerging from the darkness and flames: flesh of his flesh, unholy and blood-driven, encircling him like a demonic chorus. He was kneeling before them, his face streaked with tears. He felt no fear, only astonishment.

They are yours, Grey. The ones I give to you.

—Yes. They are mine.

Save her. Do it.

He needed something sharp. His hands searched the ground, lighting upon a sliver of metal, some broken shard from a world of broken, piecemeal things. Eight inches long, the edges ragged as a saw. Positioning it lengthwise across his wrist, he closed his eyes and slashed a deep gash into his flesh. The blood spurted forth, a wide, dark river, filling his palm. The blood of Grey, the Unleasher of Night, Familiar of the One Called Zero. Lila was moaning, dying. Any breath might be her last. A moment's hesitation—some last, extinguishing human light inside him—and Grey placed his wrist against her lips, tenderly, like a mother easing her breast to the mouth of a newborn babe.

"Drink," he said.

Grey never even saw it: the chunk of concrete, thirty-four pounds of solid rock, that Guilder, with all the strength he could muster, hoisted into the air above Grey's head and then brought down upon him.

22

They made their way into Chicago as the sun was setting, filling the sky with a golden light. First the outer ring of suburbs, empty and still; then, rising before them like a promise, the shape of the city. The lone survivors, their lives joined by the mysterious bond of their survival: they traveled in silence, dreamers in a forgotten land, their progress marked only by the grumble of the bus's engine, the hypnotic whoosh of asphalt beneath their wheels. Ghosts sat beside them, the people they had lost.

As the city came into focus, Pastor Don bent forward from his seat behind Danny. Helicopters were floating over the city, buzzing among the skyscrapers like bees around a hive; high above, the contrails of aircraft cast ribbons of color against the deepening blue. A zone of safety, it seemed, but this couldn't last. In their hearts they knew there was none.

"Let's pull off a minute."

Danny drew the bus to the side of the roadway. Pastor Don rose to address the group. The decision was upon them. Should they stop or continue? They had the bus, water, food, fuel. No one knew what lay ahead. Take a minute, Pastor Don said.

A murmur of agreement, then a show of hands. The verdict was unanimous.

"Okay, Danny."

They circled the city to the south and continued east on a rural blacktop. Night fell like a dome snapping down on the earth. By daybreak they were somewhere in Ohio. A landscape of pure anonymity; they could have been anywhere. Time had slowed to a crawl. Fields, trees, houses, mailboxes streaming by, the horizon always unreachable, rolling away. In the small towns, a semblance of life continued; people had no idea where to go, what to do. The highways, it was said, were jammed. At a mini-mart where they stopped for supplies, the cashier, glancing out the window at the bus, asked, Can I go with you? On the wall behind her head, a television screen showed a city in flames. She spoke in a hushed tone so as not to be overheard. She didn't ask where they were going; their destination was simply away. A quick phone call and minutes later her husband and two teenage sons were standing by the bus, holding suitcases.

Others joined them. A man in overalls walking alone on the highway with a rifle over his shoulder. An elderly couple, dressed as if for church, their car expired on the side of the road with its hood standing open, steam exhaling from its cracked radiator. A pair of cyclists, Frenchmen, who had been riding across the country when the crisis began. Whole families squeezed aboard. Many were overcome, weeping with gratitude as they took their places. Like fish joining a school, they were absorbed into the whole. Cities were bypassed, one after the other: Columbus, Akron, Youngstown, Pittsburgh. Even the names had begun to feel historical, like cities of a lost empire. Giza. Carthage. Pompeii. Customs evolved among them, as if they were a kind of rolling town. Some questions were asked but not others. Have you heard about Salt Lake, Tulsa, St. Louis? Do they know what it is yet, have they discovered the answer? Only in motion was there safety; every stop felt fraught with peril. For a time they sang. "The Ants Go Marching," "On Top of Spaghetti," "A Hundred Bottles of Beer on the Wall."

The landscape rose and fell, enfolding them in a green embrace: Pennsylvania, the Endless Mountains. Signs of human habitation were few and far between, the leavings of an era long passed. The battered coal towns, the forgotten hamlets with a single factory shuttered for years, red-brick smokestacks forlornly poking a blue summer sky. The air smelled strongly of pine. By now they numbered over seventy, bodies crammed into the aisles, children on laps, faces pressed to the windows. Fuel was a constant worry, yet somehow they always found more in the nick of time, their passage protected by an unseen hand.

By the afternoon of the third day, they were approaching Philadelphia. They had traveled half the width of a continent; ahead lay the eastern seaboard, with its barricade of cities, a wall of humanity pressed to the sea. A feeling of finality had taken over. There was no place else to run. They homed in on the city along the Schuylkill River, its surface as dark and impenetrable as granite. The outer towns felt to be in hiding, houses boarded, roads empty of cars. The river widened to a broad basin; heavy trees, dappled with sunlight, draped like a curtain over the road. A sign read: CHECKPOINT 2 MILES. A brief conferral and all were agreed: they had come to the end. Their fates would find them here.

The soldiers gave them directions. Curfew was two hours away, but already the streets were quiet, virtually without movement except for Army vehicles and a few police cars. Narrow, sun-drenched lanes, ramshackle brownstones, the infamous corners where packs of young men had once lingered; then suddenly the park appeared, an oasis of green in the heart of the city.

They followed the signs past the barricades, masked soldiers waving them through. The park was teeming with people, as if for a concert. Tents, RVs, figures curled on the ground by their suitcases as if lodged there by a tide. When the crowds grew too thick they were forced to abandon the bus by the side of the road and continue on foot. A terminal act: to leave it behind felt disloyal, like putting down a beloved dog who could no longer walk. They moved as one, unable to let go of one another yet, to fade into a faceless collective. A long line had formed; the air was as heavy as milk. Above them, unseen, armies of insects buzzed in the darkening trees.

"I can't do this," said Pastor Don. He had halted on the path, a look of sudden horror on his face.

Wood had stopped, too. Twenty yards ahead lay a series of chutes, harshly lit by spotlights on poles; people were being patted down, giving their names. "I know what you mean."

"I mean, Jesus. It's like we only just came from here."

The mob was streaming past. The two Frenchmen moved by with barely a glance, their meager belongings bundled under their arms. They could all feel it: something was being lost. They stepped to the side.

"Do you think we can find gas?" Jamal asked.

"I just know I'm not going in there," Pastor Don said.

They returned to the bus. Already a man was trying to jimmy the ignition. He was skinny, his face blackened with grime, his eyes roving in their sockets like he was on something. Wood seized him by the scruff of the neck and hurled him down the steps. Get the fuck out of here, he said.

They boarded. Danny turned the key; the engine roared under them. Slowly they backed away, the crowd parting around them like waves around a ship. The air was drinking up the last of the light. They turned in a wide circle on the grass and pulled away.

"Where to?" Danny asked.

No one had an answer. "I don't think it matters," Pastor Don said.

It didn't. They spent the night in Valley Forge park, sleeping on the ground by the bus, then headed south, staying off the highways. Maryland, Virginia, North Carolina: they kept on going. The journey had acquired its own meaning, independent of any destination. The goal was to move, to keep moving. They were together; that was all that mattered. The bus jostled beneath them on its tired springs. One by one the cities fell, the lights went out. The world was dissolving, taking its stories with it. Soon it would be gone.

Her name was April Donadio. The child that even now had taken root inside her would be a boy, Bernard. April would give him the last name Donadio, so that he might carry a piece of each of them in name; and across the years she spoke to the boy often of his father, the kind of man he was—how brave and kind and a little sad, too, and how, though their time together was brief, he had imparted to her the greatest gift, which was the courage to go on. That's what love is, she told the boy, what love does. I hope some-day you love somebody the way that I loved him.

But that came later. This bus of survivors, twelve in sum: they could have continued that way forever. And in a sense, they did. The green fields of summer, the abandoned, time-stilled towns, the forests thick with shadow, the bus endlessly rolling. They were like a vision, they had slipped into eter-nity, a zone beyond time. There and not there, a presence unseen but felt, like stars in the daytime sky.

III

THE FIELD

NORTH AGRICULTURAL COMPLEX
ORANGE ZONE, EX-MURUS
KERRVILLE, TEXAS
JULY 79 A.V.

*For he today that sheds his blood with me
shall be my brother.*

—SHAKESPEARE,
HENRY V

WARNING

YOU ARE ENTERING THE <u>ORANGE ZONE</u>.

WATCH THE CLOCK.
KNOW THE LOCATION
OF THE NEAREST HARDBOX.

DO NOT ENTER UNSWEPT AREAS.

IF YOU MISS THE LAST TRANSPORT,
DO NOT EXPECT TO BE RESCUED.
SHELTER IN PLACE.

OBEY ALL COMMANDS
OF THE DOMESTIC AUTHORITY.

VIOLATORS SUBJECT TO FINE
AND/OR IMPRISONMENT
UNDER ARTICLE 694, SECTION 12 OF THE
TEXAS REPUBLIC CODE OF MODIFIED
MARTIAL LAW.

WHEN IN DOUBT, RUN.

23

It was Dee Vorhees who said she wanted to bring the children.

Though she was not the only one. All the women, as her husband, Curtis, was soon to discover, were in on the plan. Dee's cousin Sally, and Mace Francis, and Shar Withers and Cece Cauley and Ali Dodd and even Matty Wright—the permanently nervous, twittering Matty Wright—told their husbands the same thing. A veritable ambush, the women flanking their men from left and right with a wifely insistence that could not be refused: *A few hours in the sunshine,* they all said, lying in bed or washing the dishes or readying the children for school. *What's the harm? Let's bring the children this time.*

And it wasn't as if they hadn't taken the girls ex-murus before, Dee reminded him, the two of them sharing a quiet moment in the kitchen after putting the girls to sleep. There was that time, she said—how long ago?—when they'd gone to Green Field for Nitia's birthday. Little Siri just a toddler, Nitia still dragging that filthy blanket wherever she went. Those peaceful hours under the spillway, and the butterflies—did he remember? The way they seemed to float along an airborne river, their bright wings falling and pumping to rise again, and the one that, surprising them all, had alighted on Nitia's nose. Dee said: Could you not feel God's presence in a thing like that? The sweet, free feeling of it, the little girls laughing and laughing, the warning siren hours off, some distant future time, and the blue sky suspended like heaven itself above their heads and the four of them being ex-murus together. The Green Zone, it was true, she didn't say it wasn't, but they could *see* the perimeter from there, the watchtowers and the sentries and the fences with their curling razor wire, and who decided these things, anyway? Who decided where one zone ended and the next began? How was an outing to North Ag any different, any more dangerous, really? Cruk would be there, and Tifty as well (the name had popped out before she could stop herself, but what could you do?); there were the hardboxes if anything happened, but why would it? In the middle of a summer day? The traps had gone empty for months, not even any dopeys around. Everyone was saying so. A few hours in the sunshine, away from the gray and grime of the city. A summer picnic in the field. That was all she was asking.

Would he do it, this one thing? For the girls? But why not just come out and say it. Would he do it for her, the wife who loved him?

Which was how, two days later, on a sultry July morning, the temperature already rising through the eighties and headed for a hundred, Curtis Vorhees, age thirty-two, foreman of the North Agricultural Complex, his father's old .38 tucked into his waistband with three rounds in the cylinder (his father had shot the other three), found himself on a transport full of whole families, and not just families: children. Nitia and Siri and their cousin Carson, just turned twelve but still so slight his feet dangled three inches above the floor; Bab and Dunk Withers, the twins; the Francis girls, Rena and Jules, seated at the rear so they wouldn't have to pay attention to the boys; little Jenny Apgar, riding on her older brother Gunnar's lap; Dean and Amelia Wright, the two of them old enough to act bored and put out; Merry Dodd and her baby brother, Satch, and little Louis Cauley, still in a basket; Reese Cuomo and Dash Martinez and Cindy-Sue Bodine. Seventeen in all, a concentrated mass of childlike heat and noise as distinct to Vorhees's senses as a buzzing swarm of bees. It was common for the wives to join their husbands for planting, and of course at harvesttime, when every pair of hands found work to do; but this was something new. Even as the bus cleared the gate, its old diesel engine roaring and sputtering, its tired chassis swaying under them, Curtis Vorhees felt it. A hot, dull job had suddenly become an occasion; the day possessed the hopeful spirit of a tradition being born. Why hadn't they thought of this before, that bringing the children would remake the day into something special?

Past the dam and fuel depot and fence line, with its sentries waving them through and down, down into the valley they went, into the golden light of a July morning. The women, seated at the rear with the hampers and supplies, were gossiping and laughing among themselves; the children, after a fruitless attempt by one of the mothers—of course it would be Ali Dodd—to organize them into a rousing chorus of the Texas anthem, the only song everyone knew (*Texas, our Texas! All hail the mighty State! Texas, our Texas! So wonderful, so great!*), had sorted themselves into various warring factions, the older girls whispering and giggling and elaborately ignoring the boys, the boys elaborately pretending not to care, the little ones bouncing on the benches and darting through the aisle to launch their various assaults; the men up front were sitting in their customary guarded silence, communicating only through the occasional exchange of a wry look or a single raised eyebrow: *What have we gotten ourselves into?* They were men of the fields, their hands thickened from work; hair shorn close, crescents of dirt under their nails, no beards. Vorhees withdrew his timepiece from his pocket and checked the hour: 7:05. Eleven hours until the siren, twelve for the last transport, thirteen until dark. *Watch the clock. Know the location of the nearest hardbox. When in doubt, run.* Words imprinted on his consciousness as indelibly as a childhood rhyme, or one of the sisters' prayers. Vorhees twisted in his seat to catch Dee's eye. She was balancing Siri on her lap, the little girl's nose pressed to the window to watch the passing world. Dee gave him a weary smile, made of words: *Thank you.* Siri had begun to bounce, pumping her knees with pleasure. The little girl pointed a chubby finger out the window, squealing with delight. *Thank you for this.*

And then, before they knew it, they'd arrived. Through the windshield of the transport, the fields of North Ag Complex leapt into view, its vast patchwork laid out below them like the squares of a motley quilt: corn and wheat, cotton and beans, rice and barley and oats. Fifteen thousand acres stitched together by a fretwork of dusty roads, and, at their edges, windbreaks of cottonwood and oak; the watchtowers and pump houses with their catch basins and nests of pipe and, dispersed at regular intervals, the hardboxes, marked by tall orange banners, hanging limply in the breathless air. Vorhees knew their locations cold, but when the corn was tall, you couldn't always find them quickly without the flags.

He rose and moved to the front, where Dee's brother, Nathan—everybody called him Cruk—was standing behind the driver. Vorhees was foreman, but it was Cruk, as the senior Domestic Security officer, who was really in charge.

"Looks like we've got a good day for this," Vorhees said.

Cruk shrugged but said nothing. Like the field hands, he was dressed in whatever he had: patched jeans and a khaki shirt frayed at the collar and wrists. Atop this he wore a plastic vest, bright orange, with the words TEXAS DEPARTMENT OF TRANSPORATION printed on the back. He was holding his rifle, a long-barreled .30-06 with a sniper scope, across his chest; a reconditioned .45 was holstered to his thigh. The rifle was standard issue, but the .45 was something special, old military or maybe police, with an oiled black finish and a polished wood grip. He even had a name for it; he called it Abigail. You had to know somebody to get a weapon like that, and Vorhees didn't have to think too hard to figure out who this person might be; it was pretty much common knowledge that Tifty was on the trade. Vorhees's .38, with its paltry three rounds, felt meager in comparison, but there was no way he could have afforded a weapon like that.

"You can always say it was Dee's idea," Cruk said.

"So you don't think this is smart."

His brother-in-law gave a stifled laugh. It was at such moments that Cruk's resemblance to his sister was the most striking, though it was also true that this was more suggestion than actual physical similarity, and something only Vorhees would have noticed. Most people, in fact, remarked on how different the two of them looked.

"Doesn't matter what I think. You know that as well as I do. Dee sets her mind to something, you might as well just hang up your balls and call it a day."

The bus gave a bone-jarring bang; Vorhees fought to stay upright. Behind them, the children shrieked with happiness.

"Hey, Dar," Cruk said, "you think maybe you can miss some of those?"

The old woman at the wheel responded with a wet *harrumph;* telling Dar what to do with her bus was tantamount to an act of war. All the transport drivers were older women, usually widows; there was no rule about this—it was just how things were done. With a face ossified into a permanent scowl, Dar was a figure of legendary cantankerousness, as no-nonsense a woman as ever walked the earth. She kept time with a stopwatch hung around her neck and would leave you standing in a cloud of dust if you were so much as one minute late for the last transport. More than one field hand had spent a night in a hardbox scared out of his wits, counting the minutes till dawn.

"A busload of kids, for Christ's sake. I can barely think with all this noise." Dar shot her eyes to the pitted mirror above the windshield. "For the love of it, pipe down back there! Duncan Withers, you get down off that bench this instant! And don't think I can't see you, Jules Francis! That's right," she warned with an icy glare, "I'm talking to you, young lady. You can wipe that smirk off your face right now."

Everyone fell abruptly silent, even the wives. But when Dar returned her eyes to the road, Vorhees realized her anger was false; it was all the woman could do not to break out laughing.

Cruk clapped a big hand on his shoulder. "Relax, Vor. Just let everyone enjoy the day."

"Did I say I was worried?"

Cruk's expression sobered. "Look, I know you'd rather Tifty wasn't coming along. Okay? I get it. But he's the best shot I've got. Say what you like, the guy can punch out a hanger at three hundred yards."

Vorhees wasn't aware that he'd been thinking about Tifty at all. But now that Cruk had brought the subject up, he wondered if maybe he was.

"So you think we'll need him."

Cruk shrugged. "Summer day like this, we'll have no problems. I'm just being careful is all. They're my girls too, you know." He broke the mood with a grin. "Just so long as Dee doesn't make a habit of this. I had to call in about fifty favors to put this little party together, and you can tell her I said so."

The bus drew into the staging area. The last of the sweepers were emerging from the corn, dressed in their bulky pads and heavy gloves and helmets with cages obscuring their faces. An assortment of weapons hung off their persons: shotguns, rifles, pistols, even a few machetes. Cruk instructed the children to remain where they were; only when the all clear was given would they be permitted to exit the bus. As the adults began carting out the supplies, Tifty descended from the platform on the bus's roof, rendezvousing with Cruk at the rear to confer with the DS officer in charge of the sweeping squad, a man named Dillon. The rest of Dillon's team, eight men and four women, had gone to take water from the trough by the pump house.

Cruk strode back to where Vorhees was waiting with the rest of the men. Already the sun was blazing; the morning's humidity had burned away.

"Clean as a whistle—the windbreaks, too." He shot Vorhees a wink. "That'll cost Dee extra."

Before Cruk could even finish making the announcement, the children were bolting from their seats and streaming off the bus, clearing space for the sweepers, who would return to the city. Watching the children as they fanned over the grounds, their bodies and faces lit with excitement, Vorhees was momentarily transfixed, his mind caught in a tide of memory. For many, the youngest especially, the day's excursion represented their first trip beyond the walls; he'd known this from the start. Yet to witness the moment was something else. Did the air feel different in their lungs, he wondered, the sun on their faces, the ground beneath their feet? Had these things felt different to him, stepping from the transport the first time, all those years ago? And of course they had: to go ex-murus was to discover a world of limitless dimensions—a world you knew existed but had never believed yourself to be a part of. He recalled the sensation as a kind of weightless physical joy, but frightening too, like a dream in which he had been given the gift of flight but found himself unable to land.

By the watchtower, Fort and Chess were sinking poles to erect a sunshade; the women were toting out the tables and chairs and hampers of food. Ali Dodd, her face shaded beneath the brim of her wide straw hat, was already trying to organize some of the children into a game of take-away. All just as Dee had foreseen when she'd broached the subject of bringing the children along.

"It's something, isn't it?"

Vorhees's cousin, Ty, was standing beside him, holding a hamper to his chest. Over six feet, with a narrow, mournful face, he always reminded Vorhees of a particularly sad-looking dog. Behind them, Dar gave three beeps of the horn; with a belch of oily smoke, the bus pulled away.

"I ever tell you about my first time out?"

"I don't think so."

"Trust me," Ty said, shaking his head in a way that told Vorhees the man had no intention of elaborating. "That's a story."

When everything had been unloaded, Cruk called the children under the tarp to review the rules, which everybody already knew. The first thing, Cruk began, was that everyone needed a buddy. Your buddy could be anyone, a brother or sister or friend, but you had to have one, and you had to stay with your buddy at all times. That was the most important thing. The open ground at the base of the watchtower was safe, within those boundaries they could go wherever they liked, but they were not to venture into the corn under any circumstances; the stand of trees at the south end was also off-limits.

Now, do you see those flags? Cruk asked, gesturing over

the field. The orange ones, hanging down like that? Who can tell me what those are?

Half a dozen hands went up; Cruk's eyes roamed the group before landing on Dash Martinez. Seven years old, all knees and elbows, with a mop of dark hair; under the beam of Cruk's attention, he froze. He was seated between Merry Dodd and Reese Cuomo, who were covering their mouths, trying not to laugh. The hardboxes? the boy ventured. That's right, Cruk replied, nodding. Those are the hardboxes. Now tell me, he continued, addressing all of them, if the siren goes off, what should you do?

Run! someone said, then another and another. *Run!*

"Run where?" Cruk asked.

A chorus of voices this time: *Run to the hardboxes!*

He relaxed into a smile. "Good. Now go have fun."

They darted away, all except the teenagers, who lingered an extra moment by the awning, seeking to separate themselves from the younger children. But even they, Vorhees knew, would find their way into the sunshine. The playing cards came out, and skeins of yarn for knitting; before long, the women were all occupying themselves, watching the children from the shade, fanning their faces in the heat. Vorhees called the men around to hand out salt tablets; even drinking constantly, a man working in this heat could become dangerously dehydrated. They filled their bottles at the pump. There was no need to explain the task before them; detassling was a grueling if simple job they had all done many times. For every three rows of corn, a fourth row had been planted of a second strain. That row would be stripped of its tassles to prevent self-pollination; come harvesttime, it would produce a new, crossbred strain, more vigorous, to be used as seed corn for the following year. When Vorhees's father had first explained this process to him, years ago, it had seemed exciting, even vaguely erotic. What they were doing was, after all, part of the reproductive process, even if it was only corn. But the physical discomforts of the job—the hours in the grueling sun, the ceaseless rain of pollen on his hands and face, the insects that buzzed around his head, seeking any opportunity to bore into his ears and nose and mouth—had quickly disabused him of this notion. His first week in the field, one man had collapsed from heat stroke. Vorhees couldn't recall who that was or what had become of him; they'd put him on the next transport and gotten back to work. It was entirely possible the man had died.

Heavy canvas gloves and wide-brimmed hats and long-sleeved shirts buttoned to the wrists: by the time the men were ready to go, they were sweating profusely. Vorhees cast his gaze to the top of the watchtower, where Tifty had taken his position, scanning the tree line with his scope. Cruk was right; Tifty was the man to have up there. Whatever else was true about Tifty Lamont, his skills as a marksman were inarguable. Yet even to hear the man's name spoken, so many years later, aroused in Vorhees a fresh turning of anger. If anything, the passage of time had only magnified this feeling; each year that slipped past was one more year of Boz's unlived life. Why should Tifty grow to be a man when Boz had not? In more circumspect moments, Vorhees understood his emotions to be irrational; Tifty might have been the instigator on that fateful night, but any one of them could have said no, and Boz would be alive. Yet no matter what Dee said, or Cruk, or Tifty himself—who even now, sweeping the tree line with his rifle, was offering a silent promise to protect Vorhees's children—nothing could dissuade Vorhees from the belief that Tifty bore a singular blame. In the end, he was forced to accept his feelings as a failure of his own character and keep them to himself.

He divided the workers into three teams, each responsible for four rows. Then they made their way to the shelter to say their goodbyes. A game of kickball was under way in the field; from the far side of the watchtower came the ring of horseshoes in the pit. Dee was resting in the shade with Sally and Lucy Martinez, playing a round of hearts. Their games were epic, sometimes lasting for days.

"Looks like we're ready to go."

She laid down her cards, lifting her face toward him. "Come here."

He removed his hat and bent at the waist to receive her kiss.

"God, you stink already," she laughed, wrinkling her nose. "That's your last one for the day, I'm afraid." Then: "So, should I tell you to be careful?"

It was what they always said. "If you want."

"Well, then. Be careful."

Nit and Siri had wandered into the tent. Bits of grass were caught in their hair and the weave of their jumpers. Like puppies who'd been rolling around in the dirt.

"Hug your father, girls."

Vorhees knelt and took them into his arms as a warm bundle. "Be good for Mommy, all right? I'll be back for lunch."

"We're each other's buddies," Siri proclaimed.

He brushed the grass from their sweat-dampened hair. Sometimes just the sight of them moved him to a rush of love that actually brought tears to his eyes. "Of course you are. Just remember what your uncle Cruk told you. Stay where Mommy can see you."

"Carson says there are monsters in the field," Siri said. "Monsters who drink blood."

Vorhees darted his eyes to Dee, who shrugged. It wasn't the first time the subject had come up.

"Well, he's wrong," he told them. "He's trying to scare you, playing a joke."

"Then why do we have to stay out of the field?"

"Because those are the rules."

"Do you promise?"

He did his best to smile. Vorhees and Dee had agreed to keep this matter vague as long as they could; and yet they both understood that they could not keep the girls in the dark forever.

"I promise."

He hugged them again, each in turn and then together, and went to join his crew at the edge of the field. A wall of green six feet tall: the corn rows, a series of long hallways, receded to the windbreak. The sun had crossed an invisible border toward midday; nobody was talking. Vorhees checked his watch one last time. *Watch the clock. Know the location of the nearest hardbox. When in doubt, run.*

"All right, everybody," he said, drawing on his gloves. "Let's get this done."

And with these words, together, they stepped into the field.

In a sense, they had all become who they were because of a single night—the last night of their childhood. Cruk, Vorhees, Boz, Dee: they ran together in a pack, their daily orbits circumscribed only by the walls of the city and the watchful eyes of the sisters, who ran the school, and the DS, who ran everything else. A time of gossip, of rumor, of stories traded in the dust. Dirty faces, dirty hands, the four of them lingering in the alley behind their quarters on the way home from school. What was the world? *Where* was the world, and when would they see it? Where did their fathers go, and sometimes their mothers as well, returning to them smelling of work and duty and mysterious concerns? The outside, yes, but how was it different from the city? What did it feel like, taste like, sound like? Why, from time to time, did someone, a mother or a father, leave, never to return, as if the unseen realm beyond the walls had the power to swallow them whole? Dopeys, dracs, vampires, jumps: they knew the names but did not feel the full weight of their meanings. There were dracs, which were the meanest, which were the same thing as jumps or vampires (a word only old people used); and there were dopeys, which were similar but not the same. Dangerous, yes, but not as much, more like a nuisance on the order of scorpions or snakes. Some said that dopeys were dracs that had lived too long, others that they were a different sort of creature altogether. That they had never been human at all.

Which was another thing. If the virals had once been people like them, how had they become what they were?

But the greatest story of all was the great Niles Coffee: Colonel Coffee, founder of the Expeditionary, fearless men who crossed the world to fight and die. Coffee's origins, like everything about him, were cloaked in myth. He was a thirdling, raised by the sisters; he was an orphan of the Easter Incursion of 38 who had watched his parents die; he was a straggler who had appeared at the gate one day, a boy warrior dressed in skins, carrying a severed viral head on a pike. He had killed a hundred virals singlehandedly, a thousand, ten thousand; the number always grew. He never set foot inside the city; he walked among them dressed as an ordinary man, a field hand, concealing his identity; he didn't exist at all. It was said that his men took an oath—a blood oath—not to God but to one another, and that they shaved their heads as a mark of this promise, which was a promise to die. Far beyond the walls they traveled, and not just in Texas. Oklahoma City. Wichita, Kansas. Roswell, New Mexico. On the wall above his bunk, Boz kept a map of the old United States, blocks of faded color fitted together like the pieces of a puzzle; to mark each new place, he inserted one of their mother's pins, connecting these pins with string to indicate the routes Coffee had traveled. At school, they asked Sister Peg, whose brother worked the Oil Road: What had she heard, what did she know? Was it true that the Expeditionary had found other survivors out there, whole towns and even cities full of people? To this the sister gave no answer, but in the flash of her eyes when they spoke his name, they saw the light of hope. That's what Coffee was: wherever he came from, however he did it, Coffee was a reason to hope.

There would come a time, many years later, long after Boz was gone, and their mother as well, that Vorhees would wonder: why had he and his brother never spoken of these things with their parents? It would have been the natural thing to do; yet as he searched his memory he could not recall a single instance, just as he could not recall his mother or father saying one word about Boz's map. Why should this be so? And what had become of the map itself that in Vorhees's memory it should be there one day and gone the next? It was as if the stories of Coffee and the Expeditionary had been part of a secret world—a boyhood world, which, once passed, stayed passed. For a period of weeks these questions had so consumed him that one morning over breakfast he finally worked up the nerve to ask his father, who laughed. *Are you kidding?* Thad Vorhees was not an old man yet, but he seemed so: his hair and half his teeth gone, skin glazed with a permanent sour dampness, hands like nests of bone where they rested on the kitchen table. *Are you serious? Now, you, you weren't so bad, but Boz—the boy could not shut up about it. Coffee, Coffee, Coffee, all day long. Don't you remember?* His eyes clouded with sudden grief. *That stupid map. To tell you the truth, I didn't have the heart to tear it down, but it surprised me that you did. Never seen you cry like that in your life. I guessed you'd figured out it was all bullshit. Coffee and the rest of them. That it would come to nothing.*

But it wasn't nothing; it had never been, could never be, nothing. How could it be nothing, when they'd loved Boz like they did?

It was Tifty, of course—Tifty the liar, Tifty the teller of tales, Tifty who wanted so desperately to be needed by someone that any fool thing would leave his mouth—who professed to have seen Coffee with his own two eyes. *Tifty,* they all laughed, *you are so full of shit. Tifty, you never saw Coffee or anybody else.* Yet even in the midst of their mockery, the idea was staking its claim; from the start, the boy possessed that talent, to make you believe one thing while simultaneously knowing another. So stealthily had he inserted himself into their circle that none could say just how this had occurred; one day there was no Tifty, and the next there was. A day that began like any other: with chapel, and school, and three o'clock's agonizingly slow approach; the sound of the bell and their sudden release, three hundred bodies streaming through the halls and down the stairs, into the afternoon; the walk from school to their quarters, faces winnowing as their classmates' paths diverged, until it was just the four of them.

Though not exactly. As they made their way into the alley,

its jumble of old shopping carts and sodden mattresses and broken chairs—people were always tossing their junk back there, no matter what the quartermaster said—they realized they were being followed. A boy, stick thin, with a gaunt face topped by a cap of red-blond hair that looked as if it had fallen from a great height onto his head. Though it was January, the air raw with dampness, he wore no coat, only a jersey and jeans and plastic flip-flops on his feet. The distance at which he trailed them, his hands buried in his pockets, was just close enough to encourage their curiosity without seeming to intrude. A probationary distance, as if he were saying: I might be someone interesting. You might want to give me a chance.

"So what do you think *he* wants?" Cruk said.

They had reached the end of the alleyway, where they had erected a small shelter from scraps of wood. A musty mattress, springs popping out, served as the floor. The boy had halted at a distance of thirty feet, shuffling his feet in the dust. Something about the way he held himself made it seem as if the parts of his body were only vaguely connected, as if he'd been pieced together from about four different boys.

"You following us?" Cruk called.

The boy gave no reply. He was looking down and away, like a dog trying not to make eye contact. From this angle, they could all see the mark on the left side of his face.

"You deaf? I asked you a question."

"I ain't following you."

Cruk turned to the others. The oldest by a year, he was the unofficial leader. "Anybody know this kid?"

No one did. Cruk looked back at the boy again. "You. What's your go-by?"

"Tifty."

"Tifty? What kind of name is Tifty?"

His eyes were inspecting the tips of his sandals. "Just a name."

"Your mother call you that?" Cruk said.

"Don't got one."

"She's dead or she left you?"

The boy was fidgeting with something in his pocket. "Both, I guess. You ask it like that." He squinted at them. "Are you like a club?"

"What makes you say that?"

The boy lifted his bony shoulders. "I've seen you is all."

Cruk glanced at the others, then looked back at the boy. He huffed a weary sigh.

"Well, no point in you standing there like a dumbass. Come over so we can have a look at you."

The boy made his way toward them. Vorhees thought there was something familiar about him, his hangdog look. Though maybe it was just the fact that any one of them could have been alone like he was. The mark on his face, they saw, was a large purple shiner.

"Hey, I know this kid," Dee said. "You live in Assisted, don't you? I saw you moving in with your daddy."

Hill Country Assisted Living: a warren of apartments, families all crammed in. Everybody just called it Assisted.

"That right?" Cruk said. "You just move in?"

The boy nodded. "From over in H-town."

"That's who you're with?" Cruk said. "Your daddy?"

"I got an aunt, too. Rose. She looks after me mostly."

"What you got in your pocket there? I see you fooling with it."

The boy withdrew his hand to show them: a foldaway knife, fat with gizmos. Cruk took it, the other three pressing their faces around. The usual blades, plus a saw, a screwdriver, a pair of scissors, and a corkscrew, even a magnifying glass, the lens clouded with age.

"Where'd you get this?" Cruk asked.

"My daddy gave it to me."

Cruk frowned. "He on the trade?"

The boy shook his head. "Nuh-uh. He's a hydro. Works on the dam." He gestured at the knife. "You can have it if you want."

"What I want your knife for?"

"Hell, he doesn't want it, I'll keep it," Boz said. "Give it here."

"Shut up, Boz." Cruk eyed the boy slowly. "What you do to your face?"

"I just fell is all."

His tone was not defensive. And yet all of them felt the hollowness of the lie.

"Fell into a fist is more like it. Your daddy do that or somebody else?"

The boy said nothing. Vorhees saw his jaw give a little twitch.

"Cruk, leave him be," Dee said.

But Cruk's eyes remained fixed on the boy. "I asked you a question."

"Sometimes he does. When he's on the lick. Rose says he doesn't mean to. It's on account of my mama."

"Because she left you?"

"On account of she died having me."

The boy's words seemed to hang in the air. It was true, or it wasn't true; either way, now his plea was nothing they could refuse.

Cruk held out the knife. "Go on, take it. I don't want your daddy's knife."

The boy returned it to his pocket.

"I'm Cruk. Dee's my sister. The other two are Boz and Vor."

"I know who you are." He squinted uncertainly at them. "So am I in the club now?"

"How many times I have to tell you," Cruk said. "We're not a club."

Just like that, it was determined: Tifty was one of them. In due course they all came to know Bray Lamont, a fierce, even terrifying man, his eyes permanently lit with the illegal whiskey everyone called lick, his drink-thickened voice roaring Tifty's name from the window every night at siren. *Tifty, goddamnit! Tifty, you get in here before I have to come looking for you!* On more than one occasion the boy appeared in the alley with a fresh shiner, bruises, once with his arm in a sling. In a sodden rage, his father had hurled him across the room, dislocating his shoulder. Should they tell the DS? Their parents? What about Aunt Rose, could she help? But Tifty always shook his head. He seemed to possess no anger over his injuries, only a tight-lipped fatalism that they could not help but admire. It seemed a kind of strength. Don't tell anyone, the boy said. It's just how he is. No changing a thing like that.

There were other stories. Tifty's great-grandfather, or so he claimed, had been one of the original signatories of the Texas Declaration and had supervised the clearing of the Oil Road; his grandfather was a hero of the Easter Incursion of 38 who, mortally bitten in the first wave, had led the charge from the spillway and sacrificed himself on the battlefield in front of his men, taking his own life on the point of his blade; a cousin, whose name Tifty refused to give ("everybody just calls him Cousin"), was a wanted gangster, the operator of the biggest still in H-town; his mother, a great beauty, had received nine separate proposals of marriage before she was sixteen, including one from a man who would later become a member of the president's staff. Heroes, dignitaries, criminals, a vast and colorful pageant of assorted higher-ups, both in the world they knew and in the one that lurked below it, the world of the trade; Tifty knew people who knew people. Doors would fly open for Tifty Lamont. Never mind that he was the son of a drunken hydro from H-town, another skinny kid with bruises on his face and ill-fitting clothing he never washed, who was looked after by a maiden aunt and lived in Assisted, just like they did; Tifty's stories were too good, too interesting, *not* to believe.

But seeing Coffee—that was simply too much. Such a claim flew in the face of the facts. Coffee was unknowable; Coffee was, like the virals, a creature of the shadows. And yet Tifty's story possessed the tincture of reality. He had gone with his father to H-town, its lawless, shantied streets, to meet Cousin, the gangster. There, in the back room of the machine shed where the still was located—a colossus of a thing, like a living dragon of wires and pipes and huffing cauldrons—among men with dangerous eyes and greasy smiles of blackened teeth and pistols tucked into their belts, the money changed hands, the jug of lick was procured. These excursions were routine, Tifty had described them many times before, yet on this occasion something was different. This time there was a man. He was distinct from the others, not on the trade—Tifty could tell that right away. Tall, with the erect bearing of a soldier. He stood to the side, his face obscured, wearing a dark overcoat belted at the waist. Tifty saw that his head was shorn. Evidently this man, whoever he was, was there on urgent business; usually Tifty's father lingered, drinking and trading stories of H-town days with the other men, but not tonight. Cousin, his great round form wedged behind his desk like an egg in its nest, accepted his father's bills without comment; no sooner had they arrived, it seemed, than they were hustling out the door. It wasn't until they were well clear of the shed that his father said, *Don't you know who it was you saw in there, boy? Huh? Don't you? I'll tell you who that was. That was Niles Coffee himself.*

"I'll tell you something else." The five of them were crowded into the shelter in the alleyway. Tifty was carving in the dust with the pocketknife, which had, after all, stayed his. "My old man says he keeps a camp below the dam. Right out in the open, like being outside was nothing. They let the dracs come to them, then crisp 'em in the traps."

"I knew it!" Boz burst out. The younger boy's face practically glowed with excitement. He swiveled on his knees toward Vorhees. "What did I tell you?"

"No fucking way," Cruk scoffed. Of all of them, his role was the skeptic's; he wore this mantle like a duty.

"I'm telling you, it was him. You could just *feel* it. The way everybody was."

"And what would Coffee want with a bunch of traders? You tell me that."

"How should I know? Maybe he buys lick for his men." A new idea came into Tifty's face. He leaned forward, lowering his voice. "Or guns."

Cruk gave a sarcastic laugh. "Listen to this kid."

"Joke all you want, I've seen them. I'm talking real Army weapons, from before. M16s, automatic pistols, even grenade launchers."

"Whoa," Boz said.

"Where would Cousin get guns like that?" Vorhees asked.

Tifty eased up on his knees to look around, as if making sure no one could hear them. "I'm not sure I should be telling you this," he continued. "There's a bunker, an old Army base near San Antone. Cousin runs patrols up there."

"I can't listen to this another second," said Cruk. "You didn't see Coffee or anybody else."

"You saying you don't believe he exists?"

The idea was sacrilege. "I'm not saying that. You just didn't see him is all."

"What about you, Vor?"

Vorhees felt caught. Half of what Tifty said was pure bullshit—maybe more than half. On the other hand, the urge to believe was strong.

"I don't know," he managed. "I guess . . . I don't know."

"Well *I* believe him," Dee proclaimed.

Tifty's eyes widened. "See?"

Cruk waved this away. "She's a girl. She'll believe anything."

"Hey!"

"Well, it's true."

Tifty leveled his eyes at the older boy. "What if I said you could see Coffee for yourself?"

"Just how would I do that?"

"Easy. We can go through one of the spillway tubes. I've been down there lots of times. This time of year, they don't release until dawn. The vents go right to the base of the dam—we should be able to see the camp from there."

The challenge had been laid down; there was no way to say no.

"There's no goddamn camp, Tifty."

* * *

It took them three days to work up the nerve, and even then Cruk forbade his sister from coming. The plan was to sneak out after their parents were asleep and rendezvous at the shelter; Tifty had plotted a route to the dam that would keep them out of sight of the DS patrols.

It was after midnight by the time Tifty arrived. The others were already waiting. He appeared at the end of the alley-way and made his way toward them quickly, the hood of his jacket drawn up over his head, hands stuffed in his pockets. As he ducked into the shelter, he withdrew a plastic bottle.

"Liquid courage." He unscrewed the cap and passed it to Vorhees.

It was lick. Vorhees and Boz's parents, prayerful people who went to church at the sisters' every Sunday, wouldn't have it in the house. Vorhees held the open bottle under his nose. A clear liquid with a harsh chemical odor, like lye soap.

"Give it here," Cruk commanded. He snatched the bottle and sipped, then handed it back to Vorhees.

"You ain't never drunk lick before?" Tifty asked Vorhees.

Vorhees did his best to look offended. "Sure I have. Lots of times."

"When did you ever drink lick?" Boz scoffed.

"There's plenty you don't know, brother." Wishing he could hold his nose, Vorhees took a cautious sip, swallowing fast to avoid the taste. A blast of stinging heat filled his sinuses; a river of fire tumbled down his throat. God, it was awful! He finished with a wheezing cough, tears swarming his eyes, everybody laughing.

Boz drank next. To Vorhees's embarrassment, his little brother managed to take a respectable sip without much more than a wince. Three more times the bottle traveled around the circle. By the fourth pass, even Vorhees had gotten the hang of it and managed a solid swallow without coughing. He wondered why he wasn't feeling anything, but the moment he stood he realized he was; the ground lurched beneath his feet, and he had to put out a hand to steady himself.

"Let's go," Tifty said.

By the time they reached the dam, they were all giggling like maniacs. The passage of minutes had altered somehow; it seemed as if they had spent a long time getting there, and no time at all. Vorhees had a fragmented memory of hiding from a DS patrol under a truck but couldn't remember the exact circumstances, nor how they had avoided capture. He knew he was drunk, but this fact was nothing his mind could focus on. They paused in the shadows while somebody—Boz, Vorhees realized, who was the drunkest of them all—vomited into a stand of weeds. And Dee, what was she doing here? Had she followed them? Cruk was barking at her to go home, but Dee was Dee: once she'd fixed her mind to something, you might just as well try to pull a bone from a dog's mouth. The fact was, Vorhees loved Dee. He always had. It was suddenly overwhelming, this love, like an expanding balloon of emotion inside his chest, and he was working up the nerve to confess his feelings when Tifty stepped toward them from wherever he'd gone and told them to follow.

He led them to a small concrete building with a flight of metal stairs descending belowground. At the bottom was a maintenance shaft, dank and gloomy, the walls dripping with moisture. They were inside the dam, somewhere above the spillway vents. Bulbs in metal cages cast elongated shadows on the walls. A building rush of adrenaline had started to bring Vorhees's senses back into focus. They came to a hatch in the wall, sealed with a rusted metal ring. Cruk and Tifty positioned themselves on opposite sides and heaved with all their might, but the wheel wouldn't budge.

"We need a lever," said Tifty.

He disappeared down the tunnel and returned with a length of pipe. He threaded it through the spokes of the ring and leaned in. With a squeal, the wheel began to turn; the door swung open.

Inside was a vertical shaft and a ladder leading down. Tifty produced a cap flare, scraped the striker, and dropped it into the hole. Tifty descended first, then Vor, Dee, and Boz, with Cruk bringing up the rear.

They found themselves in a wide tube. A spillway vent, one of six. Through these vents, water was released from the impoundment once a day and funneled down the spillway to the fields. Behind them lay a million gallons of water held in place by the dam. The air was cold and smelled of stone. A trickle of water ran the length of the floor toward the outlet, a pale disk of moonlit sky. They crept toward it, away from the light of Tifty's flare. Vorhees's heart was thudding in his chest. The world of night, outside the walls: it was beyond imagining. Ten feet from the outlet, Tifty dropped to a crouch; the others followed suit. Bars of heavy steel guarded the opening.

"I'll go first," Tifty whispered.

He moved on his hands and knees toward the end of the

tunnel. Everyone else held absolutely still. In Vorhees's drunken mind, seeing Coffee's camp had become an ancillary purpose; the evening was a pure test of courage, its object irrelevant. The bars were sturdy enough to keep out a viral, but that wasn't the danger; Vorhees half-expected a clawed hand to reach through and grab their friend and tear him to pieces. Through the lingering haze of the lick, the thought came to him that Dee must be afraid too, and that he might offer her some reassurance, but he couldn't think of what to say, and the idea died in his mind.

At the tunnel's mouth, Tifty eased up onto his knees, gripping the bars, and peered out.

"What do you see?" Cruk whispered.

A pause. Then, from their friend, two words: "Holy . . . shit."

The tone hit Vorhees as wrong. Not an exclamation of discovery but of sudden fear.

"What is it?" Cruk whispered, more harshly. "Is Coffee there?"

"I want to look!" Boz cried out.

"Quiet!" Cruk barked. "Tifty, goddamnit, what is it?"

Vorhees felt it through his knees. A rumbling, like thunder, followed by a shrieking groan of metal gears engaging. The sound was coming from behind them.

Tifty jumped to his feet. "Get out of here!"

It was water. The sound Vorhees was hearing was water being released from the impoundment. One vent and then the next and then the next, moving in a line. That's what Tifty had seen.

They would be smashed to pieces.

Vorhees rose and grabbed Boz by the arm to yank him away, but the boy wriggled free.

"I want to see him!"

"There's nothing there!"

The boy's voice cracked with tears. "There is, there is!"

Boz made a dash for the outlet. Tifty and the others were already racing toward the ladder. The sound of thunder was closer now. The adjacent tube had released; theirs would be next. In another few seconds, a wall of water would slam into them. At the tunnel's mouth Vorhees gripped his brother around the waist, but the boy held fast to the bars.

"I see him! It's Coffee!"

With all his might, Vorhees pulled; the two of them crashed to the floor. The others were calling: *Come on, come on!* Vorhees gripped his brother by the hand and began to run. Cruk was waving at them from the base of the ladder. Vorhees felt a pop of pressure in his ears; an ice-cold wind was pushing in his face. As Cruk disappeared up the ladder, Vorhees began to ascend, his brother right behind him.

Then the water arrived.

It slammed him like a fist, a hundred fists, a thousand. Below him, Boz cried out in terror. Vorhees managed to keep his grasp on the ladder, but could do nothing more; to release even one hand was to be swept away. Water swarmed his nose and mouth. He tried to call his brother's name, but no sound came. This was how it ends, he thought. One mistake and everything was over. It was so simple. Why didn't people die like this more often? But they did, he realized, as his grip on the ladder began to fail. They died like this all the time.

It was Cruk who pulled him free. Cruk, who would forever be his friend; who would one day stand with him while he married Dee; who would watch over his children on the day when everyone had brought the children for a summer picnic in the field; who would join him in the final battles of their lives, many miles and years away. As Vorhees's hands tore away, Cruk reached down and seized him by the wrist and yanked him upward, and the next thing Vorhees knew they were climbing, they were ascending the shaft to safety.

But not Boz. The boy's body wouldn't be recovered until the next morning, crushed against the bars. Maybe he'd seen Coffee and maybe he hadn't. Tifty never gave them an answer. Over time, Vorhees came to think it didn't matter. Even if he had, there'd be no comfort in it.

By midday, the detassling crew had covered sixteen acres. The sun was blazing, not a cloud in the sky; even the children, after a morning of games and laughter, had retreated to the shelter. At the pump, Vorhees removed his hat, filled a cup and drank, then filled it again to pour the water over his face. He removed his sweat-sodden shirt and wiped himself down with it. God almighty, it was hot.

The women and children had already eaten. Beneath the shelter, the work crew gathered for lunch. Bread and butter, hard-boiled eggs, cured meat, blocks of cheese, pitchers of water and lemonade. Cruk came down from the tower to fill a plate; Tifty was nowhere to be seen. Well, so what? Tifty could do as he liked. They ate heartily, without speaking. Soon all of them would be dozing in the shade.

"One hour," Vorhees said after a while, rising from the table. "Don't get too comfortable."

He ascended the stairs to the top of the tower, where he found Cruk scanning the field with the binoculars. His rifle was resting against the rail.

"Anything interesting out there?"

For a second, Cruk didn't answer. He passed Vorhees the binoculars. "Six o'clock, through the tree line. Tell me what that is."

Vorhees looked. Nothing at all, just trees and the dry brown hills beyond. "What do you think you saw?"

"I don't know. Something shiny."

"Like metal?"

"Yeah."

After a moment, Vorhees drew the binoculars away. "Well, it's not there now. Maybe it was just the sun flaring in the lenses."

"Probably that's it." Cruk took a sip of water from his bottle. "How's it going down there?"

"They'll all be asleep soon enough. A lot of the kids are down already. I don't think anybody expected it to be this hot."

"July in Texas, brother."

"Gunnar wanted to know if he could help. That boy is all heart and no sense."

Cruk took up his rifle. "What did you tell him?"

"Just you wait. Someday you'll realize how crazy you sound."

Cruk laughed. "And yet we were the same. Couldn't wait to get out into the world."

"Maybe you couldn't."

Cruk fell silent, gazing out over the rail. Vorhees sensed that something was troubling his friend.

"Listen," Cruk began, "I made a decision, and I wanted you to hear it from me. You know there's talk about the Expeditionary getting back together."

Vorhees had heard these rumors, too. It was nothing new; rumors circulated all the time. Since Coffee and his men had disappeared—how many years ago?—the subject had never really died completely.

"People are always saying that."

"This time it's not just talk. The military's taking volunteers from the DS, looking to build a unit of two hundred men."

Vorhees searched his friend's face. What was he telling

him? "Cruk, you can't be seriously thinking about it. That was all kid stuff."

Cruk shrugged. "Maybe it was, back then. And I know how you feel about it, after what happened to Boz. But look at my life, Vor. I never married. I don't have a family of my own. What was I waiting for?"

The meaning sank in all at once. "Jesus. You already signed on, didn't you?"

Cruk nodded. "I turned in my resignation from the DS yesterday. It won't be official until I take the oath, though."

Vorhees felt stunned.

"Look, don't tell Dee," Cruk pressed. "I want to do it."

"She'll take it hard."

"I know. That's why I'm telling you first."

The conversation was broken by the sound of a pickup coming down the service road. It drew into the staging area and pulled up to the shelter; Tifty climbed out. He stepped to the rear of the truck and drew down the tailgate.

"Now, what's he got?"

They were watermelons. Everyone crowded around; Tifty began to carve them up, passing fat, dripping wedges to the children. Watermelons! What a treat, on a day like this!

"For Christ's sake," Vorhees groaned, watching the performance. "Where the hell would he get those?"

"Where does Tifty get anything? You got to hand it to the guy, though. He's not going to die friendless."

"Did I say that?"

Cruk looked at him. "You don't have to like him, Vor. That's not for me to say. But he's trying. You've got to give him that."

The door to the stairs opened. Dee stepped out, carrying two plates, each bearing a pink wedge of melon.

"Tifty brought—"

"Thanks. We saw."

Her face fell with an expression Vorhees knew too well. *Let it go. Please, just for today. They're only watermelons.*

Cruk took the plates from her. "Thanks, Dee. That'll really hit the spot. Tell Tifty thanks."

She glanced at Vorhees, then returned her eyes to her brother. "I'll do that."

Vorhees knew he looked like a resentful fool, just as he knew that if he didn't say something, change the subject, he'd carry this sour feeling inside him for the rest of the day.

"How are the kids?"

Dee shrugged. "Siri's out like a light. Nit's gone off with

Ali and some of the others. They're picking wildflowers."
She paused to wipe her brow with the back of her wrist.
"Are you really going back out there? I don't know how you
stand it. Maybe you should wait until the sun's a little lower."

"There's too much to do. You don't have to worry about
me."

She regarded him for another moment. "Well, like I said.
Anything else I can bring you, Cruk?"

"Not a thing, thanks."

"I'll leave you to it then."

When Dee was gone, Cruk held out one of the plates. But
Vorhees shook his head.

"I'll pass, thanks."

The big man shrugged. He was already wolfing down his
slice, rivers of juice running down his chin. When all that
remained was the rind, he gestured toward the second plate,
resting on the parapet. "You mind?"

Vorhees shrugged in reply. Cruk finished off the second
slice, wiped his face on his sleeve, and tossed the rinds over
the side.

"You should tell Dee soon," Vorhees said.

Three o'clock, the day draining away. A faint breeze had
picked up late in the morning, but now the air had stilled
again. Under the tarp, Dee was playing a halfhearted game
of roundabout with Cece Cauley, little Louis resting at their
feet in his basket. A plump, good-natured baby, fat fingers
and fat toes and a soft, pursed mouth: despite the heat, he
had barely fussed all day and now was sound asleep.

Dee remembered those days, baby days. Their distinctive
sensations, the sounds and smells, and the feeling of profound physical attachment, as if you and the baby were a
single being. Many women complained about it—*I can't get
a moment to myself, I can't wait until she's walking!*—but Dee
never had; just thirty, she would have gladly had another,
maybe even two. It would be nice, she thought, to have a son.
But the rules were clear. Two and done, was the saying. The
governor's office was discussing an extension of the walls,
and maybe then the ban would be lifted. But probably that
would come too late, and until then, there was only so much
food and fuel and space to go around.

And Vor—well, what could she do? Boz's death was an
intractable barrier in the man's mind, the truth distorted and
enlarged over the years until it was the singular injury of his
life. Tifty was Tifty, he always would be. One day he was

being tossed into the stockade for putting a man's head through a window in a barroom brawl, the next he was producing, through a kind of Tifty magic, a truck of black-market watermelons on a scorching summer afternoon. Probably it was just a matter of time before he ended up in the stockade for good. Yet there was no denying it: Tifty would always be a part of them, and Dee most of all. There were times when Dee looked at her older daughter and honestly didn't know what the truth was. It could be one thing, or it could be the other. In a certain light Nitia was all Vor, but then the little girl would smile in a particular way or do that squinty thing with her eyes and there was Tifty Lamont.

A single night, not even. The whole thing, the entirety of their affair, had been more like ninety minutes, start to finish. How was it possible for ninety minutes to make so much difference in a life? Dee and Tifty had agreed in the aftermath that it had been a terrible mistake—inevitable, perhaps, a force of years that neither could refuse, but nothing to repeat. They both loved Vor, did they not? They'd made a big joke of it, even shaking hands to seal the deal like the two old friends they were, though of course it wasn't a joke at all: not at the time and not nine months later; it wasn't a joke now.

I will never let any harm come to you, Tifty had told her, not just that night but many times, many nights. *Not you or the girls or Vor. Whatever else is true, that's my solemn promise, my vow before God. I'll be the ground beneath your feet. Always know I'm there.* And Dee did; she knew. If she allowed herself to admit it, it was only because Tifty had agreed to accompany them that the idea of today, of a summer picnic in the field, had come about at all.

Did Dee love him? And if she did, what kind of love was it? Her feelings for Tifty were different from her feelings for Vor. Vor was steady, reliable. A creature of duty and endurance, and a good father to the girls. Solid where Tifty was vaporous, a man composed of rumor as much as actual fact. And there was no question that she and Vor belonged together; that had never been an issue. Alone in the dark, in private moments together, he spoke her name with such longing it was almost like pain; that's how much Vor loved her. He made her feel . . . what? More real. As if she, Dee Vorhees—wife and mother; daughter of Sis and Jedediah Crukshank, gone to God; citizen of Kerrville, Texas, last oasis of light and safety in a world that knew none—actually existed.

So why should she find herself, once again, thinking of Tifty Lamont?

But the cards, and this hot-hot-hot afternoon in July, when they had brought the children to the field. Dee's mind had wandered so badly, she hadn't realized what Cece was doing. Before she knew it, the woman, grinning with victory, had successfully maneuvered her into taking the queen. Two tricks, three, and it was over. Cece gleefully jotted the tally on a pad.

"Another?"

Ordinarily Dee would have said yes, if only to occupy the hours, but in the heat the game had begun to feel like work.

"Maybe Ali wants to play."

The woman, who had come back into the tent for water, waved the offer away, the ladle poised at her lips. "Not a chance."

"C'mon, just a couple of hands," Cece said. "I'm on a hot streak."

Dee rose from the table. "I better go see what the girls are up to."

She stepped away from the shelter. In the distance, she could see the tops of the cornstalks quivering where the men were working. She angled her face toward the tower's apex, positioning a hand over her eyes against the glare. A ghostly moon, daytime white, was hovering near the sun. Well, that was strange. She hadn't noticed that before. Cruk and Tifty were both on station, Cruk with his binoculars, Tifty sweeping the field with his rifle. He caught sight of her and gave a little wave, which flustered her; it was almost as if he knew she'd been thinking about him. She waved guiltily in reply.

A group of a dozen children were playing kickball, Dash Martinez waiting at the plate. Acting as pitcher was Gunnar, who had become an unofficial babysitter over the course of the afternoon.

"Hey, Gunnar."

The boy—a man, really, at sixteen—looked toward her. "Hey, Dee. Want to play?"

"Too hot for me, thanks. Have you seen the girls anywhere?"

Gunnar glanced around. "They were here just a second ago. Want me to look?"

Dee's weariness deepened. Where could they have gone? She supposed she could climb the tower and ask Cruk to track them down with the binoculars. But the hike up the stairs, once she imagined it, seemed too effortful. Easier, on the whole, to find the girls herself.

"No, thanks. If they come back, tell them I want them out of the sun for a while."

"Gunnar, pitch the ball!" Dash cried.

"Hang on a second." Gunnar met Dee's eye. "I'm sure they're nearby. They were here, like, two seconds ago."

"That's fine. I'll find them myself."

The wildflower field, she thought; probably that's where they had gone. She felt more irritated than concerned. They weren't supposed to wander off without telling anyone. Probably it had been Nit's idea. The girl was always into something.

They had five minutes left.

From the observation deck, Tifty watched Dee walk away.

"Cruk, pass me the binoculars."

Cruk handed them over. The wildflower field was located on the north side of the tower, adjacent to the corn. That's where she appeared to be headed. Probably she just wanted to get away for a few minutes, Tifty thought, away from the children and the other wives.

He passed the binoculars back to Cruk. He scanned the field with his rifle, then lifted the scope toward the tree line.

"The shiny thing is back."

"Where?"

"Dead ahead, ten degrees right."

Tifty peered hard into the scope: a distant rectangular shape, brilliantly reflective, through the trees.

"What the hell is that?" Cruk said. "Is it a vehicle?"

"Could be. There's a service road on the far side."

"Nothing should be out there now." Cruk drew down the binoculars. He paused a moment. "Listen."

Tifty willed his mind to clear. The creak of crickets, the breeze moving through his ears, the trickle of water through the irrigation system. Then he heard it.

"An engine?"

"That's what I hear, too," Cruk said. "Stay put."

He descended the stairs. Tifty pressed his eye to the rifle's scope. Now the image was clear: a big semi, the cargo compartment covered with some kind of galvanized metal.

He took out his walkie-talkie. "Cruk, it's a truck. Far side of the trees. Doesn't look like DS."

The line crackled. "I know. Double up."

He saw Cruk emerge from the base of the tower and stride

toward the shelter, waving to Gunnar to bring the children over. Tifty dragged his scope across the field: the men working, the rows of corn, the marker flags for the hardboxes drooping in the afternoon stillness. All just as it should be.

But not exactly. Something was different. Was it his vision? He lifted his face. A blade of shadow was moving over the field.

Then he heard the siren.

He turned toward the sun; instantly he knew. It had been many years since he'd felt afraid, not since that night in the dam. But Tifty felt fear now.

One minute.

Vorhees first experienced the altering illumination as a diminishment of visual detail, a sudden dimming like premature twilight. But because he was wearing dark glasses, a defense against the rain of pollen and the afternoon brightness, his mind did not initially compute this change as anything noteworthy. It was only when he heard the shouts that he removed his glasses.

A great round shape, wrapped with a glowing penumbra, was sliding over the sun.

An eclipse.

As the sirens went off, he tore down the row. Everyone else was running, too, yelling, *Eclipse! Eclipse! The hardboxes, get to the hardboxes!* He burst from the corn, practically running straight into Cruk and Dee.

"Where are the girls?"

Dee was frantic. "I can't find them!"

The darkness was spreading like ink. Soon the whole field would be enveloped.

"Cruk, get these people in the boxes. Dee, go with him."

"I can't! Where are they?"

"I'll find them." He drew his pistol from his waistband. "Cruk, get her out of here!"

Vorhees raced back into the field.

Tifty, his heart pounding with adrenaline, was sweeping the field from the tower. No sign yet, but it was only a matter of time. And the truck: what was it? Still it idled on the far edge of the windbreak. He tried to get Cruk on the walkie but couldn't raise him. In all the chaos, probably the man couldn't hear him.

He tightened the stock against his shoulder. Where would they come from? The trees? An adjacent field? Everything had been swept by Dillon's team. Which didn't mean the virals weren't there, only that he couldn't see them.

Then: at the periphery of his vision, a faint movement of the cornstalks, no more than a rustling, near one of the flags at the edge of the field. He swung the scope in close and pressed his eye to the lens. The hatch of the hardbox stood open.

It was the one place they hadn't looked. They'd never checked the hardboxes.

Everyone was running, grabbing their children, dashing into the field toward the flags. Tifty emerged from the base of the tower at a dead sprint.

"No!"

Cruk was carrying two children, Dash Martinez and Reese Cuomo, under his arms. Dee was running beside him, Cece and Ali just steps behind—Cece hugging little Louis to her chest, Ali with Merry and Satch.

"The hardboxes!" Cruk was yelling. "Get to the hardboxes!"

"They're *in* the hardboxes!"

A burst of gunfire exploded in the field. Dee saw Tifty drop to a knee and fire off three quick rounds. She turned as the first of the virals burst from the corn.

It landed right on top of Ali Dodd.

Dee felt an urge to vomit. Suddenly she couldn't make her feet move. The viral, which had finished with Ali, was now burying its jaws in Cece's neck. The woman was twitching, shrieking, arms and legs flailing like an overturned insect's. The image seared Dee's vision like a burst of light; all she could do was watch in helpless horror.

Cruk stepped forward, shoved the barrel of his rifle against the side of the creature's head, and fired.

Where was Satch? The boy was suddenly nowhere. Merry was standing in the dust, screaming. Dee hoisted the little girl to her waist and began to run.

The virals were everywhere now. In blind panic, people were dashing for the tent, a pointless gesture; it could offer no safety at all. The virals swarmed over it, tearing it to pieces, the air filling with screams. "The tower!" Tifty was yelling. "Head for the tower!" But it was too late; nobody was listening. Dee thought of her daughters, saying goodbye. How stark everything became, at the end, all the wishes for one's children distilled by the world's swift cruelty into the desperate hope that death would take them fast. She prayed they would not suffer. Or, worse, be taken up. That was the worst thing: to be taken up.

An immense force careened into her from behind. Dee tumbled to the ground, little Merry rocketing from her arms. Face-down in the dirt, she lifted her eyes to see her brother, twenty feet away, pointing his rifle at her. Shoot me, Dee thought. Whatever's about to happen, I don't want it. A prayer of childhood found her lips and she closed her eyes and muttered it quickly, into the dust.

A shot. Behind her, something fell with an animal grunt. Before her mind could process this, Cruk was yanking her to her feet, his mouth moving incomprehensibly, saying words she couldn't quite make out. His rifle was gone; all he had was the pistol, Abigail. Why would a man name a gun Abigail? Why would he name it at all? Something must have happened to her head, she realized, because here she was, worrying over Cruk's gun, when everyone was dying. Other thoughts came to her, strange things, awful things. How it would feel to be ripped in two, like Ali Dodd. Her daughters, in the field, and what was happening to them now. How terrible, Dee thought, to live one second longer than one's own babies. In a world of terrible things, surely that was the most terrible of all. Cruk was dragging her toward the door. He was doing what he thought she wanted, but she didn't, not at all—she couldn't die fast enough, in fact—and with a burst of strength Dee tore away from him, racing into the field, calling to her children.

Vorhees could hear his daughters, laughing in the corn. They were, he knew, too young to be afraid. They had snuck away to do exactly what they'd been told not to, and it was all a kind of game to them, this funny thing with the light. Vorhees raced down the rows, shouting their names, his breath heaving with panic, trying to home in on their voices. The sound was behind him, it was ahead, it was on either side. It seemed to be coming from everywhere, even inside his head.

"Nit! Siri! Where are you?"

Then there was a woman. She was standing in the middle of the row. She was draped in a dark cloak, like a woman in a fairy tale, some dweller of the forest; her head was covered by a hood, her eyes by dark glasses that concealed the upper half of her face. So total was Vorhees's surprise that for a moment he thought he might be imagining her.

"Are they your daughters?"

Who was she, this woman of the corn? "Where are they?" he panted. "Do you know where they are?"

With a languid gesture she removed her glasses, revealing a face sensuously smooth and youthfully beautiful, with eyes that glinted in their sockets like diamonds. He felt a surge of nausea.

"You're tired," she said.

Suddenly, he was. Curtis Vorhees had never been so tired in his life. His head felt like an anvil; it weighed a thousand pounds. It took every ounce of will for him to remain standing.

"I have a daughter. Such a beautiful daughter."

Behind him he heard the final, random pops of panicked gunfire. The field and sky had sunk into an unearthly darkness. He felt the urge to weep, but even this seemed beyond his command. He had dropped to his knees; soon he would fall.

"Please," he choked.

"Come to me, beautiful children. Come to me in the dark."

Somebody yanked him to his feet: Tifty. His face was very close. Vorhees could barely focus on it. The man was pulling him by the arm.

"Vor, come on!"

His tongue was thick in his mouth. "The woman . . ." But there was no one; the place where she had stood was empty. "Did you see her?"

"There's no time! We have to get to the tower!"

Vorhees would have none of it; with the last of his strength he jerked away.

"I have to find them!"

It was the butt of Tifty's rifle that brought everything to a halt. A single, crisp blow to the head, expertly aimed; Vorhees's vision swarmed with stars. Then the world turned upside down as Tifty grabbed him by the waist and hurled him to his shoulder and began to run. Fat leaves streamed past, slapping his face. Vorhees was calling, "Nit! Siri! Come back!" But he had no strength to resist. His family was dead, he knew that; Tifty would not have come for him if they were still alive. More gunfire, the shouts of the dying all around. The hardboxes, a voice said. They came from the hardboxes. Who would survive this day? And Vorhees knew, to his infinite sorrow, that once again he would be one of the lucky ones.

They burst from the corn onto open ground. The shelter was wrecked, the tarp torn away, everything scattered. Bodies strewn everywhere, but he saw no children; the little ones were gone. *Come to me, beautiful children. Come to me in the dark.* And as the door of the tower slammed behind him and he tumbled to the floor, slipping at last into a merciful unconsciousness, his final thought was this:

Why did it have to be Tifty?

IV

THE CAVE

AUTUMN, 97 A.V.

No light, but rather darkness visible
Served only to discover sights of woe.

—MILTON,
PARADISE LOST

Slide No. 2: Map of the Western Territories,
Army of the Republic of Texas
Presented at the Third Global Conference
on the North American Quarantine Period
Center for the Study of Human Cultures and Conflicts
University of New South Wales, Indo-Australian Republic
April 16-21, 1003 A.V.

To Northern Territories

Perryton

Perryton Depot

Gateway

Borger

Perryton Road

Pampa

Amarillo

Clarendon Depot

Childress

Clovis Supply Base
Under Construction

West Texas Territory

Dalhart

Dumas

Tulia

Plainview

Amarillo Road

Littlefield

Lubbock

Levelland

Slaton

Kerrville Road North

Sewell Road

Brownfield

Fort Workers Western H.Q.

Seminole

Lamesa

Snyder

Sweetwater

Abilene

Andrews

Big Spring

Midland

West Odessa

Odessa Oil Fields

San Angelo

Kerrville Road South

⊞ =	Western H.Q.
◯ =	Hardbox
⊗ =	Depot

Tucumcari

HARDING

QUAY

Clovis

Portales

ROOSEVELT

Roswell Road

Fort Workers

Lovington

Hobbs

LEA

Kermit

Wink

LOVING

Monahans

REEVES

24

Wolgast had come to Amy at last. He had come to her in dreams.

They were sometimes in one place and sometimes another. They were stories of things that had happened, events and feelings from the past replayed; they were a jumble, a pastiche, an overlap of images that in their reconfiguration felt entirely new. They were her life, her past and present commingling, and they occupied her consciousness with such completeness that upon awakening she would startle to discover herself existing in a simple reality of firm objects and ordered time. It was as if the waking world and the sleeping world had exchanged positions, the latter possessing a superseding vividness that did not abate as she moved into the traces of her day. She would be pouring water from a pot, or reading to the children in circle, or sweeping leaves in the courtyard, and without warning her mind would drown with sensation, as if she had slipped beneath the surface of the visible world into the currents of an underground river.

A carousel, its gyring lights and ringing, bell-like music falling. A taste of cold milk and the dust of powdered sugar on her lips. A room of blue light, her mind floating with fever, and the sound of a voice—Wolgast's voice—gently leading her out of the darkness.

Come back to me, Amy, come back.

Most powerful of all was the dream of the room: dirty, stale-smelling, clothing scattered in piles, containers of old food atop every surface, a television blaring with meaningless cruelty in the corner, and the woman Amy understood to be her mother—she experienced this awareness with a gush of hopeless longing—moving through the cramped space with panicked energy, scooping things from the floor, tossing them into sacks. *Come on, honey, wake up now. Amy, we got to go.* They were leaving, her mother was leaving, the world had cleaved in two with Amy on one side of the gap and her mother on the opposite, the moment and its sentiments of parting unnaturally prolonged, as if she were watching her mother from the stern of a boat as it sailed away from the pier. She understood that it was here, in this room, that her life had actually begun. That she was witnessing a kind of birth.

But it wasn't just the two of them. Wolgast was there as well. This made no sense; Wolgast had entered her life later. Yet the logic of the dream was such that his presence was intrinsically unremarkable; Wolgast was there because he was. At first Amy experienced his presence not as a bodily reality but a vaporous glow of emotion hovering over the scene. The more she felt her mother moving away from her, into a private urgency Amy neither shared nor comprehended—something terrible had happened—the more vivid became her sense of him. A deep calm infused her; she watched with a feeling of detachment, knowing that these events, which seemed to be occurring in a vivid present, had actually happened long ago. She was simultaneously experiencing them for the first time while also remembering them—she was both actor and observer—with the anomaly of Wolgast, whom she now discovered was sitting on the edge of the bed, her mother nowhere to be seen. He was wearing a dark suit and tie; his feet were bare. He was gazing absorbedly at his hands, which he held before him with the tips of his fingers touching. *Here is the church,* he intoned, weaving all but his index fingers together, *and here is the steeple. Open the door*—his thumbs separated to reveal his wriggling digits—*and see all the people. Amy, hello.*

—Hello, she said.

I am sorry I have been away. I've missed you.

—I've missed you, too.

The space around them had altered; the room had dispersed into a darkness in which only the two of them existed, like a pair of actors on a spotlit stage.

Something is changing.

—Yes. I think that it is.

You will need to go to him, Amy.

—Who? Who should I go to?

He's different from the others. I could see it the first time I laid eyes on him. A glass of iced tea. That was all he wanted, to cool himself off in the heat. He loved that woman with his whole heart. But you know that, too, don't you, Amy?

—Yes.

An ocean of time, that's what I told him. That's what I can give you, Anthony, an ocean of time. A sudden bitterness came into his face. *I always did hate Texas, you know.*

He had yet to look at her; Amy sensed that the conversation neither required nor even allowed this. Then:

I was thinking just now about the camp. The two of us, reading together, playing Monopoly. Park Place, Boardwalk, Marvin Gardens. You always beat me.

—I think you let me.

Wolgast chuckled to himself. *No, it was always you, fair and square. And Jacob Marley.* A Christmas Carol, *that was your favorite. I think you had the whole book memorized. Do you remember?*

—I remember all of it. The day it snowed. Making the snow angels.

He wore the chains he forged in life. Wolgast frowned in sudden puzzlement. *It was such a sad story.*

Here was the river, Amy thought. The great, coursing river of the past.

I could have gone on that way forever. Wolgast angled his eyes upward, addressing the darkness. *Lila, don't you see? This was what I wanted. It was all I ever wanted.* Then: *Do you . . . know this place, Amy?*

—I don't think it's anywhere. I think that I'm asleep.

He considered these words with a faint nod. *Well. That does sound right to me. Now that you say it, that makes a lot of sense.* He took a long breath and let the air out slowly. *It's strange. There's so much I can't remember. That's what it's like, you know. Like there's only this little bit of yourself you get to keep. But things are coming clearer now.*

—I miss you, Daddy.

I know you do. I miss you, too, sweetheart, more than you'll ever know. I don't think I've ever been happier than I was with you. I wish I could have saved you, Amy.

—But you did. You saved me.

You were just a little girl, alone in the world. I never should have let them take you. I tried, but not hard enough. That's the real test, you know. That's the true measure of a man's life. I was always too afraid. I hope you can forgive me.

A wave of sorrow broke inside her. How she longed to comfort him, to take him in her arms. Yet she knew that if she attempted this, were she to move even one step closer, the dream would dissolve, and she would be alone again.

—I do. Of course I do. There's nothing to forgive.

There's so much I never told you. He was staring intently at his hands. *About Lila, and Eva. Our own little girl. You were so much like her.*

—You didn't have to, Daddy. I knew, I knew. I always knew.

You filled my heart, Amy. That's what you did for me. You filled the place where Eva had been. But I couldn't save you any more than I could save her.

As if these words had willed it, the image of the room had begun to recede, the space between the two of them elongating like a hallway. A sudden desperation took her in its grip.

It's good to remember these things with you, Amy. If it's all right, I think I'll stay here for a while.

He was leaving her, he was telescoping away.

—Daddy, please. Don't go.

My brave girl. My brave Amy. He's waiting for you. He's been waiting all this time, in the ship. The answers are there. You need to go to him when the time comes.

—What ship? I don't know any ship.

But her pleas were no use; the dream was fading, Wolgast was almost gone. He was poised at the very edge of the enveloping darkness.

—Please, Daddy, she cried. Don't leave me. I don't know what to do.

At last he turned his face toward her and found her with his eyes. Bright, shining, piercing her heart.

Oh, I don't think I will ever leave you, Amy.

25

CAMP VORHEES, WEST TEXAS
Western Headquarters of the Expeditionary

Though Lieutenant Peter Jaxon was a decorated military officer, a veteran of three separate campaigns and a man about whom stories were told, he sometimes felt as if his life had stopped.

He waited for orders; he waited for chow; he waited for the latrine. He waited for the weather to break, and when it didn't, he waited some more. Orders, weapons, supplies, news—all were things he waited for. For days and weeks and sometimes even months he waited, as if his time on earth had been consecrated to the very act of waiting, as if he were a man-sized waiting machine.

He was waiting now.

Something important was happening in the command tent; he had no doubt in his mind. All morning Apgar and the others had been sealed away. Peter had begun to fear the worst. For months they'd all heard the rumors: if the task force didn't kill one soon, the hunt would be abandoned.

Five years since his ride up the mountain with Amy. Five years hunting the Twelve. Five years with nothing to show for it.

Houston, home of Anthony Carter, subject Number Twelve, would have been the logical place to start, if the place hadn't been an impenetrable swamp. So, too, New Orleans, home of Number Five, Thaddeus Turrell. Tulsa, Oklahoma, seat of Rupert Sosa, had yielded nothing but disaster; the city was a vast ruin, dracs everywhere, and they'd lost sixteen men before making their escape.

There were others. Jefferson City, Missouri. Oglala, South Dakota. Everett, Washington. Bloomington, Minnesota. Orlando, Florida. Black Creek, Kentucky. Niagara Falls, New York. All distant and unreachable, many miles and years away. Tacked to the inside of the lid of his locker Peter kept a map, each of these cities circled in ink. The seats of the Twelve. To kill one of the Twelve was to kill his descendants, to free their minds for the journey into death. Or so Peter believed. That was what Lacey had taught him when she'd exploded the bomb that killed Babcock, subject Number One; what Amy had showed him, stepping from Lacey's cabin into the snowy field, where the Many had lain in the sun to die.

You are Smith, you are Tate, you are Dupree, you are Erie Ramos Ward Cho Singh Atkinson Johnson Montefusco Cohen Murrey Nguyen Elberson Lazaro Torres . . .

They had been a group of ten then. Now they were six. Peter's brother was gone, and Maus, and Sara, too. Of the five that had made the trip to Roswell Garrison, only Hollis and Caleb had escaped—"Baby Caleb," though he was hardly a baby anymore, now in the orphanage in Kerrville, being raised by the sisters. When the virals had broken through the Roswell Garrison's perimeter, Hollis had run with Caleb to one of the hardboxes. Theo and Maus were already dead. No one knew what became of Sara; she had vanished into the melee. Hollis had looked for her body in the aftermath but found nothing. The only explanation was that she'd been taken up.

The years had scattered the others like the wind. Michael was at the refinery in Freeport, an oiler first class. Greer, who had joined them in Colorado, was in the stockade, sentenced to six years for deserting his command. And who knew where Hollis was. The man they'd known and loved like a brother had broken under the weight of Sara's death, his grief casting him into the dark underbelly of the city, the world of the trade. Peter had heard he'd risen through the ranks to become one of Tifty's top lieutenants. Of the original group, only Peter and Alicia had joined the hunt.

And Amy. What of Amy?

Peter thought of her often. She looked very much as she always had—like a girl of fourteen, not the 103 she actually was—but much had changed since their first meeting. The Girl from Nowhere, who spoke only in riddles when she spoke at all, was no more. In her place was a person much more present, more *human*. She spoke often of her past, not just her lonely years of wandering but her earliest memories of the Time Before: of her mother, and Lacey, and a camp in the mountains and the man who had saved her. Brad Wolgast. Not her real father, Amy said, she had never known who that was, but a father nonetheless. Whenever she spoke of him, a weight of grief entered her eyes. Peter knew without asking that he had died to protect her, and that this was a debt she could never repay, though she might spend her life—that infinite, unknowable span—trying to do just that.

She was with Caleb now, among the sisters, having taken up the gray frock of the Order. Peter didn't think Amy shared their beliefs—the sisters were a dour lot, professing a philosophical and physical chastity to reflect their conviction that these were the last days of humanity—but it was a more than adequate disguise, one Amy could easily pass off. Based on what had happened at the Colony, they'd all agreed that Amy's true identity, and the power she carried, was nothing anybody outside the leadership should know.

Peter walked to the mess, where he passed an empty hour. His platoon, twenty-four men, had just returned from a reconnaissance sweep to Lubbock to scout up salvageables; luck had been on their side, and they'd completed their mission without incident. The biggest prize had been a junkyard of old tires. In a day or two they'd return with a truck to take as many as they could carry for transport back to the vulcanizing plant in Kerrville.

The senior officers had been in the tent for hours. What could they be talking about?

His mind drifted back to the Colony. Odd that he wouldn't think about it for weeks or even months at a time, and then, without warning, the memories would sail into his mind. The events that had precipitated his departure now seemed as if they had happened to somebody else—not Lieutenant

Peter Jaxon of the Expeditionary or even Peter Jaxon, Full Watch, but a kind of boy-man, his imagination circumscribed by the tiny patch of ground that defined his entire life. How much energy had he devoted to nurturing his own feelings of inadequacy, manifested in his petty rivalry with his brother, Theo? He thought with wistful pride of what his father, the great Demitrius Jaxon, Head of the Household, Captain of the Long Rides, would have said to him now. *You've done well. You've taken the fight to them. I'm proud to call you son.* Yet Peter would have given it all back for just one more hour in Theo's company.

And whenever he looked at Caleb, it was his brother he saw.

He was joined at the table by Satch Dodd. A junior officer like Peter, Satch had been a toddler when his family had been killed in the Massacre of the Field. As far as Peter was aware, Satch never said anything about this, though the story was well known.

"Any idea what it's all about?" Satch asked. He had a round, boyish face that made him appear completely earnest at all times.

Peter shook his head.

"Good haul up in Lubbock."

"Just tires."

Both their minds were elsewhere; they were simply filling time. "Tires are tires. We can't do much without them."

Satch's squad would be departing in the morning to do a hundred-mile sweep toward Midland. It was bad duty: the area was a cesspool of oil, bubbling up from old wells that had never been capped.

"I'll tell you something I heard," Satch said. "The Civilian Authority is looking into whether or not some of those old wells can still be operated, for when the tanks go dry. We may find ourselves garrisoning down there before too long."

Peter was startled; he'd never considered this possibility. "I thought there was enough oil in Freeport to last forever."

"There's forever and forever. In theory, yeah, there's plenty of slick down there. But sooner or later everything runs out." Satch squinted at him. "Don't you have a friend who's an oiler? One of your crew from California, wasn't it?"

"Michael."

Satch shook his head. "Walking all the way from California. That's still the craziest story I ever heard." He placed his palms on the table and rose. "If you hear anything from upstairs, let me know. If I had to bet, they'll be sending all of us down to Midland to wade in the slick before too long."

He left Peter alone. Satch's words had done nothing to cheer him; far from it. A half dozen enlisted clomped into the mess, talking among themselves with the rough-edged, profanity-laced familiarity of men looking for chow. Peter wouldn't have minded a little company to take his mind off his worries, but as they moved from the line in search of a table, none glanced in his direction; the tarnished silver bar on his collar and the poor spirits he was radiating were evidently enough to ward them away.

What could the senior officers be talking about?

To abandon the hunt: Peter couldn't imagine it. For five years he had thought of little else. He'd signed on with the Expeditionary right after Roswell; a lot of men had. For every person who'd perished that night, there was a friend, or brother, or son who had taken his place. The ones motivated solely by a need for revenge tended to wash out early or get themselves killed—you had to have a better reason—and Peter had no illusions about himself. Payback was a factor. But the roots of his desire went deeper. All his life, since the days of the Long Rides, he'd longed to be part of something, a cause larger than himself. He'd felt it the moment he'd taken the oath that bound him to his fellows; his purpose, his fate, his person—all were now wedded to theirs. He'd wondered if he'd be somehow less himself, his identity subsumed into the collective, but the opposite had proved true. It was nothing he could speak of, not with Theo and the others gone, but joining the Expeditionary had made him feel alive in a way he never had before. Watching the soldiers eat—laughing and joking and shoveling beans into their mouths as if it were the last meal of their lives—he recalled those early days with envy.

Because somewhere along the way, the feeling had left him. As campaigns were waged and men died and territory was taken and lost, none of it seeming to amount to anything, it had slowly slipped away. His bond to his men remained, a force as abiding as gravity, and he would have sacrificed himself for any one of them without a flicker of hesitation, as, he believed, they would have done for him. But something was missing; he didn't quite know what it was. He knew what Alicia would have told him. *You're just tired. This is a long slog. It happens to everyone, be patient.* Not wrong, but not the whole story, either.

Finally Peter could stand it no longer. He exited the tent

and marched across the compound. All he needed was some pretext for knocking; with any luck, they'd let him inside, and he could glean some sense of what they were up to.

He needn't have bothered. As he made his approach, the door swung open: Major Henneman, the colonel's adjutant. Trim, a bristle of blond hair, slightly crooked teeth he showed only when he smiled, which was never.

"Jaxon. I was just going to look for you. Come inside."

Peter stepped into the shade of the tent, pausing in the doorway to let his eyes adjust. Seated around the broad table were all the senior staff—Majors Lewis and Hooper, Captains Rich, Perez, and Childs, and Colonel Apgar, the officer in charge of the task force—plus one more.

"Hi, Peter."

Alicia.

"There are two entrances I could find, here and here."

Alicia was directing everyone's attention to a map spread over the table: U.S. GEOLOGICAL SURVEY, SOUTHERN NEW MEXICO. Beside it was displayed a second map, smaller and faded with age: NATIONAL PARK SERVICE, CARLSBAD CAVERNS.

"The main opening to the cave is about three hundred yards wide. There's no way we can seal it even with our largest ED, and the terrain is too rugged to haul a flusher up there anyway."

"So what are you proposing?" Apgar asked.

"We box him in." She pointed to the map again. "I scouted another entrance, about a quarter mile away. It's an old elevator shaft. Martínez has to be somewhere between these two entrances. We set off a package of H2 at the base of the main entrance, inside the tunnel that leads toward the shaft. This should drive him toward the bottom of the elevator, where we position a single man to meet him on the way out."

"A single man," Apgar repeated. "Meaning you."

Alicia nodded.

The colonel leaned back in his chair. Everyone waited.

"Don't get me wrong, Lieutenant. I know what you're capable of. We all do. But if this thing is anything like the one you saw in Nevada, it sounds to me like a one-way trip."

"Anybody else will just slow me down."

He frowned skeptically. "And you're positive Martínez is down there?"

"It all makes sense, sir. Babcock used a cave, too. And El Paso is just a hundred miles from Carlsbad. It's his home turf."

Apgar thought a moment. "I agree, the pattern fits, but how can you be so sure?"

Alicia hesitated. "I can't really explain it, Colonel. I just know."

Peter was seated at the far end of the table. "Permission to speak, sir."

Apgar rolled his eyes. "Fine, Jaxon, go ahead and say what we all know you're going to say."

"I'm the only other person here who's seen one of the Twelve. I trust Lieutenant Donadio. If she says Martínez is down there, he's down there."

"We're all aware of your history, Lieutenant. That doesn't change the fact that we're just playing a hunch here. I don't see risking anyone unless we know for sure."

"So maybe there's another way. All of the original test subjects were chipped, like Amy. We can use the signal to locate him."

"I already thought of that. Just one problem. Radio waves can't pass through rock. How do you propose to get a signal from a thousand feet underground?"

"We don't get it from the surface. We get it from the cave."

Peter drew their attention to the diagram again. "We do like Alicia says, positioning an H2 pack inside the tunnel that leads from the base of the main entrance into the other chambers. The Twelve are big, but in tight quarters that ought to be enough to get Martínez's attention. The package is wired back to the base of the main entrance, where it's connected to the surface by a radio detonator, so we can blow it at a safe distance. Call that Blue Squad."

Apgar nodded. "I'm with you so far."

"Okay, but we don't send a single man down the elevator shaft to meet Martínez on the way out. We send two, with a radio direction finder. Call that Red Squad. The first thing Red Squad does is plant a second pack of H2 near the base of the shaft. We put it on a short timer, say fifteen seconds. Man one proceeds into the cave, using the RDF to locate Martínez, but man two holds his position at the elevator. The trick will be keeping lines of sight to maintain radio contact with the surface, so that's man two's job. He's the go-between. Basically we use a daisy-chain system. Man one is connected by radio to man two, who's connected to who-ever's positioned at the top of the shaft, call him man three, who's connected to Blue Squad. That way we can coordinate all the elements of the operation. No guesswork."

Apgar nodded. "Fair enough, but I'm already seeing the

problems, Lieutenant. It's a maze down there. What if men one and two lose contact? The whole thing collapses."

"It's a risk, but there's no reason they should, so long as the first man doesn't go any farther than these three junctures." Peter showed them on the map. "It won't give us a whole view of the cave, but we should be able to survey most of it."

"Go on."

"So. We set the two packages, man one goes looking for Martínez, man two waits to hear. After that it's just a question of the timing. Once man one locates Martínez, he radios back to man two, who contacts the surface. Blue Squad blows the hole. Martínez is pissed. Man one beats it back to the shaft, drawing him toward the elevator. Man two sets the timer. Up they go, the second package blows, Martínez is history." He clapped his hands. "Simple."

Apgar considered this. "Not a lot of margin for error there. I know Donadio's fast, but fifteen seconds won't be much to get clear of the blast. I don't know if we can winch anybody up that quickly."

"We won't have to. The shaft itself will offer enough protection. Fifty feet should do it."

"Just to be clear, you're talking about using man one as a decoy."

"Correct, sir."

"Sounds like you've done this before."

"Not me. Sister Lacey."

"Your mystic nun."

"Lacey was a lot more than that, Colonel."

Apgar placed the tips of his fingers together, glanced at the map, then raised his eyes to Peter's face. "Man one is Donadio, obviously. Any idea who this other suicidal character might be?"

"Yes, sir. I'd like to volunteer."

"And why am I not surprised?" Apgar turned to the others. "Anybody else want to chime in here? Hooper? Lewis?"

Both men were agreed.

"Donadio?"

She glanced at Peter—*Are you sure about this?*—and then gave a tight nod. "I'm good with it, Colonel."

A brief pause, followed by a sigh of surrender. "All right, Lieutenants, this is your show. Henneman, you think two squads should do it?"

"I believe so, Colonel."

"Brief Lieutenant Dodd and put a detail together to outfit

the portables. And let's see about that RDF. I'd like to move on this within forty-eight hours." Apgar looked at Peter again. "Last chance to change your mind, Lieutenant."

"No, sir."

"I didn't think so." He lifted his eyes to the room. "All right, everybody. Let's show Command what we're made of and kill this bastard."

Two nights later, they made camp at the base of the mountain. A pair of portables, twenty-four men sleeping on racks; they awoke at dawn to prepare their ascent. The ground around the portables was littered with tracks in the dust, the nighttime visitors, drawn by the scent of two dozen dozing men, a grand feast denied by walls of steel. The mountain was too steep for vehicles, the path winding. Anything they brought they would have to hump on their backs. Without the portables to protect them on the mountaintop, there would be no second chance. In the bright light of morning, the terms of their mission were starkly defined. Find Martínez and kill him, or die in the dark.

Henneman was the senior officer—an irregularity. Rarely did he go outside the walls of the garrison. But he had made his way, over the years, to this position of relative safety by doing just the opposite. Tulsa, New Orleans, Kearney, Roswell—Henneman had ascended through the ranks on a ladder of battle and blood. No one doubted his capabilities, and his presence meant something. Peter would lead one squad, Dodd the other. Alicia was Alicia: the scout sniper, the odd man, the one who didn't quite fit and seemed, by and large, to answer to no one. Everyone knew what she could do, yet her status was a source of unease among the men. No one ever said anything that Peter was aware of—if they spoke of their concerns, it wasn't to him—yet their discomfort was evident in the way they kept their distance, the cautious glances they gave her, as if they could not quite bring themselves to meet her eye. She was a bridge between the human and the viral, situated somewhere between: where did she fall?

They set out just after dawn. Now it was a race against the hours. They would need to set the charges and have everybody in position before sunset. The cool desert night had yielded to a scorching sun, its thrumming rays hitting their backs, then their shoulders, then the tops of their heads. There was no time to rest; rations were passed down the lines as they climbed, Alicia leading the way, occasionally doubling back to confer with Henneman. By the time they reached the mouth of the cave, it was late afternoon.

"Jesus, you weren't kidding," Henneman said.

They were standing at the cave's mouth. The western sun lit the interior, though its rays traveled only so deeply; beyond lay a maw of blackness. The amphitheater with its curved stone benches, the spaces between them littered with dry leaves and other debris, was inexplicable; if an audience sat here, what did they watch? Metal banisters framed a curving trail that switchbacked down into the cave. They had three usable hours of daylight left.

They reviewed the plan a final time. Dodd's squad would set the charges at the base of the cave. According to Alicia's map, the switchbacks ended two hundred feet belowground, where a narrow tunnel descended another three hundred feet to the first of several large chambers. The charges would be laid inside this tunnel, wired to a radio detonator with a clear line of sight to the cave's mouth. The explosion would shoot a compression wave through the tunnel, its destructive force magnified exponentially by its trip through the narrow space—in theory, sending whatever was down there running toward the elevator shaft. Once the charges were in place and Dodd's men had returned to the surface, Peter and Alicia would commence their descent. The elevator car was resting at the bottom, seven hundred feet below the surface, held in place by its counterweights, which were lodged at the top. A winch would lower Peter and Alicia by rope to the base of the shaft and pull them back up when they made their escape.

Dodd and his team set out. Fifteen minutes later, he radioed from the bottom. They'd made it to the mouth of the tunnel.

"Creepy as hell down here," Dodd said. "You've got to see this for yourself."

They would, soon enough. Dodd's squad had three hundred feet of cable to connect the detonator to the package. A five-minute silence ensued; then Dodd's voice returned. The bomb and the cable were laid; his team had begun their ascent. Peter and Alicia were waiting at the top of the elevator shaft, which was located a quarter mile away, in a structure that once had housed the park's offices. The winch was in place. The time was 1700 hours; they were cutting it close.

Dodd's voice on the radio: "Blue Squad, good to go."

Alicia and Peter clipped into their harnesses; Henneman wished them good luck. They balanced at the edge of the shaft and pushed off, dropping into the blackness like coins into a well. Portable fluorescents clipped to their vests bathed the walls in a yellowish glow. Peter's mind was clear, his senses acute. There was a kind of fear that deepened aware-ness, bringing focus to the mind; his was that kind. The tem-perature dropped swiftly, prickling the hair on his arms. A hundred feet, two hundred, three, their downward passage swift, their weight suspended by the harnesses, as if they were descending in two cupped hands. The elevator's cables—a thick trunk of twined steel and two smaller lines wrapped in plastic—flowed past. A dark shape emerged below: the top of the elevator. The cables were bolted to a plate on the roof. They landed with a soft thunk.

"Red Squad down."

Alicia pried loose the hatch, and they dropped inside. The doors of the car stood open. A feeling of immeasurable space beyond, as if they were standing at the entrance to a cathedral. The air was damp and cold with a strong earthen smell, vaguely ureic. They scanned the space with the lights of their rifles, their beams volleying into the immense black-ness. All around were strange, organic-looking forms, as if the walls were made of crumpled flesh.

"Flyers, get a load of this place," Alicia said.

Alicia had removed her glasses; she was in her element now, a zone of permanent night. By the glow of the fluores-cents, she knelt and removed two objects from her rucksack. The first was the explosives pack—eight sticks of HEP wired to a mechanical timer. She gingerly placed this on the floor of the cave. The second was the radio direction finder, a small, boxy object with a directional antenna and a meter to register the strength of an incoming signal at 1432 mega-hertz. She flicked the power switch and stepped from the car, holding the RDF before her to sweep the space beyond. It began to issue a faint but regular beeping. The needle nudged to life.

"Gotcha."

Peter radioed the surface: the target was present. He'd had no cause to doubt Alicia's claim, yet suddenly the situation had acquired a more potent reality. Somewhere in these cav-erns, Julio Martínez, Tenth of Twelve, lay in wait.

"Tell Dodd to stand ready and wait for my signal," Peter told Henneman.

"Acknowledged. All eyes, Lieutenants."

The moment had come. A final look passed between Peter and Alicia, freighted with meaning. Once again, here they were, the two of them poised at the precipice. There was no need to acknowledge this with words; all had been said. Neither could exist without the other, yet the distance between them could never be crossed. They were who they were, which was soldiers at war. The bond transcended all others but one, the one thing they could not have. Alicia was wearing, as ever, her trademark bandoliers, but she'd given up the cross for an M4 rifle with the fat tube of a grenade launcher fixed under the barrel. Martínez would receive no mercy from her, no final benediction.

"See you soon."

She faded into the darkness.

At the mouth of the cave, Satch Dodd's squad had formed a firing line along the lowest tier of the amphitheater. The sky had begun a discernible darkening, an enrichment of its colors as day spilled toward night. Dodd was clutching the detonator. Its signal, transmitted to the receiver at the base of the cave, would close a simple electric circuit, sending a jolt of current down the wire to the bomb.

Even at this distance, it would make a hell of a boom.

Though it was nothing he could let his men see, the journey to the bottom of the cave had rattled him. Dodd had never experienced any place like it in his life—an unearthly world of alien shapes, strange colors, and distorted dimensions, pockets of darkness everywhere he looked, spiraling down into nothingness. The trip down the tunnel had felt like crawling into his own grave. In the orphanage, Dodd had learned about hell, a realm of everlasting gloom where the souls of the wicked writhed forever in agony. Although the idea had initially terrified him, something about it had struck him, even then, as faintly unbelievable. Though only a boy, he'd sensed that hell was just a story the sisters had concocted to keep the children in line, not unlike the fables they read the children to teach simple moral lessons. Dodd's status as the youngest survivor of the Massacre of the Field had always afforded him a slightly elevated rank among the children, as if this experience had somehow made him wise. This, of course, was completely misplaced—having never really known his parents, he did not feel the loss of them, and he remembered nothing of that day—but under the spell of his playmates' admiration for the imaginary mantle of his grief, Dodd came to see himself as a boy with special powers of perception, especially where the sisters' mystical proclamations were concerned. God, okay, Dodd was good with that, it made a kind of sense. Heaven was a pleasant idea he was happy to go along with, since believing in it cost him nothing. But that was as far as he was willing to go. Hell: it was pure nonsense.

Now, standing at the mouth of the cave, detonator in hand, Dodd wasn't so sure.

The waiting was never easy. Once the shooting started a feeling of clarity always took over. You'd die or you wouldn't, you'd kill or be killed—it was one or the other and nothing in between. You knew where you stood, and for those violent, heart-pumping minutes, Dodd felt himself lifted on a wave of adrenaline that eradicated virtually everything about him that was even vaguely personal. It could be said that in the chaos of combat, the man known as Satch Dodd ceased to exist, even to himself; and when the dust cleared, and he found himself still standing, he experienced a rush of raw existence, as if he'd been shot from a cannon back into the world.

It was in the waiting that a person experienced too much of himself. Memories, doubts, regrets, anxieties, the whole range of possibilities the future contained—they all swirled together in the mind like a soup. While half of Dodd's attention was intently focused on the situation at hand—the detonator in his grip and the presence of his men around him and the walkie clipped to his shoulder, through which Henneman's command to blow the hole would come—the other half was ricocheting through the chambers of his private self. Only when Henneman gave the signal to explode the bomb would this feeling, a kind of whole-body psychological nausea, abate, igniting his power to act.

The major's voice crackled through the radio: "Blue Squad, all eyes. Donadio's going in."

Something tensed inside him; he felt himself returning to the moment. "Acknowledged."

It couldn't happen soon enough.

Seven hundred feet below, in the lightless caverns left behind when sulfide-rich waters had leached upward into the fissured limestone deposits of an ancient reef, Alicia Donadio was advancing on the signal. That this signal emanated from the chip implanted in the neck of Julio Martínez, one of twelve death row inmates infected with the CV virus created by Project NOAH at the dawn of the present age, she had no doubt.

Louise, she thought, *Louise.*

The moment they'd touched down in the cave, this name had taken ahold of her mind. Which was strange: according to the records they had salvaged from the NOAH compound, Martínez had been sentenced to death for killing a policeman, not the rape and murder of a woman. Perhaps her death had gone unrecorded, or else had never been connected to him. The shooting of the policeman was present also, a flash of violence like a white-hot spark, but within each of the Twelve lay a singular story—the one story that was the true essence, the core of who they were. For Martínez, that story was Louise.

According to her map, two tunnels led from the elevator to individual caves, marked with names suggesting their grandeur. King's Palace. Hall of Giants. Queen's Chamber. And, simply, the Big Room. To maintain a line of sight with Peter, and thus stay in communication with the surface, Alicia could go no farther than the junctures at the far end of each passageway. Beyond that, she would be on her own.

King's Palace, she thought. Somehow, that sounded like him.

"Going left."

As she proceeded down the passageway, the meter of the RDF leapt, the beeping accelerating in kind. She'd guessed right. The walls pressed around her, shards of some bright substance embedded in their surface glinting under the raking beam of her rifle. There were virals here, a great horde, like buried treasure, Martínez presiding. Alicia could see it all plainly now; the images deepened with every step, taking hold of her mind. Louise, the tightening cord encircling her neck; the precise demarcation of color above and below, her neck milky white, the skin of her face rosy and swollen with blood; the look of astonished terror in her eyes, and the cold finality of death's approach. It was all as clear as if Alicia had lived it herself, but then something shifted. Now Alicia was experiencing this event in two directions simultaneously. She was looking at Louise while also looking *from* her. How was this possible? When had she acquired this attunement to the unseen world? Through Louise's eyes she saw Martínez's face. A well-groomed man of precise features, silver hair swept back from his forehead to form a delicate widow's peak. A human face, though not precisely: there was nothing you could call a person behind his eyes, only a soulless vacancy. The pleasure he was taking was an animal's. Louise was nothing to him. She was an organization of warm surfaces created only for his desire and dispatch. Her name was written plainly on her blouse, and yet his mind could not connect this name to the human person he was strangling in the midst of raping, because the only thing real to him was himself. She felt Louise's terror, and her pain, and then the dark moment when the woman understood that death was imminent, her life at its end; that she would die without any acknowledgment from the universe that she had existed in the first place, and the last thing she would feel as she departed the world would be Martínez, raping her.

Alicia had reached the juncture, a place called the Boneyard. A strong smell of urine tanged in her nostrils, coating the membranes of her mouth and throat. In the moist air, her breath puffed before her in an icy cloud. The beep of the RDF, steadily accelerating, had become a continuous stream of sound.

She knew then what she intended to do. She had intended it all along. The plan was a cover, an elaborate ruse to conceal her purpose.

She wanted to kill Martínez herself. She wanted to feel him die.

At the elevator, Peter became aware that something wasn't as it should be just a few seconds before Alicia stepped from his line of sight. There was no rational explanation for this knowledge; it simply came to him out of the stillness, a feeling deep in his bones.

"Lish, come in."

No answer.

"Lish, can you read me?"

A hiss of static, then: "Stay there."

There was something unsettling in her voice. A feeling of resignation, as if she were severing a rope that held her over an abyss. Before he could respond, her voice returned: "I mean it, Peter."

Then she was gone.

He radioed the surface. "Something's wrong, I've lost her."

"Hold your position, Jaxon."

Had she said the left tunnel? Yes, the left.

"I'm going after her," he told Henneman.

"Negative. Stand pat—"

But Peter failed to hear the rest of Henneman's message. He was already moving away.

* * *

At the same time, Lieutenant Dodd had commenced a mad dash down the switchback into the cave. He was unaware that the chain of radio transmission had been broken and that neither Peter nor, by extension, Alicia knew that the bomb at the base of the main entrance had disarmed itself— the first mishap in a cascade of events that would never be fully reassembled to the satisfaction of Command. Somehow—a short in the line, a mechanical defect, a whim of fate—the receiver at the base of the cave had lost contact with the surface. A first-class, A1 screwup if ever there was one, and now Dodd was racing into the mouth of hell.

His first descent had taken fifteen minutes; moving at what counted as a dead sprint down the treacherous, hairpinning pathway, he made it to the bottom in fewer than five. At the edge of his vision he perceived a scuttle overhead, accompanied by a high-pitched squeaking, but in his haste he failed to process this; if Henneman's order to blow the package came before he'd made it back out, his team would fire it anyway, killing him in the blast. The only thing on his mind was reaching the bottom, repairing the detonator, and getting back out.

There it was. The receiver. Dodd had left it on a smooth, tablelike boulder situated at the tunnel's mouth; now it lay on the ground, tipped onto its side. What force had knocked it away? Dodd dropped to his knees, his breath heaving in his chest. Rivers of perspiration spilled down his face. A ghastly stink was in the air. He gently took the device in his hand. The receiver had two switches, one to arm the detonator, another to close the circuit and fire the bomb. Why wasn't it working? But then he understood that the antenna had come loose, knocked askew in the fall. He withdrew a screwdriver from his pack.

The ceiling began to move.

Alicia noticed the bones first. The bones and the smell, an overpowering stench—rank, biological, like the bottled gas of a grave. She took a step forward. As her boot touched down she felt, then heard, a crunch of bone. The skeleton of something small. The tininess of the skull, its mocking grin of teeth: a kind of rodent? Her field of view widened. The floor was carpeted with the brittle remains, in many places piled knee- or even waist-high, like drifts of snow.

Where are you? she thought. *Show yourself, you bastard. I've got a message from Louise.*

Martínez was close, very close. She was practically on top

of him. For the first time in many years Alicia knew the taste of fear, but more than that: she knew hatred. A pure force, binding and suffusing every part of her. All her life seemed called to this moment. Martínez was the great misery of the world. It was not glory she sought or even justice. It was vengeance; not killing but the act of killing. To say, *This is from Louise.* To feel his life leaving him under her hand.

Come to me. Come to me.

From out of the gloom a shape appeared, a flash of white skin in the beam of her rifle. Alicia froze. What the hell . . . ? She took a step forward, then another.

It was a man.

Ruined and sagging, old beyond old, his figure emaciated, a sketch of bones; his skin was bleached of all color, almost translucent. He was huddled in nakedness on the floor of the cave. As the light of her rifle passed over his face, he did not flinch; his eyes were like stones, inert with blindness. A bat was writhing in his hands. Its long, kitelike wings, the sheerest membranes stretched over the attenuated fans of fingered bone, fluttered helplessly. The man brought the bat to his face and, with a shocking energy, enveloped its dainty head in his mouth. A final, muffled squeal and a tremor of the creature's wings and then a snapping sound; the man twisted the body away and spat its head to the floor. He pressed the body to his lips and began vigorously to suck, his body rocking with the rhythm of his inhalations, a faint coo, almost childlike, pulsing from his throat.

Alicia's voice sounded clumsily huge in the cavernous space. "Who the hell are you?"

The man pointed his blind, rigid face toward the source of the sound. Blood slicked his lips and chin. Alicia noticed for the first time a bluish image crawling up the side of his neck: the figure of a snake.

"Answer me."

A faint puff, more air than speech: "Ig . . . Ig . . ."

"Ig? Is that your name? Ig?"

". . . nacio." His brow crumpled. "Ignacio?"

From behind her came a sound of footsteps; as Alicia spun around, the beam of Peter's rifle swept her face.

"I told you to wait."

Peter's face was a blank, transfixed by the image of the man huddled on the floor.

Alicia pointed her rifle to the man's forehead. "Where is he? Where's Martínez?"

Tears swelled from his sightless eyes. "He left us." His voice was like a moan of pain. "Why did he leave us?"

"What do you mean, he left you?"

With a searching gesture, the man raised one hand to the barrel of Alicia's rifle, wrapped it in his fist, and pulled the muzzle hard against his forehead.

"Please," he said. "Kill me."

They were bats. Bats by the hundreds, the thousands, the millions. They exploded from the roof of the tunnel, a solid airborne mass, swarming Dodd's senses with the heat and weight and sound and smell of them. They blasted into him like a wave, sealing him inside a vortex of pure animal frenzy. He waved his arms madly, trying to deflect them from his face and eyes; he felt but did not yet wholly experience the sting of their teeth, drilling into his flesh, like a series of distant pinpricks. They are going to tear you to pieces, his mind was telling him; that's how this is going to end; your awful fate is that you're going to die in this cave, torn to shreds by bats. Dodd screamed, and as he screamed his awareness of the pain became the thing itself, attaining its full dimensions, his mind and body instantly achieving a unity of pure annihilating agony, and as he pitched forward toward the detonator, with its glowing lights and switches, his physical person assuming in that elongated instant the properties of a hammer, falling, his one thought—*oh, shit*—was also his last.

The blast wave from the prematurely detonated first package, rocketing from the tunnel into the cave's complex of halls and cavities with the energy of a runaway locomotive, reached the King's Palace as a terrific bang, overlapped by a pop of pressure and a deep subterranean trembling. This was followed by a second lurch underfoot, like the deck of a boat tossed by a giant wave. It was an event in equal measures atmospheric, auditory, caloric, and seismic; it had the power to rouse the very core of the earth.

They were known as hangers: sleeping virals who, their metabolic processes suppressed, existed in a state of extended hibernation. In this condition they could endure for years or even decades, and preferred, for reasons unknown—perhaps an expression of their biological kinship to bats, a buried memory of their race—to dangle upside down, arms folded over their chests with a curious tidiness, like mummies in their sarcophagi. In the various chambers of Carlsbad Caverns (though not the King's Palace; this was Ignacio's alone) they awaited, a dozing storehouse of biological stalactites, a somnolent army of glowing icicles excited to consciousness by the bomb's detonation. Like any species, they perceived this adjustment to their surroundings as a mortal threat; like virals, they instantly snapped to the scent of human blood in their midst.

Peter and Alicia began to run.

Alicia, had she been alone, might have stood her ground. Though she would have been swallowed by the horde, it was so embedded in her nature to turn and fight that this impossible task would have felt oddly satisfying: a thing of fate, and an honorable exit from the world. But Peter was with her; it was his blood, not hers, that the virals wanted. The creatures were funneling toward them, filling the underground channels of the cavern like the undammed waters of a flood. The distance to the elevator, roughly a hundred yards, possessed a feeling of miles. The virals roared behind them. Peter and Alicia hit the elevator at a sprint. There was no time to set the charge; their initial strategy was now moot. Alicia scooped the package from the floor of the elevator, seized Peter by the wrist, kneed him through the hatch, and launched herself behind him, touching down with a clang.

"Grab a cable!" she yelled.

A moment of incomprehension.

"Do it and hold on!"

Did he understand what she had in mind? It didn't matter; Peter obeyed. Alicia dropped the package to the roof of the elevator, pointed her rifle downward at the cable plate, and pulled the trigger.

Freed from the mass of the elevator car, the counterbalancing weights plunged downward. A hard yank and then a massively accelerating force rocketed them skyward: Peter experienced their ascent in a blur, a sense of pure motion that focused on his hands, his only link to life. He would have lost his grip entirely if not for Alicia, who, below him, her grasp unassailable, acted as backstop, preventing him from slithering down the cable and plunging into the maw. In a confusion of arms and legs, they spun wildly, overwhelmed by a bombardment of physical data beyond Peter's ability to compute; he did not see the virals leaping up the shaft behind them, ricocheting from wall to wall, each jolt of movement propelling them upward, narrowing the gap.

But Alicia did. Unlike Peter, whose senses were merely human, she possessed the same internal gyroscopes as their pursuers; her awareness of time and space and motion was capable of constant recalculation, enabling her not only to maintain her grip but also to point her rifle downward. It was the grenade launcher she intended; her target was the package on the elevator's roof.

She fired.

26

FEDERAL STOCKADE, KERRVILLE, TEXAS

Major Lucius Greer, late of the Second Expeditionary, now known only as prisoner no. 62 of the Federal Stockade of the Texas Republic—Lucius the Faithful, the One Who Believed—was waiting for someone to come.

The cell where he lived was twelve feet square, just a cot and a toilet and sink and a small table with a chair. The room's only illumination came from a small window of reinforced glass set high on the wall. This was the room where Lucius Greer had spent the last four years, nine months, and eleven days of his life. The charge was desertion—not completely fair, in Lucius's estimation. It could be said that by abandoning his command to follow Amy up the mountain to face Babcock, he had simply followed orders of a deeper, different kind. But Lucius was a soldier, with a soldier's sense of duty; he had accepted his sentence without question.

He passed his days in contemplation—a necessity, though Lucius knew there were men who never managed it, the ones whose howls of loneliness he could hear at night. The prison had a small courtyard; once a week the inmates were allowed outside, but only one at a time, and only for an hour. Lucius himself had spent the first six months of his incarceration convinced he would go mad. There were only so many push-ups a man could do, only so much sleep to be had, and barely a month of his imprisonment had passed before Lucius had begun to talk to himself: rambling monologues about everything and nothing, the weather and the meals, his thoughts and memories, the world beyond the walls of the stockade and what was happening out there now. Was it summer? Had it rained? Would there be biscuits with dinner tonight? As the months had passed, these conversations had focused increasingly on his jailers: he was convinced that they were spying on him, and then, as his paranoia deepened, that they intended to kill him. He stopped sleeping, then eating; he refused to exercise, even to leave his cell at all. All night long he crouched on the edge of his cot, staring at the door, the portal of his murderers.

After some period of time in this tortured condition, Lucius decided he could endure it no longer. Only the thinnest vestige of his rational self remained; soon it would be lost to him completely. To die without a mind, its patterns of experience, memory, personality—the prospect was unendurable. Killing yourself in the cell wasn't easy, but it could be accomplished. Standing on the table, a determined suicide could tuck his head to his chest, tip forward, and break his neck in the fall.

Three times in a row Lucius attempted this; three times he failed. He began to pray—a simple, one-sentence prayer seeking God's cooperation. *Help me die.* His head was chiming from its multiple impacts on the cement floor; he had cracked a tooth. Once more he stood on the table, calibrated the angle of his fall, and cast himself into the arms of gravity.

He returned to consciousness after some unknown interval. He was lying on his back on the cold cement. Again the universe had refused him. Death was a door he could not open. Despair gripped him utterly, tears rising to his eyes.

Lucius, why have you forsaken me?

They were not words he heard. Nothing so simple, so commonplace, as that. It was the *feeling* of a voice—a gentle, guiding presence that lived beneath the surface of the world.

Don't you know that only I can take this from you? That death is mine alone to make?

It was as if his mind had opened like the covers of a book, revealing a hidden reality. He was lying on the floor, his body occupying a fixed point in space and time, and yet he felt his consciousness expanding, joining with a vastness he could not express. It was everywhere and nowhere; it existed on an invisible plane the mind could see but the eyes could not, distracted as they were by ordinary things—this cot, that toilet, these walls. He plunged into a peacefulness that flowed through his being on waves of light.

The work of your life is not done, Lucius.

And, just like that, his incarceration was over. The walls of his cell were the thinnest tissue, a ruse of matter. Day by day his contemplations deepened, his mind fusing with the force of peace and forgiveness and wisdom he had discovered. This was God, of course, or could be called God. But even that term seemed too small, a word made by men for that which had no name. The world was not the world; it was an expression of a deeper reality, as the paint on the canvas was an expression of the artist's thoughts. And with this awareness came the knowledge that the journey of his life was not complete, that his true purpose had yet to be unveiled.

Another thing: God seemed to be a woman.

He had been raised in the orphanage, among the sisters; he had no memories of his parents, of any other life. At sixteen he had enlisted in the DS, as nearly all the boys in the orphanage did in those days; when the call had gone out for volunteers to join the Second Expeditionary, Lucius had been among the first. This was right after the event known as the Massacre of the Field—eleven families ambushed on a picnic, twenty-eight people killed or taken—and many of the men who had survived that day had joined up as well. But Lucius's motives were less decisive. Even as a boy he had never been swayed by the stories of the great Niles Coffee, whose heroics seemed transparently impossible. Who in his right mind would actually *hunt* the dracs? But Lucius was young, restless as are all young men, and he had wearied of his duties: standing watch on the city walls, sweeping the fields, chasing down kids who broke curfew. Of course there were always dopeys around (picking them off from the observation platforms, though frowned upon as a waste of ammunition, was generally allowed if you didn't overdo it) and the diversion of the occasional bar brawl in H-town to break up. But these things, distracting though they were, could not compensate for the weight of boredom. If signing on with a bunch of death-loving lunatics was the only other option for Lucius Greer, then so be it.

Yet it was in the Expeditionary that Lucius found the very thing he needed, that had been absent from his life: a family. On his first detail he'd been assigned to the Roswell Road, escorting convoys of men and supplies to the garrison—at the time, just a threadbare outpost. In his unit were two new recruits, Nathan Crukshank and Curtis Vorhees. Like Lucius, Cruk had enlisted straight out of the DS, but Vorhees was, or had been, a farmer; as far as Lucius knew, the man had never even fired a gun. But he'd lost a wife and two young girls in the field, and under the circumstances, nobody was going to say no. The trucks always drove straight through the night, and on the return trip to Kerrville, their convoy was ambushed. The attack came just an hour before dawn. Lucius was riding with Cruk and Vor in a Humvee behind the first tanker. When the virals rushed them, Lucius thought: That's it, we're done. There's no way I'm getting out of this alive. But Crukshank, at the wheel, either didn't agree or didn't care. He gunned the engine, while Vorhees, on the fifty-cal, began to pick them off. They didn't know that the driver of the tanker, taken through the windshield, was already dead. As they ran alongside, the tanker swerved to the left, clipping the front of the Humvee. Lucius must have been knocked cold, because the next thing he knew, Cruk was dragging him from the wreckage. The tanker was in flames. The rest of the convoy was gone, vanished down the Roswell Road.

They'd been left behind.

The hour that followed was both the shortest and the longest of Lucius's life. Time and time again, the virals came. Time and time again, the three men managed to repel them, saving their bullets until the last instant, often when the creatures were just steps away. They might have tried to make a run for it, but the overturned Humvee was the best protection they had, and Lucius, whose ankle was broken, couldn't move.

By the time the patrol found them, sitting in the roadway, they were laughing till the tears streamed down their faces. He knew that he'd never feel closer to anyone than the two men who'd walked with him down the dark hallway of that night.

Roswell, Laredo, Texarkana; Lubbock, Shreveport, Kearney, Colorado. Whole years passed without Lucius's coming in sight of Kerrville, its haven of walls and lights. His home was elsewhere now. His home was the Expeditionary.

Until he met Amy, the Girl from Nowhere, and everything changed.

He was to receive three visitors.

The first came early on a morning in September. Greer had already finished his breakfast of watery porridge and completed his morning calisthenics: five hundred push-ups and sit-ups, followed by an equivalent number of squats and thrusts. Suspended from the pipe that ran along the ceiling of his cell, he did a hundred chin-ups in sets of twenty, front and back, as God ordained. When this was done, he sat on the edge of his cot, stilling his mind to commence his invisible journey.

He always began with a rote prayer, learned from the sisters. It was not the words that mattered, rather their rhythm; they were the equivalent of stretching before exercise, preparing the mind for the leap to come.

He had just begun when his thoughts were halted by a thunk of tumblers; the door to his cell swung open.

"Somebody to see you, Sixty-two."

Lucius rose as a woman stepped through—slight of build, with black hair threaded with gray and small dark eyes that radiated an undeniable authority. A woman you could not help but reveal yourself to, to whom all your secrets were an open book. She was carrying a small portfolio under her arm.

"Major Greer."

"Madam President."

She turned to the guard, a heavyset man in his fifties. "Thank you, Sergeant. You may leave us."

The guard was named Coolidge. One got to know one's jailors, and he and Lucius were well acquainted, even as Coolidge seemed to possess no idea of what to make of Lucius's devotions. A practical, ordinary man, his mind earnest but slow, with two grown sons, both DS, as he was.

"You're sure?"

"Yes, thank you. That will be all."

The man departed, sealing the door behind him. Stepping farther inside, the president glanced around the boxy room.

"Extraordinary." She directed her eyes at Lucius. "They say you never leave."

"I don't see a reason to."

"But what can you possibly do all day?"

Lucius offered a smile. "What I was doing when you arrived. Thinking."

"Thinking," the president repeated. "About what?"

"Just thinking. Having my thoughts."

The president lowered herself into the chair. Lucius followed her lead, sitting on the edge of the cot, so that the two were face-to-face.

"The first thing to say is that I'm not here. That's *official*. Unofficially, I will tell you that I am here to seek your help on a matter of crucial importance. You have been the subject of much discussion, and I am relying on your discretion. No one is to know about our conversation. Is that clear?"

"All right."

She opened the portfolio, withdrew a yellowed sheet of paper, and handed it to Lucius.

"Do you recognize this?"

A map, drawn in charcoal: the line of a river, and a hastily sketched road, and dotted lines marking the fringes of a compound. Not just a compound: an entire city.

"Where did you find it?" asked Lucius.

"That's not important. Do you know it?"

"I should."

"Why?"

"Because I drew it."

His answer had been expected; Lucius discerned it in the woman's face.

"To answer your question, it was in General Vorhees's personal files at Command. It took a little digging to figure out who else had been with him. You, Crukshank, and a young recruit named Tifty Lamont."

Tifty. How many years since Lucius had heard the name spoken? Though, of course, everybody in Kerrville knew of Tifty Lamont. And Crukshank: Lucius felt a twinge of sadness for his lost friend, killed when the Roswell Garrison had been overrun, five years ago.

"This place on the map, do you think you could find it again?"

"I don't know. It was a long time ago."

"Have you ever told anyone about this?"

"When we reported it to Command, we were told in no uncertain terms not to speak about it."

"Do you remember where the order originated?"

Lucius shook his head. "I never knew. Crukshank was the officer in charge of the detail, and Vorhees was second. Tifty was the S2."

"Why Tifty?"

"In my experience, nobody could track like Tifty Lamont."

The president frowned again at the mention of this name: the great gangster Tifty Lamont, head of the trade, the most wanted criminal in the city.

"How many people do you think were there?"

"Hard to say. A lot. The place was at least twice the size of Kerrville. From what we could see, they were well armed, too."

"Did they have power?"

"Yes, but I don't think they were running on oil. More likely hydroelectric and biodiesel for the vehicles. The agricultural and manufacturing complexes were immense. Barracks housing. Three large structures, one at the center, a kind of dome, and a second to the south that looked like an old football stadium. The third was on the west side of the river—we weren't sure what it was. It looked like it was under construction. They were working on the thing day and night."

"And you made no contact?"

"No."

The president directed Lucius's attention to the perimeter. "This here . . ."

"Fortifications. A fence line. Nothing insubstantial, but not enough to keep the dracs out."

"Then what do you think it was for?"

"I couldn't say. But Crukshank had a theory."

"And what was that?"

"To keep people in."

The president glanced at the map, then back at Lucius. "And you've never spoken about this? Not to anyone."

"No, ma'am. Not until now."

A silence fell. Lucius had the impression that no more questions were forthcoming; the president had gotten what she'd come for. She returned the map to her portfolio. As she rose from the chair, Lucius said:

"If I may, Madam President, why are you asking me about this now? After all these years."

The president stepped to the door and knocked twice. As the tumblers turned, she turned back to Lucius.

"They say you've become a prayerful man."

Lucius nodded.

"Then you might want to pray that I'm wrong."

27

Peter was in the medical bay for ten days. Three cracked ribs, a dislocated shoulder, burns on his legs and feet, his hands scraped raw like slabs of meat; bruises and gashes and cuts all over, too many to count. He'd been knocked cold but had apparently failed, despite his best efforts, to crack his skull. Every movement hurt, even breathing.

"From what I hear, you're goddamn lucky to be alive," the doctor said—a man of about sixty with a bulbous nose veined from years on the lick and a voice so coarse it sounded drugged. His bedside manner involved using the same tone, more or less, that a person might take with a hopelessly disobedient dog. "Stay on your back, Lieutenant. You're mine until I say otherwise."

Henneman had debriefed Peter the day the team had returned to the garrison. He was still a little out of it, doped up on painkillers; the major's questions glided over his brain with the disassociated contours of a conversation occurring in another room among people he only vaguely knew. A man, a very old man, with a tattoo of a snake on his neck. Yes, Peter confirmed, nodding his head heavily against the pillow, that was what they saw. Did he tell them who he was? Ignacio, Peter replied. He told us his name was Ignacio. The major obviously had no idea what to make of these answers; neither did Peter. Henneman seemed to be asking the same questions again and again, in only slightly altered forms; at some point, Peter drifted off. When he opened his eyes again—as he would soon discover, a day and a night having passed—he was alone.

He saw no one else except the doctor until the afternoon of the fourth day, when Alicia appeared at his bedside. By this time Peter was sitting up, his left arm dressed in a sling to hold his shoulder in place. That afternoon he'd taken his first walk to the latrine, a milestone, though the voyage of just a few shuffling steps had left him enervated, and now he was faced with the problem of trying to feed himself with hands encased in mittenlike bandages.

"Flyers, you look like hell, Lieutenant."

The light in the tent was dim enough that she'd removed her glasses. The orange color of her eyes was something Peter was accustomed to, though she rarely let others see them. She slid into a chair at his bedside and gestured toward the bowl of cornmeal mush that Peter, without much success, was attempting to spoon in his mouth.

"Want a little help with that?"

"Don't you wish."

She flashed a smile. "Well, it's good to see you've still got your pride. Henneman grill you?"

"I barely remember it. I don't think he liked the answers very much." The spoon slipped from his grip, dragging a glob of the gluey paste onto his shirt. "Shit."

"Here, let me."

He was now endeavoring to clamp the spoon between his thumb and the edge of the bowl to wedge it into his palm. "I told you, I've got this."

"Will you? Just stop."

Peter sighed and let the spoon drop to the tray. Alicia dipped it into the bowl and aimed for his mouth. "Open up for mama."

"You know, you never struck me as the maternal type."

"In your case, I'm willing to make an exception. Just eat."

Bite by bite, the bowl was emptied. Alicia took a rag and wiped his chin.

"I can do that myself, you know."

"Nuh-uh. Comes with the service." She leaned back. "There, good as new." She put the rag aside. "We had the service for Satch this morning. It was nice. Henneman and Apgar both spoke."

Though Satch was presumed killed in the explosion, Henneman had led a squad back up the mountain to look for him. The gesture was symbolic; still, it had to be made. In any case, they'd found nothing. What had happened at the base of the cave would never be known.

"So that's that, I guess."

"Satch was a good guy. Everybody liked him."

"We always say that."

Alicia shrugged. "Doesn't make it any less true."

Peter knew they were thinking the same thing: the plan had been theirs, and now Satch was dead.

"Seeing as you're fed, I should be heading off. Apgar's sending me south to recon some of those oil fields."

"Lish, how did you know something was down there?"

The question seemed to catch her short. "I don't really have an answer, Peter. It was just . . . a feeling."

"A feeling."

She was staring past him. "I don't really know how to put it into words."

"I thought only Amy could do that."

Alicia shrugged, pushing the subject aside: *Don't press.* "I guess I owe you for going out on a limb for me like that. Nice to have a little company in the doghouse at least."

"This whole thing has had it, hasn't it?" he said glumly.

"Apgar's going to do what he's going to do. I'm not a mind reader."

"Do you think he believes us?"

Alicia said nothing. Her eyes had gone away again. Then, with a quizzical expression:

"Peter, do you remember that movie *Dracula*?"

The memory called him back five years. Peter had been watching it with Vorhees's men in the Colorado garrison on the night Alicia had returned from the mission that had found the nest of virals in an old copper mine.

"I didn't know you saw it."

"Saw it? Hell, I *studied* it. The thing is like a viral owner's manual. Never mind the cape and castle and all that nonsense. It's the rest that fits. A human being whose life has been 'unnaturally prolonged.' Using the stake in the heart to kill him. The way he has to sleep in his native soil. The whole business with the mirrors—"

"Like the pan in Las Vegas," Peter cut in. "I thought the same thing."

"It's as if their reflection, I don't know, screws them up somehow. The whole movie is like that."

"Lish, where are you going with this?"

She hesitated. "Something always nagged at me, a piece I couldn't place. Dracula has a sort of adjutant. Somebody who still looks human."

Peter remembered. "The crazy one who eats the spiders."

"That's the guy. Renfield. Dracula infects him, but he doesn't flip, at least not completely. He's more like somebody caught in the early stages of infection. It got me wondering, what if they all have somebody like that?" She was looking at him keenly now. "Do you remember what Olson said about Jude?"

Olson was the leader of the community they'd found in Nevada, the Haven—a whole town of people who would sacrifice their own to Babcock, First of Twelve. Olson had been nominally in charge, but the fact had emerged that it was Jude who really ran the place. He had some kind of special relationship to Babcock, though its nature had gone unexplained.

"'He was . . . familiar,'" Peter quoted. "I never understood what Olson meant. It didn't really make sense. And you *were* pointing a gun at his head."

"So I was. And believe me, there are days when I wish I'd gone ahead and pulled the trigger. But I don't think it was gibberish. I looked up the word at the library back in Kerrville. The dictionary said the definition was archaic, so I had to look that up too, which basically just means old. It said that a familiar is a kind of helper demon, like a witch's cat. A sort of assistant. Maybe that's what Olson was talking about."

Peter allowed himself several seconds to process this. "So what you're saying is that Ignacio was Martínez's . . . familiar."

Alicia shrugged. "Okay, it's a stretch. I'm sort of cobbling things together here. But the other thing to consider is the signal. Ignacio had a chip in him, just like Amy and the Twelve. That means he's connected to Project NOAH."

"Did you tell Apgar any of this?"

"Are you serious? I'm in enough trouble as it is."

Peter didn't doubt that. Nor did he doubt that whatever blame she had incurred for the botched raid on the cave was his as well.

Alicia rose to go. "Either way, we should know more about where we stand by the time I get back from Odessa. No point in worrying for now. I know you think you're indispensable, but we can get along without you for a few days."

"You're not making me feel any better."

She smiled. "Just don't expect me to come back to feed you again, Lieutenant. You only get that once."

As she moved toward the door, Peter said, "Lish, hold up a second."

She spun to look at him.

"What Ignacio said. 'He left us.' What do you think it means?"

"I don't have an answer for that. All I know is he should have been there."

"Where do you think he went?"

She didn't answer right away. A shadow moved over her face, a darkening from within. It wasn't anything Peter had seen before. Even in the most perilous circumstances, her composure was total. She was a woman of absolute focus, always giving her attention to the task at hand. This was similar, but the energy wasn't the same. It seemed to come from a deeper place.

"I wish I knew," she said, and slipped her glasses on. "Believe me."

Then she was gone, the flaps of the tent shifting with her departure. Peter felt her absence immediately, as he always did. It was true: they were always leaving each other.

Peter did not see her again. Six days later, he was released. His ribs would need longer to heal, and he would have to take it easy for a couple of weeks, but at least he was out of bed. Making his way across the garrison to report for duty, a surge lifted his steps. The sensation reminded him of a time many years ago when, just a boy, he'd been sick with a high fever, and after the fever had broken how just being up and about made even ordinary things seem charged with a fresh vitality.

Yet something else was different; Peter could feel it. Everything appeared normal—the soldiers on the catwalks, the roar of generators, the ordered movements of military activity all around—yet he sensed a shift, a discernible lessening of intensity.

He entered the command tent to find Apgar standing behind his desk of battered metal, scowling at a stack of papers.

"Jaxon. I didn't expect to see you for a couple more days. How are you feeling?"

The question struck Peter as uncharacteristically personal. "Fine, sir. Thank you for asking."

"Take a seat, won't you?"

For a while Apgar continued to shift his papers. Though not a large man—Peter stood at least two hands taller—the colonel exuded a strong, physical presence, his movements precise, nothing wasted. After a period of time that might have been two full minutes, he appeared to achieve a satisfactory ordering to the documents and lowered himself into his chair to face Peter across the desk.

"I have new orders for you. They came this morning in the pouch from Kerrville. Before you say anything, I want you to know this has nothing to do with what happened in Carlsbad. I've been expecting this for some time, actually."

The last of Peter's hopes sank beneath the waves. Going, going, gone. "We're abandoning the hunt, aren't we?"

"'Abandoning' would be too strong a word. Putting under review. There's a feeling at Command that some of our resources have to shift. For the time being, you're being transferred to the Oil Road."

It was worse than Peter had expected. "That's a job for Domestic Security."

"Generally, yes. But this isn't without precedent, and it comes from the president's office. Apparently she's of the opinion that security for oil shipments has been too lax, and she wants the Army to take a role. A transport leaves at the end of the week for Kerrville, and I want you on it. From there you'll report to the DS in Freeport."

Despite what Apgar said, Peter knew the decision had everything to do with Carlsbad. He was being demoted—if not in rank, then in responsibility.

"You can't do that, sir."

A lift of his eyebrows, no more. "Perhaps I misheard you,

Lieutenant. I could swear you just told me what I could and could not do."

Peter felt his face grow warm. "Sorry, Colonel. That's not what I meant."

Apgar studied Peter a moment. "Look, I get it, Jaxon. Tell me something. How long have you been out here?"

Of course the colonel knew the answer; he was asking only to make a point. "Sixteen months."

"A long time in the sticks. You should have been rotated out a while ago. The only reason you haven't is that you always put in a request to stay. I've let it go because I know what the hunt means to you. In a way, you're the reason all of us are here."

"There's no place else I want to be, sir."

"And you've made that abundantly clear. But you're only human, Lieutenant. Frankly, you need the break. I'm headed back to Kerrville after we button things up, and as soon as I can, I'll put in a request at Division to move you back out to the territories. I'm not in the habit of making deals, so I suggest you take this one."

There was nothing to do but agree. "If I may ask, Colonel, what about Lieutenant Donadio?"

"She's got new orders, too. This isn't just you. As soon as she returns from the slicks, she's going north to Kearney."

Fort Kearney was the northernmost outpost of the Expeditionary. With a supply line stretching all the way from Amarillo, it was typically shut down before the first snowfall.

"Why there? Winter's only a couple of months away."

"Command doesn't tell me everything, but from what I hear it's gotten pretty thick up there. Given her talents, I'm guessing they want a new S2 to help clear out the hostiles before they evac."

The explanation felt thin, but Peter knew better than to press.

"I'm sorry about Satch," Apgar continued. "He was a good officer. I know you were friends."

"Thank you, sir."

"Dismissed, Lieutenant."

Peter spent the rest of the week in a state of suspension. With nothing else to occupy his time, he mostly stayed in his quarters. The map on the inside lid of the locker, once a badge of purpose, now felt like a bad joke. Maybe there was something to Alicia's theory, and maybe there wasn't. It seemed likely they would never find out. He thought of the time before he'd joined the Expeditionary, wondering if he'd made a mistake by enlisting. Back then, the fight had been his alone. Now it belonged to a larger enterprise, one with rules and protocols and chains of command in which he had little, if any, say. He had surrendered his freedom to become just another junior officer about whom people would someday remark, "He was a good guy."

The morning of his departure arrived. Peter carted his locker to the staging area where the transport awaited, a semitrailer loaded with the tires Peter's men had brought down from Lubbock. He hoisted his baggage into the cargo compartment of the escort vehicle and climbed into the passenger seat.

"Good to be going home, sir?"

Peter merely nodded. Anything he might have said would have sounded peevish, and the driver, a corporal from Satch's squad, didn't deserve to bear the brunt of his bad mood.

"I'll tell you the first thing I do after I collect my scrip," the corporal said, his exuberance barely contained. "I'm going straight to H-town to spend half of it on lick and the other half in a whorehouse." Suddenly embarrassed, he glanced at Peter with a flustered look. "Um, sorry, sir."

"That's all right, Corporal."

"Anybody at home for you, Lieutenant? If you don't mind my asking."

The answer was too complicated to even begin. "In a way."

The corporal gave a knowing smile. "Well, whoever she is, I'm sure she'll be happy to see you."

The order was given; with a belch of diesel fumes, the convoy began to pull away. Peter was already settling into the trancelike state he hoped to maintain for the next three days when he heard someone yelling over the racket of engines.

"Hold at the gate!"

Alicia was jogging toward the Humvee. Peter drew down the window.

"I just got back an hour ago," she said. "Who do you think you are, leaving without saying goodbye?"

Her face was a mask of oily grime; she smelled faintly of petroleum. But the thing that caught his eye was a glint of metal on her collar: a pair of captain's bars.

"Well, look at that," he said, managing a wry grin that he hoped masked his envy. "I guess I'll have to start calling you 'sir.'"

"I like the ring of that. About time, if you ask me."

"Apgar's cycling me out."

"I know. The Oil Road." There was no reason to elaborate. "It's easy duty, Peter. You've earned it."

"That's what they tell me."

"Say hi to the Circuit for me. And Greer, if you see him."

Peter nodded. There was only so much that could be said with the driver present. "When do you leave for Kearney?"

"Two days."

"All eyes up there. Apgar says it's gotten pretty thick."

"You, too." She glanced at the driver, who was studying the wheel with his eyes, then back at Peter. "Don't worry. What we were talking about before. It's not over, okay?"

He felt, inside her words, the pressure of something unstated. From behind them rose an impatient roar of engines. Everyone was waiting.

"Sir, we really have to be going," the driver said.

"That's okay, we're done here." Alicia regarded Peter one last time. "I mean it, Peter. It'll be all right. Just go see your boy."

28

The first pain arrived, like a late train roaring into the station, on an afternoon in late September of warm Texas sunshine and a high blue sky. Amy was in the courtyard, watching the children play; in another few minutes the bell would sound, summoning them inside to finish their lessons, and Amy would return to the kitchen to help make dinner. An island of rest in the midst of the day's never-ending rhythm of tasks done and, just as swiftly, undone; always, when lunch was concluded and the dishes put away and the children set loose to burn off the morning's accumulated antsiness, Amy followed them outside and took up a position at the edge of the playground that was near enough for her to enjoy the bright energy of their activity while not so close as to allow the children to draw her in. These were her favorite thirty minutes of the day, and Amy had just closed her eyes and tilted her face to receive the warm rays of the early autumn sun when the pain hit: a powerful clenching in her midriff that caused her to bend sharply at the waist, stagger forward, and exhale a soft cry of shock that even in the busy hubbub of the courtyard could not fail to go unnoticed.

"Amy? Are you all right?"

The image of Sister Catherine—pale, long-faced, irises as blue as cornflowers—came into Amy's focus. The sweat was pouring off her; her hands and feet had turned to cold jelly. Everything below her waist seemed to have lost some essential density; in another moment Amy would, literally, melt to the ground. Part of her wanted to vomit while another part refused, creating an internal stalemate that rendered her unable to speak.

"Maybe you better sit down. You're white as a ghost."

Sister Catherine steered her to a bench against the wall of the orphanage—a distance of twenty feet that could have been a mile. By the time they reached it, Amy couldn't have taken another step without collapsing. With a bustle of concern, Sister Catherine left her, then returned with a cup of water, which she pressed into Amy's hand. Activity on the playground seemed to have proceeded without interruption, but Amy could sense that some of the children were watching her. The pain had dissipated into a more general nausea, but not the feeling of weakness. She felt both hot and cold. More sisters had crowded around, all speaking in hushed, earnest voices, questioning Sister Catherine. Amy didn't want the water but everyone was insistent. She took a small sip.

"I'm sorry," she managed to say. "One minute I was perfectly fine . . ."

"Over here, Sister," Catherine said, waving toward the doors to the orphanage. "Come quickly."

The small crowd parted as Sister Peg strode forward. The old woman studied Amy with a pinched expression that managed to seem both worried and irritated at the same time.

"Well? Will somebody tell me what happened here or will I have to guess?"

"I don't know," said Sister Catherine. "She just . . . collapsed."

The playground had been brought to a standstill. All the children were staring at her now. Amy looked for Caleb, but her view was blocked by Sister Peg. She couldn't recall a time when she'd ever felt ill; she understood the principle but had never experienced the reality. Almost worse than the pain was the embarrassment. It made her want to say something, say anything, to get everyone to stop looking at her.

"Amy? Is that what happened?"

"I just felt dizzy. My stomach hurt. I don't know what it was."

The old woman pressed her palm to Amy's forehead. "Well, I don't think you have a fever."

"It was probably something I ate. I'm sure if I sit here another minute I'll be okay."

"She doesn't look good," Sister Catherine chimed in, and the others nodded. "Honestly, Amy, I thought you were going to pass out."

A general murmuring ensued. No, she didn't look good, not good at all. Could it be the flu? Something worse? If it was something the girl had eaten, would they all become sick, too?

Sister Peg allowed the group its moment of conjecture, then brought them to silence with a raised hand. "I don't see a reason to take chances. Off to bed with you, Amy."

"But I'm really feeling much better. I'm sure I'll be all right."

"I'll be the judge of that, thank you. Sister Catherine, will you assist her to the dormitory?"

Catherine helped her to her feet. She felt a little unsteady, and her stomach wasn't quite what it should be. But the worst of it had passed. Catherine led her into the building and up the stairs to the room where all the sisters slept, except for Sister Peg, who, being in charge, had quarters of her own. Amy undressed and got into bed.

"Can I do anything else?" Sister Catherine was drawing the shades.

"I'm fine." Amy did her best to smile. "I think I just need to rest a bit."

Standing at the foot of the cot, Catherine regarded her for a moment. "You know what this could be, don't you? A girl your age."

Your age. If Sister Catherine only knew, thought Amy. Yet Amy also understood what the woman was suggesting. The idea took her by surprise.

Sister Catherine smiled with sympathy. "Well, if it is, you'll know soon enough. Believe me, we've all been through it."

Making Amy promise to call her if she needed anything, Catherine made her departure. Amy leaned back on her cot and closed her eyes. The afternoon bell had rung; downstairs, the children would be filing in for their lessons, smelling of sun and sweat and fresh afternoon air, some of them, perhaps, wondering what all the fuss on the playground had been about. Surely Caleb would be worried about her; Amy should have told Sister Catherine to say something to the boy. *She's just tired. She was feeling out of sorts. She'll be right as rain in a jiff, you'll see.*

And yet: *A girl your age.* Was it possible? All the sisters complained about the "ordeal," as they called it; it was a common joke of the orphanage that living in such tight quarters, everybody menstruated at the same time, making one week of every four a nightmare of bloody rags and quick tempers. For a hundred years Amy had lived in complete innocence of these basic facts; even now she could not have said she understood the phenomenon completely, but she grasped the gist. You bled, not a lot but some, and this would be uncomfortable, extending over a period of days. For a while Amy had regarded the prospect with horror, but over time this feeling had yielded to a fierce, almost biological yearning, and the fear that none of this would ever happen to her, that this door of human belonging would always stay closed and she would live in a child's body forever.

She checked: no, she wasn't bleeding. If Sister Catherine was correct, how long before it started? She wished she'd taken the opportunity to ask Catherine more. How much blood would there be, how much pain, how would she feel different? Though in her case, Amy reasoned, nothing would quite be the same. Maybe it would be worse; maybe it would be better; maybe it would never happen at all.

She would have liked to be a woman. To see it reflected in another's eyes. For her body to know what her heart already did.

A scratchy mewing interrupted her train of thought. Of course Mouser would come to check on her. The old gray cat ambled to her bedside. A pitiful sight he was—eyes fogged with cataracts, fur matted and tacky, his tail dragging with age. "Did you come to look in on me? Did you, boy? Well, come here." Amy lifted him from the floor, leaned back on her cot, and balanced him on her chest. She ran her hands through his coat; he replied in kind, butting his head against her neck. *The sun is out, why are you in bed?* He circled three times before settling down on her chest, loudly purring. *It's fine. You sleep. I'll be right here.*

Amy closed her eyes.

Then it was night, and Amy was outside.

How had she gotten outside?

She was still wearing her nightgown; her feet were bare and damp with dew. The hour was impossible to know but felt late. Was she dreaming? But if she was still asleep, why did everything feel so real? She took measure of her surroundings. She was near the dam on the upstream side. The air was cool and moist. She felt a lingering urgency, as if she'd awoken from a dream of being chased. Why was she here? Had she been sleepwalking?

Something brushed her leg, making her startle. She looked down to see Mouser, staring at her with his clouded eyes. He began, loudly, to meow, then trotted toward the dam, stopping a few feet away to look at her again.

His meaning was clear; Amy followed. The old cat led her toward a small concrete structure at the base of the dam. Something mechanical? Mouser was standing at the door, meowing.

She opened the door and stepped inside. The darkness was total; how would she find her way? She felt along the wall, searching for a switch. There. A bank of lights flickered to life. At the center of the small room was a metal rail guarding a circular staircase. Mouser was standing on the top step. He turned to look at her, issued one more insistent meow, and descended.

The stairs spiraled down. At the bottom she found herself once again in blackness. Another fumbling search for a light switch; then she saw where she was. A wide tube, leading in only one direction, forward. Mouser was well ahead of her, dragging elongated shadows over the walls. His urgency was contagious, drawing her deeper into this underground world. They came to a second hatch, sealed with a ring. A length of pipe lay on the floor beside it. Amy threaded it between the spokes and turned; the door swung open, revealing a ladder. She turned to consult Mouser, who met her gaze with a skeptical look.

Not for me, I'm afraid. You're on your own now.

She descended. Something awaited her at the bottom; she felt its presence, deep in her bones. Something terrible and sad and full of longing. Her feet touched down. Another shaft, wider than the first. Water trickled along the floor. At the far end, she saw a circle of light. Now she knew where she was: one of the spillway tubes. It was moonlight she was seeing. She moved toward its penumbral glow just as a shadow moved across it. Not a shadow: a figure.

She knew.

Amy, Amy, daughter of my heart.

He reached toward her through the bars: a long, crooked claw, the digits distended, tipped with curving talons. As their palms touched, his fingers curled first through and then around her own. She felt no fear, only a spreading lightness. Her vision blurred with tears.

Amy, I remember. I remember everything.

Their hands held fast. The feel of his touch had dispersed to every part of her, bathing her in its warmth—a warmth of love, of home. It said: *Always I will be here. I will be the one to keep you safe.*

My brave girl. My brave Amy. Don't cry now.

A great sob shook her, a flood of pure emotion. She was happy, she was sad, she felt the weight of her life.

—What's happening to me? Why do I feel like I do? Please, tell me.

His face made no expression, for there could be none; all that he was, was in his eyes.

All your questions will be answered. He is waiting for you, in the ship. I will show you the way when the time comes.

—When? When will it come?

But Amy knew the answer even as she spoke the words.

Soon, said Wolgast. *Very, very soon.*

V

THE OIL ROAD

Can I see another's woe,
And not be in sorrow too?
Can I see another's grief,
And not seek for kind relief?

—WILLIAM BLAKE,
"ON ANOTHER'S SORROW"

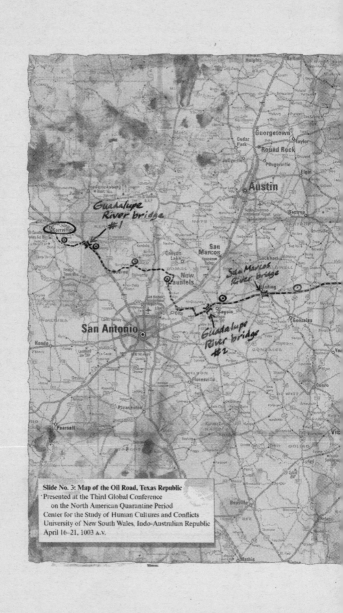

Guadalupe
River bridge
#1

San Marcos
River bridge

Guadalupe
River bridge
#2

Slide No. 3: Map of the Oil Road, Texas Republic
Presented at the Third Global Conference
on the North American Quarantine Period
Center for the Study of Human Cultures and Conflicts
University of New South Wales, Indo-Australian Republic
April 16–21, 1003 A.V.

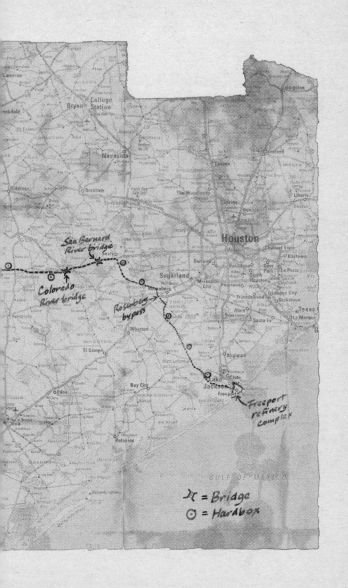

San Bernard
River bridge

Colorado
River bridge

Rosenberg
bypass

Houston

Sugarland

Lake
Jackson

Freeport
refinery
complex

)(= Bridge
⊙ = Hardbox

GULF OF MEXICO

29

Michael Fisher, oiler first class—Michael the Clever, Bridger of Worlds—aroused from a deep and dreamless sleep to the sensation, unmistakable, that somebody was fucking him.

He opened his eyes. Lore was straddling him, her spine bowed forward, her brow glazed with a glinting, sex-fired sweat. Flyers, he thought, hadn't they just done this? Most of the night, in fact? Hugely, hilariously, in every position allowable to human physiology in a sleeping berth the approximate dimensions of a coffin?

"Good morning," she announced with a grin. "I hope you don't mind I got started without you."

Well, so be it, Michael thought. There were certainly worse ways to face the day. From the flush of her cheeks, he could tell that Lore was well on the way, and, come to think of it, he wasn't far behind. She had begun to rock her hips, the weight of her sex lapping against him like waves on a beach. In and out went the waves.

"Not so fast, mister."

"For Christ's sake, keep it down!" a voice barked from above.

"Shut up, Ceps," Lore replied, "I'm working in here."

"You're making me hard! It's disgusting!"

This conversation seemed to Michael to be occurring in some distant orbit. With everyone bunked together, nothing but thin curtains for privacy, you learned to tune things out. But the feeling was more than that. Even as his senses sailed away into pure physicality, something about sex, its hypnotic rhythms, prompted in him a kind of disassociation. It was as if his mind were lagging three steps behind his body, sight-seeing its way through a landscape of various concerns and sadnesses and emotionally neutral images that rose before him like bubbles of expanding gas in the boiler. A decaying gasket that needed replacing. The delivery schedule of fresh crude down from the depot. Memories of the Colony, which he never otherwise thought about. Above him, Lore continued on her journey, while Michael drifted in this current of mental disloyalty, trying to will his attentions into alignment with hers. It seemed the least he could do.

And in the end, he did. Lore's accelerating passion won the day. By the time they pulled the curtain back, Ceps was gone. The clock above the hatch read 0630.

"Shit."

Michael swung his feet to the floor and yanked on his jumpsuit. Lore, behind him, wrapped her arms around his chest.

"Stay. I'll make it worth your while."

"I'm first shift. If I'm late again, Karlovic will chew my ass for breakfast." He stuffed his feet into his boots and swiveled his face to kiss her: a taste of salt, and sex, and something all her own. Michael wouldn't have said it was love between them, exactly. Sex was a way to pass the time, but over the months their relationship had evolved, little by little, into something more than habit.

"You were thinking again, weren't you?"

"Who, me?"

"Don't lie." Her tone wasn't bitter, merely correcting. "You know, someday I'm going to fuck all the worries out of you." She sighed and relaxed her grip. "It's all right. Go."

He rose from the berth and took his hard hat and gloves from the post. "I'll see you later?"

She had already lain back down on the cot. "That you will."

As Michael exited the barracks, the sun was just lifting over the Gulf, making its surface shimmer like a sheet of hammered metal. It might have been the first week of October, but the heat was already building, the ocean air tart as ever with salt and the sulfurous stench of burning butane. With his stomach growling—food would have to wait—he strode at a brisk clip across the compound, past the commissary and weight cages and DS barracks to the Quonset hut, where the workers on the morning shift had gathered. Karlovic, the chief engineer, was calling out assignments from the roster. He shot Michael a cold glance.

"Are we interrupting your beauty sleep, Fisher? Our mistake."

"Right." Michael was zipping his jumpsuit. "Sorry."

"You'll be even sorrier. You'll be firing up the Bomb. Ceps will be your second. Try not to blow up your crew."

Distillation Tower No. 1, known as the Bomb, was the

oldest of the lot, its rusty bulk held together by a combination of patch welds, baling wire, and prayer. Everybody said it was a matter of time before she was either decommissioned or launched a cooking crew halfway to Mars.

"Thanks, boss. That's swell of you."

"Don't mention it." Karlovic swept his gaze over the group. "All right, everyone. Seven days until we ship. I want those tankers full, people. And Fisher, hang back a minute. I want a word with you."

The crews dispersed to their towers. Michael followed Karlovic into the hut. Christ, what now? He hadn't been late by more than a couple of minutes, hardly worth a dressing down.

"Listen, Dan, I'm sorry about this morning—"

Karlovic didn't let him finish. "Forget it, that's not what I want to talk to you about." Hitching up his pants, he lowered his bulk into the chair behind his desk. Karlovic was heavy in the true sense, not fat but large in every aspect, a man of weight and heft. Tacked on the wall over his head were dozens of sheets of paper—duty rosters, work flows, delivery schedules. "I had you on the Bomb anyway. You and Ceps are the best I've got for hotwork. Take it as a compliment I'm putting the pair of you on that cranky old bitch. If I had my druthers, that thing would be in the scrap pile."

Michael didn't doubt that this was so; on the other hand, he knew strategically timed praise when he heard it. "So?"

"So this."

Karlovic slid a sheet of paper across his desk. Michael's eyes fell quickly to the signature at the bottom: Victoria Sanchez, President, Texas Republic. He quickly scanned the letter's three short paragraphs. *Well, I'll be,* he thought.

"Any idea what this is about?"

"What makes you think I would?"

"You were the last crew chief on the offload. Maybe you caught wind of something while you were up there. Talk around the depot, extra military hanging around."

"Nothing that rings a bell." Michael shrugged. "Have you spoken to Stark? Maybe he knows."

Stark was the refinery's chief security officer. He was something of a loudmouth and liked the lick too much, but he generally commanded respect among both the oilers and DS, if for no other reason than his prowess at the poker table. His caginess with the cards had cost Michael a bundle, not that the scrip was any big loss—within the fences of the refinery, there was nothing to spend it on.

"Not yet. This won't sit well with him, though." Karlovic studied Michael. "Aren't you guys friends? That whole California thing."

"I know him, yeah."

"So maybe you can grease the gears a bit. Act as a sort of, I don't know, unofficial liaison between DS and the military."

Michael allowed himself a few seconds to probe his feelings. He'd be glad to see someone from the old days, but at the same time he was aware of an inner disturbance, a sense of exposure. The self-contained life of an oiler had, in many ways, rescued him from the grief of losing his sister, occupying the mental space she had left behind. Part of him knew he was hiding, but the rest of him didn't care.

"It should be no problem."

"I'll count it as a favor. Handle it how you like." Karlovic angled his head toward the door. "Now get out of here, you've got oil to cook. And I meant what I said. Watch your ass with that thing."

Michael arrived at the distillation tower to find his crew, a dozen roughnecks, standing around wearing expressions of puzzlement. The tanker with its cargo of fresh slick sat idle. Ceps was nowhere to be seen.

"Okay, I'll bite. Why aren't you people filling this thing?"

Ceps crawled from beneath the heating element at the base of the tower. His hands and bare arms were caked with black goo. "We'll have to flush her first. We've got at least two meters of residuum in the base."

"Fuck sake, that will take all morning. Who was the last crew chief?"

"This thing hasn't been fired in months. You'd have to ask Karlovic."

"How much crude will we have to drain off?"

"A couple of hundred barrels anyway."

Eight thousand gallons of partially refined petroleum that had been sitting for who knew how long: they would need a large waste tanker, then a pumper truck and high-pressure steam hoses to flush the tower. They were looking at twelve hours minimum, sixteen to refill it and light the heating element, twenty-four before the first drop came out of the pipe. Karlovic would pop an aneurysm.

"Well, we better get started. I'll call in the order, you get the hoses ready." Michael shook his head. "I find who did this, I will kick his sorry ass."

The draining took the rest of the morning. Michael declared the leftover oil unusable and sent the truck to the waste pools for burning. Bleeding off the junk was the easy part; flushing the tank was the job everyone dreaded. Water injected into the top of the tower would clean out most of the residuum—the sticky, toxic residue of the refining process—but not all; three men would have to suit up and go inside to brush down the base and flush out the asphalt drain. The only way in was a blind port, a meter wide, through which they'd have to crawl on their hands and knees. The term for this was "going up the anus"—not an inaccurate description, in Michael's opinion. Michael would be one of the three. There was no rule about this; it was simply his habit, a gesture toward morale. For the other two, the custom was to draw straws.

The first to pull a short straw was Ed Pope, the oldest man on the crew. Ed had been Michael's trainer, the one to show him the ropes. Three decades on the cookers had taken their toll; the man's body read like a logbook of catastrophes. Three fingers sheared off by the thrown blade of a rebar cutter. One side of his head and neck seared to a hairless pink slab by a propane explosion that had killed nine men. He was deaf in that ear, and his knees were so shot that watching him bend made Michael wince. Michael thought about giving him a pass, but he knew Ed was too proud to accept, and he watched as the man made his way to the hut to suit up.

The second short straw was Ceps. "Forget it, I need you out here on the pumps," said Michael.

Ceps shook his head. The day had left them all impatient. "The hell with it. Let's just get this done."

They wriggled into their hazard suits and oxygen packs and gathered their gear together: heavy brushes on poles, buckets of solvent, high-pressure wands that would feed back to a compressor. Michael pulled his mask down over his face, taped the seals on his gloves, and checked his O_2. Though they'd vented the tower, the air inside it was still as lethal as it got—an airborne soup of petroleum vapors and sulfides that could sear your lungs into jerky. Michael felt a positive pop of pressure in the mask, switched on his head-lamp, and knelt to unbolt the port.

"Let's go, hombres."

He slithered through, dropping down to find himself in three inches of standing muck. Ed and Ceps crawled in behind him.

"What a mess."

Michael reached down into the sludge and opened the asphalt drain; the three of them began to sweep the residuum toward it. The temperature inside the tower was at least a hundred degrees; the sweat was raining off them, the trapped moisture of their breath fogging their faceplates. Once they'd cleared the worst of it, they dumped the solvent, hooked up their wands, and commenced spraying down the walls and floor.

Inside their suits, with the roar of the compressor, conversation was just about impossible. The only thing to think about was finishing the job and getting out. They'd been at it for only a couple of minutes when Michael felt a tap on his shoulder. He turned to see Ceps pointing at Ed. The man was just standing there, facing the wall like a statue, his wand held loosely at his side. While Michael watched, it slipped from his hand, though Ed seemed not to notice.

"Something's wrong with him!" Ceps yelled over the racket.

Michael stepped forward and turned Ed by the shoulders. All he got was a blank stare.

"Ed, you okay?"

The man's face startled to life. "Oh, hey, Michael," he said, too brightly. "Hey-hey, hey-hey. Woo-woo."

"What's he saying?" Ceps called out.

Michael drew a finger over his throat to tell Ceps to cut the compressor. He looked at Ed squarely. "Talk to me, buddy."

A girlish giggle escaped the man's lips. He was heaving for breath, one hand lifting toward his faceplate. "Ashblass. Minfuth. Minfuth!"

Michael saw what was about to happen. As Ed reached for his mask, Michael seized him by the arms. The man was no kid, but he was no weakling either. He wriggled fiercely in Michael's grasp, trying to break free, his face blue with panic. Not panic, Michael realized: hypoxia. His body convulsed with a massive twitch, his knees melting under him, his full weight crashing into Michael's arms.

"Ceps, help me get him out of here!"

Ceps grabbed the man by his feet. His body had gone limp. Together they carried him to the port.

"Somebody take him!" Michael yelled.

Hands appeared to pull from the far side; Michael and Ceps shoved his body through. Michael scrambled into the port, tearing off his faceplate and gloves the moment he hit fresh air. Ed was lying face-up on the hardpan; someone had stripped off his mask and backpack. Michael dropped to his knees beside the body. An ominous stillness: the man wasn't breathing. Michael placed the heel of his right hand at the center of Ed's chest, positioned the left on top, laced his fingers together, and pushed. Nothing. Again and again he pushed, counting to thirty, as he had learned to do, then slipped one hand behind Ed's neck to tip his airway open, pinched his nose, and pressed his mouth over the man's blue lips. One breath, two breaths, three. Michael's mind was clear as ice, his thoughts held in the grip of a singular purpose. Just as all seemed lost, he felt a sharp contraction of the diaphragm; Ed's chest inflated, taking in a voluminous breath of air. He turned his face to the side, gasping and coughing.

Michael rocked back on his heels, landing ass-down in the dust, his pulse pounding with adrenaline. Somebody handed him a canteen: Ceps.

"You okay, pal?"

The question didn't even make sense to him. He took a long drink, swishing the water inside his mouth, and spat it away. "Yeah."

Eventually somebody helped Ed to his feet. Michael and Ceps escorted him into the hut and sat him down on one of the benches.

"How you feeling?" Michael asked.

A bit of color had flowed back into Ed's cheeks, though his skin was damp and clammy-looking. He shook his head miserably. "I don't know what happened. I could have sworn I checked my oxygen."

Michael had already looked; the bottles were empty. "Maybe it's time, Ed."

"Jesus, Michael. Are you firing me?"

"No. It's your choice. I'm just saying there's no disgrace in calling it a day." When Ed made no reply, Michael rose to his feet. "Give it some thought. I'll back you, whatever you want to do. You want a ride to the barracks?"

Ed was staring disconsolately into space. Michael could read the truth in his face: the man had nothing else.

"I think I'll sit here a while. Get my strength back."

Michael stepped from the hut to find the rest of the crew hovering by the door. "What the hell are you all standing around for?"

"The shift's over, Chief."

Michael checked his watch: so it was.

"Not for us it isn't. Show's over, everybody. Get your lazy asses back to work."

It was past midnight when Lore said to him, "Lucky thing, about Ed."

The two of them were curled in Michael's berth. Despite Lore's best efforts, his mind had been unable to move on from the day's events. All he kept seeing when he closed his eyes was the look on Ed's face in the hut, like someone being marched to the gallows.

"What do you mean, lucky?"

"That you were there, I mean. That thing you did."

"It wasn't anything."

"Yes, it was. The man could have died. How did you know how to do that?"

The past loomed up inside him, a wave of pain.

"My sister taught me," said Michael. "She was a nurse."

30

THE CITY
Kerrville, Texas

They arrived behind the rain. First the fields, sodden with moisture, the air rich with the smell of dirt, then, as they ascended out of the valley, the walls of the city, looming eight stories tall against the brown Texas hills. At the gate they found themselves in a line of traffic—transports, heavy mechanicals, DS pickups crowded with men in their thick pads. Peter climbed out, asked the driver to deposit his locker at the barracks, and showed his orders to the guard at the pedestrian tunnel, who waved him through.

"Welcome home, sir."

After sixteen months in the territories, Peter's senses were instantly assaulted by the vast, overwhelming humanness of the place. He'd spent little time in the city, not enough to adjust to its claustrophobic density of sounds and smells and overflowing faces. The Colony had never numbered more than a hundred souls; here there were over forty thousand.

Peter made his way to the quartermaster to collect his pay. He'd never really gotten used to the idea of money, either. "Equal share," the governing economic unit of the Colony, had made sense to him. You had your share, and you used it how you liked, but it was the same as everybody else's, never less or more. How could these slips of inked paper—Austins they were called, after the man whose image, with its high, domed forehead and beaked nose and perplexing arrangement of clothing, adorned each bill—actually correspond to the value of a person's labor?

The clerk, a civilian, doled out the scrip from the lockbox, snapping the bills onto the counter, and shoved a clipboard toward him through the grate, all without once meeting his eye.

"Sign here."

The money, a fat wad, felt odd in Peter's pocket. As he stepped back into the brightening afternoon, he was already scheming how to be rid of it. Six hours remained until curfew—barely enough time to visit both the orphanage and the stockade before reporting to the barracks. The afternoon was all he had; the transport to the refinery was leaving at 0600.

Greer would come first; that way Peter wouldn't have to disappoint Caleb by leaving before the horn. The stockade was located in the old jailhouse on the west edge of downtown. He signed in at the desk—in Kerrville you were always signing things, another oddity—and stripped off his blade and sidearm. He was about to proceed when the guard stopped him.

"Have to pat you down, Lieutenant."

As a member of the Expeditionary, Peter was accustomed to a certain automatic deference—certainly from a junior domestic, not a day over twenty. "Is that really necessary?"

"I don't make the rules, sir."

Irritating, but Peter didn't have time for an argument. "Just be quick about it."

The guard ran his hands up and down Peter's arms and legs, then produced a heavy ring of keys and led him back into the holding area, a long hall of heavy steel doors. The air was dense and smelled of men. They came to the cell marked with the number 62.

"Funny," the guard remarked, "Greer doesn't see anyone in close to three years, and now he's had two visitors in just a month."

"Who else was here?"

"I wasn't on duty. You'd have to ask him."

The guard located the correct key, inserted it into the tumbler, and swung the door open to a sound of groaning hinges.

Greer, shoeless, clothed only in a pair of rough canvas trousers cinched at his waist, was seated on the edge of his bunk. His broad chest gleamed with perspiration; his hands were serenely folded in his lap. His hair, what remained of it, a silvering white, fanned to his massive shoulders, while a great tangle of beard—the beard of a prophet, a wanderer in the wilderness—straggled halfway up his cheeks. A deep stillness radiated off him; the impression he communicated was one of composure, as if he had reduced his mind and body to their essences. For an unsettling moment, he gave no indication that he was aware of the two figures standing in the doorway, causing Peter to wonder if the isolation had done something to his mind. But then he lifted his eyes, his face brightening.

"Peter. There you are."

"Major Greer. It's good to see you."

Greer laughed ironically, his voice thick with disuse. "Nobody's called me that in some time. It's just Lucius now. Or Sixty-two, if you prefer. Most people seem to." Greer addressed the guard. "Give us a few minutes, will you, Sanders?"

"I'm not supposed to leave anyone alone with a prisoner."

Peter shot him a cold glare. "I think I can take care of myself, son."

A moment's hesitancy; then the guard relented. "Well, seeing as it's you, sir, I guess ten minutes would be okay. After that my shift ends, though. I don't want to get in trouble."

Peter frowned. "Do we know each other?"

"I saw your signature. Everybody knows who you are. You're the guy from California. It's, like, a legend." All pretense of his authority was gone; suddenly he was just a starstruck kid, his face beaming with admiration. "What was it like? Coming all that way, I mean."

Peter wasn't quite sure how to respond. "It was a long walk."

"I don't know how you did it. I would have been scared shitless."

"Take my word for it," Peter assured him, "that was a big part of it."

Sanders left them alone. Peter took the room's only chair, straddling it backward across from Greer.

"Looks like you made quite an impression on our boy there. I told you it would be a hard story to keep quiet."

"It's still strange to hear it," Peter said. "How are you doing?"

Greer shrugged. "Oh, I get by. And you? You look well, Peter. The uniform suits you."

"Lish says hello. She just got bumped to captain."

Greer nodded equably. "A remarkable girl, our Lish. Destined for big things, I'd say. So how goes the fight? Or do I have to ask?"

"Not so good. We're oh-for-three. The whole Martínez thing was a catastrophe. Now it looks like Command is having second thoughts."

"That's always what they've been best at. Not to worry, the winds will turn. One thing you learn in here is patience."

"It's not the same without you. I can't help thinking it would be different if you were there."

"Oh, I very much doubt that. This has always been your show. I knew it the moment I met you. Caught upside down in a spinning net, wasn't it?"

Peter laughed at the memory. "Michael puked all over us."

"That's right, I remember now. How is he? I imagine he's not the same kid I knew back then. Always had an answer to everything."

"I doubt he's changed much. Either way, I'll find out tomorrow. They're posting me down to the refinery."

Greer frowned. "Why there?"

"Some new initiative to secure the Oil Road."

"DS will love that. I'd say you've got your hands full with that lot." He gave his knees a slap to change the subject. "And Hollis, what do you hear of him?"

"Nothing good. He took Sara's death hard. The story is he's on the trade."

Greer considered this news for a moment. "On the whole, I can't say I blame him. That may seem strange to say, knowing Hollis, but more than one man has gone that way under those circumstances. I imagine he'll come around sooner or later. He's got a good head on his shoulders."

"And what about you? You're getting out soon. If you want, I can put a word in with Command. Maybe they'd let you reenlist."

But Greer shook his head. "I'm afraid those days are over for me, Peter. Don't forget, I'm a deserter. Once you cross that line, there's no going back."

"What will you do?"

Greer smiled mysteriously. "I imagine something will come along. It always does."

For a while they talked of the others, bits of news, stories from the past. Being with Greer, Peter felt a warm contentment, but accompanying that, a sense of loss. The major had entered his life just when Peter needed him; it was Greer's steadfast presence that had given him the will to move forward in the days when his resolve had wavered. It was a debt that Peter could never fully repay: the debt of borrowed courage. Peter sensed that Greer's incarceration had changed him. He was still the same man, although something inside him ran deeper, a river of inner calm. He seemed to have drawn strength from his isolation.

As the end of the ten minutes approached, Peter told the major about the cave, and the strange man, Ignacio, and Alicia's theory about what he was. Even as he spoke the words, he realized how far-fetched the idea sounded; and yet he felt its rightness. If anything, his feeling that the information was important had grown over the days.

"There may be something to that," Greer agreed. "He said, 'He left us'?"

"Those were his words."

Greer fell silent, stroking his long beard. "The question, of course, is where did Martínez go. Did Alicia have any ideas about that?"

"Not that she told me."

"And what do you think?"

"I think finding the Twelve is going to be more complicated than we planned on."

He waited, watching Greer's face. When the major made no reply, he said, "My offer still stands. We could really use you."

"You overestimate me, Peter. I was always just along for the ride."

"Not to me. Alicia would say the same thing. All of us would."

"And I accept the compliment. But it doesn't change a thing. What's done is done."

"It still doesn't seem right that you're in here."

Greer shrugged carelessly. "Maybe it is, maybe it isn't. Believe me, I've brooded plenty on the subject. The Expeditionary was my whole life, and I miss it. But I did what I thought was right in the moment. In the end, that's all a man has to measure his life, and it's plenty." His eyes narrowed on Peter. "Which isn't something I need to tell you, is it?"

The major had him dead to rights. "I suppose not."

"You're a good soldier, Peter. You always have been, and I wasn't lying about that uniform. It does suit you. The question is, do you suit it?"

The question wasn't accusing—if anything, the opposite. "Some days I wonder," Peter confessed.

"Everybody does. The military is what it is. You can hardly take a trip to the latrine without filling out a form in triplicate. But in your case, I'd say the question runs deeper. The man I met hanging upside down in that spinner—he wasn't following anybody's orders but his own. I don't think he would have even known how. Now here you are, five years later, informing me that Command wants to give up the hunt. Tell me, are they right?"

"Of course not."

"And can you make them understand that? Make them change their minds?"

"I'm just a junior officer. They're not going to listen to me."

Greer nodded. "And I agree. So there we are."

A silence followed. Then Greer said, "Maybe this will help. Do you remember what I said to you that night in Arizona?"

"There were lots of nights, Lucius. A lot of things got said."

"So there were. But this one in particular—I'm not sure where we were exactly. A couple of days out from the Farmstead, anyway. We were sheltering underneath a bridge. Crazy-looking rocks everywhere. I remember that part because of the way the light hit them at sunset, like they were lit from the inside. The two of us got to talking. It was the night I asked you what you intended to do with the vials Lacey gave you."

It was all coming back. The red rocks, the deep silence of the landscape, the easy flow of conversation as the two of them sat by the fire. It was as if the memory had been floating in Peter's mind for five years, never quite touching the surface until now. "I remember."

Greer nodded. "I thought you might. And let me just say, when you volunteered to be injected with the virus, that was, hands down, the ballsiest thing I'd ever seen, and I've seen some ballsy things. It was nothing I ever could have done myself. I had a lot of respect for you before that, but after . . ." He paused. "That night, I said something to you. 'Everything that's happened, it feels like more than chance.' I was really just talking to myself at the time, trying to put something into words I couldn't quite figure out, but I've given the matter a lot of thought. You finding Amy, me finding you, Lacey, Babcock, everything that happened on that mountain. Events can seem random while you're living them, but when you look back, what do you see? A chain of coincidences? Plain old luck? Or something more? I'll tell you what I see, Peter. A clear path. More than that. A *true* path. What are the chances these things would have just happened on their own? Each piece falling into place exactly when we needed it? There's a power at work here, something beyond our understanding. You can call it what you like. It doesn't need a name, because it knows yours, my friend. So you wonder what it is I do all day in here, and the answer is very simple. I'm waiting to see what happens next. Trusting in God's plan." He gave Peter an enigmatic smile; the film of sweat that dampened his face and his bare, muscled chest sharpened the air of the room. "Does it seem strange to hear me say that?" His manner lightened. "Probably you're thinking, *That poor guy, all alone in this little box, he must have lost his mind.* You wouldn't be the first."

It took Peter a moment to answer. "Actually, no. I was thinking how much you reminded me of someone."

"Who was that?"

"Her name was Auntie."

Now it was Greer's turn to remember. "Of course. The woman we buried when we got back to the Colony. You never told me anything about her, and I wondered. But I didn't want to pry."

"You could have. You could say we were close, though with Auntie it was hard to tell. Half the time I think she thought I was somebody else. I used to go around to check up on her. She liked to talk about God, too."

"Is that right?" Greer seemed pleased. "And what did she have to say?"

How strange, thought Peter, to find himself thinking of Auntie now. Like Greer's story of their night in Arizona, his memory of the old woman, and the time they'd spent together, emerged in his mind as if it were yesterday. Her overheated kitchen, and the awful cups of tea; the precise, even reverential arrangement of objects in her cramped house, furniture and books and pictures and mementos; her gnarled old feet, always shoeless, and her puckered, toothless mouth and the vaporous tangle of white hair that seemed to hover in the air around her head, not even really attached to anything. As Auntie herself was unattached; alone in her shack at the edge of the glade, the woman seemed to exist in a wholly different realm, a pocket of accumulated human memory, outside of time. Now that Peter considered it, probably that was what had drawn him to her. In Auntie's presence, the daily struggles of his life always felt lighter.

"More or less the same. She wasn't the easiest woman to make sense of." A specific recollection bubbled to the surface. "There is one thing. It was the same night Amy appeared outside the gate."

"Oh?"

"She said, 'The God I know about wouldn't give us no chance.'"

Greer was watching him with studious intensity. "She said that to you."

He was still a little surprised by the clarity of the memory. "At the time I just thought it was, you know, Auntie."

Greer broke the mood with a sudden, flashing smile. "Well," he said, "it sounds to me like the woman knew a thing or two. I'm sorry I never met her. I bet the two of us would have gotten on just fine."

Peter laughed. "You know, I think you would have."

"So maybe it's time for you to trust a little more, Peter. That's really all I'm saying. Let things come to you."

"Like Martínez, you mean."

"Maybe, maybe not. There's no way to know until you know. I've never asked you what you believe, Peter, and I'm not going to. Every man gets to decide that for himself. And don't get me wrong—I'm a soldier, too, or at least I was. The world needs its warriors, and the day will come when very little else is going to matter. You'll be there for the fight, my friend, I have no doubt. But there's more to this world than meets the eye. I don't have all the answers, but I know that much."

"I wish I had your confidence."

The major shrugged this away. "Oh, you're just trying to work things out, same as the rest of us. When I was growing up in the orphanage, the sisters always taught us that a person of faith is someone who believes something he can't prove. I don't disagree, but that's only half the story. It's the end, not the means. A hundred years ago, humanity just about destroyed itself. It'd be easy to think that God doesn't like us very much. Or that there *is* no God, there's no rhyme or reason to anything and we might just as well hang it up and call it a day. Thanks, planet Earth, it was nice knowing you. But that's not you, Peter. For you, hunting the Twelve isn't an answer. It's a question. Does anybody out there care? Are we worth saving? What would God want from me, if there is a God? The greatest faith is the willingness to ask in the first place, all evidence to the contrary. Faith not just in God, but in all of us. It's a hard place you're in, and my guess is you'll be in it for a while. But it's the right one, and it's yours."

It was then that Peter understood what he was seeing. Greer was free, a free man. The walls of his cage held no meaning for him at all; his life was entirely elsewhere, unbounded by physical things. How surprising, to envy a man whose whole life was conducted in a prison cell not much larger than a good-sized latrine.

The sound of turning tumblers; their time was at an end. As Sanders entered the cell, the two men rose.

"So," Greer said, and clapped his hands conclusively. "A little downtime in Freeport, courtesy of Command. Not the best-smelling town, but the view is nice. A good place to get a little thinking done. You've certainly earned it."

"That's what Colonel Apgar said."

"Smart fellow, Apgar." Greer extended his hand. "It was good to see you, my friend."

They shook. "Take care of yourself, all right?"

Greer grinned through the pocket of his beard. "You know what they say. Three hots and a cot. It's not such a bad life when you get down to it. And as for the rest, I know you, Peter. You'll figure things out when the time is right. That's a lesson you taught me, actually."

Sanders escorted him into the hall. Only then did it occur to Peter that he'd forgotten to ask Greer about his other visitor. And something else: the major had never asked about Amy.

"Listen," Sanders said as they were passing through the second door, "I hope you don't mind my asking, but could you sign this?"

He was holding out a scrap of paper and a stub of pencil.

"It's for my wife," he explained. "To prove I met you."

Peter accepted the paper, scrawled his name, and handed it back. For a moment Sanders just looked at it.

"Wow," he said.

"Uncle Peter!"

Breaking away from the other children, Caleb flew toward him across the playground. At the last instant he took three bounding steps and catapulted into Peter's arms, nearly knocking him over.

"Whoa now, easy."

The boy's face was lit with joy. "Amy said you were coming! You're here! You're here!"

Peter wondered how she had known. But he quickly corrected himself; Amy simply seemed to know things, as if her mind were linked to the world's hidden rhythms. Holding Caleb in his arms, Peter was washed with his distinctive physical presence: his boyish weight and heat; the warmth of his breath; the milky smell of his hair and skin, moist with exertion, mixed with the lingering scent of the harsh lye soap the sisters used. Across the playground, the other children were watching. Peter caught a glimpse of Sister Peg eyeing him coolly from the monkey bars, his unannounced presence a disruption to her beloved routine.

"Let me have a look at you."

He lowered Caleb to the ground. As always, Peter was struck by the boy's uncanny resemblance to Theo. He felt a stab of regret at the time he'd carelessly allowed to pass.

"You're getting so big. I can hardly believe it."

The little boy's chest puffed with pride. "Where have you been, what did you see?"

"Lots of stuff. I was in New Mexico."

"New Mexico!" The look of wonder on his face was total; Peter might just as well have told him he'd visited the moon. Although the prevailing custom in Kerrville was not to shelter the children from knowledge of the virals, as had been done in the Colony, his child's mind had yet to absorb the ramifications. To Caleb, the Expeditionary was a grand adventure, like pirates crossing the seas or tales of the knights of old that the sisters read to them from storybooks. "How long can you stay?" the boy pleaded.

"Not long, I'm afraid. But we have the rest of the afternoon. And I'll be back soon, probably just a week or so. What would you like to do?"

Caleb's answer was instantaneous: "Go to the dam."

"Why there?"

"You can see everything!"

Peter smiled. At such moments he felt something of himself in his nephew, the same undeniable force of curiosity that had governed his life. "The dam it is."

Sister Peg came up behind the boy. Possessing a birdlike slightness, Sister Peg was nonetheless an intimidating figure, her dark eyes capable of shrinking your insides with a single censorious glance. Peter's comrades who had been raised in the orphanage—men who weathered horrible conditions and constant peril—spoke of her with an awe verging on terror. *My God,* they all said, *that woman scared the living shit out of us.*

"Hello, Sister."

Her face, a weathered topography of deep crevices and arid planes, possessed the immobility of judgment withheld. She had taken a position just beyond a normal conversational distance, a small but significant alteration that magnified her commanding presence. Her teeth were stained a yellowish brown from puffing on corn silk—an incomprehensible habit, widespread in Kerrville, that Peter regarded with a combination of wonder and revulsion.

"Lieutenant Jaxon, I didn't expect you."

"Sorry, it was all pretty sudden. Do you mind if I take him for the rest of the day?"

"It would have been better if you could have sent word. Things here run a certain way."

Caleb's body was jangling with energy. "Please, Sister!"

Her imperious gaze flicked down toward the boy, taking accounts. Delta-like fans of wrinkles deepened at the corners of her mouth as she sucked in her cheeks. "I suppose under the circumstances it would be all right. An exception, you understand, and keep an ear to the horn, Lieutenant. I know you Expeditionary feel yourselves to be above the rules, but I can't allow it."

Peter let the barb pass; it did, after all, possess an element of truth. "I'll have him back by six." Under her withering gaze, he found himself, with the next question, attempting to sound curiously offhanded. "Is Amy around? I'd like to visit with her before we go."

"She's gone to the market. You've just missed her." This declaration was followed by a tart sigh. "I suppose you'll want to stay for dinner."

"Thank you, Sister. That's kind of you."

Caleb, bored by these formalities, was tugging at his hand. "Please, Uncle Peter, I want to *go.*"

For a breadth of time no longer than half a second, the woman's stern countenance appeared to crack. A look of almost maternal tenderness flickered in her eyes. But it just as quickly vanished, leaving Peter to wonder if he'd imagined it.

"Mind the clock, Lieutenant. I'll be watching."

The dam was, in many ways, the heart of the city and its mechanisms. Along with the oil that powered the generators, Kerrville's mastery of the Guadalupe River, which provided both water for irrigation and a barrier to the north and west—nobody had ever seen a viral even attempt to swim; it was widely believed that they either had a phobia of water or simply could not stay afloat—accounted for its longevity. The river itself had been a feature of scant dimension in the early days, thin and inconsequential, falling to barely a trickle in summer. But a devastating flood in the spring of 22, a harbinger of a meteorological shift that would raise the river permanently by as much as ten feet, had necessitated its taming. It had been, by all accounts, a massive project, requiring the temporary diversion of the river's currents and the movement of huge quantities of earth and limestone to dig the bowl-like depression that would form the impound-ment, followed by the erection of the dam itself, a feat of engineering on a scale Peter had always associated with the Time Before, not the world he knew. The day of the water's first release was regarded as a foundational occurrence in the history of the Republic; more than anything else in Kerr-ville, the dam's corralling of natural forces had impressed upon him how flimsy the Colony had been in comparison. They were lucky to have made it as long as they had.

Grated steel stairs ascended to the top. Caleb took them at a dash over Peter's shouted protests to slow down. By the time Peter made the final turn, Caleb was already gazing over the water, toward the undulating ridge of hills at the horizon. Thirty feet below, the face of the impoundment possessed a stunning transparency. Peter could even see fish down there, white shapes piloting lazily in the glassy waters.

"What's out there?" the boy asked.

"Well, more Texas mostly. That ridge you're looking at is only a few miles away."

"Where's New Mexico?"

Peter pointed due west. "But it's really, really far. Three days on a transport, and that's without stopping."

The boy chewed on his lower lip. "I want to see it."

"Maybe someday you will."

They walked along the dam's curving top to the spillway. A series of vents released water at regular intervals into a wide pool, from which gravity pumps piped it down to the agricultural complex. Looming in the distance, regularly spaced towers marked the Orange Zone. They paused again, absorbing the view. Peter was once again struck by the elab-orateness of it all. It was as if in this one place, human his-tory still flowed in an uninterrupted continuum, undisturbed by the stark separation of eras that the virals had brought down upon the world.

"You look like him."

Peter turned to see Caleb squinting at him. "Who do you mean?"

"Theo. My father."

The statement caught him short; how could the boy possibly know what Theo had looked like? Of course he couldn't, but that wasn't the point. Caleb's assertion was a kind of wish, a way to keep his father alive.

"That's what everyone said. I can see a lot of him in you, you know."

"Do you miss him?"

"Every day." A somber silence passed; then Peter said, "I'll tell you something, though. As long as we remember a person, they're not really gone. Their thoughts, their feelings, their memories, they become a part of us. And even if you think you don't remember your parents, you do. They're inside you, the same way they're inside me."

"But I was just a baby."

"Babies most of all." A thought occurred to him. "Do you know about the Farmstead?"

"Where I was born?"

Peter nodded. "That's right. There was something special about it. It was like we would always be safe there, like something was looking after us." He regarded the boy for a moment. "Your father thought it was a ghost, you know."

The boy's eyes widened. "Do you?"

"I don't know. I've thought a lot about it over the years. Maybe it was. Or at least a kind of ghost. Maybe places have memories, too." He rested a hand on the boy's shoulder. "All I know is that the world wanted you to be born, Caleb."

The boy fell silent. Then, his face blooming with the mischievous grin of a plan unveiled: "You know what I want to do next?"

"Name it."

"I want to go swimming."

It was a little after four by the time they reached the base of the spillway. Standing by the edge of the pool, they stripped to their shorts. As Peter stepped out onto the rocks, he turned to find Caleb frozen at the edge.

"What's the matter?"

"I don't know how."

Somehow Peter had failed to foresee this. He offered the boy his hand. "Come on, I'll teach you."

The water was startlingly cold, with a distinct mineral taste. Caleb was fearful at first, but after thirty minutes of splashing around, his confidence grew. Another ten and he was moving freely on his own, dog-paddling across the surface.

"Look at me! Look at me!"

Peter had never seen the boy so happy. "Hold on to my back," he said.

The boy climbed aboard, gripping Peter by the shoulders. "What are we going to do?"

"Just take a deep breath and hold it."

Together they descended. Peter blew the air from his lungs, stretched out his arms, and with a whip kick sent them gliding along the stony bottom, the boy clutching him tightly, his body pulled like a cape. The water was as clear as glass. Memories of splashing in the grotto as a boy filled Peter's mind. He had done the same thing with his father.

Three more kicks and they ascended, bursting into the light. "How was that?" Peter asked.

"I saw fish!"

"I told you."

Again and again they dove this way, the boy's pleasure inexhaustible. It was past five-thirty, the shadows lengthening, when Peter declared an end. They stepped gingerly onto the rocks and dressed.

"I can't wait to tell Sister Peg we went outside," Caleb said, beaming.

"It's probably best if you don't. Let's keep that between us, okay?"

"A secret?" The boy spoke the word with illicit pleasure; they were part of a conspiracy now.

"Exactly."

The boy slid his small, moist hand into Peter's as they made their way to the hydro gate. In another few minutes, the horn would sound. The feeling came upon him in a rush of love: *This is why I'm here.*

He found her in the kitchen, standing before a massive stove covered with boiling pots. The room roared with heat and noise—the clatter of dishes, sisters racing to and fro, the accumulating racket of excited voices as the children gathered in the dining hall. Amy's back was to him. Her hair, iridescent and dark, descended in a thick braid to her waist. He hesitated in the doorway, observing her. She appeared totally absorbed in her work, stirring the contents of the nearest pot with a long wooden spoon, tasting and correcting with salt, then nimbly stepping to one of the room's several red-brick ovens to withdraw, on a long paddle, half a dozen loaves of freshly risen bread.

"Amy."

She turned, breaking into a smile. They met in the middle of the busy room. A moment of uncertainty, then they embraced.

"Sister Peg told me you were here."

He stepped back. He had sensed it in her touch: there was something new about her. Long departed was the voiceless, traumatized waif with the matted hair and scavenged clothes. The progress of her aging seemed to occur in fits and starts, not so much a matter of physical growth as a deepening self-possession, as if she were coming into ownership of her life. And always the paradox: the person standing before him, though to all appearances a young teenager, was in reality the oldest human being on earth. Peter's long absence, an era to Caleb, was for Amy the blink of an eye.

"How long can you stay?" Her eyes did not move from his face.

"Just tonight. I ship out tomorrow."

"Amy," one of the sisters called from the stove, "is this soup ready? They're getting loud out there."

Amy spoke briskly over her shoulder: "Just a second." Then, to Peter, her smile widening: "It turns out I'm not such a bad cook. Save me a place." She quickly squeezed his hand. "It really is so good to see you."

Peter made his way to the dining hall, where all the children had gathered at long tables, sorting themselves by age. The noise in the room was intense, a free-flowing energy of bodies and voices like the din of some immense engine. He took a place on the end of a bench beside Caleb just as Sister Peg appeared at the front of the room and clapped her hands.

The effect was like a lightning bolt: silence tensed the room. The children joined hands and bowed their heads. Peter found himself joined in the circle, Caleb on one side, on the other a little girl with brown hair who was seated across from him.

"Heavenly Father," the woman intoned, her eyes closed, "we thank you for this meal and our togetherness and the blessing of your love and care, which you bestow upon us in your mercy. We thank you for the richness of the earth and the heavens above and your protection until we meet in the life to come. And lastly we thank you for the company of our special guest, one of your brave soldiers, who has traveled a perilous distance to be with us tonight. We pray that you will keep him, and his fellows, safe on their journeys. Amen."

A chorus of voices: "Amen."

Peter felt genuinely touched. So, perhaps Sister Peg didn't mind his presence so much after all. The food appeared: vats of soup, bread cut into thick, steaming slices, pitchers of water and milk. At the head of each table, one of the sisters ladled the soup into bowls and passed them down the line as the pitchers made their way around. Amy slid onto the bench beside Peter.

"Let me know what you think of the soup," she said.

It was delicious—the best thing he'd eaten in months. The bread, pillowy and warm in his mouth, nearly made him moan. He silenced the urge to ask for seconds, thinking it would be rude, but the moment his bowl was empty one of the sisters appeared with another, placing it before him.

"It's not often we have company," she explained, her face rosy with embarrassment, and scurried away.

They talked of the orphanage and Amy's duties—the kitchen, but also teaching the youngest children to read and, in her words, "whatever else needs to be done"—and Peter's news of the others, though they phrased this information in a general way; it wouldn't be until after the children had gone to bed that the two of them would be able to talk in earnest. Beside him, Caleb was engaged with another boy in a vigorous conversation that Peter was only passingly able to follow, something about knights and queens and pawns. When his companion left the table, Peter asked Caleb what it was all about.

"It's chess."

"Chest?"

Caleb rolled his eyes. "No, *chess*. It's a game. I can teach you if you want."

Peter glanced at Amy, who laughed. "You'll lose," she said.

After dinner and dishes, the three of them went to the common room, where Caleb set up the board and explained the names of the various pieces and the moves they could make. By the time he got to the knights, Peter's head was spinning.

"You really can keep all this straight in your mind? How long did it take you to learn to play?"

He shrugged innocently. "Not long. It's pretty simple."

"It doesn't sound simple." He turned to Amy, who was wearing a cagey smile.

"Don't look at me," she protested. "You're on your own."

Caleb waved over the board. "You can go first."

The battle commenced. Peter had considered taking it easy on the boy—it was, after all, a children's game, and no doubt he would quickly get the hang of it—but he instantly discovered how badly he had underestimated his young opponent. Caleb seemed to anticipate his every tactic, responding without hesitation, his moves crisp and assured. In growing desperation Peter decided to attack, using his knight to take one of Caleb's bishops.

"Are you sure you want to do that?" the boy asked.

"Um, no?"

Caleb was studying the board with his chin resting on his hands. Peter could sense the complex movements of his thoughts: he was assembling a strategy, imagining a series of moves and countermoves projected forward in time. Five years old, Peter thought. Amazing.

Caleb advanced a rook three spaces, taking Peter's other knight, which he had inadvertently left open. "Watch," he said.

A quick exchange of pieces and Peter's king was boxed in. "Checkmate," the boy declared.

Peter stared hopelessly at the board. "How did you do that so fast?"

Beside him, Amy laughed—a warm, infectious sound. "I told you."

Caleb's grin stretched a mile wide. Peter understood what had happened; first the swimming, now this. His nephew had effortlessly turned the tables on him, showing Peter what he was capable of.

"You just have to think ahead," Caleb said. "Try to see it like a story."

"Tell me the truth. How good are you at this?"

Caleb gave a modest shrug. "A few of the older kids used to beat me. But not anymore."

"Is that so? Well, set it up again, youngster. I want my revenge."

Caleb had racked up his third straight victory, each more mercilessly decisive than the last, when the bell sounded, summoning him to the dormitory. The time had passed too quickly. Amy departed for the girls' quarters, leaving Peter to escort the boy to bed. In the large room of cots, Caleb exchanged his clothing for a nightshirt, then knelt on the stone floor at the side of his bed, hands pressed together, to say his prayers, a long series of "God bless"es that began with "my parents in heaven" and concluded with Peter himself.

"I always save you for last," the boy said, "to keep you safe."

"Who's Mouser?"

Mouser was their cat. Peter had seen the poor creature lounging on a windowsill in the common room—a pitiful rag of a thing, flesh drooping over his brittle old bones like laundry on a line. Peter drew the blanket up to Caleb's chin and bent to kiss him on the forehead. Sisters were moving up and down the lines of cots, shushing the other children. The room's lights had already been extinguished.

"When are you coming back, Uncle Peter?"

"I'm not sure. Soon, I hope."

"Can we go swimming again?"

A warm feeling spread through his entire body. "Only if you promise we can play more chess. I don't think I have the hang of it yet. I could use a few pointers."

The boy beamed. "I promise."

Amy was waiting for him in the empty common room, the cat nosing around her feet. He had to report to the barracks at 2100; he and Amy would have only a few minutes together.

"That poor thing," Peter said. "Why doesn't anybody put him down? It seems cruel."

Amy ran a hand along the animal's spine. A faint purr trembled from him as he arched his back to receive her touch. "It's past time, I suppose. But the children adore him, and the sisters don't believe in it. Only God can take a life."

"They've obviously never been to New Mexico."

A joke, but not entirely. Amy regarded him with concern. "You look troubled, Peter."

"Things aren't going very well. Do you want to know about it?"

She considered the question. She seemed a little pale; Peter wondered if she was feeling all right.

"Maybe some other time." Her eyes searched his face. "He loves you, you know. He talks about you all the time."

"You're making me feel guilty. Probably I deserve it."

She lifted Mouser to settle him on her lap. "He understands. I'm only telling you so you know how important you are to him."

"What about you? Are you doing okay here?"

She nodded. "On the whole, it suits me. I like the company, the children, the sisters. And of course there's Caleb. Maybe for the first time in my life I actually feel . . . I don't know. Useful. It's nice to be just an ordinary person."

Peter was struck by the frank, easy flow of the conversation. Some barrier between them had dropped. "Do the other sisters know? Besides Sister Peg, I mean."

"A few do, or maybe just suspect. I've been here for five years, and they'd have to notice I'm not aging. I think I'm a bit of a wrinkle to Sister Peg, something that doesn't really fit her view of things. But she doesn't say anything about it to me." Amy smiled. "After all, I make a mean barley soup."

Too quickly, the moment of his departure was at hand. Amy walked him to the entrance, where Peter pulled the wad of bills from his pocket and held it out to her.

"Give this to Sister Peg, all right?"

Amy nodded without comment and slid the scrip into the pocket of her skirt. Once again she pulled him into a hug, more forcefully this time. "I really have missed you." Her voice was soft against his chest. "Be safe, all right? Promise you'll do that."

There was something fraught in her insistence, a feeling, almost, of finality, a graver parting. What wasn't she saying? And something else: her body was giving off a feverish heat. He could actually feel it pulsing through the heavy fabric of his uniform.

"You don't have to worry about me. I'll be fine."

"I mean it, Peter. If anything happened, I couldn't . . ." Her voice trailed away, as if pulled to the currents of a hidden wind. "I just couldn't is all."

Now he was certain: there was something Amy wasn't telling him. Peter searched her face for what it was. A faint glaze of perspiration shone on her brow.

"Are you okay?"

Taking his hand in her own, she lifted them in concert, pressing her palm against his so that the pads of their fingers were just touching. It seemed a gesture with equal measures of togetherness and parting, connection and separation.

"Do you remember when I kissed you?"

They had never spoken of this—her quick, birdlike peck

at the mall, the virals streaming toward them. Much had happened, but Peter had not forgotten. How could he?

"I always wondered about that," he confessed.

Their raised hands seemed to hover in the darkened space between them. Amy studied them with her eyes. It was as if she were attempting to divine a meaning she herself had made. "I'd been alone so long. It's nothing I can even describe. But all of a sudden, there you were. I couldn't believe it." Then, as if jarred from a trance, she withdrew her hand, her face suddenly flustered. "That's all. You better go—you'll be late."

He didn't want to. Like the kiss, the feeling of her hand seemed to possess a unique power to linger in his senses, as if it had taken up a permanent residence in his fingertips. He wanted to say more but couldn't find the words, and the moment slipped away.

"You're sure you're all right?"

Her face assembled a smile. "Never better."

She really did look ill, he thought. "Well, I'll be back in ten days."

Amy said nothing.

"I'll see you then, right?" He wondered why he was asking this.

"Of course, Peter. Where would I go?"

After Peter had left, Amy made her way to the sisters' residence, a smaller version of the dormitories where the children slept. The other sisters were all asleep, a few of the older ones softly snoring. She stripped off her tunic and lowered herself onto her cot.

Sometime later she awoke with a start. A cold sweat glazed her body, drenching her nightshirt. The turbulence of uneasy dreams still roiled through her.

Amy, help him.

She froze.

He is waiting for you, Amy. In the ship.

—Father?

Go to him go to him go to him go to him . . .

She rose, seized with a sudden purposefulness. The moment had come.

Yet one duty remained, one final task to be performed in these last days of a life she had loved, if briefly. Through the silent hallways she padded her way to the common room. She found Mouser just where she had left him, resting on the couch. Exhaustion radiated from his eyes; his limbs were limp, he could barely raise his head.

Please, his eyes said. *I'm in pain. It's all gone on too long.*

Gently she lifted him to her chest. Running a hand along his back, she turned so he could face the window, with its view of the starry night.

"See the pretty world, Mouser?" she murmured, close to his ear. "See the pretty stars?"

It's . . . beautiful.

His neck broke with a snap, the body going limp in her arms. Amy stayed that way for a few minutes while his presence faded, stroking his fur, kissing his head and face. *Goodbye, Mouser. Godspeed to you. The children love you; you will be with them again.* Then she carried him outside to the garden shed to see about a shovel.

3 1

"Will you look what the wind blew in."

A grease-stained man had directed Peter to the commissary, where he'd found Michael sitting with a group of a dozen men and women, using forks grasped in filthy hands to shovel plates of beans into their mouths. Michael leapt off the bench and clapped him on the shoulder.

"Peter Jaxon, as I live and breathe."

"Flyers, Michael. You're enormous."

His friend's chest seemed to have doubled in size, straining the fabric of his jumpsuit; his arms were roped with muscle. A robust growth of blond stubble roughened his cheeks.

"Tell you the truth, there's not much else to do around here besides cook oil and lift weights. And word to the wise, nobody uses that word around here. It's all 'fuck this' and 'fuck that.'" He gestured toward the table. "This here's my crew. Say hello to Peter, hombres."

Introductions all around. Peter did his best to record the names but knew they'd be gone within minutes.

"Hungry?" Michael asked. "The chow's not bad if you breathe through your mouth."

"I should report to the head of DS first."

"He can keep. Since it's past twelve hundred, odds are good Stark is pie-eyed anyway. It's Karlovic you really need to see, but he's gone up to the reserve. Let me get you a plate."

They shared their news over lunch, returned their trays to the kitchen, and stepped outside.

"Does it always smell this bad?" Peter inquired.

"Oh, this is a good day. When the wind switches around you'll be crying. Blows all the crap down from the channel. Come on, I'll give you the grand tour."

Their first stop was the barracks, a cinder-block box with a rusty tin roof. Curtained sleeping berths lined the walls. A huge, long-faced man was sitting at the table in the middle of the room, shuffling and reshuffling a deck of cards.

"This here is Juan Sweeting, my second," Michael said. "Goes by Ceps."

They shook, the man greeting him with a grunt.

"How'd you get the name Ceps?" Peter asked. "I haven't heard that before."

The man curled his arms, popping a pair of biceps like two large grapefruits.

"Ah," said Peter. "I see."

"Not to worry," Michael said, "his manners aren't the best and his lips move when he reads, but he pretty much behaves himself as long as you don't forget to feed him."

A woman had emerged from one of the berths, wearing only her underclothes. She yawned into her fist. "Jesus, Michael, I was trying to get some rack." To Peter's astonishment, she draped her arms around Michael's neck, her face lighting with a greedy smile. "Unless, of course . . ."

"Not the time, *mi amiga.*" Michael gently freed himself. "In case you didn't notice, we've got company. Lore, Peter. Peter, Lore."

Her body was lean and strong, her hair, bleached by the sun, cut short. Attractive but in an unconventional, slightly masculine way, radiating a frank, even carnivorous sensuality.

"You're the guy?"

"That's right."

She gave a knowing laugh. "Well, good luck to you, friend."

"Lore's fourth-generation oiler," Michael said. "She practically drinks the stuff."

"It's a living," Lore said. Then, to Peter: "So you guys go way back, I guess. Let a girl in on the secret. What was he like?"

"Pretty much the smartest guy around. Everybody called him the Circuit. It was sort of his nickname."

"And a stupid one, too. Thanks a bunch, Peter."

"The Circuit," Lore repeated, seeming to taste the word in her mouth. "You know, I think I kind of like that."

At the table, Ceps, who had said nothing, gave a feminine moan. *"Oh Circuit, oh Circuit, make me feel like a woman . . ."*

"Shut up, the both of you." Michael was blushing to a degree at odds with his newfound muscularity, though Peter could also tell that part of him enjoyed the attention. "What are you, thirteen? Come on, Peter," he said, steering him toward the door, "let's leave these children."

"See you later, Lieutenant," Lore called merrily as they made their exit. "I'll want to hear *stories.*"

In the intensifying heat of the afternoon, Michael gave Peter the lay of the land, taking him to one of the towers and explaining the refining process.

"It sounds pretty dangerous," Peter said.

"Things happen, it's true."

"Where's the reserve?" The oil, Peter knew, came from a holding tank deep underground.

"About five miles to the north of here. It's actually a natural salt dome, part of the old Strategic Petroleum Reserve. Oil floats, so we pump in seawater and out it comes."

His friend had acquired a bit of Texas in his voice, Peter noted. Not "oil" but "awhl."

"How much is left down there?"

"Well, a shitload, basically. By our estimates, enough to fill the cookers for another fifty years."

"And once it's gone?"

"We go looking for more. There are plenty of tanks spread along the Houston ship channel. It's a real toxic swamp up there, and the place is crawling with dopeys, but it could tide us over awhile. The next closest dome is Port Arthur. It wouldn't be easy to move the operation up there, but with enough time we could do it." He gave a fatalistic shrug. "Either way, I doubt I'll be around to worry about it."

Michael announced that he had a surprise to show Peter. They walked to the armory, where Michael retrieved a shotgun, then to the motor pool for a pickup. Michael clipped the shotgun into a stand on the floor of the cab and told Peter to get in.

"Where are we going?"

"You'll see."

They drove out of the compound, then turned south on a cracked blacktop that ran parallel with the water. A salty wind gusted through the truck's open windows, taking the edge off the heat. Peter had seen the Gulf only a couple of times; its ancient span, too huge to hold in his mind, unfailingly took his breath away. Most entrancing were the waves, long tubes gathering size and momentum as they approached, falling in a curl of brown foam at the water's edge. He couldn't take his eyes off them. Peter knew he could sit on the sand for hours, just watching the waves.

Stretches of the beach were swept clean, while others still bore the evidence of catastrophe on a grand scale: mountains of rusting metal twisted into incomprehensible shapes; beached ships of every size, their hulls bleached and pitted or else stripped to the struts, tilted on the sand like exposed rib cages; ridges of undifferentiated debris, pushed inshore on the tide.

"You'd be surprised how much stuff still washes in," Michael said, gesturing out the window. "A lot of it comes down the Mississippi, then curves along the coast. The heavy stuff's mostly gone, but anything plastic seems to last."

Michael had veered off the road and was now driving close to the water's edge. Peter stared out the window. "Do you ever see anything bigger?"

"Once in a while. Last year, a barge still loaded with big containers washed in. The damn thing had been drifting for a century. We were all pretty excited."

"What was in them?"

"Human skeletons."

They came to an inlet and turned west, following the edge of a tranquil bay. Ahead was a small concrete structure perched on the water's edge. As Michael brought the truck to a halt, Peter saw that the building was just a shell, although a sign in the window still read, in faded letters, "Art's Crab Shack."

"Okay, I'll bite," Peter said. "What's the surprise?"

His friend smiled mischievously. "Leave that smoke poker here," he said, gesturing to the Browning strapped to Peter's thigh. "You're not going to need it."

Wondering what his friend had in mind, Peter deposited the gun in the glove compartment, then followed Michael to the rear of the building. A small dock on concrete piers, perhaps thirty feet long, jutted out over the water.

"What am I seeing?"

"A boat, obviously."

A small sailboat was tied up at the end of the pier, gently bobbing in the swells.

"Where did you get it?"

Michael's face shone with pride. "A lot of places, actually.

The hull we found in a garage about ten miles inland. The rest we cobbled together or made ourselves."

"We?"

"Lore and me." He cleared his throat, his face suddenly flustered. "I guess it's pretty obvious—"

"You don't owe me an explanation, Michael."

"I'm just saying it's not quite what it looks like. Well, maybe it is. But I wouldn't say we're together, exactly. Lore's just . . . well, she's just like that."

Peter found himself taking perverse pleasure in his friend's embarrassment. "She seems nice enough. And she obviously likes *you*."

"Yeah, well." Michael shrugged. " 'Nice' wouldn't necessarily be the first word I'd choose, if you know what I mean. To tell you the truth, I can barely keep up with her."

As Michael stepped aboard, Peter suddenly became aware how meager the boat looked.

"What's the problem?" Michael asked.

"We're actually going to sail that thing?"

Michael had started busily coiling lines and setting them in the bottom of the hull. "Why'd you think I brought you out here? Quit your worrying and get in."

Peter cautiously lowered himself into the cockpit. The hull moved strangely under him, responding to his weight with a sluggish shift. He gripped the rail, willing the boat to stay still. "And you actually know how to do this."

His friend laughed under his breath. "Don't be such a baby. Help me raise the sail."

Michael quickly ran through the basics: sail, rudder, tiller, mainsheet. He cast off the line, scrambled aft to the tiller, did something to make the sail abruptly fill with air, and suddenly they were off and running, streaming away from the dock with astonishing speed.

"So what do you think?"

Peter nervously eyed the receding shoreline. "I'm getting used to it."

"Here's a thought," Michael offered. "For the first time in your life, you're in a place where a viral can't kill you."

"I hadn't considered that."

"For the next couple of hours, you, my friend, are out of a job."

They tacked across the bay. As they moved into deeper water, the color changed from a mossy green to a rich blue-black, the sunlight ricocheting off the irregularities of its surface. Under the tightness of the sail, the boat possessed a more solid feel, and Peter began to relax, though not completely. Michael seemed to know what he was doing, but the ocean was still the ocean.

"How far out have you taken this thing?"

Michael looked ahead, squinting into the light. "Hard to say. Five miles anyway."

"What about the barrier?"

It was generally held that in the early days of the epidemic, the nations of the world had banded together to enforce a quarantine of the North American continent, laying mines all along the coastlines and bombing any vessels that attempted to leave shore.

"If it's out there, I haven't found it yet." Michael shrugged. "Part of me thinks it's all bullshit, you want to know the truth."

Peter eyed his friend cautiously. "You're not looking for it, are you?"

Michael didn't answer, his face telling Peter that he had hit the mark.

"That's insane."

"So is doing what you do. And even if the barrier exists, how many mines could still be floating around out there? A hundred years in the ocean would eat just about anything. And all the debris would have set them off by now, anyway."

"It's still reckless. You could blow yourself to bits."

"Maybe. And maybe tomorrow one of those cooking towers will launch me into outer space. The standards for personal safety around these parts are pretty low." He shrugged. "But that's beside the point. I don't think the damn thing was ever there to begin with. The whole coast? If you include Mexico and Canada, that's almost two hundred and fifty thousand miles. Impossible."

"What if you're wrong?"

"Then someday I may, as you say, blow myself to bits."

Peter let the matter drop. A lot had changed, but Michael was still Michael, a man of insatiable curiosity. They were moving through the inlet into open water; the breeze had picked up, casting jeweled waves over the bow. Something in his stomach dropped. It wasn't just the lurching of the boat. So much water, everywhere.

"Maybe just this once you could keep us close to land."

Michael adjusted the sail, stiffening his grip on the tiller. "I'm telling you, it's a whole other deal out there, Peter. I can't even explain it. It's like all the bad stuff just drops away. You really should see it for yourself."

"I should be getting back. Let's save it for another time."

Michael glanced at him and laughed. "Sure," he said. "Another time."

32

Alicia made her way northward, into the wide-open countryside. The Texas Panhandle: a landscape of limitless flatness like a great becalmed sea, wind drifting over the tips of the prairie grasses, the sky immense above her in its autumnal blueness, the encircling horizon broken only by the occasional creekside stand of cottonwoods or pecans or long-armed willows, their melancholy fronds bowing in submission as she passed. The days were warm but at night the temperature plunged, weighing the grass with dew. Using fuel from caches spread along her route, she'd complete the journey in four days.

She arrived at the Kearney garrison on the morning of November 6. It was as Command had feared when the resupply convoy had failed to return: not a living soul remained to greet her. The garrison was an open grave. The echoes of the soldiers' dying cries seemed to hover on the air, locked into the windswept stillness. Alicia spent two days loading the desiccated remains of her fellows into the bed of a truck and carrying them to the place she had selected, a clearing on the banks of the Platte. There she lay them in a long row, so they could be together, doused them with fuel, and set them alight.

It was the following morning that she saw the horse.

He was standing just beyond the barricades. A blue-roan stallion, his long, masculine neck bent to graze upon the heavy grasses at the edge of the parade ground—his presence unaccountable, like a single house left untouched by a tornado. He stood eighteen hands at least. Cautiously Alicia approached him, palms upturned. The animal seemed prepared to spook, nostrils flaring, ears pinned back, one great eye roving toward her. Who is this strange being, it was saying, what does she intend? Alicia advanced another step; still he did not move. She could feel the wildness that coursed in his blood, his explosive animal power.

"Good boy," she murmured. "See? I'm not so bad. Let's be friends, the two of us, what do you say?"

When an arm's length separated them, she eased her open

palm beneath his nose. His lips pulled back, revealing the yellow wall of his teeth. His eye was like a great black marble taking in the sight of her. A moment of decision, his body tense and alert; then he lowered his head, filling her open hand with the warm moistness of his breath.

"Well, I think I just found my ride." The animal was nuzzling her hand now, bobbing his head. Flecks of foam stood at the edges of his mouth. She stroked his neck, his glossy, sweat-dampened coat. His body was like something chiseled, hard and pure, yet it was his eyes that radiated the full measure of his strength. "You need a name," Alicia said. "What shall I call you?"

She named him Soldier. From the moment she swung up onto his back, they belonged to each other. It was as if they were old friends, long separated, who had found each other again; lifelong companions who could tell each other the truest stories of themselves but who could also, if they chose, say nothing at all. In the empty garrison she lingered three more days, taking stock, planning the journey ahead. She sharpened her blades to their finest point. Her orders were in her pouch. To: Alicia Donadio, Captain of the Expeditionary. Signed: Victoria Sanchez, President, Texas Republic.

On the morning of November 12 they rode out, headed east.

One bridge over the Missouri still stood, fifty miles north of Omaha, at the town of Decatur. They reached it on the sixth day. The mornings were glazed with frost, winter in the air. The trees had given up their bashfulness, showing their bare limbs. As they made their approach Alicia sensed in Soldier's gait a notch of hesitation: *The river, really?* They came to the bluffs; below them, the water churned in its broad course. Eddies swirled upon its face, dark as stone. A quarter mile north, the bridge traversed its width on massive concrete pilings, as if bestriding the river on giant legs. *Yes,* Alicia said. *Really.*

There were moments when it seemed that this decision had been hasty. In places the concrete surface had fallen away, revealing the churning waters below. She dismounted and took Soldier by the reins. Painstakingly, every step fraught with the possibility that the bridge would collapse under them, they threaded their way across. Whose stupid idea was this? Soldier seemed to ask. Oh, yours.

On the far side they halted. It was just evening; the sun

had begun its descent behind the bluffs. Alicia's rhythms had reversed: on foot, she would have been free to sleep during the day and travel at night, her habit. But not on horseback. Alicia lit a fire on the bank of the river, filled her pan, and set it to boil. She took the last of her stores from her saddlebag: a fistful of dried beans, paste in a can, a wedge of hardtack dense as a rock. She was in the mood to hunt but did not want to leave Soldier alone. She ate her meager supper, washed her pot in the river, and lay down on her bedroll to watch the sky. She had discovered that if she looked long enough, she would see a shooting star. As if responding to her thoughts, a bright streak blazed across the heavens, then two more in quick succession. Michael had told her once, many years ago, that some were leftover creations of mankind from the Time Before, called satellites. He had attempted to explain their function—something to do with the weather—but Alicia had either forgotten what he'd said or else tuned it out as yet another instance of know-it-all Michael lording his intelligence over other people. What had stuck in her mind was an abstract sense of them, their marriage of light and force: unaccountable objects of unknowable purpose that swung around the earth like stones in a sling, locked in their trajectories by counterbalancing influences of will and gravity until they gave up their trials and plunged to earth in a blaze of glory. More stars fell; Alicia began to count. The more she looked, the more she saw. Ten, fifteen, twenty. She was still counting when she fell asleep.

The day broke fresh and clear. Alicia slipped on her glasses and stretched, the pleasurable energy of a night's rest flowing through her limbs. The sound of the river seemed louder in the morning air. She had saved some hardtack for breakfast. She polished off half and fed the rest to Soldier and rode on.

They were in Iowa now; their journey was halfway done. The landscape changed, rising and falling in loamy hills with a slumped appearance and, between them, flat-bottomed valleys of rich black soil. Low clouds had moved in from the west, tamping the light. It was late afternoon when Alicia detected movement from the ridgeline. On the wind, a scent of animals; Soldier could sense it, too. Willing herself into stillness, Alicia waited for the source to reveal itself.

There. A herd of deer appeared in silhouette at the top of the ridge, twenty head in all, and, among them, a single large buck. His rack was massive, like a tree stripped for winter. She would have to make her approach from the downwind side; it was a wonder they hadn't detected her already. She placed her rifle in its holder, took up her crossbow and a sling of bolts, and dismounted. Soldier eyed her warily.

"Now, don't give me that look. A girl's got to eat." She patted his neck in assurance. "No wandering off, all right?"

She circled the ridge to the south. The deer still appeared oblivious to her presence. On knees and elbows she inched her way up the incline. She was fast, but they were faster; one shot of the cross, maybe two, would be all she had. After long minutes of patient climbing, she reached the top. The deer had fanned out into a V shape along the ridge. The buck stood forty feet away. Alicia, still pressed to the ground, pulled a bolt into her cross.

A puff of wind, perhaps. A moment of deep animal perception. The deer exploded into movement. By the time Alicia had risen to her feet, they were bounding down the ridge, away.

"Shit."

She flung the cross to the ground, drew a blade, and took off after them. Her mind was firmly locked onto the task now; nothing would deny her. Fifty feet down the ridge the ground abruptly fell away, and Alicia saw her chance: a convergence of lines that her mind beheld with absolute precision. As the buck darted below the drop-off, she raised her blade and launched herself into the air.

She fell upon him like a hawk, swinging the blade forward in a long-armed arc to drive it upward into the base of his throat. A spurt of blood and his front legs folded under him. Too late Alicia realized what was about to happen. As she pitched over his neck, her body was snatched by gravity, and the next thing Alicia knew she was tumbling head over heels down the hillside.

She came to rest at the base of the ridge. Her glasses had been stripped away. She rolled quickly onto her stomach, burying her face in her arms. Fuck! Would she be forced to lie here, utterly helpless, until dark? She eased one arm free and began to pat the ground around her. Nothing.

The only thing to do was open her eyes and look. Her face still nestled in the crook of her arm, Alicia rose to her knees. Her heart was hammering against her ribs. Well, she thought, here goes nothing.

At first she perceived only whiteness—an obliterating whiteness, as if she were staring into the heart of the sun. The shock was like a needle in her skull. But then, with unexpected swiftness, something began to change. Her vision was resolving. Colors and shapes emerged like figures from a fog. She was peering through the barest slits; she allowed her eyes to open just a little more. Bit by bit, the brightness receded to unveil more of her surroundings.

After five long years in shadow, Alicia Donadio, captain of the Expeditionary, beheld the daylit world.

Only then did she realize where she was.

She called it the Field of Bones. Though neither was it a field, in the strictest sense, nor were they bones, exactly. Rather, the crumbling, sun-blasted remains of a viral multitude, covering the tableland to a far horizon. How many was she seeing? A hundred thousand? A million? More? Alicia stepped forward, taking her place among them. From each footfall rose a cloud of ash. The taste was in her nose and throat, painting the walls of her mouth like a paste. Tears rose to her eyes. Of sadness? Of relief? Or simple amazement at this unaccountable event? It was not their fault what they were. It had never been their fault. Dropping to one knee, she drew a blade from her bandolier and touched it to herself, head and heart. Eyes closed, she bowed her head and cast her mind outward in prayer. *I send you home, my brothers and sisters, I release you from the prison of your existence. You have departed the earth to unlock the truth of what lies beyond this life. May your strength pass into me that I may face the days ahead. Godspeed to you.*

Soldier was just where she'd left him. His eyes flashed with irritation at her approach. I thought we had a deal, they said. Where the hell have you been? But as she neared, his gaze deepened knowingly. Alicia stroked his withers, kissed his long, wise face. His muscular tongue licked the tears from her bare eyes. You are my good boy, she said. My good, good boy.

She would have liked to press on, but her prize wouldn't wait. She pitched her tarp between the trees, sat on the ground, and removed her pack. Inside, wrapped in oilcloth, lay the quivering, bloody lump of the buck's liver. She pressed it to her nose and inhaled deeply, drawing in its delicious, earthen, blood-tinged smell. There would be no cooking fire tonight; it was perfect as it was.

Something was changing; the world was changing. Alicia could feel it, deep in the bone. A profound shift—seismic, seasonal—like the earth tipping on its axis. But there would be time to worry over this later.

Now, on this night, she would eat.

33

Peter saw little of Michael for the next three days. The deadline of departure loomed; all the cooking crews were running double shifts. With no scrip to spend at the card table, Peter passed his time sleeping, taking restless walks around the compound, and milling about the commissary. Karlovic he liked, but Stark was a different matter. Peter's arrival had elicited all the resentment Greer had predicted. The man would barely speak to him. Fine, Peter thought, let him stew. It's not like I wanted this duty, anyway.

His most interesting time was spent with Lore. Her appetite for information about the Colony, and Michael in particular, was as robust as everything else about her. Between shifts she would seek him out in the commissary, taking him to an empty table where they could speak out of earshot. No matter what Michael had said, it was plain that beneath her bawdy exterior her attachment to him was serious. Her inquiries possessed a probing quality, as if Michael were a lock she couldn't quite open. What had he been like back in those days? Smart, yes—that was obvious to anyone who knew him—but what else? What could Peter tell her about Sara? And their parents, what was the story? Of their journey from California, the woman knew only the public account: with the Colony's power source failing, they had made their way east in search of others, stumbling by sheer chance on the Colorado garrison. Of Amy, and what had occurred on the mountain in Telluride, she knew nothing at all, and Peter left it that way.

The most surprising turn in the conversation was Lore's interest in Alicia. Evidently Michael had spoken of her a good deal. Beneath the surface of Lore's questions, Peter detected an undercurrent of rivalry, even jealousy, and in hindsight he suspected that much of the discussion had been circling toward this subject. Peter even went so far as to assure Lore that she had nothing to worry about. Michael and Alicia were like oil and water, he said. Two more different people you'd never meet in your life. Lore responded with a confident laugh. What gave you the idea I was worried? Some crazy woman in the Exped, way the hell and gone?

Believe me, she said, waving the notion away, that's the last thing on my mind.

Peter spent his last day conferring with Karlovic and Stark, going over the details of the trip. Ten tankers full of fuel, evenly mixed between diesel and high-octane, were parked by the gate. Before morning there would be two more. The convoy would travel with an escort of six security vehicles, Humvees and 4x4s with fifty-cals mounted in the beds. The distance was three hundred miles: north from Freeport on Route 36, west on Highway 10 at Sealy, a straight shot to the outskirts of San Antonio, where they would circumnavigate the city on a mix of rural highways, then back on I-10 for the final fifty miles. Hardboxes were dispersed at regular intervals along the route, but the practice was to drive without stopping. Traveling at an average speed of twenty miles an hour, they would pull into Kerrville a little after midnight.

Peter's attention was drawn to five major chokepoints on the route: a bridge over the San Bernard River west of Sealy; another at Columbus, where they would cross the Colorado; the San Marcos bridge at Luling; and a pair spanning the Guadalupe, the first just west of Seguin, the second at the town of Comfort. The first three were a small concern—the convoy would be crossing in daylight—but they wouldn't reach Seguin until after sunset. Virals had been seen moving up and down the rivers as they hunted, and the sound of idling diesel engines was a known attractor. To make matters worse, the San Marcos bridge was in such poor repair that only one tanker would be permitted to cross it at a time. Flaring the area would provide a measure of protection, but the convoy would be broken up for nearly an hour.

Everyone gathered at the tankers in the predawn darkness. The air was damp and cold. For nearly all of them, the trip was old hat. They had become inured to it, even a little bored. Cups of chicory coffee were passed. As ranking oiler, Michael would ride in the lead Humvee, with Peter. Ceps would drive the first tanker, Lore the second. Peter had planned for Stark to ride up front, as a gesture of goodwill, but to Peter's relief the man had declined, choosing instead to remain at the refinery with the remaining DS detachment.

With the first rays of light, the gates were opened. A dozen big diesels roared to life, clouds of dense black exhaust chuffing from their smokestacks. Michael moved up the line from the rear, distributing the walkies and conferring with each of the drivers a final time. He took his place at the wheel of the Humvee and radioed each of the drivers in turn.

"Tanker One."

"Good to go."

"Tanker Two."

"Good to go."

"Tanker Three . . ." And so on. Michael handed Peter the radio and put the Humvee in gear.

"You'll see," he said. "The whole thing is a big yawn. One time, I slept most of the way."

They moved out, into the breaking day.

By late morning they had moved through the Rosenberg bypass and were angling west toward I-10. The state highways were a series of potholes, forcing the tankers to move at a creep, but once they picked up the interstate their speed would improve.

Ceps's voice came over the radio: "Michael, I've got a problem back here."

Peter swiveled in his seat. The convoy had come to a halt behind them. Michael braked the Humvee and backed up. Ceps had exited the cab of the truck and was standing on the front bumper, jimmying the hood.

"What's the problem?" Michael called.

Ceps slapped at the engine with a rag, pushing the steam away. "I think it's the coolant pump. It could take a while to fix. A couple of hours, anyway."

Two options: wait for the repair to be completed or leave the tanker behind. To complicate matters, the land on either side was an impenetrable thicket. The closest turnout was six miles back. They would have to back the convoy up all the way to Wallis.

"Can he do it?" Peter asked.

"We've got the parts. I don't see why not."

Peter gave the go-ahead. Michael took up the walkie again. "Okay, everybody, let's power down."

"Are you serious?" Lore came back. "Tell Ceps to move that hunk of junk out of the way."

"Yes, I'm serious. Kill your engines, people."

Peter positioned the security teams on either side of the convoy, their guns trained on the walls of trees and scrub. It was highly unlikely anything would happen in the middle of the day, but a tangle like that was perfect viral cover. Ceps and Lore got to work on the engine. Most of the drivers had climbed from their cabs. The cards came out as the minutes ticked away.

By the time Ceps declared the cooling system fixed, it was past three o'clock. The repair had taken nearly four hours. Kerrville was still twelve hours away—more, since they'd be doing more of the trip in the dark.

"It's not too late to go back," Michael said. "We can use the Columbus exit on the interstate to turn around. The ramps are in good shape."

"What's your call?"

They were standing by the Humvee, away from the others. "If you ask me, I think we should go. A few more hours in the dark, what's the difference? It's not like this hasn't happened before. These old junkers break down all the time. And we've got wide lanes all the way to Seguin." Michael shrugged. "It's really your decision."

Peter took a moment to think. It was a risk, but what wasn't? And Michael's logic seemed sound.

He nodded. "We go."

"That's the spirit. All eyes, brother."

The exit markers, pitted and rusting, leaning like drunks; the ancient highway with its tipping guardrails, calling them forward; the cratered roadside restaurants and filling stations and motels, some with their signs still standing against the wind, declaring incomprehensible names. McDonald's. Exxon. Whataburger. Holiday Inn Express. Peter watched the scenery flow past. They were making better time, but that wouldn't last. Darkness was coming on.

The light gave out at Flatonia. They were thirty miles east of the third bridge, moving at a steady twenty-five. The radio, which had crackled all day with banter between the vehicles, fell silent. As they approached the town of Luling there appeared, in the cones of light from the Humvee's headlamps, an exit sign marked with a red X. A hardbox. Peter glanced at Michael, looking for any change in his face, but detected none. They were moving on.

They were approaching the bridge when Michael suddenly leaned forward in his seat, peering intently over the wheel.

"What in the hell . . . ?"

Peter braced himself against the dash as Michael slammed on the brakes. The cab filled with light as the second Humvee nearly careened into them from behind, braking just in time. They skidded to a halt.

Michael was staring out the windshield. "Am I seeing things?"

Lore's voice crackled on the radio. "What's going on? Why did we stop?"

Peter snatched the radio off the dash. "DS three and four, up front on the double. One and two, hold position. Everybody else stay in your cabs."

A figure was standing in the road. Not viral: human. It appeared to be a woman, head bowed, wearing a kind of cloak.

"What's she doing?" said Michael. "She's just standing there."

"Wait here."

Peter climbed from the cab. The woman had yet to move or otherwise acknowledge their existence. The two floater DS vehicles, 4x4s, had pulled into position alongside the Humvees. Drawing his sidearm, Peter stepped cautiously forward.

"Identify yourself."

The woman was standing at the front edge of the bridge. Its iron struts carved lines of darkness against the sky. Peter raised his weapon, inching closer. She was clutching something in her hand. "Hey," he said, "I'm talking to you."

The woman raised her head. Her face filled with the light of the trucks' headlamps. Peter couldn't tell what he was seeing. Woman? Girl? Crone? The image of her face seemed to flutter in his mind, forming and re-forming like something seen through fast-moving water. He felt a jostle of nausea.

"We know where you are." Her voice was as ethereal as tissue. "It's just a matter of time."

Peter cocked his weapon, aiming at her head. "Answer me."

Her eyes shone an intense, twinkling blue. As they locked onto his own, Peter realized that what he was seeing was a beautiful woman, maybe the most beautiful of his life. The plump, pillowy lips. The delicately upswept nose. The proportionate arrangement of the facial bones and the glowing skin of her cheeks. To look at her was to be swept into a current of almost unbearable sensuality. His mouth was suddenly dry.

"You're tired," she said.

The statement, utterly baffling, jarred him from his stupor. He was what?

"I said," the woman repeated, "you're tired."

"I don't know what you're talking about."

Her face fell with puzzlement; it appeared he had disappointed her. Peter's eyes fell to the object clutched in her hand. A metal box. With her free hand she withdrew a long, metal rod from its side.

Peter knew what it was.

He leapt toward her as her finger found the switch. A sheen of light and a crack of sound like the slamming of an enormous door: a wall of scalding heat blew him backward, off his feet. The bridge, Peter thought. Whoever she is, this woman has blown the bridge. Peter was on his back, blinking at the sky. Time had briefly slipped its moorings. Something large, on fire, was descending toward him from the heavens in a languid arc.

The burning road tie crashed to the ground a few feet from his head. As Peter rolled away he felt someone's hands upon him, and suddenly he was on his feet again; Michael was pulling him toward the Humvee.

"Back up!" One arm wrapping Peter's waist, Michael was yelling into the walkie. "Everybody back up now!"

Lights were blazing at them from all directions. Before Peter could fully process the information, a pickup barreled out of the brush, its great mud-choked tires bounding over the ditch. It swerved to a halt before them, angled sideways. Four figures rose like dark apparitions from the truck's bed, simultaneously raising long, cylindrical objects to their shoulders.

"Oh, shit," said Michael.

They flung themselves to the ground as the rockets, in a white burst, jetted from their tubes. Behind them, the sound of gunfire was instantly swallowed by the DS vehicles' detonation. Flaming debris whizzed over their heads.

"Ceps," Michael barked into the walkie, "get out of there!"

The figures in the truck had paused to reload. Ceps's tanker would be next. Peter reached for his sidearm, but it was gone; he'd lost it in the first explosion. From the rear of the convoy came another tremendous bang. The oilers were leaping from their trucks, running, shouting. The attack was coming from both ends of the convoy now. They were trapped between the river and whatever was approaching from the rear, presumably more pickups with RPGs. Their fuel was forfeit, the only thing to do was run. Peter and Michael broke for the first tanker just as Ceps leapt down from the cab, tossing Peter a rifle. He snatched it from the air, swung around, took aim at the pickup, and released a barrage of strafing fire, sending the figures diving for cover.

He'd bought them a moment, but that was all. Michael grabbed Lore by the wrist as she emerged from her cab and swung her to the ground. He was shouting, waving toward the rear of the convoy. "Get away from the trucks!"

The apparitional figures rose again. One clean shot at the first tanker and it would all be over. Three thousand gallons per truck, thirty-six thousand gallons in all. The entire convoy would go up, detonating like sticks of dynamite in a line. Peter realized that one of the figures was the cloaked woman. He lifted his rifle again and squeezed the trigger, only to hear the click of an empty chamber.

The woman raised her arms and spread them wide.

At the tail end of the convoy, an altogether different sort of vehicle had appeared. It swooped upon them at high speed, engine roaring, banks of sodium vapor lights blazing from the roof of its cab. A six-wheeled semitractor: daisy-chained behind it were two large cargo boxes constructed of galvanized metal buffed to a highly reflective finish. In the weeks to come, this curious aspect—it resembled nothing so much as two mirrored boxes rolling down the highway—would emerge as a matter of significance, a clue in a sequence of clues; but at the moment of the truck's air-braking descent upon the scene, no one paid that much attention. Some of the fleeing oilers, their panicked brains washed clean of logic, and failing to notice that the smaller vehicles that had taken out the rear guard had conveniently vanished into the undergrowth, even permitted themselves the hope of rescue. They were under attack. The attack, mercilessly discombobulating, had come from nowhere. The containers, in their fortified appearance and shining bulk, resembled portables.

Which they were. Though toting a cargo of an altogether different kind.

One to see this was OFC Juan Sweeting. Despite his off-putting manner and intimidating muscularity, Ceps was a man with the soul of a poet. Alone in his rack at the end of each day, he privately put pen to paper, rendering his deepest thoughts in lines of uncommon sensitivity and verbal music. Despite the trials of his life, he steadfastly believed the world to be a beautiful, God-touched place worthy of human hopefulness; he wrote a great deal about the sea, whose companionship he treasured. Though he had never shown anyone these poems, they formed the heart of his life, like a secret lover. Sometimes, scraping oily gunk from a cooker or hurling a bulk of iron above his head in the weight cages,

Ceps was so inflamed by the desire to write a poem that it was all he could do not to abandon his task and race back to his rack to celebrate the magnificence of creation.

The arrival of the gleamingly reflective semitruck coincided with his blossoming suspicion, like Peter's, that not all was as it appeared. Indeed, nothing about the attack made sense. Why would human beings prey upon one another in this manner? Did they not possess a common foe? Why destroy an energy source that maintained the very existence of their species? The idea taking shape in his mind was the correct one, that their attackers were not in league with their own kind, and as the first of the two shining compartments released its cargo, his suspicions became certainty. But by then it was too late; it had always been too late.

The virals swarmed over the convoy. There were hundreds. But in the moment that followed, Ceps realized that the virals were not, in fact, killing everyone. Some were set upon with merciless, blood-splashing swiftness, but others were snatched bodily, flailing and screaming as the virals seized them around their waists and leapt away.

A far worse fate, to be taken. To be taken up.

He made a quick decision.

The semi had come to a halt less than twenty yards from the last tanker in the line. Ceps had seen a tanker blow before. The destruction was instant and total, a great fiery wallop, but in the preceding tenth of a second something interesting occurred. Seeking the weakest point in the structure, the expanding fuel sent the tanker's end plates shooting horizontally like corks from a bottle. In essence, an exploding tanker truck was a gun before it was a bomb. Ceps had reached the last tanker now. The silver truck was parked twenty yards straight behind him, well within range. With his massive arms, Ceps unscrewed the cap of the offload port and opened the valve. Gasoline spouted from the pipe in a glistening gush. He stood in this current, soaking his clothes. He filled his hands and splashed his hair. This ravishing world, he thought, his senses filling with the smell of fuel, like bottled fire. This achingly bittersweet, ravishing world. Perhaps someone would find his sheaf of poems tucked beneath his mattress and read in its pages the hidden truths of his heart. The words of a poem he loved came back to him. Emily Dickinson: a boy of eight, he had found a book of her poems in the Kerrville Library, in a room nobody ever went to. Because it seemed no one had any use for it, and in a state of anthropomorphic sympathy for its lone-

liness on the shelf, Ceps had tucked it into his coat and stolen off to an alleyway, where, sitting on an ash can, he'd
discovered a voice long gone from the earth, that seemed to
strike straight to his most secret self. Now, standing in the
path of the gushing port, he closed his eyes to let its words,
etched in memory, pass through him one last time:

Beauty crowds me till I die
Beauty, mercy have on me
But if I expire today
Let it be in sight of thee—

He removed his lighter from his pocket and flicked it open
to balance his thumb upon its flinted wheel.

A hundred yards away, in the cab of the third tanker, Peter
was attempting to put the thing in gear. The knob, its markings long since worn off, told him nothing. Each attempt
was met with a grinding sound.

"Move over."

The door swung open and Lore scrambled in, Michael following. Peter slid across the bench to let him take the wheel.

"Our plan is?" Michael asked.

"We don't have one."

Michael glanced into the side-view. His eyes widened.
"Now we do."

He jammed the gearshift into first, swung the wheel all the
way to the left, and hit the gas, clipping the second tanker.
Instead of reversing, Michael pressed the accelerator again.
A screech of metal and suddenly they were free, a fifteen-ton
wheeled missile bounding into the undergrowth.

Behind them, the world exploded.

The truck shot forward like a rocket; Peter was thrust
back in his seat. The rear of the truck lifted, swerved, then
somehow found traction again. The cab was bouncing so
fiercely it seemed certain they would shake apart. Michael
worked through the gearbox, still accelerating. Brush swept
over the windshield; they were flying blind as bats. He turned
the wheel left again, guiding them in a long arc across the
tangled field, and then with a second toss they were on the
highway again, racing east.

Their flight had not escaped attention. In the side-view,
Peter saw a bank of pale green light gathering behind them.

"We can't outrun them in this thing," Michael said. "The
only chance is the hardbox."

Peter jammed a magazine into his rifle. "What have you got?" he asked Lore, and she showed him a pistol.

"That's not the only problem," Michael said. "We've lost our brake coupler."

"Meaning what?"

"I can't slow down or she'll jackknife. We'll have to jump."

The virals were closing. Peter guessed two hundred yards, maybe less.

"Can you get us up the exit ramp?"

"At this speed, there's no way I'll make the turn at the overpass. It's ninety degrees."

"How far's the box from the top of the ramp?"

"A hundred yards straight south."

There was no way they would make it if they jumped at the base of the ramp. A hundred yards would be cutting it close as it was, and that was assuming they escaped the fall uninjured.

The hardbox marker appeared in Michael's headlights. Lore climbed over the bench and took a place by the door as Michael downshifted, cutting their speed to thirty, and veered to the right, guiding them up the ramp. They flung the doors wide, filling the cab with swirling wind.

"Here we go."

As they hit the top of the ramp, Michael and Lore leapt from the cab, Peter just behind them. He hit the ground on his feet, knees flexed to absorb the impact, then rolled end over end on the pavement. The air poured from his chest. He came to a stop just in time to see the taillights of the tanker barreling through the guardrail. For the thinnest instant, the vehicle, all thirty thousand pounds of it, seemed on the verge of taking flight. But then it sank from sight, its disappearance followed by one more titanic explosion on a night of them, a roiling cloud with a white-hot center that blazed like an enormous flare.

From his left, the sound of Lore's voice: "Peter, help me!"

Michael was unconscious. His hair was slick with blood, his arm twisted in a way that seemed broken. The first virals were at the foot of the ramp now. The light of the burning truck had bought them a moment, but that was all. Peter hoisted Michael over his shoulder. Christ, he thought, his knees buckling under the weight, this would have been easier a few years ago. The hardbox flag stood in dark silhouette against the stars.

They ran.

34

She appeared in the doorway as Lucius was concluding his evening devotions. From her hand dangled a chiming ring of keys. Her plain gray tunic and tranquil demeanor did nothing to communicate the impression of someone in the midst of a jailbreak, though Lucius noted a glaze of perspiration on her face, despite the evening chill.

"Major. It's good to see you."

His heart was full of a feeling of events set in motion, circles closing, a destiny unveiled. All his life, it seemed, he had been anticipating this moment.

"Something's happening, isn't it?"

Amy nodded evenly. "I believe it is."

"I've prayed on it. I've prayed on *you.*"

Amy nodded. "We will have to move quickly."

They stepped from the cell and continued down the dark hallway. Sanders was asleep at his desk in the outer room, his face turned sideways over neatly folded arms. The second guard, Coolidge, was snoring on the floor.

"They won't awaken for a while," Amy explained, "and when they do, they'll have no memory of this. You will simply be gone."

Lucius reached down to withdraw Sanders's pistol from its holster, then glanced up to see Amy regarding him with a look of caution.

"Just remember," she warned. "Carter's one of us."

Lucius chambered a round and set the safety and tucked the gun into his waistband. "Understood."

Outside, they walked with measured briskness toward the pedestrian tunnel, keeping to the shadows. At the portal, three domestics were idly standing around a fire burning in an ash can, warming their hands.

"Good evening, gentlemen," said Amy.

They melted to their knees, looks of mild surprise stamped on their faces. Lucius and Amy eased their bodies to the ground.

"That's some trick," said Lucius. "You'll have to teach me sometime."

On the far side of the tunnel, a pair of saddled horses

waited. Lucius gave Amy a leg up, then climbed aboard the second horse, taking the reins loosely in his hand.

"One thing I need to ask," he said. "Why me?"

Amy thought a moment. "Each of us has one, Lucius."

"And Carter? Who does he have?"

An inscrutable look came into her eyes, as if her thoughts were carrying her far away. "He is different from the rest. He carries his familiar inside him."

"The woman in the water."

Amy smiled. "You've done your homework, Lucius."

"Things have a way of coming."

"Yes, they do. He loved her more than life but could not save her. She is the heart of him."

"And the dopeys?"

"They are his Many, his viral line. They kill only because they must. It goes hard with them. As he thinks, they think. As he dreams, they dream. They dream of her."

The horses were tamping the dust. It was just past midnight, a moonless sky the only witness to their departure.

"As I of you," said Lucius Greer. "As I of you."

They rode into the darkness.

35

Brothers, brothers.

And away, into the night. Julio Martínez, Tenth of Twelve, his legions discarded, cast to the wind. Julio Martínez, answering the call of Zero.

It is time. The moment of rebuilding has come. You will remake the world again; you will become the true masters of the earth, commanders not only of death but of life. You are the seasons. You are the turning earth. You are the circle within the circle within the circle. You are time itself, my brothers in blood.

In life Martínez had been an attorney, a man of law. He had stood before judges, defended the accused before juries of their peers. Death row cases were his specialty, his professional forté. He had acquired a particular brand of fame. The calls had come from everywhere: Would the great Julio Martínez, Esq., come to the aid of such-and-such? Could he be persuaded to swoop into action? The rock star who had bashed his girlfriend's brains out with a lamp. The state senator with the dead whore's blood on his hands. The suburban mother who had drowned her newborn triplets in the tub. Martínez took them all. They were insane or they were not; they pled or they didn't; they went to the needle, or the tiny cell, or scot-free. The outcome was irrelevant to Julio Martínez, Esq.; it was the drama he loved. To know one was going to die and yet struggle against its inevitability—that was the fascination. Once, as a boy, in the field behind his house, he had come upon a rabbit in a trap, the kind with a spring and teeth. Its iron jaws had clamped onto the animal's hind legs, flaying flesh to bone. The creature's small, dark eyes, like beads of oil, were full of death's wisdom. Life ebbed from it in a series of spasmodic scuffles. The boy Martínez could have watched for hours, and did just that; and when the rabbit failed to perish by nightfall, he carried it to the barn and returned to the house and ate his supper and went to bed in his room of toys and trophies, waiting for morning, when he could watch the rabbit die some more.

It had taken three days. Three glorious days.

Thus, his life and its dark investigations. Martínez had his reasons. He had his rationale. He had his particular method—the rag of spirits, the loyal cord and infinitely pliable duct tape, the dank, unseen compartments of dispatch. He chose low women, those lacking learning or culture, not because he despised them or secretly wanted them but because they were easy to ensnare. They were no match for his beautiful suits and movie-star hair and silken courtroom tongue. They were bodies without name or history or personality, and when the moment of transport approached, they offered no distraction. The timing was all, the orchestrated, simultaneous release. The old choir of sex and death singing.

A certain amount of practice had been required. There had been misfires. There had been, he was forced to admit, a certain amount of accidental comedy. The first one had died well but too soon, the second had kicked up such a ruckus that the whole thing had dissolved into farce, the third had wept so pitiably that he could hardly pay attention. But then: Louise. Louise, with her corny waitress uniform and sensible waitress shoes and unsexily supportive waitress hose. How beautifully she'd left her life! With what exquisite rapture in the taking! She was like a door opening into the great unknowable beyond, a portal into the infinite blackness of unbeing. He had been eradicated, pulverized; the winds of eternity had blown through him, beating him clean. It was everything he'd imagined and then some.

After that, frankly, he couldn't get enough of it.

As for the highway patrolman, the universe was not without its ironies. It gave and took away. To wit: the Jag with a broken taillight, and Martínez with the woman's bagged body in the trunk; the cop's slow saunter toward the car, his hand resting manfully on the butt of his pistol, and the downward glide of the driver's window; the patrolman's face pressed close, sneering with bored righteousness, his lips saying the customary words—*Sir, could I see . . . ?*—and never finishing. In the harried aftermath, Martínez had managed to dispose of the body in the trunk, his nighttime practices thus to remain forever unknown, unconnected to his fate. But a dead policeman by the side of the highway, everything recorded by his dashboard video camera, well. In the end, the only thing to do, as the saying went, was for the great Julio Martínez, Esq., champion of the unchampionable, defender of the loathsomely defenseless, to pour himself a glass of thirty-year-old single-malt and toss it over his tongue while the windows of the house twirled with the lights of justice and come out with his hands dutifully up.

Which, given the way things had worked out, hadn't turned out to be such an unlucky turn of events, actually.

Martínez couldn't say he cared much for his fellows. With the exception of Carter, who struck him as purely pitiable— the man didn't even seem to know what he was or what he'd done; Martínez hadn't heard so much as a squeak from the man in years—they were nothing more than common criminals, their deeds random and banal. Vehicular homicide. Armed robbery gone bad. Barroom shenanigans with a body on the floor. A century marinating in their own psychological waste had done nothing to improve them. Martínez's existence was not without its irritating aspects. The never quite being alone. The endless hunger always needing to be filled. The ceaseless talk-talk-talk inside his head, not just his brothers but Zero, too. And Ignacio: there was a piece of work. The man was a litany of self-pitying excuses. *I didn't mean to do half those things. It's just the way I was built.* After a hundred years listening to the man's whining, Martínez wouldn't miss him one bit.

There had been something attractively berserk about Babcock, though. You had to hand it to the man for metaphor. Carving out his mother's larynx with a kitchen knife; in another life, he surely would have been a poet. Over the decades, Martínez had mentally sat in that foul kitchen about a million times, and it was true: the woman would *not* shut up. There was a kind of person in this world who needed you to paint a picture, and Babcock's mother was that kind.

And then one day Babcock was simply gone, his signal silenced, like a television station suddenly off the air. The corner of Martínez's mind where Babcock stood, endlessly gouging out the gristly nubbin of his mother's voice box, was empty. All of them knew what had happened; their collective, blood-borne existence ordained it. One of their brothers had fallen.

God bless and keep you, Giles Babcock. May you find in death the peace that eluded you in life, and what came after.

And so from Twelve, Eleven. A loss, a chink in the armor, but ultimately a matter of lesser concern in the vital period to come. It had been a good century, on the whole, for Julio Martínez. He recalled the early days with poignant fondness. The days of blood and mayhem and the great unleashing of his kind upon the earth. To kill was one thing, one glorious thing; to take was another. A banquet richer still in its satisfactions. From each one Martínez had taken a flavorful bite of soul, drawing them into the fold, expanding his dominion. His Many were not merely *part* of him, an *extension* of him; they *were* him. As he, Julio Martínez, was one of Twelve and the Zero also, concomitant and coextensive, united with one another and with the darkness in which they permanently dwelled.

Brothers, brothers, it is time. Brothers, brothers, the hour is at hand.

For it was inevitable; they had built a race of pure rapaciousness. Their Many, created to protect them, had devoured the earth like locusts, leaving nothing in their wake. Feast had yielded to famine, summer's bounty to winter's scarcity; they would need a home, a zone of protection, of rest. To dream their dreams. To dream of Louise.

My brothers, your new home is waiting. They will bow before you; you will live as kings.

Martínez liked the sound of that.

He discarded them without ceremony. His Many, millionsfold. He called them together from all the hidden places and said to them: *Die.* Dawn was reaching its red-fingered hand over the horizon. They pointed their faces blindly toward it. They showed no hesitation; all that he commanded, so did they. The sun was moving toward them like a blade of light over the earth. *Lie down, my sons and daughters; lie down in the sun and die.*

There followed a certain amount of screaming.

Night by night he made his way east, across the exhausted land. His instincts were acute. The world rippled with sensuousness, caressing him with its sounds and smells. The grass. The wind. The subtlest movements of trees. He lingered, tasting all. He had been away too long. He called to his fellows, their voices threading with darkness as they made their way from every corner to the place of their renewal.

—We are Morrison-Chávez-Baffes-Turrell-Winston-Sosa-Echols-Lambright-Martínez-Reinhardt-Carter. Eleven of Twelve, one brother lost.

And Zero replied in kind:

Oh, my brothers, my pain is as great as your own. But you will be Twelve again. For I have made another, one to watch and keep you in your place of rest.

—Who? they asked, each as one and then together. —Who is the other you have made?

And Zero spoke from out of the darkness:

Our sister.

VI

THE INSURGENT

FORT POWELL, IOWA
POP. 69,172
97 A.V.

Night, you who gather in your lovely lap
The things the shining dawn flung far and wide,
The ewe-lamb you bring back, the straying goat,
The child you lead unto its mother's side.

—Sappho, c. 612 b.c.,
Fragment 120

ATTENTION

A MESSAGE FROM THE DIRECTOR

Citizens of the Homeland!
There are traitors among us!

The disgraceful methods of the so-called "insurgency" have reached new lows. Dozens of your fellow citizens, including innocent women and children, have been murdered in cold blood by these cowardly conspirators, who act without mercy.

We must defend ourselves!
Stand with your Director!
End the plague of violence!

We call on all citizens to help bring these despicable traitors to justice. The safety of our Homeland is at stake.

Everyone must do his part!

- Be vigilant. The person standing beside you might at this very moment be plotting the deaths of hundreds.
- Report any suspicious activities at once to Human Resources personnel.
- Maintain discipline in your lodging and workplace.
- Stand ready. At any time you may be called upon to assist with defense.
- Anyone offering aid to the insurgency or interfering with the duties of the Homeland Authority will be seen as an **enemy** of the state.

Watch! Listen! Stay on guard!
Together we can restore peace and
security to our beloved Homeland!

36

Everywhere people were whispering: there had been another bombing in the market.

The November morning broke gray and cold, tasting of the winter to come. Sara awoke to the blare of the horn, followed by a chorus of coughing, throats clearing, bones cracking ambivalently to life. Her eyes and mouth were as dry as paper. The room smelled of unwashed skin and stale breath and delousing powder, a biological vapor of human decay, though Sara barely noticed. Some of the smell, she knew, was herself.

Another pitiless sunrise, she thought. Another morning as a citizen of the Homeland.

She had learned not to linger on her bunk. One minute late to the ration line and you could find yourself dragging through the day without a scrap in your stomach. A bowl of corn mush trumped a few slender minutes of tormented half sleep every time. With her stomach growling, she unwrapped her threadbare blanket and swung her weight around, ducking her head, to plant her sneakered feet on the floorboards. She always slept wearing her sneakers, such as they were— a ragged pair of Reeboks inherited from a bunkmate who had died—because footwear was always being stolen. *Who took my shoes!* a voice would cry out, and the victim would go charging through the lodge, begging and accusing and eventually crumpling to the floor in hopeless tears. *I'll die without them! Somebody help me, please!* It was true: a person would die without shoes. Though she worked at the biodiesel plant, word had gotten out in the flatland that Sara was a nurse. She had seen the blackened nuts of frozen toes, the scabs of worms burrowed in; she'd pressed her ear to the sunken chests and listened to the pneumonic rattles of lungs slowly drowning; she'd felt beneath her fingertips the drum-taut bellies of septic appendicitis, or malignancy, or simple starvation; she'd palmed the foreheads blazing with fever and dressed the weeping wounds that would devour the body with rot. And to each person, Sara said, with the taste of a lie in her teeth: You'll be fine. Not to worry. In another few days you'll be right as rain, I promise. It wasn't medical care she was giving; it was a sort of blessing. You will die, and it will hurt, but you will do it here, among your own kind, and the last touch you feel will be one of kindness, because it will be mine.

Because you didn't want the cols to know you were sick, let alone the redeyes. Nothing was ever said aloud, but people in the flatland had few illusions what the hospital was actually for. Man or woman, old or young, it didn't matter; you passed through those doors and nobody saw you again. Off to the feedlot you went.

The lodges varied in size; Sara's was one of the largest. The bunks were stacked four high, twenty bunk lengths in each row, ten rows: eight hundred souls crammed into a room the approximate dimensions of a feed shed. People were rising, jamming their children's heads into hats, murmuring to themselves, their limbs moving with the heavy docility of livestock as they shambled to the door. Quickly scanning the area to make sure she wouldn't be observed, Sara knelt by her bunk, lifting the mattress with one hand while sliding the other beneath it. She removed the piece of carefully folded paper from its hiding place and secreted it in the pocket of her tunic. Then she drew herself upright.

"Jackie," Sara said quietly, "wake up."

The old woman was curled in a fetal position with the blanket drawn to her chin. Her rheumy eyes stared dully at the wash of gray descending from the high windows of the lodge. Sara had listened to her coughing all night.

"The light," Jackie said. "It looks like winter."

Sara felt her forehead. No trace of fever; if anything, the woman felt cold. It was hard to say how old Jackie was. She'd been born in the flats, but her parents had come from somewhere else. Jackie wasn't one to speak of the past, but Sara knew she had outlived three children and a husband, the last sent to the feedlot for the crime of coming to the aid of a friend who was being sticked by a col.

The room was rapidly emptying out. "Jackie, please." Sara shook her by the shoulder. "I know you're tired, but we've really got to go."

The woman's eyes drew Sara into focus. She trembled with a dry cough.

"I'm sorry, hon," she said, when the spasm had passed. "I don't mean to be uncooperative."

"I just don't want to miss breakfast. You need to eat."

"There you go, looking out for me like you always do. Help an old lady down, will you?"

Sara gave Jackie a shoulder for balance and eased her to the floor. Her body was practically weightless, a form of sticks and air. Another cough hacked through her chest, a sound like pebbles being shaken in a sack. She slowly drew herself erect.

"There now." Jackie took a moment to swallow. Her face was flushed; beads of dampness had risen on her forehead. "All better."

Sara pulled the blanket off her bunk and draped it over the woman's shoulders. "It's going to be a cold one. Stay by me, okay?"

Her lips stretched into a toothless smile. "Where else would I go, hon?"

Sara retained only fleeting images of her capture. A sense of certain death, everything over and done, and then a huge force, merciless in its energy, seizing her bodily. A glimpse of the ground dropping away as the viral hurled her into the air—why hadn't it just killed her?—and then another massive jolt as she was snatched once more, plucked from the air by the second viral, and then the third, and so on, each aerial vault catapulting her farther away from the walls and lights of the garrison and into the enveloping blackness, her person passed from airborne hand to airborne hand like a ball in a children's game, all of it beyond the boundaries of her comprehension, and then the final brain-battering impact as she was slammed into the truck. The awful coming to consciousness, like climbing a ladder from hell into hell. Days without water, without food. The endless bone-banging hours and whispered, unanswerable questions. Where were they going? What was happening to them? Nearly all the captives were women, part of the civilian corps stationed at Roswell, though a handful of soldiers were among them. The cries of the injured and frightened. The smothering darkness.

Sara's mind had not returned to full awareness until their arrival. It was as if time had stretched for the duration of their journey only to snap back into shape when the door opened onto a disorienting splash of daylight. Revealing . . . what? Half of the truck's human cargo had perished—a few dead at the outset and filling the compartment with a stink of gray decay, others from injuries sustained in their capture, the rest from some combination of hunger and thirst and suffocating hopelessness. Sara was lying on the floor, as they all were, both the living and the dead, inertly limbed and thick-tongued, her back propped against the wall, her eyes clenched against the unaccustomed brightness. An inversion of her physical proportions seemed to have occurred, such that most of her mass had lodged in her head. Over her lifetime, she had seen a lot of people die; lying among them was a first. The boundary separating her from them seemed a membrane as permeable as gauze. Through stinging slits, she watched as a half dozen expressionless men in ragged khaki and heavy, floor-banging boots boarded the compartment and commenced a perfunctory toting away of the deceased. She gathered that the unstructured weight of a dead body was something these men were accustomed to, its purposeless association of parts warranting no more consideration than any other awkward object a person might be forced to carry. Body after body, unceremoniously hauled away. When they came for her, Sara lifted a hand in protest; she might have said something like "Please" or "Wait" or "You can't do this." But these meager efforts were instantly silenced by a hot slap across her cheek, followed, for good measure, by the thrust of a boot that would have caught her midsection had Sara not protectively folded around herself.

"Shut. The fuck. Up."

She did. She shut the fuck up. The man who had struck her was a col Sara would come to know as Sod. Among the citizens of the flatland, all the cols had nicknames. Sod was Sod because he liked raping people. A lot of them did, it was like a game to them, but Sod distinguished himself by the breadth of his appetites. Women, men, children, livestock. Sod would have raped the wind if it had a hole in it.

Sara's turn in the shed would come: brief, brutal, over. In the near term, the pain of his blows had the counterintuitive effect of restoring her senses. Strategies began to form; priorities stepped into line. On balance, staying alive seemed desirable, and the shutting-the-fuck-up seemed the best way to accomplish this. Be quiet, she told herself. Blend in. See what you can see without seeming to. If they want to kill you, they'll do it anyway.

Don't mention the baby.

The clubs came out, poking and prodding as they were marched into the sunshine. They were someplace green. Its lushness mocked her, the cruelest of jokes. The truck had parked in a kind of holding area, a wired compound of stubby concrete buildings with glinting metal roofs; adjacent to this, at a distance of several hundred yards, was a massive, tiered structure, unlike anything Sara had ever seen. It looked like an enormous bathtub. Tall banks of lights lifted from its curving walls, ascending hundreds of feet into the air. While Sara watched, a gleaming silver semitruck, identical to the one they'd just disembarked, drew up to the building's base. Men were jogging alongside, carrying rifles. They wore bulky pads; caged masks were drawn down over their faces. As the truck approached the wall, it seemed to sink into the earth—a ramp, Sara realized, taking it belowground. A gate opened, and it was gone.

"Eyes down. No talking. Two lines, women to the left, men to the right."

Inside one of the huts, they were told to strip and deposit their clothes in a pile. Now they stood naked, twenty-three women in identically reflexive postures of self-protection, one arm held horizontally to shield their breasts, the other extended downward over their genitals. Three of the uniformed men looked on, rocking on their heels, alternating frank leers with laughing faces of disgust. There were gutters in the floor, drains. Slants of light descended from a series of long, barred windows at the roofline. Twenty-three naked women wordlessly staring at the floor, most of them in tears: to speak would be to violate some implied contract to go on living. Whatever was headed their way seemed to be taking its time getting there.

Then, the hose.

The water blasted them like a jet of ice. Water as weapon; water as battering fist. Everyone was yelling, women were tumbling, bodies were sliding on the floor. The hose's operator enjoyed himself spectacularly, whooping like a rider on a galloping horse. He picked off one and then another. He swept them in a line. He zigzagged his pummeling probe from their faces to their breasts and farther down. The water hit you and then it stopped and then it hit you again. There was nowhere to run, nowhere to hide; all you could do was endure.

It stopped.

"Everybody on your feet."

They were led outside again in their shivering nakedness. Water was streaming down their faces, running in rivulets from their hair. Their skin puckered with its evaporation. A single wooden chair had been placed in the middle of the compound. One of the guards stood beside it, languidly sharpening a razor on a leather strop. Four more approached, each bearing a large plastic tub.

"Get dressed."

Clothing was tossed their way—loose pants with draw-string waists, long-sleeved tunics that hung to the hips, all made of scratchy wool with a harsh chemical smell—followed by a random assortment of shoes: sneakers, plastic sandals, boots with the soles split away. Sara found her feet swimming in a pair of leather lace-ups.

"You, step forward."

The man with the razor was pointing at Sara. The other women parted around her. There was something disloyal about this, though Sara hardly blamed them; she might have done the same. Doom weighing in her chest, she approached the chair and sat. She was facing the other women now. Whatever was about to happen, Sara would see it first in their eyes. The man swept her hair into his fist and yanked it taught. A single slice and it was gone. He began to chop indiscriminately at the remains, hewing close to her scalp. There was no pattern to his efforts; he might just as well have been slashing his way through a forest. Sara's hair fell to her feet in golden ribbons.

"Go stand with the others."

She returned to the group. When she touched her head, her fingers came away tacky with blood. She studied its texture with her fingertips. *This is my blood,* Sara thought. *Because it is my blood, it means that I'm alive.* The second woman was in the chair now. Sara thought her name was Caroline. She had met her briefly in the infirmary at the Roswell Garrison; like Sara, she was a nurse. A tall, impressively big-boned girl who radiated health, good cheer, competence. She wept into her hands as the barber hacked away.

One by one they were shorn. So much came down to hair, Sara realized. In their disfigured semibaldness, something private had been stolen, melding them into an indistinguishable collective, like animals in a herd. She was so light-headed with hunger she didn't see how she could continue standing. None of them had had a scrap to eat—no doubt to keep them compliant, so that when food was offered they would feel some gratitude to their captors.

When the cutting was done, they were told to march across the holding area to a second concrete building for something called "processing." They were marshaled into a line before a long table, where one of the guards, radiating the sense of being in charge, sat with a look of irritation on his face. As each was called forward, he reloaded a clipboard.

"Name?"

"Sara Fisher."

"Age?"

"Twenty-one."

He eyed her up and down. "Can you read?"

"I can read. Yes."

"Special skills?"

She hesitated. "I can ride."

"Ride?"

"Horses."

His eyes rolled a little. "Anything useful?"

"I don't know." She tried to think of something safe. "Sew?"

He yawned. His teeth were so bad, they appeared to wiggle in his mouth. He jotted something onto the clipboard and tore off the bottom half of the page. From a bin beneath the table he retrieved a ratty blanket, a metal plate, a battered cup and spoon. He passed these to her, the paper balanced on top. Sara quickly glanced at it: her name, a five-digit string of numbers, "Lodge 216," and, below that, "Biodiesel 3." The handwriting had the blockiness of a child's.

"Next!"

One of the guards took her by the arm and led her down a hallway of sealed doors. A tiny box of a room and another chair, though not like any chair Sara had seen before: a menacing contraption of cracked red leather and steel, its back reclined at a forty-five-degree angle, with straps at the chest, feet, and wrists. Lurking above it, like the legs of a spider descending on silken threads, was an armature of gleaming metal instruments. The guard shoved her toward it.

"Sit down."

He strapped her to the chair and departed. From without the room, the sound muffled by the thick walls, came a burst of ominously high-pitched sound. Was it screaming? Sara thought she might be ill. She would have been, if there had been anything in her stomach to come up. The last of her defenses were collapsing. She would beg. She would plead. She had no strength to resist.

The door opened behind her. A man stepped into her field of vision, dressed in a gray smock. He had a little round belly and clouded glasses perched at the tip of his nose and bushy eyebrows that curled like wings at the tips. Something about his face was kind, almost grandfatherly. Like the guard at the table, he was looking at a clipboard. He raised his eyes and smiled.

"Sara, is it?"

She nodded, tasting bile.

"I'm Dr. Verlyn." He glanced at the straps, frowning as he shook his head. "Those people are idiots. I bet you're famished. Let's see if we can get you out of here."

She experienced a flash of hope that he intended to release her, but as he drew a stool beside the chair, snapping on a pair of rubber gloves, she realized he meant something else. He placed his hand beneath her chin to open her jaw. He peered inside her mouth, then held up two fingers before her face.

"Follow with your eyes, please."

Sara traced his fingers as they made a figure eight and pulled away. He took her pulse, then produced a stethoscope from the pocket of his smock and listened to her heart. He sat up straight and returned his attention to the clipboard, squinting through his glasses.

"Any health problems you're aware of? Parasites, infection, night sweats, difficulty urinating?"

Sara shook her head.

"How about menstruation?" He was checking off boxes. "Any problems there? Excessive bleeding, for example."

"No."

"It says here you're . . ." He paused, flipped through pages. "Twenty-one. Is that correct?"

"Yes."

"Ever been pregnant?"

Something clenched inside her.

"It's a simple question."

She shook her head. "No."

If he detected her lie, he gave no sign. He let the clipboard fall to his lap. "Well, you appear to be in perfect health. Wonderful teeth, if you don't mind my saying so. Nothing to be done there."

Was she supposed to say thank you? Above her face the spider still loomed, gleaming ominously.

"Now then, let's see if we can't finish up quickly and get you on your way."

Suddenly something changed. Sara sensed it in a quick hardening of his features, but not just there; it was as if the air of the room had undergone some subtle alteration. The doctor began vigorously pumping a pedal beneath her chair, producing a whirring sound, then reached above her face to draw down one of the spider's legs. At its tip, spinning in time to his foot strokes, was a buzzing drill bit.

"This will be easier if you don't move."

* * *

Some minutes later, Sara found herself standing outside, clutching her meager belongings to her chest. When she'd started to scream, the doctor had given her a leather strap to bite on. On the pale skin of the inside of her forearm, first gouged and then cauterized in place, was a shiny metal tag, engraved with the same string of digits she'd seen on the paper: 94801. That's who you are now, the doctor had explained, removing the strap, now with its embedded impressions of her teeth. He'd stripped off his gloves and stepped to the sink to wash his hands. Whoever you thought you were, you're not that person anymore. You're flatlander number 94801.

The semi was gone, replaced by an open-backed five-ton. Sara saw the words IOWA NATIONAL GUARD imprinted on the driver's door—the first evidence of where she was. A guard motioned for Sara to board; a second guard was standing at the front of the cargo bay, his back braced against the cab, idly spinning his club on its leather strap. Some of the women were already there and a few of the men as well. Everyone was slumped on the benches, their faces carrying the stunned weight of all that had occurred.

She took a place beside one of the men, a young officer she knew as Lieutenant Eustace. He had been the scout who had brought them into Roswell. As she lowered herself to the bench, he angled his shorn head close to Sara's.

"What the hell is this place?" he whispered.

Before Sara could answer, the guard sparked to attention. "You," he barked, gesturing at Eustace with the end of his club. "No talking."

"Who are you people? Why won't you tell us anything?"

"I said, keep quiet."

Sara understood what was about to happen. It was the implied climax of the day's design, the one demonstration of their powerlessness that had yet to be delivered.

"Yeah?" Eustace's face lit with defiance, the last of his energy spitting from his lips. He knew what he was asking for; he didn't care. "Go to hell, all of you."

The guard took a long stride forward and, with a look of absolute boredom, brought the club crashing down on Eustace's knees. Eustace rocked forward, clenching his teeth in barely contained agony. Nobody moved a muscle; everyone was gazing intently at the floor.

"Mother . . . *fucker*," he gasped.

The guard spun the club around and backhanded the

heavy end into Eustace's nose. A wet exoskeletal crunch, like the sound of an insect stamped underfoot; a crimson spray arced into the air, spattering Sara across the face. Eustace's head snapped back, his eyes fluttering in their sockets. He ran his tongue along the inside of his upper lip and spat a shard of a tooth away.

"I said . . . *fuck* . . . *you.*"

Blow after hammering blow: his face, his head, the bony joints of his hands. By the time Eustace toppled over, his eyes rolled back into his skull, his features crushed into a pulpy mass, blood had rained down on them all.

"Get used to it." The guard paused to wipe his baton on his pant leg and dragged his eyes over the group. "It's pretty much how we do things."

As the truck pulled away, Sara drew Eustace toward her to cradle his ruined face in her lap. The man was barely conscious, his breath gurgling in his throat. Perhaps he would die; it seemed likely. And yet there was a feeling of victory in what he'd done. She bent at the neck and whispered into his ear:

"Thank you."

Thus, in blood, it began.

"One People! One Director! One Homeland!"

How many times had Sara been forced to shout these words? With the morning roll call and the singing of the anthem complete, everyone dispersed to their designated transports. Sara helped Jackie up, then climbed aboard. She saw a new face, one she recognized: Constance Chou, Old Chou's wife. They acknowledged each other with tight nods, but that was all. What had happened at the Colony had come to Sara in bits and pieces over the years. The story was no different from the others she'd heard and differed from the events at Roswell only by degree; in many ways, the greater shock had been that so many other islands of humanity had existed at all. By the time Sara arrived, the Colony's survivors had already dispersed across the flatland. The number Sara heard was fifty-six. How easy it was for fifty-six people to be subsumed into the masses; with their chopped hair and identical tunics, everybody looked the same. Yet every now and then, a familiar face leapt out. She had glimpsed a woman she thought was Penny Darrell, and another who she swore was Belle Ramirez, Rey's wife, though when Sara had called her name, the woman hadn't answered. One morning in the ration line, her bowl had been filled by a man she had seen many times without recognizing as Russell Curtis, her own cousin. He appeared so much older than the man Sara recalled that when their eyes met, it took her a moment to place him. For the better part of a year she had been housed in the same lodge as Karen Molyneau, Jimmy's widow, and her two daughters, Alice and Avery. It was from Karen that Sara took the most information, including the names of the dead. Ian Patal, who had been killed defending the power station. Hollis's sister-in-law, Leigh, and her baby, Dora, who had perished on the trip to the Homeland; Other Sandy, who had died shortly after arrival, Karen wasn't sure how; Gloria and Sanjay Patal. As dark as this news was, Sara still regarded her year with Karen and her girls as a brief respite, a period in which she'd felt connected to the past. But they were always moving people around between the lodges, and one day the three of them were gone, strangers sleeping in the bunks where they had lain their heads for a year. Sara hadn't seen them since.

The ride to the biodiesel plant took them along the river, through a maze of squalid lodges to the industrial zone at the north edge of the flatlands. The day gave no promise of improvement; a bitter wind spit kernels of rain into their faces. The air was ripe with the stenches of the flatland, pooling animal waste and a compressed and filthy humanity and, behind it, like a curtain of scent, the dark earthiness of the river. They passed through a juggernaut of checkpoints, fences opening and closing, the cols with their clipboards and pens and inexhaustible appetite for paperwork and the structures of authority waving them through. The far side of the river gave onto open floodplain, denuded and colorless, the crops long picked for winter; to the east, ascending in steps above the river, rose the Hilltop, where all the redeyes lived, and at its apex the Capitol Dome, capped with its crown of gold. It was said that this structure, and those surrounding it, had at one time been a university, which was a kind of school, though with only the Sanctuary for comparison, Sara had difficulty absorbing this fact. Sara had never been up the hill, let alone inside the Dome. Some workers were allowed inside, gardeners and plumbers and kitchen help, and of course the attendants, who were women selected to serve the Director and his staff of redeyes. Everybody said the attendants were the lucky ones, that they lived in luxury with good food and hot water and soft beds to sleep in, but the information was all secondhand. No attendant had ever returned to the flatland; once they went in, the Dome became their lives.

"Get a look at that," Jackie murmured.

Sara's thoughts had wandered off, her awareness blunted by the cold. They were cutting away from the river on the access road; to the north, beyond the boundaries of the Homeland, Sara could make out the shape of the cranes spiking through the treetops like a pair of huge, skeletal birds. The Project, it was called: a decades-long undertaking to erect a massive steel-and-concrete structure of unknown purpose. Flatlanders who worked there, nearly all of them men, were searched each day going to and coming from the site; even to talk about what they did there was regarded as treason and could get you sent to the feedlot, though rumors abounded. One theory would hold sway for a time before yielding to another and then to a third, the first eventually reemerging to start the cycle anew. Even the men who worked there, when they could be convinced to speak of it at all, did not appear to know what they were constructing. There was talk of mazelike hallways, vast chambers, foot-thick doors of solid steel. Some claimed it was a monument to the Director, others that it was a factory. A few claimed it was nothing at all, merely a distraction concocted by the redeyes to keep the flatlanders occupied. A fourth hypothesis, one that had gained currency in recent months, was that the Project was an emergency bunker. Should the Director's mysterious power to keep the virals at bay ever fail, the structure could serve as a refuge for the population. Whatever it was, the work appeared to be approaching completion; fewer and fewer men would board the transports to the site each morning, and they were all older, most having worked there for years.

But the cranes weren't the object of Jackie's attention. As the five-ton drew toward the last guardhouse, Sara saw two words imprinted on the perimeter wall, painted in broad, dripping strokes of white:

SERGIO LIVES!

A pair of flatlanders were dousing long-armed brushes in buckets of soapy water, preparing to scrub it off. A col stood beside them with a rifle cradled over his chest. He glowered as the transport passed, meeting Sara's eye for an icy instant. She looked away.

"Fisher, you see anything that interests you?"

The voice belonged to one of the two cols riding in the back of the truck, a trim man of twenty-five or so, who went by the name Vale.

"No, sir."

For the final five minutes of the ride, she kept her eyes glued to the floor. Sergio, Sara thought. Who was Sergio? The name, rarely spoken in the open, possessed an almost incantatory power: Sergio, leader of the insurgency, bomber of markets and police stations and guardhouses, who, with his unseen fellows, seemed to glide like ghosts through the Homeland, igniting weapons of destruction. Sara understood the words on the fence to be a kind of taunt. *We were here,* they said, *we stood right where you are standing now, we are everywhere among you.* Sergio's methods were marked by an almost incomprehensible cruelty. The insurgents' targets were anywhere the cols might gather, a program of assassination and disruption, but if you were in the wrong place at the wrong time, your presence made no difference. A man or woman would open their coat to reveal the rows of dynamite strapped to their chest, and that would be the end of you. And always, in the final instant, as their thumb found the trigger on the detonator, sending themselves and anyone within the blast radius into oblivion, they would utter these two words: Sergio lives.

The transport pulled up to the plant, and the workers disembarked. A yeasty odor hung in the air. Four more trucks of workers pulled in behind them. Sara and Jackie were assigned to the grinders, as were most of the women. Why this should be so, Sara had never understood—the job was neither more nor less arduous than anything else—but that's how things were done. Corn would be mashed, then combined with fungal enzymes and fermented to make fuel. The smell was so intense that it seemed to be part of Sara's very skin, though she had to admit there were far worse jobs: tending the hogs, or working at the waste treatment plant or slurry pens. They got into line to check in with the foreman, tied their kerchiefs around their faces, then made their way through the cavernous space to their workstations. The corn was stored in large bins with spouts at the bottom; from these openings they would retrieve one bushel at a time and load it into the grinders, where rotating paddles pummeled the kernels into meal. As the moisture in the corn was released it formed a gluey paste, which adhered to the interior walls of the grinder; it was the operator's job to dislodge it, a task requiring great dexterity and quickness, as the paddles did not stop rotating. The difficulty was compounded by the cold, which made even the simplest movements feel sluggish and imprecise.

Sara set to work. The day that loomed ahead would pass in a kind of trance. It was a skill she'd acquired as the years had passed, employing the hypnotic rhythms of work to drain her mind of thought. Not to think: that was the goal. To occupy a purely biological state, her senses absorbing only the most immediate physical data: the whir of the grinder's paddles, the stink of fermenting corn, the nubbin of cold emptiness in her belly where the measly bowl of watery gruel that passed for breakfast had long since been absorbed. For these twelve hours, she was flatlander no. 94801, nothing less or more. The real Sara, the one who thought and felt and remembered—Sara Fisher, First Nurse, citizen of the Colony, daughter of Joe and Kate Fisher and sister of Michael; beloved of Hollis, friend to many, mother of one—was hidden away in a folded slip of paper, tucked like a talisman in her pocket.

She did her best to keep an eye on Jackie. The woman had her worried; a cough like hers was nothing good. In the flatlands a person didn't really have friends, not in the way that Sara had known friendship. There were faces you knew and people you trusted more than others, but that was the extent of it. You didn't talk about yourself, because you weren't really anybody, or your hopes, since you had none. But with Jackie she had allowed her defenses to drop. They had formed a mutual pact, an unstated pledge to watch out for each other.

At noon they were given a fifteen-minute break, just enough time to race to the latrine—a wooden platform suspended above a ditch, with holes to squat over—and gobble another bowl of gruel. There was no place to sit, so you ate standing up or on the ground, using your fingers for a spoon, then got in a second line for water, which was dispensed with a ladle that all the women shared. All the while they were watched by the cols, who stood to the side, twirling their sticks. Their official title was Human Resources Officers, but nobody ever called them that in the flatland. The word was short for "collaborators." Nearly all were men but there were some women, often the cruelest of the lot. One female col, whom they called Whistler for the deep cleft in her upper lip, a congenital deformity that gave her voice a distinctive, reedlike sound, seemed to take special delight in inventing new and subtle ways to inflict discomfort. It was her habit to single out one person, most often a woman, as if she were performing an experiment. Whistler set her sights on you and the next thing you knew you would be pulled out of the latrine line for a pat-down just when it was your turn, or assigned some impossible and pointless job, or switched to a different crew just as your break was coming. The only thing you could do was take it, gritting your teeth through the misery of your aching bladder or empty stomach or exhausted limbs, knowing that soon Whistler's attention would pass to another, though this only made things worse and seemed to be the point of the entire exercise; you found yourself wishing for the suffering to befall somebody else, and thus you became complicit, part of the system, a cog in a wheel of torment that never stopped turning.

She looked for Jackie at the break, but the woman was nowhere to be seen. Sara moved quickly through grinding stations, searching for her friend. The foreman's whistle would blow at any moment, summoning them back to work. She had nearly given up when she turned a corner to find Jackie sitting on the ground, her face damp with sweat, her kerchief balled to her mouth.

"I'm sorry," she managed. "I just couldn't stop coughing."

The cloth was stained with blood. Sara knew what was happening; she'd seen it before, the effects of years of dust in the lungs. One minute a person was fine, the next they were drowning in it.

"We have to get you out of here."

She pulled the woman to her feet just as the whistle blew. One hand wrapped around Jackie's waist, Sara steered her toward the exit. Her goal was to get outside before anyone noticed; what would happen after that, Sara had no idea. Vale was the col in charge. Not the best, but not the worst, either. More than once, Sara had caught him watching her in a way that made it seem like he had something in mind for her, something personal, though he had never acted on it. Perhaps now would be the time. A shuddering nausea passed through her at the thought, yet she knew she was capable of it. She would do what she had to.

They had nearly reached the exit when a figure stepped into their path. "Where do you think you're going?"

Not Vale: Sod. Backlit by the open door, he loomed before them. Sara's stomach dropped.

"She just needs some air. The dust—"

"Is that right, old woman? The dust bothering you?" With

the butt of his stick he tapped the woman's chest, igniting a strangled cough. "Get back to work."

"It's all right, Sara," Jackie wheezed, freeing herself from Sara's arm. "I'll be fine."

"Jackie—"

"I mean it." She looked at Sara, her eyes saying, *Don't.* "She's just a busybody, that's all. Thinking she knows what's best for me."

Sod's eyes flicked the length of Sara's body. "Yeah, I heard that about you. Think you're some kind of doctor, do you?"

"I never said that."

"Sure you didn't." With his free hand Sod cupped his crotch, rocking his hips forward. "Hey, Doctor, I've got a pain right here. What do you say you get a closer look at it?"

The moment caught and held; Sara thought of Eustace, in the truck. The blood on his face, his shattered hands and teeth. His broken smile of triumph. Standing before Sod, she willed herself to say the words, to utter the curse that would unleash him upon her. It was all so simple, so stark. She could see the scene unfolding in her mind. Just two words, and the flare of anger in Sod's eyes, and then the crash of the stick. These were the terms of her life, a thousand humiliations enacted daily. They had taken everything from her. To accept the worst—no, to embrace it—that was the only resistance.

"Sara, *please.*" Jackie was staring at her. *Not like this. Not for me.*

Sara swallowed. Everyone was looking at her.

"Okay," she said.

She turned and walked away. The space around her had grown strangely quiet. All she could hear was her heart.

"Don't worry, Fisher," Sod called after her with a leering laugh. "I'll know where to find you. It'll be as good as the last time, I promise."

It was later, as Sara lay in her cot, that she permitted herself to consider the full measure of these events. Something had changed within her. She was on the verge, a figure standing at the precipice, waiting to jump. Five long years: it could have been a thousand. The past was disappearing inside her, rinsed away by the wash of time, the bitter cold of her heart, the sameness of days. She had plunged down inside herself for too long. Winter was coming. Winter light.

She had somehow gotten Jackie through the day. Now the old woman slept above her, the straps of her bunk sagging with her restive turning. Jackie's death, when it came, would come badly, in long agonal hours, a strangling from within, before the final stilling. Would her fate be Sara's own? To stumble blindly through the years, a being without purpose or connection, a hollow shell of nothing?

Sara had not returned the makeshift envelope to its hiding place under the mattress. Seized by a sudden loneliness, she withdrew it from beneath the lump of rags that served as her pillow. It had been given to her by the midwife's assistant in the birthing ward—the same woman who had told her that the baby, arriving early in a gush of blood, had not survived. It was a girl, the woman had told her. I'm sorry. Then she'd slipped the envelope into Sara's hand and vanished. Through the haze of grief and pain Sara had ached to hold her daughter, but this hadn't happened; the child had been taken away. She'd never seen the woman again.

Carefully she unfolded the pocket of brittle paper with the tips of her fingers. Inside lay a coiled lock of hair—a baby curl. The room was sunk in darkness, and yet its pale golden color was vivid to her eyes. She brought it to her face, inhaling deeply, trying to capture its scent. Sara could never have another, the damage was too great; Kate was the only one. That was what she'd named her, Kate. How she wished she'd told Hollis. She had wanted to save her news, to choose the perfect moment to give him the present of the two of them conjoined. How foolish she'd been. She thought: I know you're better off, my darling. Wherever you are now, I hope it is a place of light and sky and love. If only I could have held you, just one time, to tell you how much I loved you.

37

This Sergio thing: it had simply gone on too long.

Not that there hadn't been uprisings before. The year 31, wasn't it? And again in 68? Not to mention the hundred little brushfires of defiance put down over the years. And wasn't it true that the problem inevitably boiled down to a single individual, a lone renegade, who simply failed to get the *point*? That when this man was taken care of (it was always a man), the flames of resistance, deprived of their essential oxygen, would extinguish of their own accord?

And yet this Sergio: he didn't feel like the others. Standing in the window at the base of the cupola, his gaze directed over the grimy stain of the flatland and the colorless, winter fields beyond, Director Horace Guilder took stock. The man's methods were different, for starters, not merely in quantity but in kind. People blowing themselves up! Strapping sticks of dynamite to their chests, or pipe bombs crammed with shards of glass and broken screws, and actually mustering the will to blow themselves and everyone around them to a bloody mist! It was beyond madness, a full-blown psychosis that could only mean that this Sergio, whoever he was, held a deeper psychological sway over his followers than any who had come before. The flatlanders had safety, they had food to warm their bellies, they slept in beds at night without fear of the virals. They were allowed to live their lives, in other words, and this was the thanks he got? Couldn't they see that everything he'd done, he'd done for them? That he had built a home for mankind so that it might, against the prevailing winds of history, continue?

True, there was a certain . . . unfairness to things. An uneven distribution of resources, one could say, a partitioning of management from labor, of haves from have-nots, us from them. An unpleasant reliance on the human capacity for pulling the ladder up behind oneself, and the time-tested tools—icy showers, endless lines to stand in, the excessive use of proper nouns, loudspeakers blaring a constant stream of inanities, etc.—of broad social compliance. "One People! One Homeland! One Director!" The words made him wince, but a certain amount of stage-managed demagoguery went with the territory. Nothing really new, in other words, all of it warranted under the terms of the present age. But sometimes, such as now, on this icy Iowa morning, the first arctic front of the season bearing down on them like a runaway train of ass-hammering cold, Guilder had a hard time maintaining his enthusiasm.

His expansive suite of offices, which also functioned as his living quarters, had served, at various times in its two-hundred-year history, as the office of the Iowa territorial governor, the headquarters of the state historical museum, and a storage room. Its last old-world occupant had been the provost of Midwest State University, a man named August Frye (so read the man's stationery), who, from its generous windows, had no doubt passed many happy hours soaking in the heartwarming sight of cheerful corn-fed undergraduates flirting like maniacs as they strolled their way to class upon its well-kept Iowa lawns. On the day Guilder had assumed residency, he'd been surprised to discover that

Provost August Frye had decorated the place with a nautical theme: ships in bottles, maps with serpents, overwrought oil paintings of lighthouses and oceanscapes, an anchor. A strikingly incongruous choice, given that Midwest State (go Bearcats!) was hard aground in about the most landlocked place on earth. After nearly a hundred years, what Guilder wouldn't have given for a smidgen of scenery.

Hence the major problem with immortality, apart from the peculiar diet: everything began to bore you.

At such moments, the only thing that cheered him was taking stock of his accomplishments. Which were not inconsiderable; they had constructed a city literally from nothing. What excitement he'd felt in the early days. The ceaseless ring of hammers. The trucks returning from their journeys across an unmanned continent, bursting with the abandoned treasures of the old world. The hundreds of tactical decisions made daily, and the buzzing energy of the staff— men handpicked from among the survivors for their expertise. They had, in short, built a veritable brain trust from the human leavings of catastrophe. Chemists. Engineers. City planners. Ag scientists. Even an astronomer (who had come in surprisingly handy) and an art historian, who had advised Guilder (who, to be perfectly honest, couldn't tell Monet's water lilies from dogs playing poker) on the proper preservation and display of a major haul of masterworks from the Art Institute of Chicago, which now decorated the walls of the Dome, including Guilder's office. What fun they'd had! Granted, there was a certain frat-house mentality to the way they'd conducted themselves, minus the sexual shenanigans, of course. (The virus pretty much gutted that part of your brain like a trout; most of the staff couldn't even bring themselves to look at a woman without making a face.) But in the main, decorum and professionalism had ruled the day.

Such happy memories. And now: Sergio. Now: pipe bombs. Now: the bloody mist.

Guilder's train of thought was broken by a rap on the door. He heaved a weary sigh. Another day of forms to fill out, duties to be parceled, edicts to be issued from on high. Taking a seat behind his desk, an expanse of eighteenth-century polished mahogany the approximate dimensions of a ping-pong table, as rightly befit his station as Beloved Director of the Homeland, Guilder braced himself for another morning's ceaseless appetite for his opinions—a thought that gave rise almost instantly to the first inklings of an appetite of a more physical and pressing nature, a burble of acid-tasting emptiness that ascended from his gut. So soon? Was it that time of the month already? The only thing worse than the burps were the farts that came after, room-clearing jets of oniony gas that even the farter himself could not enjoy.

"Come."

As the door swung open, Guilder drew up his necktie and hastened to make himself look occupied, shifting documents around the desktop with manufactured intensity. He selected one arbitrarily—it turned out to be a report on repairs at the sewage treatment plant, a page literally about shit—and pretended to study it for a full thirty seconds before lifting his eyes with directorial fatigue toward the dark-suited figure waiting in the doorway, holding a clipboard chunky with paper.

"Got a second?"

Guilder's chief of staff, whose name was Fred Wilkes, advanced into the room. Like all residents of the Hilltop, his eyes had the bloodshot look of a chronic pot smoker's. He also possessed the glossily sleek appearance of a twenty-five-year-old—a far cry from the wiry septuagenarian of Guilder's first acquaintance. Wilkes had been the first to come aboard; Guilder had discovered the man hiding out in one of the college's dormitories in the first days after the attack. He was holding—hugging, really—the body of his late wife, whose hefty proportions had not been improved by three days of gaseous decomposition in the Iowa heat. As Wilkes related, the pair had fled the refugee-processing center on foot when the buses had failed to arrive; they'd made it all of three sweltering miles before his wife had clutched her chest, rolled her eyes heavenward, and toppled over, dead of a heart attack. Unable to leave her behind, Wilkes had scavenged a wheelbarrow and carted her mountainous form to the college, where he'd taken refuge with only her corpse, and his memories of a lifetime shared, for company. Despite the horrendous smell (which Wilkes either didn't notice or much care about), the two of them made for a genuinely heartrending sight that might have moved Guilder to tears if he were a certain kind of man, which he might have once been but was no longer.

"Listen," Guilder had said, kneeling before the grief-stricken man, "I'd like to make you a proposition."

And so it had begun. It was that very day, that very hour in fact, even as he'd watched Wilkes take his first disgusted sip, that Guilder had heard the Voice. As far as he could tell, he was still the only one; none of the other staffers gave so much as a hint of experiencing Zero's mental presence. And as for the woman, who knew what was going on inside her head?

Now, the width of one and a half human lifetimes later, his grand design coming to fruition and the last of humanity having been gathered at his feet (the Kerrville thing, like the Sergio thing, being a small but significant irritant, a pea under the mattress of the Plan), here was Wilkes with his omnipresent clipboard and a facial expression, evidently, of not-good news.

"I just thought you should know the gathering party's back. What's, ah, left of it."

With this disconcerting introduction, Wilkes withdrew the top sheet of paper from his clipboard and placed it on Guilder's desk and backed away, as if he were happy to be rid of the thing.

Guilder scanned it quickly. "What the hell, Fred."

"I guess you could say things didn't go exactly as planned."

"*Nobody*? Not one of them? What is *wrong* with these people?"

Wilkes gestured toward the paper. "The flow of oil has been at least temporarily disrupted. That's a plus. It opens a lot of doors."

But Guilder was beyond consolation. First Kearney, now this. There had been a time when scooping up survivors had proved a relatively clear-cut undertaking. The woman appeared; the gates swung open, the wheel of the vault began to turn, the drawbridge descended over the moat; the woman did her stuff, like a lion tamer at the circus; and the next thing you knew, the trucks were galloping back to Iowa, packed with human cargo. The Kentucky caves. That island in Lake Michigan. The abandoned missile silos in North Dakota. More recently, the California raid had been a bona-fide bonanza, fifty-six survivors taken, most of whom had marched like lambs into the truck once the power was cut and the terms were set. (Get in or you're meat.) The usual attrition rate—some died en route, others failed to adapt to their new circumstances—but a solid haul nonetheless.

Since then, it had been one out-of-control bloodbath after another, starting with Roswell.

"Apparently there wasn't much of a negotiation phase. The convoy was pretty heavily armed."

"I don't care if they had a nuclear missile. We knew that going in. These are *Texans*."

"In a manner of speaking, that's true."

"We're about to go on-line here, and this is what you tell me? We need bodies, Fred. Living, breathing bodies. Can't she control these things anymore?"

"We could go in the old-fashioned way. I said so from the start. We'd take some casualties, but if we keep hitting their oil supply, sooner or later their defenses will weaken."

"We *collect* people, Fred. We don't lose them. Have I failed to make myself clear? Can you not do basic math? People are the *point*."

Wilkes shrugged defensively. "You want to talk to her?"

Guilder rubbed his eyes. He supposed he'd have to make the gesture, but talking to Lila was like playing handball by yourself: the ball came right back no matter how hard you slapped it. One of the most significant aggravations of the job was dealing with the woman's peculiar fantasies, a wall of delusion that Guilder could penetrate only by the roughest sort of insistence. Of all the experts he'd harvested through the years, why hadn't he thought to get a shrink? Keeping her in babies made her calm; the woman's special talent was an indispensable commodity that needed to be managed with care. But in the throes of motherhood she was virtually unreachable, and Guilder worried about further damaging her fragile psyche.

Because that was the thing about Lila. Of everyone who had tasted the blood, only she was endowed with the ability to control the virals.

More than control: in Lila's presence, they became like pets, docile and even affectionate. The feeling was a two-way street; put the woman within two hundred yards of the feedlot, and she turned into a purring cat with a litter of kittens. The effect was nothing Guilder had been able to replicate on his own, though Lord knows he'd tried. Back in the early days, he'd been downright obsessed. Time after time he'd donned the pads and gone into the feedlot, thinking that if he could only find the right mental trick or ingratiating body language or soothing tone of voice they'd fall at his knees the way they did with her, like dogs waiting for their ears to be scratched. But this never happened. They'd tolerate his presence for a whopping three seconds before one of them tossed him in the air—he didn't register as food, more like a man-sized toy—and the next thing Guilder knew he'd be flying around the place until somebody hit the lights to get him out.

He'd long since stopped trying, of course. The sight of

Horace Guilder, Director of the Homeland, being batted around like a beach ball wasn't exactly the kind of confidence-inspiring image he wanted to broadcast. Nor could anybody on the medical staff explain to his satisfaction just what it was that made Lila different. Her thymus cycled faster, needing the blood every seven days, and her eyes looked different, displaying none of the retinal stain that marked the senior staffers'. But her sensitivity to light was just as pronounced, and as far as Suresh could tell, the virus in her blood was the same as theirs. In the end, the man had thrown up his hands and attributed her abilities to the less than subtle fact that Lila was a woman—the only woman in the fold, which was how Guilder wanted it.

Maybe that's all there is to it, Suresh had said. *Maybe they just think she's their mother.*

Guilder became aware that Wilkes was looking at him. What had they been talking about? Lila? No, Texas. But Wilkes had told him there was something else.

"Which brings me to, um, the second thing." And that was when Wilkes told Guilder about the bombing in the market.

Fuck! Fuck, fuck, fuck!

"I know, I know," Wilkes said, shaking his head in his Wilkesian way. "Not the best turn of events."

"He's one man. One!"

Guilder's face, his whole body, tingled with righteous anger. Another volleying burp arose. He wanted vengeance. He wanted things to settle the hell down. He wanted this Sergio, whoever he was, with his head on a goddamn *pike.*

"We've got people working on it. HR is asking around, and we've offered double rations to anybody who comes forward with a solid lead. Not everyone down the hill is so enamored."

"And somebody please tell me how he's moving through the flatland like it's a goddamn expressway? Do we not have patrols? Do we not have checkpoints? Can somebody please shed some light on this little detail?"

"We have a theory about that. The evidence points to an organization that's classically cellular. Clusters of just a few individuals operating within a loose operational framework."

"I am perfectly aware what a terrorist cell is, Fred."

His chief of staff made a flustered gesture with his hands. "I'm simply saying that looking for one man may not be the answer. That it's the *idea* of Sergio, not Sergio per se, that we're up against. If you follow me."

Guilder did, and it wasn't a cheering thought. He'd been down this road before, first in Iraq and Afghanistan and then Saudi, after the coup. You lopped off the head but the body didn't die; it simply grew another head. The only useful strategy in these situations was psychological. Killing the body was never enough. You had to kill the spirit.

"How many do we have in custody?"

Thus more paper. Guilder read the full report. According to eyewitnesses, the market bomber had been a female agricultural worker in her thirties. There'd never been any problems with her; by all accounts she was as meek as a lamb, a quality that to a disconcerting extent matched the profiles of other suicide bombers. She had no living family except for a sister; her husband and son had died six years ago, in an outbreak of salmonella. She'd apparently gotten past the checkpoints disguised in a col's uniform (the original wearer's body had been found stuffed into a dumpster, her throat slashed, one arm mysteriously severed at the elbow), though where she'd procured the explosives was unknown. None had been reported missing from the armory or the construction depot, but a full inventory had yet to be completed. Nine of her lodgemates plus her sister's family, including two young children, had been detained for questioning.

"Nobody seems to know anything," Wilkes said with a toss of his hand. He'd taken a seat on the far side of the desk while Guilder read. "Apart from the sister, it's like they barely knew her. We can take it up a notch, but I don't think it's going to produce much in the way of useful intelligence. These people would have caved already."

Guilder placed the file aside, among the many others. The burps, which continued unabated, had painted the walls of his mouth with a foul taste of animal decay, not unlike the stench of the decomposing Mrs. Wilkes. A fact that, if the barely concealed look of olfactory distaste on his chief of staff's smoothly youthful face gave any indication, had not failed to escape the man's attention.

"No need," Guilder said.

Wilkes frowned doubtfully. "You want us to release them? I don't think that's wise. At least let's make them cool their heels a couple more days. Rattle a few chains, see where it takes us."

"You said yourself that if they knew anything, they would have already talked."

Guilder paused, aware that he was about to cross a line.

The thirteen flatlanders sitting in the detention center were, after all, people, human beings, probably not guilty of anything. More to the point, they were tangible physical assets in an economy of scarcity. But given the frustrating intractability of the Sergio situation, and the debacle in Texas, and the time-sensitive nature of Guilder's grand designs, which were at long last coming to complex fruition; and in the grip of his own rapidly burgeoning physical need, a titanic biological imperative that, as he regarded Wilkes from across the burnished prairie of his oversized desk, was blossoming inside him like a flower in a time-lapse video, he didn't think for too long. He came to the line, gave it one quick look, and stepped over.

"It seems to me," said Director Horace Guilder, "the time has come to sell this thing."

Guilder waited a few minutes after Wilkes was gone to stage his departure. As he had reminded himself many times, a great deal of his authority boiled down to a sense of dignity in his public movements, and it was better for people not to witness him in such an agitated state. He took the ring of keys from his desk and stepped out. Strange, how the hunger had come on so quickly. Usually it crept up on him over a period of days, not minutes. From the base of the cupola, a winding flight of stairs descended to the ground floor, its downward passage flanked by oil portraits of various dukes and generals and barons and princes of the realm, a parade of disapproving, heavy-jawed faces in period costume. (At least he hadn't resorted to having his picture painted—though, come to think of it, why not?) He peered over the rail. Fifty feet below were the tiny figures of the uniformed security detail; members of the leadership, in their dark suits and ties, scuttling briskly to and fro with their officious briefcases and clipboards; even a couple of attendants, flowing diaphanously across the polished stone floor in their nunnish costumes, like a pair of paper boats. It was Wilkes he was looking for, and there he was: by the massive front door with its inlaid carvings of assorted prairie kitsch (a fist gripping wheat, a plow merrily tilling the bountiful Iowa topsoil), his loyal chief of staff had paused to confer with two of the leadership, Ministers Hoppel and Chee. Guilder supposed that Wilkes was already setting the day's orders in motion, bringing them up to speed, but this assumption was belied when Hoppel reared back his head, clapped his hands together, and barked a laugh that ricocheted through the marbled space like a bullet in a submarine. Guilder wondered what the fuck was so funny.

He turned from the rail and made his way to the second, more conventional, and highly unobservable stairway that was his alone to use. By now his insides were roaring. It was all he could do not to take the stairs three at a time, which in his present condition would have probably resulted in some bone-breaking pratfall that would heal within hours but still hurt like hell. Bearing himself like a crystal chalice that might at any moment spill its contents to the floor, Guilder descended one cautious step at a time. The salivation had started, a veritable waterfall he had to suck back between his teeth. Vampire bibs, he thought wryly; now, that would be a moneymaker.

The basement at last, with its heavy, vaultlike door. Guilder withdrew the keys from the pocket of his suit coat. Hands trembling with anticipation, he keyed the door, turned the heavy wheel, and shouldered it aside.

By the time he was halfway down the hall he'd stripped to the waist and was kicking off his shoes. He was riding this thing full-bore now, a surfer skimming down a wave. Door after door sailed past. Guilder could hear the muffled cries of the damned coming from within, a sound that had long since ceased to arouse even a grain of pity within him, if it ever had. He blasted past the warning signs—ETHER PRESENT, NO OPEN FLAME—hit the freezer room at a dead sprint, turned the final corner, and narrowly avoided collision with a lab-coated technician. "Director Guilder!" he gasped. "We didn't know . . . !" But these words were cut short as Guilder, with more violence than was called for, applied the full swinging weight of his left forearm to the side of the man's head, sending him crashing into the wall.

It was blood he wanted, and not just any blood. There was blood and there was *blood*.

He came to the final door, skidding to a halt. With fumbling hands he undid his trousers and tossed them away, then keyed the door and opened it.

"Hello, Lawrence."

38

In the morning, Jackie was gone.

Sara awoke to find the woman's cot empty. Lit with panic,

she tore through the lodge, cursing herself for sleeping so deeply. The old woman who bunked in the second row? Had anyone seen her? But no one had, or so they said. At morning roll, Sara detected only the smallest hitch of silence in the space where Jackie's number should have been. Everyone was looking down. Just like that, the waters had closed over her friend. It was as if she'd never existed at all.

She moved through the day in a fog, her mind teetering on the razor-thin edge between desperate hope and outright despair. Probably there was nothing to be done. People disappeared; that was the way of things. And yet Sara could not talk herself out of the idea that if the woman was still in the hospital, if she hadn't been taken to the feedlot yet, there might be a chance. But how could Jackie have been taken right from under Sara's nose like that? Wouldn't she have heard something? Wouldn't the woman have protested? It simply didn't add up.

That was when Sara figured it out. She hadn't heard anything, because there had been nothing to hear. *Not like this. Not for me.* Jackie had left the lodge of her own accord.

She'd done it to protect Sara.

By midafternoon she knew she had to do something. Her guilt was excruciating. She never should have tried to get Jackie out of the plant, never confronted Sod the way she had. She'd all but painted a target on the woman's back. The minutes were ticking away. The virals in the feedlot ate just after dusk; Sara had seen the trucks. Livestock carriers crammed with lowing cows, but also the windowless vans that were used to move prisoners from the detention center. One was always parked at the rear of the hospital, its meaning plain to anyone who cared to consider it.

The cols supervising the grinding teams were Vale and Whistler. Vale she thought she could have worked with, but with Whistler watching, Sara didn't see how. There was only one solution she could think of. She topped off her bushel basket, lifted it from the ground, took three steps toward the grinder, and stopped.

"Oh," Sara cried. She let the basket drop, clutching her stomach. "Oh. Oh."

She melted, moaning, to her knees. For a moment it seemed that amid the noise of the grinders her demonstration had gone unnoticed. She amplified her cries, curling her legs to her chest, hugging her midriff.

"Sara, what is it?" One of the other women—Constance Chou—was crouching over her.

"It hurts! It hurts!"

"Get up or they'll see you!"

Another voice broke through: Vale's. "What's going on here?"

Constance backed away. "I don't know, sir. She just . . . collapsed."

"Fisher? What's wrong with you?"

Sara didn't answer, just kept up with the moaning, rocking at the waist and throwing in a few spastic kicks for good measure. A circle of onlookers had formed around her. "Appendix," she said.

"What did you say?"

She clenched her face with manufactured pain. "I think . . . it's my . . . appendix."

Whistler charged through the crowd, pushing onlookers aside with her baton. "What's her problem?"

Vale was scratching his head. "She says something's wrong with her pendix."

"What are you people looking at?" Whistler barked. "Get back to work." Then, to Vale: "What do you want to do with her?"

"Fisher, can you walk?"

"Please," she gasped. "I need a doctor."

"She says she needs a doctor," Vale reported.

"Yeah, I heard that, Vale." The woman huffed a sigh. "All right, let's get her out of here."

They helped her to a pickup parked behind the plant and laid her in the back. Sara kept up the rocking and moaning. A brief negotiation ensued: should one of them take her or should they call for a driver?

"Fuck it, I'll take her," Whistler said. "Knowing you, you'll dither all day."

The trip to the hospital took ten minutes; Sara used them to formulate a plan. All she'd been thinking about was getting to the hospital, to find Jackie before the van took her away; she hadn't considered the next step. It seemed to her now that she held only two good cards. First, she wasn't really sick; once she experienced a miraculous recovery, it didn't seem likely that they'd ship a perfectly able-bodied woman off to the feedlot. Second, she was a nurse. Sara wasn't sure how she'd put this fact to use—she'd have to improvise—but she might be able to use her medical knowledge to convince the person in charge that Jackie wasn't as ill as she appeared.

Or maybe nothing she did would matter. Maybe once she

passed through the hospital doors, she'd never come out. This prospect, as she weighed it, did not appear entirely bad, thus giving her a third card to play: the card of not caring anymore if she lived or died.

Whistler pulled up to the hospital entrance, strode back to the cargo bed, and drew down the tailgate.

"Out with you. Let's go."

"I don't think I can walk."

"Well, you'll have to try, because I'm not carrying you."

Sara sat up. The sun had peeked from behind the clouds, sharpening the scene with its cold brightness. The hospital was a three-story brick building, part of a cluster of low, workaday structures at the southern edge of the flatland. At a distance of twenty yards stood one of three major HR substations. A dozen cols guarded the entrance, which was flanked by concrete barricades.

"Am I talking to myself here?"

She was; Sara was barely listening. She was focused on the car, a small sedan of the type the cols used to move among the lodges. It was headed toward them at high speed, dragging a boiling plume of dust. Sara clambered down from the bed. Simultaneously, she sensed a figure rushing at her from behind. The car was bearing down, its speed unabated. There was something odd about it, and not just the wild velocity of its approach. The windows were blacked out, obscuring the driver; something was written on the hood, the letters scrawled in streaks of white paint.

SERGIO LIVES

As the vehicle sailed toward the barricades, somebody smashed her from behind. In the next instant she was flat on the ground, her body smothered, as the truck exploded with a blast of sound and a wave of superheated pressure she didn't believe could actually exist in the world. The air was sucked from her lungs. Things were falling. Things were sailing through the air and impacting like meteors around her, flaming, heavy things. There was a screeching sound of metal, a rain of tinkling glass. The world was noise and heat and the weight of a body on top of her, and then a sudden silence and a wash of warm breath close to her ear and a voice saying:

"Come with me now. Do exactly as I say."

Sara was on her feet. A woman, no one she knew, was pulling her by the hand against the inertia of her wonderment. Something had happened to her hearing, bathing the scene around her in a milky unreality. The substation was a smoking crater. The pickup was gone; it lay on its side where the entrance to the hospital was, or had been. Something wet was on Sara's hands and face. Blood. She was covered in it. And sticky things, biological things, and a fine, jeweled dust she realized was composed of tiny bits of glass. How amazing, she thought, how very amazing everything was, especially what had happened to Whistler. It was striking, what a body looked like when it wasn't one thing anymore but had been dispersed in recognizably human pieces over a wide area. Who would have guessed that when a body blew apart, as had evidently happened, it actually did that: it blew apart.

She broke away, first her vision and then the rest of her; the woman was running and so was she, running and also being dragged, the energy of her rescuer—for Sara understood that this woman had protected her from the blast—passing into her body through their gripping hands. Behind them the silence had given way to a chorus of screams and shouts, a weirdly musical sound, and the woman skidded to a halt behind a building that somehow still stood (hadn't all the buildings in the world just blown up?) and dropped on the ground. In her hand was a kind of hook, and with this hook she drew aside the manhole cover.

"Get in."

Sara did. She got in. She lowered herself into the hole where a ladder waited. Something smelled bad. Something smelled like shit because it was. As Sara's feet touched the bottom, her sneakers filling with the horrible water, the woman reached over her head and resealed the manhole with a clank, plunging Sara into an absolute darkness. Only then did it occur to her in fullest measure that she had been in an explosion of many deaths and much destruction and that in its immediate aftermath, an interval of probably less than a minute, she had given herself completely to a woman she did not know, and that this woman had whisked her into a kind of nonexistence: that Sara had, in effect, disappeared.

"Wait."

The glow of a small bluish flame igniting: the woman was holding a lighter, touching it to the head of a torch. A blaze leapt forth, illuminating her face. Somewhere in her twenties, with a long neck and small, dark eyes, full of intensity. There was something familiar about her, but Sara couldn't fix her mind on it.

"No more talking. Can you run?"

Sara nodded yes.

"Come on."

The woman began to move at a trot down the sewer pipe, Sara following. This went on for some time. At each of many intersections, the woman decisively chose a direction. Sara had begun to take stock of her injuries. The explosion had not occurred without effect. There was a variety to her pains, some of them quite sharp, others more like a generally dispersed thudding. Yet none was so severe as to prevent her from keeping up with the woman. After more time had passed, Sara realized that the distance they had traveled must have surely placed them beyond the wired boundaries of the Homeland. They were escaping! They were free! A ring of light appeared before them: an exit. Beyond it lay the world—a dangerous world, a lethal world where virals roamed unchecked, but even so it loomed before her like a golden promise, and she stepped into the light.

"Sorry about this."

The woman was behind her. She had reached one hand around Sara's waist, drawing her into stasis; the other hand, holding a cloth, rose to Sara's face. What in the world? But before Sara could utter a single sound of protest, the cloth was covering her mouth and nose, flooding her senses with an awful choking chemical smell, and a million tiny stars went off inside her head; and that was the end of that.

39

Lila Kyle. Her name was Lila Kyle.

Though, of course, she knew that the face in the mirror had other names. The Queen of Crazy. Her Loony Majesty. Her Royally Unhinged Highness. Oh, yes, Lila had heard them all. You'd have to get up pretty early in the morning to pass one over on Lila Kyle. Sticks and stones, she always said (her father said), sticks and stones, but what galled her, really, was the whispering. People were always whispering! As if they were the adults and she the child, as if she were a bomb that might go off at any second. How strange! Strange and not a little disrespectful, because in the first instance, she wasn't crazy, they were one hundred percent wrong about that; and in the second, even if she were, even if, for the sake of argument, she liked to strip naked in the moonlight and howl like a dog (poor Roscoe), what concern of it was theirs? How crazy she was or was not? (Though she had to confess, there were days, certain difficult days when her thoughts would not cooperate, like an armful of autumn leaves she was attempting to shove into a bag.) It wasn't *nice*. It was beyond the *pale*. To speak behind a person's back, to make such vile insinuations—it was outside the bounds of common decency. What had she ever done to deserve such treatment? She kept to herself, she never asked for anything, she was quiet as a mouse; she was wholly content to bide her time in her room with her lovely little things, her bottles and combs and brushes and her dressing table, where now she sat—it seemed she had been sitting there for some time—brushing out her hair.

Her hair. As she shifted her attention to the face in the mirror, a wave of warm recognition flowed through her. The sight always seemed to take her by surprise: the rosy, pore-free skin, the dewy glistening of her eyes, the humid plumpness of her cheeks, the delicate proportionality of her features. She looked . . . amazing! And most amazing of all was her hair. How lustrous it was, how abundant to the touch, how rich with its molassesy thickness. Not molasses: chocolate. An excellent dark chocolate from someplace wonderful and special, Switzerland, maybe, or one of those other countries, like the candies her father had always kept in his desk; and if she was good, *very* good, or sometimes for no reason at all, simply because he loved her and wanted her to know it, he would summon her to the sanctified quarters of his masculine-smelling study, where he wrote his important papers and read his inscrutable books and conducted his generally mysterious fatherly business, to bestow upon her the symbol of this love. *Only one now,* he would say to her, the oneness amplifying the specialness because it implied a future in which further visits to the study would occur. The golden box, the lifting lid, the moment of suspense: her little hand hovered over the rich bounty of its contents like a diver poised at the edge of a pool, calculating the perfect angle for her plunge. There were the chocolate ones, and the ones with nuts, and the ones with the cherry syrup (the only ones she didn't like; she'd spit them out into a Kleenex). But best of all were the ones with nothing, the pure chocolate nuggets. That was what she craved. The singular treasure of milky melting sweetness that she was attempting to divine from among its fellows. This one? This one?

"Yolanda!"

Silence.

"Yolanda!"

In a flurry of skirts and veils and windy fabric, the woman came bustling into the room. Really now, Lila thought, what a ridiculous getup *that* was. How many times had Lila instructed her to dress more practically?

"Yolanda, where have you been? I've been calling and calling."

The woman was looking at Lila as if she'd lost her mind. Had they gotten to her, too? "Yolanda, ma'am?"

"Who else would I call?" Lila sighed exorbitantly. The woman could be so dense. Though her English was not the best. "I would like . . . something. If you please. *Por favor.*"

"Yes, ma'am. Of course. Would you like me to read to you?"

"Read? No." Though the thought was suddenly appealing; a little Beatrix Potter might be the very thing to soothe her nerves. Peter Rabbit in his little blue jacket. Squirrel Nutkin and his brother Twinkleberry. The two of them could get into such mischief! Then she remembered.

"Chocolate. Do we have any chocolate?"

The woman still appeared totally out of it. Maybe she'd gotten into the liquor. "Chocolate, ma'am?"

"Leftover Halloween candy, maybe? I'm sure we have some somewhere. Anything will do. Hershey's Kisses. Almond Joy. A Kit Kat. Whatever is fine."

"Um . . ."

"*¿Sí?* A little choc-o-LAH-tay? Check the cabinet over the sink."

"I'm sorry, I don't know what you're asking for."

Now, this was annoying. The woman was pretending not to know what chocolate was!

"I fail to see what the problem is, Yolanda. I have to say, your attitude has begun to trouble me. A great deal, in fact."

"Please don't be angry. If I knew what it was, I'd be glad to get it for you. Maybe Jenny knows."

"That's my point, you see. That is precisely what I'm saying." Lila sighed heavily. A pity, but there was really nothing left to be done. Better to rip the band-aid off than drag things out.

"I'm afraid, Yolanda, I'm going to have to let you go."

"Go?"

"Go, yes. *No más.* We no longer require your services, I'm afraid."

The woman's eyes seemed practically to pop from her head. "You can't!"

"I'm truly sorry. I wish things had worked out. But under the circumstances, you really leave me with no alternative."

The woman hurled herself at Lila's knees. "Please! I'll do anything!"

"Yolanda, get ahold of yourself."

"I'm begging you," the woman blubbered into her skirt. "You know what they'll do. I'll work harder, I swear!"

Lila had expected her to take it badly, but this undignified display was wholly unexpected. It was positively embarrassing. The urge to offer some consoling touch was strong, but Lila resisted it, lest this draw things out, leaving her hands hovering awkwardly in the air. Maybe she should have waited until David got home. He was always better at this sort of thing.

"We'll provide you with a reference, of course. And two weeks' pay. You really shouldn't take it so hard."

"It's a death sentence!" She hugged Lila's knees as if she were clinging to a life raft. "They'll send me to the basement!"

"I hardly think this qualifies as a death sentence. You're completely overreacting."

But the woman was beyond appeals to reason. Unable to form words through the storm of her uncontrollable sobs, she had given up her pleading, soaking Lila's skirt with mucusy tears. The only thing on Lila's mind was extricating herself from the situation as quickly as possible. She hated things like this, she *hated* them.

"What's going on in here?"

Lila lifted her gaze toward the figure standing in the door, at once breathing a sigh of relief. "David. Thank God. We seem to have a bit of a situation here. Yolanda, well, she's a little bit upset. I've decided to let her go."

"Christ, another one? What's the matter with you?"

Now, wasn't this typical. Wasn't this typical David. "That's fine for you to say, gone all day, leaving me stuck in the house. I'd think you'd back me up."

"Please, don't do this!" Yolanda wailed.

Lila made a get-this-woman-off-me gesture with her hands. "A little help here?"

Which did not prove quite as easy as it might have. As David (not David) bent to extricate the sobbing Yolanda (not Yolanda) from Lila's knees, the woman redoubled her hold and commenced, unbelievably, to scream. What a scene she was making! For goodness sake, you'd think being fired from a housekeeping job really *was* a death sentence from the way she was acting. With a hard yank at the waist, David pulled her free and hoisted her bodily into the air. She kicked and screamed in his arms, flailing like a crazy person. It was only through his superior strength that he managed to contain her. One thing about David: he'd kept himself in shape.

"I'm sorry, Yolanda!" Lila called as he whisked her away. "I'll mail you a check!"

The door slammed behind them. Lila released a breath she realized she'd been holding in her chest. Well, wasn't that something. Wasn't that just about the most uncomfortable business she'd ever had to endure. She felt completely rattled, and not a little guilty besides. Yolanda had been with them for years, and for everything to end so badly. It left a sour taste in Lila's mouth. Though admittedly, Yolanda had never been the best housekeeper, and recently she'd really let things go. Probably some personal difficulties. Lila had never even been to the woman's house, though; she knew nothing of her life. How curious was that? All these years, Yolanda coming and going, and it was as if Lila didn't know the woman at all.

"Well, she's gone. Congratulations."

Lila, who had resumed brushing her hair, examined David coolly through the mirror as he paused in the doorway to straighten his tie.

"And how is this my fault, exactly? You saw her. She was completely out of control."

"That's the third one this year. Good attendants don't grow on trees."

She took another long, luxurious stroke with the brush. "So call the service. It's really not such a big deal, you know."

David said nothing more, evidently content to let the matter drop. He moved to the divan, drawing up the knees of his suit pants to sit down.

"We have to talk."

"Can't you see I'm busy? Don't they need you back at the hospital or something?"

"I don't work at a hospital. We've been over this a million times."

Had they? Sometimes her thoughts were autumn leaves, sometimes they were bees in a jar, little buzzing things going round and round.

"What happened in Texas, Lila?"

"Texas?"

He sighed grumpily. "The convoy. The Oil Road. I thought my instructions were clear."

"I haven't the foggiest idea what you're talking about. I've never been to Texas in my life." She paused her brushing, meeting David's eyes through the mirror. "Brad always hated Texas. Probably you don't want to hear anything about that, though."

Her words, she saw, had hit their mark. Bringing up Brad was her secret weapon. Though she knew she shouldn't, she took a perverse delight in the expression on David's face whenever she spoke the name—the deflated blankness of a man who knew he could never measure up.

"I don't ask much of you. What I'm beginning to wonder is if you can control these things anymore."

"Yes, well." Buzz, buzz.

"Are you listening to me? We can't have any more disasters like this. Not when we're this close."

"I don't see what you're so upset about. And to be perfectly honest, I don't care for the way you're speaking to me."

"Goddamnit, put that fucking brush *down*!"

But before she could do this, he snatched it from her hand and sent it pinwheeling across the room. He seized her by the hair, yanking her head back, and jammed his face so close to hers it wasn't even a face but a *thing,* a monstrous distorted sluglike thing, bathing her with its rotten bacterial breath.

"I've had it with your bullshit." Spittle splashed her cheeks, her eyes; it launched revoltingly from his mouth into hers. The edges of his teeth were etched with a dark substance, giving them a terrifying vividness. Blood. His teeth were lined in blood. "This *act* of yours. This stupid game."

"Please," she gasped, "you're hurting me!"

"Am I?" He twisted her hair, hard. A thousand pinpoint agonies screamed from her scalp.

"David," she pleaded, tears drowning her vision, "I'm begging you. Think about what you're doing."

The slug face roared in anger: "I'm not David! I'm Horace! My name is Horace Guilder!" Another twisting yank. "Say it!"

"I don't know, I don't know! You're confusing me!"

"Say it! Say my name!"

It was the pain that did it. In a cyclonic rush, her consciousness collapsed upon itself.

"You're Horace! Please, just stop!"

"Again! All of it!"

"Horace Guilder! You're Horace Guilder, Director of the Homeland!"

Guilder released her, stepping away. She was lying backward over her dressing table, shaking with sobs. If only she could go back. *Go back,* she thought, clamping her eyes tight to hide this horror of a man, this Horace Guilder, from her sight. *Lila, go back. Send yourself away again.* She shook with a nausea that rose from a place so deep it had no name, a sickness not of the body but of the soul, the metaphysical core of her fractured self, and then she was on her knees, vomiting, gasping and choking and spewing the vile blood that she herself had drunk that very morning.

"Okay, then," said Guilder, wiping his hands on his suit coat. "Just so that's clear."

Lila said nothing. So powerful was her longing to will herself away, she couldn't have formed words if she'd tried.

"Big days ahead, Lila. I need to know that you're on board. No more of your nonsense. And please, try not to fire any more attendants. These girls don't grow on trees."

With the back of her wrist, she wiped the rancid spittle from her chin. "You said that already."

"I'm sorry?"

"I said, you said that already." Her voice didn't even sound like her own. "About attendants not growing on trees."

"Did I?" He gave a little laugh. "So I did. Funny when you think about it. Something along those lines would sure come in handy, given the exigencies of the food chain and all. I'm sure your pal Lawrence would agree. I tell you, that man can *eat.*" He paused a moment, enjoying this thought, before his eyes hardened on her again. "Now clean yourself up. No offense, Lila, but you've got vomit in your hair."

40

"Sara? Can you hear me?"

A voice was floating toward her. A voice and also a face, one she knew but couldn't place. A face in a dream, which was what she was certain she was having: an unsettling dream in which she was running and all around her were bodies and parts of bodies, and everything on fire.

"She's still completely out of it," the voice said. It seemed to reach her across an impossible distance. A continent. An ocean. It seemed to come from the stars. "How much did you use?"

"Three drops. Well, maybe four."

"*Four*? Were you *trying* to kill her?"

"It was rushed, okay? You told me you wanted her out. So, she's out."

A heavy sigh. "Get me a bucket."

A bucket, thought Sara, what did the voices want with a bucket? What did a bucket have to do with anything? But no sooner had she thought this than a force of cold wetness crashed into her face, blasting her into consciousness. She was choking, drowning, waving her arms in panic, her nose and throat filling with the icy water.

"Easy now, Sara."

She sat upright, too fast; her brain sloshed in its casing, swirling her vision.

"Ooo," she moaned. "Ooo."

"The headache's bad, but it won't last. Just breathe."

She blinked the water from her eyes. Eustace?

It was. His top front teeth were gone, shorn at the root; his right eye was clouded with blindness. With a gnarled hand, he was holding out a metal cup.

"It's good to see you again, Sara. You've already met Nina, here. Say hello, Nina."

Standing behind him was the woman from the pipe. A rifle was slung across her chest, her arms folded casually over it. "Hello, Sara."

"Don't worry," Eustace said. "I know you have a lot of questions, and we'll get to them. Just drink."

Sara took the cup and gulped the water down. It was astonishingly cold and tasted vaguely metallic, as if she were licking a bar of iron.

"I thought you were—"

"Dead?" Eustace grinned, showing his ruined mouth. "In point of fact, everybody here is dead. Nina, remind me, how exactly did you die?"

"I believe it was pneumonia, sir. That or something very heavy fell on me. I can never remember how we did the paperwork."

The explosion, the dash through the pipe; it was all coming back now. Sara drained the cup and took a moment to inspect her surroundings. She appeared to be in some kind of bunker, although there were no windows; she sensed they were someplace underground. The room's only illumination came from a stand of flickering torches.

"Where are we?"

"Someplace the redeyes can't find us." He had a way of looking at her, angling his face to aim his good eye, that somehow added to the penetrating seriousness of his gaze. "Beyond that, I can't tell you. The important thing is you're safe here."

"Are you . . . Sergio?"

Another broken-toothed smile. "I'm flattered you would think so. But no. There is no Sergio. Not in the way you mean."

"But I thought—"

"And you're supposed to. The name is short for 'insurgency.' Nina, if I'm not mistaken, that was your idea, wasn't it?"

"I believe it was."

"People need a name. Something to focus on, a face to attach to the idea. That's our face. Sergio."

She looked at the woman, who was regarding her coolly, then back to Eustace.

"The explosion. That was you, wasn't it?"

Eustace nodded. "Our early reports indicate seventeen cols dead, including your friend Whistler, and two members of the staff who were visiting for an inspection. Not a bad day's work, I'd say. But that's not the real prize."

"It's not?"

"No. The real prize is you, Sara."

Eustace was looking at her intently now. Both of them were. Sara shivered in the cold. A shift had occurred, an inversion of the conversation's energies; he was trying to draw her out. Could they trust her? More to the point, could she trust them?

"This is the part where you ask me why."

Not wanting to concede too much, Sara nodded.

"As of this morning, there is no Sara Fisher. Sara Fisher, flatlander number 94801, was killed in a suicide bombing that took the lives of nineteen loyal security officers of the Beloved Homeland. The only recognizable part of Sara Fisher that remains intact is, conveniently, an arm with your tag on it. This was procured from a female col who, not twenty-four hours ago, was employing it to beat women and children in the dairy barns. We thought that under the circumstances it had better uses, though she seemed not to agree. Put up rather a struggle, Nina, did she not?"

"The woman was a fighter. I'll give her that."

He regarded Sara again. "I see in your expression that our methods come as a shock. They shouldn't."

It was all going by her too fast. "You kill people. Not just the cols. Innocent bystanders."

Eustace nodded evenly. His face was unreadable, almost emotionless. "That's true. Fewer than our glorious director would have you believe, but these things never come without cost."

She was appalled by his casual tone. "That doesn't justify it."

"Oh, I think it does. Let me ask you something. What do you think the redeyes will do after today's attack?"

Sara said nothing.

"All right, I'll tell you. Reprisals. They'll crack down hard. It won't be pretty."

Sara looked at Eustace, then Nina, then Eustace again. "But why would you want that?"

Eustace took a long breath. "I'll put it as simply as I know how. This is a war, Sara. Nothing more or less. And in this war, we're badly outnumbered. We've managed to infiltrate nearly every level of their operation, but the numbers are still on their side. We could never defeat them if we engaged them directly. Our theater of operations is psychological. Rattle the leadership. Draw them out. Every person who's hauled into detention is somebody's father, somebody's wife, somebody's son or daughter. For each one the redeyes send to the feedlot, two more will join us. It may seem brutal. But there it is." He paused, allowing his words to sink in. "Maybe this doesn't make sense to you. Soon enough it will, if my hunch about you is correct. In any event, the upshot of the afternoon's attack is that you no longer exist. And that makes you extremely valuable to us."

"Are you telling me you planned this?"

He shrugged in a manner that suggested the question was more complex than she'd intended. "There's planning and there's planning. A lot of what we do is a matter of timing and luck. But in your case, a great deal of thought went into your extraction. We've been watching you for some time, waiting for the right moment. It was Jackie who put the pieces together and gave the go-ahead. The episode at the biodiesel plant was staged, as was her sudden disappearance from the lodge last night. She knew you would come looking for her at the hospital. Frankly, I found the whole thing a little elaborate, and I had my doubts, but her confidence in you won the day. And I'm pleased to say she was right."

Sara's mind was swimming with disbelief. No, drowning. "Jackie is . . . one of you?"

Eustace nodded. "The woman was with us from the beginning, a senior operative. I can't tell you how many attacks she engineered. Her final mission was to bring you in."

Sara groped for words but found none. She simply couldn't square the woman Eustace was describing with the one she knew. Jackie? A member of the insurgency? For more than a year, the woman had barely been out of Sara's sight. They'd slept three feet from each other, worked side by side, eaten every meal in each other's company. They'd told each other everything. It made no sense; it wasn't possible. Then:

"What do you mean by 'final'?"

Something changed in the air. "I'm sorry," he said. "Jackie's dead."

His words were like a slap. "She can't be!"

"I'm afraid it's true. I know she meant a lot to you."

"They don't move people from the hospital until dark! I've seen the van! We have to get her!"

"Listen to me—"

"There's still time! We have to do something!" She darted her eyes to Nina, still standing impassively with her arms folded over her rifle, then back at Eustace. "Why aren't you doing anything?"

"Because it's too late, Sara." His expression softened. "Jackie was never in the hospital. That's what I'm telling you. Jackie was the driver of the car."

The sensation was of something breaking. That was how it felt. Something broke inside her. A final severing, the last thread binding her to the life she knew cut away. She was floating, floating away.

"She knew how sick she was. At most she would have lasted a few more months before they sent her to the feedlot." Eustace leaned closer. "It was how she wanted it. The crowning moment of a glorious career. She wouldn't have had it any other way."

"She's dead," Sara said, to no one.

"She did what she had to do. Jackie was a hero of the insurgency. And here you are, ready to pick up where she left off."

She couldn't seem to make herself cry. She wondered why this was, and then she knew: the last tears of her life had fallen; there were no more left inside her. How strange, not to be able to cry. To love someone the way she'd loved Jackie and find no mourning in her heart.

"Why me?"

"Because you hate them, Sara. You hate them and you're not afraid of them. I saw it in you that day in the truck. Do you remember?"

Sara nodded.

"There are two kinds of hatred. One gives you strength, the other takes it away. Yours is the first kind. I've always known that about you. Jackie knew it, too."

It was true; she hated them. She hated them for their leering eyes, their easy, laughing cruelty. She hated them for their watery gruel and icy showers; she hated the lies they made her shout; she hated their battering batons and the smiles on their smug faces. She hated them with her bones and blood, each cell of her body; her nerves fired with hatred, her lungs breathed hatred in and out, her heart pumped an elixir of pure hatred through her veins. She was alive because she hated them, and she hated them, most of all, for taking her daughter away.

She became aware that Eustace and Nina were waiting for her to speak. She understood that all they'd done and said had been arranged for this one purpose. Step by careful step, they had led her to the edge of an abyss. Once she stepped off, she'd be herself no more.

"What do you want me to do?"

VII

THE OUTLAW

As flies to wanton boys are we to th' gods;
They kill us for their sport.

—Shakespeare,
King Lear

41

The three of them were rescued the next afternoon by a DS patrol sent to look for them when the tankers failed to arrive in Kerrville. By this time, Peter, Michael, and Lore had left the hardbox and returned to the scene of the attack. The blast had gouged out a wide crater, fifty yards at least; heaps of twisted wreckage lay spread over the adjacent fields. Oily smoke poured forth from still-burning pools of petrol, smearing a sky already inhabited by a cloud of airborne scavengers. Bodies, charred to blackened crusts, mingled with the debris. If any of the grisly remains belonged to their attackers, it was impossible to tell. All that was left of the mysterious gleaming truck were a few sheets of galvanized metal, proving nothing.

Michael was a wreck. His physical injuries—a dislocated shoulder he had rammed back into place against the wall of the hardbox, a sprained ankle, a gash above his right ear that would need stitches—were the least of it. Eleven oilers and ten DS officers: men and women he had lived with, worked with. Michael had been the one in charge, somebody they trusted. Now they were gone.

"Why do you think he did it?" Peter asked. He was speaking of Ceps; during their long night in the hardbox, Michael had told Peter what he'd seen in the side-view mirror. The two of them were sitting on the ground at the edge of the river; Lore had moved upstream. Peter could see her squatting by the water, shoulders shaking with tears she didn't want them to witness.

"I guess he thought there was no other way." Michael squinted upward, watching the circling birds, though he seemed not to be really looking at anything. "You didn't know him like I did. There was a lot to the guy. No way he'd let anybody be taken up. I only wish I'd had the guts to do it myself."

Peter could read the pain and doubt in his friend's face: the disgrace of the survivor. He had known this emotion himself. It wasn't the kind of thing that ever left you. "It wasn't your fault, Michael. If the blame is anyone's, it's mine."

If his words were any comfort, Peter couldn't see it. "Who do you think those people were?" Michael said.

"I wish I knew."

"What the hell, Peter? A truckload of virals? Like they were pets or something? And that woman?"

"I don't get it, either."

"If it was the oil they wanted, they could have just taken it."

"I don't think that's what they were after."

"Yeah, well. Neither do I." A ripple of anger tensed his body. "One thing I do know. If I ever find those people, I'm going to make it hurt."

They spent the night with the search party in a hardbox east of San Antonio and arrived in Kerrville the next morning. Once inside the city, they were separated into different chains of command: Peter to Division Headquarters and Michael and Lore to the Office of the Domestic Authority, which oversaw all ex-murus assets, including the Freeport oil complex. Peter was given time to clean up before his debriefing. It was midday, the barracks mostly empty. He stood in the shower for a long time, watching the greasy soot swirl down at his feet. He knew himself well enough to understand that the full emotional impact of events hadn't quite sunk in. Whether this was a weakness or a strength he could never decide. He knew he was in a lot of trouble, but this concern seemed petty. Most of all, he felt sorry for Michael and Lore.

He dressed in his cleanest fatigues and made his way to Command, a former office complex adjacent to city hall. When he entered the conference room, he was startled to see a face he knew: Gunnar Apgar. But if he'd expected any word of reassurance from the man, it quickly became evident that none was forthcoming. As Peter snapped to attention, the colonel shot him a cold glance, then returned his attention to the papers resting on the long table before him—no doubt the report from the DS patrol.

But it was the second man of the three that gave Peter the most pause. To Apgar's right sat the imposing figure of Abram Fleet, general of the Army. Peter had laid eyes on the man only once in his life; it was tradition that the GA administer the oath of induction for all Expeditionary. There was nothing physically remarkable about the general's appearance—everything about him communicated an almost perfect physical averageness—yet he was who he was, a man whose presence altered a room, seeming to make the molecules of air vibrate at a different frequency. The third person seated at the table Peter didn't recognize, a civilian with a trim gray beard and hair like brushed wheat.

"Have a seat, Lieutenant," the general said. "Let's bring this to order. You know Colonel Apgar. Mr. Chase is here as a representative of the president's staff. He will serve as her eyes and ears in this"—he hunted for the correct phrase—"unfortunate development."

For over two hours, they pounded Peter with questions. The general did most of the talking, followed by Chase; Apgar was largely silent, occasionally scribbling a note or asking for clarification. The tenor of the whole thing was disquietingly peremptory, as if they were trying to ensnare Peter in a contradiction. The underlying suggestion seemed to be that his story was a cover-up for some man-made catastrophe for which Peter, one of only three survivors, including the convoy's head oiler, bore the blame. Yet as the grilling continued, he began to sense that this suspicion was hollow, a front for some deeper concern. Again and again they returned to the matter of the woman. What was she wearing, what did she say, how did she look? Had there been anything odd about her appearance? To each of these repeated probings, Peter related the order of events as accurately as he could. She was wearing a cloak. She was remarkably beautiful. She said, *You're tired.* She said, *We know where you are. It's just a matter of time.* "We," the general repeated. We who? *I don't know.* You don't know because you don't remember? *No, I'm positive. She didn't say anything else.* Round and round, until even Peter began to doubt his own account. By the time it was over—his questioning came to a close with an abruptness in keeping with its hectoring tone—he felt not just emotionally but physically exhausted.

"A word of warning, Lieutenant," the general concluded. "You are not to discuss what happened on the Oil Road, or the contents of these proceedings, with anybody. That includes the surviving members of the convoy and the search party that brought you in. The determination of this body is that for reasons unknown, one of the tankers exploded, destroying the convoy as well as the San Marcos bridge. Is that clear?"

So, the truth. What had happened on the Oil Road was not the whole story; it was a piece of a larger puzzle the three men were trying to wedge into place. Peter stole a glance at

Apgar, whose expression communicated only the manufactured neutrality of someone obeying the orders of his superior.

"Yes, General."

Fleet paused, then continued with a note of caution: "One last matter, Jaxon, and this is also to be treated with the utmost confidence. It seems that your friend Lucius Greer has escaped from detention."

For an instant Peter doubted that he'd heard the general correctly. "Sir?" He darted his eyes toward the others. "How did he—?"

"That's not known at this point. But it seems very likely he had help. The same night Greer went missing, one of the sisters left the orphanage and failed to return. A DS at the western pickets reported seeing two people leaving on horseback just after oh three hundred hours. A man—Greer, obviously—and a teenage girl, wearing the tunic of the Order."

"Are you talking about . . . Amy?"

"So it would seem." Fleet hunched over the table. "Greer is not my first concern. He's an escaped prisoner, and he'll be dealt with. But Amy is a different matter. Though I've always regarded your claims about her with considerable skepticism, she is nevertheless an important military asset." Fleet was looking at Peter with renewed intensity. "We know you visited both of them before departing for the refinery. If you have anything to say, I suggest you say it now."

It took Peter a moment to parse the question's meaning. "You think I know about this?"

"Do you, Lieutenant?"

Peter's mind wrestled with three ideas simultaneously. Amy had broken Lucius out of jail; the two of them had fled the city, their destination unknown; the general suspected him of being an accomplice. Any one of these would have been enough to knock him flat; together, they had the effect of focusing his thoughts on the immediate problem of defending himself. And, rising in the back of his mind, was a new question: what did Amy's disappearance have to do with the woman on the Oil Road? Surely the three men before him were wondering the same thing.

"Absolutely not, General. They didn't tell me anything."

"You're certain? I remind you, this goes into the record as your official statement."

"Yes, I'm certain. I'm as amazed as you are."

"And you have no idea where the two of them might have gone?"

"I wish I did."

Fleet regarded Peter for another moment, his face set. He looked toward Chase, who nodded.

"Very well, Jaxon. I'll take you at your word. Colonel Apgar has relayed your wishes to return to Fort Vorhees as soon as possible. I'm inclined to grant that request. Report to the duty officer at the motor pool, and he'll give you a space on the next transport."

Suddenly this was the last thing Peter wanted. The general's intentions were clear: Peter was being banished to guarantee his silence.

"If it's all right, sir, I'd like to return to the refinery."

"That's not an option, Lieutenant. You have your orders."

A thought occurred to him. "Permission to speak freely, sir."

Fleet sighed heavily. "My understanding is that's what you do, Lieutenant. You might as well get it over with."

"What about Martínez?"

"What about him?"

Apgar quickly met Peter's eye. *Tread carefully.*

"The man in the cave. 'He left us'—those were his words."

"I'm aware of that, Jaxon. I've read the report. What's your point?"

"He wasn't where he was supposed to be, either. Maybe Greer and Amy went searching for him." He looked at each of the three men in turn, then together. "Maybe they know where he is."

A frozen moment followed. Then, from Fleet: "It's an interesting idea, Lieutenant. Is there anything else?"

Just like that, the idea had been put aside. Or maybe not. Either way, Peter sensed that his words had hit the mark.

"No, sir."

The general's eyes darkened with warning. "As I said, you're not to discuss these matters with anyone. I don't think I have to tell you that any indiscretion would not be looked on kindly. You're free to go, Lieutenant."

"I'm sorry, Sister Peg is away for the day."

Sister Peg was never away for the day. The defensive posture of the woman in the doorway made it plain: Peter wasn't getting past her.

"Will you at least tell Caleb I was here?"

"Of course, Lieutenant." Her eyes darted past him in the

manner of someone conscious of being observed. "Now, if you will excuse me . . ."

Peter returned to the barracks to pass a restless afternoon on his bunk, gazing at the ceiling. His transport would be leaving the next morning at 0600; he had no doubt that such a swift departure was by design. Men came and went, banging through the room in their heavy boots, yet their presence scarcely registered in his consciousness. Amy and Greer—where could they have gone? And why the two of them together? How could she have broken him out, and how had they made it past the sentries at the portal? He scoured his memory for anything either of them had done or said to indicate they were planning such an escape. The only thing he could come up with was the strange serenity that had radiated from the major—as if the walls that caged him were inconsequential, their substance illusory. How could that be so?

It was a mystery, like everything else about the last thirty days. The whole thing left the impression of figures drifting just beyond the barriers of a heavy fog, there and not there.

As the empty hours wore on, Peter's thoughts were borne back to his evening among the sisters: his time with Caleb, the boy's youthful energy and cleverness; the joy in Amy's face as she turned from the oven to see him standing there; the quiet moment they'd shared as he made his departure, their hands touching in space. The gesture had felt entirely natural, an involuntary reflex without hesitation or resistance; it seemed to have risen from both a deep well inside him and someplace far away, like the forces that propelled the waves he loved to look at, curling onto the beach. Of all the events of the last few days, their moment in the doorway stood most vividly in his recollection, and he closed his eyes, replaying it in his mind. The warmth of her cheek against his chest, and the bright force of her embrace; the way Amy had looked at their joined hands. *Do you remember when I kissed you?* He was still hearing these words in his mind as he fell asleep.

He awoke in darkness; his mouth tasted of dryness and dust. He was surprised he'd slept so long; he was surprised he'd slept at all. He was reaching to lift his canteen from the floor when he noticed a figure sitting on the adjacent bunk.

"Colonel?"

Apgar was facing him, his feet resting on the floor, hands braced on his knees. He took a long breath before speaking. Peter understood that the man's presence was what had awakened him.

"Listen, Jaxon, I didn't feel right about what happened in there today. So what I'm about to tell you is just between us, is that understood?"

Peter nodded.

"The woman you described was seen once before, years ago. I didn't see her myself, but others did. You know about the Massacre of the Field?"

Peter frowned. "You were there?"

"I was just a kid, sixteen. It's not something I talk about. None of us do. I lost my parents and my little sister. My mother and father were killed outright, but I never knew what happened to her. I suppose she was taken up. To this day, I still have nightmares about it. She was four years old."

Apgar had never told Peter anything so personal; he'd never told him anything personal at all. "I'm sorry, Colonel."

The pain of this memory, and the effort that went into telling it: these were plainly written on the man's face. "Well, it was a long time ago. Condolences noted, but that's not why I'm here, and I'm sticking my neck out telling you any of this. If Fleet found out, he'd have my commission. Or send me to the stockade."

"You have my word, sir."

Apgar paused, then began again: "Twenty-eight souls were lost that day. Of those, sixteen, like my sister, were never accounted for. Everybody knows about the eclipse. What they don't know is that the virals were hiding in the hardboxes, like they knew about it in advance. Just before the attack began, a young DS officer in the tower reported seeing a large truck like the one you described waiting just beyond the tree line. You see where I'm going with this?"

"You're saying it was the same people."

Apgar nodded. "Two men saw the woman. The first was the DS officer I mentioned. The other was a field hand, the foreman of the North Ag complex. His wife and daughters were among those lost that day. His name was Curtis Vorhees."

Another surprise. "*General* Vorhees?"

"I expected you would find this interesting, especially given his friendship with Greer. Vorhees signed on right after the massacre. Half the leadership of the Second Exped came from that day. Nate Crukshank was the other DS in the tower. I'm sure you recognize the name. Did you know he was Vorhees's brother-in-law?"

Crukshank had been the commanding officer at Roswell.

The sudden alignment of players felt like pieces snapping together. Peter recalled his days with Greer and Vorhees at the Colorado garrison—the two men's warm, easy friendship, and the stack of charcoal sketches Greer had shown him after the general had been killed. Vorhees had drawn the same image again and again, a woman and two little girls.

"What about the first DS? Who was he?"

"Well, that's a name everybody knows. Tifty Lamont."

This made no sense. "Tifty Lamont was DS?"

"Oh, Tifty was more than that. I owe that man my life many times over, and I'm not alone. After the massacre, he signed on with the Exped too, a scout sniper, maybe the best there ever was. Made captain before he busted out. Vorhees, Crukshank, and Tifty went way back. I don't know the story, but there was one."

Tifty Lamont as Expeditionary, an officer even. From everything Peter had heard about the man, this fact seemed completely incongruous. "So what happened to him?"

"Tifty?"

"The man's an outlaw."

A new look came into Apgar's face. "I don't know, Lieutenant. You'd have to ask him. That is, if you could find him. If, say, you knew somebody who knew somebody."

A silence caught and held. Apgar was looking at him expectantly. Then:

"How many people did you say were in this colony of yours in California?"

"Ninety-two."

"Ninety-two souls, gone without a trace. Pretty puzzling, if you ask me. Doesn't exactly fit the typical MO of a viral attack. Put the sixty-seven at Roswell into the mix and you've got close to two hundred people pretty much vanished into thin air. And now Amy takes off, just when this woman reappears and effectively severs our oil supply. I could see why the brass would be concerned. Even more so when you consider the fact that the only other living soul who's seen this woman is . . . what was the term you used?"

"An outlaw."

"Exactly. Persona non grata. A politically touchy situation, to say the least. On the one hand, you have the military, who want nothing to do with the man. On the other, you have the Civilian Authority, which can't, at least not *officially.* Are you with me here, Lieutenant?"

"I'm not much for politics, sir."

"That makes two of us. Bunch of people covering their

asses. Which is why we find ourselves where we are. Just the sort of circumstances that would benefit from a third party. Somebody with a history of, let's say, personal initiative, who can think around the corners. I'm not alone in this opinion, either. Certain confidential discussions have been had in high places. Civilian, not military. Apparently, being your CO makes me an expert on your character. Yours and Donadio's."

Peter frowned. "What does Alicia have to do with this?"

"That I don't know. But I can tell you two things, and the math is up to you. The first is that nobody's heard from Fort Kearney in three months. The second is that Donadio had two sets of orders. I was only privy to the first, which came from Division and were just as I told you. The second came in a sealed pouch from Sanchez's office, eyes only."

"I don't understand. Why wouldn't they want you to know what her orders were?"

"An excellent question. Just who knows what seems to be the crux of the matter. There seems to be a certain interest in questions of confidentiality, and it doesn't only apply to you. So Fleet wants you out of the picture, I'm not telling you anything you don't already know. But just between us, Fleet and Sanchez haven't always seen eye to eye, and the chain of command isn't as clear as you might think. The Declaration leaves a lot of room open to interpretation, and things can get pretty murky. This business of the woman on the Oil Road isn't a matter of, shall we say, general consensus among military and civilian authorities. Nor is Martínez, who, as you succinctly put it, wasn't where he was supposed to be, just when Amy somehow breaks Greer out of the stockade and takes off. All very interesting."

"So you think Martínez is part of this."

Apgar shrugged. "I'm just the messenger. But Fleet has never been what you might call a true believer. As far as he's concerned, Amy is a distraction and the Twelve are a myth. Donadio he can't argue with—she's obviously different— but in his book, that doesn't prove a thing. He tolerated the hunt only because Sanchez made such a fuss it wasn't worth the fight, and what happened in Carlsbad is his opportunity to finally shut it down. There are those who believe different."

Peter took a moment to digest this. "So, Sanchez is going behind Fleet's back."

Apgar frowned ironically. "I wasn't aware I'd said anything of the kind. Talk like that would be above my rank. Be that as it may, I would consider it a personal favor if you could assist me in locating the appropriately resourceful individual to connect a few dots here. Know anybody who fits the bill, Lieutenant?"

The message was clear. "I think I do, Colonel."

"Excellent." Apgar paused before continuing: "Funny thing about that transport. The damnedest coincidence, actually. It seems the paperwork has been misplaced. You know how these things are. Should take about forty-eight hours to sort out, seventy-two at the outside."

"That's good to know, sir."

"I thought you might share that opinion." The colonel slapped his knees. "Well, it seems I'm needed elsewhere. I've been assigned to a presidential task force to deal with this . . . unfortunate development. Don't know how much I can contribute, but I go where I'm told." He rose from the bunk. "Glad you got your rest, Lieutenant. Busy days ahead."

"Thank you, Colonel."

"Don't mention it. And I do mean that literally." He looked at Peter again. "Just be careful with him, Jaxon. Lamont is nobody you want to cross."

They rode through the night and into another. They were east of Luling now. They had no map but didn't need one; Interstate 10 would lead them straight to Houston, into its jungled heart. Greer had been there once before—just the outskirts, but they'd told him enough. The city was an impenetrable swamp, a miasma of tree-tangled muck and sodden ruins, crawling with dopeys. If they didn't get you, the alligators would. They cruised the befouled waters like half-submerged boats, many having grown to gargantuan dimensions, their powerful jaws endlessly searching. Huge clouds of mosquitoes blanketed the air. Your nose, your mouth, your eyes: always they were looking for the body's door, seeking out the soft spots. Houston, what remained, was not a place for humankind; Greer wondered why anyone had ever thought it habitable to begin with.

They would face that soon enough. Now they found themselves in a prairie land of tall grasses and thickets, reclining mile by mile toward the sea. This far to the east, the highway hadn't been cleared. It seemed more suggestion than structure, its surface cracked and subsumed under washes of heavy clay soil. Graveyards of ancient cars frequently blocked the way. Few words had passed between the two of them since their departure: conversation was simply not necessary. Across the days, Greer had sensed a change in Amy, an aura of physical distraction. She was perspiring heavily; at times he caught her wincing, as if in pain. But when he expressed his concern, the girl peremptorily dismissed it. *I'm fine,* she insisted. *It's nothing.* Her tone was almost angry; she was telling him not to press.

As darkness fell, they made their camp in a clearing within sight of a ruined motel. The sky was clear, the temperature falling, calling forth dew from the air. Greer knew they were safe for the night; in Amy's presence he was in a zone of protection. They unrolled their bedrolls and slept.

He awakened later with a start; something was wrong. He rolled to the side and saw that Amy's bedroll was empty.

He did not allow himself to panic. A gibbous moon had risen as they'd slept, slicing the darkness into spaces of light and shadow, a landscape of menacingly elongated forms and pockets of blackness. The horses were obliviously chewing on a stand of weeds. Greer removed the Browning from his pack and moved cautiously into the gloom. He willed his eyes to parse shape from shape. Where had she gone? Should he call out to her? But the silence of the scene and its hidden dangers forbade it.

Then he saw her. She was standing just a few yards from their encampment, facing away. The rhythms of conversation touched his ears. Was she speaking to someone? It seemed so, and yet there was no one.

He approached her from behind. "Amy?"

No reply. She had given up her murmuring; her body was absolutely still.

"Amy, what is it?"

She turned then to face him with a look of mild surprise. "Oh. I see."

"Who were you talking to?"

She gave no answer. She seemed to be only partially present. Was she sleepwalking?

Then: "I suppose we should go back."

"Don't scare me like that."

"I'm sorry. I didn't mean to." She flicked her eyes downward at the gun. "What are you doing with that?"

"I didn't know where you'd gone. I was worried."

"I thought I made myself clear, Major. Put it away now." She walked past him, headed back to camp.

42

Time interminable; time without end. His existence was a nightmare from which he couldn't awaken. Thoughts floating past like glinting dust motes, darting from wherever he looked. Every day they came. The men with their glowing, blood-red eyes. They unhooked the bloated bags and bore them away on their rattling cart and hung fresh ones on their stands. Always the bags, endlessly needful, constantly filling with their drip-drip-drip of Grey.

They were men who enjoyed their work. They told little jokes, they kept themselves amused. They enjoyed themselves at his expense, like children taunting an animal at the zoo. Here now, they cooed, extending the fragrant dropper toward his mouth, does baby need his bottle? Is baby hungry?

He tried to resist them. He clenched his muscles against the chains, he turned his face away. He mustered every ounce of will to deny them, yet always he succumbed. The hunger soared inside him like a great black bird.

—Say it for Mama. Say, I'm a baby who needs his bottle, I promise to be good. Be a good baby, Grey.

The tip of the dropper wafted enticingly under his nose, the scent of blood like a bomb exploding in his brain, a million neurons firing in an electrical storm of pure desire.

—You'll like this one. An excellent vintage. You like the young ones, don't you, Grey?

Tears squeezed from his eyes. Tears of longing and revulsion. The tears of his too-long life, a century of lying naked in chains. The tears of being Grey.

—Please.

—Say it. I like the young ones.

—I'm begging you. Don't make me.

—The words, Grey. A wave of sour breath close to his ear. Let me . . . hear . . . the . . . words.

—Yes! Yes, I like the young ones! Please! Just a taste! Anything!

And then at last the dropper, its delicious earth-rich squirt on his tongue. He smacked his lips. He rolled the thick muscle of his tongue around the walls of his mouth. He suckled like the baby they said he was, wishing he could make the feeling last, though he never could: an involuntary bob of his throat and it was gone.

—More, more.

—Now, Grey. You know there can't be any more. A dropper a day keeps the doctor away. Just enough to make you keep churning out the viral goodness.

—Just one taste, that's all. I promise I won't tell.

A dark chuckle: And supposing I did? Supposing I gave you just one more dropper? What would you do then?

—I won't, I swear, I just want . . .

—I'll tell you what you want. What you want, my friend, is to rip those chains right out of the floor. Which, I have to say, is pretty much what I'd want in your situation. That's what I'd be thinking about. I'd want to kill the men who put me here. A pause, then the voice coming closer: Is that what you want, Grey? To kill all of us?

He did. He wanted to rip them limb from limb. He wanted their blood to flow like water; he ached to hear their final cries. He wanted this even more than death itself, though just a little. Lila, he thought, Lila, I can feel you, I know that you are near. Lila, I would save you if I could.

—See you tomorrow, Grey.

And on and on. The bags came empty and went away full, the dropper did its work. It was his blood that sustained them, the men with their glowing eyes. They fed on Grey's blood and lived forever, as he lived forever. Grey eternal, in chains.

Sometimes he wondered where the blood they fed him came from. But not very often. It wasn't the kind of thing he wanted to think about.

Occasionally he still heard Zero, though it wasn't like Zero was talking to him anymore. That part of the deal seemed to have expired, long ago. The voice was muffled and far away, as if Grey were eavesdropping on a conversation taking place on the other side of a wall, and all things considered, he counted it a small mercy to be left alone with only his own thoughts for company, no Zero and his talk-talk-talk filling up his head.

Guilder was the only one who took his blood straight from the source. That was what they called Grey, the Source, like he wasn't even a person but a thing, which he supposed he was. Not always but sometimes, when he was feeling especially hungry, or for other reasons Grey couldn't guess at,

Guilder would appear at the door in his underclothes, so as not to get blood on his suit. He would unhook the bag from its tube, viscous fluid spurting over him, and place the IV in his mouth, sucking up Grey's blood like a kid taking soda pop from a straw. *Lawrence,* he liked to say, *you're not looking so hot. Are they feeding you enough? I worry about you all alone down here.* Once, long ago, years or even decades, Guilder had brought a mirror with him. It was in what used to be called a lady's compact. Guilder popped the lid and angled it to Grey's face, saying, *Why don't you take a look?* An old man's face gazed back at him, wrinkled as a prune—the face of someone sitting on the fence of death.

He was permanently dying.

Then one day he awoke to find Guilder straddling a chair, looking at him. His tie was undone around his neck, his hair askew; his suit was rumpled and stained. Grey could tell he was late in his cycle. He could smell the rot coming off the man—a dumpstery, corpselike, slightly fruity stink—but Guilder made no move to feed. Grey had the sense that Guilder had been sitting there for some time.

"Let me ask you something, Lawrence."

The question was going to be asked one way or another. "Okay."

"Have you ever . . . now, how do I put this?" Guilder shrugged vaguely. "Have you ever been in love?"

Coming from the man's mouth, the word seemed completely alien. Love was the property of a different age; it was positively prehistoric.

"I don't understand what you're asking."

Guilder's face bunched with a frown. "Really, it seems like a perfectly simple question to me. Choirs of angels singing in their heaven, your feet levitating three inches off the ground. You know. In love."

"I guess not."

"It's a yes or no thing, Lawrence. It's one or the other."

He thought of Lila. Love was what he felt for her, but not the way Guilder meant. "No. I've never been in love."

Guilder was looking past him. "Well I was, once. Her name was Shawna. Though that wasn't her real name, of course. She had skin like butter, Lawrence. I'm totally serious here. That was how it tasted. Something a little Asian about her eyes, you know that look? And her body, well." He rubbed his face and exhaled a melancholy breath. "I don't feel that part anymore. The sex part. The virus pretty much takes care of that. Nelson thought the steroids you were taking might have been the reason the virus was different in you. There might have been some truth to that. But you make your bed, you have to lie in it." He chuckled ironically. "Make your bed. That's funny. That's a laugh."

Grey said nothing. Whatever mood Guilder was in, it seemed to have nothing to do with him.

"I suppose it's not such a bad thing on the whole. I can't honestly say that sex ever did me any favors. But even after all these years, I still think about her. Little things. Things she said. The way the sun looked, falling over her bed. I kind of miss the sun." He paused. "I know she didn't love me. It was all a big act was what it was. I knew that from the start, even if I couldn't admit it to myself. But there you have it."

"Why are you telling me this?"

"Why?" His gaze narrowed on Grey's face. "That should be obvious. You can be pretty obtuse, if you'll pardon my saying so. Because we're *friends,* Lawrence. I know, you probably think I'm the worst thing that ever happened to you. It could certainly appear that way. I'm sure this all might feel a little unfair. But you really left me no choice. Honestly, Lawrence? As odd as it seems, you're the oldest friend I have."

Grey held his tongue. The man was completely delusional. Grey found himself involuntarily flexing against his chains. The greatest happiness of his life, short of dying, would be to pop Guilder's head clean off.

"What about Lila? I don't mean to pry, but I always thought there was something between you two. Which was pretty surprising, given your history."

Something twisted inside him. He didn't want to talk about this, not now, not ever. "Leave me alone."

"Don't be like that. I'm just asking."

"Why don't you go fuck yourself?"

Guilder inched his face a little closer, his voice lowered confidentially. "Tell me something. Do you still hear him, Lawrence? The truth now."

"I don't know who you're talking about."

Guilder shot him a correcting frown. "Please, can we not? Do this? He's real is what I'm asking you. It's not some bullshit in my head." He was peering at Grey intently. "You know what he's asked me to do, don't you?"

There seemed no point denying it. Grey nodded.

"And on the whole, taking everything into consideration, you think it's a good idea? I feel like I need your input here."

"Why does it matter what I think?"

"Don't sell yourself short. You're still his favorite, Lawrence, no doubt about that. Oh sure, I may be the one in charge. I'm the captain of this ship. But I can tell."

"No."

"No what?"

"No, it's not a good idea. It's a terrible idea. It's the worst idea in the world."

Guilder's eyebrows lifted, like a pair of parachutes catching the air.

"Look at you." For the first time in eons, Grey actually laughed. "You think he's your *friend*? You think any of them are your friends? You're their bitch, Guilder. I *know* what they are. I know what Zero is. I was *there*."

He'd obviously struck a nerve. Guilder began clenching and unclenching his fists; Grey wondered, in a lazy way, if the man was about to hit him. The prospect didn't concern him in the least; it would break the monotony. It would be something different, a new kind of pain.

"I have to say, your response is more than a little disappointing, Lawrence. I was hoping I could count on a little support. But I'm not going to stoop to your level. I know you'd like that, but I'll be the bigger man. And just a little FYI: the Project was completed today. A real ribbon cutter. I was saving that as, you know, a surprise, something I thought you'd enjoy hearing about. You could be a part of this if you wanted. But apparently I've misjudged you."

He rose and headed for the door.

"What do you want, Guilder?"

The man turned back, leveling his blood-red eyes.

"What's in it for you? I never could figure that out."

A long silence, then: "Do you know what they are, Grey?"

"Of course I know."

But Guilder shook his head. "No, you don't. If you did, you wouldn't have to ask. So I'll tell you. They're the freest things on earth. Without remorse. Without pity. Without love. Nothing can touch them, hurt them. Imagine what that would be like, Lawrence. The absolute freedom of it. Imagine how wonderful that would be."

Grey made no reply; there was none to be made.

"You ask me what I want, my friend, and I'll give you my answer. I want what they have. I want that little whore out of my head. I want to feel . . . *nothing*."

The vase hit the wall in a satisfying explosion of glass. The car bombing was the last straw. This had to end *now*.

Guilder summoned Wilkes to his office. By the time his chief of staff entered the room, Guilder had managed to calm himself a little.

"Round up ten more per day."

Wilkes seemed taken aback. "Um, anybody in particular?"

"It doesn't matter!" Jesus, sometimes the man could be thick as a plank. "Don't you get it? It *never* mattered. Just pull them out of morning roll."

Wilkes hesitated. "So you're saying it should just be, you know, arbitrary. Not people we suspect of having ties to the insurgency, necessarily."

"Bravo, Fred. That's exactly what I'm saying."

For a second Wilkes just stood there, staring at Guilder with a bewildered look on his face. Not bewildered: disturbed.

"Yes? Am I talking to myself here?"

"If you say so. I can work up a list and send it down the hill to HR."

"I don't care how you do it. Just put it together." Guilder tossed a hand toward the door. "Now get out of here. And send an attendant to clean up this mess."

43

The route to Hollis was more circuitous than Peter had anticipated. The trail had taken them first to a friend of Lore's, who knew someone who knew someone else; always they seemed to be one step away, only to find that the target had moved.

Their last lead directed them to a Quonset hut where an illegal gambling hall operated. It was after midnight when they found themselves walking down a dark, trash-strewn alley in H-town. Curfew had long passed, but from everywhere around them came little bits of noise—barking voices, the crash of glass, the tinkling of a piano.

"Quite a place," Peter said.

"You haven't been here much, have you?" said Michael.

"Not really. Well, never, actually."

A shadowy figure stepped from a doorway into their path. A woman.

"Oye, mi soldadito. ¿Tienes planes esta noche?"

She moved forward from the shadows. Neither young nor

old, her body so thin it was nearly boyish, yet the sensual confidence of her voice and the way she stood—shifting from one foot to the other, her pelvis pushing gently against her tiny skirt—combined with the heavy-lidded declivity of her eyes, as they trolled the length of Peter's body, to give her an undeniable sexual force.

"¿Cómo te puedo ayudar, Teniente?"

Peter swallowed; his face felt warm. "We're looking for Cousin's place."

The woman smiled a row of silk-stained teeth. "Everybody's somebody's cousin. I can be your cousin if you want." Her eyes drifted to Lore, then Michael. "And what about you, handsome? I can get a friend. Your girlfriend can come if she wants, too. Maybe she'd like to watch."

Lore gripped Michael by the arm. "He's not interested."

"We're really just looking for someone," Peter said. "Sorry to have troubled you."

She gave a dark laugh. "Oh, it's no trouble. You change your mind, you know where to find me, Teniente."

They moved along. "Nice fellow," Michael said.

Peter glanced back down the alley. The woman, or what he'd assumed was a woman, had faded back into the doorway.

"I'll be damned. Are you sure?"

Michael chuckled ruefully, shaking his head. "You really have to get out more often, hombre."

Ahead they saw the Quonset hut. Blades of light leaked from the edges of the door, where a pair of beefy men stood guard. The three of them paused in the shelter of an overflowing trash bin.

"Better let me do the talking," Lore said.

Peter shook his head. "This was my idea. I should be the one to go."

"In that uniform? Don't be ridiculous. Stay with Michael. And the two of you, try not to get picked up by any trannies."

They watched her march up to the door. "Is this such a good idea?" Peter asked quietly.

Michael held up a hand. "Just wait."

At Lore's approach the two men tensed, moving closer together to bar her entry. A brief conversation ensued, beyond Peter's hearing; then she returned.

"Okay, we're in."

"What did you tell them?"

"That the two of you just got paid. *And* you're drunk. So try to act it."

The hut was crowded and loud, the space partitioned by large, hexagonal tables where cards were being dealt. Clouds of silk smoke choked the air, consorting with the sour-sweet aroma of mash; there was a still nearby. Half-dressed women—at least Peter took them to be women—were seated on stools at the periphery of the room. The youngest couldn't have been a day over sixteen, the oldest nearly fifty, haggish in her clownish makeup. More were moving in and out of a curtain at the back, usually in the arm-draped company of a visibly intoxicated man. As Peter understood it, the whole idea of H-town was to overlook a certain amount of illegal vice but to cordon it off within a specific area. He could see the logic—people were people—but staring it in the face was a different matter. He wondered if Michael was right about him. How had he gotten so prim?

"Not go-to they're playing, is it?" he asked Michael.

"Texas hold 'em, twenty-dollar ante from the looks of it. A bit rich for my blood." His eyes, like Peter's, were patrolling the room for Hollis. "We should try to blend in. How much scrip do you have?"

"Nothing."

"Nothing?"

"I gave it all to Sister Peg."

Michael sighed. "Of course you did. You're consistent, I'll give you that."

"The two of you," Lore said. "What a couple of pussies. Watch and learn, my friends."

She strode up to the closest table and took a chair. From the pocket of her jeans she withdrew a wad of bills, peeled off two, and tossed them into the pot. A third bill produced a shot glass, the contents of which she downed with a toss of her sun-bleached hair. The dealer laid out two cards for each player; then the betting began. For the first four hands Lore seemed to take very little interest in her cards, chatting with the other players, folding quickly with a roll of her eyes. Then, on the fifth, with no discernible change in her demeanor, she began to drive up the bet. The pile on the table grew; Peter guessed there were at least three hundred Austins sitting there for the taking. One by one the others dropped out until just a single player remained, a skinny man with pockmarked cheeks who was wearing a hydro's jumpsuit. The last card was dealt; stone-faced, Lore put down five more bills. The man shook his head and folded his cards.

"Okay, I'm impressed," said Peter, as Lore raked in the pot. They were standing off to the side, close enough to watch without seeming to. "How did she do that?"

"She cheats."

"Really? I don't see how."

"It's pretty simple, actually. The cards are all marked. It's subtle, but you can figure it out. One player at the table is playing for the house so it always comes out ahead. She used the first few hands to figure out who it was and how to read the cards. It also doesn't hurt that she's a woman. In here, no one's taking her seriously. They assume she'll bet when she has good cards, that she'll fold when she doesn't. Three-quarters of the time she's bluffing."

"What happens when they realize what she's doing?"

"They won't, not right away. She'll throw a hand or two."

"And then?"

"Then it's time to leave."

A sudden commotion drew their attention to the rear of the room. A dark-haired woman, her dress torn from her shoulders, arms crossed over her exposed breasts, burst through the curtain, screaming incoherently. A second later a man emerged, his pants bunched comically around his ankles. He seemed to be floating a foot off the floor—suspended, Peter realized, by a man gripping him from behind. As the first man hurtled through the air, Peter recognized him; it was the young corporal from Satch's squad who had driven the transport from Camp Vorhees. The second man, mountainous, the lower half of his face buried in a salt-and-pepper beard, was Hollis.

"Aha," said Michael.

With impressive nonchalance, Hollis hauled the man to his feet by his collar. The woman was shrieking profanities, jabbing a finger at the two of them—*Kill this fucker! I don't have to put up with this shit! Do you hear me? You're fucking dead, you asshole!*—as Hollis half-shoved, half-levitated him toward the exit.

"That's our cue," Peter said.

At a quickstep they made their way for the door, Lore coming up behind them as they exited the hut. The corporal, crying desperate apologies, was simultaneously trying to pull up his pants and scamper away. If Hollis was moved by the man's appeals, he gave no sign. While the two guards looked on, laughing uproariously, Hollis hoisted the corporal by the waistband and propelled him farther down the alley. As he pulled the man upright again, Peter called his name.

"Hollis!"

For a perplexing instant the man seemed not to recognize them. Then he made a small sound of surprise. "Peter. *Hola.*"

The corporal was still squirming in his grip. "Lieutenant, for God's sake do something! This monster's trying to kill me!"

Peter looked at his friend. "Are you?"

The big man shrugged drolly. "I suppose, since he's one of yours, I could let it go this one time."

"Exactly! You could let me go and I'll never come back, I swear it!"

Peter directed his attention to the terrified soldier, whose name, he recalled, was Udall. "Corporal. Where are you supposed to be? Don't bullshit me."

"West Barracks, sir."

"Then get there, soldier."

"Thank you, sir! You won't regret it!"

"I already do. Now get out of my sight."

He scampered away, holding up his pants.

"I wasn't going to really hurt him," Hollis said. "Just put a scare into him."

"What did he do?"

"Tried to kiss her. That's not allowed."

The offense seemed minor. Given all Peter had seen, it didn't seem like an offense at all. "Really?"

"Those are the rules. Pretty much anything goes except for that. It's mostly up to the women." He glanced past Peter. "Michael, it's good to see you. It's been a while. You're looking well."

"Same here. This is Lore."

Hollis smiled in her direction. "Oh, I know who you are. It's nice to finally have a proper introduction, though. How were the cards tonight?"

"Not too bad," Lore replied. "The plant at table three is a real chump. I was just getting started."

The man's expression hardened a discernible notch. "Don't judge me for this, Peter. That's all I'm asking. Things work here in a certain way, that's all."

"You have my word. We all know . . . ." He searched for the words. "Well. What you went through."

A moment passed. Hollis cleared his throat. "So, I'm thinking this isn't a social call."

Peter glanced over his shoulder at the two doormen, who were making no effort to conceal their eavesdropping.

"Is there someplace we could talk?"

Hollis met them two hours later at his house, a tarpaper shack on the western edge of H-town. Though the outside was anonymously decrepit, the interior possessed a surprising homeyness, with curtains on the windows and sprigs of dried herbs hanging from the ceiling beams. Hollis lit the stove and put on a pan of water for tea while the others waited at the small table.

"I make it with lemon balm," Hollis remarked as he placed four steaming mugs on the table. "Grow it myself in a little patch out back."

Peter explained what had happened on the Oil Road and the things Apgar had told him. Hollis listened thoughtfully, stroking his beard between sips.

"So can you take us to him?" Peter asked.

"That's not the issue. Tifty's no one you want to mix yourself up with—your CO's right about that. I can vouch for you, but those guys are nobody to fool with. My say-so will only go so far. Military isn't exactly welcome."

"I don't see a lot of options. If my hunch is right, he may be able to tell us where Amy and Greer went. All of this is connected. That's what Apgar was telling me."

"Sounds a bit thin."

"Maybe. But if Apgar's right, the same people might be responsible for what happened at Roswell, too." Peter hated to press, but the next question needed to be asked. "What do you remember?"

A look of sudden pain swept Hollis's face. "Peter, there's no use in this, okay? I didn't see anything. I just grabbed Caleb and ran. Maybe I should have done things differently. Believe me, I've thought about it. But with the baby . . ."

"No one's saying different."

"Then leave it alone. Please. All I know is that once the gates were open, they just poured in."

Peter glanced at Michael. Here was something they hadn't known, a new piece of the puzzle.

"Why were the gates open?"

"I don't think anyone ever figured that out," said Hollis. "Whoever gave the order, they must have died in the attack. And I've never heard anything about some woman. If she was there, I didn't see her. Or these trucks of yours." He took a heavy breath. "The fact is, Sara's gone. If I allowed myself to think different for one second, I'd go crazy. I'm sorry to say it, believe me. I won't pretend I've made my peace with it. But the best thing to do is accept reality. You too, Michael."

"She was my sister."

"And she was going to be my wife." Hollis looked at Michael's shocked face. "You didn't know that, did you?"

"Flyers, Hollis. No, I didn't."

"We were going to tell you when you got to Kerrville. She wanted to wait for you. I'm sorry, Circuit."

No one seemed to know what to say next. As the silence stretched, Peter looked around the room. For the first time he understood what he was seeing. This little shack, with its stove and herbs and snug feeling of home—Hollis had made the house that he and Sara would have had together.

"That's all I've got," said Hollis. "That will have to satisfy you."

"I can't accept it. Look at this place. It's like you're waiting for her to come home."

Hollis's grip visibly tightened on his mug. "Let it go, cuz."

"Maybe you're right. Maybe Sara's dead. But what if she's still out there?"

"Then she was taken up. I'm asking you nicely. If our friendship means anything to you, don't make me think about this."

"I have to. We all loved her, too, Hollis. We were a family, *her* family."

Hollis rose and returned his mug to the sink.

"Just take us to Tifty. That's all I'm asking."

Hollis spoke with his back to them. "He's not what you think. I owe that man."

"For what? A job in a brothel?"

His head was bowed, his hands clutching the edge of the sink, as if he'd taken a blow. "Jesus, Peter. You never change."

"You didn't do anything wrong. You did what you had to. And you got Caleb out."

"Caleb." From Hollis, a heavy sigh. "How is he? I keep meaning to visit."

"You should see for yourself. He owes you his life, and it's a good one."

Hollis turned to face them again. The tide had turned; Peter could see it in the man's eyes. A small flame of hope had been lit.

"What about you, Michael? I know what Peter thinks."

"Those were my friends that got killed. If there's payback, I want it. And if there's a chance my sister's alive, I'm not going to just do nothing."

"It's a big continent."

"It always was. Never bothered me any."

Hollis looked at Lore. "So what's your opinion?"

The woman startled a little. "What are you asking me for? I'm just along for the ride here."

The big man shrugged. "I don't know, you're pretty good with the cards. Tell me what the odds are."

Lore shifted her gaze to Michael, then back at Hollis. "This isn't a question of odds. Of all the men in the world, that woman chose you. If she's still out there, she's waiting for you. Staying alive any way she can until you find her. That's all that matters."

Everybody waited for what Hollis would next say.

"You're a real ballbuster, you know that?"

Lore grinned. "Famous for it."

Another silence fell. Then:

"Let me pack a few things."

44

The first snow fell on Alicia's third night scouting the fringes of the city, fat flakes spiraling from an inky sky. A clean, wintry cold had settled onto the earth. The air felt hard and pure. It moved through her body like a series of small exclamations, bursts of icy clarity in her lungs. She would have liked to set a fire, but it might be seen. She warmed her hands with her breath, stamped her feet on the frozen earth when she felt sensation receding. There was something suitable about it, this shock of cold; it had the taste of battle.

Soldier was beside her no more. Where Alicia was going, he could not follow. There had always been something celestial about him, she thought, as if he'd been sent to her from a world of spirits. In his deep awareness, he had seen what was happening to her, the dark evolution. The fierce taste uncoiling inside her since the day she had sunk her blade into the buck on the ridge, prying forth the living heart of him. There was an exhilarating power in it, a flowing energy, but it came at a cost. She wondered how much time remained before it overwhelmed her. Before her human surface stripped away and she became one thing only. Alicia Donadio, scout sniper of the Expeditionary, no more.

Go now, she had told him. *You're not safe with me.* Tears floated on the surface of her eyes; she longed to look away from him but couldn't. *You great lovely boy, I will never forget you.*

She had traveled the final miles on foot, tracing the river. Its waters still flowed easily but this wouldn't last; ice had begun to crust at the edges. The landscape was treeless and bare. The image of the city bristled from the horizon as dusk was falling. She had been smelling it for hours. Its vastness startled her. She withdrew the yellowed, hand-drawn map from her pack and took the lay of the land. The dome rising from the hilltop, the bowl-like stadium, the bisecting river with its hydro dam, the massive concrete building with its cranes, the rows of barracks hemmed by wire—all just as Greer had recorded, fifteen years ago. She took out the RDF and adjusted the gain with fingers numb with cold. She swept it back and forth. A wash of static; then the needle nudged a fraction of an inch. The receiver was pointing at the dome.

Somebody was home.

She no longer needed her glasses except in the brightest hours of the day. How had this come to pass? What had happened to her eyes? She examined her face in the surface of the river; the orange light had continued to fade. What did it mean? She looked almost . . . normal. An ordinary human woman. Would that were true, she thought.

She passed the first two days circling the perimeter to gauge its defenses. She took inventories: vehicles, manpower, weaponry. The regular patrols that left from the main gate were easy to avoid; their efforts felt perfunctory, as if they perceived no real threat. At first light trucks would disperse from the barracks to thread through the city, carting workers to the factories and barns and fields, returning as darkness fell. As the days of observation passed, it came to Alicia that she was seeing a kind of prison, a citizenry of slaves and slave masters, yet the structures of containment seemed meager. The fences were thinly manned; many of the guards didn't even appear to be armed. Whatever force held the populace in check, it came from within.

Her focus narrowed to two structures. The first was the large building with the cranes. It possessed the blocky appearance of a fortress. Through her binoculars Alicia could discern a single entrance, a broad portal sealed by heavy metal doors. The cranes sat idle; the building's construction seemed complete, and yet to all appearances it went unused. What purpose did it serve? Was it a refuge from the virals, a shelter of last retreat? That seemed possible, though nothing else about the city communicated a similar sense of threat.

The other was the stadium, situated just beyond the southern perimeter of the city in an adjacent fenced compound. Unlike the bunker, the stadium was the site of daily activity. Vehicles came and went, step vans and some larger trucks, always at dusk or shortly after, disappearing down a deep ramp that led, presumably, to the basement. Their contents were a mystery until the fourth day, when a livestock carrier, full of cattle, descended the ramp.

Something was being fed down there.

And then shortly after noon on the fifth day, Alicia was resting in the culvert where she'd made her camp when she heard the distant wallop of an explosion. She pointed her binoculars to the heart of the city. A plume of black smoke was uncoiling from the base of the hill. At least one building was on fire. She watched while men and vehicles raced to the scene. A pumper truck was brought in to douse the flames. By now she had learned to distinguish the prisoners from their keepers, but on this occasion a third class of individuals appeared. There were three of them. They descended upon the site of the catastrophe in a sleek black vehicle utterly unlike the salvaged junkers Alicia had seen, straightening their neckties and fussing with the creases of their suits as they emerged into the winter sunshine. What strange costumes were these? Their eyes were concealed by heavy dark glasses. Was it just the brightness of the day or something else? Their presence had an instantaneous effect, the way a stone cast ripples across the surface of a pond. Waves of anxious energy radiated from the others on the scene. One of the suited men appeared to be taking notes on a clipboard while the other two shouted orders, gesturing wildly. What was she seeing? A leadership caste, that was apparent; everything about the city implied one's existence. But what was the explosion? Was it an accident or something deliberate? A chink in the armor, perhaps?

Her orders were clear. Scout the city, assess the threat, report back to Kerrville in sixty days. Under no circumstances was she to engage the inhabitants. But nothing said she had to stay outside the wires.

The time had come to take a closer look.

*　*　*

She chose the stadium.

For two more days, she observed the comings and goings of the trucks. The fences were no problem; getting into the basement would be the tricky part. The door, like the portal on the bunker, looked impenetrable. Only when a truck hit the top of the ramp would the door ascend, sealing quickly as the vehicle passed through, all of it perfectly timed.

Dusk of the third day: behind a stand of scrub, Alicia stripped herself of weapons—all but the Browning, snug in its holster, and a single blade sheathed against her spine. She had scouted a spot in the wires where her ascent would be concealed by one of several buildings that appeared unused. A hundred yards of open ground separated these buildings from the ramp. Once the driver of the van rounded the corner, Alicia would have six seconds to cross the distance. Easy, she told herself. Nothing to it.

She took the fence with a single toehold, scuttled against the building's rear wall, and peered around the corner. There it was, right on time, churning toward the stadium: the van. The driver downshifted as he approached the turn.

Go.

When the vehicle hit the top of the ramp, Alicia was just twenty feet behind it. The door, ascending on clattering chains, approached its apex. With a vaulting stride she took to the air, alighting on the van's roof and dropping face-down within half a second of passing beneath the door.

Flyers, was she *good*.

Already she was feeling it, feeling *them*. The too-familiar prickling along her skin and, deep inside her skull, a watery murmuring, like the caress of waves upon a distant shore. The van, at reduced speed, was moving through a tunnel. Ahead she saw a second door. The driver beeped the horn; the door rose to let them through. Another three seconds: the van drew to a halt.

They were in a wide, open space, fifty feet on a side. Peeking over the top of the windshield, Alicia counted eight men. Six were armed with rifles; the other two wore heavy backpacks with tanks and long steel wands. At the far end of the room was a third door, different from the others: a heavy steel contraption with thick crossbars set into the frame.

One of the men sauntered toward the van, holding a clipboard; she pressed herself as flat against the roof as she could.

"How many you got?"

"The usual."

"Are we supposed to do them as a group?"

"Hell if I know. What does the order say?"

A shuffling of paper. "Well, it doesn't," the second man answered. "A group, I suppose."

"Is the betting pool still open?"

"If you want."

"Give me seven seconds."

"Sod has seven. You'll have to pick something else."

"Six, then." The driver's door creaked open; Alicia heard his feet hit the concrete floor. "I like the cows better. It takes longer."

"You are one sick bastard, you know that?" There was a pause. "You're right, though. It is pretty cool." He directed his voice away from the van. "Okay, everybody, showtime! Let's dim the lights!"

With a thunk the lights extinguished, replaced by a twilight-blue glow emanating from caged bulbs along the ceiling. All the men were backing away from the door at the far end of the room. There could be no doubt what lay on the other side; Alicia sensed it in her bones. A metal gate began to drop from the ceiling, then jolted to a stop. The men with the backpacks had taken up positions on the near side of the gate, wicks of flame dancing at the tips of their wands. The driver strode to the rear of the van and opened it.

"Come on, out with you."

"Please," a man's voice pleaded, "you don't have to do this! You're not like them!"

"It's okay, it's not what you think. Be a good fellow now."

A woman this time: "We haven't done anything! I'm only thirty-eight!"

"Really? I could have sworn you were older." The click of a cocking revolver. "All of you, let's move."

One by one they were hauled from the van, six men and four women, shackled at the wrists and ankles. They were sobbing, pleading for their lives. Some could barely stand. While two men kept their rifles trained, the driver moved among them with a ring of keys, unlocking the chains.

"What are you unshackling them for?" one of the other guards asked.

"Please, don't do this!" the woman cried. "I'm begging you! I have children!"

The driver backhanded the woman, knocking her to the ground. "Did I tell you to shut up?" Then, holding up a pair of shackles to the guard: "You want to clean these things later? I sure don't."

Do not engage the inhabitants, Alicia told herself. *Do not engage the inhabitants. Do not engage the inhabitants.*

"Sod?" the driver called. "Are we ready over there?"

A piggish-looking man stood off to the side at some kind of control panel. He moved a lever, and the gate gave a little twitch. "Hang on a second, it's jammed."

Do not engage, do not engage, do not engage . . .

"There, that's got it."

The hell with it.

Alicia rolled off the roof to find herself standing face-to-face with the driver. "Howdy."

"Son of a . . . bitch?"

She drew her blade and shoved it under his ribs. With a sharp exhalation he staggered backward.

"All of you," Alicia yelled, "hit the floor!"

Alicia unholstered the Browning and moved forward into the room, the weapon cupped in her hands, firing methodically. The guards seemed too stunned to react: one by one she began to pick them off in rusty spurts of blood. The head. The heart. The head again. Behind her, the prisoners had erupted in a torrent of wild screaming. Her mind was focused, clear as glass. The air grew suffused with a sweet intoxication of blood. She popped them off their feet. She lit them up like lightning. Nine bullets in her magazine; she'd finish them off with one to spare.

It was one of the men with the flamethrowers that got her. Though he certainly didn't intend to. At the instant Alicia pulled the trigger, he was trying only to protect himself—an instinctive gesture, to duck his head and turn his back to her.

45

"Papers."

Willing her fingers to stop trembling, Sara held the forged pass out for the guard. Her heart was hammering so hard against her ribs, it was a wonder the woman couldn't hear it. She snatched the pass from Sara's hands and looked it over quickly, darting her eyes to Sara's face before examining it a final time and shoving it back without expression.

"Next!"

Sara pushed through the revolving wire door. A final act: once on the other side, she was on her own. Beyond it lay a fenced chute, like something in a slaughterhouse. A column of day laborers was shuffling through—groundskeepers, kitchen workers, mechanics. More cols stood watch on either side of the chute, holding back snarling dogs on chains, laughing among themselves whenever one of the flatlanders flinched. Bags were searched, everyone was patted down. Drawing her shawl around her head, Sara kept her eyes averted. The real danger was being seen by someone who knew her—flatlander, col, it didn't matter. Not until she was wearing the veil of an attendant would she be safely anonymous.

How Eustace had managed to place her in the Dome, Sara didn't know. *We're everywhere* was all he would say. Once she was inside, her contact would find her. An exchange of code words, ordinary remarks of hidden meaning, would establish their identities. She moved up the hill, trying to make herself invisible by keeping her eyes to the ground, though on second thought, should she? Would it seem more natural to look around? Even the air seemed different here—cleaner, but in a way that seemed laden, humming with danger. At the periphery of her downcast vision she detected a heavy presence of HR personnel, moving in twos and threes. Probably they had ramped up security because of the car bombing, but who knew? Maybe it was always like this.

The Dome was ringed by concrete barricades. She showed her pass at the guardhouse and ascended the wide staircase that led to the entrance, a pair of massive doors set in a bronze frame. At the threshold she drew air into her chest. Here goes, she thought.

The doors were flung open, forcing her to dodge to the side. Two redeyes brushed past, the collars of their suits turned up against the cold, leather briefcases swinging from their hands. She thought she had escaped their notice when the one on the left halted on the top step and turned to look at her. "Watch where you're going, flatlander."

She was staring at the ground, doing anything to avoid their eyes. Even behind their dark lenses, they had the power to make her insides twist. "Sorry, sir. My mistake."

"Look at me when I'm speaking to you."

It felt like a trap. "I meant no offense," she murmured. "I have a pass." She held it out.

"I said, *look at me.*"

Against all instincts, Sara slowly raised her face. For a fraught moment, the redeye considered her from behind the inscrutable shield of his glasses, making no move to accept the pass. The second one's attentions appeared elsewhere; he was merely indulging his companion with this interruption in their day. There was something distinctly infantile about them, thought Sara. With their soft, unblemished faces and boyishly limber bodies, they were like overgrown children playing dress-up. Everything was a game to them.

"When one of us tells you to do something, you do it."

The other one puffed his cheeks impatiently. "What the hell is with you today? She's nobody. Can we please just go?"

"Not until I'm done here." Then, to Sara: "Have I made myself clear?"

Her blood felt like ice in her veins. It took every ounce of her will not to look away. Those demonic eyes. That curling sneer. "Yes, sir," she stammered. "Completely."

"Tell me. What is it that you do?"

"Do?"

A flicker of a smile, like a cat with a mouse in its paws. "Yes, what do you do. What's your job."

She offered an obsequious shrug. "I just clean, sir." When he made no reply, she added, "I'm going to be an attendant."

The redeye studied her another moment, deciding if this was a satisfactory answer or not. "Well, here's a little word to the wise, flatlander. You go through those doors, you best watch yourself. It doesn't take much."

"I will, sir. Thank you, sir."

"Now get the fuck to work."

Sara waited for the pair to complete their descent before she allowed her body to unclench. *Flyers,* she thought. *For the love of God, get ahold of yourself. You're about to walk into a building full of these things.*

She screwed up her courage and opened the door.

She was instantly overwhelmed by a feeling of expansiveness, her sense of dimension distorted by a vertical vastness of space. She'd never seen anyplace like it: the gleaming marble floor, the tiers of balconies, the massive, curving stairs. The ceiling soared far above. Diminished sunlight descended from the high, curtained windows of the cupola, dimming the interior to a kind of twilight. Everything seemed both loud and quiet at once, the tiniest sounds reverberating before being absorbed by the void. Cols were stationed both around the room's periphery and at regular intervals on the stairs. A line of workers, ten deep, waited at the processing desk in the middle of the room. She assumed her place behind a man with a bag of tools over his shoulder. The desire to glance past him to see what lay ahead was intense but nothing to indulge. The line crept forward as each pass was stamped. She was fifth in line, then third, then second. The man with the tool bag stepped to the side, revealing the figure seated behind the desk.

It was Vale.

Sara's heart jolted with adrenaline. She couldn't move; she couldn't breathe. It would all be over before it had even begun. Her orders were clear: she couldn't be taken alive. Nina had spared nothing in describing exactly what the redeyes would do to her. *It will be like nothing you've ever experienced. You'll beg them to kill you. You can't hesitate.* What could she use? Should she just run and pray they'd shoot her?

"Are you feeling all right, miss?"

Vale was looking at her expectantly, extending a hand to receive her pass.

"What did you say?"

"Are . . . you . . . feeling . . . all right?"

She felt as if she'd been yanked from the edge of a cliff. She fumbled for the correct response. "I'm just a little nervous."

If Vale was surprised to see her, his face did not betray it. Vale was simply a better actor than she was. All those years Sara had known him, and she'd never detected a thing.

"The Dome can be a little overwhelming the first time you see it. You must be the new girl, Dani. Is that correct?"

She nodded. Dani, that was her name now. Not Sara.

"Display your tag, please."

She drew up her sleeve and extended her arm. Eustace, using an insider in the records department, had arranged to have Sara's number assigned to her new, fictitious identity. Vale made a small show of checking it against his paperwork.

"It seems you're to report to Deputy Director Wilkes." He gestured for another col to take his place at the desk. "Come with me."

Sara didn't know the name. But a deputy director—he had to be a member of the senior staff. Vale escorted her down a short hallway to an elevator with reflective metal doors. They stood in silence, both looking forward, as they waited for the car.

"Step inside, please."

Entering behind her, Vale pushed the button for the sixth floor. The car began its upward climb. Still he wasn't looking at her. She wondered if he was going to say anything. Then, as they passed the fourth floor, he reached toward the panel again and flipped a switch. The car abruptly halted.

"We only have a second," Vale said. "You've been assigned to the woman, Lila. This is better than anything we could have hoped for."

"Who's Lila?"

"She's the one who controls the virals. A major target. She's under heavy guard and almost never leaves her rooms."

Sara's mind raced to encode every word he said. "What am I supposed to do?"

"For now, just watch her. Try to win her trust. You and I won't have any more direct contact. Any messages will go through the serving girl who brings you your meals. If the spoon on your tray is upside down, there's a note under your plate. Return any messages the same way, but only do this in an emergency. Got that?"

Sara nodded.

"I always liked you, Sara. I'd like to think I did what I could to protect you. But none of that matters now. If the redeyes figure out who you are, I won't be able to help you." He slid his fingers under his waistband and withdrew a small square of metal foil and pressed it into her hand. "Always keep this hidden on your person. There's a piece of blotter paper inside. It's soaked in the same compound Nina used to knock you out but at a much higher concentration. Put it under your tongue. It won't take more than a couple of seconds. Believe me, it's better than going to the basement."

Sara slid the envelope into the pocket of her trousers. Death was with her now. She hoped she'd have the nerve if the time came.

Vale's hand was on the switch. "Ready?"

With a lurch the car resumed its upward course, then decelerated as they approached their destination. Vale, snapping back into character, placed his hand on her arm, gripping her just above the elbow. The doors slid open to reveal a col, heavyset with dark teeth, glaring at them with his hands on his hips.

"What the hell is going on with this elevator?" Then, locating Sara with his eyes: "What's she doing up here?"

"New attendant. I'm taking her to Wilkes."

The col examined her up and down. His eyebrows wagged suggestively. "Pity. She's a nice one."

Vale led her down a hall lined with heavy wooden doors. Stationed at eye level beside each was a brass plate bearing a name and title, some of which Sara recalled from broadsheets posted in the flatlands: "Aidan Hoppel, Minister of Propaganda," "Clay Anderson, Minister of Public Works," "Daryl Chee, Minister of Material Resource Recovery," "Vikram Suresh, Minister of Public Health." They came to the final door: "Frederick Wilkes, Chief of Staff and Deputy Director of the Homeland."

"Come."

The office's occupant was bent forward over a stack of papers on his desk, scribbling with a fountain pen. A muted winter light filtered through the draped windows behind him. A moment passed; then he looked up.

"Dani, is it?"

Sara nodded.

The redeye shifted his gaze to Vale. "Wait outside, please."

The door clicked shut. Wilkes rocked back in his chair. An air of weariness radiated from him. He pulled a sheet of paper from the pile and looked it over.

"The dairy barns. That was where you worked?"

"Yes, Deputy Director."

"And you have no immediate family."

"No, Deputy Director."

Wilkes returned his attention to the page on his desktop. "Well, it seems this is your lucky day. You're to be Lila's companion. Does the name mean anything to you?"

Sara meekly shook her head.

"Heard rumors, perhaps? We have no illusions that security isn't always what it could be. You can tell me if you have."

With monumental effort, she forced herself to look him in the eye. "No, I haven't heard anything."

Wilkes let a moment pass before continuing. "Well. Suffice it to say that Lila is one of a kind. The job is pretty straightforward. Basically, do whatever she asks. You will find she can be—how do I put this? Unpredictable. Some of the things she asks of you will seem odd. Think you're up to this?"

She returned a crisp nod. "Yes, sir."

"The one thing you must do is get her to eat. This takes some coaxing. She can be extremely stubborn."

"You can count on me, Deputy Director."

He leaned back in his chair again, folding his hands in his lap. "You will find life in the Dome much more comfortable than the flatland. Three square meals a day. Hot water for bathing. Very little will be asked of you other than the duties I've described. If you do a good job, there's no reason you can't enjoy our largesse for years to come. One last matter. How are you with children?"

"Children, sir?"

"Yes. Do you like them? Get on with them? Personally, I find them rather trying."

Sara felt a familiar pang. "Yes, Deputy Director. I like them fine."

She waited for further explanation from Wilkes, but none was evidently forthcoming. He inspected her for another few seconds from across his desk, then picked up the telephone.

"Tell them we're on the way."

Roughly an hour later, Sara found herself garbed in an attendant's robe, standing at the threshold of a room so sumptuously decorated that its volume of detail was difficult to absorb. Heavy drapes were drawn over the windows; the only sources of light were several large silver candelabras positioned around the room. Gradually the scene came into focus. The sheer volume of furniture and bric-a-brac made it seem less like a place where someone lived than a storage room of miscellaneous objects. A voluminous sofa covered in fat, tasseled pillows, as well as a pair of equally overstuffed chairs, stood to one side, facing a low square table of polished wood, its surface piled with books. More pillows of various colors were scattered on the floor, which was dressed by an ornately patterned rug. The walls were covered with oil paintings in heavy gilt frames—landscapes, pictures of horses and dogs, as well as a great many portraits of women and their children in curious costumes, the images possessing a disturbing half reality. One in particular caught Sara's attention: a woman in a blue dress and an orange hat, sitting in a garden beside a little girl. She moved toward it to have a closer look. A small plaque at the bottom of the frame read, "Pierre-Auguste Renoir, *On the Terrace,* 1881."

"Well, there you are. It's about time they sent someone."

Sara pivoted. A woman, arms folded over her chest, was standing in the bedroom doorway. She was both more and less than the image Sara had assembled from the things Vale and Wilkes had said. The person she had envisioned was at the very least a substantial presence, but the figure before her appeared quite frail. She was perhaps as old as sixty. Deep fissures lined her face, cutting borders between its various regions; crescents of drooping skin hung like hammocks beneath her watery eyes. Her lips were so pale they were practically nonexistent, like ghost lips. She was wearing a shimmering robe of some thin, shiny fabric, a thick towel encircling her head like a turban.

"*¿Hablas inglés?*"

Sara stared dumbly, unable to formulate a reply to this incomprehensible question.

"Do . . . you . . . speak . . . English?"

"Yes," Sara stated. "I speak English."

The woman gave a little start. "Oh. So you do. I have to say, that's a surprise. How many times have I asked the service to send somebody who spoke even a little English? I don't even want to tell you." She made a distracted gesture with her hands. "I'm sorry, your name again?"

Never mind that she hadn't told her to begin with. "It's Dani."

"Dani," the woman repeated. "Where are you from, exactly?"

The most general answer seemed the wisest. "I'm from here."

"Of course you're from *here*. I meant *originally*. Your tribe. Your people. Your clan." Another agitated flutter of her hands. "You know. Your *familia*."

With each exchange, Sara felt herself being pulled deeper into the quicksand of the woman's oddness. Yet something about her was almost endearing. She seemed quite helpless, a twittering bird in a cage.

"California, actually."

"Ah. Now we're getting somewhere." A pause; then, with a dawning look: "Oh, *I* see. You're working your way through school. Why didn't you say so?"

"Ma'am?"

"Please," she chirped, "call me Lila. And don't be so modest. It's an admirable thing you're doing. A great show of character. Of course, that doesn't mean I'll be paying you more than the other girls. I made that clear with the service. Fourteen an hour, take it or leave it."

Fourteen what? Sara wondered. "Fourteen is fine."

"And, of course, the Social Security. We'll be paying that, and filing the 1099. David is very particular about these things. He's what you'd call a rule follower. A big ol' stick in the mud. No health insurance, I'm afraid, but I'm sure you get that through your school." She beamed encouragingly. "So, are we good?"

Sara nodded, completely dumbfounded.

"Excellent. I have to say, Dani," the woman, Lila, continued, gliding into the room, "you've come just in the nick of time. Not a moment too soon, in fact." She had taken a box of matches from her robe and was lighting a large candelabra near her dressing table. "Why don't you just put that over there?"

She was referring to the tray Wilkes had given her. On it was a metal flask and cup. Sara placed the tray on the table the woman had indicated, adjacent to an ornately carved wardrobe draped with scarves. Lila had positioned herself in front of a standing mirror and was turning her shoulders this way and that, examining her reflection.

"So what do you think?"

"I'm sorry?"

She placed one hand on her stomach and pressed inward as she filled her chest with air. "This awful diet. I don't think I've ever been so famished in my life. But it really does seem to be doing the trick. What would you say, Dani? Another five pounds? You can be honest."

Standing in profile, the woman was just skin and bones. "You look fine to me," she said gently. "I wouldn't lose any more."

"Really? Because when I look in this mirror what I'm thinking is, who is this blimp? This zeppelin? *Oh God, the humanity.* That's what I'm thinking."

Sara remembered Wilkes's orders. "I think you're supposed to eat, actually."

"So I'm told. Believe me, I've heard *that* before." She placed her hands on her hips, scrunched up her face, and dropped her voice an octave. "Lila, you're too skinny. Lila, you've got to put some meat on those bones. Lila this, Lila that. Blah, blah, blah." Then, her eyes widening with sudden panic: "Oh my goodness, what time is it?"

"I guess it's . . . about noon?"

"Oh my goodness!" The woman began to dart around the room, snatching up various belongings and putting them down again in a manner that seemed arbitrary. "Don't just stand there," she implored, grabbing a pile of books and shoving them into the bookcase.

"What would you like me to do?"

"Just . . . I don't know. *Anything.* Here—" She filled Sara's hands with pillows. "Put these over there. On the whoozi-whatzis."

"Um, you mean the sofa?"

"Of course I mean the sofa!"

And just like that, a light seemed to switch on in the woman's face. A wondrous, happy, shining light. She was staring over Sara's shoulder, toward the door.

"Sweetheart!"

She dropped to a crouch as a young child, a girl in a plain smock, blond ringlets bouncing, dashed past Sara into the woman's outstretched arms. "My angel! My sweet, sweet girl!"

The child, who was holding a sheet of colored paper, pointed at the woman's turbaned head. "Did you take a bath, Mummy?"

"Why, yes! You know how Mummy likes her baths. What a clever little girl you are! So, tell me," she continued, "how were your lessons? Did Jenny read to you?"

"We read *Peter Rabbit*."

"Wonderful!" the woman beamed. "Was it funny? Did you like it? I'm sure I've told you how much I adored him when I was your age." She turned her attention to the paper. "And what do we have here?"

The little girl held it up. "It's a picture."

"Is that me? Is it a picture of the two of us?"

"They're birds. That one is named Martha, the other one is Bill. They're building a nest."

A flicker of disappointment; then she smiled again. "Why, of course they are. Anyone could see that. It's as plain as the nose on your pretty little face."

And on and on. Sara barely ingested any of it. An intense new sensation had come over her, a feeling of biological alarm. Something deep and atavistic, tidal in its weight and movement, accompanied by a focusing of her senses on the back of the little girl's blond head. Those curls. The precise and singular dimensions that the little girl's body occupied in space. Sara already knew without knowing, a fact she also knew, the paradox building a kind of hallway inside her, like images reflected infinitely in two opposing mirrors.

"But how awful of me," the woman, Lila, was saying, her voice at some impossible remove from reality, a transmission from a distant planet. "I've totally forgotten my manners. Eva, I need to introduce you to someone. This is our new friend . . ." She paused, drawing a blank.

"Dani," Sara managed.

"Our wonderful new friend Dani. Eva, say how do you do."

The child turned. Time collapsed as Sara beheld her face. A unique amalgamation of form and features that was the only one in all the universe. There was no doubt in Sara's mind.

The little girl sent her a shining, closed-lip smile. "How do you do, Dani?"

Sara was looking at her daughter.

But in the next second something changed. A shadow fell, a dark presence descending. It jolted Sara back to the world.

"Lila."

Sara turned. He was standing behind her. His face was a man's, ordinary, forgettable, one of thousands like it, but from it radiated an invisible force of menace as incontrovertible as gravity. To behold him was to feel oneself plunging.

He looked at Sara contemptuously in the eye, piercing her utterly. "Do you know who I am?"

Sara swallowed. Her throat was as tight as a reed. For the first time, her mind darted to the foil package secreted in the deep folds of her robe; it would not be the last.

"Yes, sir. You're Director Guilder."

His mouth curled downward with distaste. "Put down your veil, for God's sake. Just the sight of you makes me sick."

With trembling fingers, she did so. Now the shadow became a shadow literally, his features mercifully blurred behind the blush of fabric, as if in mist. Guilder strode past her, to where Lila still crouched with Sara's daughter. If his presence meant anything to the little girl, Sara couldn't see it, but Lila was a different story. Every part of her tightened. Clutching the child in front of her like a shield, she rose to her feet.

"David—"

"Just stop it." His eyes flicked disagreeably over her. "You look like hell, you know that?" Then, turning to face Sara once more: "Where is it?"

He was, she understood, speaking of the tray. Sara pointed.

"Bring it here."

Her hands, somehow, managed this.

"Get rid of them," Guilder said to Lila.

"Eva, sweetie, why doesn't Dani take you outside?" She looked quickly at Sara, her eyes beseeching. "It's such a beautiful day. A little fresh air, what do you say?"

"I want *you* to take me," the girl protested. "You *never* go outside."

Lila's voice was like a song she was being made to sing. "I know, sweetheart, but you know how sensitive Mummy is to the sun. And Mummy has to take her medicine now. You know how Mummy gets when she takes her medicine."

Reluctantly, the child complied. Breaking away from Lila, she moved to where Sara was standing beside the door.

With excruciating miraculousness, she took Sara by the hand.

Flesh meeting flesh. The unbearable corporeal smallness of it, its discrete power, its infusion of memory. All of Sara's senses molded around the exquisite sensation of her child's tiny hand in her own. It was the first time their bodies had touched since one was inside the other, though now it was the opposite: Sara was the one inside.

"Run along, you two," Lila croaked. She gave a wave of absolute misery toward the door. "Have fun."

Without a word, Kate—Eva—led Sara from the room. Sara was floating; she weighed a million pounds. Eva, she thought. I have to remember to call her Eva. A short hallway and then a flight of stairs: a pair of doors at the bottom pushed into a small, fenced yard with a teeter-totter and a rusted swing set. The sky looked down with a solemn, snow-filled light.

"Come on," the child said. And broke away.

She climbed aboard a swing. Sara took her place behind her.

"Push me."

Sara drew back the chains, suddenly nervous. How much was safe? This precious and beloved being. This holy, miraculous, human person. Surely three feet was more than enough. She released the chains, and the girl arced away, vigorously pumping her legs.

"Higher," she commanded.

"Are you sure?"

"Higher, higher!"

Each sensation a piercing. Each a painless engraving in the heart. Sara caught her daughter at the small of her back and thrust her away. Up and out she rose, into the December air. With each arc her hair volleyed backward, suffusing the air behind her with the sweet scent of her person. The girl swung silently; her happiness was bound into a pure occupation of the act itself. A little girl, swinging in winter.

My darling Kate, thought Sara. *My baby, my one.* She pushed, and pushed again; the girl flew away, always returning to her hands. *I knew, I knew, I always knew. You are the ember of life I blew on, a thousand lonely nights. Never could I let you die.*

46

Houston.

The liquefied city, drowned by the sea. The great urban quagmire, none but its skyscrapered heart left standing. Hurricanes, drenching tropical rains, the unchecked slide of a continent's waters seeking final escape to the Gulf: for a hundred years the tides had come and gone, filling the lowlands, carving out grimy bayous and contaminated deltas, erasing all.

They were ten miles from the city's central core. The last days of travel had been a game of hopscotch, seeking out the dry places and segments of passable roadway, hacking their way through thickets of spiny, insect-infested vegetation. In these quarters, nature unveiled its true malevolent purpose: everything here wanted to sting you, swarm you, bite you. The air creaked with its saturated weight and miasma of rot. The trees, gnarled like grasping hands, seemed like something from another age entirely. They seemed positively made up. Who would invent such trees?

Darkness came on with a chemically yellowish dimming. The trip had compacted to a crawl. Even Amy had begun to show her irritation. Her signs of illness had not abated; rather, the opposite. When she thought Greer wasn't looking, he caught her pressing her palms to her stomach, exhaling with slow pain. They quartered that night on the top floor of a house that seemed outrageous in its ruined opulence: dripping chandeliers, rooms the size of auditoriums, all of it spattered with a black, off-gassing mold. A brown line three feet above the marble floor circumscribed the walls where floodwaters had once risen. In the massive bedroom where they took shelter, Greer opened the windows to clear the air of the ammonic stench: below him, in the vine-clotted yard, lay a swimming pool full of goo.

All night long, Greer could hear the dopeys moving in the trees outside. They vaulted from limb to limb, like great apes. He listened to them rustling through the foliage, followed by the sharp animal cries of rats and squirrels and other small creatures meeting their demise. Amy's injunction notwithstanding, he dozed fitfully, pistol in hand. *Just remember. Carter's one of us.* He prayed it was true.

Amy was no better in the morning.

"We should wait," he said.

Even standing seemed to take all the strength she could muster. She made no effort to hide her discomfort, gripping the flat of her belly, her head bowed in pain. He could see the spasms shuddering her abdomen as the cramps moved through her.

"We go," she said, speaking through gritted teeth.

They continued east. The skyscrapers of downtown emerged in their particularity. Some had collapsed, the clay soil having expanded and contracted over the years to pulverize their foundations; others reclined against each other like drunks stumbling home from a bar. Amy and Greer traced a narrow spit of sand between weed-choked bayous. The sun was high and bright. Seaborne wreckage had begun to appear: boats, and parts of boats, splayed on their sides in the shallows as if in a swoon of exhaustion. When they reached the place where the land ended, Greer dismounted, retrieved the binoculars from his saddlebag, and pointed them across the stained waters. Dead ahead, wedged against a skyscraper, lay a vast ship, hard aground. Her stern rose impossibly high in the air, massive propellers visible above the waterline. On it was written the vessel's name, dripping with rust: CHEVRON MARINER.

"That's where we'll find him," said Amy.

There was no dry path across; they would have to find a boat. Luck favored them. After backtracking a quarter mile, they discovered an aluminum rowboat overturned in the weeds. The bottom appeared sound, the rivets tight. Greer dragged it to the lagoon's edge and set it afloat. When it failed to sink, he helped Amy down from her mount.

"What about the horses?" he asked her.

Her face was a mask of barely bottled pain. "We should be back before dark, I think."

He stabilized the craft as Amy boarded, then lowered himself onto the middle bench. A flat board served as a paddle. Seated in the stern, Amy had been reduced to cargo. Her eyes were closed, her hands wrapped her waist, sweat dripping from her brow. She made no sound, though Greer suspected her silence was for his benefit. As the distance narrowed, the ship expanded to mind-boggling dimensions. Its rusted sides loomed hundreds of feet over the lagoon. It was listing to one side; the surrounding water was black with oil. Greer paddled their craft into the lobby of the adjacent building and brought them to rest beside a bank of motionless escalators.

"Lucius, I think I'm going to need your help."

He assisted her from the boat and up the nearest escalator, supporting her by the waist. They found themselves in an atrium with several elevators and walls of smoked glass. ONE ALLEN CENTER a sign read, with a directory of offices beneath. The ascent that lay ahead would be serious; they'd need to climb ten stories at least.

"Can you make it?" Greer asked.

Amy bit her lip and nodded.

They followed the sign for the stairs. Greer lit a torch, gripped her at the waist again, and began to climb. The trapped air of the stairwell was poisonous with mold; every few floors they were forced to step out just to clear their lungs. At the twelfth floor, they stopped.

"I think we're high enough," said Greer.

From the sealed windows of a book-lined office they looked down on the tanker's decking, wedged hard against the building ten feet below. An easy drop. Greer took the desk chair, hoisted it over his head, and flung it through the window.

He turned to look at Amy.

She was studying her hand, holding it before her like a cup. A bright red fluid filled her palm. It was then that Greer noticed the stain on her tunic. More blood was trickling down her legs.

"Amy—"

She met his eye. "You're tired."

It was like being wrapped in an infinite softness. A blanketing, whole-body sleep.

"Oh, damn," he said, already gone, and folded to the floor.

47

Peter and the others entered San Antonio on Highway 90. It was early morning; they had passed the first night in a hardbox in the city's outer ring of suburbs, a sprawl of collapsed and scoured houses. The room lay beneath a police station, with a fortified ramp at the rear. Not a DS hardbox, Hollis explained; one of Tifty's. It was larger than the hardboxes Peter had seen, though no less crude—just a stuffy room with bunks and a garage bay where a fat-tired pickup awaited, cans of fuel in the bed. Crates and metal military lockers were stacked along the walls. What's in these? Michael asked, to which Hollis said, one eyebrow raised, I don't know, Michael. What do you think?

They drove out at first light beneath a heavy sky, Hollis at the wheel beside Peter, Michael and Lore riding in the truck's bed. Much of the city had burned in the days of the epidemic; little remained of the central core save for a handful of the taller buildings, which stood with forlorn austerity against the backdrop of bleached hills, their scorched facades telegraphing the blackened and collapsed interiors where an army of dopeys now dozed the day away. "Just dopeys," people always said, though the truth was the truth: a viral was a viral.

Peter was waiting for Hollis to turn off, to take them north or south, but instead he drove them into the heart of town, leaving the highway for narrow surface streets. The way had been cleared, cars and trucks hauled to the sides of the roadway. As the shadows of the buildings engulfed the truck, Hollis slid the cab's rear window open. "You better weapon up," he cautioned Michael and Lore. "You'll want to watch yourself through here."

"All eyes, hombre," came the man's reply.

Peter gazed at the destruction. It was the cities that always turned his thoughts to what the world had once been. The buildings and houses, the cars and streets: all had once teemed with people who had gone about their lives knowing nothing of the future, that one day history would stop.

They moved through without incident. Vegetation began to crowd the roadway as the gaps between the buildings widened.

"How much longer?" he asked Hollis.

"Don't worry. It's not far."

Ten minutes later they were skirting a fence line. Hollis pulled the vehicle to the gate, removed a key from the glove box of the pickup, and stepped out. Peter was struck by a sense of the past: Hollis might have been Peter's brother, Theo, opening the gate to the power station, all those years ago.

"Where are we?" he asked when Hollis returned to the truck.

"Fort Sam Houston."

"A military base?"

"More like an Army hospital," Hollis explained. "At least it used to be. Not a lot of doctoring goes on here anymore."

They drove on. Peter had the sense of driving through a small village. A tall clock tower stood to one side of a quadrangle that might have once been the center of town. Apart from a few ceremonial cannons, he saw nothing that seemed military—no trucks or tanks, no weapon emplacements, no fortifications of any kind. Hollis brought the pickup to a halt before a long, low building with a flat roof. A sign above the door read, AQUATICS CENTER.

"Aquatics," Lore said, after they'd all disembarked. She squinted doubtfully at the sign, a rifle balanced across her chest in a posture of readiness. "Like . . . swimming?"

Hollis gestured at the rifle. "You should leave that here. Wouldn't want to make a bad impression." He shifted his attention to Peter. "Last chance. There's no way to undo this."

"Yes, I'm sure."

They entered the foyer. All things considered, the building's interior was in good shape: ceilings tight, windows solid, none of the usual trash.

"Feel that?" Michael said.

A basal throbbing, like a gigantic plucked string, was radiating from the floor. Somewhere in the building a generator was operating.

"I kind of expected there to be guards," Peter said to Hollis.

"Sometimes there are, when Tifty wants to put on a show. But basically we don't need them."

Hollis led them to a pair of doors, which he pushed open to reveal a great, tiled space, the ceiling high above and, at the center of the room, a vast, empty swimming pool. He guided them to a second pair of swinging doors and a flight of descending stairs, illuminated by buzzing fluorescents. Peter thought to ask Hollis where Tifty got the gas for his generator, but then answered the question for himself. Tifty got it where he got everything; he stole it. The stairs led to a room crowded with pipes and metal tanks. They were under the pool now. They made their way through the cramped space to yet another door, though different from the others, fashioned of heavy steel. It bore no markings of any kind, nor was there an obvious way to open it; its smooth surface possessed no visible mechanisms. On the wall beside it was a keypad. Hollis quickly punched in a series of digits, and with a deep click the door unlatched, revealing a dark corridor.

"It's okay," Hollis said, angling his head toward the opening, "the lights go on automatically."

As the big man stepped through, a bank of fluorescents flickered to life, their vibrancy intensified by the hospital-white walls of the corridor. Peter's sense of Tifty was radically evolving. What had he imagined? A filthy encampment, populated by huge, apelike men armed to the teeth? Nothing he had seen even remotely conformed to these expectations. To the contrary: the display so far indicated a level of technical sophistication that seemed well beyond Kerrville's. Nor was he alone in this shifting of opinion; Michael, too, was frankly gawking. *Some place,* his face seemed to say.

The corridor ended at an elevator. A camera was poised above it. Whoever was on the other side knew they were coming; they'd been observed since they'd entered the hall.

Hollis tilted his face upward to the lens, then pressed a button on the wall adjacent to a tiny speaker. "It's all right," he said. "They're with me."

A crackle of static, then: "Hollis, what the fuck."

"Everyone's unarmed. They're friends of mine. I'll vouch for them."

"What do they want?"

"We need to see Tifty."

A pause, as if the voice on the other end of the intercom was conferring with somebody else; then: "You can't just bring them here like this. Are you out of your mind?"

"I wouldn't ask if it wasn't important. Just open the door, Dunk."

An empty moment followed. Then the doors slid open.

"It's your ass," the voice said.

They entered; the elevator commenced its downward creep. "Okay, I'll bite," Michael ventured. "What is this place?"

"You're in an old USAMRIID station. It's an annex to the main facility in Maryland, activated during the epidemic."

"What's USAMRIID?" asked Lore.

It was Michael who answered. "It stands for 'United States Army Medical Research Institute of Infectious Diseases.'" He frowned at Hollis. "I don't get it. What's Tifty doing here?"

And then the doors of the elevator opened to the sound of weapons being cocked, and each of them was staring down the barrel of a gun.

"All of you, on your knees."

There were six. The youngest appeared to be no more than

twenty, the oldest in his forties. Scruffy beards and greasy
hair and teeth clotted with grime: this was more like it. One
of them, a giant of a man with a great bald head and ridges
of soft fat folded at the base of his neck, had bluish tattoos
all over his face and the exposed flesh of his arms. This, apparently, was Dunk.

"I told you," Hollis said, kneeling on the floor like the rest
of them, hands on top of his head, "they're friends of mine."

"Quiet." His clothing was a hodgepodge of different uni-
forms, both military and DS. He holstered his revolver and
crouched in front of Peter, sizing him up with his intense
gray eyes. Viewed up close, the images on his face and arms
became clear. Virals. Viral hands, viral faces, viral teeth.
Peter had no doubt that beneath his clothes, the man's body
was covered with them.

"Expeditionary," Dunk drawled, nodding gravely. "Tifty's
going to like this. What's your name, Lieutenant?"

"Jaxon."

"Peter Jaxon?"

"That's right."

Maintaining his crouch, Dunk swiveled on the heels of his
boots toward the others. "How about that, gentlemen. It's
not every day we get such distinguished visitors." He focused
on Peter again. "We don't get visitors at all, actually. Which
is a bit of a problem. This isn't what you'd call a tourist destination."

"I need to see Tifty."

"So I hear. Tifty, I'm afraid, is indisposed at the moment.
A very private fellow, our Tifty."

"Cut the bullshit," Hollis said. "I told you, I'll vouch for
them. Tifty needs to hear what they have to say."

"This is your mess, my friend. I don't think you're exactly
in a position to be making demands. And what about you
two?" he asked, addressing Lore and Michael. "What do
you have to say for yourselves?"

"We're oilers," Michael replied.

"Interesting. Did you bring us any oil?" His gaze narrowed on Lore; a smile, bright with menace, flickered over
his face. "Now, you I think I know. Poker, wasn't it? Or dice.
Probably you don't remember."

"With a mug like yours, how could I forget?"

Grinning, Dunk rose and rubbed his meaty hands together. "Well, it's been very nice meeting all of you. A real
pleasure. Before we kill you, does anyone have anything else
to say? Goodbye, maybe?"

"Tell Tifty it's about the field," said Hollis.

Something changed; Peter could sense it at once. The words fell over Dunk's face like a shadow.

"Tell him," Hollis said.

The man appeared stunned into inaction. Then he drew his pistol.

"Let's go."

Dunk and his men escorted them down a long corridor. Peter took stock of their surroundings, though there wasn't much to see, just more halls and closed doors. Many of the doors had keypads on the walls beside them like the one beneath the pool. Dunk brought them to a halt before one such door and gave it three hard raps.

"Enter."

The great gangster Tifty Lamont. Once again Peter found his expectations overturned. He was a physically compact man, with glasses perched on the tip of his long, hooked nose. His pale hair flowed over his neck, thin at the top with a crown of pink scalp beneath. Seated behind a large metal desk, he was performing the improbable act of constructing a tower out of wooden sticks.

"Yes, Dunk?" he said, not looking up. "What is it?"

"We've captured three intruders, sir. Hollis brought them in."

"I see." He continued with his patient stacking. "And you did not kill them because . . . ?"

Dunk cleared his throat. "It's about the field, sir. They say they know something."

Tifty's hands halted over the model. After several seconds, he lifted his face, peering at them over his glasses.

"Who says?"

Peter stepped forward. "I do."

Tifty studied him a moment. "And the others? What do they know?"

"They were with me when I saw her."

"Saw who, exactly?"

"The woman."

Tifty said nothing. His face was as rigid as a blind man's. Then: "Everyone out. Except for you . . ." He wagged a finger toward Peter. "What's your name?"

"Peter Jaxon."

"Except for Mr. Jaxon."

"What do you want me to do with the others?" Dunk asked.

"Use your imagination. They look hungry—why don't you give them something to eat?"

"What about Hollis?"

"I'm sorry, did I mishear you? Didn't you say he brought them in?"

"That's the thing. He showed them where we are."

Tifty sighed heavily. "Well, that is a wrinkle. Hollis, what am I going to do with you? There are rules. There's a code. Honor among thieves. How many times do I have to say it?"

"I'm sorry, Tifty. I thought you needed to hear what he had to say."

"Well, sorry doesn't cut it. This is a very awkward position you've put me in." He cast his eyes wearily around the room, as if his next sentence could be found somewhere among its shelves and files. "Very well. Where are you on the roster?"

"Number four."

"Not anymore. You're suspended from the cage until I say otherwise. I know how much you like it. I'm being generous here."

Hollis's face showed nothing. What was the cage? Peter thought.

"Thank you, Tifty," Hollis said.

"Now all of you get the hell out."

The door sealed behind them. Peter waited for Tifty to speak first. The man rose from behind his desk and stepped to a small table with a pitcher of water. He poured himself a glass and drank it down. Just when the silence had begun to strain, he addressed Peter with his back turned.

"What was she wearing?"

"A dark cloak and glasses."

"What else did you see? Was there a truck?"

Peter recounted the events on the Oil Road. Tifty let him talk. When Peter had concluded, the man moved back to his desk.

"Let me show you something."

He opened the top drawer, removed a sheet of paper, and slid it across the desktop. A charcoal drawing, the paper stiffened and slightly discolored, of a woman and two little girls.

"You've seen one of these before, haven't you? I can tell."

Peter nodded. The picture wasn't anything he could easily pull his eyes from. It possessed an overwhelming haunted-ness, as if the woman and her children were gazing out of the page from someplace beyond the ordinary parameters of time and space. Like looking at a ghost, three ghosts.

"Yes, in Colorado. Greer showed it to me, after Vorhees was killed. A big stack of them." He lifted his eyes to find Tifty watching him keenly, like a teacher giving a test. "Why do you have a copy?"

"Because I loved them," Tifty replied. "Vor and I had our difficulties, but he always knew how I felt. They were my family, too. That's why he gave this to me."

"They died in the field."

"Dee, yes, and the little one, Siri. Both were killed outright. It was fast, though you know the saying: Make it quick, but not today. The older girl, Nitia, was never found." He frowned. "You're surprised by all this? Not quite what you expected?"

Peter couldn't even begin to answer.

"I'm telling you these things so you understand who and what we are. All these men have lost someone. I give them a home, a place to put their anger. Take Dunk, for instance. He may be imposing now, but when I look at him, do you know what I see? An eleven-year-old kid. He was in the field, too. Father, mother, sister, all gone."

"I don't see what running the trade has to do with that."

"That's because it's only part of what we do. A way of paying the bills, if you like. The Civilian Authority tolerates us because it has to. In a way, it needs us as much as we need it. We're not so very different from your Expeditionary, just the other side of the same coin."

Tifty's logic felt too convenient, a way to justify his crimes; on the other hand, Peter could not deny the meaning of the picture.

"Colonel Apgar said you were an officer. A scout sniper."

Tifty's face lit with a quick smile; there was a story there. "I should have known Gunnar would have something to do with this. What did he tell you?"

"That you made captain before you busted out. He called you the best S2 there ever was."

"Did he? Well, he's being kind, but only a little."

"Why did you resign?"

Tifty shrugged carelessly. "Many reasons. You could say that military life didn't suit me on the whole. Your presence here makes me think it may not suit you particularly well, either. My guess would be you've gone off the reservation, Lieutenant. How many days are you AWOL?"

Peter felt caught. "Just a couple."

"AWOL is AWOL. Believe me, I know all about that. But in answer to your question, I left the Expeditionary because of the woman in the field. More specifically, because I told Command where she came from, and they refused to do anything about it."

Peter was dumbstruck. "You *know* where she comes from?"

"Of course I know. So does Command. Why do you think Gunnar sent you here? Fifteen years ago, I was part of a squad of three sent north to locate the source of a radio signal somewhere in Iowa. Very faint, just little scratches of noise, but enough to catch it with an RDF. We didn't know why, the Exped wasn't in the business of chasing down every random squeak, but it was all very hush-hush, very top-down. Our orders were to scout it out and report back, nothing more. What we found was a city at least two, maybe three times the size of Kerrville. But it had no walls, no lights. By any reckoning, it shouldn't have existed at all. And you know what we saw? Trucks like the one I saw in the field just before the attack. Like the one you saw three days ago."

"So what did Command say?"

"They ordered us never to tell anyone."

"Why would they do that?" Though, of course, they had told Peter exactly the same thing.

"Who knows? But my guess would be the order came from the Civilian Authority, not the military. They were scared. Whoever those people were, they had a weapon we couldn't match."

"The virals."

The man nodded evenly. "Stick your fingers in your ears and hope they never came back. Maybe not wrong, but it wasn't anything I could sit with. That was the day I resigned my commission."

"Did you ever go back?"

"To Iowa? Why would I do that?"

Peter felt a mounting urgency. "Vorhees's daughter could be there. Sara, too. You saw those trucks."

"I'm sorry. Sara. Do I know this person?"

"She's Hollis's wife. Or would have been. She was lost at Roswell."

A look of regret eased across the man's face. "Of course. My mistake. I believe I knew that, though I don't think he ever mentioned her name. Nevertheless, this changes nothing, Lieutenant."

"But they could still be alive."

"I don't think it's likely. A lot of time has passed. Either way, there wasn't anything I could do about it. Not then and not now. You'd need an army. Which the CA more or less guaranteed we didn't have. And in the leadership's defense, these people, whoever they are, never returned. At least until now, if what you're saying is true."

Something was missing, Peter thought, a detail lurking at the edge of his awareness. "Who else was with you?"

"On the scouting party? The officer in charge was Nate Crukshank. The third man was a young lieutenant named Lucius Greer."

The information passed through Peter like a current.

"Take me there. Show me where it is."

"And what would we do when we got there?"

"Find our people. Get them out somehow."

"Are you listening, Lieutenant? These aren't just survivors. They're in league with the virals. More than that—the woman can control them. Both of us have seen it happen."

"I don't care."

"You should. All you'll accomplish is getting yourself killed. Or taken. My guess is, that would be a good deal worse."

"Then just tell me how to find it. I'll go on my own."

Tifty rose from behind his desk, returned to the table in the corner, and poured himself another glass of water. He drank it slowly, sip by sip. As the silence lengthened, Peter got the distinct impression that the man's mind had taken him elsewhere. He wondered if the meeting was over.

"Tell me something, Mr. Jaxon. Do you have children?"

"What does that have to do with anything?"

"Indulge me."

Peter shook his head. "No."

"No family at all?"

"I have a nephew."

"And where is he now?"

The questions were uncomfortably probing. And yet Tifty's tone was so disarming, the answers seemed to spring forth of their own accord. "He's with the sisters. His parents were killed at Roswell."

"Are you close? Do you matter to him?"

"Where are you going with this?"

Tifty ignored the question. He placed his empty glass on the table and returned to his desk.

"I suspect he admires you a great deal. The great Peter Jaxon. Don't be so modest—I know just who you are, and more than the official account. This girl of yours, Amy, and this business with the Twelve. And don't blame Hollis. He's not my source."

"Who then?"

Tifty grinned. "Perhaps another time. Our subject at hand is your nephew. What did you say his name was?"

"I didn't. It's Caleb."

"Are you a father to Caleb, is what I'm asking. Despite your gallivanting around the territories, trying to rid the world of the great viral menace, would you say that's true?"

Suddenly Peter had the sense of having been perfectly maneuvered. It reminded him of playing chess with the boy: one minute he was drifting in the current of the game; the next he was boxed in, the end had come.

"It's a simple question, Lieutenant."

"I don't know."

Tifty regarded him another moment, then said, with a note of finality, "Thank you for your honesty. My advice to you would be to forget about all of this and go home and raise your boy. For his sake, as much as your own, I'm willing to give you a pass and let you and your friends go free, with the warning that speaking of our whereabouts will not, how shall I put this, bring happy things your way."

Checkmate. "That's it? You're not going to do anything?"

"Consider it the greatest favor anybody's ever done you. Go home, Mr. Jaxon. Live your life. You can thank me later."

Peter's mind scrambled for something to say that might convince the man otherwise. He gestured toward the drawing on the desk. "Those girls. You said you loved them."

"I did. I do. That's why I'm not going to help you. Call me sentimental, but I won't have your death on my conscience."

"Your *conscience*?"

"I do have one, yes."

"You surprise me, you know that?" Peter said.

"Really? How do I surprise you?"

"I never thought Tifty Lamont would be a coward."

If Peter had expected to get a rise, he saw none. Tifty rocked back in his chair, placed the tips of his fingers together, and looked at him coolly over the tops of his spectacles. "And you were thinking maybe that if you pissed me off, I'd tell you what you want to know?"

"Something like that, yeah."

"Then you mistake me for somebody who cares what others think. Nice try, Lieutenant."

416 | JUSTIN CRONIN

"You said one of them was never found. I don't see how you can sit here if she could still be alive."

Tifty sighed indulgently. "Perhaps you didn't get the news, but this isn't a what-if world, Mr. Jaxon. Too many what-ifs are just a way to keep yourself up at night, and there's not enough decent sleep to go around. Don't get me wrong, I admire your optimism. Well, maybe not admire—that might be too strong a word. But I do understand it. There was a time when I wasn't so very different. But those days are passed. What I have is this picture. I look at it every day. For now, that's what I have to content myself with."

Peter picked up the drawing again. The woman's shining smile, the lift of her hair on an unseen breeze, the little girls, wide-eyed, hopeful like all children, waiting for their lives to unfold. He had no doubt that this picture was the center of Tifty's life. Looking at it, Peter sensed the presence of a complex debt, allegiances, promises made. This picture: it wasn't just a memorial; it was the man's way of punishing himself. Tifty wished he'd died with them, in the field. How strange, to find himself feeling sorry for Tifty Lamont.

Peter returned the picture to its place on Tifty's desk. "You said the trade was only part of what you do. You never told me what else."

"I didn't, did I?" Tifty removed his glasses and rose. "Fair enough. Come with me."

Tifty manipulated another keypad and the heavy door swung open, revealing a spacious room with large metal cages stacked against the walls. The air was rank with a distinctly animal scent, of blood and raw meat, and the high-noted aroma of alcohol. The light glowed a cool, violety blue—"viral blue," Tifty explained, with a wavelength of four hundred nanometers, at the very edge of the visible spectrum. Just enough, he told Peter, to keep them calm. The builders of the facility had understood their subjects well.

Michael and Lore had joined them. They passed through the room of cages and ascended a short flight of stairs. What awaited them was obvious; it was just a question of how it would be revealed.

"And this," said Tifty, opening a panel to reveal two buttons, one green, one red, "is the observation deck."

They were standing on a long balcony with a series of catwalks jutting over a metal shelf. Tifty pushed the green button. With a clatter of gears and chain, the shelf began to withdraw into the far wall, revealing a surface of hardened glass.

"Go on," Tifty urged. "Look for yourselves."

Peter and the others stepped onto the catwalk. Instantly one of the virals hurled itself upward against the glass, crashing into it with a thump before bouncing off and rolling back to the corner of its cell.

"Fuck . . . *me*," Lore gasped.

Tifty joined them on the catwalk. "This facility was built with one purpose in mind: studying the virals. More accurately, how to kill them."

The three of them were staring at the containers below. Peter counted nineteen of the creatures in all; the twentieth container was empty. Most appeared to be dopeys, barely reacting to their presence, but the one who had leapt at them was different—a full-blown female drac. She eyed them hungrily as they moved along the catwalks, her body tense and her clawed hands flexing.

"How do you get them?" Michael asked.

"We trap them."

"With what, spinners?"

"Spinners are for amateurs. The gyrations immobilize them, but such devices are no good, really, unless you want to crisp them on-site. To take them alive, we use the same baited traps the builders of this facility used. A tungsten alloy, incredibly strong."

Peter tore his gaze away from the drac. "So what have you learned?"

"Not as much as I'd like. The chest, the roof of the mouth. There's a third soft spot at the base of the skull, though it's very small. They bleed to death if you dismember them, but it's not easy cutting through the skin. Heat and cold don't seem to have much effect. We've tried a variety of poisons, but they're too smart for that. Their sense of smell is incredibly acute, and they won't eat anything we've laced no matter how hungry they get. One thing we do know is that they'll drown. Their bodies are too dense to keep them afloat, and they can't hold their breath very long. The longest any of them lasted was seventy-six seconds."

"What if you starve them?" Michael asked.

"We tried that. It slows them down, and they enter a kind of sleep state."

"And?"

"As far as we can tell, they can stay that way indefinitely. Eventually we stopped trying."

Suddenly Peter understood what he was seeing. The work of the trade was really just a cover. The man's true purpose was right here, in this room.

"Tifty, you are full of shit."

Everybody turned. Tifty crossed his arms over his chest and gave Peter a hard look.

"You have something on your mind, Lieutenant?"

"You always meant to go back to Iowa. You just couldn't figure out how."

Tifty's expression didn't change. His face looked suddenly older, worn down by life. "That's an interesting theory."

"Is it?"

For five seconds the two men stared at each other. No one else said anything. Just when the silence had gone on too long, Michael broke the tension.

"I think she likes you, Peter."

Fifteen feet below, the big drac was looking up at him, her head rolling lazily on her gimballed neck. She uncocked her jaw like someone yawning and drew back her lips to display her glinting teeth. *These are for you.*

Tifty stepped forward. "Our latest addition," he said. "We're all very proud of this one—we've been tracking her for weeks. It's not often we get a full-blown drac anymore. We call her Sheila."

"What are you going to do to her?" Michael asked.

"We haven't decided. More or less the usual, I suppose. A little of this, a little of that. She's too mean for the cage, though."

Peter recalled Hollis's punishment. "What's the cage?"

Tifty's face lit with a smile. "Ah," he said.

Midnight. During the intervening hours, the three of them had been confined to a small, unused room, with one of Tifty's men outside. Peter had finally managed to fall asleep when a buzzer sounded and the door opened.

"Come with me," said Tifty.

"Where are we going?" Lore asked.

"Outside, of course."

Why "of course"? thought Peter. But this seemed to be Tifty's way. The man had a taste for drama. "Where's Hollis?" Peter asked.

"Not to worry, he'll be joining us."

A cloudy, starless night. A truck was waiting for them, parked at the steps. They climbed into the bed while Tifty got into the cab with the driver. They weren't guarded, but unarmed, in the dark, where would they go?

A few minutes passed before the truck drew up to an immense rectangular building, like an airplane hangar. Several other vehicles were present, including a large flatbed. Men milled about in torchlight, conspicuously armed with pistols and rifles, some smoking corn silk. From inside the building came a buzz of voices.

"Now you'll see what we're really all about," said Tifty.

The building's interior was a single cavernous space, lit by torches. A huge American flag, tattered with age, hung from the rafters. At the center was the cage, a domed structure approximately fifty feet in diameter with a hooked chain descending to the floor from its apex. Surrounding it were bleachers packed with men, all talking loudly, urgently waving Austins at a figure moving up and down the rows. At Tifty's entrance a cheer shot up from the crowd, accompanied by a thunder of pounding feet. He did nothing to acknowledge this, escorting the three of them to an empty region on the lower tier of the bleachers, just a few feet from the crisscrossing bars of the cage.

"Five minutes till the betting closes!" a voice rang out. "Five minutes!"

Hollis took a place beside them. "Is this what I think it is?" Peter said.

He nodded tersely. "Pretty much."

"They're actually betting on the outcome?"

"Some are. With dopeys, mostly it's just how many minutes it will take."

"And you've actually done this."

Hollis looked at him strangely. "Why wouldn't I?"

The conversation was cut short as a second, louder cheer erupted. Peter looked up to see a metal crate being toted into the room on a forklift. A figure entered from the other side, walking with a manful swagger: Dunk. He was wearing heavy pads and carrying a pike; a sweeper's mask rode on top of his head, leaving his tattooed face exposed. He raised his right fist and pumped it in the air, summoning a frenzied stamping from the bleachers. The forklift operator dropped the box in the middle of the cage and backed away while a second man hooked the latch to the chain. As he moved clear, Dunk stepped inside. The door was locked behind him.

A hush fell. Tifty, seated beside Peter, got to his feet, holding a megaphone. He cleared his throat and directed his voice over the crowd. "All please rise for the national anthem."

Everyone clambered to their feet, placed their right hands over their hearts, and began to sing:

Oh, say can you see, by the dawn's early light,
What so proudly we hailed, at the twilight's last gleaming?
Whose broad stripes and bright stars, through the perilous
fight,
O'er the ramparts we watched, were so gallantly streaming?

Peter, standing too, struggled to recall the words. It was a song from long ago—from the Time Before. Teacher had taught them in the Sanctuary. But the melody had been tricky and the words had made no sense his boyhood self could discern, and he'd never gotten the hang of it. He glanced at Michael, whose eyebrows lifted in shared surprise.

The last screeching note extinguished itself in another detonation of cheers. From the aural chaos emerged a repeated refrain, the beat established by thundering feet: *Dunk, Dunk, Dunk, Dunk* . . . Tifty let it run its course, then raised a hand for silence. He faced the cage again.

"Dunk Withers, do you stand ready?"

"Ready!"

"Then . . . start the clock!"

Pandemonium. Dunk drew his mask down, a horn sounded, the chain was pulled. For a moment nothing happened; then the dopey popped free of the crate and skittered up the cage with a quick, insectile movement, like a roach scurrying up a wall. It could have been looking for a way out or a vantage point for attack; Peter couldn't tell. The crowd had its opinion. Instantly the cheers turned to boos and catcalls. At the top of the cage, the dopey grasped one of the bars with its feet and unfurled its body so that the top of its head was pointed toward the floor, arms held away from its sides. Dunk stood below it, shouting unhearable taunts and waving the pike, daring it to drop. *Meat!* the crowd chanted, clapping in syncopation. *Meat! Meat! Meat!*

The dopey seemed disoriented, almost dazed. Its bland gaze darted about the room randomly, as if the racket and commotion had short-circuited its instincts. Its features had a blurry appearance, as if its human characteristics had been dissolved by strong acid. For five more seconds it hung there, then ten.

Meat! Meat! Meat! Meat!

"Enough already." Tifty rose to his feet, taking up the megaphone. "Throw in the meat!"

From without the bars huge, blood-saturated chunks were lobbed into the cage, landing with smeary splats. This was all it took. The creature released the steel bar and dove for the nearest hunk. The upper section of a cow's leg: the dopey scooped it off the floor and shoved its jaws into the fatty folds, not so much drinking the fluids it contained as inhaling them. Two seconds and it was drained; the creature flung the desiccated remains away.

It swiveled toward Dunk. Now the man meant something. The dopey lowered itself to a crouch, balanced on its prehensile toes and massive splayed hands. The telltale cock of the head, the moment of regard.

It charged.

As the viral leapt toward him, arms extended, claws aiming for his throat, Dunk dropped to the floor and came up swinging the pike. The crowd went wild. Peter felt it too, the raw excitement of the contest surging in his veins. Dodging the pike, the dopey scampered back up the wall of the cage. No dazed retreat this time: its intentions were clear. When they came, they came from above. Twenty feet up, the dopey pushed itself backward off the bars, tucking its body into a headfirst aerial roll, twisting like a corkscrew as it descended in a rush of movement, and alighted on its feet ten feet from Dunk. The same engagement reversed: Dunk lunged; the dopey dropped. The pike speared the empty air above its head. As Dunk fell forward, carried by his own momentum, the dopey shot from its crouch and rammed headlong into his padded midsection, blasting him across the cage.

Dunk wound up propped upright against the bars, obviously shaken. The pike lay on the floor to his left; the mask had been torn away. Peter saw him reaching for the weapon, but the gesture was weak, his hand scrabbling with fogged inaccuracy. His chest was heaving like a bellows, a trickle of blood running from his nose to his upper lip. Why hadn't the dopey taken him yet?

Because it was a trap. The dopey seemed to suspect as much; as it contemplated the fallen warrior, Peter could sense the creature's interior conflict. The drive to kill versus an inchoate tactical suspicion that not all was as it appeared—a vestige, perhaps, of the human capacity for reason. Which would win out? The crowd was chanting Dunk's name, trying to rouse him from his stupor. That or goad the dopey into action. Any death would do. Just by going into the cage, Dunk had already secured the most important victory: to be human. To deny the virals' dominion over himself, over his fellows, over the world. The rest would fall as it fell.

Blood won.

The dopey went airborne. Simultaneously, the wandering hand found and secured the pike. As the creature fell, Dunk lifted the pike to a forty-five-degree angle, aligning it with the center of the dopey's descending chest, bracing the butt against the floor between his knees.

Did the dopey know what was about to happen? Did it experience, in that sliver of time in which the outcome was ordained, an awareness of its race toward death? Was it happy? Was it sad? And then the tip of the pike found its mark, spearing the creature so thoroughly that life breathed out of it in a single, grand, instantaneous exhalation of death.

Dunk shoved the body to the side. Peter had joined the crowd on its feet. His energy was a part of theirs; it flowed in the collective current. His voice rang with the multitude:

Dunk, Dunk, Dunk, Dunk!
Dunk, Dunk, Dunk, Dunk!

Why was this different? Peter wondered, while another part of his brain refused to care, adrift in his unanticipated elation. He had faced the virals on the rampart, in cities and deserts, forests and fields. He had dropped seven hundred feet into a crawling cave. He had given himself to death's likelihood hundreds of times, and yet Dunk's courage was something more, something purer, something redeeming. Peter glanced at his friends. Michael, Hollis, Lore: there was no mistaking it. They felt just as he did.

Only Tifty looked different. He'd gotten on his feet like the rest of them, but his face was emotionless. What was he seeing in his mind's eye? Where had he gone? He had gone to the field. Not even the cage could lighten this burden. Here was Peter's opening. He waited for the cheering to die. In the stands, bets were being counted and paid.

"Let me go in there."

Tifty studied him with one raised eyebrow. "Lieutenant, what are you asking?"

"A wager. My life against your promise to take me to Iowa. Not just tell me where this city is. You have to go with me."

"Peter, this is not a good idea," Hollis warned. "I know what you're feeling. We call it cage fever."

"That's not what this is."

Tifty folded his arms over his chest. "Mr. Jaxon, how dumb do I look? Your reputation precedes you. I don't doubt a dopey is well within your abilities."

"Not a dopey," he said. "Sheila."

Tifty weighed him with his eyes. Behind him, Michael and Lore said nothing. Maybe they understood what he was doing, and maybe they didn't. Maybe they were too dumbstruck by his apparent loss of his faculties to formulate a response. It didn't matter either way.

"All right, Lieutenant, it's your funeral. Not that there'll be anything to bury."

Peter was escorted to a small room at the rear of the arena by Tifty and two of his men. Michael and Hollis were with him; Lore waited in the stands. The room was bare except for a long table displaying armored pads and an array of weapons. Peter suited up. He had initially been concerned that the pads would slow him down too much, but they were surprisingly light and pliable. The mask was a different matter; Peter couldn't see how it would be any help, and it cut down his peripheral vision. He put it aside.

Now for armaments. He was permitted two. No firearms were allowed, only piercing weapons. Blades, crossbows, pikes and swords and axes of various lengths and weights. The cross was tempting, but in such close quarters it would take too long to reload. Peter chose a five-foot pike with a barbed steel tip.

As for the second: he cast his eyes around for something that would serve his purpose. In the corner of the room was a galvanized trash can. He removed the lid and examined it.

"Somebody give me a rag."

A rag was produced. Peter wet it with spit and rubbed the inside of the lid. His reflection began to emerge—not with any distinctiveness, barely more than a blurry shape; but it would have to suffice.

"This is what I want."

Tifty's men burst into laughter. *A trash can lid! Some pathetic little shield against a full-blown drac! Did he intend to commit suicide?*

"Your foolishness is one thing, Lieutenant," said Tifty. "But this. I can't allow it."

Michael looked at him with a quizzical frown. "Like . . . Las Vegas?"

Peter gave him the barest nod, turned to Tifty again. "You said anything in the room."

"That I did."

"Then I'm ready."

He was led into the arena. The crowd erupted in roars and stamping, but the sound was different than it had been with Dunk. Their allegiances had reversed. Peter wasn't one of them; they were excited to watch him die, this arrogant soldier of the Expeditionary who dared to think he could take on a drac. The box was already in position at the center of the ring. As Peter approached, he thought he could see it shaking. He heard, from the bleachers, "All bets now closing!"

"Not too late to back out," Hollis said. "We could make a run for it."

"What kind of odds are they giving me?"

"Ten to one you survive thirty seconds. A hundred to one you make it a minute."

"You get one down?"

"Took you to win in forty-five. I'll be set for life."

"The usual arrangement, okay?" Peter didn't need to elaborate: *If I'm bitten but survive, don't let me. Make it fast.*

"You don't have to worry."

"Michael? Hold him to that."

The man's face was bereft. "Jesus, Peter. You did it *once.* Maybe it was something else that slowed them down. Did you think about that?"

Peter looked at the box in the middle of the ring. It was shuddering like an engine. "Thanks—I'm thinking about it now."

They shook hands. A grave moment, but they had been through similar ones before. Peter stepped inside the cage; one of Tifty's men sealed the door behind him. Hollis and Michael took their places on the bleachers with Lore. Tifty rose with his megaphone.

"Lieutenant Jaxon of the Expeditionary, do you stand ready?"

A chorus of boos. Peter did his best to tune them out. He had been running on pure conviction, but now that the moment was here, his body had begun to doubt his mind. His heart was racing, his palms damp. The pike felt absurdly heavy in his hand. He filled his chest with air. "Ready!"

"Then . . . start the clock!"

* * *

In the aftermath, Peter was to learn that the contest had lasted a grand total of twenty-eight seconds. This seemed both long and short; it had happened slowly and all at once, a blur of events that didn't correspond to the ordinary course of time.

What he would remember was this:

The drac's explosion from the box, like water shot from a hose; her majestic airborne leap, a force of undiluted nature, straight to the top of the cage, and then three quick ricochets as she bounded side to side, too fast for Peter's eyes to follow; the picture in his mind's eye of her anticipated release and the arc her body would employ as she fell upon him, and then the moment of its occurrence, exactly as he'd foreseen; the blast of force as their bodies collided, one stationary, one in headlong flight; the drac sending him careening across the cage, and his body—breathless, broken, his own for a moment or two more but no longer—rolling and rolling and rolling.

He was on his stomach. The trash can lid and pike were gone. He rolled onto his back and scrabbled backward on his hands and feet, and then he found what was left of the pike. The pole had snapped two feet from its pointed steel end. He wrapped it with his fist and rose. He would go down swinging; he would die on his feet at least. On a distant planet, crowds were cheering. The viral was moving toward him in a manner he would have described as leisurely, almost sauntering. She cocked her head and opened her jaws to give him a good, long look at her teeth.

Their eyes met.

Really *met*. A bona fide, soul-searching gaze. The moment locked, and in that moment Peter felt his mind plunging into hers: its sensations and memories, thoughts and desires, the person she'd been and the pain of the terrible thing she'd become. Her expression had softened, her posture relaxed a discernible notch. The ferocity of her expression contained something else now: a profound melancholy. A human being was still inside her, like a tiny flame in the dark. *Don't look away,* Peter told himself. *Whatever you do, don't break her gaze.* The pike was in his hand.

He took one step, then another. Still she did not move. He felt a kind of quiet shuddering within himself, not of fear but of longing; this was what she wanted. The crowd had silenced. It was as if the two of them were alone in some immense, still space. An empty church. An abandoned theater.

A cave. He drew back the pike, placing his free hand on her shoulder for balance. *Please,* her eyes said.

Then it was over.

The crowd was absolutely still. Peter realized he was shaking. Something irrevocable had happened, beyond knowing. He looked down at the body. He had felt her soul leaving her. It had brushed him like a breeze, only the breeze was inside him, made of words. *Thank you, thank you. I am free.*

Tifty was waiting for him when he exited the cage.

"Her name wasn't Sheila," Peter said. "It was Emily."

Tifty said nothing, wearing an expression of pure bewilderment.

"She was seventeen when she was taken up. Her last memory was of kissing a boy."

"I don't understand."

Hollis, Michael, and Lore were coming down the bleachers. Peter moved toward them, stopped, then turned back to Tifty.

"You want to know how to kill them?"

The man nodded, slack-jawed.

"Look them in the eye."

48

Amy's mind was full of him. Full of Carter and the woman, whose name was Rachel. Rachel Wood.

Amy felt it, felt it all. She felt and saw and knew. The woman's arms around him, pulling him down and down. The taste of pool water, like demon's breath. The soft thunk as they reached the bottom, their bodies entwined like lovers'.

How Carter had loved her. That was what Amy felt most keenly: his love. The man's life had stopped right there, at the bottom of the pool, his mind forever trapped in a loop of sorrow. *Oh please, let me,* thought Anthony Carter. *I'll die if you want me to, I would die for you if you asked, let me be the one to die instead.* And then the bubbles rising as the woman took the first breath, her lungs filling with the awful water, the deep spasm of death moving through her; and then the letting go.

His was the sadness at the center of the world. The *Chevron Mariner:* that's what this place was. It was the very beating heart of grief.

Blood was dripping from her as she made her way aft across the tilted deck. Amy could feel the change coming, a rumbling in the hills above. It would sweep down upon her like an avalanche. It would obliterate her, fashion her anew. She descended into the bowels of the ship, its maze of halls, its listing passages of pipe. Her feet sloshed through standing water the color of rust. Rainbow shimmers danced upon its surface. She moved by instinct. She homed in. She was the receiver to Carter's beacon, which inexorably drew her down and down and down.

The pump room.

They were hanging everywhere, filling the space with their glow. They clung to every surface. They lay curled upon the floor like children. Here was the reservoir, the lair. The nest of Anthony Carter, his doleful legions suspended in abeyance. *Where are you?* she thought, and as she did her body shook, and in the wake of this convulsive jolt came a massive tightening in her abdomen, as if she'd been clenched by a giant fist. She staggered, fighting to remain upright. Blots of blackness swelled across her vision. It was happening. It was happening now.

I am here.

—Where? Where are you? Please, I think that I am . . . dying.

Come to me, Amy. Come to me come to me come to me . . .

A door stood before her. Had she opened it? She stumbled forward, down the narrow passageway beyond. The floor was slick with oil, the blood of the earth, time's distillate, compressed by a planet. She came to a second portal. T1, it was marked: Tank No. 1. She knew what lay beyond. It had ever been thus. With all her strength she gripped the rusted ring and turned. Space flew open wide around her, as if she'd entered an immense cathedral.

And there he was. Anthony Carter, Twelfth of Twelve. Wizened and small, a wisp of a thing, no larger than the man he'd been and, in his heart, still was. A being of refusal made flesh. He lay on the floor, in the waste of the world; slowly he unfurled himself, rising to meet her. Carter the Sorrowful, the One Who Could Not, locked in the prison that he himself had made.

"Help me," said Amy, a last great shudder moving through her, taking her over, and she fell into his arms.

And then she was somewhere else.

She was under a highway overpass. Amy knew this place,

or so it felt. Its sights and sounds and smells were laden with a weight of memory. The echoing roar of cars passing overhead; the *click-click-click* of the roadway's joints; the drifting trash and grime and heavy, smoke-choked air. Amy was standing at the edge of the road, holding a cardboard sign: HUNGRY, ANYTHING WILL HELP, GOD BLESS YOU. Traffic streamed by, cars, trucks, no one even looking her way. She was dressed in rags; her hands were black with grime. Her stomach was a stone of cold emptiness. The heedless vehicles flew past. Why would no one stop?

Then, the car. A large SUV, dark and gleaming: it slowed, then stopped, not so much drawing to the curb as alighting, like a great black bird. Its tinted windows fashioned squares of perfect reflection, doubling the world. With a soft mechanical whir, the passenger window drew down.

"Amy, hello."

Wolgast was sitting at the wheel, dressed in a navy suit and dark tie. He was smoothly shaved, his hair swept back from his forehead, shining faintly, as if it were still damp from the shower. "You're right on time." Smiling, he leaned across to open the door. "Why don't you get in?"

Amy placed her sign on the ground and climbed onto the passenger seat. The air inside the car was cool, with a leathery smell.

"It's wonderful to see you," Wolgast said. "Don't forget to buckle up, sweetheart."

Her amazement was such that she could barely form words. "Where are we going?"

"You'll see."

They drove clear of the underpass, into summer sunshine. Around them the shops and houses and cars flowed past, a world of busy humanity. The car bounced agreeably under them on its cushioning springs.

"How far is it?"

Wolgast shrugged vaguely. "Not very. Just up the road a bit." He glanced sidelong. "I have to say, you're looking very well, Amy. So grown up."

"What . . . is this place?"

"Well, Texas." He made a face of distaste. "All of this is Houston, Texas." A memory took hold of his face. "Lila got so sick of hearing about it. 'Brad, it's just a state like any other,' she always said."

"But how are we here?"

"The how, I don't know. I don't think there's an answer to

that. As for the why . . ." He glanced at her again. "I'm one of his, you understand."

"Carter's."

Wolgast nodded.

"Are you in the ship, too?"

"The ship? No."

"Where, then?"

He didn't respond right away. "I think it's best if he explains it to you." His eyes shifted quickly to Amy's face again. "You really do look wonderful, Amy. The way I always imagined. I know he'll be happy to see you."

They had moved into a neighborhood of large houses, lush trees, and wide, well-kept lawns. Wolgast pulled into the driveway of a white-brick colonial and stopped the car.

"Here we are. I guess I'll leave you to it, then."

"You're not coming with me?"

"Oh, I'm afraid I'm just the messenger this time. Not even. More like the deliveryman. Just go around back."

"But I don't want to go without you."

"It's all right, sweetheart, he won't bite you." He took her hand and gently squeezed. "Go on now, he's waiting. I'll see you again soon. Everything will be all right, I promise."

Amy exited the car. Locusts were buzzing in the trees, a sound that somehow deepened the stillness. The air was heavy with moisture and smelled of freshly mown grass. Amy turned to glance at Wolgast, but the car had disappeared. This place, she understood, was different in that way; things could simply disappear.

She made her way up the driveway, through a trellised gate wreathed with flowering vines, into the backyard. Carter was sitting at a table on the patio, wearing jeans and a dirty T-shirt and heavy, unlaced boots. He was rubbing his neck and hair with a towel; his mower was parked nearby, exuding a faint aroma of gasoline. At Amy's approach he looked up, smiling.

"Well, there you are." He gestured toward the two glasses of liquid on the table. "I just got done here—come and sit a spell. I thought you might like some tea." The smile broadened to a wide, white grin. "Ain't nothing as good as a glass of tea on a hot June day."

Amy took the chair across from him. He had a small, smooth face and gentle eyes and close-cropped hair, like a cap of dark wool. His cocoa-colored skin was speckled with black spots; flecks of grass were on his shirt and arms. Adjacent to the patio, the pool was a presence of cool, inviting blueness, the water gently lapping at its tiled edges. It was only then that Amy realized it was the same house where she and Greer had spent the night.

"This place," said Amy. She angled her face toward the buzzing trees. Rich sunlight warmed her skin. "It's so beautiful."

"It rightly is, Miss Amy."

"But we're still inside the ship, aren't we?"

"In a manner," Carter replied evenly. "In a manner."

They sat in silence, sipping the cold tea. Beads of moisture dribbled down the sides of the glasses. Things were coming clearer now.

"I think I know why I'm here," said Amy.

"I'm expecting you do."

The air had suddenly chilled; Amy shivered, drawing her arms around herself. Dry leaves, like bits of brown paper, were blowing across the patio; the light had lost its color.

"I been thinking on you, Miss Amy. All the while. Me and Wolgast, we had us a talk. A good talk, like you and me is having now."

Whatever Carter was going to tell her, she suddenly didn't want it. It was the leaves that made her think it: she was afraid.

"He said he's yours. That he belongs to you."

Carter nodded in his mild way. "Man says he owes me, and I reckon that's right, but I set store by him, too. He's the one give me the time to figure it. An ocean of time, Anthony, that's what he said. I took me some there at the start, never said I didn't. Was the hunger made me. But I never could set with it. Wolgast was the one give me the chance to make things right."

"He's the one who sealed you in the ship, isn't he?"

"Yes'm. Asked him to do it when the hunger got too bad. He would have sealed his own self up too, except for you. Go look after your girl, I said. That man, he loves you with his whole heart."

Amy became aware that something was in the pool. A dark shape slowly rising, parsing the surface of the water to take its place among the floating autumn leaves.

"She always there." Carter gave his head a slow, sorrowful shake. "That's the pity of it. Every day I cut the lawn. Every day she rise."

He fell quiet for a moment, his kind face adrift in grief. Then he gathered himself and faced her squarely again. "I know it ain't fair to you, the things you got to face. Wolgast

know it, too. But this here's our chance. Never come another."

Her doubt became certainty then, like a seed breaking
open inside her. She had felt it for days, weeks, months. The
voice of Zero, summoning her. *Amy, go to them. Go to them,
our sister in blood. I have known you, felt you. You are the
omega to my alpha, the one to watch and keep them.*

"Please," she said, her voice trembling. "Don't ask me to
do this."

"The asking ain't mine to do. Telling, neither. This here's
just about what *is.*" Carter hitched up in his chair, removed
a handkerchief from his back pocket, and held it out to her.
"You go on and cry if you want to, Miss Amy. You owed
that at least, I reckon. Cried me a river myself."

She did; she wept. In the orphanage she had tasted life.
With Caleb, and the sisters, and Peter, and all the others. She
had become a part of something, a family. She had made a
home in the world. Now it would be gone.

"They'll kill us both."

"I reckon they'll try. I known it from the start." He leaned
over the table and took her hand. "Ain't right, I know it, but
this here is ours to carry. Our one chance. Ain't never come
another."

There was no way to refuse; fate had found her. The light
was fading, the leaves were blowing down. In the pool, the
woman's body continued on its slow passage, floating and
turning in the eternal current.

"Tell me what to do."

VIII

THE CHANGELING

I'm Nobody! Who are you?
Are you—Nobody—too?
Then there's a pair of us!
Don't tell! They'd advertise, you know.

—EMILY DICKINSON

49

The first real snow of winter arrived, as it always seemed to, in the middle of the night. Sara was sleeping on the sofa when she was roused by a tapping sound. For some stretch of time this sound mingled in her mind with a dream she was having, in which she was pregnant and trying to tell Hollis about it. The scene of this dream was a perplexing jumble of overlapping locations (the porch of the house in First Colony where she had grown up; the biodiesel plant, among the roar of the grinders; a ruined theater, wholly imagined, with tattered purple curtains suspended over a stage), and though other characters drifted at the periphery (Jackie, Michael, Karen Molyneau and her daughters), its sense was one of isolation: she and Hollis were alone, and the baby, tapping away inside her—Sara understood this to be a form of code—was asking to be born. Each time she tried to explain this to Hollis, the words came out as different words entirely—not "I'm pregnant" but "It's raining," not "I'm having a baby" but "Today is Tuesday"—causing Hollis to look at her first with confusion, then amusement, and finally outright laughter. "It's not funny," Sara said. Tears of frustration filled her eyes as Hollis laughed in his warm, big-throated way. "It's not funny, it's not funny, it's not funny . . ." and on and on, and in this state the dream dissolved, and then she was awake.

She lay still a moment. The tapping was coming from the window. She pushed the blanket aside and crossed the room, and drew the drapes aside. The grounds of the Dome were kept lit at night, an island of luminescence in a sea of darkness, and through the beams of these lights an icy snow was pouring down, tossed on gusting winds. It seemed more ice than snow, but as she lingered, something changed. The particles slowed and fattened, becoming snowflakes. They descended upon every surface, building a mantle of white. In the other two rooms of the apartment Lila slept, and Sara's daughter, snug in her little bed. How Sara longed to go to her, to lift her child into her arms and carry her back to the couch and hold her as she slept. To touch her hair, her skin, to feel the warm brush of her breath. But this thought was an empty dream, nothing she dared allow herself to imagine was actually possible. Aching with longing, Sara watched the falling snow, welcoming its slow erasure of the world, though down in the flatland, she knew, it meant something else. Frozen fingers, frozen toes, bodies racked with cold. The months of dark and misery. *Well,* Sara thought with a shiver. *The winter. So it begins. At least I'll be inside.*

But when she awoke in the morning, something changed again.

"Dani, look! Snow!"

A glittering light blasted into the room. The little girl, dressed in her nightshirt, had perched on a chair to draw back the drapes and was pressing her nose to the frosted window. Sara rose quickly from the couch and yanked them shut.

"But I want to see!"

From the inner room: "Dani! Where are you? I need you!"

"Just a minute!" Sara looked into the girl's pleading eyes. "I'm sorry, sweetheart. You know the rule."

"But she can stay in bed!"

"Dani!"

Sara heaved a sigh. Lila's mornings were difficult, beset by focusless anxiety and nameless dread. The effect was magnified with each day that passed since her last feeding. Under the blood's restorative spell, she became cheerful and affectionate to both of them, even a little giddy, though her interest in Kate felt more abstract than personal; she seemed not to comprehend fully the child's age, often speaking to her as if she were an infant. On these good days, Lila appeared fully persuaded that she was living in some place called Cherry Creek, married to a man named David—though she also spoke of someone named Brad, the two seeming interchangeable—and that Sara was a housekeeper sent by "the service," whatever that was. But as the effect of the blood waned, over a period of four or five days, she became abrupt and panicky, as if this elaborate fantasy was increasingly difficult to maintain.

"Let me get her in the bath. Then I'll see if I can take you outside to play. Do we have a deal?"

The little girl nodded vigorously.

"Now get dressed."

Sara found Lila sitting up in bed, clutching the folds of her thin nightgown over her chest. If Sara had to guess her age, she would have said the woman looked about fifty; tomorrow it would be more, the lines of her face deepening, her muscles sagging, her hair graying and growing thin. Sometimes the change was so precipitous Sara could actually watch it happening. Then Guilder would bring the blood, Sara would be banished from the room with Kate, and by the time they returned, Lila would be a lush-haired, smooth-skinned twenty-five-year-old once more, the cycle starting over.

"Why didn't you answer me? I was worried."

"I'm sorry, I overslept."

"Where's Eva?"

Sara explained that the girl was getting dressed and excused herself to prepare Lila's bath. Like the woman's dressing table, the bath was a place of totemic importance. In its deep, lion-clawed cocoon, the woman could soak for hours. Sara opened the tap and laid out Lila's soaps and oils and little jars of cream with two fat, freshly laundered towels. Lila liked to bathe by candlelight; Sara took a box of wooden matches from the vanity and lit the candelabra. By the time Lila appeared in the doorway, the air was opaque with steam. Sara, in her heavy attendant's robe, had begun to sweat. Lila closed the door and turned away to remove her dressing gown. Her upper body was thin, though not as thin as it would become, its mass redistributing downward over the days, into her hips and thighs. She turned to face Sara again and regarded the tub with a look of caution.

"Dani, I'm not really feeling myself today. Could you help me in?"

Sara took Lila by the hand as she stepped gingerly over the railing and lowered herself into the steaming water. Once she was immersed, the woman's expression softened, tension departing her face. Sinking down to her chin, she took a long, happy breath, moving her hands like paddles to shift the water to and fro across her body. She leaned back to wet her hair, then shimmied up, bracing her back against the side of the tub. Freed of gravity, the woman's breasts floated over her chest in a pantomime of restored youth.

"I do love the bath," she murmured.

Sara took her place on the stool beside the tub. "Hair first?"

"Mmmmmm." Lila's eyes were closed. "Please."

Sara began. As with everything, there was a certain way Lila liked it done. First the crown of her head, Sara's hands vigorously massaging, then moving downward to smooth the long strands of hair between her fingers. The soap, then a rinse, then the same order of events repeated with the scented oil. Sometimes she had Sara do this more than once.

"It snowed last night," Sara ventured.

"Hmmmm." Lila's face was relaxed, her eyes still closed. "Well, that's Denver for you. If you don't like the weather, just wait a minute, it will change. That's something my father always said."

Lila's father's sayings, duly noted as such, were a prominent feature of their conversations. Sara used a pitcher dipped in bathwater to pour the soap away from Lila's forehead and began to work in the oil.

"So I suppose everything will be closed," Lila continued. "I really wanted to get to the market. We're practically out of everything." Never mind that, as far as Sara was aware, Lila never set foot from the apartment. "You know what I'd like, Dani? A long, lovely lunch. Someplace special. With good linens and china and flowers on the table."

Sara had learned to go along. "That sounds nice."

Lila gave a protracted sigh of memory, sinking deeper into the bath. "I can't tell you how long it's been since I had a long, lovely lunch."

A few minutes passed, Sara working the oil into the woman's scalp. "I think Eva would enjoy some time outside." It felt like a monstrous lie to say this name, but sometimes it was unavoidable.

"Yes, I suppose she would," Lila said noncommittally.

"I was wondering, are there any other children she can play with?"

"Other children?"

"Yes, someone her own age. I thought it would be good for her to have some friends."

Lila frowned uncomfortably. Sara wondered if she'd pressed too far. "Well," she said, with a tone of concession, "there's that neighbor girl, little what's-her-name. With the dark hair. But I hardly ever see her. Most of the families around here keep to themselves. Bunch of sticks-in-the-mud, if you ask me." Then: "But you're a good friend to her, aren't you, Dani?"

A friend. What stinging irony. "I try to be."

"No, it's more than that." Lila smiled drowsily. "There's something different about you, I can tell. I think it's wonderful for Eva, having a friend like you."

"So I can take her outside," Sara said.

"In a minute." Lila closed her eyes again. "I was hoping you could read to me. I do so love to be read to in the bath."

* * *

By the time they escaped, it was nearly noon. Sara bundled Eva in a coat and mittens and rubber galoshes and a woolen cap, pulling it down over the little girl's ears. For herself she had only the robe, and nothing for her feet but her ratty sneakers and wool socks, but she hardly cared. Cold feet, so what? They took the stairs to the courtyard and emerged into a world so remade it felt like an entirely new place. The air had a sharp, fresh smell, and the sun was rebounding off the snow with eye-searing intensity. After so many days in the enforced gloom of the apartment, Sara had to pause at the threshold to give her vision a moment to adjust. But Kate had no such difficulty. With a snap of energy she released Sara's hand and bolted from the doorway, propelling herself across the courtyard. By the time Sara had slogged toward her—she might have erred about the sneakers; they were going to be a problem—the child was scooping handfuls of downy snow into her mouth.

"It tastes . . . cold." Her face beamed with happiness. "Try some."

Sara did as instructed. "Yum," she said.

She showed the girl how to build a snowman. Her mind was full of sweet nostalgia; it was as if she were a Little again, playing in the courtyard of the Sanctuary. But this was different; Sara was the mother now. Time had turned its inexorable circle. How wonderful to feel her daughter's infectious happiness, to experience the sense of wonder that passed between them. For the time being, all pain was banished from Sara's mind. They could have been anywhere. The two of them.

Sara thought of Amy, too, the first time in years she had done this. Amy, who had never been a little girl, or so it seemed, but somehow always was; Amy, the Girl from Nowhere, in whose person time was not a circle but a thing stopped and held, a century cupped in the hand. Sara felt a sudden, unexpected sadness for her. She had always wondered why Amy had destroyed the vials of virus that night at the Farmstead, casting them into the flames. Sara had hated them, not just what they represented but the very fact of their existence, but she had also known what they were: a hope of salvation, the one weapon powerful enough to use against the Twelve. (*The Twelve,* she thought; how long had it been since that name had crossed her mind as well?) Sara had never known quite what to think of Amy's decision; now she had her answer. Amy had known that the life those vials had denied her was the only true human reality. In Sara's daughter, this triumphantly alive little person that Sara's body had made, lay the answer to the greatest mystery of all—the mystery of death, and what came after. How obvious it was. Death was nothing, because there was no death. By the simple fact of Kate's existence, Sara was joined to something eternal. To have a child was to receive the gift of true immortality—not time stopped, as it had stopped in Amy, but time continuing and everlasting.

"Let's make snow angels," she said.

Kate had never done this. They lay down side by side, their bodies enveloped in whiteness and the tips of their fingers just touching. Above them the sun and sky looked down in witness. They moved their limbs back and forth and rose to inspect the imprints. Sara explained what angels were: they're us.

"That's funny," said Kate, smiling.

The serving girl, Jenny, would be bringing lunch; their time in the snow was at an end. Sara imagined the rest of the day: Lila lost in fantasy, leaving the two of them alone; wet clothing drying on racks by the fire, Sara and her daughter snuggled on the sofa and the sweet exchange of heat where their bodies touched and the hours of stories she would read—*Peter Rabbit* and *Squirrel Nutkin* and *James and the Giant Peach*—before the two of them drifted together into a sleep of intertwining dreams. Never had she been so happy.

They were walking back to the entrance when Sara glanced up to the window and saw that the drapes were pulled aside. Lila was watching them, her eyes concealed behind dark glasses. How long had she stood there?

"What's she doing?" Kate asked.

Sara summoned a smile to her face. "I think she was just enjoying watching us." But inside she felt a spark of fear.

"Why do I have to call her Mummy?"

Sara stopped in her tracks. "What did you say?"

For a moment the girl was silent. Melted snow was dripping off the branches.

"I'm tired, Dani," Kate said. "Can you pick me up?"

Unbearable joy. The girl's weight was nothing in her arms. It was the missing part of her, come home. Lila was still watching from the window, but Sara didn't care. Kate wrapped her arms and legs tightly around her, and in this manner, Sara carried her daughter out of the snow and back to the apartment.

* * *

Sara had received no messages; every day she looked for the inverted spoon, the note tucked under the plate, finding none. Jenny came and went, depositing her trays of bread and cornmeal and soup and wordlessly scurrying away. Having virtually never left the apartment except to take Kate to the courtyard, Sara had glimpsed Vale only once, when Lila had sent her to look for a maintenance worker to unplug the tub's drain. He was walking down the corridor in the company of two other cols, including the jowly one who had met them at the elevator on Sara's first day. Vale had passed right by her. As ever, his disguise—which was really just a way of carrying himself, the confident saunter of his rank—was absolutely seamless. No recognition occurred between them; if Vale knew who she was, he gave no sign.

She wasn't supposed to send a message on her own except for an emergency, but the lack of contact left her anxious. Finally she decided to risk it. There was no loose paper in the apartment, but of course there were the books. One night after Lila had gone to bed, Sara tore a small piece from the back of *Winnie-the-Pooh*. The larger problem was finding something to write with; there were no pens or pencils in the apartment. But in the bottom drawer of Lila's dressing table she found a sewing kit with a cushion of needles. Sara selected the one that looked the sharpest, jabbed it into the tip of her index finger, and squeezed, summoning a bead of blood. Using the needle as a makeshift pen, she scrawled her message onto the paper.

Need meeting. D.

The following day, when Jenny came to collect her lunch tray, Sara was waiting. Rather than allow the girl to simply whisk it away as usual, Sara lifted the tray from the table and held it out to her, making eye contact and then darting her glance downward, lest the point be missed.

"Thank you, Jenny."

Two days later came the reply. Sara secreted the note into the folds of her robe, waiting for a private moment. This didn't happen until later in the day, when Lila napped. She was close to the end of her cycle now, parched and infirm and out of sorts; soon Guilder would be coming with the blood. In the bathroom Sara unfolded the slip of paper, on which was written a time and place and a single sentence of instruction. Sara's heart sank; she hadn't realized she'd have to leave the Dome. She would need to secure Lila's permission under some credible pretext; if she didn't get it, she had no idea what she'd do. With Lila in her impaired state, Sara wondered if the woman would even comprehend the request.

She broached the subject the next day while she was washing Lila's hair. A few hours off, was how she put it. An outing to the market. It would be good to see a few new faces, and while she was there she could look for some special oils or soaps. The request aroused in Lila a palpable anxiety; she'd become more clingy recently, barely letting Sara out of her sight. But in the end she yielded to the gentle force of Sara's argument. *Just don't be too long,* said Lila. *I never know what to do without you, Dani.*

Vale had paved the way; at the front desk, the col handed her the pass with a perfunctory warning that it was only for two hours. Sara stepped into the wind and headed toward the market. Only cols and redeyes were allowed to barter there; currency took the form of small plastic chips in three colors, red, blue, and white. In the pocket of Sara's robe were five of each, part of the compensation that Lila doled out to her every seven days, furthering the fiction that Sara was a paid employee. The snow had been pushed from the sidewalks in what had once been the town's small commercial area, three blocks of brick buildings adjacent to the college. Most of the city went unused and abandoned, fading into soft decay; nearly all of the redeyes, except for senior staff, lived in a mid-rise apartment complex at the south end of downtown. The market was the heart of the city, with checkpoints at either end. Some of the buildings still bore signs indicating their original function: Iowa State Bank, Fort Powell Army-Navy, Wimpy's Café, Prairie Books and Music. There was even a small movie theater with a marquee; Sara had heard that cols were sometimes permitted to go, to watch the handful of movies that were shown over and over again.

She displayed her pass at the checkpoint. The streets were vacant save for the patrols and a handful of redeyes, strolling in their luxuriously heavy coats and sunglasses. Shielded by her veil, Sara moved in a bubble of anonymity, though this sense of security was, she knew, a dangerous illusion. She walked at a pace that was neither fast nor slow, her head down against the cold gusts that whipped up from the streets and around the corners of the buildings.

She came to the apothecary. Bells tinkled as she stepped inside. The room was warm and fragrant with wood smoke and herbs. Behind the counter, a woman with a scrim of gray hair and a puckered, toothless mouth was bent over a scale, measuring out minute quantities of a pale yellow powder and funneling them into tiny glass vials. She lifted her eyes as Sara entered, then darted them to the col lingering by a display of scented oils. *Be careful. I know who you are. Don't approach until I get rid of him.* Then, speaking in an elevated, helpful voice: "Sir, perhaps you were looking for something special."

The col was sniffing a bar of soap. Mid-thirties, not unhandsome, broadcasting an air of vanity. He returned the soap to its place on the display. "Something for a headache."

"Ah." A smile of assurance; the solution was in hand. "Just a moment."

The old woman selected a jar from the wall of herbals behind her, spooned the dry leaves into a paper package, and handed it to him over the counter. "Dissolve this in warm water. Just a pinch should do it."

He surveyed the package uneasily. "What's in it? You're not trying to poison me, old woman?"

"Nothing more than common dillonweed. I use it myself. If you want me to sample it first, I'd be glad to."

"Forget it."

He paid her with a single blue chip; the woman followed him with her eyes as he departed to a chime of bells.

"Come with me," she said to Sara.

She led her to a storage room in the back with a table and chairs and a door to the alleyway. The woman told Sara to wait and returned to the front of the store. Several minutes passed; then the door opened: Nina, dressed in a flatlander's tunic and dark jacket and a long scarf that wrapped the lower half of her face.

"This is incredibly dumb, Sara. Do you know how dangerous this is?"

Sara stared into the woman's steely eyes. Until this moment, she hadn't realized how angry she was.

"You knew my daughter was alive, didn't you?"

Nina was unwinding the scarf. "Of course we knew. That's what we *do,* Sara: we know things, then we put the information to use. I'd think you'd be happy about it."

"How long?"

"Does that matter?"

"Yes, damnit, it matters."

Nina gave her a hard look. "All right, suppose we've known all along. Supposing we'd told you. What would you have done? Don't bother to answer. You would have gone off half-cocked and done something stupid. You wouldn't have made it ten steps into the Dome without blowing your cover. If it's any consolation, there was a good deal of discussion about this. Jackie thought you should know. But the prevailing opinion was that the success of the operation came first."

"Prevailing opinion. Meaning yours."

"Mine and Eustace's." For a moment, Nina's expression seemed to soften. But only for a moment. "Don't take it so hard. You got what you wanted. Be happy."

"What I want is to get her out of there."

"Which is what we're counting on, Sara. And we'll get her out, in time."

"When?"

"I think that should be obvious. When all of this is over."

"Are you *blackmailing* me?"

Nina shrugged off the accusation. "Don't misunderstand me—it's not something I'm particularly averse to. But in this case, I don't have to." She looked at Sara carefully. "What do you think happens to those girls?"

"What do you mean, 'girls'? My daughter's the only one."

"She is *now*. But she's not the first. There's always another Eva. Giving Lila a child is the only way Guilder can keep her calm. Once they reach a certain age, though, the woman loses interest, or else the child rejects her. Then they get her a new one."

A wave of dizziness filled Sara's head; she had to sit down. "How old?"

"Five or six. It varies. But it always happens, Sara. That's what I'm telling you. The clock is ticking. Maybe not today, or even tomorrow, but soon. Then off to the basement she goes."

Sara forced herself to the next question: "What's in the basement?"

"It's where they make the blood for the redeyes. We don't know all the details. The process starts with human blood, but then something happens to it. They change it somehow. There's a man down there, a kind of viral, or so it's said. They call him the Source. He drinks a distillate of human blood, it changes in his body, something different comes out. You've seen what happens to the woman?"

Sara nodded.

"It happens to all of them, but it's slower in the men. The blood of the Source rejuvenates them. It's what keeps them alive. But once your daughter goes down there, she'll never come out."

A storm of emotions roiled inside Sara. Anger, helplessness, a fierce desire to protect her daughter. It was so intense she thought she might be ill.

"What am I supposed to do?"

"When the time comes, we'll tell you. We'll get her out. You have my word."

Sara understood what Nina was asking. Not asking: telling. They had maneuvered her perfectly. Kate was the hostage, and the ransom would be paid in blood.

"Hate her for it, Sara. Think about what she does. The moment will come for all of us, myself included, just like it came for Jackie. I'll go willingly when I'm asked. And unless this thing comes off, your daughter is on her own. We'll never be able to reach her."

"Where is it?" Sara asked. She didn't have to be clearer than that; her meaning was obvious.

"It's better if you don't know yet. You'll receive a message the usual way. You're the linchpin, and the timing matters."

"What if I can't do it?"

"Then you die anyway. And so does your daughter. It's just a matter of when. I've told you about the how." Her eyes were looking deep into Sara's. There was no compassion anywhere inside them, only an icy clarity. "If this goes according to plan, it will be the end of the redeyes. Guilder, Lila, all of them. Do you understand what I'm saying to you?"

Sara's mind had gone utterly numb. She felt herself nodding, then saying, in a faint voice, "Yes."

"Then do your duty. Do it for your daughter. Kate, is that her name?"

Sara was dumbstruck. "How did you—?"

"Because you told me. Don't you remember? You told me her name the day she was born."

Of course, she thought. So much made sense now. Nina was the woman from the birthing ward who'd given her the lock of Kate's hair.

"You may not believe me, Sara, but I'm trying to right a wrong here."

Sara wanted to laugh. She would have, if such a thing were still possible. "You have a funny way of showing it."

"Maybe so. But those are the times we live in." Another searching pause. "You have this inside you. I know it when I see it."

Did she? The question was meaningless. Somehow she would have to find the strength.

"Do it for your daughter, Sara. Do it for Kate. Otherwise she has no chance."

50

The things they were doing were endurable. Not without pain, and pain's cousin, which was the anticipation of it. But able to be borne. For a long time they asked her nothing. They made no demands of any sort. This was simply the sort of thing they liked to do, and they would go on doing it, taking their dark pleasure, which Alicia did not surrender easily. She silenced her cries, she bore it all stoically, she laughed whenever she could, saying: *Do your damnedest, my friends. I'm the one who must be kept in chains. Do you think this fact, in and of itself, is not a kind of victory?*

The water was the worst of it. Strange, because Alicia had always liked the water. She'd been a fearless swimmer as a child, diving deep into the grotto at the Colony, holding her breath as long as she could, touching the bottom as her ears thudded and watching the bubbles of her exhaled breath ascending from darkness into sunlight far above. Sometimes they funneled the water into her mouth. Sometimes they pulled her down from the chains, strapped her to a board, and dunked her headfirst into an icy tub. Each time she thought, *Here goes,* and counted the seconds until it was over.

Her strength had ebbed discernibly as the days passed. A slight downward adjustment on the whole, but enough. They offered her food, pasty gruel of soy or corn and over-smoked strips of meat hardened to the consistency of leather, their unstated intention being to keep her alive so that they could enjoy themselves for as long as possible, but without the others . . . well. She made a silent vow: when at last she tasted human blood, the unambiguous final act of her transformation, the blood would be theirs. To surrender her membership in the human race was a heavy thing, but there was some consolation in this thought. She would drink the bastards dry.

There was no way to gauge the march of days. Left to herself, she adopted the mental practice of retracing events of her past, moving through her memory as if it were a hall-way of pictures: standing the watch at First Colony; her journey with Peter and Amy and the others across the Darklands to Colorado; her strange, arid childhood with the Colonel. She had always called him "sir," never "Daddy" or even "Niles"; from the start he had been her superior officer, not a father or friend. Strange to think of that now. Her memories of her life carried a range of emotions, grief and happiness and exhilaration and loneliness and to some degree love, but the feeling they shared was of belonging. She was her memories, and her memories were her. She hoped she'd get to keep them when all was said and done.

She had begun to wonder if all they had in mind for her was an endless repetition of their painful ministrations when the rhythm of her captivity was disrupted by the arrival of a man who bore the appearance of being in charge. He did not introduce himself, and for at least a minute he didn't say anything at all, just stood before her where she was suspended from the ceiling, examining her with the expression of someone reading a puzzling book. He was dressed in a dark suit and tie and stiff white shirt; he didn't look a day over thirty. His skin was pale and tender, as if it never saw the sun. But it was his eyes that told the real story. Why should she be surprised?

"You're . . . different." Stepping closer, he breathed sharply through his nose, darting it at the air around her like a dog.

"Yeah, I get that a lot."

"I can smell it on you."

"Can't say I've had much of a chance to clean up." She offered her boldest grin. "And you might be . . . ?"

"I'll ask the questions."

"You know, you shouldn't read in the dark like that. It's hell on your eyes."

He reared back and struck her, open-palmed, across the face.

"Wow," Alicia said, waggling her jaw. "Ouch. That kind of stings."

He moved forward again and violently twisted her upraised arm. "Why don't you have a tag?"

"That's a nifty outfit you're wearing. Makes a girl feel a little underdressed."

Another blow to the face, like the crack of a whip. Alicia blinked her watering eyes and ran her tongue over her teeth, tasting blood. "You know, you guys have been doing that a lot. It's not very welcoming. I don't think I like you very much."

His bloodshot eyes narrowed with rage. Now she was getting somewhere. "Tell me about Sergio."

"Can't say that rings a bell."

He struck her again. Little scraps of light twinkled in her vision. She could tell that he was saving the full measure of his strength. He would dole it out one drop at a time, a slow escalation.

"Why don't you cut me down from here and we can have us a real chat? Because this obviously isn't working for you."

Wham went his hand, a fist this time. It was like being hit by a board. Alicia shook it off, spitting blood.

"Tell me."

"Go piss yourself."

A hammering blow to her gut. Her breath froze in her chest as her diaphragm compressed like a vise. The airless seconds passed. The moment her lungs finally expanded, he hit her again.

"Who . . . is . . . Sergio?"

Alicia was having a little trouble focusing. Focusing and breathing and thinking. She braced herself for another blow, but none arrived; she became aware that the man had opened the door. Three figures stepped through. They were carrying a kind of bench, waist-high, with a broad frame at its base.

"I'd like to introduce you to a friend of mine. This is Sod. You've actually already met."

Alicia's vision gradually sharpened. Something was wrong with the man's face. Or, rather, one side of his face, which looked like a slab of inconsistently cooked meat, raw at the center and blackened at the edges. Half the man's hair had burned away, as had most of his nose. His left eye looked melted, vulcanized to a runny jelly.

"Yuck," Alicia managed to reply.

"Sod here was in the holding area when you decided to shoot a tank full of liquid propane. He's not so happy about it."

"All in a day's work. Nice to meet you, Sod. That's quite a name, 'Sod.'"

"Sod is a man of special enthusiasms. You could say the name is well earned. He has a bit of a bone to pick with you." The man in the suit addressed the other two: "Tie her down. On second thought, wait a second."

The blows fell and fell. The face. The body. By the time the man had exhausted himself, Alicia was barely feeling any of it. Pain had become something else—distant, vague. A rattle of chains and a release of pressure on her wrists. She was facing the floor, her waist straddling the bench and her feet bound to its frame, spread wide. Her trousers were yanked from her body.

"A little privacy for our friend here," the first man said, and Alicia heard the door closing, and then the sound, ominous and final, of tumblers turning in the lock.

5 1

Every night, as Amy and Greer journeyed northward, she dreamed of Wolgast. Sometimes they were on the carousel. Sometimes they were driving in a car, the little towns and the green spring countryside flowing past, mountains looming in the distance, their faces shining with ice. Tonight they were in Oregon, at the camp. They were in the main room of the lodge, sitting across from each other on the floor, their legs folded Indian-style, and on the floor between them was the Monopoly board with its squares of faded color and money in ordered piles and Amy's little hat and Wolgast's little automobile and Wolgast tossing the dice from a cup and moving his piece forward to St. Charles Place, site of one of Amy's six (six!) hotels. The room was warm from the stove, and outside the windows a dry snow was falling through the velvety darkness and the deep winter cold.

"For Pete's sake," he groaned.

He doled out the bills. His exasperation was false; he wanted to lose. He told her she was lucky, making it so with his words. You're lucky, Amy.

Round and round their pieces traveled. More money changed hands. Park Place, Illinois Avenue, Marvin Gardens, the hilariously named "B. & O." Amy's stack of money grew as Wolgast's shrank toward zero. She bought railroads and utilities, she had built her houses and hotels everywhere, a gauntlet of ownership that enabled her to erect more, blanketing the board. Understanding this accelerating mathematics was the key to the game.

"I think I need a loan," Wolgast confessed.

"Try the bank." She was grinning with victory. Once he borrowed money, the end would fall swiftly; he would toss up his arms in surrender. Then they would assume their customary places on the sofa, a blanket drawn up to their chests, and take turns reading to each other. Tonight's book: H. G. Wells, *The Time Machine*.

He spilled the dice onto the board. A three and a four. He

moved his car ahead and landed on "Luxury Tax," with its little diamond ring.

"Not again." He rolled his eyes and paid up. "It's so wonderful to be here with you." He lifted his eyes past her, to the window. "It sure is snowing out there. How long has it been snowing?"

"I think it's been snowing a long time."

"I've always loved it. It makes me remember being a kid. It always feels like Christmas when it snows."

The wood in the stove crackled. All through the dense forest the snow fell and fell. Morning would break with a soft white light and silence, though in the place they were, morning would not come.

"Every year my parents took me to see *A Christmas Carol*. Wherever we were living, they'd find a theater and take me. Jacob Marley always scared me something awful. *He wore the chains he forged in life.* It's so sad. But beautiful, too. So many stories are like that." He thought for a moment. "Sometimes I wish I could stay here forever with you. Silly of me, I know. Nothing lasts forever."

"Some things do."

"What kind of things?"

"The things we like to remember. The love we've felt for people."

"The way I love you," said Wolgast.

Amy nodded.

"Because I do, you know," he said. "Did I ever tell you that?"

"You didn't need to say it. I always knew. I knew it from the start."

"No, I should have said it." His tone was regretful. "It's better when it's said."

A silence descended, deep as the forest, deep as the snow that fell upon it.

"Something is different about you, Amy." He was studying her face. "Something's changed."

"I think that it has, yes."

A soft darkness was moving in from the edges. It always happened this way, like lights going down on a stage until all that remained was the two of them.

"Well, whatever it is," he said, and grinned, "I like it." A moment passed, then: "Did you tell Carter how sorry I was?"

"He knows."

Wolgast was gazing past her. "That's something I can

never forgive myself for. I knew it just to look at him. He loved that woman with his whole heart." He dropped his eyes to the Monopoly board. "Looks like we're done here. I don't know how you do it. I'll get you next time."

"Would you like to read?"

They took their place on the couch beneath the woolen blanket. Mugs of hot cocoa sat on the table, having arrived, like everything else, of their own accord. Wolgast lifted the book and riffled the pages until he found the right one.

"*The Time Machine,* chapter seven." He cleared his throat and turned his face toward her. "My brave girl. My brave Amy. I really do, you know."

"I love you, too," said Amy, nestling against him.

And in this manner they passed an infinity of hours, the barest blink of an eye, until the darkness, a blanket in its own right, settled down upon them.

52

They followed the eastern supply line north to Texarkana, taking food and fuel and sleeping in the hardboxes. Their vehicle was one of Tifty's, a small cargo truck retrofitted as a portable, which they would soon need: north of Little Rock they'd be sheltering in the open. Fuel was a problem they didn't have, Tifty explained. The truck could carry an extra two hundred gallons in reserve, and on his trip north with Greer and Crukshank, fifteen years ago, they'd scouted sources all the way to the Iowa line—airfields, diesel power plants, large commercial depots with their fields of mushrooming tanks. The truck was equipped with a filtering system they could use to strip out the contaminants, and an oxidizing compound. A slow process, but with luck and good weather, they could reach Iowa by the middle of December.

Their first night in the portable occurred a hundred miles south of the Missouri border. As twilight fell, Tifty retrieved a large plastic jug from the cargo bed, pulled a rag over his face, and poured the contents, a clear liquid, in a line around the vehicle.

"What's in that stuff?" Lore asked. The stink was eye-watering.

"Old family recipe. The dracs hate it—plus, it covers our smell. They won't even know we're in there."

They ate their dinner of beans and hardtack and bedded down on the racks. Soon Hollis was snoring away. Hollis? Peter thought. No, Lore. She slept the way she did everything: however she liked. Peter could understand why Michael was drawn to her—her attraction was powerful—but also why his friend wouldn't come out and say so. Who could withstand being wanted so badly? Even if the quarry wanted to be caught, it put up a struggle. During their days of waiting at the refinery, Peter had wondered, more than once, if Lore was flirting with him. She was, he decided; but it was only a tactic. She was trying to draw herself deeper into Michael's world. Once she got to the heart of it, he'd have no defenses left; Michael would be hers.

Peter shifted on his rack, trying to make himself comfortable; he always had difficulty getting to sleep in a portable. Just when he would begin drifting off, a noise from outside would jar him into wakefulness. One time near Amarillo, the virals had pounded on the walls all night. They'd actually lifted the frame and attempted to turn it over. To keep their spirits up, the men of Peter's squad had passed the hours playing poker and telling jokes, as if nothing of importance were happening. *Hell of a racket out there* was the most anyone would say. *How am I supposed to concentrate on the cards?* Peter would miss that life; he was AWOL nine days, as much of an outlaw as Hollis or Tifty. No matter what Gunnar might offer in Peter's defense, the man's message had been clear: you do this on your own; no one's going to say they knew you.

The next thing he was aware of, Hollis was shaking him awake. They disembarked into the cold. This far north, there could be no doubt of the change of seasons. The sky set low with heavy gray clouds like formations of airborne stone.

"See?" Tifty said, gesturing at the ground around the truck. "No tracks at all."

They drove on. The absence of virals nagged at Peter's mind. Even outside the hardboxes they'd seen no tracks, no scat. A welcome turn of events, but so unlikely as to be disturbing, as if the virals were saving something special for them.

Their progress slowed, the roads becoming vague; frequently Tifty had to stop the truck to recalculate their course, using a compass and maps and sometimes a sextant, a device Peter had never seen before. Michael showed him how it worked. By measuring the sun's angle to the horizon, and taking into account the time and date, it was possible to compute their location without any other points of reference. The instrument was typically used on ships at sea, Michael explained, where the horizon was unobstructed, but it could work on land, too. How do you know this stuff? Peter asked, but realized as he posed the question what the answer was. Michael had taught himself to use a sextant for that day when he would sail out to find, or not find, the barrier.

The days of travel passed, and still no virals. By now they were openly puzzling over this, though the discussion never advanced beyond noting its oddness. *Strange,* they said. *I suppose we should consider ourselves lucky.* Which they were, but luck had a way of betraying you in the end. Eleven days in, Tifty announced that they were approaching the Missouri-Iowa line. They were dirty and exhausted; tempers were short. For two full days they'd been stymied by a nameless river, backtracking mile after mile, trying to find a bridge still standing. Their fuel supply was getting low. The landscape had changed again, not quite as flat as Texas but close, with gently undulating hills subsumed under waist-high grass. The hour was approaching noon when Hollis, at the wheel, brought the truck to a halt.

Peter, who had been dozing in the back, roused to the sound of the truck's doors opening. He drew upright to find himself alone in the cab. Why were they stopping?

He retrieved his rifle and climbed down. Everything was coated with a fine, pale powder—the grass, the trees. Snow? The air had a tart smell, like something burnt. Not snow. Ashes. Little clouds of whiteness puffed underfoot as Peter advanced to where the others were standing, at the crest of a hill. There he stopped, as his companions had stopped, pinned in place by what they saw.

"For the love of God," Michael said. "What the hell are we looking at?"

53

This woman: who was she?

A spy. An insurgent. That much was obvious; her attempt to free the hostages had all the trademarks, and she had killed six men before making her fatal mistake. But the absence of a tag on her arm didn't add up. That curious odor Guilder had detected; what did it mean? They'd recovered her weapon, a Browning semiautomatic with two bullets remaining in the magazine. Guilder had never seen one like it; it wasn't one of theirs. Either the insurgency had stockpiled a cache of weapons from a source he didn't know about, or the woman came from someplace else entirely.

Guilder didn't like mysteries. He liked them even less than he liked the idea of Sergio.

The woman seemed unbreakable. She hadn't told them so much as her name. Even Sod, that psychopath, a man of notoriously revolting appetites, had failed to extract a scrap of information. The decision to employ the man's services had come about with curious ease. Sending people to the feedlot was one thing; the virals made mercifully short work of it, and the creatures needed to be fed. It wasn't anything nice, but it was over fast. And as for a few blows in detention, or the cautious application of the waterboard, well, sometimes such measures were simply unavoidable. What had the term been, back in the day? Enhanced interrogation.

But sanctioned rape: that was something new. That was a bit of a head-scratcher. It was the kind of thing that happened in small, brutal countries where men with machetes hacked people to bits for no reason other than the fact that they'd been born in the wrong village, or had slightly different ears, or preferred chocolate to vanilla. The thought should have repelled him. It should have been . . . beneath him. This was what Sergio had driven him to. Strange how something could seem completely crazy one day and entirely reasonable the next.

These were the thoughts running through Guilder's mind as he sat at the head of the conference table. If he'd had the option, he would have skipped these weekly meetings, which inevitably devolved into convoluted procedural squabbling, a classic example of too many cooks in the kitchen. Guilder was a firm believer in a clear chain of command and the dispersed authorities of the pyramidal bureaucracy. It tended to create a bloat of busywork at the bottom and an excessive appetite for paperwork and precedent, but it kept everybody in his own corner. Still, the pretense of shared governance needed to be maintained, at least for now.

"Does anybody have anything to say?"

No one seemed to. After an uncomfortable silence, Propaganda Minister Hoppel, who was seated to Guilder's immediate left, next to Suresh, the Minister of Public Health, and directly across from Wilkes, cleared his throat and said, "I think what everybody is worried about, well, not so much worried as concerned, and I think I'm speaking for everyone here—"

"For God's sake, spit it out. And take off your glasses."

"Oh. Right." Hoppel slid the smoke-colored lenses from his face and placed them with nervous delicacy on the conference table. "As I said," he continued, and cleared his throat again. "Is it possible that, maybe, things are getting a little out of hand?"

"You're damn right they are. That's the first intelligent thing anybody has said to me all day."

"What I mean is, the strategies we've employed don't seem to be getting us where we want to be."

Guilder sighed with irritation. "What are you suggesting?"

Hoppel's eyes darted involuntarily at his colleagues. *You better back me up here—I'm not going out on this limb by myself.*

"Perhaps we should de-escalate. For a time."

"De-escalate. We're getting hammered out there."

"Well, that's the thing. There's a lot of talk in the flatland, and it's not going our way. Maybe we should try ratcheting things down a bit. See where that leaves us."

"Have you lost your mind? Have all of you lost your minds?"

"You said yourself that things aren't really working out the way we'd like."

"I didn't say that, you did."

"Be that as it may, a few of us were talking—"

"That's the worst-kept secret in this room."

"Right. So, okay. What we came up with was the idea that maybe we should go in the opposite direction. More of a hearts-and-minds approach. If you follow."

Guilder took a calming breath. "So what you're suggesting, and excuse the paraphrase, is that we should look like pussies."

"Director Guilder, if I may." This was Suresh. "The pattern of a successful insurgency—"

"They're killing people. They're killing *flatlanders*. What about this isn't clear? These people are butchers."

"No one is saying different," Suresh continued with a bland look. "And for a while that worked in our favor. But the roundups haven't produced any usable intelligence. We still don't know where Sergio is or how he moves. No one's come forward. And in the meantime, the reprisals have been an effective recruitment tool for the insurgency."

"Do you know how you sound? I'll tell you how you sound. You sound rehearsed."

Suresh ignored the barb. "Let me show you something."

From a folder on the table he withdrew a sheet of paper, which he slid toward Guilder. One of their own propaganda bulletins, but on the other side was scrawled a different message.

Flatlanders, Rise Up!

The Last Days of the Redeyes Are at Hand!

Join Your Brethren in the Insurgency!

Every Act of Disobedience Strikes a Blow Against the Regime!

And so on, in that vein. Guilder lifted his head to find everyone staring at him, as if he were a bomb that might go off.

"So? What does this prove?"

"HR personnel have found fifty-six of these so far," Suresh replied. "I'll give you an example of the problem this is causing. This morning at roll call, an entire lodge refused to sing the anthem."

"And were they beaten?"

"There were over three hundred of them. And we can only hold half that number in detention. We simply don't have the room."

"So cut their rations in half."

"The flatlanders are on a subsistence diet already. We reduce it any further and they won't be able to work."

It was maddening. Every point Guilder made was instantly parried. He was looking down the barrel of nothing less than an organized insurrection among the senior staff.

"Get out, all of you."

"I think," Suresh pressed with infuriating composure, "that we should come to some consensus on a strategy."

A hot rush of blood shot to Guilder's face. The veins were pounding in his head; he was practically apoplectic. He picked up the paper and waved it in the air.

"Hearts and minds. Do you hear what you're saying? Did you read this?"

"Director Guilder—"

"I have nothing more to say to you. Go."

Papers were gathered, briefcases closed, anxious glances

exchanged around the table. Everybody rose and started moving toward the exit. Guilder put his head in his hands. Jesus Christ, this was all he needed. Something had to be done, and it had to be done immediately.

"Wilkes, wait a second."

The man turned, eyebrows raised.

"You stay."

The others departed. His chief of staff lingered by the door.

"Sit."

Wilkes returned to his chair.

"You mind telling me what the hell that was about? I've always trusted you, Fred. Relied on you to keep things running. Don't bullshit me now."

"They're just worried."

"Worried is one thing. I won't tolerate division in the ranks. Not when we're so close. They could get here any day now."

"Everybody understands that. They just don't want . . . well, for things to get out of control. They caught me by surprise, too."

Save your excuses, thought Guilder. "What do you think? Have they gotten out of control?"

"Do you really want to ask me that?" When Guilder said nothing, Wilkes shrugged. "Maybe a little."

Guilder rose, removed his glasses from his jacket pocket, and pulled the drapes aside. This dismal place. This middle of goddamned nowhere. He found himself suddenly nostalgic for the past, the old world of cars and restaurants and stores and dry cleaners and tax returns and traffic jams and waiting in line at the movies. He hadn't felt this depressed in a long time.

"People are going to have to have more babies."

"Sir?"

He spoke with his back to the man. "Babies, Fred." He shook his head at the irony. "Funny, I've never really known much about them. Never really felt the urge. You had a couple, didn't you?"

It was an unwritten rule not to ask about their former lives. Guilder could feel Wilkes's hesitation in his answer. "The missus and I had three. Two boys and a girl. Seven grandkids, too."

"Do you think about them?"

Guilder turned from the window. Wilkes had put on his glasses, too. Was it the light or something else?

"Not anymore." One corner of Wilkes's mouth gave a little twitch. "Are you testing me, Horace?"

"Maybe I am, a little."

"Don't."

The word had more force behind it than Guilder had ever heard from the man. He couldn't decide if this was reassuring or not.

"We're going to have to get everybody on the same page, you know. Can I count on you?"

"Why do you even have to ask that?"

"Humor me, Fred."

A hitch of time; then Wilkes nodded.

The right answer, but Wilkes's hesitancy nagged. Why *was* Guilder asking? It wasn't just the juvenile tenor of the meeting that bothered him; he'd dealt with that before. Somebody was always stepping on somebody else's toes. *Ouch! That hurt! No fair! I'm telling!* Something deeper and more troubling was brewing. It was more than a failure of resolve; it had the feeling of an insurrection in the making. All his instincts told him so, as if he were perched over a widening crevasse, one foot on this side, one on the other.

He closed the drapes and returned to the table. "What's the situation with the feedlot?"

The muscles in Wilkes's face visibly relaxed; they were back on familiar ground. "The blast tore the place up pretty good. It will take at least three more days to repair the gates and lighting."

Too long, thought Guilder. They'd have to do it in the open. Maybe it was better that way; he could kill two birds with one stone. A bit of theater, to get the troops in line. He pushed his notepad across the table to his chief of staff.

"Write this down."

54

"It's just so . . . strange."

Lila had just come off her feeding and was deep within its throes. The blood had been delivered, by Guilder presumably, while Sara and Kate were playing in the courtyard. After two successive days above freezing, the snow had turned into a sticky skin, perfect for snowballs. They'd thrown them at each other for hours.

Now they were playing a game of beans and cups on the

floor by the fire. The game was new to Sara; Kate had taught her. Another pleasure, to learn a game from one's own child. Sara tried not to think how fleeting this would be. Any day the message from Nina could come.

"Yes, well," Lila said, as if she and Sara had been having a conversation, "I'm going to have to be going on an errand soon."

Sara paid this little attention. Lila's mind seemed adrift in reverie. An errand to where?

"David says I have to go." Facing the mirror, Lila made the scowly face she always adopted when speaking of David. "Lila, it's for charity. I know you don't like opera, but we absolutely have to go. Lila, this man is the head of a major hospital, all the wives will be there, how will it look if I have to go alone?" She sighed resignedly, her brush pausing on its journey through her lustrous mane of hair. "Maybe just once he'd think about what *I* want to do, the places *I* want to go. Now, *Brad* was thoughtful. Brad was the kind of man who listened." Her eyes met Sara's through the mirror. "Tell me something, Dani. Do you have a boyfriend? Someone special in your life? If you don't mind my asking. My gosh, you're certainly pretty enough. I bet you have dozens of them just beating down your door."

Sara was momentarily disoriented by the question; Lila rarely, if ever, asked Sara anything about herself. "Not really."

Lila considered this. "Well, that's smart. You have lots of time yet. Play the field, don't settle. If you meet the right man, you'll know." The woman resumed her careful brushing. Her voice was suddenly sad. "Remember that, Dani. There's someone waiting out there for you. Once you find him, don't let him out of your sight. I made that mistake, and now look at the fix I'm in."

The remark, like so many, seemed to float in the ether, unable to touch down on any firm surface. Yet over the days of their confinement, Sara had begun to detect a pattern of meaning to these oblique utterances. They were shadows of something real: an actual history of people, places, events. If what Nina said about the woman was true—and Sara believed it to be so—Lila was every inch the monster the red-eyes were. How many Evas had been sent to the basement because Lila had . . . what were Nina's words? *Lost interest.* And yet Sara could not deny that there was something pitiable about the woman. She seemed so lost, so frail, so laden with regret. *Sometimes,* Lila had remarked once, apropos of nothing, and with the heaviest of sighs, *I just don't see how things can go on like this.* And, one evening while Sara was rubbing lotion into her feet, *Dani, did you ever think about just running away? Leaving your whole life behind and starting over?* More and more she let Sara and Kate go their own way, as if she were abdicating her role in the little girl's life— as if, at some level, she knew the truth. *I look at the two of you and I think, How perfect you are together. That little girl adores you. Dani, you're the piece of the puzzle that was missing.*

"So what do you think?"

Sara's attentions had returned to the game. She glanced up from the floor to see Lila looking earnestly at her.

"Dani, it's your turn," said Kate.

"Just a minute, sweetheart." Then, to Lila: "I'm sorry. What do I think about what?"

An effortful smile was plastered to her face. "Coming with me. I think you'd be a great help. Jenny can look after Eva."

"Come where?"

Sara could see it in Lila's eyes: whatever their destination was, the woman absolutely didn't want to go alone. "What does it matter, really? One of David's . . . *things.* They're usually just deadly, to be honest. I really could stand the company." She bent forward from her stool and addressed the child. "What do you say, Eva? How about an evening with Jenny while Mummy goes out?"

The girl refused to meet her eye. "I want to stay with Dani."

"Of course you do, pumpkin. We all love Dani. There's no more special person in the world. But once in a while grown-ups have to go off to be by themselves, to do grown-up things. That's just how it is sometimes."

"Then you go."

"Eva, I don't think you're listening to what I'm saying."

The girl was tugging at the sleeve of Sara's robe. "Tell her."

Lila frowned. "Dani? What's this about?"

"I don't . . . know." She looked at Kate, who had scuttled beside her on the floor, protectively wedging her body against Sara's. Sara put an arm around her. "What is it, honey?"

"Eva," Lila interjected, "what do you want Dani to tell me? Speak up, now."

"I don't like you," the girl murmured into the folds of Sara's robe.

Lila drew back, the color draining from her face. "What did you say?"

"I don't like you! I like *her!*"

Lila's expression was beyond shock. It was a portrait of absolute rejection. Sara suddenly understood viscerally what had happened to the other Evas. *This* was what had happened.

"Well." Lila cleared her throat, her wounded eyes roaming restlessly about the room, seeking some object to attach her attentions to. "I see."

"Lila, she didn't mean it." The girl had resumed her protective huddle against Sara's body, pressing her face into her robe while simultaneously watching Lila warily from the corner of her eye. "Tell her, sweetheart."

"That won't be necessary," Lila said. "She couldn't have made herself more clear." The woman rose unsteadily from her stool. Everything was different now; the words had been spoken. "If you will excuse me, I think I'll lie down for a bit. David will be here soon."

She didn't so much walk as stumble toward her bedroom. Her back was bent forward, as if she'd suffered a physical blow.

"Do you still want me to come with you?" Sara asked gently.

Lila halted, clutching the frame for balance. She didn't look at Sara as she gave her answer.

"Of course, Dani. Why wouldn't I?"

They drove to the stadium in darkness. A convoy of ten vehicles, pickups front and rear, each carrying a detail of armed cols in the bed, with eight sleek SUVs in between for the senior staff. Lila and Sara rode in the backseat of the second car. Lila was dressed in a dark cloak with the hood gathered at her neck, oversized dark glasses covering the upper half of her face like a shield. The driver was someone Sara recognized without being able to place, a skeletally thin man with lank brown hair and pale roving eyes that met Sara's through the mirror as they pulled away from the Dome.

"You. What's your name?"

"Dani."

He shot a grin through the mirror. Sara felt a jolt of apprehension. Did he know her? Had his gaze somehow penetrated the obscuring curtain of her veil?

"Well, you're in for a treat tonight, Dani."

Guilder had initially refused to let Sara come, but Lila wouldn't budge. *David, how do you think I feel, being dragged around to all your silly parties with your silly friends? I'm simply not going without her, like it or lump it.* On and on like this until Guilder, with a huff, had relented. Fine, he'd said. Have it your way, Lila. Maybe one of your attendants should see what you really are. The more the fucking merrier.

They were passing the flatland now, following the river, becalmed under a skin of winter ice. Something was happening to Lila. With each minute that passed, the lights of the Dome fading behind them, her personality receded. She was stretching her back like a cat, making little humming sounds at the back of her throat, touching her face and hair.

"Mmmm," Lila purred with an almost sexual pleasure. "Can you feel them?"

Sara had no answer.

"It's . . . *won*derful."

They passed through the gate. Ahead Sara saw the stadium, lit from within, glowing in the winter night. She felt not so much fear as a spreading blackness. The caravan slowed as it ascended the ramp and emerged onto a brilliantly lit field surrounded by bleachers. The vehicles stopped behind a silver cargo truck where a dozen cols were waiting, fidgeting with their batons and stamping their feet in the cold. A tall stake had been tamped into the ground in the middle of the field.

"Mmmm," said Lila.

Doors flew open; everybody disembarked. Standing beside the car, Lila lifted Sara's veil and tenderly touched her cheek. "My Dani. My sweet girl. Isn't it marvelous? My babies, my beautiful babies."

"Lila, what's happening here?"

She rocked her head on her neck with sensuous delight. Her eyes were soft and distant. The Lila Sara knew was nowhere inside them. She moved her face toward Sara's and, astonishingly, kissed her dryly on the lips.

"I'm so glad you're with me," she said.

The driver took Sara by the elbow and led her to the bleachers. Twenty men in dark suits were seated in two rows, chatting energetically among themselves, blowing on their fists. "This is so cool," Sara heard one of them say as she was shown to her place in the fourth row, among a group of cols. "I *never* get to see this."

Down front, Guilder faced the group. He was wearing a black overcoat, a dark tie visible at his throat. He was holding something in his gloved hand: a radio.

"Gentlemen of the senior staff, welcome," he declared with a buoyant grin. His breath puffed before his face, punctuating the words. "A little present for you tonight. A show of gratitude for all your hard work as we near the climax of all our labors."

"Bring 'em on!" one of the redeyes hooted, eliciting cheers and laughter.

"Now, now," Guilder said, waving them to silence. "All of you are well acquainted with the spectacle that is about to unfold. But tonight, we have something very special planned. Minister Hoppel, would you please come forward?"

A redeye in the second row got to his feet and joined Guilder at the front. Tall, with a square-jawed face and brush-cut hair. Grinning with embarrassment, he said, "Gosh, Horace, it's not even my birthday."

"Maybe he's about to demote you!" another voice yelled.

More laughter. Guilder waited for it to die down. "Mr. Hoppel here," he said, placing a fatherly hand on the man's back, "as everyone knows, has been with us from the very beginning. As Minister of Propaganda, he has provided us with a key element in support of our efforts." His expression abruptly hardened. "Which is why, with the greatest regret, I must tell you all that incontrovertible evidence has come to my attention that Minister Hoppel is in league with the insurgency." He darted a hand toward the man's face, stripping off his glasses and tossing them away. Hoppel gave a shriek of pain as he drew his arm up over his eyes. "Guards," said Guilder, "take him."

A pair of cols grabbed Hoppel by the arms; more quickly surrounded him, weapons drawn. A moment of confusion, voices buzzing through the bleachers. *What? What is he saying? Hoppel, could it really be . . . ?*

"Yes, my friends. Minister Hoppel is a traitor. It was he who passed crucial intelligence to the insurgency that led to last week's bombing, in which two of our colleagues were killed."

"Jesus, Horace." The man had gone weak at the knees. His eyes were squeezed tight. He tried to shrug the men's grip off, but he seemed to have lost all strength. "You know me! All of you know me! Suresh, Wilkes, somebody—tell him!"

"I'm sorry, my friend. You've done this to yourself. Take him to the field."

He was dragged away. Beside the silver truck, Hoppel was bound to the stake with heavy rope. One of the cols produced a bucket and poured the contents over him with a crimson splash, soaking his clothing, hair, face. He wriggled helplessly, uttering the most pitiful cries. *Don't do this. Please, I swear, I'm no traitor. You bastards, say something!*

Guilder cupped his mouth. "Is the prisoner secure?"

"Secure!"

He lifted the radio to his mouth. "Hit the lights."

The thunk of tumblers, the screech of the opening door.

Alicia was hanging from the ceiling, her bound wrists stretched above her head, holding aloft her slowly creaking weight. She was tired, so tired. Rivulets of dried blood ran down her naked legs. The man known as Sod, through the days of his dark business, had left no part of her untouched. He had filled her ears and nose with the hot stench of his grunting exhalations. He had scratched her, struck her, bitten her. Bitten, like an animal. Her breasts, the soft skin of her neck, the insides of her thighs, all embedded with the marks of his teeth. Through it all, she had not wept. Cried out, yes. Screamed. But she would not give him the satisfaction of her tears. And now here he was again, lazily swinging the chiming ring of keys around his finger, dragging his one good eye down the length of her body, wearing a greedy, bestial smile on his half-cooked face.

"I thought, since everybody's all off at the stadium for the big show, we might have a little bit of alone time."

What was there to say? There was nothing.

"Now, I'm thinking that the two of us might try something new. The bench feels so . . . impersonal."

He began to undress, a complicated business of leather and buckles. He kicked off his boots, his pants. As he went about his grand unveiling, Alicia could only watch in mute revulsion. She felt like she had about ten different Alicias in her head, each with a single scrap of information lacking any reference to the others. And yet: *alone time.* That was new, she thought. That was a definite wrinkle in the proceedings. Usually there were four of them: one to operate the winch, two to take her down, plus Sod. Where were the others?

Alone time.

"I'm begging you," she croaked, "just don't make it hurt. I'll make it good for you."

"That's very sporting."

"Let me down and I'll show you how good."

He considered this.

"Just tell me what you want and I'll give it to you."

"You're full of shit."

"You can leave the shackles on. I promise I'll cooperate. I'll give you everything you want."

In his face, she saw the idea taking hold. She was naked, beaten. What could a woman in her condition do? The keys were clipped to the belt loop of his trousers, lying on the floor behind him. Alicia forced herself not to look at them.

"There might be something to that," Sod said.

The chains, which ran through a block hung from the ceiling, were operated by a lever affixed to the wall. Pantless, engorged, Sod stepped toward it and unlocked the brake. A rattle overhead; Alicia's feet touched down.

"More slack," she said. "I'll need to move."

A sleepy, sexual grin. "I like your thinking."

The pressure on her wrists released. "A little more."

Her tactic had to be obvious, but the man's anticipation trumped the last of his judgment. Alicia's arms fell to her sides. She now had eight feet of slack to play with.

"No funny stuff, now."

She lowered herself to all fours in invitation. Sod moved behind her, joining her on the floor.

"I'll make it good for you," she said. "I promise."

As he placed his hands on her hips, she drew her right foot to her chest and smashed it into his face. A crack and then a yelp; Alicia shot to her feet and swung around. He was sitting on the floor, holding his nose, dark blood gushing through his fingers.

"You fucking bitch!"

He lurched toward her, going for her throat. The question was who got to whom first. Alicia stepped back, arced one hand from her side, forming a lasso with the chain, and tossed it forward.

The loop dropped over his head. She yanked him toward her, stepping aside and using his momentum to spin him around. Now she had him from behind. With the other hand she formed a second loop of chain and dropped it around his neck. A quick hop and she had her legs around his waist. He was making a gurgling noise, his arms flailing at the air. *Die, you pig,* she thought, *just die,* and with all her strength she rocked her weight backward, tugging the chains like the reins of a horse, sending them pitching toward the ground until with a hard jolt the slack ran out, the block above them caught and held, and Alicia heard the sound she longed for: a satisfying pop of bone.

They were suspended eighteen inches off the floor. Two hundred pounds of dead weight now lay on top of her. She tucked her legs beneath her, arched her back, and pushed. Sod's body folded forward onto its knees, pitching face-first onto the concrete as she unlooped the chains from his neck. She scooped the keys from the floor and undid the shackles and tore them from her wrists.

Then she was kicking him, stomping on his head, smashing his face into the concrete with the hard nub of her heel. Her mind collapsed in a roar of hatred. She seized him by the hair and dragged his lifeless form across the cell and propped him upright to hammer his head against the wall. "How do you like that, you piece of shit? You like that broken neck? You like me killing you?"

Maybe there was somebody outside the cell, and maybe there wasn't. Maybe more men would rush in and chain her to the ceiling and start it all again. But that didn't matter. All that mattered was Sod's head. She would smash it until he was the deadest thing in the history of the world, the deadest man who'd ever been. She was yelling, over and over, "God damn you! God damn you! God damn you!"

Then it was over. Alicia let him go. The body tipped sideways to the floor, leaving a glistening smear of brains on the wall. Alicia slumped to her knees, drinking great gulps of air into her lungs. It was over, but it didn't feel over. There was no over, not anymore.

She needed clothes. She needed a weapon. Strapped to Sod's calf she discovered a heavy-handled knife. The balance was poor, but it would do. She gathered up his trousers and his shirt. Dressing herself in the man's clothing, ripe with his stench, filled her with disgust. Her skin crawled, as if he were touching her. She rolled up the sleeves and the legs of his trousers and cinched the waist. The boots, far too large, would only slow her down; she would have to travel barefoot. She dragged the body away from the door and banged on the metal with the butt of her knife.

"Hey!" she yelled, cupping her mouth to lower the register of her voice. "Hey, I'm locked in here!"

The seconds passed. Maybe no one was out there. What would she do then? She hammered on the door, louder this time, praying someone would come.

Then the tumblers turned. Alicia darted behind the door as the guard stepped into the room.

"What the hell, Sod, you told me I had thirty minutes—"

But these sentiments went unfinished as Alicia, darting behind him, drew one hand over his mouth and used the other to ram the knife into the small of his back, swishing the handle as the tip drove upward.

She eased the body to the floor. Blood was releasing from it in a wide, dark pool. Its rich scent rose to her nostrils. Alicia recalled her vow. *I will drink those bastards dry. I will baptize myself in the blood of my enemy.* The thought had sustained her through the days of torment. But as she looked at the two men, first the guard and then Sod, his pale, naked body like a stain of whiteness on the concrete, she shuddered with disgust.

Not now, she thought, *not yet,* and she slipped into the hallway.

The field sank into darkness. For a moment, all was still. Then, from high overhead, a cool aquatic light pulsed down onto the field, bathing it in an artificial moonglow.

Lila had appeared at the rear of the silver truck. All the redeyes were pocketing their sunglasses. Hoppel had given up his pleas and begun to sob. A van drove onto the field. Two cols disembarked and trotted to the rear of the vehicle and opened the doors.

Eleven people stumbled out, six men and five women, shackled at the wrists and ankles and to each other. They were stumbling, weeping, begging for their lives. Their terror was too great; all their resistance was gone. A cold numbness had taken hold of Sara; she thought she might be ill. One of the women looked like Karen Molyneau, but Sara couldn't be certain. The cols dragged them toward Hoppel and instructed them to get down on their knees.

"This is so awesome," a nearby voice said.

All but one of the cols jogged away, remaining with Lila at the rear of the large truck. Her body was swaying, her head rocking side to side, as if she were floating in an invisible current or dancing to unheard music.

"I thought there were supposed to be ten," the same voice said. One of the redeyes, two rows below.

"Yeah. Ten."

"But there's eleven of them."

Sara counted again. Eleven.

"You better go down there and tell Guilder."

"Are you kidding? Who knows what's on his mind these days?"

"You should check that at the door. He hears you say that, you'll be next."

"The guy has slipped a gear, I'm telling you." A pause. "I always knew there was something off about Hoppel, though."

These words touched Sara like a distant wind. Her attention was now solely focused on the field. Was that Karen? The woman looked older, and too tall. Most of the prisoners had adopted a defensive posture, their bodies folded where they knelt in the crusted snow, hands held over their heads; others, kneeling upright, faces washed by the blue light, had begun to pray. The last col was strapping on armored pads. He wedged a helmet over his head and waved toward the bleachers. Every muscle in Sara's body clenched. She wanted to look away but couldn't. The col moved to the door of the silver truck's cargo compartment, fumbling loudly with keys.

The doors swung open; the col dashed away. For a second, nothing happened. Then the virals emerged, popping from the truck's interior like man-sized insects, landing on all fours in the snow. Their lean figures, striated with muscle, throbbed with glowing vividness. Eight, nine, ten. They moved toward Lila, whose arms were held open at her sides, palms raised. A gesture of invitation, of welcome.

At her feet, they bowed.

She touched them, stroked them. She ran her hands over their smooth heads, cupped their chins like children's to gaze adoringly into their eyes. *My lovelies,* Sara heard her say. *My wonderful beauties.*

"Will you look at that? She fucking loves them."

From the hostages came only a sound of quiet weeping. The end was inevitable; they had no choice but to accept it. Or perhaps it was simply the strangeness of the scene that stunned them into silence.

My sweet pets. Are you hungry? Mama will feed you. Mama will take care of you. That's what Mama will do.

"No, I'm certain there's supposed to be ten."

A new voice this time, coming from the right: "Did you say ten? That's what I heard, too."

"So who's the eleventh?"

One of the redeyes shot to his feet, pointing at the field. "There's one too many!"

All heads swiveled toward the voice, including Guilder's.

"I'm not kidding! There are eleven people out there!"

Go now, my darlings.

The virals broke away from Lila. Simultaneously, one of the hostages shot to his feet, exposing his face. It was Vale. The virals were encircling the group; everyone was screaming. Vale tore the flaps of his jacket aside to reveal rows of metal tubes strapped to his chest. He yanked his arms skyward, his thumb poised on the detonator.

"Sergio lives!"

IX

THE ARRIVAL

And I looked, and behold a pale
Horse; and the name that sat on him
Was Death; and Hell followed with him.

—REVELATION 6:8

55

Lila's dressing table detonated with a splintering crash. Guilder hauled her to her feet again and slapped her across the face with the back of his hand, sending her flying back, toward the sofa.

"How could you let this happen?" His face boiled with rage. "Why didn't you call the virals back? Tell me!"

"I don't know, I don't know!"

From the collar of her bathrobe this time: with terrifying effortlessness, Guilder hurled her, face-first, into the bookshelf. A thud of impact, things falling, Lila screaming. Sara was huddled on the floor, her body curled around Kate, the little girl wilted with fear.

"Every last viral! Nine of my men, dead! Do you know how this makes me look?"

"It wasn't my fault! I don't remember! David, please!"

"There is no David!"

Sara clenched her eyes tight. Kate was whimpering softly in her arms. What would happen if Guilder killed Lila? What would become of the two of them then?

"Stop it! David, I'm begging you!"

Lila was lying face-up on the floor, Guilder straddling her, one hand holding her by her collar. The other was balled into a fist, pulled back, ready to strike. Lila's arms lay across her eyes like a shield, though this effort would come to nothing; Guilder's fist would crush her face like a battering ram.

"You . . . disgust me."

He loosened his hold and stepped away, wiping his hands on his shirt. Lila was sobbing uncontrollably. Blood bulged from a cut along her cheekbone. More was in her hair. Guilder flicked his eyes toward Sara, dismissing her with a glance. *You're nothing,* his eyes said. *You're a character in a game of pretend that's gone on far too long.*

Then he stormed from the room.

Sara went to where Lila was whimpering on the floor. She knelt beside her, reaching for her face to examine the cut. In an unexpected burst of energy, Lila shoved Sara's hand away and scampered backward.

"Don't touch it!"

"But you're hurt—"

The woman's eyes were wild with panic. As Sara moved toward her, she waved her hands in front of her face.

"Get away! Don't touch my blood!"

She leapt to her feet and ran to the bedroom, slamming the door behind her.

6:02 A.M.

The vehicles made their way into the flatland in the pre-dawn darkness, gates flying open as they passed. At the head of the line, like the point of an arrow, was the sleek black SUV of the Director, followed by a pair of open trucks, full of uniformed men. Into the maze of lodges they roared, hurling clots of dirty snow from their mudchoked tires, their passage observed by the workers filing from the buildings to assemble for morning roll—weary faces, weary eyes, dully noting the vehicles sailing past. But their glances were brief; they knew better than to look. *Something official; it has nothing to do with me. At least, it better not.*

Guilder watched the flatlanders from the passenger window, full of contempt. How he loathed them. Not just the insurgents, the ones who defied him—all of them. They plodded through their lives like brute animals, never seeing beyond the next square of earth to be plowed. Another day in the dairy barns, the fields, the biodiesel plant. Another day in the kitchen, the laundry, the pigsties.

But today wasn't just another day.

The vehicles halted before Lodge 16. The eastern sky had softened to a yellowish gray, like old plastic.

"This is the one?" Guilder asked Wilkes.

Beside him, the man gave a tight-lipped nod.

The cols disembarked and took up positions. Guilder and Wilkes stepped clear of the car. Before them, in fifteen evenly spaced lines, three hundred flatlanders stood shivering in the cold. Two more trucks pulled in and parked at the head of the square. Their cargo bays were draped by heavy canvas.

"What are those for?" Wilkes asked.

"A little extra . . . persuasion."

Guilder strode up to the senior HR officer and snatched the megaphone from his hand. A howl of feedback; then his voice boomed over the square.

"Who can tell me about Sergio?"

No reply.

"This is your only warning. Who can tell me about Sergio?"

Again, nothing.

Guilder gave his attention to a woman in the first row. Neither young nor old, she had a face so plain it could have been made of paste. She was clutching a filthy scarf around her head with hands covered by fingerless gloves black with soot.

"You. What's your name?"

Eyes cast down, she muttered something into the folds of her scarf.

"I can't hear you. Speak up."

She cleared her throat, stifling a cough. Her voice was a phlegmy rasp. "Priscilla."

"Where do you work?"

"The looms, sir."

"Do you have a family? Children?"

She nodded weakly.

"So? What do you have?"

Her knees were trembling. "A daughter and two sons."

"A husband?"

"Dead, sir. Last winter."

"My condolences. Come forward."

"I sang the hymn yesterday. It was the others, I swear."

"And I believe you, Priscilla. Nevertheless. Gentlemen, can you assist her, please?"

A pair of cols trotted forward and grabbed the woman by her arms. Her body went slack, as if she were on the verge of fainting. They half-carried, half-dragged her to the front, where they shoved her onto her knees. She made no sound; her submission was total.

"Who are your children? Point them out."

"Please." She was weeping pitifully. "Don't make me."

One of the cols lifted his baton over her head. "This man is going to bash your brains out," Guilder said.

She shook her bowed head.

"Very well," Guilder said.

Down went the baton; the woman toppled forward into the mud. From the left came a sharp cry.

"Get her."

A young teenager, with her mother's face. Onto her knees she went. She was crying, trembling; snot was running from her nose. Guilder raised the megaphone.

"Does anybody have anything to say?"

Silence. Guilder drew a pistol from beneath his coat and

racked the slide. "Minister Wilkes," he said, holding out the gun, "will you please do the honors?"

"Jesus, Horace." His face was aghast. "What are you trying to prove?"

"Is this going to be a problem?"

"We have *people* for this kind of thing. That wasn't part of the deal."

"What deal? There is no deal. The deal is what I say it is." Wilkes stiffened. "I won't do it."

"You won't or you can't?"

"What difference does it make?"

Guilder frowned. "Not very much, now that I think about it." And with these words, he stepped behind the girl, pushed the muzzle of the gun to the back of her head, and fired.

"Good Christ!"

"You know what the biggest problem with never growing old is?" Guilder asked his chief of staff. He was wiping down the blood-tinged barrel with a handkerchief. "I've given this a lot of thought."

"Fuck you, Horace."

Guilder pointed the pistol at Wilkes's colorless face, leveling its sights at the spot between his eyes. "You forget that you can die."

And Guilder shot him, too.

A change came over the crowd, their fear turning to something else. Murmurs moved up and down the lines, whispered calculations, the building energy of people who knew they had nothing to lose. Things had moved rather more briskly than Guilder would have liked—he'd hoped to get something useful before the hammer came down—but now the die was cast.

"Open the trucks."

The canvas was pulled away. An eruption of volcanic screaming: no mystery now. Guilder walked briskly to his car, got in, and told the driver to go. They pulled away in a plume of mud and dirty snow as, behind them, the orchestra unleashed its mortal symphony: a melody of shouts and screams, high and wild and full of fear, punctuated by the syncopated rhythm of automatic weapon fire, fading to the final pops as the cols moved through the fallen bodies, silencing the last.

56

Iowa. The ashy bones.

They'd exhausted their fuel near the town of Millersburg, sheltered the night in a roofless church, and set out the next morning on foot. Another seventy miles, said Tifty, perhaps a little more. They'd encountered two more bone fields like the first, the number of dead virals unimaginable. Thousands, millions even. What did it mean? What impulse had led them to lie down on the open earth, waiting for the sun to take them away? Or had they perished first, their corpses reclaimed by the morning light? Even Michael, the man of theories, had no answer.

They walked. Trudged, through snow that now rose in places to their knees. Their rations were scarce; they saw no game. They had been reduced to eating their final stores—strips of dried meat and suet that left a coating of grease on the roofs of their mouths. The earth felt crystallized, the air held in suspension, like bated breath. For hours, no wind at all, and then it came howling. Daylight came and left in the blink of an eye. Heavy parkas with fur-lined hoods, woolen hats pulled down to their brows, gloves with the tips of the fingers cut away in case they needed to use their weapons, though Peter wondered if they could actually manage this. He'd never felt so cold. He hadn't known cold like this existed. How Tifty maintained his bearings in this desolate place, he had no idea.

They passed their eighteenth night in an auto-repair shop that contained, miraculously, a potbellied woodstove of cast iron with a soapstone top. Now, what to burn? As darkness came on, Michael and Hollis returned from the house next door, carrying a pair of wooden chairs and armfuls of books. The *Encyclopaedia Britannica,* 1998. A shame to burn it, it went against the grain, but they needed the heat. Two more trips and they were supplied for the night.

They awoke to brilliant sunlight, the first in days, although the temperature had, if anything, dropped. A hard north wind rattled the branches of the trees. They allowed themselves the luxury of setting one last fire and huddled around it, savoring every bit of heat.

"Like . . . molting."

It was Michael who had spoken. Peter turned toward his friend. "What did you say?"

Michael's eyes were focused on the door of the stove. "How many do you think we've seen?"

"I don't know." Peter shrugged. "A lot."

"And they all died at the same time. So let's suppose what's happening is supposed to happen, that it's part of the viral life cycle. Birds do this, insects, reptiles. When part of the body is worn out, they cast it off and grow a new one."

"But we're talking about whole virals," Lore said.

"That's how it *looks*. But everything we know about them says they function as a group. Each one connected to its pod, each pod connected to its member of the Twelve. Never mind the mumbo jumbo about souls and all the rest. I'm not saying it isn't true, but that's Amy's turf. From my point of view, the virals are a species like any other. When Lacey killed Babcock, all of his virals died. Like bees, remember?"

"I do," said Hollis, nodding along. "Kill the queen and you kill the hive. That's what you said."

"And what we saw on that mountain bore it out. But suppose each one of the viral families is actually a single organism. Each of the Twelve is like a major organ—the heart, the brain. The rest are like the feathers on a bird, or the carapace of an insect. When it wears out, the organism sheds it, in order to grow a new one."

"They don't *feel* like feathers," Lore said acidly.

"Okay, not feathers, but you get the idea. Something peripheral, expendable. I've always wondered what was keeping so many alive. What's left to eat? We know they can go a long time without feeding—Tifty, you proved that—but nothing can survive indefinitely without food. From the standpoint of species longevity, it makes no sense to devour your entire food supply. As predators, they're actually *too* successful. The idea has always bothered me, because everything else about them is so organized."

"I'm not sure I'm following," Tifty said. "Are you saying they're dying out?"

"Obviously something's happening. The fact that it's occurring all at once implies that it's a natural process, built into the system. Here's another analogy. When the human body goes into shock, it draws blood away from the periphery and redirects it to the major organs. It's a defense mechanism. Protect what's important, forget the rest. Now imagine that each of the viral tribes is one animal, and that it's going into shock from starvation. The logical thing would be to radically reduce the numbers and let the food supply come back."

"And then what?" Peter asked.

"Then you start the cycle over."

For a moment, nobody spoke.

"Anyway," Michael continued, "it's just an idea I had. I could be full of shit."

Peter knew different. "So why is it happening here?"

"That," said Michael, "is what worries me."

The time for leaving was at hand; they'd stayed too long as it was. They gathered their gear and zipped up their parkas, bracing themselves for the blast of frigid air that would assail them the second they stepped through the door.

"Six days if the weather holds," said Tifty, hitching up his pack. "Seven at the most."

"Why do I wish it were more?" said Lore.

Grey. Grey.

His eyes popped open.

Can you feel them, Grey?

"Who's there? Guilder, is that you?"

I'm sorry I have been away. You are still my favorite, Grey. Since the very first day we met. Do you remember?

His stomach clenched: the voice of Zero.

"Stop it." His wrists yanked reflexively at the chains. He was lying in his own filth, his body stank, his mouth tasted permanently of blood. "Go away. Leave me alone."

You told me everything about yourself. You didn't even know you were doing it. Did you feel me in your mind even then?

—Get out, he thought. Get out get out get out. Wake up, Grey.

Oh, you're not sleeping. I've always been here. Even as you have lain in chains a hundred years, I have lain with you. Like the story of Job, who lay in the ashes, cursing his fate. God tested him, as I have tested you.

—I don't know you. I don't know what you are.

You don't, Grey? How can you not know? I am the God who abides with you. The one true God of Grey. Can you not feel my love? Can you not feel my wings of love spreading over you, forever and ever?

He had begun to weep.

—Let me die. Please. All I want to do is die.

You love her, don't you, Grey?

He swallowed, tasting the foulness of his mouth. His body was a cave of filth and rottenness.

—Yes.

The woman. Lila. She means everything to you.

—Yes.

Yours is the blood that flows in her veins, as mine flows in yours. Do you see? Do you understand? We are all of a piece, Grey. You lie in chains, but you are not alone. The God of Grey abides with you. The God of all that is, and all that is to come. The God of the next new world. There will be a special place for you in that world, Grey.

—The next new world.

They are coming, Grey.

—Who? Who is coming?

But even as he asked the question, he knew.

Our brothers.

57

And suddenly, she was free. Alicia Donadio, Last of the First, the New Thing and captain of the Expeditionary, was bounding over the wires, into the night, away.

She ran. She ran and kept on running.

She'd killed a few men along the way. Some women, too. Alicia had never killed a human woman before; it seemed not so very different, on the whole. Because in the end, everybody left their life in the same manner. The same surprise upon their faces, their fingers touching the wound with exploratory tenderness, the identical ethereal gaze, aimed into eternity. There was a certain grace to it.

Maybe that's why Alicia liked it as much as she did.

She found her gear where she'd left it hidden in the brush. A pike and cross. The RDF. Her bandoliers of blades. A change of clothes, a blanket, shoes. A hundred rounds of ammo but no gun to fire it. She'd left Sod's knife behind, embedded in the left kidney of a man who had commanded her to stop, as if she might actually do this. Racing from the detention center, she hadn't even known if it would be day or night. Time had been annihilated. The world she found was a changed place. No, that wasn't right. The world was the same; it was she who had changed. She felt apart from everything, spectral, almost bodiless. Above her the winter stars shone hard and pure, like chips of ice. She needed shelter. She needed sleep. She needed to forget.

She took refuge in a shed that at one time might have contained chickens. Half the roof was gone; only the barest form remained: a single wall left standing, the little cages encrusted with fossilized droppings, a floor of hard-packed earth. She wrapped herself in the blanket, her broken body shaking with the cold. *Louise,* she thought, *was it like this?* Her mind tossed with memories, bright flashes of torment that split her thoughts like lightning. When would it stop, when would it stop.

It was still dark when she awoke, her mind climbing slowly to awareness. Something warm was brushing the back of her neck. She rolled and opened her eyes to discover an immense dark form looming above her.

My good boy, she thought, and then she said it: "My good, good boy." Soldier dipped his face to hers, his great nostrils flaring, bathing her face with his breath. He licked her eyes and cheeks with his long tongue. It was a miracle. There was no other word. Someone had come. Someone had come, after all. Alicia had longed for this without knowing it, one soul to comfort her in this comfortless world.

Then, stepping improbably from the gloom, a figure, and a woman's voice, strange and familiar at once:

"Alicia. Hello."

The woman crouched before her, drawing down the hood of her long, wool coat. Her long black tresses tumbled free.

"It's all right," she said softly. "I'm here now."

Amy? But it was not the Amy she knew.

This Amy was a woman.

A strong, beautiful woman with thick, dark hair and eyes like windowpanes lit from behind with golden light. The same face but different, deeper; the impression was one of completeness, a coming into the self. A face, thought Alicia, of wisdom. Her beauty was more than appearance, more than a collection of physical details; it came from the whole.

"I don't . . . understand."

"Shhhh." She took Alicia's hand. Her touch was firm but tender, like a mother's, comforting her child. "Your friend. He showed us where you were. Such a handsome horse. What do you call him?"

Her mind felt heavy, benumbed. "Soldier."

Amy cupped Alicia's chin and lifted it slightly. "You're hurt."

How was this possible? How was anything possible? Beyond the shed Alicia saw a second figure, holding a pair of horses by the reins. A windblown swirl of white hair and a great pale beard masked his features. But it was the way he held himself, with a soldier's bearing, that told Alicia who he was; that this man in the snow was Lucius Greer.

"What did they do to you?" Amy whispered. "Tell me."

That was all it took. Her will collapsed, a wave of sorrow came undammed inside her. She did not speak so much as shudder the word: "Everything."

And at long last, a great sob shook her—a howl of purest pain and grief cast skyward to the winter stars—and in Amy's arms, Alicia began to weep.

Guilder. It's time.

Guilder, rise.

But Guilder did not hear these words. Director Horace Guilder was asleep and dreaming—a terrible, oft-repeated dream in which he was in the convalescent center, smothering his father with a pillow. Contrary to history, this did not proceed without a struggle. His father thrashed and flailed, his hands clawing at the air, fighting to break free as he issued muffled cries for mercy. Only when his resistance ceased, and Guilder removed the pillow from his face, did Guilder see his error. It wasn't his father he had killed, but Shawna. Oh, God, no! Then Shawna's eyes popped open; she began to laugh. She laughed so hard that tears came to her eyes. Stop laughing! he yelled. Stop laughing at me! Guilder, she said, you're so funny. You should see the look on your face. You and your crappy bracelet. Your mother was a whore. A whore a whore a whore . . .

Prepare the way, Guilder. Rise to meet them. The moment is at hand.

He jolted awake.

Our moment, Guilder. The birth of the next new world.

The information hit his brain like voltage. He bolted upright in his vast bed, its preposterous acreage of pillows and blankets and sheets, realizing, with faint embarrassment, that he'd fallen asleep with his clothes on. And why, he thought absurdly, did he need, of all things, a canopy bed? A bed so huge it made him feel like a doll? But he shook the question away. They were coming! They were here! He swiveled his feet to the floor and jammed them into the leather lace-ups that he had, apparently, possessed the energy to remove before passing out with exhaustion. Ramming his shirttail into his pants, he dashed to the door and down the hall.

"Suresh!"

The sound of his pounding caromed down the empty hall-way.

"Suresh, wake up!"

The door to Suresh's quarters opened to reveal his new chief of staff's sleepy, bronze-colored face. He was wearing a puffy white bathrobe and slippers, blinking like a bear exiting its cave.

"Cripes, Horace, you don't have to yell." He yawned into his fist. "What time is it?"

"Who cares what time it is? They're *here.*"

Suresh startled. "Right now, you mean?"

Rise up and meet them, Guilder. Bring them home.

"Don't just stand there, get dressed."

"Right, okay. I'm on it."

"Move, goddamnit!"

Guilder returned to his apartment and stepped into the bathroom. Should he shave? Wash his face at least? Why was he thinking like this, like a boy on prom night? He ran a damp hand through his hair and brushed his teeth, trying to calm himself. Was this what passed for toothpaste around this place? This awful-tasting gritty goo? For the love of God, why, in ninety-seven years, had they never managed to come up with a decent toothpaste?

He removed a fresh suit from the wardrobe. The blue tie, the red, the green and yellow stripes: he didn't know. He was suddenly so nervous his fingers could barely manage the knot. And hungry. A stone of cold emptiness sat in his gut. A visit with his old friend Grey would have been just the ticket to settle his nerves, but he should have thought of that earlier.

Standing before the mirror, he took a steadying breath. Easy, Guilder, easy. You know what to do. It's just another day at the office. It can't be any worse than a meeting with the Joint Chiefs, can it?

In point of fact, it could. But there was no use in dwelling on the prospect.

By the time he reached the lobby, Suresh was waiting with Guilder's driver. "The trucks are on their way," Suresh said as Guilder drew on his gloves. "You want a full detail to escort you?"

Guilder declined; he would go on his own. Best to keep things simple. The two men shook hands.

"Good luck," said Suresh.

As the car glided down the hill, Guilder's anxiety began to lessen. He was moving into the moment now. At the river they turned north and headed toward the Project. Its dark shape heaved from the earth like a headstone, a square of deeper blackness against the night sky. The portal was open, waiting.

They didn't stop but turned east on the service road. At one time it had been used to move equipment to the site: the quarried blocks of stone, the twirling cement mixers from the concrete plant, the flatbeds with their stacked girders of harvested steel. Now it would carry an altogether different delivery. They passed through the auxiliary gate. Five more minutes and they drew up to where the two semis were waiting in a field of frozen corn stubble.

Guilder told the driver to go. The semis' cabs were empty; their drivers, too, had departed. Guilder pressed his ear to the side of one of the trucks. He heard muffled murmurings inside, interspersed with a female sound of frightened weeping.

The voice in his head was silent. A profound stillness encased him like the anticipatory stillness before a storm. They would be coming from the west. He waited.

Then:

The first one appeared, then another and another, eleven points of glowing phosphorescence spaced at equal intervals on the horizon. The gaps between them narrowed as they neared, like the lights of a giant aircraft approaching.

Come to me, Guilder thought. *Come to me.*

Details began to emerge. Not so much to emerge as to enlarge. One was smaller than the rest—that would be Carter, of course, he thought; the unknowable, anomalous Anthony Carter—but the others took his breath away. In their powerful forms and graceful movements and absolute mastery of themselves they seemed to shrink the space around them, to bend dimensions, to rewrite the course of time. They flowed toward him like a glowing river, bathing him in the light of their majestic horror.

Come to me, he thought. *Come to me. Come to me.*

The moment of their arrival possessed a feeling of absolute completeness. A baptism. The closing covers of a book. A long dive into blue water and the instant of entry, the world wiped away. They stood before him, great and terrible. He drank the majestic, terrifying images of their memories as if dipped into a pool of purest madness. A weeping girl on a dirty mattress. A shopkeeper, hands raised, and the bony press of a gun's muzzle at the vertical crease between his eyebrows. A sensation of utter drunkenness, and a boy on his bicycle glimpsed through a windshield, and the thud of contact followed by a sharp jolt as his little body passed beneath the vehicle's wheels. A delicious feeling of sex, and a woman's eyes expanded to impossible wideness as the cord tightened around her neck. A chorus of terror, depravity, black evil.

I am Morrison-Chávez-Baffes-Turrell-Winston-Sosa-Echols-Lambright-Martínez-Reinhardt-Carter.

Guilder unlatched the cargo door of the first truck. The prisoners tried to run, of course. Guilder had ordered no shackles; he wanted nothing to constrict them. Most made it only a few steps. The few that got farther experienced, perhaps, a fleeting hope of salvation. Their pointless flight was part of the rapture. The moment unfolded in great splashes of blood and abruptly severed screams and living tissue torn asunder, and in the silence that followed Guilder stepped to the rear of the second truck and opened its door in welcome.

"Welcome, my friends. You are home at last. We will see to your every need."

X

THE ASSASSIN

I go, and it is done; the bell invites me.

—SHAKESPEARE,
MACBETH

58

Vale was gone, which could mean only one thing. Sara's turn would come next.

Jenny had disappeared as well. Two days after the bombing in the stadium, a new girl had taken her place. Was she with them? No, Sara would have detected it. A message under the plate, an exchange of reassuring glances. Something. But the girl—pale, nervous, whose name Sara didn't know and was never to learn—came and went in silence.

Lila had taken to her bed. All day long and into the night she tossed and turned. She roused only to bathe but shooed Sara's offers of help away. Her voice was drained; even speaking seemed to require all her energy. "Leave me be," she said.

Sara was alone, cut off. The system was collapsing.

She passed the days with Kate, but this time together felt different, final. The child could sense it too, as children did. What was the source of their powers of perception? Everything was colored by a mood of pointlessness. They played the usual games, not caring who won. Sara read the usual stories, but the child listened only vaguely. Nothing helped. The end of their time was approaching. The days were long and then too short. At night they slept together on the sofa, melded as one. The soft warmth of the girl's body was torment. Sara lay awake for hours listening to her quiet breathing, drinking in her scent. What are you dreaming? she wondered. Are you dreaming of goodbye, as I am? Will we see each other again? Is there such a place? Holding Kate close, she remembered Nina's words. *We'll get her out. Otherwise she has no chance.* My child, thought Sara, I will do what I must to save you. I will go when asked. It's the only thing I have.

On the third morning, Sara took Kate outside. The cold was biting, but she welcomed it. She pushed Kate on the swing for a time, then rode the teeter-totter with her. Kate had said nothing about Lila since the night Guilder had beaten her. Whatever cord had connected them had been severed. When the cold grew too fierce, they headed back inside. Just as they reached the door, Kate stopped.

"Somebody gave this to me," she said, and showed Sara. In her hand was a pink plastic egg.

"Who did?"

"I don't know. She was over there."

Sara followed the girl's gesture across the courtyard. There was no one. Kate shrugged. "She was there a second ago."

For just a few minutes, not more than five, Sara had let Kate wander off by herself.

"She told me to give it to you," Kate said, and held the egg out to her.

The woman had to be Nina, of course. Sara tucked the egg into the pocket of her robe. Her body felt numb. When Jenny had disappeared, she had allowed herself the faint hope that this burden would pass from her. How foolish she'd been.

"Let's keep this a secret—would that be okay?"

"She said the same thing." Then, her face brightening, Kate asked, "Is it a secret message?"

Sara did her best to smile. "That's it exactly."

She didn't open the egg right away; she was afraid to. When they returned to the dark apartment, they found Lila lighting the candelabras with a long match. Her face was drained of color, her hair brittle and askew. She called them over to the sofa and held out a book.

"Would you read to me?"

Little Women: Sara opened the cover to a puff of dust from its yellowed pages.

"I haven't heard this one in ages," Lila sighed.

Sara was made to read for hours. Part of her mind registered the story as interesting, but the rest was in a fog. The language was difficult, and she often lost her place. Kate's attention waned; eventually she fell asleep. It seemed entirely possible that Lila was going to make Sara read the entire book.

"I need to go to the bathroom," Sara said finally. "I'll be right back."

Before Lila could say anything, she stepped briskly to the lavatory and closed the door. She pulled up her robe and sat on the toilet and withdrew the egg from her pocket. Her heart was beating wildly. A flicker of hesitation; then she opened it and unfolded the paper.

The package is in the garden shed at the edge of the court-yard. Look beneath the floorboards to the left of the door. The target is the senior staff meeting in the conference room, to-

morrow 1130 hrs. Take the central elevator to the fourth floor, then the first hallway on the right. The last door on the left is the conference room. Tell the guard that Guilder sent for you. Sergio lives.

She had returned the paper to the egg when there came an urgent rapping on the door. "Dani! I need you!"

"Just a second!"

The handle jiggled. Had she locked it?

"I have the key, Dani! Please, open the door!"

Sara lurched off the toilet, sending the egg skittering across the floor. Shit! The key was turning in the lock. She had just enough time to shove the egg into the bottom drawer of the vanity before turning to see Lila standing in the open doorway.

"All done," she said. She heaved a smile onto her face. "What do you need, Lila?"

The woman's face blanched with confusion. "I don't know. I thought you'd gone somewhere. You scared me."

"Well, I did. I went to the bathroom."

"I didn't hear the toilet flush."

"Oh. Sorry." Sara turned and pulled the chain. "That was rude of me."

For a moment Lila said nothing. She seemed completely disconnected from reality.

"Could you do something for me? A favor."

Sara nodded.

"I would like some . . . chocolate."

"Chocolate." What was chocolate? "Where would I get that?"

Lila stared incredulously. "The kitchen, of course."

"Right. I guess that was obvious." Maybe someone in the kitchen would know what Lila was talking about. Sara didn't think it would be a good idea to come back empty-handed. "I'll go right away."

Lila's face relaxed. "Anything would be fine. Even a cup of cocoa." Her eyes unfocused; she gave a little sigh. "I always loved a cup of cocoa on a winter afternoon."

Sara stepped from the apartment. How much had Lila seen? Why hadn't Sara thought to flush the note down the toilet? Had she closed the drawer? She replayed the moment in the mind; yes, she had. There was no reason for Lila to go looking there, though to be safe, Sara would have to retrieve it before the serving girl returned.

The kitchen was located on the far side of the building; she'd have to cross the atrium, which was always full of cols.

Still riding a wave of adrenaline, she aimed her eyes at the floor and made her way down the hall.

As she entered the lobby she became aware of a commotion. An attendant was being escorted by two guards, her pitiful cries amplified by the room's expansive acoustics.

"Don't! Please, I'm begging you! I'll do better! Don't take me to the basement!"

The woman was Karen Molyneau.

"Sara! Help me!"

Sara halted in her tracks. How could Karen see her face? And then she realized that she'd made the one fatal error, the one thing she could never forget to do. She'd neglected to pull down her veil.

"Sara, please!"

"Stop."

The command had come from a third man. As he stepped forward, Sara recognized him immediately. The round belly, the fogged glasses riding the tip of his nose, the winglike eyebrows. The third man was Dr. Verlyn.

"You." He was examining her face intently. "What's your name?"

Her mouth had gone dry. "Dani, sir."

"She called you Sara."

"I'm sure she's mistaken." Her eyes flicked reflexively toward the exit. "I'm Dani."

"Sara, why are you doing this?" Karen was wriggling like a fish in a net. "Tell them I'm no insurgent!"

Verlyn's gaze hardened. The corners of his mouth lifted in a smile. "Oh, I remember you. The pretty one. I never forget a face, not one like yours."

Sara bolted for the door. Three strides and she went blasting through it. She tore down the steps, into the sun and wind, shouts rising behind her. "Stop her! Stop that woman!" Where could she run to? But there was no place; cols were racing toward her from all directions, hemming her in like a tightening noose. Sara's hand went to her pocket and found the little envelope of folded foil. Here it was, the end. She stopped on the path; there was no use running anymore—she had only a second or two. The package opened to reveal its lethal contents. She took the blotter between her thumb and index finger and raised it to her mouth. *Goodbye, my child, how I love you, goodbye.*

But it was not to be. As she brought the blotter to her lips, someone rammed her from behind, rocketing her off her feet; the ground fell away and rose again, slowly and then quickly and finally all at once, her skull collided with the pavement, and everything went black.

59

The three of them were lying with their bellies pressed to the upward slope of the culvert, Greer scanning the scene with the binoculars. The late afternoon sun was lighting fires in the clouds.

"You're *sure* this is the place," Amy said.

Alicia nodded. They had lain there for nearly three hours. Their attentions were focused on a wide-mouthed drainage pipe jutting from the base of a low hillside. The snow around the opening was crisscrossed with tire tracks.

The minutes passed. Alicia had begun to doubt herself when Greer raised his hand. "Here we go."

A figure had emerged from the pipe, wearing a dark jacket. Man or woman, Alicia couldn't tell. A scarf covered the lower half of the person's face; a wool cap was pulled down to the tops of the eyes. The figure paused, looking south with a hand to its brow.

"Looks like he's waiting for someone," Greer said.

"How do you know it's a man?" Alicia asked.

"I don't." Greer handed the binoculars to Amy, who pushed a strand of hair aside and pressed the lenses to her eyes. It was amazing to see, Alicia thought; in every aspect, even the smallest gesture, Amy was both the girl she'd always been and someone entirely new. As Greer told the story, Amy had gone into the belly of the ship, the *Chevron Mariner,* as one thing and had come out another. Even Amy couldn't provide an explanation. To Alicia, the oddest thing about it was the fact that it didn't seem odd at all.

"I can't tell either. But whoever's supposed to meet him is running late." Amy drew down the binoculars. Beneath her oversized wool coat, she still wore the shapeless tunic of the Order. Her legs were covered in thick woven leggings, her feet shod in laced boots of crinkled leather. "If we're going to find Sergio, I don't think we're going to get a better chance."

Alicia nodded. "Agreed. Major?"

"No objection here."

The only cover to conceal their approach was a line of brush on the east side of the pipe and a stand of bare trees on the hillside above it. Amy and Alicia left Greer to stand lookout and moved at a crouch along the culvert in opposite directions. Amy would take the right, at ground level; Alicia would drop down from above. Once they were in position, Greer would whistle, diverting the man's attention, and they would make their move.

Everything unfolded according to plan. Alicia scuttled on her belly to the top of the pipe. The crown of the man's capped head was right below her. From this angle, she wouldn't be able to see Amy, but Greer would. She waited for the signal, then:

Where did he go?

Rising to her knees, Alicia rotated in time to receive his full weight slamming into hers. Not *his* weight. Hers. In an airborne embrace they tumbled over the lip, the woman crashing down upon her as Alicia landed on her back in the snow.

"Who the hell are you?" The woman had pinned Alicia's arms with her knees and was holding a knife to her throat, the blade just nicking her skin. Alicia had no doubt that she would use it.

"Steady there. I'm a friend."

"Answer the question."

"Amy? A little help here?"

Amy had moved in from behind. Her approach had been absolutely soundless. Before the woman could react, Amy grabbed her by the collar and flung her sideways; as the woman leapt to her feet and lunged forward with the knife, Amy slapped it away, darted behind her, and locked her in a half nelson, the other arm gripping her around the waist. Alicia's only thought was: *I'll be goddamned.*

"Stop it," Amy said. "We want to talk, that's all."

The woman spoke through gritted teeth. "Go to hell."

"Don't you think I could break your neck if I wanted to?"

"Be my guest. Tell Guilder I said, Fuck you, too."

Amy glanced at Alicia, who had collected the woman's knife and was dusting snow from her pants. Greer was trotting toward them. "Does that name mean anything to you?" Amy asked.

Alicia shook her head.

"Who's Guilder?" she asked the woman.

"What do you mean, who's Guilder?"

"What's your name?" Amy asked. "You might as well tell me."

A moment's hesitation, then: "Nina, okay? It's Nina."

"I'm going to let you go now, Nina," Amy said. "Promise me you'll listen to what we have to say. That's all I'm asking."

"Fuck off."

Amy tightened her grip to make the point. "Do. You. Promise."

Another burst of struggle; then the woman relented. "Okay, okay. I promise."

Amy released her. The woman stumbled forward and spun around. A young face, not much older than twenty, but her eyes told a different tale—hard, almost ferocious.

"Who are you people?"

"That was a nice move," Alicia said to Amy. She twirled the knife around her index finger and passed it to her. "Where'd you learn that?"

"Where do you think? By watching you." She pointed her eyes at Greer. His long beard was clotted with snow, like the muzzle of a dog. "Lucius, could I ask you to stand lookout again? Let us know when the vehicle approaches."

"That's all? Just let you know?"

"It would be good if you could . . . delay them a little. Until we're done talking."

Greer jogged up the ridge. Amy addressed the woman again, making a small but meaningful gesture with the knife. "Take a seat."

Nina glared with defiance. "Why would I do that?"

"Because you'll be more comfortable. This is going to take some time." Amy slid the knife into her belt. *I'm done with this, if you behave.* "We're not at all who you think we are. Now sit."

Reluctantly, Nina lowered herself to the snow. "I'm not going to tell you anything."

"I very much doubt that," said Amy. "I believe you'll tell me everything I need to know, once I explain what's about to happen here."

"I want to play with Dani!"

"Eva, sweetheart—"

The little girl's face was flushed with anger. She snatched one of the leather cups off the floor and hurled it at Lila, missing narrowly.

"You go to bed!" Lila shouted. "You go to bed this instant!"

The girl was immovable. Her face was bright with loathing. "You can't make me!"

"I'm your mother! You do as I say!"

"I want Dani!"

She had filled a hand with dry beans. Before Lila could react, the little girl reared back and launched them with astonishing, hate-fueled force into Lila's face. More beans spattered on the floor behind her, a clattering rain. She leapt to her feet and began to tear through the apartment—yanking books from the shelves, batting things off tables, hurling pillows into the air.

"Stop it this instant!"

The girl picked up a large ceramic vase.

"Eva, no—"

The little girl heaved it over her head and brought it down like somebody slamming the trunk of a car. Not a crack but a detonation: the vase exploded into a million ricocheting shards.

"I hate you!"

Something was happening, something final. Lila knew this, just as she sensed, in a deeper layer of her brain, that all of this had happened before. But the thought went no further; the hard edge of something hit her head. The girl was throwing books.

"Go away!" she screamed. "I-hate-you-I-hate-you-I-hate-you!"

But as Lila watched her mouth forming these terrible words, they seemed to be coming from somewhere else. They were coming from inside her head. She lurched forward and grabbed the little girl around the waist and hoisted her off her feet. The girl kicked and screamed, wriggling in Lila's grip. All Lila wanted was—what? To calm the girl down? To get ahold of the situation? To silence the screaming that was tearing through her brain? For every ounce of force Lila applied, the girl replied in kind, shrieking at the top of her lungs, the scene ballooning to grotesque dimensions, a kind of madness, until Lila lost her footing, their combined centers of gravity tilted backward, and they went down hard, crashing into the dressing table.

"Eva!"

The little girl was scooting away from her. She came to a stop against the base of the sofa, glaring furiously. Why wasn't she crying? Was she hurt? What had Lila done? Lila approached her on her hands and knees.

"Eva, I'm sorry, I didn't mean it . . ."

"I hope you die!"

"Don't say that. Please. I'm begging you not to say that."

And with these words tears came at last to the little girl's eyes, though not tears of pain, or humiliation, or even fear. *I will despise you forever. You are not my mother and never were, and you know that as well as I.*

"Please, Eva, I love you. Don't you know how much I love you?"

"Don't say that! I want Dani!" Her tiny lungs expelled an amazing amount of sound. "I-hate-you-I-hate-you-I-hate you!"

Lila clamped her hands over her ears, but nothing would block the child's cries.

"Stop it! Please!"

"I-hope-you-die-I-hope-you-die-I-hope-you-die!"

Lila tore into the bathroom and slammed the door. But this accomplished nothing: the screaming seemed to come from everywhere, an obliterating roar. She fell to her knees, sobbing into her hands. What was happening to her? *My Eva, my Eva. What have I done, to make you hate me so?* Her body shook with pain. Her thoughts were swirling, tumbling, shattering; she was a million broken pieces of Lila Kyle spread across the floor.

Because the girl wasn't Eva. No matter how hard Lila wished to make it so, there was no Eva; Eva was gone forever, a ghost of the past. The knowledge poured through her like acid, burning the lies away. *Go back,* Lila thought, *go back.* But she could never go back, not anymore.

Oh, God, the terrible things she'd done! The terrible, awful, unpardonable acts! She wept and shook. She cried, as her father always said, stroking paint on his little boats, a river. She was an abomination. She was a stain of evil on the earth. Everything was revealed to her, everything was of a piece, time stopped and moved again in a reassembled continuum inside her, telling its history of shame.

I hope you die. I hope you die I hope you die I hope you die.

Then something else was happening. Lila found herself sitting on the edge of the tub. She had entered a state beyond volition; she chose nothing, everything was choosing her. She opened the tap. She dipped her hand into its current, watching the water flow through her fingers. So here it was, she thought. The dark solution. It was as if she'd always known; as if, in the deepest recesses of her mind, she'd been performing this final act, over and over, for a hundred years. Of course the tub would be the means. For hours she'd sunk into its warmth; whole decades had passed in its comforting immersion, its delicious erasure of the world, yet always it had whispered to her: *Here I am. Lila, let me be your last deliverance.* The steam swirled upward, clouding the room with its moist breath. A perfect calm encased her. She lit the candles, one by one. She was a doctor; she knew what she was doing. *Soy médico.* She stripped and examined her naked body in the mirror. Its beauty—for it *was* beautiful— filled her with memories: of being young, a child herself, emerging from the bath. You are my princess, her father had teased, rubbing her hair to dry it and hugging her in the soft warmth of a freshly laundered towel. You are the fairest in the land. The recollections flowed through the water. She was a child, and then a teenager, in her blue taffeta dress with a fat corsage pinned to the shoulder, each picture morphing into the next until finally she beheld a woman, full of maturely youthful strength, standing before the mirror in her mother's wedding gown. The bodice of delicate lace, the descending curtain of shimmering white silk: how her life in all its promise had seemed captured in that image. *Today is the day I will marry Brad.* Her hand fell to her belly; the wedding dress was gone, replaced by a vaporous nightgown. A morning sun was streaming through the windows. She turned and, in profile, cupped the voluptuous curve of her belly. *Eva. That's who you'll be; that is who you are. I will name you Eva.* The steam was rising, the tub nearly full.

Brad, Eva, I am coming. I have been away too long. I am coming to be with you now.

Three blue lines pulsed at the base of each wrist: the cephalic vein, winding upward around the radial border of the forearm; the basilic, commencing in the dorsal venous network before ascending the posterior surface of the ulnar side to join the vena mediana cubiti; the accessory cephalic, arising from the tributory plexus to merge with the cephalic at the back of the elbow. She needed something sharp. Where were the scissors? The ones Dani, and all the others who had come before, employed to trim her hair? She tried one drawer of the vanity and then the next, and when she came to the bottom, there they waited, gleaming with sharpness.

But what was this?

It was an egg. A plastic Easter egg, like the ones she'd hunted in the grass when she was just a girl. How she'd loved the ritual: the wild dash over the field, her little basket swinging in her hand, the dew on her feet and the slow accumulation of treasure, her mind envisioning the great white rabbit whose nocturnal visitation had left behind this bounty. Lila cupped the egg in her palm. She felt the faintest rattling within. Could it be . . . ? Was it possible . . . ? But what else *could* it be?

There was only one answer. Lila Kyle would die with the taste of chocolate on her tongue.

60

Treachery. *Treachery.*

How had the insurgency gotten so close? Could somebody please tell him that? First the redhead, then Vale, and now Lila's attendant, too? That quaking mouse? That anonymous nobody who looked at the floor whenever he entered the room? How deep inside the Dome did the conspiracy reach?

To Guilder's vast irritation, the redhead was still at large. She'd killed eleven people making her escape; how was that even *possible*? They'd never even learned her name. *Call me what you like,* she'd said, *just don't call me early in the morning.* Jokes, from a woman who'd been beaten continuously for days. As for Sod, Guilder, in hindsight, was forced to concede his error. Letting a man like that off his leash had been a one-way ticket to disaster.

Guilder supervised the attendant's interrogation himself. Whatever it was that gave the redhead her strength, this one was made of softer stuff. Three dunks in the tub were all it took to make her talk. The bomb in the shed. The serving girl, Jenny, though nobody had seen her in days. A hideout she didn't know the location of because they'd knocked her out, which made sense; that's what Guilder would have done. A woman named Nina, though the only Nina in the files had died four years ago, and a man named Eustace, whom they had no record of at all. All very interesting, but nothing he could make real use of.

Do you want us to try harder? the guard asked. We could, you know, go a few more rounds. Guilder looked down at the woman, who was still strapped to the board, her hair drenched by the ice-cold water, the last wet gasps shuddering through her. Sara Fisher, No. 94801, resident of Lodge 216, a worker in Biodiesel Plant 3. Verlyn remembered her from the haul they'd brought in from Roswell. So, one of those infernal Texans. Now that the eleven virals had arrived, he'd really have to do something serious about the Texas situation. The woman hardly seemed the type; he had to remind himself that she'd intended to kill him. Though, of course, there was no type; that's what the last violent months had taught him. The insurgency was everyone and no one.

Never mind, he told the guard. Get her hooked up. I think Grey will enjoy what this one has to offer. He always likes the young ones.

He took the stairs from the basement to his office, donned his glasses, and opened the drapes. The sun had just dipped below the horizon, jetting the clouds with ribbons of bright color. The sight was pretty, sort of. Guilder supposed it was the kind of thing he might have enjoyed, a century ago. But a person could only look at so many sunsets in a lifetime and muster an opinion. The problem of living forever, etc., etc., etc.

He missed Wilkes. The man hadn't always been the best company—he'd been far too eager to please—but at least he'd been somebody to talk to. Guilder had trusted him, confided in him. Across the years there wasn't much they hadn't gotten around to saying. Guilder had even told him about Shawna, though he'd masked the story in irony. *A whore, can you believe it? What a jackass I was!* My, but they'd had a good, long laugh at that. The thing was, this was just the sort of unconstructed, vaguely anxious hour when Guilder would have stuck his head from the door, summoning his friend into his office on some pretense—"Fred, get in here!"—but really just to talk.

His friend. He supposed they were. Had been.

Darkness came on. Guilder's gaze traveled down the hill to the Project. It would need a new name now. Hoppel would have been the guy for that; no doubt about it, he'd had a way with words. In his former life he'd been an ad guy with a big Chicago agency, experience he'd put to plentiful use concocting the catchphrases and jingles that kept the troops in rhetorical line, right down to the words of the anthem. *Homeland, our Homeland, we pledge our lives to thee. Our labors do we offer, without recompense or fee. Homeland, our Homeland, a nation rises here. Safety, hope, security, from sea to shining sea.* Corny as hell, and Guilder hadn't been so keen on the word "recompense"—it seemed a little bookish—but the thing scanned nicely and was, by the standards of its genre, not too hard on the ears.

So, what should they call it there? "Bunker" was too martial. "Palace" had the right general ring, but there was nothing palatial about the place. It looked like a big concrete box. Something religious? A shrine? Who would not go willingly into a shrine?

Just how many of the flatlanders would have to go, and at what frequency, remained to be seen; Guilder had yet to receive specific instructions from Zero on this point, the general sense being that things would come out in the wash. The Twelve—or rather, Eleven—might be different from your garden-variety viral, but they were what they were—eating machines, basically. No matter what directives came down from on high, a century of gobbling up everything with a pulse would be a hard habit to shake. But in the main, their diet would consist of a combination of donated human blood and domestic livestock. The right ratios needed to be scrupulously maintained; the human population had to grow. Generation by generation, human and viral, working together—which was, come to think of it, not a bad way to sell the thing. It was positively Hoppelesque. What was the term? Rebranding? That's what Guilder needed. A fresh point of view, a new lexicon, a new vision. A rebranding of the viral experience.

He might have really hit on something with this shrine business. The establishment of something rather like an official religion, with all the mumbo jumbo and ritualistic trappings, might be just the lubricant the gears of human psychology required. State worship was all stick and no carrot; it produced only an arid obedience to authority. But hope was the greatest social organizer of all. Give people hope, and you could make them do just about anything. And not just your average, everyday kind of hope—for food or clothes or the absence of pain or good suburban schools or low down payments with easy financing. What people needed was a hope beyond the visible world, the world of the body and its trials, of life's endless dull parade of *things*. A hope that all was not as it appeared.

And there it was, the name. How simple it was, how elegant. Not a shrine; a temple. The Temple of Life Everlasting. And he, Horace Guilder, would be its priest.

So, not such a worthless day after all. Funny how things could just come like that, he thought with a smile—his first in weeks. Screw Hoppel and his ditties. And while he was at it, screw Wilkes, that ingrate. Guilder had everything in hand.

First the injection, and the wooziness, and Sara, lying on a wheeled gurney, observed the ceiling flowing past.

"Alley . . . *oop.*"

Now she was somewhere else. The room was dim. Hands were lifting her onto a table, tightening straps around her arms and legs and forehead. The metal was chilly beneath her. At some point her robe had been removed and replaced by a cotton gown. Her mind moved with animal heaviness through these facts, noting them without emotion. It was hard to care about anything. Here was Dr. Verlyn, peering down at her through his tiny glasses in his grandfatherly way. His eyebrows struck her as extraordinary. He was holding a silver forceps; a wad of cotton soaked in brown fluid was clinched between the tines. She supposed that since he was a doctor, he was doing something medical to her.

"This may feel a little cold."

It did. Dr. Verlyn was swabbing down her arms and legs; at the same time, somebody else was positioning a plastic tube beneath her nose.

"Catheter."

Now, that was not so nice. That wasn't nice at all. A moan rose from her throat. Other things began to happen, various pokings and intrusions, the alien sensation of foreign objects sliding under her skin—her forearms, the insides of her thighs. There was a beeping sound, and a hiss of gas, and a peculiar odor under her nose, strikingly sweet. Diethyl ether. It was manufactured at the biodiesel plant, though Sara had never seen how this was done. All she remembered were tanks with the word FLAMMABLE stenciled in red on the sides, and their clattering bulk as they were rolled on dollies to a waiting truck.

"Just breathe, please."

What a strange request! How could she not breathe?

"That's it."

She was borne aloft on the softest cloud.

61

Two days had passed since they'd made contact with the insurgency. At first, Nina had failed to believe them, as anyone would. The story was too fantastic, the history too complex. It was Alicia who had finally come up with a way to prove their case. She retrieved the RDF from her pack and led the woman up the ridge and pointed it toward the Dome. Greer was watching the valley below. At this distance, Alicia worried that she wouldn't get a signal. What would they do then to convince the woman? But there it was, fat and clear, a continuous pulsation. Alicia was relieved but also perplexed: if anything, the signal was stronger. Amy was silent a moment, then said, We'll have to hurry now. That sound you're hearing: it means the remaining Twelve are already here. She drew the knife from her belt and passed it to Nina and told Alicia and Greer to disarm as well. We're surrendering to you, said Amy. The rest is up to you.

The truck arrived, carrying two armed men. Alicia and the others met them with arms raised. Their wrists were bound, black hoods drawn over their heads. An interval of time passed, the three of them freezing in the bouncing cargo bed; then they heard the sound of a garage door opening. They were escorted from the truck and told to wait. A few minutes passed; footsteps approached.

"Take them off," a man's voice said.

The hoods were removed, revealing half a dozen men and women standing before them with raised weapons—all but one.

"Eustace?"

"Major Greer." Eustace shifted his broken face toward Alicia. "And Donadio, too." He shook his head. "Why am I surprised?" He turned to the others and gestured for them to lower their guns. "It's all right, everyone."

"You *know* them?" Nina asked.

Eustace looked them over again, noticing Amy. "Now, you I don't think I've seen before."

"Actually," said Amy, "that's not precisely true."

They had arrived on the eve of Eustace's people making their move. Years of painstaking infiltration had reached the moment of culmination. First, the decapitation of the leadership, followed by simultaneous attacks on a range of major targets: HR stations, industrial infrastructure, the power station, the detention center, the apartment complex on the edge of downtown where most of the redeyes lived. Weapons and explosives had been cached throughout the city. Their forces were small, but once the attack was under way, they believed, their numbers would grow. The slumbering giant of seventy thousand flatlanders would awaken and rise. Once that happened, the insurrection would become an avalanche, unstoppable. The city would be theirs.

But something had gone wrong. Their operative in the

Dome had been found out. They knew she'd been taken alive, but not where—in all likelihood, the basement.

"I'm afraid there's something I must tell you," Eustace said, and explained who this operative was.

Sara was here. It strained belief. No, it went hurtling past it. And her daughter, too. Sara's. Hollis's. In some deep way, the child belonged to all of them. Their purpose had magnified, but so had the situation's complexity. They would have to get the two of them out.

Amy repeated the story she had told Nina. There could be no doubt that the virals were present somewhere in the city, or what this meant. Here was where they would begin rebuilding their legions. Eustace regarded their tale with skepticism, but then something clicked.

"Guilder will want to protect them," Amy said. "Is there someplace in the city that's unusually fortified? It would have to be large."

Eustace sent a man to retrieve the blueprints of the Project. Three people died to get these, Eustace said, and he unrolled the paper over the table.

"We never knew what this place was for. Lots of stories, but never anything that really added up. The place is a fortress. The redeyes have been building it for years."

Amy examined the blueprints, her eyes making swift calculations. "This is where we'll find them."

"I don't know how you can be so certain."

"Count the chambers."

Eustace bent over the paper. With his index finger, he traced each corridor to its destination. Then he looked up.

Thus their cause was joined to another. The building known as the Project was now the focus. Its design played in their favor: like the cave in New Mexico, the Project's tight quarters could amplify the explosive force of a single bomb detonated at the heart of the structure. But could they get inside? Doubtful—and even if they could, it would be like walking into a lion's den. Their losses would be heavy, and too many men would have to be diverted from other targets.

"So we don't go in to get them," Amy said. "We make them come to us."

"What do you have in mind?"

Amy thought a moment. "Tell me what kind of man Guilder is."

Eustace shrugged. Throughout the proceedings he had

taken no umbrage at their presence. It was good, he said, to be among Expeditionaries again.

"He's a monster. Cruel, obsessive, monomaniacal in the extreme. He's absolutely fixated on Sergio."

"What would he do if he captured him?"

"Have the time of his life, probably. But Sergio doesn't exist. It's just a name."

"But what if he did?"

Eustace rubbed a hand over his chin. "Well, the man likes a show. Probably he'd stage a public execution, make a big display."

"Public. Meaning everybody."

"I suppose." Eustace's expression shifted. "Oh. I see."

"Where would he do that?"

"The stadium's the only place large enough. It can hold seventy thousand easily. Which would—"

"Leave the rest of the Homeland undefended. Resources spread thin, major targets exposed."

Eustace was nodding now. "And if he's really interested in making a demonstration of power—"

"Exactly."

Bewildered glances were exchanged around the table. "Somebody, please enlighten me," said Nina.

Amy leaned forward in her chair. "Here's what we do."

It took another twenty-four hours to make ready. Nina returned to the city to contact the leaders of the various cells with new instructions. The insurgency's hideout would be forfeit, of course. They rigged it with trip-wire explosives—barrels of ammonium nitrate fertilizer and diesel fuel connected to sulfur igniters. Nothing would remain but an ashy hole; with luck, Guilder would presume that all inside had been killed, a mass suicide, the insurgency's final blaze of glory.

They prepared the vehicles for departure. Alicia would drive Amy to the pipe, then rendezvous with the rest of Eustace's men to continue to their fallback location. Now all they were waiting on was the weather—they needed snow to cover their tire tracks. It might be tomorrow; it might be a week; it might be never. An hour before sunset on the third day, a tantalizing dust of flurries began to fall. It stopped, then started up again, slowly gathering force, as if the weather had cleared its throat and spoken. *Go now.*

They drove out, a convoy of nine trucks carrying forty-seven men and women. Alicia peeled away and aimed her vehicle north. The snow formed a dense, whirling mass in the truck's headlights. Beside her, Amy, wearing an attendant's robe, was silent. Alicia had warned her what she would be facing; there was no reason to discuss it further, especially now.

Thirty minutes later they arrived at the pipe. Despite her better judgment, Alicia said, "You know what they'll do to you."

Amy nodded. A brief silence; then: "There's a purpose to everything. A shape. Do you believe that?"

"I don't know."

Amy pulled Alicia's hand off the wheel and took it in her own, twining their fingers together. "We're sisters, you know. Blood sisters. I know what's happening to you, Lish."

Amy's words felt like something falling inside her. And yet: of course she would know. How could Amy not know?

"Can you control it?"

Alicia swallowed with difficulty. Over the last two days, the desire had become intense. It was reaching its dark hand inside her, taking her over. Her mind was fogged with it. Soon it would overwhelm her will to resist.

"It's getting . . . harder."

"When the time comes—"

"I'm not going to let it."

All around, the snow was falling. Alicia knew that if she didn't leave soon, she might get stuck. One last thing needed to be said. It took all her courage to form the words.

"Take care of Peter. You can't let him know what happened to me. Promise me that."

"Lish—"

"You can tell him anything else. Make up a story. I don't care. But I need your word."

A deep quiet ensued, encasing the two of them. Alicia had been alone with this knowledge for too long; now it was shared. She searched her emotions. Loss, relief, the feeling of crossing a border into a dark country. She was giving him up.

"In a way, I've always known this would happen. Even before I met you. There was always somebody else."

Amy made no reply. Her silence told Alicia all she needed to know.

"You should go," Alicia said.

Still Amy said nothing. Her face was uncertain. Then: "There's something I haven't told you, Lish."

* * *

Gray day into gray day. The continent's vast inland empire of weather. Would it snow? Would the sun ever come out again? Would the wind blow at their backs or into their frozen faces? They walked and walked, hunched forward against the weight of their packs. There were no signs, no landmarks. The roads and towns were gone, subsumed like sunken ships beneath the waves of snowy prairie. Tifty confessed that he didn't know exactly where they were. Central Iowa, northeast of Des Moines, but anything more specific . . . He made no apologies; the situation was what it was. Why couldn't you have decided to do this in summer? he said.

They were almost out of food. They'd cut their rations in half, but half of nothing would be nothing. As they huddled inside a ruined farmhouse, Lore doled out the meager slices on the blade of her knife. Peter placed his beneath his tongue to make it last, the hardened fat dissolving slowly in the warmth of his mouth.

They went on.

Then, late on the afternoon of the twenty-eighth day, a vision appeared: materializing slowly from a colorless sky, a tall sign, rocking in the wind. They made their way toward it; a cluster of buildings emerged. What town was this? It didn't matter; the need for shelter trumped every other concern. They passed through the outer commercial ring, with its husks of supermarkets and chain stores, flat roofs long collapsed under the weight of winter snow, and continued into the old town. The usual remnants and rubble, but at the heart they came to two blocks of brick buildings that appeared sound.

"Don't suppose we'll find anything to eat in there," Michael said.

They were standing before a storefront, the front windows of which were amazingly unbroken. Faded lettering on the glass read, FANCY'S CAFÉ.

Hollis said, "Looks like they've been out of business for a while."

They forced the door and entered. A narrow space, with booths of cracked vinyl opposite a counter with stools; except for the dust, which caked every surface, it was remarkably undisturbed. From time to time one found such a place, a museum of the past where the passage of decades had somehow failed to register, more eerie than ruins.

Michael lifted a menu from a stack on the counter and opened it. "What's meatloaf? I get the meat part, but a loaf of it?"

"Jesus, Michael," Lore said. She was shivering, her lips blue. "Don't make it worse."

Hollis and Peter scouted the back. The rear door and windows had been sealed with plywood; a hammer and nails lay on the floor.

"We're not going to get much farther without food," Hollis said gravely.

"You don't have to remind me."

They returned to the front of the café, where the others were bundling themselves in blankets on the floor. Darkness was falling. The room was freezing, but at least they were out of the wind.

"I'm going to look around," Peter said. "Maybe I can figure out where we are."

He slogged his way across the street, then moved down the block, peering in the storefronts. He tried some of the doors, but all were locked. Well, they could come back in the morning and open a few to see what was there.

At the end of the second block he tried a handle without looking—he was just going through the motions now—and was startled when the door swung open. Stepping inside, he holstered his pistol and removed a match from the box in the breast pocket of his parka and struck the tip, cupping the flame against the breeze coming from the open door.

Well, son of a bitch.

Peter knew a supply cache when he saw one. Burlap bags were stacked against the walls of the otherwise bare room. He knelt and opened the nearest bag with a flick of his blade: dried beans. In another he found potatoes, in a third apples. He lit another match and raised it over the floor; there were footprints all around in the dust. Who had left this here? What did it mean?

Their situation was dire, but at least they wouldn't starve. Better to think about what to do next on a full stomach. He sank his teeth into an apple. It was flavorless, hard as a chunk of ice. He polished it off in a frenzy, jammed more into his pockets, and scanned the room for something he could use to carry food back to the others. In the corner he found a bucket full of copper wire. He dumped the wire on the floor, filled the bucket with apples and potatoes, and returned to the street.

He was instantly aware of something odd. The night seemed brighter. The moon? But there was no moon. A prickle of alarm danced over his skin, then he heard the sound. He turned his face away from the wind, listening hard. A distant rumbling. The sound was coming closer, becoming more distinct by the second.

Engines.

He dropped the pail and raced up the block toward the café. A line of vehicles was roaring toward him. He heard voices yelling, then a series of pops. Jets of snow flew up around him.

Somebody was shooting at him.

He tore through the door of the café just as a phalanx of guns opened fire, exploding the windows. *Get down!* he yelled, *Get down!*, but everybody already had. He dove over the counter, landing on top of Lore, who was holding her hands over her head. The blaze of the vehicles' headlights filled the room. Things were splintering, crashing, round after round being pumped into the tiny room.

"Michael! Where are you?"

His voice came from under one of the banquettes: "Who are they? What do they want?"

The question was rhetorical: whoever they were, they wanted to kill them.

"Tifty? Hollis?"

Michael again: "They're with me! Tifty's cut, but he's okay!"

"I've got Lore!"

A pause in the shooting; then they opened fire again.

"Can anybody see anything?"

"Three vehicles straight outside," Hollis called. "More down the street!"

"Maybe we should surrender!" Michael yelled.

"I don't think these are the sort of people you surrender to!"

The room was being pummeled. Peter had only his pistol; he'd left his rifle by the door. They'd never make it to the back, and the doors and windows were boarded up, anyway. The café was a death trap.

"What do you want to do?" Hollis called.

"Can Tifty move on his own?"

"I'm okay!"

Flattened to the floor, Peter swiveled his face to Lore. "What do you have?"

She showed him her knife. "Just this."

He aimed his voice over the counter: "We go on three! Somebody toss us a gun!"

It arrived from Michael's direction, dropping on top of

them. Lore took it and racked the slide. The guns outside had fallen silent again. Nobody out there was in any hurry.

"Shooting our way out of here isn't much of a plan," Lore said.

"I'd be happy to hear a better one."

Peter was rising to his knees when Lore stopped him with a hand. "Listen," she whispered.

He heard footsteps crunching snow, followed by a tinkle of glass underfoot. He raised a finger to his lips. How many were there? Two? A hostage, he thought suddenly. It was their only chance. There was no way to communicate with the others; he'd have to go on his own. He pointed to Lore, gesturing toward the far end of the counter, away from the door. He mouthed: *Make a noise.*

Lore slithered along the floor. Peter holstered his pistol and compressed his body to a crouch. When Lore was in position she looked at him, her face set, and nodded.

"Help me," she moaned.

Peter leapt to the top of the bar. As the nearest man turned, Peter drew his pistol and fired at the backlit shape and sailed down upon the second man, sending the two of them crashing to the floor. Peter's pistol clattered away. A moment of mad scrambling, arms and legs tangling; the man had a good thirty pounds on him, but surprise was on Peter's side. A semi was strapped to the man's thigh. Locking a forearm around his adversary's neck, Peter pulled him into a backward embrace, yanked the gun free of its holster, and shoved the muzzle into the curve of his jaw beneath his flowing silver hair.

"Tell them to hold fire!"

From their place on the floor, Peter found himself staring directly at Michael, hidden beneath one of the tables. His eyes grew very wide. "Peter—"

"I mean it," Peter told the man, pressing the barrel deeper. "Yell it, so everyone can hear."

The man had relaxed in his arms. Peter felt him shudder, though not with pain. The man had started to laugh.

"Stand down!" a new voice said—a woman's. "Everybody cease fire!"

The second man wasn't a man after all. She was sitting on the floor with her back braced against one of the booths, her right arm held across her chest to clutch her wounded shoulder.

"Flyers, Peter." Alicia drew her bloodied hand away. Now

she was laughing, too. "Lucius, can you believe he fucking shot me?"

62

At the base of the ladder, Amy touched the map to her torch. The paper caught instantly, snatched away in a flash of blue flame. She doused the torch in the trickle of water at her feet, ascended the ladder, and shoved the manhole cover aside.

She was in the alley behind the apothecary shop. She sealed the plate and peeked around the corner of the building; above the heart of the city, the Dome stood imperiously, its hammered surface shining with light. She drew down her veil and walked briskly from the alleyway. Men with dogs were moving along the barricades. She strode up to the guardhouse, where two men were blowing on their hands, and displayed her pass.

"This doesn't look right." He showed it to the second man. "Does this look right to you?"

The col glanced at it quickly, then looked at Amy. "Lift your veil."

She did as he asked. "Is there something wrong?"

He studied her face a moment. Then he handed back the pass. "Forget it. It's fine."

Amy threaded past them and headed up the stairs. None of the other men paid her any note; the guards at the gate had verified her presence as warranted. Inside, she marched past the guard at the desk, who barely glanced at her, crossed the lobby to the elevator, and rode it to the sixth floor.

The elevator opened on a circular balcony circumscribing the building's atrium. Four corridors led away, like spokes on a wheel. Amy made her way around the balcony to the third corridor and down its length to the last door, where the guard, a droopy-faced man with a tonsure of gray hair, was sitting on a folding metal chair, flipping through the brittle pages of a hundred-year-old magazine. On the cover was the image of a woman in an orange bikini, her hands pushed upward through her hair.

"The Director asked to see me," Amy told him, drawing up her veil.

His eyes broke from the page, finding Amy's, and that was all it took. She eased him to the floor, propped his back against the wall, and took the key from his belt. His chin was rocked forward onto his chest. She put her lips close to his ear.

"I'm going to go inside now. I want you to count to sixty—can you do that?"

His eyes were closed. He nodded slightly, making a murmur of assent.

"Good. Count to sixty, and when you get there, throw yourself off the balcony."

She unlocked the door and stepped inside. There was something deceptively benign about the room. Two wingback chairs faced an enormous desk, its polished surface gleaming faintly. The floor was covered in thick carpet, muffling everything but the sound of Amy's breathing. One whole wall was books; another displayed a large painting, lit by a tiny spotlight, of three figures sitting at a long counter and a fourth man in a white hat, all seen through a window on a darkened street. Amy paused to read the small plaque at the base of its frame: Edward Hopper, *Nighthawks,* 1942.

To her right was a pair of parlor doors with windows of leaded glass. Amy turned the knob and eased through.

Guilder was lying on top of the blankets in his underwear. A pile of cardboard folders floated in the sea of bedding beside him. Soft, windy snores were issuing from his nose. Where should she stand? She chose the foot of the bed.

"Director Guilder."

He jerked violently awake, darting a hand beneath his pillow. He pushed himself up the headboard, scrambling away from her; with both hands he leveled the pistol at her and cocked the hammer. He was trembling so profoundly Amy thought he might shoot her by accident.

"How did you get in here?"

She sensed his uncertainty. The robe of an attendant, but the face was none he knew. "The guard was very accommodating. Why don't you put that down?"

"Goddamnit, *who are you?*"

She heard voices from the hall, fists pounding on the outer door.

"I am Sergio," she said. "I've come here to surrender."

XI

THE DARKEST NIGHT OF THE YEAR

DECEMBER 21, 97 A.V.

My soul is in the midst of lions;
I lie among ravenous beasts—
men whose teeth are spears and arrows,
whose tongues are sharp swords.

—Psalm 57:4

CAPTURED!

A MESSAGE FROM THE
OFFICE OF THE DIRECTOR

The despicable murderer known as "Sergio"
is in custody!

The insurgency has been smashed!

Peace has been restored
to our beloved Homeland!

SENTENCE TO BE CARRIED OUT
BY PUBLIC EXECUTION
IN THE STADIUM

ALL WORKERS REPORT TO
HR PERSONNEL AT YOUR LODGES
2130 HRS TOMORROW

Stand together, Citizens of the Homeland!
Rejoice in this glorious day of justice!
Let all traitors know that this will be their fate!

Events had followed just as Amy had foreseen. The time and place of her execution were set; only the method had yet to be revealed—the final detail on which their plan depended. Would Guilder simply shoot her? Hang her? But if such a meager display was all he intended, why had he ordered the entire population, all seventy thousand souls in the Homeland, to observe? Amy had baited the hook; would Guilder take it?

Peter passed the next four days lurching between emotional poles—alternating states of worry and astonishment, both overlain with a powerful feeling of déjà vu. Everything possessed a striking familiarity, as if no time had passed since they'd faced Babcock on the mountaintop in Colorado. Here they all were, together once more, their fates drawn together as if by a powerful gravitational force. Peter, Alicia, Michael, Hollis, Greer: they had converged upon this place by different routes, for different reasons. Yet it was Amy, once again, who had led them.

Greer had related the story of her transformation: Houston, Carter, the *Chevron Mariner;* Amy's journey into the bowels of the ship and then her return. The full measure of what had passed between Amy and Carter, Greer couldn't tell them; all he knew was that Carter had directed them here. Beyond that, Amy either wouldn't or couldn't say.

That night at the orphanage, the two of them standing at the door, the tips of their fingers colliding in space: Had she known what was happening to her? And had he? Peter had felt in Amy's touch the pressure of something unstated. *I am going away. The girl you know will not be here when next we meet.* Which she had; the girl who Amy was had gone away. In her place was now a woman.

The group clothed their anxieties in unnecessary repetitions of their various preparations. The cleaning of weapons. The examination of blueprints and maps. The going over of checklists and the assorted mental inventories they would carry into war. Hollis and Michael became, in the last days, a kind of closed loop; their purpose had narrowed to Sara and Kate. Alicia dealt with the anxiety the way she dealt with everything—by pretending it wasn't important. The bullet from Peter's pistol had missed the bone and exited cleanly, a lucky thing, but even so. She would be healed in a day or two, but in the meantime the sling on her arm was a constant reminder to Peter of how close he'd come to killing her. When she wasn't barking orders, she retreated into unreachable silence, letting Peter know, without saying so, that she had entered the zone of battle. Greer intimated that something had happened to her in the cell, that she'd been beaten badly, but any attempt to ask her more about this, to offer comfort, was sternly rebuffed. "I'm all right," Alicia said with a peremptory tone that could only mean she wasn't. "Don't worry about me. I can take care of myself." She seemed, in fact, to be actively avoiding him, disappearing for long stretches; if he didn't know better, he would have said she was angry with him. She would return hours later smelling of horse sweat, but when Peter asked her where she'd gone, all she would say was that she'd been scouting the perimeter. He had no reason to doubt this, yet the explanation felt thin, a cover for something unstated.

Tifty, too, had undergone a subtle but significant change. His reunion with Greer had meant more than Peter had expected. They had served in the Expeditionary together, an inarguable bond, but Peter had not anticipated the depth of their friendship. A genuine warmth flowed between them. Peter puzzled over this at first, but the reason was obvious: Greer and Tifty had been here before, with Crukshank, all those years ago. The story of the field, and Dee, and the two little girls: of any man living, Greer best knew the heart of Tifty Lamont.

In this manner the hours, and then the days, moved by. Over everything two questions hovered: Would the plan work? And if it did, could they get to Amy in time?

On the third night, when Peter couldn't stand the waiting for one more second, he left the basement of the police station where everyone was sleeping, ascended the stairs, and stepped outside. The front of the building was protected by a broad overhang that kept the area clear of snow. Alicia was sitting with her back against the wall and her knees pulled to her chest. The sling had come off. In one hand she held a long, gleaming bayonet, serrated near the base; in the other was a sharpening stone. With calm, even strokes she was running the blade of the knife along the stone, first one side and then the other, pausing at the conclusion of each pass to examine her work. She seemed not to notice Peter at first, so intent was her focus; then, sensing his presence, she lifted her eyes toward him. It seemed her moment to speak, but she didn't say anything; her face bore no expression at all, beyond a kind of vague distraction.

"Mind some company?" he asked.

"Sit if you want."

He took a place beside her on the ground. Now he could feel it. The air around her seemed to prickle with barely contained rage. It flowed off her like an electric current.

"That's some knife."

She had resumed her patient sharpening. "Eustace gave it to me."

"You think it's sharp enough?"

"Just keeping my hands busy."

He groped for the next thing to say but couldn't find it. Where have you gone, Lish?

"I should be angry with you," he said. "You could have told me what your orders were."

"And then what would you have done? Follow me?"

"I'm AWOL as it is. A few more days wouldn't have made any difference."

She blew on the tip of the knife. "They weren't your orders, Peter. Don't get me wrong—I'm glad to see you. I'm not even that surprised. In a weird way, it makes sense you'd be here. You're a good officer, and we'll need you. But we all have our jobs to do."

He was taken aback. A good officer? Was that all he was to her? "That doesn't sound like you."

"It doesn't matter how it sounds. That's just how it is. Maybe it's time somebody said it."

He didn't know how to respond. This wasn't the Alicia he knew. Whatever had happened to her in that cell, it had driven her so far inside herself it was as if she wasn't there at all.

"I'm worried about you."

"Well, don't be."

"I mean it, Lish. There's something wrong. You can tell me."

"There's nothing to tell, Peter." She looked him in the eye. "Maybe I'm just . . . waking up. Facing reality. You should, too. This isn't going to be easy."

He felt stung. He searched her face, hunting for any scrap of warmth, finding none. Peter was the first to turn away.

"What do you think's happening to her?" he asked.

He didn't have to be any more specific; Alicia knew whom he was referring to.

"I'm trying not to think about it."

"Why did you let her go?"

"I didn't *let* her do anything, Peter. It wasn't up to me."

A chilly silence fell.

"I could really use a drink," Peter said.

She gave a quiet laugh. "Now, that's new. Those aren't words I believe I've ever heard you say before."

"There's a first time for everything." Then: "Do you remember that night in the bunker in Twentynine Palms when we found the whiskey?"

The bottle had been in a desk drawer. To celebrate the repair of the Humvees and their impending departure from the bunker, they'd passed it around, toasting the great adventure that awaited them on their journey east to Colorado.

Alicia said, "God, we all got so drunk. Michael was the worst. He never could hold his lick."

"No, I think it was Hightop. Remember how he broke open one of the light sticks and smeared that goo all over his face? 'Look at me, look at me, I'm a viral!' That kid was hilarious."

His mistake was instantly evident. Five years later, the boy's death was still a raw wound; in all that time, Peter had never heard Alicia so much as speak his name.

"Sorry. I didn't mean—"

A bright light flashed over the horizon. Lightning? In winter? Moments later they heard the boom, muted but unmistakable.

Eustace appeared at the foot of the steps. "I heard it too. Which direction?"

It had come from the south. It was hard to gauge the distance, but they guessed five miles.

"Well," Eustace said, nodding to himself, "I guess we'll know more in the morning."

Shortly after dawn, a messenger arrived, sent by Nina. The explosives at their hideout had done their work; their ruse had been successful. Minister Suresh, whom Guilder had sent to personally oversee their capture, was rumored to be among the dead. A taste, everyone hoped, of things to come.

But it was the second part of the message that offered the most promise. A semitruck had been parked outside the Project since the prior evening. It was guarded by a large security detachment, twenty men at least. The last piece had fallen into place; the virals were on the move. Guilder had tipped his hand.

Everybody knew the implications of what they were attempting. The plan seemed sound, but the odds were long. Guilder's orders to move the population to the stadium implied that the rest of the city would be only lightly protected, and if everything proceeded according to design, the insurgency would accomplish in one stroke a beheading of virtually every aspect of the regime. But timing would be critical; with so many elements of the resistance acting independently, and lacking the ability to communicate with one another once the siege was under way, it wouldn't take much for things to fall apart. Any variable could throw the operation into chaos.

The greatest variable was Sara. Assuming she was in the basement of the Dome, staging a rescue operation would be strategically cumbersome, and nobody knew where her daughter was. She could be in the Dome, or she could be someplace else entirely. Once they stormed the building and the shooting started, distinguishing between friend and foe would be nearly impossible. The decision they came to was that Hollis and Michael would lead an advance team to the basement. Five minutes would be all they'd have. After that, the building and all its inhabitants would be fair game.

Eustace would head up the operation against the stadium itself. The contents of the explosives package, a form of nitroglycerin, had been stolen from the Project site during construction and subsequently modified to their purpose, making it more potent but also highly unstable. It was of the same type that had been delivered to Sara in the Dome and was now presumed lost. Despite its power, the only way to guarantee the outcome was to deliver it to the eleven virals, as Eustace said, "in person, a bomb with legs." Peter failed to understand this at first; then the meaning came. The legs would be Eustace's.

Their teams would enter the city at four locations, all branched to the main storm pipe. Eustace's team, which included Peter, Alicia, Tifty, Lore, and Greer, would use the confusion at the stadium to infiltrate the crowd; elements of the insurgency under Nina's command would already be in position in the bleachers to seize control when the moment came. Weapons had been concealed in the lavatories and under the stairs to the upper bleachers. Eustace's appearance on the field would be the signal to attack.

At the first touch of darkness, they set out. There was no

point in concealing their tracks; one way or the other, they would never be returning. The night was clear, the sky wide and starlit, a vast indifferent presence gazing down. Well, Peter thought, maybe not so indifferent. He certainly hoped that someone up there cared, as Greer had said. It was hard to believe only a few weeks had passed since their conversation in the stockade. They reached the pipe and began to walk. Peter found himself thinking not only of Amy but Sister Lacey, too. Amy was one thing; she was another. The woman had faced Babcock with absolute fearlessness, a pure acceptance of the outcome. Peter hoped he would prove as worthy.

At the base of the manhole closest to the stadium, the group exchanged final words. The other teams, moving to locations throughout the Homeland, would remain concealed belowground until they heard the detonation in the stadium, which would serve as the signal to commence their assaults. Only Hollis and Michael would move sooner. There was no way to predict the moment to act; they would have to follow their instincts.

"Good luck," Peter said. The three men shook hands, then, when this seemed inadequate, embraced. Lore rose on tiptoes to kiss Hollis on his bearded cheek.

"Remember what I said," she told him. "She's waiting for you. You'll find her, I know it."

Hollis and Michael made their way down the tunnel, their images fading, then gone. With handshakes all around and wishes for luck, the other groups departed behind them. Peter and the others waited. The cold was numbing; all of them had wet feet, their shoes soaked by the fetid waters. Eustace was wearing an olive jacket, the deadly cargo concealed beneath. Nobody spoke, but the silence that encased the man ran deeper. In a private moment, Eustace had assured Peter that there was simply no other way. He was glad to do it, in fact. Many people had been sent to their deaths at his orders. It was only right that his turn should come.

It was a little after 1700 hours when, from the top of the ladder, Tifty said, "It's starting. We need to move."

They would exit one at a time at one-minute intervals. The opening lay beneath a pickup truck that a member of Nina's team had left in place on the south side of the stadium. Sooner or later it would be noticed and remarked on— *What's that doing there?*—but so far it had escaped attention. From the manhole each of them would make their way into the lines of people flowing into the stadium. A tricky moment, but only the first of many.

Eustace went first. Greer watched from the top of the ladder. "Okay," he said, "I think he made it."

Lore and Greer followed. Once inside, they would rendezvous at specific points within the structure. Alicia would be the next to last; Tifty would bring up the rear. Peter got into position at the base of the ladder. Alicia was standing behind him. Like all of them, she was disguised in a flatlander's scratchy tunic and trousers.

"Sorry about your arm," he said, for the hundredth time.

Alicia smiled in her knowing way. It was the first smile he'd seen in days. "Hell, it was probably about time one of us shot the other. We've practically done everything else. I'm just glad your aim is so bad."

"This is a touching scene," Tifty said dryly, "but we really have to *go.*"

Peter hesitated; he didn't want those words to be the last thing the two of them ever said to each other.

"I told you you'd get your chance, didn't I?" Alicia hugged him quickly. "You heard the man—get moving. I'll see you when the dust settles."

And yet she did not look at him when she spoke, averting her glance with misted eyes.

The question before him was this: what the hell should he wear?

The era of suits and ties had come to an end for Horace Guilder. That part of his life was over. A suit was the outfit of a government official, not the high priest of the Temple of Life Everlasting.

It was all a little nerve-racking. He'd never been to church much, even as a kid. His mother took him once in a while, but his father never went. But as Guilder recalled it, some kind of robe was standard. Something along the lines of a dress.

"Suresh!"

The man limped into the bedroom. What a sight he was. His face was swollen and pink; his brows and lashes had been scorched away, giving his eyes a startled appearance. He had cuts and bruises all over, puckered and raw-looking. It would all pass in a few days, but in the meantime the man looked like a cross between an Easter ham and the loser of a lopsided boxing match.

"Get me an attendant's robe."

"What for?"

Guilder waved him toward the door. "Just get it. A big one."

The summoned article was produced. Suresh lingered, evidently hoping for some explanation for Guilder's curious request, or perhaps just looking forward to the sight of Guilder wriggling into the thing.

"Don't you have someplace to be?"

"I thought you wanted me to stay here."

"Jesus, don't be dense. Go see about the car."

Suresh hobbled away. Guilder positioned himself in front of the full-length mirror with the gown held before him. For the love of God, he was going to look like a clown in this thing. But the clock was ticking; HR would be bringing the flatlanders into the stadium any minute. A little delay wasn't necessarily bad—it would ramp up the anticipation—but crowd control would get to be an issue if he dawdled for too long. Best to face the music; over his head went the robe. The image in the mirror wasn't a clown after all, more like the bride at an Amish wedding. The thing was utterly shapeless. He removed a pair of neckties from the rack in his closet, knotted them together, and cinched the waist. A definite improvement, but something was missing. The priests he recalled from his boyhood brushes with religion had always worn some kind of shawl. Guilder went to the window. The drapes were held against the window frame by heavy golden ropes with tassels at the ends. He unhooked them and balanced them over his shoulders, the tassels swaying at his waist, and returned to the mirror. Not bad for somebody who knew absolutely nothing about religion or, for that matter, fashion. What a shock it would be to historians of the future to learn that Horace Guilder, High Priest of the Temple of Life Everlasting, Rebuilder of Civilization, Shepherd of the Dawn of the New Age of Cooperation Between Human and Viral, had sanctified himself with a pair of curtain tiebacks.

He opened the door to find Suresh waiting for him. The man's bald eyes widened.

"Don't say a word."

"I wasn't going to."

"Well, don't."

They rode the elevator to the lobby. The building was strikingly silent; Guilder had sent most of his personal detachment to the stadium. This spread the cols and redeyes thin, but keeping the stadium under control was paramount.

The vehicles were waiting, chuffing exhaust into the cold: Guilder's car, the semi with its magnificent cargo, a pair of escort trucks, and a security van. He walked briskly to the van, where two cols were standing at the rear. One thing about a priest's vestment: it didn't offer much warmth on a winter night. He should have brought a coat.

"Open it."

It was hard to believe that the figure seated before him on the bench had been the source of so much trouble. She might have been considered pretty, if Guilder's thoughts ran in that direction. Not that she was dainty—she wasn't. Underneath the swelling and discoloration, she was obviously a solid specimen. Deep-set eyes, strong features, a taut, muscular frame that was nonetheless feminine. But in Guilder's imagination, Sergio had always been a man, and not just any man; the mental portrait he'd concocted was a knockoff of Che Guevara, some banana republic revolutionary with eyes like pinpricks and a scraggly beard. This was Joan of Arc.

"Anything to say for yourself?" Guilder couldn't have cared less; the question was just for fun.

Her wrists and ankles were shackled. Her split and swollen lips gave her voice a thickened quality, as if she had a bad cold. "I'd like to say I'm sorry."

Guilder laughed. Sergio was sorry! "Tell me, what are you sorry for?"

"For what's about to happen to you."

So, defiant to the end. Guilder supposed it came with the territory, but it was nonetheless irritating. He wouldn't have minded banging her around a little more.

"Last chance," the woman said.

"You have an interesting point of view," Guilder replied. He stepped back from the open door. "Seal her up."

For a long time, perched on the edge of the bed, Lila watched her. Slants of light from the window fell across the child's sleeping face, blond curls flowing over the pillow. For days she had been beyond the reach of comfort, alternating between hours of sullen refusal to speak and explosive, toy-throwing tantrums, but in sleep her defenses dissolved and she became a child again: trusting, at peace.

What is your name? Lila thought. *Who are you dreaming of?*

She reached out to touch the little girl's hair but stopped herself. The child wouldn't awaken; that wasn't the reason. It was the unworthiness of Lila's hand. So many Evas over the years. And yet there had only ever been one.

I'm sorry, little girl. You didn't deserve this; none of them did. I am the most selfish woman in the world. What I did, I did for love. I hope you can forgive me.

The child stirred, tightening the covers around herself, and pivoted her face toward Lila's. Her jaw flexed; she made a little moan. Would she awaken? But no. Her palm slid under the curve of her cheek, one dream passed into the next, and the moment slipped away.

Better that way, thought Lila. Better that I should simply fade into darkness. She rose gingerly from the bed. At the door she turned for one last look, bathed in memory: of a time when she had stood at the nursery door with Brad, in the house they had made together with their love, to watch their little girl, this swaddled newborn bundle, this miracle upon the earth, sleeping in her crib. How Lila wished she herself had died, all those years ago. If heaven were a place of dreams, that's the dream she would have passed eternity inside.

Farewell, she thought. Farewell to you, somebody's child.

The scene outside the stadium was one of ordered chaos, a human vastness on the move. Peter slid into the stream. Nobody even looked at him; he was one more anonymous face, one more shorn head and filthy body in rags.

"Keep it moving, keep it moving!"

In four lines they flowed up a ramp and passed through an iron gate into the stadium. To Peter's left, a series of concrete staircases ascended to lettered gates; ahead, a longer flight climbed to the upper decks. The crowd was being divided—two lines to the lower stands, two up the stairs. The field was brilliantly lit; light poured through the gates. Peter tried to catch a glimpse of Lore or Eustace, but they were too far ahead of him. Maybe they'd already broken away. The letters ascended. P, Q, R, then: S.

Peter dropped to one knee, pretending to tie his shoelaces. His successor in line bumped him, grunting in surprise. Whatever you did, you didn't stop.

"Sorry, go ahead."

The line bunched as it flowed around him. Through shuffling legs he glimpsed the nearest guard. He was gazing vaguely in Peter's direction from a distance of ten yards—probably attempting to discern the source of the interruption. *Look away,* thought Peter.

A flick of the col's eyes, and Peter darted into the crawl space underneath the stairs. No shouts rose behind him. Either he had gone unnoticed or the crowd didn't care, locked into their habit of obedience. The entrance to the men's room was ten feet away, at the base of the bleachers. There was no door, only a cement-block wall angled for privacy. Peter peeked around the stairs. An obscuring barrier of shuffling flatlanders marched past. *Now.*

The room was surprisingly large. On the right was a long line of urinals and stalls. He moved briskly to the last and pushed open the door to see a fierce-looking woman with short, dark hair perched on the rim of the toilet, aiming a heavy-handled revolver at his face.

"Sergio lives."

She lowered the gun. "Peter?"

He nodded.

"Nina," she said. "Let's go."

She led him to a tiny room behind the lavatory: a desk and chair, wheeled buckets with mops, and a line of metal lockers. From one of the lockers Nina withdrew a pair of guns of a type Peter had never seen before, something between a rifle and a large pistol, with an extra-long magazine and a second handle jutting from the underside of the barrel.

"Know how to use one of these?" she said.

Peter drew back the bolt to show that he did.

"Short bursts only and fire from the waist. You'll get twelve rounds per second. If you hold the trigger down, the clip will empty fast."

She handed him three extra magazines, then pulled open a drawer-like panel in the wall.

"What's that?" Peter asked.

"The garbage chute."

Peter stood on the chair, wedged himself inside, and dropped down feetfirst. The corridor was tipped like a slide, cushioning his descent, but not enough. He landed hard, his feet skidding out from under him.

"Who the hell are *you*?"

There were two of them, dressed in suits. Redeyes. Lying helplessly on his back, Peter could do nothing. He was clutching the gun over his chest, but shots would be heard. As he scrabbled away, simultaneously attempting to rise to his feet, both men drew pistols from belt holsters.

Then, Tifty. He appeared behind the one on the left and swung the butt of his rifle upward into the man's head. As the second turned, Tifty kicked his feet out from under him, dropped to his knees to straddle his back, yanked him by the hair to angle his head upward, wrapped his neck with his free arm and twisted. A crunching pop, then silence.

"Okay?" Tifty glanced up at Peter. The dead man's head, still locked by Tifty's forearm, sagged at an unnatural angle. Peter looked at the other redeye. Dark blood was seeping from his head onto the floor.

"Yeah," Peter managed.

A rattling from behind them and Nina dropped down. She landed catlike, fluidly raising her weapon to sweep it over the room.

"I see I'm late." She angled the gun to the ceiling. "You're Tifty?"

For a moment the man said nothing. He was staring at her intently.

"You can let go of him, you know," she said. "He's not going to get any more dead."

Tifty broke his gaze away. He released the dead man's head and rose to his feet. He seemed a little shaken; Peter wondered what had thrown the man off.

"We better hide these bodies," Tifty said. "Did Eustace make it in?"

"We'd have heard it if he didn't."

They were in some kind of loading area. A tunnel, wide enough to fit a good-sized truck, led to the left, presumably to the outside; to the right was a smaller hallway. An arrow painted on the wall bore the words VISITORS' LOCKER ROOM.

They dragged the corpses behind a pile of crates and moved down the hall. They were under the field now, on the south side. The hallway ended at a flight of stairs going up. The light was barely enough to see by. Overhead Peter heard the rumble of the crowd.

"We wait here till it starts," Nina said.

In the back of the van, Amy could see nothing. A small window separated the cargo area from the cab, but the driver had left it closed. Her body felt like she'd been dragged from a runaway horse, but her mind was clear and focused on the moment. The van descended the hill and leveled out, the tires spitting up mud and snow into the wheel wells.

"Hey, you back there."

The window had opened. The driver glanced at Amy through the mirror with a smile of wicked delight.

"How's it feel?"

The man in the passenger seat laughed. Amy said nothing.

"You fucking people," the driver said. His eyes narrowed in the mirror. "You know how many of my friends you killed?"

"Is that what you call them?"

"Seriously," he said with a dark laugh, "you should see these things. They are going to rip you apart."

The van was bouncing through deep potholes, jostling the chains. "What's your name?" Amy asked.

The driver frowned; it wasn't the kind of question he expected from a woman on the way to her execution.

"Go on, tell her," the other man said. Then, shifting his weight to angle his face to the opening: "He's Ween."

"Ween?" Amy repeated.

"Yeah, everyone calls him that on account of he's got a short one."

"Ha, ha," the driver said. "Ha, ha, ha, ha."

The conversation seemed over. Then the driver flicked his eyes to the mirror again.

"That thing you told Guilder," he said. Amy could read the uncertainty in his voice. "About what was going to happen. I mean, you were bullshitting, right?"

Amy hooked a foot under the bench and shot her thoughts deep into his eyes. At once the driver stomped on the brake, slamming the second man face-first into the windshield. A crash sent him jerking backward again as the vehicle behind them clipped the van's bumper with a sound of breaking glass and crunching metal.

"What the hell is wrong with you?" The second man was pressing a hand to his face. Blood dripped through his fingers. "You broke my nose, you asshole!"

The convoy had come to a halt. Amy heard a rapping on the driver's window.

"What's going on? Why did you stop?"

The driver replied sluggishly: "I don't know. My foot fell asleep or something."

"Jesus, look at this," the second guard said. He was holding out his bloodied hands for the man at the window to see. "Look what this idiot did."

"Do you need another driver?"

Amy watched the driver's face through the mirror. He gave his head a dislodging shake. "I'm okay. I just . . . I don't know. It was weird. I'm fine."

The man at the window paused. "Well, be careful, all right? We're almost there. Keep it together."

He moved away; the van began to creep forward again.

"You are an unbe*liev*able dick, you know that?"

The driver didn't answer. He darted his eyes to Amy's, their gazes ricocheting in the mirror. A split second, but she saw the fear in them. Then he looked away.

2140 hours. Hollis and Michael were crouched in the alley behind the apothecary. Using binoculars, they'd watched Amy being loaded into the van, followed by the departure of the convoy for the stadium. The assault team that would take the Dome, a dozen men and women armed with firearms and pipe bombs, was still concealed in the storm pipe, fifteen feet below.

"How long do we wait?" Michael said.

The question was rhetorical; Hollis merely shrugged. Though the city had an empty feel, the entrance to the Dome was still defended by a contingent of at least twenty men they could see from the alleyway. The thing they weren't saying was that they had no way of knowing if Sara and Kate were even in the building or how to find them if they were, assuming they could actually get past the guards—a chain of contingencies that in the abstract had seemed surmountable but that now rose before them with stark definition.

"Don't worry about Lore," Hollis said. "That girl can take care of herself, believe me."

"Did I say I was worried?" But of course Michael was. He was worried about all of them.

"I like her," said Hollis. He was still scanning the scene with the binoculars. "She'd be good for you. Better than Lish."

Michael was taken aback. "What are you talking about?"

Hollis pulled the lenses away and looked him in the eye. "Please, Circuit. You've never been a very good liar. You remember when we were kids, the way you two went at it? It couldn't have been more obvious even then."

"It was?"

"To me, anyway. All of it. You, her." He shrugged his broad shoulders and looked through the binoculars again. "Mostly you. Lish I could never read."

Michael tried to assemble a denial, but the attempt collapsed. For as long as he could remember, there had been a place in his mind where Lish stood. He'd done his best to suppress his feelings, since nothing good could come of them, but he'd never quite managed to tamp them down completely. In fact, he'd never managed it at all. "Do you think Peter knows?"

"Lore's the one to worry about. The girl doesn't miss much. But you'd have to ask him. I'd say so, but there's a way of knowing something without knowing it." Hollis tensed. "Hold up."

A vehicle was approaching. They pressed themselves into the doorway. Headlights blazed down the alley. Michael held his breath. Five seconds, then ten; the truck moved away.

"You ever shot anybody?" Hollis asked quietly.

"Just virals."

"Trust me. Once things get going, it's not as hard as you think."

Despite the cold, Michael had begun to perspire. His heart was hammering against his ribs.

"Whatever happens, just get her, all right?" he said. "Get them both."

Hollis nodded.

"I mean it. I'll cover you. Just get through that door."

"We'll both go."

"Not from the looks of things. You need to be the one, Hollis. Understand? Don't stop."

Hollis looked at him.

"Just so that's clear," said Michael.

Like the others, Lore and Greer had successfully faded into the crowd. Where the lines of flatlanders separated, they nudged their way into the stream being directed to the second tier, then the third, and finally the top of the stands. They met beneath the stairs that led to the control rooms.

"Nicely done," Greer whispered.

They retrieved their weapons: a pair of old revolvers, which they would use only as a last resort, and two blades, six inches long with curved steel pommels. The last of the crowd was being ushered into place. Greer marveled at the flatlanders' orderliness, the numb submission with which they allowed themselves to be led. They were slaves but didn't know it—or perhaps they did but had long since accepted the fact. All of them? Maybe not all. The ones who hadn't would be the deciding factor.

"Would you like to pray with me?" he said.

Lore looked at him skeptically. "It's been a while. I'm not sure I'd know how."

They were facing each other on their knees. "Take my hands," Greer said. "Close your eyes."

"That's it?"

"Try not to think. Imagine an empty room. Not even a room. Nothing."

She accepted his hands, her face faintly embarrassed. Her palms were moist with anxious sweat.

"I was kind of thinking you were going to say something, the way the sisters do. Holy this and God bless that."

He shook his head. "Not this time."

Greer watched her close her eyes, then did so himself. The moment of immersion: he felt a spreading warmth. In another moment his mind dispersed into a measureless energy beyond thought. *O my God,* he prayed, *be with us. Be with Amy.*

But something was wrong. Greer felt pain. Terrible pain. Then the pain was gone, subsumed by a darkness. It rolled over his consciousness like a shadow crossing a field. An eclipse of death, terror, black evil.

I am Morrison-Chávez-Baffes-Turrell-Winston-Sosa-Echols-Lambright-Martínez-Reinhardt . . .

He jolted away. The spell was broken; he was back in the world. What had he seen? The Twelve, yes, but what was the other? Whose pain had he felt? Lore, still kneeling, her empty hands outstretched, had experienced it, too: Greer could see it in her shocked face.

"Who's Wolgast?" she said.

Lila's feet seemed barely to touch the ground as she walked down the corridor toward the atrium. There was a feeling of invincibility to her actions; once made, certain decisions could not be undone. The stairs she sought were situated at the end of a long hallway on the opposite side of the building. As she turned the corner she broke into a run, headed for the door as if pursued. The heavyset guard rose from his chair to bar her way.

"Where do you think you're going?"

"Please," she gasped, "I'm starving. Everybody's gone."

"You need to get out of here."

Lila lifted her veil. "Do you know who I am?"

The guard startled. "I'm sorry, ma'am," he stammered. "Of course."

He pulled the key from a cord affixed to his belt and fit it into the lock.

"Thank you," Lila said, making her best show of relief. "You're a godsend."

She descended the stairs. At the bottom she faced the second guard, who was standing before the steel door that led to the blood-processing facility. She hadn't been down here in many years, but she remembered it clearly in all its mercenary horror: the bodies on tables, the vast refrigerators, the bags of blood, the sweet smell of the gas that kept the subjects in everlasting twilight. The guard was watching her with his hand resting on the butt of his pistol. Lila had never fired a gun in her life. She hoped it wasn't hard.

She stepped toward him with a confident gait, lifting her face at the last instant to look him deeply in the eyes.

"You're tired."

Concealed behind the dugout on the north side of the stadium, Alicia dropped the magazine from her semi, examined it to no purpose, blew imaginary dust from the top, and slid it back into the handle, shoving it into place with the base of her palm. She had now removed and reinserted the magazine ten times. The gun was a .45 ACP with a cross-hatched wooden handle, twelve rounds in each clip. Twelve, thought Alicia, and noted the irony. Strange, and not unpleasing, how the universe sometimes worked.

A murmur broke through the crowd. Alicia rose on her knees to peer out at the field. Had it begun? A curious object was being towed into the field—a Y-shaped steel armature, twenty feet high, affixed to a broad platform. Chains swung from the booms at the top. The truck halted in the middle of the field; two cols appeared and jogged back to the trailer. They slid blocks under the tires, winched up the nose, unhooked the trailer from the truck, and drove away.

She made her final preparation. The bayonet was tied with rough twine to her thigh. She freed it and slid it into her belt. *Amy,* she thought, *Amy, my sister in blood. All I ask is this. Let me be the one to kill Martínez.*

As the line of vehicles came to a halt outside the main ramp to the stadium, Guilder's nerves were still jangling from the collision with the van. They were lucky it hadn't been worse.

But if he'd thought their safe arrival would bring relief, the sight of the stadium, blazing with light in the winter dark, quickly disabused him of this notion. He exited the car to an immense sound of humanity. Not cheering—these people were much too cowed for that—but a crowd of seventy thousand in one place made a noise of its own, intrinsic to its mass. Seventy thousand pairs of lungs opening and closing; seventy thousand pairs of idle feet bobbing; seventy thousand backsides shifting on cement bleachers, trying to get comfortable. There were voices in the mix as well, and coughing, babies crying, but mostly what Guilder heard was a sort of subterranean rumble, like the aftershock of an earthquake.

"Get her in place," he said.

The guards yanked her from the van. Guilder didn't feel the need to look at her as they dragged her away. He signaled to Suresh to have the semi moved into position. The truck pulled forward and glided up the ramp toward the end zone.

Guilder had given extensive thought to the matter of presentation. Some pageantry was called for. He'd struggled with what to do until he'd come upon an appropriately crowd-whipping analogue: the orchestrated arrival on the field of play of a major sports franchise. Suresh would function as stage manager, coordinating the various visual and auditory elements that would lift the evening's demonstration to the level of spectacle. Together they'd gone through the items on the checklist: sound, lighting, display. They'd done a dry run that afternoon. A few problems had emerged, but nothing that couldn't be dealt with, and Suresh had assured him that everything would come off without a hitch.

They made their way up the ramp; Suresh, limping, did his best to keep up. HR personnel lined both sides of the idling semi; the staff had already been seated in the lower boxes. The noise of the crowd seemed to flow toward Guilder like a wave, immersing him in its energy. The plows had swept the field of snow, leaving behind a muddy landscape; in the center, the platform and armature awaited. A nifty device: it was Suresh who'd come up with the idea. The insurgency had nearly blown him up; who wouldn't be a little mad? As a physician he also seemed to know better than anyone interesting ways to kill people. Suspending her high in the air would give everyone a chance to see her insides unraveling; she'd feel more that way, too, and feel it longer.

While Guilder reviewed his notes, Suresh fitted him with his microphone, running the cable down his back to the transmitter, which he clipped to Guilder's improvised belt of neckties. "Flick this here," Suresh said, drawing his attention to the toggle switch, "and you're on."

Suresh backed away. He drew down his earphones, adjusted his microphone, and began the countdown:

"Sound booth."

(Check.)

"Lights."

(Check.)

"Fire teams."

(Check.)

And so on. Guilder, listening vaguely, shook out his robed arms like a boxer preparing to step into the ring. He had always wondered about this gesture, which seemed like empty showmanship. Now he understood the sense of it.

"Good to go when you are," Suresh said.

So: the moment at last. What a shock the crowd was in for. Guilder slid his glasses onto his face and took a last, long breath.

"All right, everyone," he said. "Let's look alive. It's game time."

He stepped forward, into the light.

64

"Dani, wake up."

The voice was familiar. The voice belonged to someone she knew. It drifted toward her from high above, saying this curious, half-remembered name.

"Dani, you have to open your eyes. I need you to try."

Sara sensed her mind emerging, her body taking shape around her. She felt suddenly cold. Her throat was tight and dry, sweet-tasting. She was supposed to open her eyes—that's what the voice was telling her—but her lids felt like they weighed a thousand pounds apiece.

"I'm going to give you something."

Was the voice Lila's? Sara felt a prick in her arm. Nothing. Then:

Oh!

She bolted upright, violently curling forward at the waist, her heart thudding against her rib cage. Air rushed to her lungs, expelled by a dry cough that screeched across the parched lining of her throat.

Lila pressed a cup to her lips, bracing the back of Sara's head with her palm. "Drink."

Sara tasted water, cold water. The images around her began to coalesce. Her heart was still racing like a bird's. Bits of pain, real and remembered, jabbed at her extremities. Her head felt like it was only vaguely related to the rest of her.

"You're all right," said Lila. "Don't worry. I'm a doctor."

Lila was a doctor?

"We need to be quick. I know it won't be easy, but can you stand?"

Sara didn't think she could, but Lila made her try. She swung her legs to the side of the gurney, Lila helping her by the elbow. Below the hem of Sara's gown, white bandages encircled her upper thighs. More bandages dressed her lower arms. All of this had happened without her being aware of it.

"What did they do to me?"

"It's the marrow they take. They start with the hips. That's the pain you feel."

Sara eased her feet to the floor. Only then did it occur to her that Lila's presence was an aberration—that she was freeing her.

"Why do you have a gun, Lila?"

Gone was the frail, uncertain woman Sara had come to know. Her face radiated urgency. "Come."

Sara saw the first body when they stepped into the hall: a man in a lab coat lying face-down on the floor, his arms and legs splayed in the random arrangement of swift death. The top of his skull had been blasted off, its contents splashed over the wall. Two more lay nearby, one shot in the chest, the other through the throat—though the second man wasn't dead. He was sitting upright against the wall, his hands encircling his neck, his chest moving in shallow jerks. It was Dr. Verlyn. Through the hole in his neck, his rapid breathing made a clicking sound. His lips wordlessly working, he looked at Sara with pleading eyes.

Lila was tugging her by the arm. "We need to hurry."

She didn't have to say it again. More bodies—the splashes of blood and startled postures and expressions of surprise in unseeing eyes—flowed past. It was a massacre. Was it possible that Lila had done this? They came to the end of the hall, where the heavy steel door stood open. A col lay beside it, shot in the head.

"Get her out of the building," Lila commanded. "It's the last thing I'll ask of you. Do whatever you have to."

Sara understood that she was speaking of Kate. "Lila, what are you doing?"

"What should have been done long ago." A look of peace had come into her face; her eyes glowed with warmth. "It will all be over soon, Dani."

Sara hesitated. "My name's not Dani."

"I thought perhaps it wasn't. Tell me."

"It's Sara."

Lila nodded slowly, as if agreeing that this was the right name for her to have. She took Sara's hand.

"You will be a good mother to her, Sara," she said, and squeezed. "I know it. Now run."

A hush fell over the crowd as Guilder stepped onto the field, all seventy thousand faces swiveling to look at him. He stood still a moment, drinking in the stillness as his eyes traveled the grandstands. He would make a humble entrance, like a priest's. Time seemed to stretch as he walked to the platform. Who knew it could take so long to cross fifty yards? The silence around him seemed to deepen with every step.

He arrived at the platform. He gazed out upon the crowd, first one side of the field, then the other. His hand slipped to his waist and located the toggle.

"All rise for the singing of the anthem."

Nothing happened. Had he hit the right button? He glanced toward Suresh, who was standing on the sidelines, making a frantic rolling motion with his hand.

"I *said,* please rise."

Begrudgingly, the crowd took to its feet. "Homeland, our Homeland," Guilder began to sing, "we pledge our lives to thee . . ."

Our labors do we offer, without recompense or fee. Homeland, our Homeland, a nation rises here. Safety, hope, security, from sea to shining sea . . .

With a sinking feeling, Guilder realized that almost nobody else was singing. He heard a few isolated voices here and there—HR personnel and, of course, the staff, manfully croaking the words from the fifty-yard line—but this only heightened the impression that the crowd, basically, was on strike.

Homeland, our Homeland, of peace and plenty fair. The light of heaven shines upon your beauty rich and rare. One mind! One soul! Your love is all we see. Let all combine with heart and hand: one Homeland, strong and free!

The song didn't end so much as turn a corner and fall down. Not a good sign at all. The first of several beads of sweat shot from his armpit to slither unimpeded down the length of his torso. Maybe he should have found somebody who could actually sing to warm up the crowd. Still, Guilder had a few things planned to engage the people fully in the evening's transformational festivities. He cleared his throat, glanced toward Suresh once more, received the man's approving nod, and spoke.

"I stand before you today on the eve of a new era—"

"Murderer!"

A buzz of voices shivered through the crowd. The shout had come from behind him, somewhere in the upper decks. Guilder spun around, blindly searching the sea of faces.

"Killer!"

The voice was a woman's. Guilder saw her standing at the railing. She waved a fist madly in the air.

"You butcher!"

"Somebody arrest that woman!" Guilder barked into his microphone, too loudly.

A general catcalling erupted. Objects went sailing through the air, lobbing onto the field. The crowd was throwing the only thing it had. The crowd was throwing its shoes.

"Monster! Assassin! Torturer!"

Guilder was frozen. None of this was what he'd expected at all.

"Demon! Tyrant! Swine!"

"Devil! Satan! Fiend!"

If he didn't do something fast, he'd lose them completely. He gave Suresh the signal; the switch was thrown. To an orchestrated explosion of colored light and smoke, the pickup carrying the woman in its bed bounded onto the field, the semi lumbering behind it. Simultaneously, the fire teams went racing around the edges of the field, igniting barrels of ethanol-soaked wood, making a flickering perimeter of flame. As the pickup halted at the platform, the semi turned in a wide circle and began to back up. The guards dropped the gate of the pickup, yanked the woman from the bed, and flung her to the muddy ground at the base of the platform.

"Get up."

The crowd was in an uproar—booing, whistling, hurling shoes like missiles.

"I said, get up."

Guilder kicked her hard, in the ribs. When she made no cry he kicked her again, then hauled her to her feet and shoved his face so close to hers that the tips of their noses practically touched.

"You have no idea what you're about to face."

"Actually, I do. You could say we're of a very long acquaintance."

He didn't know what to make of this curious claim, but he didn't care. He signaled to the guards to take her away. The woman offered no resistance as they dragged her to the base of the armature and pressed her to her knees. There were streaks of mud on her cheeks, her tunic, in her hair. Under the blazing lights she seemed meager, almost doll-like, and yet Guilder could still discern the defiance in her eyes, an absolute refusal to be cowed. He hoped the virals would take their time, maybe bat her around a bit. The guards unlocked her shackles, then reattached her wrists to the chains that hung from the armature.

They began to winch her up.

With every foot of her ascent, the roars of the crowd intensified. In protest? Anticipation? The pure emotional thrill of watching a person ripped apart? They hated him, Guilder understood that, but they were part of this thing now; their dark energy had joined to the night's transformative power.

The woman came to a rest high in the air, her arms held from her sides, her body swaying.

"Last words?"

She thought a moment. "Goodbye?"

Guilder laughed. "That's the spirit."

"I meant that the other way around."

Guilder had heard enough. He turned toward the rear of the semi. Two cols in heavy pads were posted by the doors. Suresh was watching him intently from the sidelines; Guilder caught his eye and nodded.

Hey, Lila, he thought, you delusional has-been, get a load of *this*.

And suddenly there was silence. A great freezing of all movement as the stadium was dipped in darkness.

A burst of blue.

The time to move had arrived. Greer and Lore burst from their hiding place and charged up the stairs. A single col was standing guard at the door to the control room. Greer got there first.

"What the fuck?" The guard noticed the knives. "Whoa," he said.

Greer gripped him by the ears—conveniently oversized, jutting from the sides of his head like a pair of handles—and rammed his own forehead into the man's skull. Down he went, felled like a tree.

They flew through the door. Again, just one man awaited, a redeye. Wearing chunky earphones with a microphone, he was seated before a panel of lights and switches. A wall of windows looked down on the field, bathed in blue. The earphones were a plus; their entry had gone unnoticed. The tacit understanding between Greer and Lore said that it was now her turn.

The redeye lifted his face. "Hey, you're not supposed to be here."

"True," said Lore, who slipped behind him, placed her left hand on his forehead, and drew her knife across his throat, cutting it like paper.

The doors of the semi swung open.

They emerged in magnificence, like kings. Their movements were stately, deliberate; they showed no haste, only the pure self-possession of their kind. No one could mistake what they were. They towered. They occupied space with a glorious immensity of height and breadth. They had fed on the blood of generations, inflating their persons to colossi. Even Carter, with his modest dimensions, seemed, in the company of his brethren, to partake of their magnificence. At the wondrous sight of them, the crowd made a collective inhalation of breath. Screams would follow, of this fact Guilder had no doubt, but in the moment of the eleven virals' emergence, a deep, anticipatory quiet reigned. The mighty beings stepped forward in rich display. Their backs were erect, their powerful claws articulating like immense devices of pain. They had the aspect of giants. They were legend made flesh, the great bestriders of the earth. The guards raced for the sidelines, to live another day, though Guilder paid this no notice. His mind was full of glory.

My brothers, Guilder thought, *I offer you this token, this foretaste. This tender morsel, this beginning. My brothers, come forward and together we will rule the Earth.*

Nina's team of assassins tore up the stairs. They surfaced at field level in a dugout situated just below the bleachers where the senior staff members were seated. Once Eustace began his run they would spring onto the field, turn to face their enemies, and unleash the contents of their short-barreled automatics.

But now, crouched in the final moments of their concealment, they, like everyone in the crowd, experienced an emotion that was one part terror, one part wonder, one part something else that lacked any point of reference in their lives. Peter was simultaneously attempting to process three competing visual facts. The last of the Twelve were before him, mere yards away; Amy, suspended in chains, was the bait that had drawn them forth; Amy was not Amy but a grown woman. Greer and Alicia had tried to prepare him, but no words could have readied him for this reality.

Where was Eustace?

Then Peter saw him. He was standing at the rail in the end zone—just another flatlander, dragooned into the role of witness. The eleven virals stood before Guilder like a platoon of soldiers awaiting orders. *Goddamnit,* Peter thought, *you're too far apart. Get closer to each other, you bastards.*

Guilder raised his arms.

Lila, alone. The Dome was silent, like a great animal holding its breath. This place, she thought. This tabernacle of pain. How could such a place be allowed to exist on the earth?

The gun was empty; she placed it on the floor and darted back down the hall. Behind each door lay a person on a slab, their life force slowly draining away. There was no time to save them, that was Lila's one regret, but at least she could release them from their torment.

Room by room she traveled, unsealing the doors with the ring of keys she'd taken from the guard. A few words of benediction for each trapped soul within; then she opened the valves on the ether tanks. A cloying sweetness filled the air. Her movements began to feel sluggish; she would have to work quickly. Leaving the doors open behind herself, she made her way down the corridor. The warning signs were posted at regular intervals on the walls of the hallway: ETHER PRESENT. NO OPEN FLAMES.

She came to the final door. She tried one key and then another and another, her fingers heavy and imprecise, the gas already inside her. The serrations bit and held.

Lila's heart shattered at the sight of him. They had chained him to the floor. He lay in naked degradation, suspended eternally at the precipice of death. Monsters! How could she have let this scene of anguish pass? How could she have waited a hundred years to alleviate his pain?

"Lawrence, what have they done to you?"

She hurled herself to her knees beside him. His eyes were open, but his stare seemed to pass through her to another world. She smoothed his wrinkled cheeks, his shriveled brow. She dipped her head to his, their foreheads touching as she stroked his face. "Lawrence," she whispered, over and over, "my Lawrence."

His lips at last formed words: "Save . . . me."

"Of course I will, my darling." The tears were pouring forth, a torrent. The gas was in the hall. From the pocket of her gown, Lila removed the box of matches. "We will save each other."

High above the field, Greer and Lore were also waiting for the eleven virals to move.

"Goddamnit," Greer said, the binoculars pressed to his eyes, "why aren't they doing anything?"

Guilder's hands were still raised. What was happening? He dropped them to his sides and lifted them again, waving with agitation. Still no response.

"Mother*fucker*!"

Lore's hand was poised on the switch. Her voice was frantic. "What should I do? What should I do?"

"I don't know!"

Then Greer saw movement on the field. A figure was racing from the end zone: Eustace.

"Do it! Turn on the lights!"

Even then, it was too late.

Sara, running: she tore across the atrium—was that gunfire outside?—and down the hall to Lila's apartment, rocketing through the door.

"Kate!"

The child was asleep in her bed. As Sara scooped her up, her eyes fluttered open. "Mummy?"

"I'm here. Baby, I'm here."

Now she was sure of it: there was shooting outside. (Though she could not be aware of this, this was the moment when her brother, Michael, rushing up the stairs, took a bullet to his right thigh, a pain he found oddly unimportant, so fueled was he by a rush of pure adrenaline. Hollis hadn't lied: once things got rolling, shooting somebody wasn't hard at all, and he picked off two more guards before his leg folded beneath him, the gun slipped from his hand— the thing was empty anyway—and his vision lit with stars.) Down the hall Sara dashed, carrying her child. *My child, my child.* They would live or they would die, but whichever it was they would do it together; never would they part again.

She hit the atrium at a sprint just as a man came blasting through the front doors. There was blood on his shirt; he was holding a gun. His bearded face was lit with a look of wild determination. Sara stopped in her tracks.

Hollis?

* * *

From her position high above the ground, Amy took in the whole of the scene. The crowd of thousands in its wild uproar; Guilder, his arms irrelevantly raised; the emergence of Nina's team from the dugout, and the subsequent unleashing of their firepower upon the rows of suited men, who screamed and dove for cover and sometimes did nothing at all, sitting with uncomprehending composure as their bodies were splashed with rosy arcs of death; Alicia appearing on the field, weapon drawn, ready to charge; Eustace streaming toward them from the end zone, the bomb clutched to his chest, and behind him the col who dropped to one knee, raised his rifle, and took him in its sights; the spurt of blood, and Eustace spinning and tumbling, the bomb squirting away. These events moved around her like planets in their orbits, a whirling cosmos of activity, yet their presence touched her only in passing, brushing her senses like a breeze. She stood at the center, she and her kinsmen, and it was there, on that stage, that all would be decided.

—My brothers, hello. It's been a while.

We are Morrison-Chávez-Baffes-Turrell-Winston-Sosa-Echols-Lambright-Martínez-Reinhardt . . .

—I am Amy, your sister.

That was when she felt him. In the midst of evil, a shining light. Amy sought out Carter with her eyes. He stood slightly apart, his body crouched in the posture of his kind.

It wasn't Carter.

—Father.

Yes, Amy. I am here.

A rush of love swelled her heart. Tears rose to her throat.

—Oh, Daddy, I'm sorry. Look away. Look away.

As the field blazed with light, Amy closed her eyes. It would be like opening a door. That was how she had imagined it. An act not of will but of surrender, to give away this life, this world. Images flashed through her mind, swifter than thought. Her mother kneeling to hug her, the bright force of her embrace, then a view of her back as she walked away; Wolgast, his big hand poised at her spine, standing beside her as she rode the carousel beneath the lights and music; a view of a starlit winter sky, on the night when they had made the snow angels; Caleb watching her with his knowing eyes as she tucked him into bed, asking, "Did anyone love you?"; Peter, standing at the door of the orphanage, their hands meeting in space, saying with touch what could not be said with words. The days flowed through her one by one, and when they had passed, Amy sent her mind outward to those she cherished, saying goodbye.

She opened the door.

At the edge of the field, Peter and the others, having emptied their magazines into the lower tiers, were dropping their clips to reload. They did not yet know that Eustace had been shot, only that the lights had come on as planned, signaling the start of his run; at any moment they expected the explosion to come from behind them.

It didn't.

Peter spun toward the platform. The virals, doused by the lights, had adopted various postures of self-protection. Some were staggering backward with their faces buried in the crooks of their arms. Others had dropped to the ground, curling in on themselves like babes in their cribs. It was an awesome sight, one Peter would remember all the days of his life, yet it paled in comparison to what was occurring above the platform.

Something was happening to Amy. She was convulsing against the chains, wracked by contractions of such violence it seemed she might shatter into pieces. Spasm after spasm, their power intensifying. With a final, bone-breaking jolt she went limp; for a hopeful moment Peter thought it was over.

It wasn't over.

With a deep animal howl, Amy threw back her head. Now Peter understood what he was seeing. Something that should have taken hours was happening in seconds. The facial features melting into fetal vagueness. The spine elongating, fingers and toes stretching into clawed prehensility. Teeth ejected in advance of the picketlike rows, and the skin hardening into its thick, crystalline carapace. The space around her had begun to glow, as if the air itself were lit by the accelerated force of her transformation. With a violent jerk Amy pulled the chains across her chest, snapping them clean from their blocks, and by the time she reached the ground, crouching with liquid grace to absorb the impact of her fall, there were not eleven virals on the field but twelve.

There were Twelve.

She rose. She roared.

Which was when, in the basement of the Dome, Lila Kyle and Lawrence Grey, their fates never to be known, joined hands, counted to three, brushed the match across the striker, and all the lights went out.

65

The explosion in the basement, fueled by the fiery ignition of thirty-two hundred pounds of highly compressed diethyl ether inhalant, produced a release of energy roughly equivalent to the crash of a small passenger jet. With nowhere else to go, its explosive force rocketed upward, seeking any alley of travel to accommodate its rapidly oxygenating expansion—stairwells, hallways, ductwork—before folding back on itself and blasting through the floor. Once it was unleashed into the larger spaces of the building, the rest was up for grabs. Windows blew. Furniture went airborne. Walls were suddenly there no longer. It rose and as it rose it expelled a gyring wake of pure destruction like a tornado in reverse, everything flung up and out from its white-hot heart, until it found the bones of the structure itself, the steel girders and meticulously chiseled limestone blocks that had suspended its roof above the Iowa prairie since the days of the pioneers, and blew them all to pieces.

The Dome began to fall.

Three miles away, the spectators in the stadium experienced the destruction of the Dome as a chain of discrete sensory occurrences: first a flash, then a boom, followed by a deep seismic rattle and a clamping down of blackness as the city's power grid collapsed. Everybody froze, but in the next instant something changed. A new force roused to life inside them. Who could say who started it? Insurgents planted in the stands had already begun their assault on the guards, but now they weren't alone. The crowd rose up in violence, a wild mob. So ferocious was their undammed fury that as they fell upon their captors it was as if their individuality had dissolved into a single animal collective. A swarm. A stampede. A pod. They became their enemy, as all must do; they ceased to be slaves, and so became alive.

On the field, Guilder was . . . dissolving.

He felt this first in the backs of his hands—an abrupt constriction of the skin, as if he were being shrink-wrapped. He held them up to his face. In numb incomprehension—the pain had yet to arrive—he watched as the flesh of his hands puckered and began to split open in long, bloodless seams.

The sensation spread, dancing over the surface of his body. His fingertips found his face. It felt like touching a skull. His hair was falling out, his teeth. His back bent inward, drawing him into an old man's stoop. He fell to his knees in the mud. He felt his bones collapsing, crumbling to dust.

"Grey, what did you do?"

A shadow fell.

Guilder lifted his face. The virals filled his darkening vision with a final image of their magnificence. *My brothers,* he thought, *what is happening to me? Help me, my brothers, I am dying.* But he saw no kinship in their eyes.

Betrayer.

Betrayer.

Betrayer betrayer betrayer . . .

Other things were occurring—gunshots, voices yelling, figures running in the dark. But Guilder's consciousness of these events was instantly subsumed into the larger awareness, cold and final, of what was about to happen to him.

Shawna, he thought, *Shawna, all I wanted was a little company. All I wanted was not to die alone.*

And then they were upon him.

The conclusive unfolding of events, which accounted for just thirty-seven seconds in the lives of the participants, occurred in overlapping frames of simultaneous movement collapsing toward the center. Illuminated only by firelight—the barrels at the periphery continued to burn—and the virals' phosphorescent glow, the scene possessed a whiff of hell. The virals, finished with Guilder, his body scattered in desiccated pieces that were more dust than corpse, had assembled in a loose line. They appeared to be regarding Amy with a look of caution. Perhaps they did not know yet what she portended; perhaps they were afraid of her. Peter, his weapon reloaded, was firing in bursts into their massive figures, though without visible effect; the bullets skimmed pointlessly off their armored bodies in bright sparks; they didn't so much as glance in his direction. From the other side of the field, Alicia was moving forward with her pistol raised, just as Nina and Tifty were racing downfield to flank them. The plan was now moot; they had only their instincts. Standing erect on the platform, Amy raised her arms. From each wrist hung a long length of chain. She jerked them into the air and began to rotate them at her wrists, swinging them in wide, accelerating arcs. Spinners, Peter realized. Amy was making spinners, to disorient the virals. Faster and faster the chains whirred in the air above her head, a hypnotic blur of movement. The creatures froze, entranced. With an avian dart, Amy's head tipped to the side; her gaze compacted, calculating the angle of attack. Peter knew what was about to happen.

Amy Harper Bellafonte, fully weaponized. Amy, the Girl from Nowhere, airborne.

As she shot forward, she let the chains fly, snapping them from her body like a pair of whips. Simultaneously she tucked her head to her chest, aligning her posture in mid-flight so that she would meet the closest among them feet-first, chest-high, her physical person transformed at the moment of impact into a battering ram with twenty-foot iron wings. She was a fraction of their size, but momentum was on her side; she sailed through the first one, blasting him backward; by the time she landed, the chains had found their targets, wrapping two others around their necks. With a hard yank she drew the left one toward her, buried her face beneath his jaw, and shook him like a dog with a rag in its mouth.

He howled.

And, with a jet of blood and a bony cracking sound, died.

She unfurled him from the chain with a snap of her wrist, rotating the body away like a top. Her attention turned to the second viral, but the balance had shifted: the element of surprise was gone; the hypnotic effect of the spinners had worn away. The creature launched toward her, their bodies meeting in an uncontrolled collision that sent them both tumbling end over end away from the platform. Amy wrenched the chain free but seemed disoriented; she crouched on her hands and knees in the dirt. A kind of whole-body rippling moved through the remaining virals, their shared consciousness reassembling, achieving focus. One more wink of time and they would fall on her like a pack of animals.

Which they might have, if not for the small one.

Peter's mind had yet to parse them as anything more than a collective; he was forced to do so now. One of the virals was different. In bulk and stature he appeared no larger than a man. In the instant before the others leapt upon Amy, he beat them to the punch; with a compact aerial bound he alighted between her and her attackers, turning to face them, claws raised, his body in a posture of challenge. His chest expanded in a massive intake of breath; his lips pulled back, exposing his teeth.

The blast of sound that followed was completely out of proportion with the size of the body that produced it. It was a howl of purest rage. It was a roar that could have felled a forest, flattened a mountain, knocked a planet off its axis. Peter literally felt himself pushed back by it; his eardrums popped with pain. The small viral had bought Amy only a second, but it was enough. As she rose to her feet, the others shot forward.

Chaos.

Suddenly it was impossible to tell what was happening or where to shoot, the images of battle too quick for human eyes to compute. Peter realized he had expended the last of his rounds, but the gun was useless anyway. He glimpsed Alicia advancing from the far side of the field, still firing her pistol.

Where were Tifty and Nina?

He looked downfield. Nina was racing toward the platform, the bomb clutched to her chest. Tifty was behind her. She waved her free arm over her head, yelling at the top of her lungs: "You bastards! Look over here! Hey!"

The one that took note—did it grasp her intentions? Did it know the meaning of what she held? It did not so much launch as lob itself toward her, dropping in a four-limbed spread like a spider on silk. Tifty saw it first. As he raised his weapon he tried to push Nina aside, but the effort came too late; as with all things falling, the leisureliness of the viral's plunge was an illusion. It crashed into the two of them, Tifty taking the brunt. Peter expected the bomb to go off, but that didn't happen. The viral seized Nina by the arm and flung her away, casting her spiraling over the dirt; then it turned toward Tifty. As Tifty raised his weapon, the creature engulfed him.

A scream. A gunshot.

It wasn't a decision. There were no pros and cons. Peter dropped his gun and made for the bomb where it lay in the dirt, running for all he was worth.

The only two people who saw it all were Lore and Greer. And even then, it was Greer alone, the man of faith, whose prayers had afforded him a deeper comprehension of the scene, who was able to make sense of it.

Viewed from the control room, the battle on the field played out with a flattened quality, rendered more decipherable by distance. At one end lay Eustace, unconscious or dead, and between him and the platform, the body of Tifty

Lamont; Nina was gone, hurled into the darkness; Alicia, on the opposite side, was the only one still firing. At the center stood the platform; Amy, having wrenched herself free from the melee, had vaulted to the top of the armature. Her tunic was in shreds, stained with the dark wetness of blood; one clawed hand clutched her side, as if to stanch a wound. Even at this distance, Greer could discern the harsh labor of her breathing. Her transformation was complete, yet one human vestige remained: her hair. Black and wild, it tumbled freely around her face. In another moment her attackers would strike in overwhelming force, yet her posture did not communicate retreat. There was something invincible about her, almost royal.

Then he saw Peter, racing downfield. Where was he going? The semi?

No.

Greer blasted from the room and down the stairs. He would part the crowd with his body, his fists, his blade if he had to. *Amy, Amy, I am coming.*

Alicia would not be denied. She had consecrated her existence to this holy fact. She had felt it since the cave: a singular longing drawing her forward, as if she were being pulled down the length of a tunnel. As she moved toward the virals, firing her weapon—her bullets, she knew, would do no actual damage; she only wanted to draw their attention—she was a being of only one thought, one vision, one desire.

Louise, I will avenge you. You have not been forgotten. Louise, you, too, are my sister in blood.

"Show yourself, you son of a bitch!"

Her bullets skimmed and flashed. She dropped her empty magazine, rammed another home, and resumed firing. Through gritted teeth she advanced, murmuring her dark prayer. He would know her, feel her; it could not be otherwise. It was a thing of destiny, that she should be the one to kill him, to wipe him from the face of the earth. He was Julio Martínez, Esq., Tenth of Twelve. He was Sod of the bench and the grunting exhalations. He was all the men in all the years of history who had violated a woman in this manner, and she would drive her blade deep into the dark heart of him and feel him die.

One of the virals swiveled toward her. Of course, Alicia thought; she would have recognized him anywhere. His physique was identical to the others', and yet there was something distinctive about him, an air of haughtiness that only

she would be able to detect. He regarded her through soulless eyes lidded with bored languor; he appeared, almost, to
smile. Alicia had never seen an expression on a viral's face
before; now she did. *I know you,* his bland, arrogant face
seemed to say. *Don't I know you? Don't tell me, let me guess.
I'm certain I know you from someplace.*

You're damn right you know me, she thought, and drew
the bayonet from her belt.

They launched toward each other simultaneously—Alicia
with the blade raised above her head, Martínez with his
great taloned hands reaching forward like a prow of knives.
An unstoppable force meeting an immovable object: their
trajectories intersected in a headlong, grappling collision,
Martínez's vastly greater mass passing both through and
under her, sending her pinwheeling over his head. In her moment of uncontrolled flight, Alicia acknowledged but did
not yet feel the lacerations on her arms and face where his
claws had torn into her flesh. She hit the dirt and rolled once,
twice, three times, each rotation defusing her momentum,
and sprang to her feet again. She was winded, stumbling, her
head chiming with the impact. Somehow she had maintained her grip on the bayonet; to lose it was to accept defeat, unthinkable.

Martínez, twenty feet away, had dropped to a froglike
squat, his hands splayed like paddles on the dirt. The smile
had morphed into something else, more playful, full of rich
enjoyment. He seemed about to laugh. Goddamn your
laughing face, Alicia thought, raising her bayonet once
more.

A shape was falling toward them.

The bomb, the bomb, where was the bomb?

Then Peter saw it, lying just a few yards from Tifty's body.
He skidded in the dirt and scooped it to his chest. The
plunger was intact, the wires still connected. How would it
feel? Like nothing, he thought. It would feel like nothing.

Something blasted him from behind, hard as a wall. For a
moment everything left him: breath, thought, gravity. The
bomb went spiraling away. The ground unfurling beneath
him and a flash of mental blackness; then Peter found himself face-up in the mud.

The viral loomed above him; their faces were mere inches
apart. The sight seemed to cross the wires of Peter's senses,
as if he were tasting nightfall, or listening to lightning. As
the creature tipped its head, Peter did the one, last thing he

could think of, believing it would be the final gesture of his life: he cocked his head in concert, willed his mind into absolute focus, and looked the viral dead in the eye.

I am Wolgast.

Then Peter saw: he was holding the bomb.

Help me.

Alicia, sister. Alicia, he is yours.

Martínez never saw it coming. In the fraction of a second before he uncoiled his massive body, Amy landed behind him. With a snap of her wrists she jetted the chains forward to encircle his frame like a pair of lassos, pinning his arms to his sides. The smile melted into a look of surprise.

Now, said Amy.

With a mighty pull she drew Martínez upright, exposing the broad meat of his chest. As Martínez tumbled backward, Alicia landed, straddling his waist, driving his body to the ground. The bayonet was poised above her head, wrapped in her fists. And yet she did not make it fall.

"Say it!" she yelled over the roaring in her ears. "Say her name!"

His eyes sought to focus. *Louise?*

And with these words, and all that she was, Alicia brought it down and drove it home, killing him in the ancient manner.

The final seconds of the battle of the field were, to the crowds in the stands, an incomprehensible blur of movement. Not so to Lucius Greer. Greer understood, as no one else could, what was about to happen. The chains that Amy had employed to restrain Martínez were now pinning her to his corpse. Alicia was struggling to turn him over in order to release her. They were sitting ducks, and yet the remaining virals had yet to fall. Perhaps Martínez's death had caused a break in their communal train of thought; perhaps the shock of seeing one of their own perish beneath a human hand had rendered them immobile; perhaps they merely wished to prolong the moment of victory, and thus extract the fullest measure of satisfaction from their final assault; perhaps it was something else.

It was something else.

As Greer charged across the field, another figure was rushing from his right. A glance was all he needed for his eyes to learn what his mind already knew. It was Peter. He was shouting, waving. But something was different. The virals sensed it, too. They snapped to attention, their noses darting, tasting the air.

"Look over here, you bastards!"

Peter was naked to the waist, his torso slick with blood—warm, fresh, living rivers of blood that coursed down his arms and chest from the long, curving wounds of the blade still clutched in his hand. His intentions were clear: he would draw the virals away from Amy and Alicia, down upon himself. He was the bait; what was the trap?

And Greer heard:

I am Wolgast.

I am Wolgast.

I am Wolgast.

Greer ran.

Alicia saw it, too.

Amy was still pinned to Martínez's body. The chains that tethered her had wound upon themselves; every pull only drew them tighter. Howling in frustration, Alicia saw Peter racing toward the virals; saw their bodies swiveling, heads cocking, eyes blazing with animal attraction, the pleasure of the kill.

Peter, no, she thought. *Not you. After everything, not you.*

She never knew how Amy got loose. One moment she was there and the next she wasn't. The empty shackles would be found just where Amy had left them, attached to chains still hopelessly lashed to Martínez's body; in the ensuing days, as each of them puzzled over the meaning of this fact, opinions would differ. To some it meant one thing, to some it meant another. It was a mystery, as Amy was a mystery; and like any mystery, it said as much about the seer as the seen.

But this came later. In the split second that remained, all Alicia knew was that Amy was gone; she was soaring away. A streak of light, like a shooting star; then she was falling, down upon Peter.

"Amy—"

But that was all she said.

Because Wolgast loved her.

Because Amy was home.

Because he had saved her, and she him.

And Peter Jaxon, lieutenant of the Expeditionary, heard and saw and felt it all; he felt it all at last. In a single meeting of their eyes, Wolgast's whole life had poured into his own. Its comprehensive sorrows. Its bitter losses and aching regrets. Its love for a forgotten girl, and its long sojourn through a hundred years of night. He saw faces, figures, pictures of the past. A baby in its crib, and a woman reaching to lift it into her arms, the two of them bathed in an almost holy light. He saw Amy as she had been, a tiny child, full of strange intensity, alone in the world, and the lights of a carousel and stars in a winter sky and the forms of angels carved in the snow. It was as if these visions had always been a part of him, like a recurring dream only lately remembered, and he felt profoundly grateful to have seen them, to give them witness in the final seconds of his life.

Come to me, he thought. *Come to me.*

He raced headlong. He cast himself into the hands of God. He sensed but did not see Greer streaming toward him, and Wolgast barreling from behind with the bomb clutched to his chest, aiming his body for the heart of the pod. And in the last instant, Peter heard the words:

Amy, run.

And: *Father—*

And: *I love you.*

And as Wolgast dove into their midst, one clawed thumb poised on the plunger; and as Amy likewise swooped down upon Peter to hurl him away, taking the brunt of the destruction in his stead; and as the last of the Twelve in their fury fell upon Wolgast—Wolgast the True, the Father of All, and the One Who Loved—a hole in space opened where he had stood, dark night burst to brightest day, and the heavens rent with thunder.

66

It came to feel as if there were two cities in the minutes that followed: the grandstands, where chaos reigned, and the field below, a zone of aftermath, of sudden calm. A beginning and an ending, standing adjacent but apart. Soon the two would merge, as the crowd, the violence of its uprising exhausted, absorbed the amazing fact of its liberty and began to disperse, going where it liked, including the field; they would find it one by one, drifting down, moving tentatively as their bodies tasted freedom. But in the near term, the combatants on the field were left to themselves, to take a final measure of the living and the lost.

It was Alicia whom Peter awakened to see. She was blackened, bruised, bloodied. Much of her hair had been burned away, tendrils of smoke still rising. *Peter,* she was saying. She hovered above him, tears streaming down her cheeks. *Peter.*

He struggled to speak. His tongue moved heavily in his mouth: *Amy? Is she—?*

Alicia, softly weeping, shook her head.

Somehow Greer had survived. The blast had flung him far away. By all rights he should have been dead, and yet they found him lying on his back, staring at the starlit sky. His clothing was shredded and seared; otherwise he appeared untouched. It was as if the force of the blast had moved not through him but around him, his life protected by an invisible hand. For a long moment he neither spoke nor moved. Then, with an exploratory gesture, he raised a hand to his chest, patting it cautiously; he lifted it to his face, tracing his cheeks and brow and chin.

"I'll be damned," he said.

Eustace, too, would live. At first they believed he was dead; his face was drenched in blood. But the shot had gone wide; the blood was from his left ear, now gone, shorn like a plant plucked from soil and replaced by a puckered hole. Of the detonation itself he had no memory, or none he could fully assemble beyond a chain of isolated sensations: a skull-cracking blast of noise, and a scorching wave of air passing above, then something wet raining down, and a taste of smoke and dust. He would escape the night with only this one additional disfigurement to a face already bearing plentiful scars of war and a permanent ringing in his ears, which would, in fact, never abate, causing him to speak in an overly loud voice that would make people think he was angry even when he wasn't. Over time, once he had returned to Kerrville and risen to the rank of colonel, serving as military liaison to the president's staff, he would come to regard this as less an inconvenience than a remarkably useful enhancement to his authority; he wondered why he hadn't thought of it before.

Only Nina would depart the field unscathed. Hurled away by the viral that had killed Tifty, she'd been thrown clear of the blast zone. She had been moving upfield when the bomb went off, its concussive force blowing her backward off her feet; but in the preceding moment she'd been the only one to witness the death of the Twelve, their bodies consumed and scattered in a ball of light. All else was a blur; of Amy, she had seen nothing.

Nothing at all.

* * *

But one of them had fallen.

They found Tifty with his gun still in his hand. He lay in the mud, broken and severed, his eyes rimmed by blood. His right arm was gone, but that was the least of it. As they gathered around him, he labored to speak through his fitful breathing. At last his lips formed words: "Where is she?"

Greer alone seemed to understand what he was asking. He turned toward Nina. "It's you he wants."

Perhaps she understood the nature of the request, perhaps not; none could tell. She lowered herself to the ground beside him. With trembling effort, Tifty lifted his hand and touched her face with the tips of his fingers, the gentlest gesture.

"Nitia," he whispered. "My Nitia."

"I'm Nina."

"No. You're Nitia. My Nitia." He gave a tearful smile. "You look . . . so much like her."

"Like who?"

Life was ebbing from his eyes. "I told her . . ." His breath caught. He had begun to choke on the blood that poured from his mouth. "I told her . . . I would keep you safe." Then the light in his eyes went out and he was gone.

No one spoke. One of their own had slipped away, into darkness.

"I don't understand," Alicia said. She glanced at the others. "Why did he call her that?"

It was Greer who answered: "Because that's her name." Nina looked up from the body. "You didn't know, did you?" he said. "There was no way you could."

She shook her head.

"Tifty was your father."

In due course, there would come a full accounting. A pickup would race onto the field; they would watch three people emerge. No, four. Michael and Hollis and Sara, holding a little girl in her arms.

But for now they stood silently in the presence of their friend, the core of his life laid bare. The great gangster Tifty Lamont, captain of the Expeditionary. They would bury him where he'd fallen, in the field. Because you never leave it, Greer explained; that's what Tifty always said. You might think you can do it, but you can't. Once you'd stood there, it became a part of you forever.

No one ever left the field.

XII

THE KISS

JANUARY 98 A.V.

On the day of victory, no man is tired.

—ARAB PROVERB

67

The weather failed to cooperate. January in Iowa—what had they expected? Bone-numbing day followed bone-numbing day. Food, fuel, water, electricity, the complex enterprise of keeping a city of seventy thousand souls running—the joy of victory had quickly been subsumed by more mundane concerns. For the time being the insurgency had assumed control, though Eustace, by his own admission, had no particular knack for the job. He felt overwhelmed by the volume of detail, and the hastily assembled provisional government, composed of appointed delegates from each of the lodges, did little to lighten his load; it was bloated and disorganized, half the room always squabbling with the other half, leaving Eustace to throw up his hands and make all the decisions anyway. A degree of docility among the population remained, but this wouldn't last. There had been looting in the market before Eustace was able to secure it, and every day there were more stories of reprisals; many of the cols had tried to slip anonymously into the populace, but their faces were known. Without a justice system to try the ones who surrendered, or those who had been captured by the insurgency in advance of the mob, it was hard to know what to do with them. The detention center was bursting at the seams. Eustace had raised the possibility of retrofitting the Project—it was certainly secure enough and had the additional advantage of isolation—but this would take time and did nothing to address the problem of what to do with the prisoners when the population began to move south.

And everybody was freezing. Well, so be it, Peter thought. What was a little cold?

He had formed a close friendship with Eustace. Some of this was their shared bond as officers of the Expeditionary, but not all; they had discovered, as the days passed, that they possessed compatible temperaments. They decided that Peter should lead the advance team that would travel south to prepare Kerrville for the influx of refugees. Initially he'd objected; it didn't seem right to be among the first to leave. But he was the logical choice, and in the end, Alicia sealed the case. Caleb is waiting for you, she reminded him. Go see to your boy.

The exodus itself would have to wait till spring. Assuming Kerrville could send enough vehicles and personnel, Eustace planned to move five thousand people at a time, the composition of each group determined by a lottery. The trip would be arduous—all but the very old and very young would have to walk—but with luck the Homeland would be empty within two years.

"Not everybody will want to go, you know," Eustace said.

The two of them were seated in Eustace's office, in the back room of the apothecary, warming themselves with cups of herbal tea. Most of the buildings in the market had been taken over by the provisional government to serve various functions. The latest project to occupy them was the tallying of a census. With all the redeyes' records having been destroyed in the Dome, they had no idea who was who, or even how many people there were. Seventy thousand was the generally accepted number, but there was no way to know precisely unless they counted.

"Why wouldn't they?"

Eustace shrugged. The left side of his head was still bandaged, giving his face a lopsided appearance, though balanced by his clouded eye. Sara had removed the last of Peter's stitches the prior day; his chest and arms now bore a road map of long, pinkish scars. In private moments, Peter couldn't stop touching them, amazed not only by the fact that he'd inflicted these wounds upon himself but also that, in the heat of the moment, he'd barely felt a thing.

"This is what they know. They've lived their entire lives here. But that's not the whole reason. It's good to right a wrong. I don't know how many will feel that way once we start moving people south, but some will."

"How will they manage?"

"I suppose how people always manage. Elections, the rough business of building a life." He sipped his tea. "It'll be messy. It might not work at all. But at least it will be theirs."

Nina came in from the cold, stamping waffles of snow from her boots. "Jesus, it's freezing out there," she said.

Eustace offered her his cup. "Here, warm yourself up."

She took it in her hands and sipped, then bent to kiss him quickly on the mouth. "Thank you, husband. You really need to shave."

Eustace laughed. "With a face like mine? Who cares?"

That the two of them were a couple was, as Peter had

learned, the worst-kept secret of the insurgency. One of the first things Eustace had done was issue an executive order permitting flatlanders to marry. In many instances this was a technicality; people had been paired up for years or even decades. But marriage had never possessed official sanction. The list of couples waiting to be married now ran to the hundreds, and Eustace had two justices of the peace operating night and day out of a storefront down the block. He and Nina had been among the first, as had Hollis and Sara.

"Good news," Nina said. "I just came from the hospital."

"And?"

"Two more babies were born this morning, both healthy. Mothers doing fine."

"Well, how about that." Eustace grinned at Peter. "See what I'm telling you? Even on the darkest night, my friend, life will have its way."

Peter made his way down the hill, hunched against the wind. As a member of the executive staff he was permitted the use of a vehicle, but he preferred to walk. At the hospital he headed for Michael's room. Power had been only partially restored, but the hospital had been one of the first buildings relit. He found Michael awake and sitting up. His right leg, encased in plaster from ankle to hip, was suspended from a sling at a forty-five-degree angle above the bed. It had been touch and go for a while, and Sara had thought he might lose the leg; but Michael was a fighter, and now, three weeks later, he was officially on the mend.

Lore was sitting by the bed, manipulating a pair of knitting needles. Eustace had put her to work as a foreman at the biodiesel plant, but any free moment found her back at the hospital, at Michael's bedside.

"What are you making?" Peter asked her.

"Hell if I can say. It was supposed to be a sweater, but it's coming out more like socks."

"You should really stick to what you know," Michael advised.

"Just you wait till you're out of that cast, my friend. I'll show you what I know. It's nothing you'll forget." She looked at Peter, slyly smiling to make sure he got the joke. "Oh, I'm sorry, Peter. Got a little carried away. I guess I forgot you were there."

He laughed. "It's okay."

She gave one of her needles a wave. "I just want to mention, in case our boy here takes a turn for the worse, I've always thought you had a very nice look to you. Plus, you're a war hero. I'd be interested in anything you had to say, Lieutenant."

"I'll give it some thought."

"Of that I have no doubt." She dropped the yarn to her lap. "As it happens, my shift begins in thirty minutes, so I'll leave you two to talk about me." She rose, bagged her knitting, patted Michael on the arm, then thought better of it and kissed him on the top of his head. "Need anything before I go?"

"I'm fine."

"You're not fine, Michael. You're far from fine. You scared the living hell out of me is what you did."

"I said I was sorry."

"Keep saying it, bub. One day I'll believe you." She kissed him again. "Gentlemen."

When Lore was gone, Peter took her seat. "Sorry about that," Michael said.

"I don't know why you keep apologizing for her, Michael. You're the luckiest guy on planet Earth, as far as I'm concerned." He tipped his head toward the bed. "So how's the leg really?"

"It hurts like hell. Nice of you to finally visit."

"Sorry about that. Eustace is keeping me busy."

"So how many have you found?"

Peter understood that Michael was asking about the other First Colonists. "The number we're hearing is fifty-six. We're still trying to track everyone down. So far we've found Jimmy's daughters, Alice and Avery. Constance Chou, Russ Curtis, Penny Darrell. The Littles are going to take some time to sort out. Everybody's spread all over the place."

"Good news, I guess." Michael stopped, leaving the rest unstated. So many others, gone.

"Hollis told me what you did," Peter said.

Michael shrugged. He looked a little embarrassed, but proud, too. "It seemed like the thing to do at the time."

"You ever want a job in the Exped, you let me know. Assuming they'll have me back. The next time we talk, I might be in the stockade."

"Peter, be serious. They'll probably make you a general for this. That or ask you to run for president."

"Then you don't know the Army like I do." And yet, for just a moment, he thought: what if? "We'll be leaving in a few days, you know."

"So I figured. Don't forget to bundle up. Say hello to Kerr-ville for me."

"We'll get you in the next trip, I promise."

"I don't know, hombre, the service here is pretty good. The place kind of agrees with me. Who's going with you?"

"Sara and Hollis and Kate, but that's obvious. Greer's staying to help with the evacuation. Eustace is putting a team together."

"What about Lish?"

"I'd ask her if I could find her. I've barely seen her at all. She's been riding out on this horse of hers. She calls him Soldier. What she's doing I have no idea."

"I'm sorry you missed her. She came by this morning."

"Lish was here?"

"Said she wanted to say hello." Michael looked at him. "Why? Is that so strange?"

Peter frowned. "I guess not. How did she seem?"

"How do you think? Like Lish."

"So there wasn't anything different about her."

"Not that I noticed. She wasn't here very long. She said she was going to help Sara with the donations."

As interim director of public health, Sara had discovered that the building that served as the hospital was, as she'd long suspected, a hospital in name only. There was almost no medical equipment, and no blood at all. With so many people injured in the siege, and babies being born and all the rest, she'd had a freezer brought over from the food-processing facility and had instituted a program of blood donation.

"Lish as a nurse," Peter said, and shook his head at the irony. "I'd like to see that."

What became of the redeyes themselves was never fully un-derstood. Those that hadn't been killed in the stadium had essentially ceased to exist. The only conclusion to be drawn, supported by Sara's story about Lila, was that the destruc-tion of the Dome, and the death of the man known as the Source, had caused a chain reaction similar to the one they'd seen in Babcock's descendants on the mountain in Colo-rado. Those who'd witnessed it described it as a rapid aging, as if a hundred years of borrowed life were surrendered in just a few seconds—flesh shriveling, hair falling out in clumps, faces withering to the skull. The corpses they'd found, still dressed in their suits and ties, were nothing but piles of brown bones. They looked like they'd been dead for decades.

As the day of departure approached, Sara found herself working virtually around the clock. As word had spread in the flatland that actual medical care could now be had, more and more people had come in. The complaints varied from the common cold to malnutrition to the broad bodily failures of old age. A few seemed simply curious about what seeing a doctor would be like. Sara treated the ones she could, comforted those she could not. In the end, the two felt not so very different.

She left the hospital only to sleep, and sometimes eat, or else Hollis would bring meals to her, always with Kate in tow. They had been quartered in an apartment in the complex at the edge of downtown—a curious place, with wide, tinted windows that created a permanent evening light within. It felt a little eerie, knowing that the former occupants had been redeyes, but it was comfortable, with large beds made with soft linens and hot water and a working gas stove, on which Hollis concocted soups and stews of ingredients she didn't want to know about but which were nonetheless delicious. They would eat together in the candlelit dark and then fall into bed, making love with quiet tenderness so as not to wake their daughter.

Tonight Sara decided to take a break; she was dead on her feet, and starving besides, and missed her family keenly. Her family: after all that had happened, how remarkable these two words were. They seemed the most miraculous in the history of human speech. When she had seen Hollis charging through the entrance of the Dome, her heart had instantly known what her eyes could not believe. Of course he had come for her; Hollis had moved heaven and earth, and here he was. How could it have been otherwise?

She made her way up the hill, past the toppled wreckage of the Dome—its charred timbers had smoldered for days—and through the old downtown. To move freely, without fear, still seemed a little unreal to her. Sara thought about stopping into the apothecary, to say hello to Eustace and whoever else was around, but her feet refused this impulse, which quickly passed. With anticipation lightening her step, she ascended the six flights to the apartment.

"Mummy!"

Hollis and Kate were sitting together on the floor, playing beans and cups. Before Sara could uncoil the scarf from her neck, the girl leapt to her feet and flew into her arms, a soft collision; Sara hoisted Kate to her waist to look her in the eye. She had never told Kate to address her by this name, not wanting to confuse her more than necessary, but this had turned out not to matter; the girl had simply done it. Having never had a father before, Kate had taken a little more time to adapt to Hollis's role in her life, but then one day, about a week after the liberation, she had started to call him Daddy.

"Well, there you are," Sara said happily. "How was your day? Did you do fun things with Daddy?"

The little girl reached toward Sara's face, wrapped her nose with her fist, and made a show of snatching it from Sara's face, popping it into her mouth, and pushing her tongue against the inside of her cheek. "I haf yur nose," she said thickly.

"Now, give that back."

Kate, beaming wildly, blond hair bouncing around her face, waggled her head with playful defiance. "Nuh-uh. It's mine."

Thus, the tickling, and laughter from all sides, and the theft of more bodily parts, and the eventual return of Sara's nose to her face. By the time the struggle was over, Hollis had joined in. Cupping the back of Kate's head, he kissed Sara quickly, his beard—warm, familiar, full of his scent—pressing like wool against her cheeks.

"Hungry?"

She smiled. "I could eat."

Hollis dished her out a bowl; he and Kate had already had their dinner. He sat with her at the little table while she dug in. The meat, he confessed, could have been just about anything, but the carrots and potatoes were passable. Sara hardly cared; never had food tasted so good as it had the last few weeks. They talked about her patients, about Peter and Michael and the others, about Kerrville and what awaited there, about the trip south, now just a few days off. Hollis had initially suggested that they wait until spring, when the travel would be less arduous, but Sara would have none of it. Too much has happened here, she'd told him. I don't know where home is, but let's let it be Texas.

They washed the dishes, set them in the rack, and readied Kate for bed. Even as Sara drew the nightshirt over the little girl's head, she was already half-asleep. They tucked her in and retreated to the living room.

"Do you really have to go back to the hospital?" Hollis asked.

Sara took her coat from the hook and wriggled her arms

into the sleeves. "It'll just be a few hours. Don't wait up." Though that was exactly what he'd do; Sara would have done the same. "Come here."

She kissed him, lingering there. "I mean it. Go to bed."

But as she put her hand on the knob, he stopped her.

"How did you know, Sara?"

She almost, but not quite, understood what he was asking. "How did I know what?"

"That it was her. That it was Kate."

It was odd; Sara had never thought to ask herself this question. Nina had confirmed Kate's identity in their clandestine meeting in the back room of the apothecary, but she needn't have; there had never been a trace of doubt in Sara's mind. It was more than the child's physical resemblance that told her so; the knowledge had come from someplace deeper. Sara had looked at Kate and instantly understood that of all the children in the world, this one was hers.

"Call it a mother's instincts. It was like . . . like knowing myself." She shrugged. "I can't explain it any better than that."

"Still, we were lucky."

Sara had never told him about the foil packet; nor would she ever. "I'm not sure if you can even call something like this luck," she said. "All I know is we're here."

It was after midnight by the time she was finishing her rounds. Yawning into her fist, her mind already halfway home, Sara stepped into the last examining room, where a young woman was sitting on the table.

"Jenny?"

"Hi, Dani."

Sara had to laugh—not only at the name, which seemed like something from a distant dream, but the girl's presence itself. It wasn't until she'd seen her that Sara had realized that she'd assumed Jenny was dead.

"What happened to you?"

She shrugged sheepishly. "I'm sorry I left. After what happened in the feedlot, I just panicked. One of the kitchen workers hid me in a flour barrel and got me out on one of the delivery trucks."

Sara smiled to reassure her. "Well, I'm glad to see you. What seems to be the trouble?"

The girl hesitated. "I think I may be pregnant."

Sara examined her. If she was, it was too early to tell. But being pregnant got you a spot in the first evacuation. She filled out the form and handed it to her.

"Take this to the census office and tell them I sent you."

"Really?"

"Really."

The girl stared at the slip of paper in her hand. "Kerrville. I can't believe it. I barely remember it."

Sara had been filling out a duplicate evacuation order on her clipboard. Her pen paused in midair. "What did you say?"

"That I can't believe it?"

"No, the other thing. About remembering."

The girl shrugged. "I was born there. At least I think I was. I was pretty small when they took me."

"Jenny, why didn't you tell anyone?"

"I did. I told the census taker."

Flyers, how had they missed this?

"Well, I'm glad you told *me*. Somebody may be looking for you. What's your last name?"

"I'm not really sure," Jenny said, "but I think that it was Apgar."

68

The day of departure arrived with a hard, bright dawn. The advance team gathered at the stadium: thirty men and women, six trucks, and two refuelers. Eustace and Nina had come to see them off, as well as Lore and Greer.

A small crowd had gathered, family and friends of those who would be departing. Sara and the others had already said goodbye to Michael the night before, at the hospital. Go on, he said, his face red, get out of here. How is a guy supposed to get his rest? But the card Kate had made for him proved his undoing. *I Love Youe Unkle Michel, Get Whell.* Aw, flyers, he said, get over here, and gripped the little girl tightly to his chest, tears rolling from his eyes.

The last supplies were loaded into the trucks; everybody climbed aboard. Peter would ride in the lead pickup, with Hollis; Kate and Sara were riding in one of the large transports at the rear. As Peter fired the ignition, Greer stepped to his window. In Peter's absence, the major had agreed to serve in his stead as Eustace's second-in-command and was now in charge of the evacuation.

"I don't know where she is, Peter. I'm sorry."

Had he been so obvious? Once again, Lish had left him standing at the altar. "I'm just worried about her. Something's not right."

"She went through a lot in that cell. I don't think she's told us even half of it. She'll bounce back—she always does."

There was nothing more to say on the subject. Nor on the other, which in the days since the uprising had hung over them with its unspoken weight of grief. The logical explanation was that Amy had been killed in the explosion, vaporized with the other virals, and yet part of him could not accept this. She felt like a ghost limb, an invisible part of him.

The two men shook hands. "Be careful okay?" Greer said. "You too, Hollis. It's a different world out there, but you never know."

Peter nodded. "All eyes, Major."

Greer allowed himself a rare smile. "I confess I like the sound of that. Who knows? Maybe they'll take me back, after all."

The moment of parting was at hand. Peter ground the truck into gear; with a throb of heavy engines, the line of vehicles drew clear of the gate. In the rearview mirror, Peter watched as the buildings of the Homeland receded from view, fading into the winter whiteness.

"I'm sure she's somewhere, Peter," Hollis said.

Peter wondered whom he meant.

From her hiding place in the culvert, Alicia watched the convoy drive away. For many days she had lived this moment in advance, attempting to prepare herself. How would it feel? Even now she couldn't say. Final, that was all. It felt final. The line of trucks cut a broad arc around the fences of the city and turned south. For a long time Alicia watched it, the image growing smaller, the sound of the engines dimming. She was still watching when it disappeared.

There was one thing left to do.

She'd taken the blood from the hospital, secreting the sloshing plastic pouch beneath her tunic when Sara's back was turned. It had taken all her resolve not to clamp her jaws into it and bathe her face and mouth and tongue in its earthy richness. But when she'd thought of Peter, and Amy, and Michael, and all the others, she had found the strength to wait.

She had buried the pouch in the snow, marking the spot

with a stone. Now she dug it free: a block of red ice, dense in her hand. Soldier was watching her from the edge of the culvert. Alicia would have told him to go, but of course he wouldn't; they belonged to each other till the end. She built a fire of crackling scrub, melted snow in a pot, waited till the bubbles rose, and dipped the bag into the steaming water—as if, she thought, she were steeping tea. Gradually the contents softened to a slush. When the blood had thawed completely, Alicia removed the bag and lay in the snow, cradling its warmth against her chest. Within its plastic casing lay a destiny deferred. Since the day the viral had bitten her on the mountain, five years ago, the knowledge of her fate had lain inside her; now she would meet it. She would meet it, and die.

The morning sun was climbing into a cloudless winter sky. The sun. Alicia squinted her eyes against its brightness. *The sun,* she thought. *My enemy, my friend, my last deliverance.* It would sweep her away. It would scatter her ashes to the wind. Be quick now, Alicia said to the sun, but not too quick. I want to feel it coming out of me.

She raised the bag to her lips, pulled the tab, and drank.

By dusk the convoy had traveled sixty miles. The town was named Grinnell. They took shelter in an abandoned store at the edge of town that apparently had once sold shoes; boxes and boxes of them lined the racks. So, a place worth returning to, someday. They ate their rations, bedded down, and slept.

Or tried to. It wasn't the cold—Peter was accustomed to that. He was simply too keyed up. The events in the stadium had been too enormous to process all at once; nearly a month later, he still found himself caught up in their emotions, his mind flashing restlessly with the images.

Peter pulled on his parka and boots and stepped outside. They'd posted a single guard, who was sitting in a metal folding chair they'd brought out from the store; Peter accepted the man's rifle and sent him to bed. The moon was shining, the air like ice in his lungs. He stood in silence, drinking in the night's stark clarity. For days after the uprising, Peter had tried to will himself into some emotion that would correspond to the magnitude of events—happiness or triumph or even just relief—but all he felt was lonely. He remembered Greer's parting words: *It's a different world out there.* It was, Peter knew that; yet it did not seem so. If anything, the world felt even more like itself. Here were the frozen fields, like a vast, becalmed sea; here was the immeasurable, starlit sky; here was the moon with its jaundiced, heavy-lidded gaze, like the answer to a question nobody had posed. Everything was just as it had been, and would go on being, long after all of them were gone, their names and memories and all they were ground like their bones into the dust of time and blown away.

A noise behind him: Sara stepped through the door, toting Kate on her hip. The girl's eyes were open and looking about. Sara moved beside Peter, her boots crunching on the snow.

"Couldn't sleep?" he asked.

She made a face of exasperation. "Believe me, *I* could. It's my fault, I let her nap too long in the truck."

"Hi, Peter," the little girl said.

"Hi, sweetheart. Shouldn't you be in bed? We've got another long day tomorrow, you know."

She pressed her lips together. "Mm-mm."

"See?" Sara said.

"Want me to take her for a while? I can, you know."

"What, out here, you mean?"

Peter shrugged. "A little fresh air should fix her right up. And I could use the company." When Sara didn't answer, Peter said, "Don't worry, I'll keep an eye. What do you say, Kate?"

"You're sure about this?" Sara pressed.

"Sure I'm sure. What else am I going to do? The minute she gets sleepy, I'll bring her inside." He propped his rifle against the building and held out his arms. "Come on now, hand her over. I'm not taking no for an answer."

Sara acquiesced, shifting Kate from her waist to Peter's. The little girl wrapped her legs around him, gripping the lapel of his parka to balance her weight.

Sara stood back a bit to regard the two of them. "I've got to say, this isn't a version of you I've seen before."

He felt himself smile. "Five years. A lot can change."

"Well, it suits you." A sudden yawn seized her. "Seriously, if she gets to be a bother . . ."

"She won't. Now, will you go? Get some sleep."

Sara left them alone. Peter lowered himself into the chair, shifted Kate to his lap, and turned her body toward the winter sky. "So what do you want to talk about?"

"I dunno."

"Not tired at all?"

"Nope."

"How about we count some stars?"

"That's boring." She shifted, making herself comfortable, then commanded: "Tell me a story."

"A story. What kind?"

"A once-upon-a-time story."

He wasn't sure how, having never done this before. Yet as he considered the girl's request, a rush of memories flowed through him: his days as a Little in the Sanctuary, sitting in circle with the other children, their legs folded under them; Teacher, her pale, moonlike face and the stories she told, of talking animals in waistcoats and skirts and kings in their castles and ships crossing the sea in search of treasure; the drowsy sensation of the words passing through him, carrying him away into distant worlds and times, as if he were leaving his own body. They were recollections of another life; they were so distant as to feel historical; yet sitting in the winter cold with Sara's daughter on his lap, they did not seem apart from him. He felt a mantle pass and, with it, a twinge of regret: he'd never told Caleb a story.

"So." He cleared his throat, stalling to assemble his thoughts. But the truth was, he had nothing; every story from his childhood had suddenly fled his mind. He'd simply have to wing it. "Let's see—"

"It needs a girl in it," Kate said, helpfully.

"So it does. I was just getting to that. So, once upon a time there was a little girl—"

"What did she look like?"

"Hmm. Well, she was very pretty. A lot like you, actually."

"Was she a princess?"

"Are you going to let me tell this or not? But now that you mention it, she was. The most beautiful princess who ever lived. But the thing is, she didn't *know* she was a princess. That's the interesting part."

Kate frowned bossily. "Why didn't she know?"

Something clicked then; he felt the contours of a story emerging in his mind.

"That is a very excellent question. What happened was this. When she was very young, not much more than a baby, her parents, the king and queen, took her on a picnic in the royal forest. It was a sunny day, and the little girl, whose name was Princess . . ."

"Elizabeth."

"Princess Elizabeth, saw a butterfly. An *amazing* butterfly. Her parents weren't paying attention, and she followed the butterfly into the woods, trying to catch it. But the thing is, it wasn't a butterfly. It was . . . a fairy queen."

"Really?"

"It's true. Now, the thing about fairies is, they don't trust people. They pretty much keep to themselves, and that's the way they like it. But the fairy queen was different. She'd always wanted a daughter. Fairies don't have children of their own. It made her very sad not to have a little girl to take care of, and when she saw Princess Elizabeth, she was so moved by her beauty that she couldn't help herself. She led the child away, deeper and deeper into the woods. Soon the little girl was lost and began to cry. The fairy queen landed on her nose, and brushed her tears away with her delicate wings, and said, 'Don't be sad. I'll take care of you. You will be my little girl now.' And she took her to the big hollow tree where she lived with all her fairy subjects, and gave her food to eat and a table to sit at and a little bed to sleep in, and before too long Princess Elizabeth had no memory of any other life, except her life among the fairies of the forest."

Kate was nodding along. "What happened then?"

"Well, nothing. Not right away. For a while they were very happy together, the fairy queen especially. How wonderful it felt for her to have a little girl of her own. But as Elizabeth grew, she began to feel that something wasn't right. Do you know what that was?"

"She wasn't a fairy?"

"Exactly. Good for you, for figuring that out. She wasn't a fairy, she was a little girl, and not so little anymore. Why am I so different? she wondered. And the taller she grew, the harder this was for the fairy queen to conceal. Why do my feet stick out from my bed, Elizabeth would ask her, and the fairy queen would say, Because beds are always small, that's just how they are. Why is my table so tiny, Elizabeth asked, and the fairy queen said, I'm sorry, it's not the table's fault, you'll just have to stop growing. Which, of course, she couldn't do. She grew and grew, and soon she barely fit inside the tree anymore. All the other fairies complained. They were afraid she'd eat all their food and there'd be nothing left. They were afraid she'd accidentally squash them. Something had to be done, but the fairy queen refused. With me so far?"

Kate nodded, enthralled.

"Now, the king and queen, Elizabeth's parents, had never stopped looking for her. They'd combed every inch of the forest, and all the lands of the kingdom besides. But the tree was very well hidden. Then one day they heard a rumor about a little girl living in the forest with the fairies. Could that be our daughter? they wondered. And they did the only thing they could think of. They ordered the royal woodsmen to cut down all the trees until they found the one with Elizabeth inside it."

"*All* of them?"

Peter nodded. "Every last one. Which was not a good idea. The woods were home not only to the fairies but to all kinds of animals and birds. But Elizabeth's parents were so desperate, they would have done anything to get their daughter back. So the woodsmen got to work, chopping down the forest, while the king and queen rode out on their horses, calling her name. 'Elizabeth! Elizabeth! Where are you?' And you know what happened?"

"She heard them?"

"Yes, she did. Only the name Elizabeth didn't mean anything to her anymore. She had a fairy name now, and had forgotten everything about her life. But the fairy queen knew what she was hearing, and she felt pretty awful about it. How could I have done this terrible thing? she thought. How could I have taken Elizabeth away? But still she couldn't make herself fly out of the tree to tell Elizabeth's parents where she was. She loved the girl too much, you see, to let her go. 'Be very still,' she said to Elizabeth. 'Don't make a sound.' The woodsmen were coming closer and closer. Trees were falling everywhere. All the fairies were afraid. 'Give her back,' they said to the fairy queen, 'please, give her back before they destroy the entire forest.'"

"Wow," Kate gasped.

"I know. It's a pretty scary story. Should I stop?"

"Uncle Peter, *please.*"

He laughed. "All right, all right. So, the woodsmen came to the tree with Elizabeth and the fairies inside. It was an especially magnificent tree, tall and wide, with a big canopy of leaves. A fairy tree. But as one woodsman reared back with his axe, the king had a change of heart. The tree, you see, was just too beautiful to cut down. I'm sure the creatures of the forest care about this tree as much as I care about my daughter, he said. It wouldn't be right to take it away from them, all because I've lost something I love. Everybody, put your axes down and go home and let me and my wife mourn for our daughter, who we will never see again. It was very sad. Everybody was in tears. Elizabeth's parents, the woodsmen, even the fairy queen, who had heard every word. Because she knew that Elizabeth could never be her real daughter, no matter how hard she wished it. So she took her by the hand and led her out of the tree and said, 'Your Majesties, please forgive me. It was I who took your daughter. I wanted a little girl of my own so much that I couldn't help myself. But I know now that she belongs with you. I'm so very, very sorry.' And you know what the king and queen said?"

"Off with your head?"

Peter stifled a laugh. "Just the opposite. Despite everything that had happened, they were so happy to have their daughter back, and so moved by the fairy queen's remorse, that they decided to reward her. They issued a royal proclamation that the fairies should be left to live in peace, and that all children of the realm should have one special fairy friend. Which is why, to this day, only children can see them."

Kate was silent a moment. "So that's the end?"

"Pretty much, yeah." He felt faintly embarrassed. "I haven't really done this before. How'd I do?"

The girl considered this, then said, with a crisp nod, "I liked it. It was a good story. Tell me another."

"I'm not sure I've got another one in me. Aren't you tired yet?"

"*Please,* Uncle Peter."

The night was clear, the stars shining down. Everything was still, not a trace of movement or sound. Peter thought of Caleb, realizing with a power that startled him how much he missed the boy, how he longed to hold him in his arms. Alicia was right, and Tifty too. But most of all, Amy. *He loves you, you know.* The truth filled him like a breath of winter air. Peter would go home and learn to be a father.

"So, okay . . ."

He talked and talked. He told her every story he knew. By the time he was done, Kate was yawning; her body had gone slack in his arms. He unzipped his coat and swiveled her on his lap, pulling the flaps around her.

"Are you cold, sweetheart?"

Her voice was soft, half gone. "Nuh-uh."

She nestled against him. Just another minute, Peter thought, and closed his eyes. Just another minute, and I'll take her inside. He felt Kate's warm breath on his neck; her chest moved gently against his own, rising and falling, like long waves on a beach. But a minute passed, and then another and another, and by that time Peter wasn't going anywhere, because he was fast asleep.

* * *

In the lavatory of the apothecary shop, Lucius Greer was shaving.

The day, and most of the night besides, had disappeared under an avalanche of duties. A meeting of the Council of Lodges, during which Eustace had attempted first to reexplain and then once more justify the lottery procedure for evacuation; the tallying of census data, which had revealed numerous duplicate forms, some made in error, others with deliberate intent by individuals trying to increase their odds of being chosen; a brawl outside the detention center when a group of three cols, half-starved after weeks of hiding in an unused warehouse, had attempted to turn themselves in, only to be intercepted by the small crowd that kept vigil outside the building; nine weddings over which he'd been asked to officiate when one of the JPs had taken ill (all Lucius had to do was read four sentences off a card, yet it surprised him, how weighty it felt to say them aloud); the first official gathering of the evacuation support teams, and the partitioning of their responsibilities in preparation for the first departure; and on and on. A day of one thing and then another and another; Lucius couldn't remember what or even if he'd eaten, he'd barely sat down all day, and yet here he was, past midnight, gazing at his grizzled, hirsute face in the mirror, holding a blade in one hand and a pair of scissors in the other.

He began with the scissors. Snip by snip the wild torrent of his hair and beard fell away, their white leavings gathering on the floor by his feet like drifts of feathered snow. When this was done he warmed a pot of water, soaked a rag and wrung it out, and lay it over his face to soften the bristles that remained. He smeared his cheeks with soap, harsh and chemical-smelling, then went to work with the blade: first his cheeks, then the long arc of his neck, and finally his head, working backward from brow to crown to the base of his skull in short, measured strokes. The first time he had shaved himself in this manner, the night before he'd taken the oath of the Expeditionary, he had cut himself in about twenty places. It was commonly said that you didn't need to look at the uniform to know a fresh recruit; all you had to do was look at his head. But with time and practice, Greer, like all of his fellows, had gotten the knack, and it pleased him to discover that he hadn't lost his touch. He could have done it blindfolded in the dark if he had to, yet there was satisfaction to be had in observing a ritual that after so many years still possessed the power of a baptism. Scrape by scrape his visage was laid bare, and when the task was complete, Greer stepped back to examine his face in the mirror, running his hand over the cool pinkness of his rediscovered flesh and nodding with approval at the image he beheld.

He wiped himself down, cleaned and dried his blade, and put his supplies away. Many days had passed since he had properly slept, and still he was not the least bit tired. He drew on his parka and boots, let himself out the back, and made his way down the alley. It was nearly one A.M., not a soul about, yet from all around Greer sensed a kind of molecular restlessness, a subaural hum of life. He moved past the ruined Dome, down the hill, through the flatland to the stadium. By the time he arrived, the moon was down. He chose not to enter the structure, rather to stand in the absolute quiet and take it in whole, this blot of darkness against the starry sky. He wondered: Would history remember this place? Would the people of the future, whoever they were, give it a name, one worthy of the events that had transpired here, to record it for posterity? A hopeful thought, a bit premature, but one worth having. And Lucius Greer took a silent vow. Should such a future come to pass, should the final battle for earth's dominion be taken in victory, he would be the one to put pen to paper, to give the story words.

He did not know when this battle would be. Amy had not told him that. Only that it would come.

He understood, then, what force had led him here. He was looking for a sign. What form this sign would take, he could not say. It might come now, it might come later, it might not come at all. Such was the burden of his faith. He opened his mind and waited. An interval of time moved by. The night, the stars, the living world; all passed through him, like a blessing.

Then:

Lucius. My friend. Hello.

And on this night of miraculous things, Peter, sitting outside the shoe store, awoke to the feeling that he was, in fact, not awake at all—that one dream had simply opened into the next, like a door behind a door. A dream in which he was sitting with Sara's daughter in his arms at the edge of the snowy fields, all else being the same—the inky sky, the winter cold, the lateness of the hour—except for the fact that they were not alone.

But it was not a dream.

She crouched before him, in the manner of her kind. Her

transformation was complete; even her raven mane was gone. Yet as their eyes met and held, the image wavered in his mind; it was not a viral he saw. It was a girl, and then a woman, and then both of these at once. She was Amy, the Girl from Nowhere; she was Amy of Souls, Last of the Twelve; she was only herself. Extending a hand toward him, Amy held her palm upright; Peter replied in kind. A force of pure longing surged in his heart as their fingers touched. It was a kind of kiss.

How long they stayed that way, Peter didn't know. Between them, in the warm cocoon of his coat, Kate slept soundly, oblivious. Time had released its moorings; Peter and Amy drifted together in the current. Soon the child would awaken, or Sara would come, or Hollis, and Amy would be gone. She would lift away in a streak of starry light. Peter would return the sleeping child to her bed, and lie down himself, even attempt to sleep; and in the morning, in the gray winter dawn, they would stretch their bones and load up their gear and continue on their long road south. The moment would pass, like all things, into memory.

But not just yet.

EPILOGUE

THE
GOLDEN HOUR

As easy might I from myself depart
As from my soul, which in thy breast doth lie.
That is my home of love.

—SHAKESPEARE,
SONNET 109

69

The driver this time was a woman. Amy put down her sign and got into the car.

"How do you do, Amy?" She offered her hand. "I'm Rachel Wood."

They shook. For a moment Amy was rendered speechless, arrested by the woman's beauty: a face of delicate, well-made bones, as if honed with the finest tools; skin that glowed with youthful health; a trim, strong body, her arms articulated with lean muscle. Her hair, pulled away from her face in a taut ponytail, was blond with golden streaks. She was wearing what Amy knew to be tennis clothes, although this knowledge seemed to come from elsewhere, the idea of tennis itself lacking any meaningful reference. Sunglasses with tiny jewels embedded in the arms were perched on top of her head.

"I'm sorry I wasn't here to get you before," Rachel continued. "Anthony thought you'd like a familiar face the first time."

"I'm very glad to meet you," Amy said.

"That's sweet of you to say." She smiled, showing her teeth, which were small and straight and very white. "Buckle up now."

They glided away from the overpass. All was the same as the last time—the same houses and stores and parking lots, the same glowing summer light, the same busy world flowing past. In the deep leather of her seat, Amy felt as if she were floating in a bath. Rachel seemed thoroughly at home at the wheel of the immense vehicle, humming a shapeless tune under her breath as she guided them confidently through traffic. As a large pickup braked ahead of them, blocking the lane, Rachel flicked on her blinker and deftly swerved to pass.

"For goodness sake," she sighed, "some people. Where do they learn to drive?" She looked at Amy hastily and returned her eyes to the road. "You know, you're not quite what I imagined, I have to say."

"No?"

"Oh, not in a bad way," Rachel assured her. "That's not

what I meant at all. Honestly, you're just pretty as a picture. I wish I had skin like that."

"So how am I different?"

She hesitated, choosing her words. "I just thought you'd be, you know. Younger."

They continued on. Amy's abrupt arrival in this place had brought about a mild disorientation and, with it, a muting of emotion. But as the minutes passed, she felt her mind opening to her circumstances, the images and her responses to them growing more defined. How remarkable everything was, Amy thought. How very, very remarkable. They were inside the ship, the *Chevron Mariner*, yet she had no physical awareness of this; as before, with Wolgast, every detail of the scene possessed an absolutely firm appearance of reality. Perhaps it was real, in some alternate sense of the word. What, after all, was "real"?

"Right there is where I stopped with him, that first time." Rachel gestured out the window to a block of stores. "Somehow I had it in my head he might like doughnuts. Doughnuts, can you imagine?" Before Amy could assemble a response, she went on: "But listen to me, giving you the grand tour. I'm sure you know all about it. And you must be tired, after such a long trip."

"It's all right," Amy said. "I don't mind."

"Oh, he was such a sight." Rachel shook her head sadly. "That poor man. My heart just went out. I said to myself, Rachel, you have to do something. For once in your little life, get your head out of the sand. But of course I was really thinking about myself, as usual. Which is the thing. I've got enough regrets on that score to last a hundred lifetimes. I didn't deserve him, not one iota."

"I don't think he believes that."

She slowed the car to turn onto a residential street. "It's really marvelous, you know. What you're doing. He's been alone so long."

Soon, they pulled up to the house. "Well, here we are," Rachel announced in a chipper voice. She had put the vehicle in park though she'd left the engine running, just as Wolgast had done. "It was a pleasure to finally meet you, Amy. You'll want to watch your step getting out."

"Why don't you come with me? I know he'd like to see you."

"Oh, no," said Rachel. "It's nice of you to ask, but that's not how this works, I'm afraid. That's against the rules."

"What rules?"

"Just . . . the rules."

Amy waited for more, but there was none; there was nothing to do but climb out of the car. By the open door she turned to look at Rachel, who was waiting with her hands on the wheel. The air was thick and warm beneath the green canopy of the trees; insects were buzzing everywhere with their bright, chaotic music, like the notes of an orchestra tuning up.

"Tell him I'm thinking about him, won't you? Tell him Rachel sends her love."

"I don't understand why you can't come with me."

Rachel directed her gaze over the dashboard, toward the house. It seemed to Amy she was searching for something, her eyes, which had clouded with a sudden grief, pausing at each of its many windows. Tears appeared at the corners of her eyes.

"I can't, you see, because it wouldn't make any sense."

"Why wouldn't it make sense?"

"Because, Amy," she said, "I'm already there."

She found him kneeling in the flowerbeds, working in the dirt. A wheelbarrow was positioned nearby; piles of dark mulch, exuding a heavy earthen smell, were dispersed among the beds. At her approach he rose to his feet, removing his broad-brimmed straw hat and drawing off his gloves.

"Miss Amy, you're right on time now. I was just setting to work on the lawn, but I reckon that'll keep." He waved his hat toward the patio, where glasses of tea awaited. "Come and sit a spell."

They took their places at the table. Amy tipped her face to the crowns of the trees, letting the sunlight warm her. The aromas of grass and flowers filled her senses.

"Thought you'd be more comfortable this way," Carter said. "The two of us can have a time, talking and such. Make the days pass."

"You knew he'd be there, didn't you?"

Carter mopped his brow with a rag. "Didn't send him, if that's what you mean. Wolgast just had his way. No talking him out of it when he set his mind on it."

"But how come the others didn't know who he was? They couldn't have. They would have killed him."

Carter shook his head. "Their kind never could read me, one way or the other. You could say we been out of touch awhile. It's a two-way street, and I ain't sent nothing back their way since the beginning. Shut my mind to all of them."

Carter hitched up in his chair and returned the cloth to his back pocket. "You done right, Miss Amy. Wolgast, too. Was a hard and terrible thing, I know that."

She was suddenly thirsty; the tea felt cool and sweet going down and left a bright, lemony taste on her tongue. Carter watched her, waving his hat in a gentle motion to push a breeze over his face.

"And Zero?"

"I expect there's time yet. But he'll be coming for us. This here's personal now. He's surely the worst of 'em. Put 'em all together and you still ain't got one Zero. Bridge we cross when we come to it."

"And until then, here we stay."

Carter nodded in his patient way. "Yes'm. Here we stay."

They sat together in silence, thinking of what would come. "I've never tended a garden before," Amy said. "Would you teach me?"

"Always lots to be done. Reckon I could use the help. Mower's fussy, though."

"I'm sure I could learn."

"I'm supposing you could, now," he said with a smile. "I reckon that's the case."

Amy remembered her promise. "Rachel told me to send her love."

"Did she, now. I was just thinkin' on her. How she look to you?"

"Beautiful, really. I'd never really had a chance to see her clearly before. But sad, too. She was looking at the house, like there was something she wanted."

Carter seemed surprised. "Why, it's her babies, Miss Amy. I thought you knew."

Amy shook her head.

"Haley and the little one. Woman can't see or touch 'em, where she is. It's her babies she's always dreamin' on. It's the most awful ache to her."

Amy finally understood. Rachel had drowned herself, leaving her children behind. "Will she ever see them again?"

"I expect she will when she ready. It's her own self she has to forgive, for leaving them like she did."

His words seemed to hover in the air, not sounds alone but things of form and substance. The temperature was dropping; the leaves had begun to fall.

"She not the only one, Miss Amy. Some folks can't find a way on they own. For some it's a bad feeling in the mind. Others just can't let go. Them's the ones that love too hard."

In the pool, the body of Rachel Wood had completed its slow ascent to float upon the surface. Amy looked down at the table; she knew what Carter was saying to her. *Every day I cut the lawn,* she thought. *Every day she rise.*

"You got to go to him," said Carter. "Show him the way."

"I just . . ." She felt his eyes on her face. "I don't know how."

He reached over the table and cupped her chin, lifting it upward. "I know you, Miss Amy. It's like you been inside me all my life. You the one was made to set this whole world right. But Wolgast's just a man. It's his time now. You got to give him back."

Tears trembled in her throat. "But what will I do without him?"

"Just like you always done," said Anthony Carter, and smiled into her eyes. "Just like you do now. You *Amy.*"

70

He came to her a final time. Or it was she who came to him. They came to each other, to say a last goodbye.

For Wolgast it began with a sensation of abstract motion. He was in a kind of nowhere, floating through an infinite space, though bit by bit the scene resolved, its spatial and temporal parameters firming, and he became aware that he was, of all things, riding a bicycle. A bicycle! Now, that was strange. Why was he on a bicycle? He hadn't ridden one in years, but he'd loved it as a boy: the feeling of pure freedom and gyroscopic lift, his body's energy flowing through this marvelous mechanism that joined him to the wind. Wolgast was on a bicycle, riding down a dusty country lane, and Amy was beside him, perched on a bicycle of her own. This fact surprised him neither more nor less than anything else about the scene, it all simply *was,* just as Amy was both a little girl and a grown woman, and for a time they rode together without speaking, though the idea of time itself felt strange. What was time? How long had they been riding like this? Some period of hours, perhaps, or even days, and yet the light was always the same—a permanent penumbral twilight that enriched the colors of everything around him with a golden glow: the fields and trees, the dust that rose under his wheels, the small white shapes of houses in the distance. Everything felt very close; everything was far away.

"Where are we going?" Wolgast asked.

Amy smiled. "Oh, it's not much farther."

"What . . . is this place?"

She said nothing more. On they rode. Wolgast's heart was full of warm contentment, as if he were a boy again: a boy riding his bicycle at sunset, waiting for the call that would summon him home.

"Are you tired?" Amy asked.

"Not at all. It feels wonderful."

"Why don't we stop at the crest of the next hill?"

They coasted to a halt. A grassy valley opened below them. In the distance, nestled by trees, was a house: small, white, like the others, with a porch and black shutters. Amy and Wolgast lowered their bicycles to the ground and stood together quietly. There was no wind at all.

"It's quite a view," Wolgast said. Then: "I think I know where I am."

Amy nodded.

"It's strange." He took a deep breath and let it out slowly. "I don't really remember how it happened, but I suppose that's for the best. Is it always like this?"

"I'm not sure. I think sometimes it is."

"I remember thinking I had to be brave."

"You were. The bravest man I ever saw."

He mulled this over. "Well, that's good. I'm glad to hear it. In the end, I guess that's all a person can ask." He sent his gaze over the valley again. "That house. I'm supposed to go there, aren't I?"

"I believe that you are."

He turned to look at her. A second passed; then he broke into a smile of discovery.

"Wait a minute. You're in *love*. I can see it in your face."

"I think I am, yes."

Wolgast shook his head with wonder. "I'll be damned. How about that. My little Amy, all grown up, in love. And does he love you back, this person?"

"I think he does," she said. "I hope he does."

"Well, he'd be a fool not to. You can tell him I said so."

For a moment neither spoke. Amy waited.

"So," he began again. His voice was thick with emotion. "I suppose that means my work here is done. I guess I always knew this day would come. I'm going to miss you, Amy."

"I'll miss you, too."

"That was always the hardest part, missing you. I think that's why I could never bring myself to leave. I always thought, What will Amy do without me? Funny how in the end it was the other way around. I suppose all parents feel that way. But it's different when it's you." The words caught in his throat. "Let's do this quickly, okay?"

She put her arms around him. She was crying too, but not with sadness. Though perhaps a little bit of sadness. "It will be all right, I promise."

"How do you know?"

At the far end of the valley, at the edge of the fields, the door to the house had opened.

"Because that's what heaven is," said Amy. "It's opening the door of a house in twilight and everyone you love is there." She hugged him tightly to her. "It's time for you to go home, Daddy. I've kept you as long as I could, but you have to go now. They're waiting for you."

"Who's waiting, Amy?"

On the porch a woman had appeared, holding a baby in her arms. Amy backed away and touched his tearstained cheek.

She said, "Go see."

71

She awoke to the cold and a vision of stars. Stars by the hundreds, the thousands, the millions. Stars in their slow turning, pinwheeling over her face, and some of them were falling. Alicia watched them fall, counting off the seconds. One one thousand, two one thousand, three one thousand. She tallied the durations of their descents as they plunged across the heavens, and in so doing she came upon the understanding that the world was where she'd left it and she was still alive.

How could she be alive?

She sat upright. Who knew what time it was. The moon had set, dipping the sky in blackness. Nothing had changed; she was just the same.

And yet:

Alicia, come to me.

The sound of her name, whispered on the wind.

Come to me, Alicia. The others are gone, you will be my one. Come to me come to me come to me . . .

She knew whose voice this was.

Alicia climbed from the culvert. Fifty feet away, Soldier

was grazing on a frosted stand of weeds. At the sound of her emergence, he lifted his head: *Ah, there you are; I was beginning to wonder.* His great hooves tossed clumps of white as he ambled toward her with his powerful gait.

—You good boy, she said. She caressed his muzzle, his breath filling her palms with a scent of earth. You splendid, noble boy. How well you know me. I guess we're not done, after all.

Her pack was lying in the culvert. She had no gun, but the bandoliers were there, blades tucked into their sheaths. She pulled the leather straps over her chest and cinched them tight to her frame. She climbed on Soldier's naked back and clicked her tongue, turning him east.

Come to me, Alicia. Come to me come to me come to me . . .

You're damn right I will, she thought. Leaning forward, his great mane filling her hands, she heeled Soldier to a trot, then a canter, and finally a gallop, wild through the snow.

You bastard. Here I come.

DRAMATIS PERSONAE

THE TWELVE

Tim Fanning, a.k.a. "The Zero." Professor of biochemistry, Columbia University. Infected by CV-0 virus on scientific expedition to Bolivia, Feb. 21, 20XX.

1. **Giles Babcock (deceased).** Sentenced to death for one count of capital murder, Nye County, Nevada, 2013.
2. **Joseph Morrison.** Sentenced to death for one count of capital murder, Lewis County, Kentucky, 2013.
3. **Victor Chávez.** Sentenced to death for one count of capital murder and two counts of aggravated sexual assault with a minor, Elko County, Nevada, 2012.
4. **John Baffes.** Sentenced to death for one count of capital murder and one count of second-degree murder with depraved indifference, Pasco County, Florida, 2010.
5. **Thaddeus Turrell.** Sentenced to death for the capital murder of a Homeland Security officer, New Orleans Federal Housing District, 2014.
6. **David Winston.** Sentenced to death for one count of capital murder and three counts of aggravated sexual assault, New Castle County, Delaware, 2014.
7. **Rupert Sosa.** Sentenced to death for one count of vehicular homicide with depraved indifference, Lake County, Indiana, 2009.
8. **Martin Echols.** Sentenced to death for one count of capital murder and one count of armed robbery, Cameron Parish, Louisiana, 2012.
9. **Horace Lambright.** Sentenced to death for two counts of capital murder and aggravated sexual assault, Maricopa County, Arizona, 2014.
10. **Julio Martínez.** Sentenced to death for the capital murder of a peace officer, Laramie County, Wyoming, 2011.
11. **William Reinhardt.** Sentenced to death for three counts

of capital murder and aggravated sexual assault, Miami-Dade County, Florida, 2012.

12. **Anthony Carter.** Sentenced to death for one count of capital murder, Harris County, Texas, 2013.

YEAR ZERO

Bernard Kittridge, a.k.a. "Last Stand in Denver." A survivor.
April. A survivor.
Timothy. Her stepbrother.
Danny Chayes. A school bus driver.
Lila Kyle. A doctor.
Lawrence Grey. A janitor, Project NOAH.
Horace Guilder. Deputy director, Division of Special Weapons ("The Warehouse").
Major Frances Porcheki. Officer of the Iowa National Guard.
Vera. A Red Cross nurse.
Ignacio. A janitor, Project NOAH.
Nelson. Chief technical officer, Division of Special Weapons.
Shawna. A prostitute.
Rita Chernow. A police detective.

OTHER SURVIVORS

Pastor Don
Wood
Delores
Jamal
Mrs. Bellamy
Joe Robinson
Linda Robinson
Boy Jr.

THE FIELD, 79 A.V.

Curtis Vorhees. Foreman of the North Agricultural Complex, Kerrville, Texas.
Delia "Dee" Vorhees. His wife.
Boz Vorhees. His brother (deceased).
Nitia and Siri Vorhees. Daughters of Curtis and Delia Vorhees.
Nathan Crukshank. Brother of Delia Vorhees; a Domestic Security (DS) officer.
Tifty Lamont. A Domestic Security officer.

OTHER FAMILIES IN THE FIELD

Tyler Vorhees family
Withers family
Dodd family
Apgar family
Cauley family
Francis family
Cuomo family
Martinez family
Wright family
Bodine family

97 A.V.

KERRVILLE, TEXAS

Amy Harper Bellafonte. The Girl from Nowhere.

Lieutenant Peter Jaxon. Officer of the Expeditionary, Army of the Republic of Texas.

Lieutenant Alicia Donadio. Officer of the Expeditionary.

Colonel Gunnar Apgar. Officer of the Expeditionary.

Major Alexander Henneman. Officer of the Expeditionary.

Lieutenant Satch Dodd. Officer of the Expeditionary.

Lucius Greer. A prisoner.

Hollis Wilson. A bouncer.

Dunk Withers. A criminal.

Abram Fleet. General of the Army.

Victoria Sanchez. President of the Republic of Texas.

Sister Peg. A nun, in charge of the orphanage.

Sister Catherine. A nun.

Caleb Jaxon. Nephew of Peter Jaxon, son of Theo Jaxon and Mausami Patal.

FREEPORT, TEXAS

Michael Fisher. Oiler first class (OFC); crew chief at Freeport refinery complex.

Lore DeVeer. An oiler.

Juan "Ceps" Sweeting. An oiler.

Ed Pope. An oiler.

Dan Karlovic. Chief engineer of Freeport refinery complex.

THE HOMELAND

Jackie. A worker.

Eustace. An insurgent.

Nina. An insurgent.

Vale. A human resources officer.

Whistler. A human resources officer.
Sod. A human resources officer.
Dr. Verlyn. A physician.
Dani. An attendant in the Dome.
Jenny. An attendant in the Dome.
Fred Wilkes. Chief of staff.
Vikram Suresh. Minister of public health.
Aidan Hoppel. Minister of propaganda.

ACKNOWLEDGMENTS

Every book needs friends, and this one has many. A big ole tip of the hat to: Ellen Levine at Trident Media Group; Mark Tavani and Libby McGuire at Ballantine Books; Bill Massey at Orion; Gina Centrello, president of the Random House Publishing Group; Claire Roberts at Trident Media; the spectacular production, publicity, marketing and sales teams at Random House, Orion, and my many publishers around the world; Jennifer ("Jenny") Smith; and the English Department of Rice University. On matters military, I am especially indebted to Adrian Hoppel. Thanks also to Rudy Ramos, sniper-dentist, and Coert Voorhees. Mark and Bill: Pour yourselves a frosty, my brothers; you've earned it. Ellen: No truer friend have I.

To the members of Team Cronin, large and small, I say: Without you, nothing. Thank you for my life.

My gratitude to you all.